1636
THE OTTOMAN
ONSLAUGHT

ERIC FLINT'S BESTSELLING RING OF FIRE SERIES

1632 by Eric Flint
1633 with David Weber
1634: The Baltic War with David Weber
1634: The Galileo Affair with Andrew Dennis
1634: The Bavarian Crisis with Virginia DeMarce
1634: The Ram Rebellion with Virginia DeMarce et al.
1635: The Cannon Law with Andrew Dennis
1635: The Dreeson Incident with Virginia DeMarce
1635: The Eastern Front
1635: The Papal Stakes with Charles E. Gannon
1636: The Saxon Uprising
1636: The Kremlin Games with Gorg Huff & Paula Goodlett
1636: The Devil's Opera with David Carrico
1636: Commander Cantrell in the West Indies with Charles E. Gannon
1636: The Viennese Waltz with Gorg Huff & Paula Goodlett
1636: The Cardinal Virtues with Walter Hunt
1635: A Parcel of Rogues with Andrew Dennis
1636: The Ottoman Onslaught

Grantville Gazette I-V, ed. by Eric Flint
Grantville Gazette VI-VII, ed. by Eric Flint & Paula Goodlett

Ring of Fire I-IV, ed. by Eric Flint

1635: The Tangled Web by Virginia DeMarce
1635: The Wars for the Rhine by Anette Pedersen
1636: Seas of Fortune by Iver P. Cooper
1636: The Chronicles of Dr. Gribbleflotz by
Kerryn Offord & Rick Boatright

Time Spike by Eric Flint with Marilyn Kosmatka

**For a complete list of Baen Books by Eric Flint,
please go to www.baen.com.**

1636
THE OTTOMAN ONSLAUGHT

ERIC FLINT

1636: The Ottoman Onslaught

Copyright © 2017 by Eric Flint

A Baen Books Original

Baen Publishing Enterprises
P.O. Box 1403
Riverdale, NY 10471
www.baen.com

ISBN: 978-1-4767-8184-6

Cover art by Tom Kidd
Maps by Michael Knopp

First printing, January 2017

Distributed by Simon & Schuster
1230 Avenue of the Americas
New York, NY 10020

10 9 8 7 6 5 4 3 2

Pages by Joy Freeman (www.pagesbyjoy.com)
Printed in the United States of America

DEDICATION

To those I stood with:

Pearl and Morris Chertov
Fred Halstead
Steve Kindred
Ken Miliner
Linda May O'Brien
Jerry O'Connell
Claudia Roberson
Kathy Shields
Ken Shilman

Gone but not forgotten

Contents

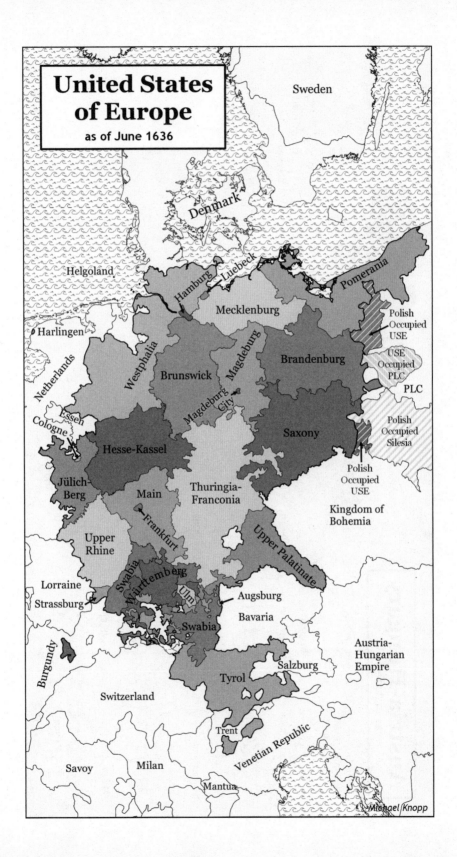

United States of Europe
as of June 1636

Sweden

Denmark

Helgoland

Hamburg
Luebeck
Pomerania

Harlingen

Mecklenburg

Polish Occupied USE

Netherlands

Westphalia

Brunswick

Magdeburg

Brandenburg

USE Occupied PLC

Essen
Cologne

Magdeburg City

PLC

Hesse-Kassel

Saxony

Polish Occupied Silesia

Jülich-Berg

Main

Thuringia-Franconia

Polish Occupied USE

Upper Rhine

Frankfurt

Kingdom of Bohemia

Lorraine

Strassburg

Swabia
Württemberg
Ulm

Upper Palatinate

Augsburg

Bavaria

Burgundy

Swabia

Austria-Hungarian Empire

Salzburg

Switzerland

Tyrol

Trent

Savoy

Milan

Venetian Republic

Mantua

Michael Knopp

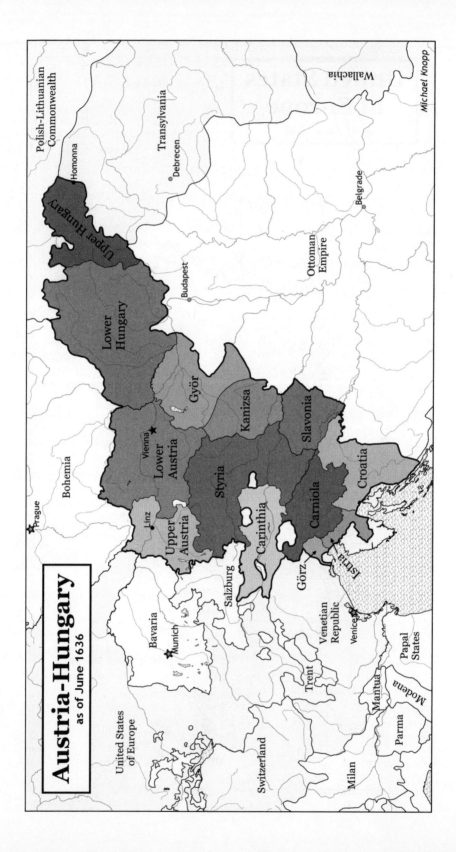

Austria-Hungary
as of June 1636

Polish-Lithuanian Commonwealth

Homonna

Upper Hungary

Transylvania

Debrecen

Wallachia

Michael Knopp

Lower Hungary

Budapest

Belgrade

Ottoman Empire

Bohemia

Győr

Kanizsa

Slavonia

Vienna

Lower Austria

Styria

Carniola

Croatia

Prague

Linz

Upper Austria

Carinthia

Görz

Istria

United States of Europe

Salzburg

Bavaria

Munich

Venetian Republic

Trent

Venice

Papal States

Switzerland

Mantua

Modena

Milan

Parma

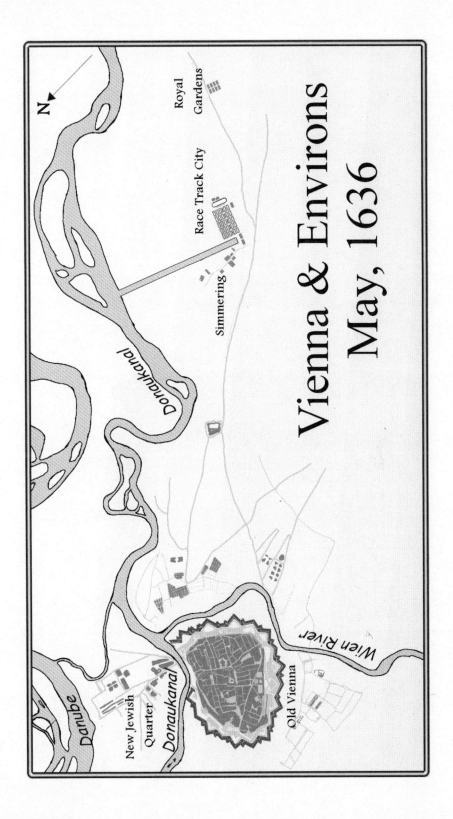

Part One

April 1636

Ah, but a man's reach should exceed his grasp,

Or what's a heaven for?

Chapter 1

Regensburg, Upper Palatinate

The march from Regensburg was supposed to have begun at dawn—and so it did, in a manner of speaking. The cavalry patrols had actually passed through the city's gates before sunrise. Right on schedule.

But now that he'd been a general for almost a year, Mike Stearns had learned that military time schedules bore precious little resemblance to what he'd considered "punctuality" in those innocent days when he'd been a civilian. In this, as in so many things, Carl von Clausewitz's old dictum applied. Perhaps better to say, the future dictum, since the man wouldn't even be born for another century and a half, and then in a different universe.

By now, Mike had memorized the damn thing: *Everything in war is simple, but the simplest thing is difficult.*

He knew Clausewitz's axiom as well as he knew Murphy's Law—which applied to military matters even more stringently than it did to the affairs of civilians.

Civilians. Those happy-go-lucky, carefree, insouciant folk in whose ranks Mike could vaguely remember himself being counted once. Back in those halcyon days when he'd been a coal miner worried about nothing more substantial than methane explosions and roof falls. Or the prime minister of a nation, whose frets over issues of war and peace, prosperity and poverty, and the schemes and plots of traitors and malcontents had never troubled what he remembered as blissful sleep.

Pfah. Tell a cabinet member to do something, be it never so problematic and ticklish, and the task would get done—started upon, at least—within the hour.

Tell an army to do something as simple and straightforward as walk out of a town—just walk, no running required—and move on down the road—fifteen miles, maybe twenty; no more—and you'd be lucky if the ass end of the army made it through the gates by noon. The camp followers coming behind wouldn't manage the feat until mid-afternoon.

He could also remember a time when he'd intended to eradicate the pernicious seventeenth-century military custom of having camp followers in the first place. He'd been brought up as a stout American lad, watching John Wayne movies. You never saw a mob of camp followers trailing after John Wayne, did you? *Sands of Iwo Jima, The Longest Day, The Fighting Seabees*—not a camp follower anywhere in sight. Not even in his civil war movie, *The Horse Soldiers.* For that matter, not even in the movie where he'd portrayed the Mongol emperor Genghis Khan, *The Conqueror,* although Mike wasn't entirely sure about that. The film had been such a turkey that he'd stopped watching it halfway through. It was possible that a stray camp follower might have wandered across the stage toward the end.

Not likely, though. And it wasn't just the movies. Mike had served a three-year stint in the United States Army. That would be the army of the United States of *America,* long before the Ring of Fire happened.

Did the U.S. Army have camp followers? Not unless you counted the families living on a military base—but that wasn't really the same thing at all. When American soldiers went on campaign back up-time, their families stayed behind. They sure as hell didn't trail after the soldiers like a gigantic caravan.

Caravan? It was more like a circus train without rails. All that was missing were elephants and a carousel.

"I'd think you'd have become accustomed to this by now, General."

Turning in the saddle, Mike saw that his aide Christopher Long had come up behind him and was now almost alongside.

"I think a grin like that on an adjutant's face when addressing his commanding officer is probably a court-martial offense," Mike said. He wondered if he sounded as sour as he felt. "I still have the occasional daydream about a lightning offensive. We even had a name for it where and when I came from: *Blitzkrieg.*"

His other aide, Ulbrecht Duerr, had ridden up in time to hear his last sentence.

"'Blitzkrieg,' is it? Lightning war. Ha! No wonder those stupid German descendants of ours lost most of their wars. Went charging out without proper consideration of what it takes to keep the supplies coming."

He now looked at Long. "Have you noticed, Christopher, that our commander is always disgruntled at the beginning of a campaign?"

Long smiled. "Oh, yes. I've come to expect it."

Mike was about to make some retort but...

Was it true? Was he really that predictable?

He thought back on previous campaigns.

Well, maybe. After the first one, anyway. Well. After the first day of the first one.

"Remind me again why I don't ban all camp followers," he said.

"First, because the men would probably mutiny," said Duerr. The cheery tone in which he said that was *surely* a court-martial offense. Court-martialable? Mike wasn't sure of the proper usage—which just went to show he was still a civilian at heart. Carefree, happy-go-lucky...

"We'd have to hope they'd mutiny," added Long, "because if they didn't, they'd soon enough start dying of hunger or exhaustion or disease—or any combination thereof."

"On account of there'd be no one to feed them or keep their clothing reasonably clean," Duerr continued, still sounding cheery.

"Or tuck them in at night and sing them lullabies," Mike grumbled.

"This sort of bitterness really doesn't suit a man as young as you are, General. Look at me! Much older than you, I am—not to mention properly scarred in a soldierly manner."

He held up a crooked forefinger, which hadn't healed quite properly after being broken at the Battle of Ostra outside Dresden. Duerr had several scars on his body which were actually more impressive, but they were covered by his uniform—and besides, he was inordinately proud of this one. He'd defeated an enemy cavalryman in hand-to-hand combat even though his injury had forced him to fight left-handed.

Mike had had his own adventures in that battle, and quite

splendid ones at that. He'd had two horses shot out from under him. Not one—two. But he'd come out of it quite unscarred, at least bodily.

Whether he'd come out of it unscarred mentally as well...

Too soon to know, he thought. He didn't think he'd developed PTSD so far, if "developed" was the proper term to use. He'd have to ask Maureen Grady the next time he saw her. She ran the Department of Social Services and was probably—no, almost certainly—the best psychologist in the world.

Having settled that issue to his momentary satisfaction, he went back to grousing about what really bothered him on this sunny day in April of 1636.

"Is it really too much to expect an army to move faster than an old lady with a walker?"

"Is a 'walker' something like a cane?" asked Christopher Long. "If so, the answer is 'yes.' A competent crone can out-hobble any army in the world."

"Taken as a whole," Duerr qualified. "A detached cavalry unit could certainly run her down. Flying artillery also."

Had he cross-checked that last assertion with the commander of the Third Division's flying artillery, Duerr would have gotten an argument. Lieutenant Colonel Thorsten Engler, normally a calm and phlegmatic officer, was having as close to an apoplectic fit as such a man could manage. He was even swearing a little. At least, by Thorsten Engler values of swearing.

Only under his breath, though. The actual swearing was being done by a lieutenant whom Thorsten was observing, since it would have been inappropriate for the commanding officer to deal with the problem directly.

"You—you miserable cruds." Angrily, the young lieutenant pointed at the wagon's undercarriage. "What in the name of—of—whatever—is wrong with you? Can't you see that the axle is broken? If you keep forcing the horses you'll lame one of them. You have to *lift* the dam—blasted thing out of the ditch."

The lieutenant was being a bit unfair—and certainly too harsh. It was true that the crew of the volley gun which was the focus of his displeasure had somehow managed to run their gun carriage into a ditch and had then broken the axle while trying to get it out. But they were almost brand new recruits, not one of Engler's experienced crews. Judging from the way they were handling the poor horses, all of them were town youngsters to boot.

Thorsten's rank was brand spanking new and he was still trying to adjust to his new status and position. General Stearns had only informed him three days before the march began that he'd succeeded in persuading the Powers-That-Be in the army's headquarters in Magdeburg—translation: he'd done an end run around the brass and gotten the emperor's ear directly—to assign the newest flying artillery company—just graduated from training camp, oh joy—to Stearns' Third Division instead of sending it to Torstensson's forces outside Poznań. (What possible use is flying artillery in a siege, after all?)

In his wisdom, Stearns had then decided to detach Engler's flying artillery company from the Hangman regiment and put Engler in charge of all the Third Division's flying artillery units. That being one very experienced veteran company—his—and the newly arrived pack of mewling infants who seemed to have trouble telling one end of a volley gun from the other and one end of a horse from the other.

Where had they trained them? On fishing boats?

There was one—minor—positive note. Thorsten had given all the new officers a lecture on the subject of avoiding undue coarseness in dealing with enlisted men. He was pleased to see that the lieutenant was doing his best to follow the guidelines.

"Yes, you heard me, you—you—soldiers and I use the term broadly. *Lift* the carriage out of the ditch. No, no, no—*after* you unload the volley gun, you—you—"

The words trailed off, partly from exhaustion—not physical but mental. Spiritual, almost.

To make things perfect, Stearns had decided to call the new formation a "squadron"—the only squadron in the USE Army—and had promoted Engler to the rank of lieutenant colonel. The promotion was itself problematic. In part because he'd been leapfrogged over a number of majors at least some of whom were bound to be resentful. More importantly—Thorsten didn't really care what envious thoughts might be infecting the odd officer here and there—because the rank of lieutenant colonel did not officially exist in the USE Army.

True, Jeff Higgins, the commanding officer of the Hangman regiment, held the rank as well.

That made two of them. In the entire army. Marvelous. Should the military hierarchy—translation: pack of wretched bureaucrats who'd put the most hidebound theologian to shame when it came to dogmatic enforcement of regulations—eventually decide to disqualify Thorsten's service on the grounds that he held no recognized rank, then should he be discharged due to injuries received he'd have neither a pension nor a valid disability claim.

Fine for Higgins to face such a plight. He was now a rich man thanks to the vagaries of the new stock market. Engler, on the other hand, was just a farmer with no farm whose betrothed had the income of a social worker—which was almost as mediocre in this universe as the one she'd come from.

One of the members of the gun crew slipped as they struggled to lift the carriage out of the ditch. Not surprising, really—it had rained the day before and the soil was still rather muddy. Thorsten was inclined to be charitable about the matter even if one of the wheels hadn't broken as a result. The carriage was now effectively ruined.

The lieutenant was not so inclined.

"You—you—you—"

Lieutenant Colonel Jeff Higgins, on the other hand, was in a fairly good mood. A bit to his surprise—certainly to his pleasure—his new adjutant Manfred Blecher was proving to be every bit as competent as Eric Krenz, who'd formerly held the post.

Not as much fun, true—not nearly as much fun, being honest. Blecher wasn't exactly a dour fellow but no one would ever mistake him for the life of the party. But Jeff would gladly settle for competence. He was by now accustomed to running an entire regiment, but it was still a task that was made much easier by having an energetic and intelligent staff, even if it was only a staff of three people: Blecher, who served as what the navy would call an executive officer, and Rudi Bayer and Ulrich Leitner. They were, respectively, in charge of personnel and logistics.

The weather was nice, too. There weren't but a few clouds in the sky and almost no wind. That probably meant there wouldn't be any rain today, which would give the soil a chance to dry out from the rains of the past week. Thankfully, those hadn't been particularly heavy.

Jeff could remember a time—a bit vaguely now, almost five years after the Ring of Fire—when he'd had accurate weather forecasts readily available on what amounted to a moment's notice. But he didn't really think much about that, any more. The seventeenth century was what it was, and all things considered he wasn't a bit sorry to be in the here and now. His wife Gretchen was enough to make up for everything he'd left behind—and then some.

He would admit to occasionally missing Ben and Jerry's ice cream. They did have ice cream now, true. But it was a long way short of Cherry Garcia.

Best of all, on this first day of what was shaping up to be a fairly brutal campaign—nobody took Bavarian armies lightly in the here and now—Jeff finally had a cavalry force he had a lot of confidence in.

Cavalry had always been the biggest weakness of the new USE Army, and of the Third Division in particular. A very high percentage of cavalrymen came from the nobility and most noblemen weren't any too fond of the new political dispensation. Not in general—and certainly not when it came to the person of Mike Stearns, whom they blamed more than anyone.

So, they'd had to make do with what they could scrape up. But here again, as with the beefed-up flying artillery, Stearns' stature with Gustav II Adolf since the Saxon and Polish campaigns the year before and the Battle of Ostra in February had paid dividends. He'd been able to persuade the emperor to free up some of the cavalry assigned to Torstensson's two divisions at Poznań and send them to join the Third Division in the Bavarian campaign.

Jeff would have been glad to get any experienced cavalry force. But to put the cherry on the cake, the emperor had sent them Alex Mackay and his unit of Scots horsemen. After Mackay had recovered from the wound he'd gotten in Scotland from would-be assassins, he'd rejoined the Swedish army and participated in the invasion of Poland the year before.

Now, he and his men had swapped uniforms and were part of the USE army's Third Division. They were out there patroling ahead, making sure there weren't any Bavarians lurking about intending to commit mischief. Jeff figured they'd all be able to sleep easy for a few nights.

Not many, of course. War was what it was also.

Chapter 2

Ingolstadt, Upper Palatinate

"And there they are," murmured Major Tom Simpson. He lowered his binoculars and leaned back from the gondola railing. Above his head, the great swollen envelope of the *Pelican* blocked out the sun.

"All four of them?" asked his aide, Captain Bruno von Eichelberg. He was still leaning over the rail, peering down at Ingolstadt. Peering toward Ingolstadt, it might be better to say. They were at least a mile away from the city walls and only a thousand feet or so high.

"Yup, all four," replied Tom. "They've got them positioned just the way I would, too. One facing each way on the river and the other two facing north."

Von Eichelberg grunted. "Don't see much point to the two facing north. Unless they've got much better carriages than I can imagine them building in the past three months, they can't swivel them much. Those guns were designed to sink ships and destroy fortifications, not fire on cavalry and infantry."

"True enough—although God help any poor bastards that do come into the line of fire. Those are ten-inch rifles. Load 'em with canister or grapeshot and they'll cut down anyone in front of them."

Von Eichelberg curled his lip. "And if General Schmidt has recently lost his mind—which didn't seem to be the case the last time we spoke to him, two days ago—he'll march his soldiers right into that line of fire. But assuming he's still the same canny bastard I seem to recall, he'll stay well away from those guns. So I still don't see the point."

Tom made a little shrugging motion. "Where else are the Bavarians going to position them, Bruno? They don't need more than one gun facing up and down the Danube. I grant you there's only a limited value to where they have the other two placed, but the only alternative is to not use them at all."

Von Eichelberg leaned back from the railing also. "Should we go closer? To see what else we might be able to."

The young pilot of the *Pelican,* Stefano Franchetti, got a worried look on his face. "Ah . . . Major Simpson, by now the Bavarians almost certainly have some sort of antiairship guns—or, well, something—in position."

Tom scratched at his beard. Like most American men since the Ring of Fire, he'd abandoned the effort to remain clean-shaven and adopted the almost universal down-time custom of men maintaining facial hair. He wasn't all that partial to beards, actually—and neither was his wife Rita. But he was even less partial to shaving regularly under seventeenth-century conditions, that being the only practical alternative almost anywhere outside of Grantville or the few other places with a reliable supply of electricity. The safety razors that had come through the Ring of Fire were long gone by now, and while most electrical razors were still functioning, they were useless for a soldier on campaign.

There were now safety razors being made down-time by several companies, the best known of which was Burmashave. Of course, they were much more expensive than the ones that had been made up-time, but the price had come down far enough that they weren't luxury items any more. Their use was still not widespread, however. Simply having safety razors wasn't enough to make daily shaving a common practice, because there were so many other obstacles.

Up-time, everyone had had easy and effectively instant access to hot running water. Down-time, they didn't—even in big cities, much less on military campaign. There was no premade shaving cream, no convenient cans of shaving foam or gel. You had to do it the old fashioned way with a shaving brush and soap. It could be done and some people did it. But most men didn't think it was worth the time and trouble.

Besides, there was one definite advantage to being able to

fiddle with a beard. It gave a man time to think. Cleanliness might or might not be next to godliness—Tom's Episcopalian upbringing made him skeptical of simplistic Methodist saws—but he was quite sure that being clean-shaven was next to being a dumb-ass. How much silly trouble had men gotten into up-time because they hadn't paused to scratch at their beards before saying something stupid?

Or, worse, doing something stupid. Witness the proverbial last words of the redneck: *Hey, guys, watch this!*

Ascribed to rednecks, anyway. Tom had known plenty of upstanding blue-blood wealthy young fellows back up-time who'd done things every bit as stupid as tease alligators or conduct drag races down city streets.

Still...

"Take us a little closer, Stefano."

"But, Major—"

Tom raised a big hand in a calming gesture. "Relax. I don't intend to fly over the city, I just want to get a better look."

He saw no reason to add that what he specifically wanted to get a better look at was precisely the thing Stefano was afraid of—whatever antiaircraft measures the Bavarians might have put in place since they seized Ingolstadt in January.

Antiairship, rather. In the here and now, no one had yet come up with any effective way to shoot down airplanes unless the pilot did something reckless. The one and only instance in which ground fire had brought down an airplane was the killing of Hans Richter in the battle at Wismar during the Baltic War.

Hans had become a national hero as a result of that action— due in large part to Mike Stearns' propaganda. But the truth was, Hans had screwed the pooch. He'd let his anger override his judgment in that battle. Even then, the shot that took him down was something of a "golden BB."

Shooting down airships—or at least damaging them, or their crews—might be more feasible, though. The speed of airplanes, even the primitive ones being built in this era, was at least an order of magnitude greater than that of airships. As much as two orders of magnitude, for an airship moving slowly enough to be a good bombing platform, which meant no more than one or two miles per hour—just enough to keep steady in the wind. The *Pelican* and her two sister ships, the *Petrel* and the *Albatross*, had delivered a terrible blow to a Bavarian cavalry force when they dropped incendiary bombs on them. But they'd been completely stationary above the village where the cavalrymen were bivouacked and their victims had either been asleep or drunk—or both, most of them.

It remained to be seen what sober and alert defenders could do, especially now that they'd had three months to develop something. Ingolstadt was one of the centers of weapons-making in central Europe, so they would have had the resources to do so.

"Fire!" ordered Major von Eckersdörfer. A moment later, the first rocket in the barrage hissed its way into the sky. Within two or three seconds, eight others had followed suit. The tenth and last rocket in the planned barrage was a misfire.

And, as such, a source of considerable apprehension to the artillerymen handling the rockets. Most likely, the fuse had simply sputtered out and could be replaced. But there'd been one apparent misfire which had ignited just as an artilleryman had come up to it, taking most of the man's face off along with his jaw. Perhaps thankfully, he'd died of the injuries within a day. Another rocket had exploded as the fuse was being withdrawn, killing another man instantly.

The standard procedure now with misfires was to wait a while, then toss a bucket of water over it—from as great a distance as possible—and wait a while longer before doing anything further. That "further" consisted of shoving it over an embankment with a long pole and waiting at least an hour before approaching the rocket.

And then…hope for the best.

Watching from a distance, Captain Johann Heinrich von Haslang thanked providence—again—that he was not assigned to the rocket unit. He was in command of a different sort of anti-airship effort, which was based on much more reliable weaponry.

He watched as the flight of rockets headed toward the still-distant airship. He thought von Eckersdörfer had given the order to fire too soon—much too soon, in fact. The rockets were of the new "Hale" design, copied from an American encyclopedia. The rockets were given a rotary motion in flight by the use of canted exhausts and small fins, which greatly improved their accuracy from the simple "Congreve" design.

But they still weren't that accurate and the airship was at the very limit of their range. Von Haslang wasn't surprised to see one, then two, then five rockets veer aside and explode harm-lessly in mid-air. Only the ninth rocket came anywhere close to the airship—and that was only "close" in relative terms. When its timed fuse set off the warhead it was much too far from the enemy craft to do any possible damage.

"They're shooting at us, Major Simpson," said Stefano, doing his best to control his anxiety and not succeeding particularly well.

Tom refrained from the obvious response: *I am not blind, thank you.* That would just hurt the youngster's feelings. Push came to shove, Franchetti was a civilian, not a soldier. He'd vol-unteered for this mission—more likely, been volunteered by his employer, Estuban Miro—and had been reasonably cooperative. But he didn't have much experience coming under enemy fire, so he had no good way to gauge how great the risk might be.

"Stop fretting, Stefano," said Bruno von Eichelberg. "They fired much too soon."

He pointed at the small smoke clouds left by the exploding rockets, which were rapidly being eddied away by the winds. "The nearest explosion—that one, see it?—is at least a quarter of a mile away and a hundred yards below us. Those warheads can't weigh more than a few pounds. One of them would have to explode within twenty yards of us—no, more like ten yards—before it could do much damage."

"It'd have to hit us here in the gondola, too," Tom added. "This is a hot air vessel, not hydrogen. There's nothing that even incendiaries could blow up."

At that, Franchetti visibly relaxed. He might not be familiar with enemy fire, but he did know airships. Unless an explosion tore a great rent in the envelope above them—which was not very likely—they wouldn't lose altitude quickly. Just punching a bunch of holes in the fabric wouldn't do much at all.

And while the gondola they were riding in wasn't armored, as such, it was still pretty tough. A big wicker basket, basically. A cannon ball striking it head on would probably punch through, as would an up-time rifle bullet fired from a heavy caliber gun. Or, even if it didn't, the impact would probably send splinters flying everywhere, which might cause even worse casualties if not structural damage. But a round musket ball probably wouldn't penetrate, unless it was fired at close range.

There was no real chance that shrapnel could penetrate. The biggest danger would be from an explosion that sent shrapnel over the rim of the gondola and struck the crew directly. But that would take a very lucky shot indeed.

Another rocket volley came their way—defining "their way" very loosely—but Tom ignored it. He'd just spotted an odd-looking portion of the city's walls and was now studying it through his binoculars.

"I will be good God—Gnu damned," he said, remembering at the last instant to modify his unthinking blasphemy. People in the seventeenth century didn't hesitate to swear like the proverbial trooper, but they avoided blasphemy.

"What is it, Major?" asked von Eichelberg.

"I do believe some Bavarian fellow has been using his noggin."

"And a 'noggin' would be..."

"Sorry. American slang. It means using his head. Thinking."

He leaned back from the railing and offered the binoculars to von Eichelberg, then pointed at something on the walls below.

"Look at that bastion," he said. "At least, I'll call it a bastion for lack of a better term. It's new. It wasn't there when we held Ingolstadt."

Von Eichelberg spent a couple of minutes studying the structure in question through the binoculars.

"It looks like...some sort of pit? But what for?"

"You see the radial design?" Tom replied. "What looks like a bunch of rails leading up to those shrouded...whatever-they-ares at the top of the pit?"

"Yes," said Bruno. He lowered the binoculars and frowned.

"I think those are gun carriages," said Tom. "Slanted up at something like thirty degrees and covering at least one-sixth of the visible sky. And the shrouds would be covering the guns themselves. I'm willing to bet that if we got closer you'd see them stripping those shrouds—they're probably canvas—right off."

Von Eichelberg issued a grunt. The sound combined surprise with something close to admiration. "Shrewd!"

Tom shrugged. "Maybe. Then again, maybe not. I'm willing to bet that design's brand new and never been tested."

His subordinate grinned. "Well, then. What better time than now?"

Franchetti was looking alarmed again—very alarmed.

"Major Simpson, what are you thinking?"

Tom pointed down to the bastion. Down—and away. They were still the better part of a mile from the city walls.

"Head toward it, Stefano. I want to see what happens."

"But—but—"

Tom clapped his hand on the young man's shoulder. "Re-*lax*, will you? Whatever that emplacement is, it's got to be some sort of prototype. That's a fancy up-time word that means 'wild-ass idea that nobody's tried out yet.' Almost no prototype ever made worked the way it was supposed to the first time out."

Little Boy and Fat Man did, he thought to himself. But he saw no reason to worry the youngster with hypotheticals. Besides, Oppenheimer and his team had spent a lot longer—not to mention a lot more money—developing the first atomic bombs than whatever Bavarian bright boys down there could have spent developing whatever this thingamajig was.

Franchetti's expression made it clear he still had his doubts, but he steered the blimp in the direction Tom had indicated. He had the four lawnmower engines going full blast now, to give the vessel maximum speed. The things were unmuffled and made an incredible racket. Anyone who wanted to say anything now would have to shout—and do it almost in someone's ear.

"How soon should we fire, Captain?" asked one of the gunners. "And shouldn't we start taking off the covers?"

Von Haslang didn't reply immediately. He was too intent on studying the oncoming airship.

"Captain?" the gunner repeated.

Von Haslang shook his head. "They're still much too far away. And leave the covers on. Once we take them off, they'll know exactly what they're facing and they'll turn aside."

He didn't add what he could have, which was that the airship wouldn't be able to turn away quickly. He'd spent quite a bit of time studying the enemy vessels in the course of the four day pursuit of the USE artillery unit that had escaped from Ingolstadt three months earlier. True, he'd never gotten a close look at any of them, but he hadn't needed to in order to determine that the airships had one great weakness. They were unwieldy. In that respect, nothing at all like the much smaller but also much faster enemy airplanes.

Those famous airplanes weren't really much of a threat as weapons, though, certainly not to land forces. They simply couldn't carry enough in the way of explosives. Their real utility in time of war was that they provided superb reconnaissance except in bad weather.

The airships, on the other hand, did have a significant capability to drop bombs. But...they were slow. Faster than infantry, certainly, and even faster than cavalry except when heading directly into a wind. But they could not change direction quickly at all. Even a man on foot below an airship could easily outmaneuver the thing.

Hence, the design of what von Haslang and the other officers and artificers who'd developed it called "the hedgehog." It was somewhat akin to a stationary and very big volley gun or organ gun. They had two inch guns on rails slanted about thirty degrees into the air and a few degrees apart from each other. The guns fired explosive shells with timed fuses. Once an airship came within range one of them would begin to fire, and if the vessel veered aside it would come into the line of sight of the adjoining guns.

Once fired, the recoil would send the gun sliding down the rail into the pit, but it would be arrested in time by pulleys and counter-weights and brakes. It could then be reloaded and hoisted back up.

Not quickly, of course. But the airships weren't that quick either.

That was the theory, at any rate. No one had any idea yet if the hedgehogs would work. They'd built two of them, so far.

"Steady," von Haslang said. "Steady...Still too soon..."

But his plans were overthrown.

"*What are you waiting for?*" demanded a voice from behind him.

Von Haslang's jaws tightened. He didn't have to look to recognize the voice of the garrison's commander, General Timon von Lintelo. Who was, in von Haslang's now-well-considered opinion, an incompetent over-bearing ass—but also, sadly, highly regarded by Duke Maximilian of Bavaria.

"Answer me, von Haslang! Why haven't you fired yet?"

Now turning, von Haslang saw that the general wasn't even going to wait for a reply. Von Lintelo was already gesturing fiercely at the crew of the gun which was—or would have been in a couple of minutes, rather—in line of sight of the airship.

"Shoot at them!" he shouted. "Quickly, before they pass us by!"

The gun crew stripped the canvas covering from the gun. Seeing that, the other gun crews did likewise.

"Shoot! Shoot! They'll get away!"

It was utterly exasperating. The USE airship was still well out of range. It wasn't even in proper line of sight, although it had gotten close.

The gun fired. The recoil sent it racing down the rails toward the bottom of the pit. Before it could reach the bottom, however, the restraining apparatus brought it to a stop.

That much, at least, had gone according to plan.

The shell's warhead exploded at just about the proper time also.

Somewhere between two and three hundred yards short of the target.

The airship began to veer aside. Slowly, slowly.

Compounding his folly, von Lintelo ordered the next three guns to fire as the airship moved into line with them. None of those shots came within three hundred yards of the enemy when the warheads exploded—the last two, not within four hundred yards.

The general shook a finger under von Haslang's nose. "If you'd been more alert, we might have had them!" The statement was ridiculous and on some level even von Lintelo had to know that. But among the general's many unpleasant traits was his invariant habit of blaming his subordinates for his own errors.

All they'd accomplished was to give the enemy advance warning of what lay in store for them.

"Interesting," said Tom.

Captain von Eichelberg was less impressed. "It seems quite ungainly."

"Oh, yeah—but then, so are we. And unlike the rockets, those shells went where they were fired."

He went back to beard-scratching. "It's more like a mine field than a weapon system. As long as you know where it is, you can stay away from it. But I could see where it might make a decent area defense system."

"I only saw one other pit like that," said von Eichelberg.

"Me, too. But I wonder how many there'll be at Munich, by the time we get there?"

Chapter 3

Magdeburg, capital of the United States of Europe

The large room in Rebecca Abrabanel's town house in Magdeburg—she much preferred that term to "mansion"—was fuller than she'd ever seen it, even at the height of the recent crisis that was often described as a semi-civil war. The room had been designed as a salon, but over the past six months it had wound up being pressed into service as the unofficial meeting place of the top leadership of the Fourth of July Party—the members of Ed Piazza's "shadow cabinet" along with whatever FoJP provincial leaders happened to be in the capital. At least one or two prominent Committee of Correspondence figures usually attended also, including Gunther Achterhof, the central figure in Magdeburg's CoC.

Every seat at the large conference table in the center was occupied except the one reserved for her at the south end. There were also people standing against all the walls except the eastern one, which had a row of windows. The windows didn't provide much of a view, since the town house was located toward the northern end of the Aldstadt, away from the river. But Rebecca still enjoyed the daylight the windows provided.

The edifice hadn't been chosen for the view, in any event. It had been chosen for much more cold-blooded reasons. The big building would be easy to defend against possible attack. Given the disastrous outcome of Oxenstierna's attempted *coup d'etat*, such an assault in the middle of the capital was now extremely unlikely. But, happily, the sunlight flooding the room remained.

19

"I apologize for my tardiness," she said, after entering the room and closing the door behind her.

"Pressing matters of state, no doubt!" said Constantin Able-idinger, grinning. As always, his voice bore a fair resemblance to a fog horn.

"Insofar as the term is defined by a three-and-a-half-year-old girl incensed by her brother's encroachment on what she considers her rightful territory, yes." Rebecca took her seat and folded her hands together on the table. "I am pleased to report that I was able to forestall the outbreak of actual hostilities."

That was good for a laugh around the table, echoed by the standing-room-only participants.

"Why was this meeting called on such short notice?" asked one of the men standing against the wall facing Rebecca. That was Anselm Keller, an MP from the Province of the Main. His tone wasn't hostile, just brusque, as was the nature of the man.

Ed Piazza, seated about midway down the table and facing the windows, provided the answer. "Wilhelm Wettin has just called for elections to be held toward the end of July. They will begin on Friday the eighteenth and conclude on Sunday the twenty-seventh. Ten days in all."

"It should be two weeks," complained another man standing against a wall. This was the wall to Rebecca's left, right next to the door she'd come in. The speaker was Werner von Dalberg, the central leader of the Fourth of July Party in the Oberpfalz—or Upper Palatinate, as it was also called. He held no position in government but that was, hopefully, about to change. Von Dalberg would be the FoJ Party's candidate for governor of the province.

Like the State of Thuringia-Franconia and Magdeburg Province, the Oberpfalz now had a republican structure. Those three were, so far, the only provinces of the United States of Europe of which that was true. All the other provinces had one or another type of hereditary executive or were still under direct imperial administration.

The Oberpfalz had also been under direct imperial administration until very recently. As part of the informal negotiations between Gustav II Adolf and Michael Stearns after the end of what was now being called either the Dresden Crisis or—by the Committees of Correspondence—the Oxenstierna Plot, the emperor had agreed to relinquish imperial administration of the Oberpfalz and accept a republican structure for the province.

Stearns had no formal standing in those negotiations. Technically speaking, he was just one of the divisional commanders in the USE army and subordinate to General Lennart Torstensson, not someone who had any business negotiating much of anything with the USE's head of state.

But formalities were one thing, realities another. After the emperor's months-long incapacitation and Stearns' defeat of the Swedish general Banér at the Battle of Ostra, which had effectively ended the Dresden Crisis, there was no way Gustav Adolf could have reestablished his authority without making a wide-ranging series of agreements with Stearns—and doing so quite openly and visibly. If the emperor didn't cut a deal with Stearns he knew he'd eventually wind up having to negotiate with the Committees of Correspondence, which he'd much rather avoid altogether.

The emperor's decision to give the Upper Palatinate a republican structure would probably cause trouble for him in the future with sections of the nobility, who were not pleased by the decision, to put it mildly. The "Upper" part of the Upper Palatinate referred to the fact that it had been traditionally part of the Palatinate, just separated geographically. The Palatinate as a whole had been ruled by Frederick V, the elector Palatine— the very same man who accepted the Bohemian offer to make him their king and thereby triggered off the Thirty Years War.

Having been driven out of Bohemia by the Austrians after the Battle of the White Mountain in 1620, Frederick—now often known as "the Winter King"—soon lost the Palatinate as well when it was conquered by Spanish forces under the command of Tilly. He spent the last ten years of his life in exile in the Netherlands, trying without success to get his lands restored.

In the universe the Americans came from, Frederick V would die of disease—something diagnosed as "a pestilential fever"—on November 29, 1632. In one of the many ironies produced by the Ring of Fire, he would die in his new universe at almost exactly the same time, on December 5, 1632. Again, the cause was disease, but the diagnosis was less imprecise. He slipped on the ice one morning and broke his collarbone. In and of itself the injury was not at all life-threatening, but he made the mistake of taking the medical advice of his doctor. This Dutch worthy was aware of the new medical theories coming out of Grantville but was a stout fellow who'd have no truck with such nonsense. So he prescribed bed rest—nonstop, and weeks of it. Soon enough, the Winter King contracted pneumonia and died.

His passing left the inheritance of his lands something of a mess. His widow, Elizabeth Stuart, was the sister of King Charles of England. She could not rule in her own right but only as regent for their children. The oldest son, Frederick Henry, had died in a boating accident in 1629. In the Americans' universe the second son, Karl Ludwig, would eventually be restored as the elector Palatine by the terms of the Treaty of Westphalia in 1648 that finally ended the Thirty Years War—but only the Lower Palatinate. The Oberpfalz, the Upper Palatinate, would remain in the hands of the Bavarians.

In the new universe, however, even that partial restoration seemed unlikely because Karl Ludwig had converted to Catholicism in the course of his exile at the court of King Fernando of the reunited Netherlands. The Palatinate was now a Calvinist region and that seemed to preclude any possibility that Karl Ludwig could ever regain the territory—barring, at least, some now-highly-unlikely conquest of the area by a Catholic power.

The next two oldest sons, Rupert and Moritz, were both teenagers and seemed more interested in the affairs of their mother's homeland than those of the Palatinate. In the universe the Americans came from, the older of the two would gain much fame as "Prince Rupert of the Rhine," the royalist partisan who figured so prominently in the English Civil War. In this universe the young man had come under the influence of the exiled Thomas Wentworth and was more inclined toward the parliamentary side in the coming conflict. In any event, he seemed to have no interest at all in regaining his ancestral lands in the Germanies.

The other teenager was a girl and therefore wasn't in line of succession. The Palatinate wasn't governed by the Salic law of France and some other principalities. There were any number of female rulers in the Germanies. The neighboring realm of Hesse-Kassel, for instance, was currently ruled by Amalie Elisabeth, the widow of Landgrave Wilhelm V, serving as regent for her oldest son. Each dynasty had its own rules when it came to the line of succession—what were called "house laws"—and those of the Palatinate excluded females.

It probably wouldn't have mattered anyway. Even if she had been eligible to rule, Elisabeth wouldn't be interested. Her life had also been changed by the Ring of Fire—in her case, by the influence of the American nurse in Amsterdam, Anne Jefferson. Elisabeth had developed a passionate interest in medicine. Her ambition was to become a doctor following up-time principles, not to get involved in the wrangles of royalty and aristocracy, which she now viewed as hopelessly medieval.

That left the youngest sons who'd survived infancy: Edward, Philip Frederick, and Gustav. But the oldest of them, Edward, was only ten. It would be some years before he was in any position to advance his claim to the Palatinate, assuming he chose to do so at all.

And in the meantime, Emperor Gustav II Adolf had Committees of Correspondence aroused by his former chancellor Axel Oxenstierna's attempted counter-revolution to deal with—not to mention the so-called "Prince of Germany," Mike Stearns, who'd just won a decisive victory over a Swedish army outside of Dresden. The emperor had come to the conclusion that a peace settlement in the hand was worth two future crises in a bush, and granted the now-very-popular demand of the Upper Palatinate's population to get rid of the be-damned electors altogether and replace them with a republic.

"Two weeks," von Dalberg repeated. "The elections should be held over two weeks, not ten days. They should run till the end of the month."

Piazza shrugged. "I don't disagree, Werner. But is it really something worth fighting with Wettin over?"

"Not in the least," chimed in Ableidinger, "I think a shorter election period actually works to our advantage. We're a lot better organized than our opponents."

A woman seated next to Piazza spoke up. "Speaking of which, does anyone know yet what our opposition is going to consist of? Are the Crown Loyalists still a single party or are they going to splinter?"

The questions came from Helene Gundelfinger. Officially, she was the vice-president of the State of Thuringia-Franconia, the most populous province in the USE. In practice, she'd been functioning for months as the actual president since Ed Piazza had moved to Magdeburg—although again, not officially. He still maintained his legal residence in Bamberg, the capital of the SoTF.

Piazza and Rebecca exchanged glances. Depending on the issue involved, one or the other of them usually had better intelligence on issues of this nature than any of the other leaders of the party.

"Judging from my recent correspondence with Amalie Elisabeth," said Rebecca, "I think what she is aiming for is to break away—or force the reactionaries to break away, so she can keep the name 'Crown Loyalist'—and form a new party. In all likelihood, if she succeeds in this effort Wettin will join with her. So would Duke George of Brunswick Province."

By the time she finished, Gunther Achterhof had a frown on his face. She had no trouble seeing the expression because he was seated directly across from her at the other end of the long conference table—which was actually six tables pushed together to form one very big one. And she had no trouble interpreting the expression because she knew from long experience that Achterhof was never happy to be reminded that political affairs sometimes required regular communication with—one of his favored phrases—"the exploiters and oppressors of the common classes."

On this occasion, though, he didn't make any open criticism. Gunther could be extraordinarily stubborn but he was not stupid. If nothing else, he'd lost enough quarrels with Rebecca over this issue to know that his was a hopeless cause. All the more hopeless now that Gretchen Richter had made it clear in her own correspondence to the CoC activists in Magdeburg that she herself engaged in regular discussions and negotiations with Ernst Wettin, who was simultaneously the imperial administrator of Saxony and a younger brother of the current prime minister.

"What should be our attitude on the subject?" asked another participant in the meeting, seated elsewhere at the table. That was Charlotte Kienitz, the FoJP's central leader in the province of Mecklenburg. "Or should we have one at all?"

A naïve and unsuspecting person—almost anyone, actually—would be quite taken in by Kienitz's innocent tone. The questions she asked seemed to derive from nothing more than simple curiosity.

In reality, the questions had been prearranged by Rebecca and Ed Piazza. Over time, Charlotte had become one of their closest confidants and political allies in the never-ending political disputes in the party. Compared to the Crown Loyalists, with their fierce—at times, violent—factional conflicts, the Fourth of

July Party was a veritable model of unity. Still, albeit not to the extent of the Crown Loyalists, it was a coalition of differing and sometimes competing interests. The leadership provided by Rebecca Abrabanel and Ed Piazza was generally accepted by most activists in the party—sometimes grudgingly—but that was at least in part due to their light-handed way of running things. They both preferred persuasion to strong-arm tactics. And if Rebecca had the ultimate strong arm available to her if she really needed it—that would be her husband Mike Stearns, the man who more than any other had created the United States of Europe in the first place, had served as its first prime minister, was now one of its most celebrated military figures and carried the unofficial title of the Prince of Germany—she preferred not to use it at all.

Which was just fine with Stearns himself. He had more than enough to deal with as a general in time of war, and he had complete confidence in his wife's political abilities and acumen.

Rebecca had asked Charlotte to pose those questions if the opportunity arose, because she'd just spent the past few weeks writing the chapters in her book on political affairs that addressed the issue. So, she responded immediately and easily.

"I think we should view ourselves as tacitly—not openly, since that would do more harm than good—allied with Amalie Elisabeth, when it comes to this question."

She forestalled the gathering protest she could see on several faces—Gunther's being one of them, but by no means the only one—by pressing on.

"Be realistic, everyone!" She said that in a sharper tone than she normally used. "If there is one absolute iron law in politics, which has applied, does apply, and will apply in any political system created by the human race, it is this."

She paused, briefly, for effect. "*There will always be a conservative faction*—and it will always be powerful. In fact, except in times of revolution and great upheaval, it will usually tend to be dominant."

The protests that followed were fierce but not particularly coherent, which was what Rebecca had expected. She was making a pronouncement that was bound to irritate revolutionaries—"rub them the wrong way," in the up-time idiom—who hadn't thought these matters through. She waited patiently until the voices of opposition died down a bit before speaking again.

And, again, used a harsher tone than she normally did—
much harsher, in fact. "*Grow up*, as my sometimes-blunt husband
would say."

That reminder of her closest associate brought quiet to the
room. "When I say 'conservative,' I am not referring to any particular political philosophy. I am using the term in lower case,
so to speak. I am referring to the basic attitude of most people
that unless conditions are intolerable it is usually better to err
on the side of caution."

She nodded toward Piazza. "The most conservative American
in our world—someone like Tino Nobili, for instance—"

That brought a sarcastic bark from Ed and a little titter of
laughter from a number of other people. Even among down-timers
in Magdeburg, the cranky up-time pharmacist in Grantville was
notorious. *He's to the right of Attila the Hun* was a common up-
time depiction of the man.

"Even someone like Nobili," Rebecca continued, "is more
progressive than most people—yes, even most commoners—in
the Europe of our time. He does not, for instance, object to
women being able to vote or hold office, whether electoral or
hereditary. Nor—unlike almost all apothecary guilds in the here
and now—does he have a problem with the idea of a woman
someday running his own pharmacy."

She let that sink in, for a moment. "In politics, things are
always relative. I can remember a time—so can many of you in
this room—when John Chandler Simpson seemed to be a bastion
of reaction. Today... not so much, does he? At least, I've never
heard anyone in this room suggest that he should be removed
from his position as the leading admiral of our navy. And my
husband Michael thinks quite highly of the man. Now. Not a
few years ago, however."

She shrugged and leaned back in her chair. "The essence of
conservatism is not a political philosophy of any kind. It is a
general attitude." Again, she nodded toward Ed Piazza. "His folk
have a plethora of saws expressing that attitude. So does every
folk. *If it ain't broke, don't fix it.* That's my personal favorite—
and, by the way, a piece of wisdom I subscribe to myself. *Better
the devil you know than the devil you don't.* That's another. A
third—I'm quite fond of this one also—is *be careful what you
wish for because you might get it.* And finally, of course, there is

the famous Murphy's Law, which perhaps encapsulates the heart of conservatism: *if something can go wrong, it will.*"

Piazza now chimed in. "I agree with Rebecca. The point she's making is that we will always have a strong conservative faction to deal with. Folks, I can even remember myself voting Republican up-time once in a while." Seeing the lack of comprehension on some faces, he waved his hand. "Republicans were our variety of Crown Loyalists—well, sort of—back in up-time America. The point is—"

He leaned forward to give emphasis to his next words. "Since we're going to have a conservative political party to deal with here in the USE, it's entirely in our interest to have it be one that's reasonable and responsible—and, yes, Gunther, that's quite possible. We had plenty of conservative politicians like that where I came from."

Rebecca picked up the thread. "We can deal with Amalie Elisabeth, without any threat or risk of violence. The same is true with Wettin himself, now that he's broken from the outright reactionaries. No, that's not really putting it the right way, is it? He didn't 'break' from them—they ousted him from office and placed him in prison because he objected to their treasonous behavior. And we all know from Gretchen's letters that Ernst Wettin conducted himself most honorably during Banér's siege of Dresden."

Smooth as silk, Charlotte Kienitz inserted herself back into the discussion. "So what you're saying is that we should do whatever we can to encourage a rupture between outright reactionaries and those conservatives who are following the principles which Alessandro Scaglia lays out in his recent book *Political Methods and the Laws of Nations.*"

Scaglia was a former Savoyard diplomat who'd become one of the chief advisers to King Fernando and his very shrewd wife Maria Anna, a former archduchess of Austria. In fact, the newly reunited Netherlands could be called the best current state practitioner of those principles. Rebecca had devoted two full chapters of her book to an analysis of Scaglia's theses—an analysis which was sometimes in agreement and never harshly critical.

"Yes, exactly," Rebecca said. She then bestowed a benign gaze upon the glowering face of Gunther Achterhof. "I realize that this course of action will not always be met with favor by the conservatives in our own movement. I speak of those folk who are generally set in their ways and dislike flexibility as a matter of course."

A big round of laughter erupted in the room. After a moment, Gunther allowed a crooked smile to come to his face. The man had virtues as well as faults, one of them being a good if usually acerbic sense of humor.

After the meeting ended and the gathering dissolved into pleasant conversation and chitchat, Charlotte sidled up to Rebecca.

"I notice you didn't bring up the issue of your retirement in Ed's favor," she said.

"No, Ed and I decided that we'd do better to keep it to one controversy at a time. We'll be holding another full meeting in a few days. I'll bring it up then."

They'd already agreed that Rebecca would resign from her seat in the House of Commons, thereby creating a slot for Piazza so he could run in the special by-election that would be called to choose her successor. She represented a district of the city of Magdeburg that was so overwhelmingly pro-Fourth of July Party that the Crown Loyalists hadn't even bothered to run a candidate. It was perhaps the safest seat in the entire Parliament and there was no doubt that Piazza would win the election.

Ed needed to be a member of Parliament if he were to serve as the USE's next prime minister. He could not do so as the president of the State of Thuringia-Franconia. That position placed him in the House of Lords and disqualified him from the nation's top executive position.

As for Rebecca, she would concentrate on the election campaign itself. Although the term wasn't being used, she would be what up-time Americans would have called Piazza's campaign manager.

And after the election, assuming Piazza won—which most people thought he would—there were at least two possibilities. Rebecca was by nature inclined toward working in the background. She was an organizer by temperament and had a positive dread of public speaking. So her own preference would be to serve Piazza as his chief of staff. That was a position that had not existed in her husband's administration, because Michael Stearns had a very hands-on approach to governing. But Piazza was a more traditional sort of executive, and he definitely preferred to work through a staff.

But there was another possibility, which she knew Piazza himself preferred. That was to appoint Rebecca as his secretary of state. She was quite adept at diplomacy—extraordinarily adept, in fact—as she'd proved in her past dealings with Cardinal Richelieu, Don Fernando both before and after he became the king in the Netherlands, and the prince of Orange, Fredrik Hendrik.

Such a position would give her more public exposure than she really cared for, but at least she wouldn't have to be giving a lot of public speeches. She could hope, anyway.

And there was this, too, which she had to admit. Among the many things she had learned from Michael Stearns was that the best way to negotiate was to make sure that the person you were dickering with saw a clear alternative to you—which was a lot worse than you were. Michael had been particularly adept at using Gretchen Richter and the Committees of Correspondence for that purpose.

As the USE's secretary of state, Rebecca could go him one better. *Would you rather negotiate with me or with my husband? That would be the one they call the Prince of Germany, who crushed the reactionaries in Saxony and—*

Hopefully, hopefully. Michael would sometimes lead from the front and he might get killed in the doing, which would crush her heart.

Still, soon enough, she thought she'd be able to add: *—and crushed the duke of Bavaria as well.*

Chapter 4

Regensburg, Bavaria

"I'm telling you, Tom, we've created a monster." Rita Simpson set down her cup and made a face. "What I wouldn't do for a cup of real coffee."

Across the table in their small kitchen, her husband leaned back in his chair and regarded his wife with a calm, level gaze. "I'm trying to figure out how 'we' comes into this. *I'm* not the one who took Ursula Gerisch under his wing—and I'm certainly not the one who sent her up to Grantville to discuss religion with Veleda Riddle."

He took a sip from his own cup. "I agree the coffee sucks. Which is not surprising since it's not exactly coffee to begin with."

Rita glared at him from beneath lowered brows. "It's *your* fucking church, that's why it's 'we.'"

Tom nodded. "Indeed, I am a member of the Episcopal church—but I remind you that its official name is the Protestant Episcopal Church in the United States of America. United States of *America*, please note. Not Europe. As churches in the here and now go, it's something of a waif. There were never very many Episcopalians in Grantville to begin with and my father and I only added two more to the number."

He took another sip from the cup. "Technically, my mother's a Unitarian, not an Episcopalian, although back up-time she probably spent more time at Dad's church than her own—and

30

now that's she's down-time she won't go near anything that might even vaguely resemble a Unitarian congregation on account of. Well. You know. Best case scenario, she'd wind up associated with Polish Socinians—to whom she's actually rather partial but given the current war with Poland and the fact that she's an admiral's wife it's a tricky political situation. Worst case scenario she gets burned at the stake somewhere, which happened pretty often to the founders of Unitarianism in this the not-altogether-enlightened Early Modern Era."

Rita frowned. "Really? *Unitarians* got burned at the stake? For Chrissake, they're about as milk toast as any religion gets."

"True—by the standards of the late twentieth century. But not today's." He shook his head. "History was never your strong suit, love."

"That's 'cause it's boring."

"How unfortunate for you, then, that you wound up living in a history book." That came accompanied by a big grin.

Her returning smile was sour, sour. "Very funny. What's your point?"

"Theologically speaking, Unitarianism can be traced all the way back to the apostolic age right after Jesus' death. Arius was one of the founders—depending on how you look at it—and Arianism was probably the first of the great heresies. There've been oodles of people burned at the stake ever since if they get associated with it. The burning parties are pretty ecumenical, too. So far as I know, Luther never set a torch to a pile of kindling himself with a Unitarian perched on it, but he denounced Unitarian ideas as being responsible for the rise of Islam—"

"*Huh?*"

"Oh, yeah. There's a reason—bunch of 'em, actually—that I'm not a Lutheran. But moving right along, Calvin—that would be *the* Calvin, the one they named Calvinism after—had Michael Servetus burned at the stake in Geneva back in the middle of the last century. Not to be outdone, the Catholics had him burned in effigy a short time afterward."

He drained the cup, made a face, and set it down on the table. "Stuff really is crappy. Anyway, to get back to where we started, the long and the short of it is that being an American Episcopalian these days means having to deal with the Anglican Church—and given the awkward relations the USE has with

England, that means in practice dickering with Archbishop Laud since he's now in exile and is at least willing to talk to us."

"Like I said!" Rita's tone was triumphant. "It's _your_ church."

"Formally speaking, yes. But I'm what you might call my father's brand of Episcopalian. Sophisticated, progressive—at least on social issues; you don't want to get my dad started on economics—and, most of all, relaxed on the subject of religion in general. Veleda Riddle, on the other hand—that would be the woman that _you_ told Ursula she ought to talk to—is what my mother calls a Samurai Episcopalian."

Rita frowned. "Isn't that a contradiction in terms?"

"I think so—but Veleda Riddle does not. And therein lies the source of your current unease. Because Ursula—who is _your_ protégée, I remind you, not mine—has returned from Grantville filled with the fanatical zeal of the convert."

"Who ever heard of a fanatic Episcopalian? And what would you call that, anyway? High church holy rolling?"

They heard the door to their apartment opening. They kept it unlocked because, first, the door had no lock; second, because Tom kept procrastinating about getting a workman to install one; and, finally, because the story of what had happened to the Bavarian soldiers who got slaughtered while breaking into Tom and Rita's apartment in Ingolstadt was by now very widespread. The odds that anyone would try to steal anything from them were so low that they didn't really need a lock anyway.

Julie Sims came into the kitchen, with her daughter Alexi in tow. "You wouldn't believe what Ursula's up to now," she said. Her expression was a peculiar mix of amusement and something very close to horror.

"Don't tell me," said Rita.

"Of course I'm going to tell you. It's _your_ fault in the first place."

"Toldya," said Tom.

Elsewhere in Regensburg, the same Ursula Gerisch that Tom, Rita and Julie had been discussing was creating a different sort of ruckus. This one, of what might be called a technical-military nature, not a theological one.

"Stefano doesn't like the new bomb pots. He says they're too heavy."

Bonnie Weaver squinted at Ursula, her expression one of

unalloyed suspicion. "You *can't* be that naïve, Ursula." A spiteful part of Bonnie's soul was tempted to add *given your own history* but that would just be cruel. Unfair, too. Whether the stories that Ursula had been not much better than a prostitute when Rita rescued her were true or not, it was indubitably true that since that rescue Ursula had led a life that was completely untainted by carnal excess. Religious excess, yes; whoring, no.

Ursula frowned. "What do you mean?"

"Oh, come on! What Stefano really cares about is that he wants Mary Tanner Barancek to stay on as his so-called 'copilot'—"

"She *is* capable of piloting their airship. Pretty well. I've seen her myself."

"Fine." Bonnie waved a rather plump hand. "Doesn't matter how good she is as a copilot. The Powers-That-Be have decreed that any member of an airship crew has to be able to double in every capacity. That means bomb-handlers have to be able to fly the ship, in a pinch—and pilots and copilots have to be able to heave bombs overboard. However much those bombs weigh."

Ursula looked a bit sulky. "Those new bombs *are* heavy."

Bonnie nodded. "So they are. Just shy of fifty pounds. I'd prefer lighter bombs myself. But the problem is that we've run out of the smaller jugs that we originally used. And this isn't the time and place I came from where you could just pick up the phone and order a new batch of jugs from some factory off in Philadelphia or Kansas City or wherever and have them delivered by UPS in a few days. Until we get some more of those smaller jugs, we've got no choice but to use the pots at hand. And if those pots make for incendiary bombs that are too big and heavy for a Size Four girl like Mary to handle easily, so be it. We can train someone else to be the *Pelican's* copilot."

She paused for a moment and contemplated Ursula. The German woman was somewhere in her late twenties, looked to be in pretty good health—and, unlike Mary Tanner Barancek, didn't have the usual American female obsession with her weight. She was attractive but on the heavy side, as was Bonnie herself.

(Well, on the heavy side, anyway. Bonnie didn't think she was as good-looking as Ursula, but she didn't care much because one Johann Heinrich Böcler didn't seem to.)

"How about you?" she asked. "You could be a bombardier, if you wanted to."

For a moment, Ursula got a look on her face that was almost longing. For whatever reason—perhaps because she'd been rescued by an airship—Ursula adored flying. She went up in one of the airships any chance she got and whenever an airplane passed overhead she wouldn't stop looking at it until it was out of sight.

She shook her head. "No, it wouldn't be right. If I were up in the air all the time I couldn't conduct my missionary work properly."

Bonnie tightened her lips in order to keep herself from saying something impolitic. Like, oh...*Who the hell ever heard of an Episcopalian missionary?*

But, sure enough, Ursula Gerisch was one—and surprisingly effective at it. In the short time since she'd returned from Grantville she'd already made seven or eight converts.

What was it about down-time Germans that made them so receptive to new up-time creeds? Bonnie had heard that the Mormons were growing by leaps and bounds over in Franconia, especially in and around Bamberg. Apparently, up-time Episcopalians were different enough from down-time Anglicans that nobody—at least, no Germans—thought of them as an English church.

Bonnie herself was a Baptist, formally speaking. But although she considered herself a Christian she was not deeply committed to any particular denomination or creed. If things continued to unfold well between her and Johann—familiarly known as "Heinz"—she'd probably eventually become a Lutheran. Just to keep peace in the family, so to speak. His father was a Lutheran pastor, and while Heinz himself shared Bonnie's indifference to theology, he had a strong attachment to respectability. Bonnie sometimes found that trait annoying, but most of the time she didn't. There had been aspects of West Virginia hillbilly culture that she'd never cared for at all, starting with the carousing and not-infrequent brawls at the bar located on U.S. Route 250, not all that far from the house where she'd grown up.

She giggled, for a moment.

"What's so funny?" asked Ursula.

"Oh...I just had a flash image of Heinz in the middle of a tavern brawl."

Ursula's laugh was an outright caw. "Not likely!" Smiling, she shook her head. "He is a nice man, Heinz is. Even if he won't listen to me about the true church."

✧   ✧   ✧

At that very moment, elsewhere in Regensburg, the nice man in question was feeling quite exasperated—and several times over.

First, he was exasperated because the wainwright he was negotiating with to supply the Third Division with wagons was being pointlessly stubborn. Böcler was operating within the tight budget constraints given to him by the Third Division's quartermaster, Major David Bartley. The offer he was making to Herr Fuhrmann was a take-it-or-leave-it proposition and the man knew it perfectly well.

Second, he was exasperated because once again he'd had to fend off Ursula Gerisch's continuing effort to convert him to her newly adopted Episcopal church. There was no chance at all that Heinz would abandon the Lutheran faith he'd been brought up in. Not because he was so devoted to that creed as a matter of theological conviction, but simply because it would cause undue and unneeded stress upon his relations with his family.

Which—point of exasperation Number Three—were already under some stress because somehow his father had discovered that he had formed an attachment of sorts with Bonnie Weaver and said father, being a conscientious pastor, was making a blasted nuisance of himself by peppering his son with letters inquiring as to the young woman's character, faith, demeanor, parentage, education, financial prospects—you name the issue and Pastor Böcler was sure to include it in his queries.

As if he wasn't busy enough already!

Which—fourth—brought him to the major, never-ending and ongoing source of his exasperation, which was the simplest of them all.

He didn't make enough money. Not to support a wife and family, at any rate. He knew from various remarks she'd made that Bonnie herself wasn't particularly concerned about the matter. She had the common—quite startling—American attitude on the issue, which Heinz thought was a perfect illustration of Aesop's fable about the ant and the grasshopper.

The up-timers didn't even have the excuse of not being familiar with the fable. They knew Aesop's fables quite well, as a matter of fact. Yet they would approvingly refer to the fable in one breath and in the very next make it clear that they considered the grasshopper to be the model for their own conduct.

The one time he'd tried to address the issue directly with Bonnie, her insouciant answer had been "the Lord will provide."

Baptists, they called themselves. Amazingly, it was quite a prominent creed among the Americans.

How had they managed to survive?

"Never mind," he finally told Herr Fuhrmann, having come to the end of his patience. "The wheelwright, Herr Becker, is willing to accept the terms I offered. I'm sure he won't object to the extra business of having to do a lot of wagon repair because you won't provide me with sufficient new ones."

And off he went, ignoring the protests coming from behind him.

Watching the scene through the window in a tavern across the street, David Bartley came to his decision. He'd been pondering it for days, much longer than he would have weighed a decision involving the stock market.

In the end, that disparity was the decisive factor for him. David simply couldn't transfer the dispassionate, even cold-blooded way he worked the stock market over to his commercial dealings with people in the flesh. He didn't think Johann Heinrich Böcler was particularly cold-blooded either, but what the young man exemplified was the best sort of German junior official. He was hard-working and conscientious almost to a fault. Best of all—David had never had any use for so-called "hard sell" artists—while Böcler would take "no" for an answer he'd keep looking until he found someone who'd say "yes." People didn't discourage him the way they could so often discourage Bartley himself.

In short, the perfect right-hand man for him. David could hire Heinz as his own employee and call him a sub-contractor for the army. No one would squawk since his salary wasn't coming out of the military's budget but David's own pocket.

Which was now deep, deep, deep. David took a great deal of pride in the uniform he wore and the contribution he was making to the war effort. The actual salary he got as a major he contributed to the soldiers' widows and orphans fund, since he hardly needed it himself. He'd already made a fortune in the stock market and expected to continue doing so indefinitely.

And after the war . . . If Heinz worked out as his quartermaster's assistant, he'd surely have a place for him in one or another of his civilian enterprises.

David finished his beer, paid for it, and left the tavern. By the time he got out on the street, Böcler was no longer in sight, but David wasn't concerned. He started walking in the direction Böcler had been going when last he saw him, listening for the sound of an earnest voice engaged in bargaining.

He'd find him soon enough. If Johann Heinrich's parents had been Puritans instead of Lutherans, they would have named him something like Reliable in the Eyes of the Lord Böcler. Or Prudence or Patience, if he'd been a girl.

Late that day, Bonnie Weaver dropped by Rita and Tom's apartment.

"Have you seen Heinz?" she asked. "I've been looking for him all afternoon."

Without waiting for an invitation, she pulled out a chair and sat down at the kitchen table. There was just enough room for her because Tom had left a couple of hours ago to deal with an issue involving the artillery train. He and his men would be marching out of Regensburg themselves the next day to join the campaign against the Bavarians.

Rita occupied her usual seat by the window—the very tiny window with a very distorted glass pane, which didn't do much except let in some sunlight and not much of that—and Julie was sitting across from her trying to keep Alexi from fidgeting, as thankless a task as it ever was with energetic three-year-olds.

Bonnie immediately relieved her of that burden. "Here, let her play with this," she said. She dug into her purse and came out with a top in her hand. The toy was made of wood and was larger than most up-time versions would have been. But the biggest difference was the carving—it almost looked like a work of art.

Alexi's attention was immediately riveted and her hands stretched out as if driven by instinct. She already knew how to use a top so no instruction was necessary. Five seconds later she was happily contemplating the joys and delights of the laws of motion.

"Bless you, Bonnie," said Julie. "I was at the point where I was either going to have to take her home or—or—"

"Don't say it! Strangulation is really not an option, as tempting as it might sometimes be."

"Would you like some coffee?" Rita asked. "I can make some."

Bonnie gave her a look full of doubt and suspicion. "Are we talking actual coffee?"

"Don't be ridiculous."

"Didn't think so. No, thanks." She turned toward Julie. "I'm curious, though—you've been living in Grantville ever since you got back from Scotland, Julie. What's the coffee situation back home, these days?"

"Sucky. You can get it, usually, but it's always expensive as hell and the quality's pretty unpredictable."

"Where's it coming from? Turkey?"

"Most of it's brought in by Italian merchants. I think they buy it from somewhere in the Ottoman Empire, but someone told me most of the coffee is actually grown farther south. Yemen and I think Ethiopia, too." Julie's expression darkened. "God knows what it gets cut with along the way, though. I've had some so-called 'coffee' that I don't want to think where it actually came from or what was really in it."

"How long are you planning to stay here in Regensburg?"

Julie shrugged. "As long as Alex is campaigning in Bavaria, I figure. He'll be close enough I might get to see him from time to time. When he was off in Poland it was hopeless so I just stayed home. In Grantville, I've got ready-made babysitters of the best persuasion."

Rita and Bonnie both grinned. "Grandparents," said Rita. "And—lucky you—one of them's a dentist so you don't have to worry about that either."

"The best medical care's still in Grantville, too," Julie said. "Even with Dr. Nichols living up in Magdeburg now. For a woman with a child in the Year 1636 in our plague-and-typhoid-fever-not-to-mention-diphtheria-infested brave new world, that's a load off."

"Regensburg's not too bad that way," Bonnie said, a bit defensively.

Rita nodded. "It's pretty good, actually. The sanitation practices are up to Magdeburg standards, anyway. A lot of that's the army's influence."

"Yeah, I know. That's part of the reason I decided to move down here."

Bonnie cocked her head slightly. "Did you bring your rifle?"

"Yeah, sure. I don't go much of anywhere without it. But I doubt very much if it'll ever come out of the case unless I go hunting."

The sounds of someone entering the apartment filtered into the kitchen.

"We're back here!" Rita half-shouted.

Böcler came into the room.

"There you are!" said Bonnie. "I've been looking all over for you."

Heinz had a peculiar expression on his face. "I was meeting with David Bartley. For a while. Then I decided it would be most appropriate to do this the up-time way—I asked David how it was done—and I've spent the past two hours negotiating with Herr Sommer."

"The jeweler?" asked Bonnie, frowning. "Why does the army need a jeweler?"

Heinz shook his head. "Not the army. Me." He took a slow, deep breath. "I have a new employer. Herr Bartley. The offer came with a large—very large—increase in remuneration. So..."

He looked around, leaned over, and gently nudged Alexi to the side. The girl was so intent on her spinning top that she didn't even seem to notice.

"Herr Bartley tells me one knee is correct. If he is not right, blame him, not me—but not to his face. I do not want to lose the job."

He got down on one knee, reached into a pocket of his coat and drew out an ornate little wooden box, then got a look of consternation on his face.

"I forgot to ask. I am not certain which one of us is supposed to open it."

He offered the box to Bonnie.

She stared at it. "Holy shit." Then she smiled very widely. "If that's what I think it is, Heinz, the answer's yes."

"And boy are you in a world of hurt, if it's not," said Rita, smiling widely herself.

When Bonnie opened the box, her smile widened still further. It threatened to split her face, in fact.

"I recommend leaving the 'holy shit' part out of your report to your dad, though," cautioned Rita. "I don't think that's technically blasphemy, but *still*..."

Chapter 5

Dresden, capital of Saxony

The look that Gretchen Richter was giving Eddie Junker fell short of friendly. Way short.

"The first and only time I flew in an airplane, you crashed the plane. I barely got out alive."

In point of fact, she'd been completely unharmed. The plane had landed on soil that was too wet and soft, causing it to upend. But there had been no great speed involved and when things settled down Gretchen and Eddie had simply found themselves suspended upside down in their safety harnesses.

Still, it had been . . . startling, to say the least.

Eddie scowled. "That wasn't my fault." Since his girlfriend wasn't there to take umbrage, he added: "Denise told me the airfield was suitable. Ha! If you have a quarrel, take it up with her. Besides, it's irrelevant."

He rose, went over to the open window and pointed to the southwest. "The new airfield is farther from the river and elevated a bit. Much better constructed, too, even if it hasn't been macadamized yet."

Gretchen didn't bother to get up and look herself. She knew there'd be nothing to see even if she did. The large chamber in the Residenzschloss—also called Dresden Castle—that she'd established as her headquarters had a nice view of the city and the countryside. But the castle was close to the Elbe, not to the city's walls. From that distance, the most she'd see on a very clear day was the elevated hut that passed for a "control tower"—which controlled nothing; ridiculous name—and possibly the outlines of the landing strip. But if the sky was overcast, as it was today, the airstrip would be indistinguishable from the surrounding farmlands.

"There won't be any problem taking off, unless it rained very recently. And there will be no problem at all landing at Magdeburg because that field is in excellent condition. A macadamized airstrip—*and* radio capability, so they can warn us ahead of time if there is any problem with the weather."

"And if there is?"

Eddie shrugged. "Then we fly back here. Or land somewhere the weather is clear. For Pete's sake, Gretchen, Magdeburg is only one hundred and twenty miles from here as the crow flies—and we fly the way crows do. In a straight line. We can be there in an hour. No weather patterns change that quickly."

Gretchen was distracted for a moment by Eddie's use of the expression "for Pete's sake." The American euphemism had become widely adopted because it allowed the speaker to skirt blasphemy.

But only skirt it. A number of theologians claimed that the expression was still inappropriate since the "Pete" in question was clearly a reference to Saint Peter. Whether taking the name of a saint in vain qualified as "blasphemy" could be disputed, of course, and there were other theologians who dismissed the argument on the grounds that "Pete's sake" was clearly a reference to "pity's sake" and therefore...

The distraction lightened her mood. She even smiled, being reminded of her husband. Jeff was known, when a theologian or cleric annoyed him, to refer to the present time as the *miserable seventeenth be-damned century and if the preachers don't like it they can kiss my rosy up-time ass.*

Despite being what people called a lapsed Catholic, Gretchen had quite a bit more in the way of religious faith than her husband did. But she didn't disagree with him very often on the subject of priests and parsons and their defects.

There was no point in her pining for her husband, however. He was off in Bavaria, leading one of the regiments in the Third Division. She had no idea when she'd see him again—leaving aside the possibility that it might be never, since he could get killed in the fighting. So, she forced her mind back to the issue at hand.

And then...forced herself to agree. She had a real dread of flying again, but the issue at stake was too important for her to be guided by fear.

Besides, it was the first time in her life that Gretchen had ever been summoned to an audience with an emperor. Somewhere underneath the hard revolutionary shell she'd constructed around her soul there was still a provincial printer's daughter. She could remember the excitement in her town in the Oberpfalz—she'd been nine years old at the time—when Archduchess Maria Christina once passed through.

Despite herself, she felt traces of that same excitement now— and cursed herself for it, of course.

But all that was irrelevant. For her to refuse to answer Gustav Adolf's summons—especially since it had been worded quite politely—would be a serious political mistake. And it would be almost as bad a mistake to delay her response by refusing to accept Francisco Nasi's offer to provide her with his private airplane to make the trip. If she insisted on traveling overland the journey would take days—maybe even a week or more, depending on the state of the roads.

The prospect of doing so wasn't attractive anyway. While Gretchen wasn't afraid of horses she didn't much like to ride them, either, any more than her husband did.

"Fine," she said curtly. "We'll leave tomorrow afternoon."

"We could leave today, if you wish. There's still plenty of daylight left and the weather's good."

"No. I have business to attend to before I leave."

Eddie shrugged. "Whatever you say."

"It may be a trap—a trick," said Georg Kresse. "When you get there, they will toss you into a dungeon."

Captain Eric Krenz shook his head. "I doubt if they even have a dungeon in Magdeburg. Most of the city is new, you know, built since the sack. That's true of the Royal Palace and Government House, for sure."

"So what?" demanded Kresse, scowling. He and Krenz didn't get along very well. The leader of the Vogtland rebels found the young officer's insouciance annoying.

Gretchen intervened before the dispute could escalate. "I'm not concerned about its being a trap, Georg. Gustav Adolf would have to be an idiot to do something like that, and whatever other faults he may have he's not stupid. What concerns me is simply what the purpose of this summons might be. I don't see what the emperor and I have to talk about."

Kresse immediately veered from being suspicious of the emperor to being suspicious of...Gretchen herself.

"He plans to suborn you. Turn you traitor to the cause."

Krenz barked a laugh. "What part of 'the emperor is not stupid' are you having trouble with, Georg?"

"It's not funny!"

"Yes, it is. The next thing you'll be saying—"

"Enough!" said Tata. She didn't quite shout, but given Tata that hardly mattered. She was a young woman and short to boot, but had a very forceful personality. "There's no point to this argument."

She gave the Vogtlander a fierce look. "Even if Gretchen were to be swayed to treachery by the emperor's mystical force of will—that would be in between his seizures, I guess—it would take a bit of time. By then she'll be back and can give us all a report and we can make up our minds whether your worries are well-grounded or—"

"Stupid beyond belief," Krenz muttered.

Tata glared at him. "I said 'enough'! I meant it! Don't try my patience, Eric!"

Krenz seemed suitably abashed. Gretchen doubted if he really was. More likely, he'd just decided that risking Tata's wrath wasn't worth the pleasure of baiting the Vogtland leader any further. When all was said and done, after all, Tata was the one in the room in position to expel Eric from her bed. Krenz might not view that possibility as a fate worse than death—not quite—but he'd certainly not be happy about it.

She herself didn't find Kresse's dark thoughts more than mildly exasperating. The leader of the Vogtland rebels was a capable man, but he tended to be rigid and prone to suspicion. He reminded her a lot of Gunther Achterhof—except Gunther at least had a good sense of humor. If Kresse had one, she'd never seen any evidence of it.

"Are we all agreed then?" she asked, looking around the table. "I will accede to the emperor's summons and go to Magdeburg tomorrow."

Her expression got rather sour. "By airplane. May God have mercy on my soul."

Which He might or might not, she thought. She hadn't been inside a church in years. In her defense—assuming it would carry any weight with the Creator, which it might or might not—she felt she'd been betrayed by the Catholic church she'd been raised in. The soldiers who broke into her father's print shop, murdered him and then subjected her to more than two years of torment had claimed to be defending the Catholic cause, had they not?

Gretchen wasn't an outright nonbeliever like her husband, but she'd never found another church that suited her. The Protestant denominations all seemed...drab. Reverential but joyless.

She gave everyone at the meeting plenty of time to register any further objections or raise any questions. Since there didn't seem to be any, she declared the meeting adjourned.

"I need to talk to Jozef before I go," she said to Tata after everyone had left the room. "Do you know where he might be found?"

Tata sniffed. "Wherever there's liquor available and young women whose tits are bigger than their brains."

Gretchen smiled. It was true that Jozef Wojtowicz was an incorrigible womanizer. The Pole was handsome, charming, quick-witted—rather tall and well-built, too—and never seemed to lack female companionship.

Well... "Incorrigible" was perhaps unfair. He wasn't stupid about it. He'd never once tried to seduce Gretchen, for instance, although it was obvious he found her attractive. He'd never chased after Tata, either. Unlike most womanizers Gretchen had known, Jozef—to use an American quip—generally thought with his big head, not his little one.

"Find him, would you?" As Tata started to leave, Gretchen stopped her with a hand on her shoulder. "Not you, yourself. You and I have other things we need to discuss before I leave. Get someone else to do it."

Tata sniffed again. "I have just the person."

"Why you?" Tata gave Eric Krenz a squinty look. "Two reasons. First, because you're handy. Second, because you know every tavern in Dresden, including the ones with the prettiest barmaids that Wojtowicz will be chasing after."

She held up a hand, forestalling Eric's protest. "I didn't accuse you of chasing after them yourself, did I? But don't tell me you don't notice these things because you do. I'm tolerant—I used to be a barmaid myself; it's a necessary skill in the job—but I'm not blind. Your hands may not roam but your eyes do."

Eric's open mouth...closed. "Um," he said.

"Be off," Tata commanded.

Wojtowicz arrived a little over an hour later. Krenz's guesswork had been good—he'd found Jozef in the second tavern he'd searched.

Then, of course, half an hour had been needed to negotiate with the fellow. Like all Poles of Eric's acquaintance, Jozef was inclined toward stubbornness. Happily, like all Poles of Eric's acquaintance, he was also inclined to drink. So, a pleasant if too brief time had passed in which a Pole and a Saxon commiserated on the unreasonableness of women.

"What does Richter want with me now?" wondered Wojtowicz.

"Don't know, but it's probably nothing good." Eric drained a fair portion of his beer stein. "As I recall, the last time she summoned you into her presence she talked you into leading a reckless sortie against besieging troops."

Jozef looked a bit apprehensive—but only a bit. "It can't be anything like that. We're not at war at the moment. Well...not *here,* at any rate." He waved his hand in a southwesterly direction. "Over there in Bavaria they are, but we're not involved with that."

Eric shrugged. "There'll be some unpleasant task that needs doing. There always is. It's because of Adam's fall, I think. Although I'm not sure. I'm not a theologian."

Jozef's laugh was a hearty, cheery thing. A passing barmaid gave him a second look. For probably the fourth time that evening, Eric suspected.

"'I'm not a theologian,'" Jozef mimicked. "Indeed, you are not. I, on the other hand, am an accomplished student of the holy texts so I know that it was all Eve's fault. It's *always* the woman's fault, you heathen."

After Gretchen explained her purpose, Jozef didn't find the quip amusing any longer.

Damned woman!

"I really think you're...what's the up-time expression?"

"'Spooking at shadows'?" Gretchen supplied. "You're probably right—but I still want to find out what's happening over there."

"Why me?" Jozef asked, trying not to whine openly. It was a stupid question, because the answer was obvious.

"Don't be stupid. You're a Pole. I want you to go into Polish territory and spy for us."

"And that's another thing! I am Polish, just as you say." He tried to put on his best aggrieved expression. "And now you're asking me to be a traitor—"

"Oh, stop it! I'm not asking you to sneak into King Władysław's palace in Warsaw and steal state secrets. I'm asking you to go just over the border—well, a bit farther—and see what that swine Holk is up to in Breslau, or wherever he is now. Holk's Danish, I think, or maybe German—and most of his men are Germans. So stop whining—which is phony and you know it—about your Polish pride. You know perfectly well you'll get most of your information from other Poles on account of Holk's men will have been plundering and raping and murdering them in the name of protecting them."

Jozef made a face. Heinrich Holk's reputation as the worst sort of mercenary commander was something of a byword by now in central Europe. What in God's name had King Wladyslaw been thinking, when he hired the bastard?

"All right, I'll do it," he said. A sudden thought came to him. Maybe...

"But I want a favor in return."

"What is it?"

"I want some batteries."

Gretchen frowned. "Batteries? You mean...the electricity things? That store the electrical power?"

"Yes. Those."

"What for?"

He tried to look simultaneously secretive and mysterious. "I'm not saying. It's my business."

That was fairly lame, but it was better than the alternative: *I want the batteries so I can start using my radio again and get back in touch with my uncle and employer Stanislaw Koniecpolski, the grand hetman of Poland and Lithuania and the commander of the army facing the forces of the USE at Poznań, so I can resume spying on you for him.*

Not wise.

After a moment, Gretchen shrugged. "I suppose I can spare one or two batteries."

Later that night, having finished her preparations for the trip to Magdeburg—that hadn't taken long; just packing a small valise—she mentioned Jozef's request to Tata.

"What in the world would he want batteries for?—that he'd be so close-mouthed about?"

Tata sniffed. "Wojtowicz? He probably got his hands on one of those up-time sex toys—what do they call them? Bilbos, or something like that—and figures if he can get it working again he can impress one of the town's—what do they call them? Bimbos, I think. Or dumbos."

Chapter 6

Vienna, capital of Austria-Hungary

Minnie Hugelmair was not easy to impress. Her best friend Denise thought that was simply a function of her personality, but Minnie herself ascribed it to her glass eye.

Well, not the glass eye so much as the absence of the real one. She'd lost that in the course of a riot in the streets of Jena which got started when some drunken Lutheran apprentices interpreted a song she was singing—a German rendition of *Toiling On*, which had followed *The Romish Lady*, whose verses were as stalwartly anti-Catholic as you could ask for—as advocacy for Popery and work righteousness.

Prior to that time, Minnie had been a foundling with no particular political or theological convictions. She'd been taken in by the American Benny Pierce and taught to play the fiddle and sing, something she discovered she had a real talent for and enjoyed doing. Then she lost her eye to a thrown cobblestone—she'd gotten a concussion out of that, too—and when she regained consciousness she came to several conclusions to which she'd held firmly since.

First, since Benny had adopted her in mid-riot to keep her from being arrested and hauled away to prison, she had a fierce attachment to him. And, by extension, to all his fellow Americans since she now considered herself one as well.

Second, all theology was idiocy and all theologians were idiots.

Third, theologians being invariably supported by the state, you had to keep a close watch on all public officials, who were also prone to being idiots.

Finally, having only one eye was an advantage in some respects. In particular, a one-eyed young woman was not likely to be fooled by swindlers, charlatans—theologians being prominent in that category—or any other manner of scoundrel, especially official ones. That, because all such rascals depended upon the illusions created by stereoscopic vision. Seeing everything in two dimensions allowed a young woman to see them for what they really were.

Still, there were times...

"Wow," she said, looking around the chamber she and Denise had been ushered into. "This is ours?"

Denise seemed a bit abashed herself—and she was normally about as easy to abash as a hippopotamus. "That's what Noelle said."

A few seconds of silence followed, as they continued to examine the room. Then Minnie said: "I don't think there's more than ten square inches of undecorated wall anywhere."

"Doesn't look like, does it? I've never seen this many portraits outside of a photographer's studio in Fairmont my mom dragged me into once. Except these are *painted*. I bet one or two of them are even by that guy Michael Angelo."

"Who's he?"

"Some famous Italian artist. He painted the...Pristine Chapel, I think it was. Or maybe it was the Vatican. I can't remember."

As they'd been talking, they'd been slowly circumnavigating the room—or it might be better to say, navigating it, since there weren't all that many open square inches of floor space either.

"It's like a furniture show room," Denise said, maneuvering her way around an expensive looking armchair. It was ornately carved but, from an American viewpoint, scantily upholstered.

Once they completed their investigation of the quarters they'd been assigned in the royal palace, they began examining the central item of furniture in the room.

"That *is* a bed, right?"

"I think so. I want this side," said Minnie, pointing.

"Yeah, sure." Denise and Minnie had shared a bed plenty of times and Minnie always wanted the side that let her good eye see what was coming.

There was a knock on the door.

"Come—" But the door was already opening before Denise could finish the invitation. Noelle Stull came through, looking simultaneously pleased and preoccupied.

Neither Denise nor Minnie had any trouble interpreting the peculiar combination. Noelle was pleased because for the past two days, since they'd arrived in Vienna, she'd been able to spend considerable time in the company of Janos Drugeth. She hadn't seen the man in person since...

Well, since she more-or-less tried to shoot him on the Danube but wound up shooting the river instead. She even had a tattoo placed on her butt to commemorate the occasion, depicting a death's head topped by a debonair feathered cap over crossed pistols and the logo *I Shot The Danube.*

That had been almost a year and a half ago. Since then they'd conducted their courtship by mail. Janos hadn't seen the tattoo yet but it was becoming increasingly obvious that he would before much longer.

Probably not before they got married, though. Both of them were devout Catholics and, allowing for some leeway in how one interpreted the phrase, pretty straitlaced.

The preoccupied part of her expression was due to the reason for Noelle's presence in Vienna. She hadn't come here simply or even primarily to conclude a courtship. That had been an excuse which everyone found convenient because it allowed the USE and Austria-Hungary to begin comprehensive negotiations without anyone having to formally admit it.

Which they weren't prepared to do yet because the diplomatic situation had any number of awkward aspects.

For the Austrian emperor—Ferdinand was still using that title even though he'd disavowed any intention of reconstructing the Holy Roman Empire—the awkwardness began with the fact that he was a Habsburg and his Spanish cousins were still enemies of the United States of Europe. That enmity was no formality, either. Spain and the USE had clashed militarily in the recent past and both nations expected such clashes to continue.

For the USE and Austria both, there was the still more awkward problem that the USE was allied to Bohemia and now wanted to make peace and if possible develop an alliance with Austria—which still officially characterized King Albrecht of

Bohemia as the traitor Wallenstein whose head needed to be removed as soon as possible. Not surprisingly, Wallenstein was adamant that any rapprochement between the USE and Austria had to include a settlement on the status of Bohemia that was acceptable to him.

For the moment, no ambassadors were being exchanged. Instead, a lovestruck American lady who just happened by coincidence to have the confidence of the current president of the State of Thuringia-Franconia and the probable future prime minister of the USE just happened by coincidence to be in Vienna visiting her betrothed who just happened by coincidence to be one of the Austrian ruler's closest friends and advisers.

Hence the mixed expression on Noelle's face. Pleased; preoccupied.

"So when does Count Dracula get to see the tattoo?" asked Denise.

Noelle gave her a look that would have been irritated if she hadn't been in such a good mood. "That joke stopped being funny at least a year ago. And it's particularly inappropriate since I just got back from spending a couple of hours at Janos' church talking to the priest who'd be officiating at the wedding assuming it happens which seems pretty likely given that Janos was right there with me discussing the same issue."

Minnie nodded solemnly. "That settles it, then. Janos Drugeth is not a vampire. Can't be if he was standing on consecrated ground and didn't burn right up on the spot."

Now she looked at Denise. "And I have to say I'm with Noelle on this. That joke stopped being funny *at least* a year ago."

Denise grinned. "Fine. I'll let it go. What's up, Noelle? I don't think you came here just to tell me that your squeeze turns out not to be undead after all."

Noelle pointed over her shoulder with a thumb. "They're going to be holding some sort of fancy formal feast tonight, officially in honor of some official but really for our sake."

"Oh, yuck," said Denise.

"Double yuck," agreed Minnie.

"Yeah, I know, it's not exactly your cup of tea. But you've got to show up, whether you like it or not."

"What the hell are we supposed to wear?" demanded Denise. "What I know about how to dress for a formal seventeenth fucking century formal dinner is—is—" She looked like a fish gasping out of water as she tried to think of a suitable analogy.

"If I took out my glass eye would they still make me come?" That was Minnie's contribution.

"Cut it out, both of you." Again, Noelle pointed over her shoulder with the thumb. "I know you don't know squat. That's why I'm taking you to see Sarah and Judy Wendell and the other Barbies. They set up shop in the palace an hour ago, so they can all get ready for the occasion."

Denise frowned. "Why are *they* coming?"

Minnie shook her head and gave Noelle a sad look. "Sometimes I worry about her, Noelle. Denise is usually pretty bright, but now and then..."

She looked at her friend. "They're stinking rich. What more does anybody need to get invited to a fancy whatever-they-call-this? Dinner, ball, soiree, whatever."

Noelle headed for the door. "Follow me. *Now,* Denise."

As it turned out, the Barbies—especially Judy Wendell—were a lot of help. Denise and Judy knew each other, of course. They were just about the same age and they'd gone to school together before the Ring of Fire. But they'd never been close—and that, for two reasons.

First, they belonged to different crowds. Simplifying a great deal—which, of course, was exactly the way kids in middle and high school categorized everyone—Denise was a bad girl and Judy was a good girl. Denise's father had been a biker who made his living as a welder; Judy's father had been an insurance agent. Denise could often be found sneaking a cigarette behind the girls' gym; Judy had never smoked in her life.

Secondly, the one thing they had in common had tended to keep them apart as well. They had been, by the generally held opinion of most girls and all boys, the two best-looking girls in their class. Neither Denise nor Judy cared very much about their appearance themselves. But the boys who clustered around them did, and that automatically tended to keep them at a distance from each other.

It was too bad, in a way, Denise was now realizing. Judy was a big help getting her and Minnie properly fitted out for the upcoming fancy event. Yet, much to their surprise, Judy was just about as irreverent and sarcastic about the whole business as they were. Looking back on it, Denise could now see where her impression of Judy as a stuck-up snot had probably been unfair. Up close, the girl had a pretty wicked sense of humor.

Besides, both Denise and Minnie had heard the famous story before they'd even arrived in Vienna.

"Pretty hard not to like a girl who knees an archduke in the balls when he gets fresh with her," was Minnie's way of putting it.

"Can't argue with that," said Denise.

The event itself went reasonably smoothly. Noelle was relieved to see that the Barbies—especially Judy Wendell—kept a close eye on her two sometime-wayward charges and steered them out of trouble.

Thankfully for her own peace of mind, she never overheard Judy's running commentary on the various royal, noble, and patrician attendees at the gala affair, which ranged from derisive remarks on personal foibles to explications of episodes far too scandalous for three teenage girls to even be discussing, much less analyzing in detail.

Ingolstadt

"How many are there?" General Timon von Lintelo lowered his spyglass and looked at the officer standing next to him on the wall. That was Lorenz Münch von Steinach, the colonel in command of the Bavarian cavalry units stationed in Ingolstadt. Two reconnaissance patrols had just returned after scouting the area north of the city.

"The exact number of the enemy forces isn't known, General." Münch used his chin to point to the north. "That area is too heavily wooded for the scouts to be sure they saw everything. But whatever the precise figure might be, there's no doubt at all that we'll be heavily outnumbered."

Lintelo grunted. The sound had something of a sarcastic flavor, but the general didn't give voice to it. Lintelo was partial to Münch. Had the cavalry colonel been another officer he might have received an open reprimand for not being able to provide an exact figure for the enemy's force—and never mind that such figures in the middle of a war were always at least partly a mirage.

That they were heavily outnumbered was the key point anyway. The exact ratio—three to one, four to one, possibly even five to one—was somewhat academic. When Duke Maximilian learned that General Stearns and the USE's Third Division were concentrating their forces at Regensburg, he immediately drew the conclusion that their plan was to march directly on Munich, rather than trying to recapture Ingolstadt first.

It would be a bold move, leaving an enemy fortress in his rear, but the American general had a reputation by now for being bold to the point of recklessness. So, the duke had ordered almost two-thirds of the soldiers who seized Ingolstadt in January to withdraw and rejoin the main Bavarian army just north of Munich.

Von Lintelo wasn't privy to Maximilian's plans, but he was sure the duke intended to meet Stearns somewhere in the open field rather than waiting for him to invest the Bavarian capital. Maximilian was given to boldness himself, and he'd recently hired the Italian general Ottavio Piccolomini to command the Bavarian army. Given the circumstances of that hiring, Piccolomini would have his own reasons to act decisively.

Piccolomini had distinguished himself during the recent Mantuan War—although more as a diplomat than a soldier—but his principal *bona fides* were peculiarly theoretical. Much like the French marshal Turenne, Piccolomini's rapid promotion was due primarily to what was said about him in the American history books. Apparently in that other universe he'd been a major figure in military affairs.

Hiring the commander of an entire army because of his otherworldly and future reputation bordered on folly, perhaps, but Maximilian didn't have many other choices. The duke's behavior since the treachery of the Austrian archduchess who was supposed to have married him had been savage and often not very sane. As a result, Bavaria had hemorrhaged experienced commanders. Just to name two of the most prominent, General Franz von Mercy and his immediate subordinate Colonel Johann von Werth had both abandoned Bavaria after Ingolstadt had been lost due to the treachery of its commander, Cratz von Scharffenstein. Von Werth had since gone to work for Grand Duke Bernhard in Burgundy and von Mercy had taken employment with the Austrians.

Piccolomini would be anxious to prove himself, therefore. And he would probably share Maximilian's assessment that Stearns was a lucky commander rather than a competent one. Von Lintelo shared that assessment himself. The American's luck was bound to run out soon, and where better to have that happen than on the hills and plains of northern Bavaria?

Regensburg

"This seems completely silly for such a risk," complained Stefano Franchetti.

"Look on the bright side," said Bonnie Weaver, grunting as she heaved another sack of leaflets over the rim of the gondola. She was in something of a foul mood because the only reason she'd gotten drafted into doing this grunt work was because she'd done Heinz the favor of picking up the leaflets at the printer's and then discovered that apparently she was expected to deliver it to the airfield herself.

That meant dickering with a nearby teamster company to provide her with a wagon and driver and then deciding she had to accompany the wagon to make sure the delivery was done properly—and *then* deciding she had no choice but to provide Stefano and Mary Tanner Barancek some help in loading the sacks of leaflets into the gondola because Franchetti was being sullen and Barancek was being Size Four.

"What's the bright side?" groused Stefano.

"These things only weigh about twenty-five pounds, which Mary ought to be able to handle well enough. Who knows? If the brass decides to list tonight's adventure as a combat mission—which they probably will, just to avoid having to wrangle with your boss Estuban over the surcharge—then Mary gets her qualifying run. One of three, anyway."

"Hey, she's right!" said Mary, looking cheerful. She went instantly from Struggling Size Four to Hefty Size Ten.

It took only a few minutes more, after that.

"Why so many sacks?" Mary wondered.

"From what Heinz told me, Major Simpson wants the streets of Ingolstadt paved with those leaflets. Have fun tossing them overboard." And with that, Bonnie headed off. Happily—no fool

she, and the teamster hadn't asked for much and it was a government job anyway, not like she was paying for it—the wagon
was waiting to take her back into town.

Six hundred feet above Ingolstadt

The rockets made a pretty sight, Tom thought. Between their
innate inaccuracy and the fact they'd had to aim by moonlight
obscured by clouds, none of the missiles got dangerously close
except one—and all that one did when it exploded was pepper
the bottom of the gondola with shrapnel that never penetrated.
And he'd stayed far enough away from both of the rail gun pits
that neither one of them ever opened fire at all.

He had Stefano slow down once they got over the city because
he wanted to make sure the leaflets didn't fall outside of the city
walls. There wasn't much chance of that happening, with the very
light wind that night, but Tom didn't want to take any chances.

This expedition was based on pure guesswork, as was true
of almost any psychological warfare tactic. But Tom thought his
guesswork was probably on the money, and if he was right he'd
be saving himself and something like twenty thousand soldiers
from the USE army and the SoTF National Guard a fair amount
of grief.

"Okay, that's the last one," said Mary. She was breathing
heavily and the moonlight shone off a sheen of sweat on her
face. Between her slenderness and the pace at which they'd been
working, she was close to exhaustion by now.

"All right, Stefano," said Tom. "You can go to full throttle."

Damn, those lawnmower engines made a racket.

For some odd reason, two rockets were sent after them when
they were at least half a mile beyond the city limits. Whoever
fired them was probably motivated by sheer frustration, because
there was no chance at all they could have done any damage.

"Do you think it was worth taking the risk?" asked Stefano,
when they were another five miles away and headed back toward
Regensburg. The young pilot was sounding quite cheerful now,
though. Combat bonus pay was nice, once you knew you'd gotten clear.

"We'll find out soon enough," Tom replied.

Ingolstadt

The battalion of Italian mercenaries had several men who could read German, and even two who could read English. But it hardly mattered since the contents of the leaflets were translated into Italian and Spanish also—as well as French, Polish and Dutch.

AMNESTY

ALL BAVARIAN SOLDIERS WHO SURRENDER
WILL BE GIVEN AMNESTY WHEN WE CAPTURE
INGOLSTADT EXCEPT THE TRAITORS IN THE
1ST BATTALION.

The 1st Battalion had been the one whose treachery had allowed the Bavarians to retake Ingolstadt.

"Well, fuck," said one of them, after his buddy translated it for him. He didn't read at all. At least half of the battalion was illiterate.

But, by daybreak, every single one of them knew what the leaflets said.

The first breakout took place just before noon. General von Lintelo didn't move quickly enough and make sure all of the guards at the gates were from reliable units. About thirty Italian mercenaries from the 1st Battalion got out through the west gate before control was restored. An hour later, another twenty or so overpowered the guards at another gate and got out of the city as well. Several dozen more—no exact count was ever made—got out right after them.

Thereafter, von Lintelo regained control of all the gates.

Until nightfall. Two hours past sundown, after a quick negotiation, the Swiss mercenaries guarding the west gate pocketed their bribe and led the Italians out of the gate themselves.

Maybe there'd be amnesty given to Swiss who weren't in that battalion . . . and maybe there wouldn't. Words were cheap. Every soldier in the garrison, no matter what his origin or what unit he belonged to or what language he spoke knew that by now, sixteen years after the White Mountain and five years after the sack of Magdeburg, there were no troops as hated in central Europe as those in the employ of Bavaria. They'd all heard of the enemy's battlecry: *"Magdeburg quarter!"*

And the Bavarian troops had behaved almost as badly when they took Ingolstadt as they had five years earlier in Magdeburg. If the USE army retook the city, there was most likely going to be another slaughter. Amnesty be damned. *Magdeburg quarter.*

Chapter 7

Vienna

"So what does Wallenstein want—besides keeping his head?" Ferdinand III, in that moment, reminded Janos Drugeth more of his pig-headed father than himself. His tone was sour; the expression on his face more sour still.

Janos glanced at Noelle. He was pleased to see that she was withstanding imperial disfavor without any seeming effort. Her own expression was polite, attentive—and in some indefinable way that was much too subtle to warrant taking any offense, it was also distant. So might a taxonomist study an interesting new insect to see how best it might be classified.

"Keeping his head suggests that he's also keeping his throne," she said evenly.

Ferdinand waved his hand. "Yes, yes, of course."

Janos decided it was time for him to intervene. Perhaps he'd be able to nudge the imperial foul mood in a more useful direction.

"I think it might be better if we considered what *we* might want from Wallenstein." Seeing the still-mulish look on his monarch's face, his tone roughened a bit and, for the first time since the audience began, he transgressed protocol by using the emperor's given name. He normally only did that when he and Ferdinand were alone.

"Ferdinand, the Turks are *coming*. There is no doubt about it any longer. They haven't begun the march from Belgrade yet but that's just because they're waiting for the spring grass to grow a bit more. And by all accounts of our spies, that army Sultan Murad has assembled in Belgrade is enormous. It's probably as big as the one Suleiman brought against us a century ago."

Ferdinand now looked weary rather than petulant. He wiped his face with his hand.

"Do you really think it's that big?"

Janos shrugged, the motion constrained both by the chair he was sitting in as well as his cumbersome dress uniform. "Who really knows? The number in the chronicles of Suleiman's siege ranged from one hundred and twenty thousand men to three hundred thousand. All I can say for sure is that we're somewhere in that same range today. If you press me—yes, I know you are—I'd guess at the lower end of the range. Spies almost always overestimate an enemy's numbers."

He sat up straighter and leaned forward, his hands planted on his knees. "But it doesn't matter, Ferdinand. Even if he only has one hundred thousand—even ninety or eighty thousand—we're badly outnumbered. In 1529, the Spanish emperor Charles V sent pikemen and musketeers to support us, and when the Turks attacked in 1683—would attack, did attack, however you put something that happens in another universe—the kingdom of Poland came to our aid. Today? Whether they admit it publicly or not, the Poles and the Spanish will be supporting the Turks. So will the Russians, most likely."

Ferdinand head came up. "The Russians also? Do you really think so?"

Janos waggled his hand back and forth. "Define who you mean by 'the Russians.' I don't doubt the czar would support us. But Mikhail's under what seems to be house arrest. Sheremetev holds the real power in Moscow and he favors the Poles and they'll favor the Turks. The point is, we're only going to have two possible allies in this coming war."

Ferdinand's expression went back to being mulish.

Janos threw up his hands. "Face it, will you? We need the United States of Europe—*and* we need Bohemia."

Noelle was simultaneously appalled, apprehensive—and, being honest, a bit thrilled. She'd known Janos was close to the Austrian emperor but she hadn't realized just how close that relationship really was. There were rulers in Europe—there'd certainly been rulers in Austria!—who'd have ordered Janos arrested for the way he was talking to his monarch. Some of the harsher and more intemperate of those rulers would have had him beheaded as well.

And . . . this was the fellow she intended to marry. Not simply marry, either, since it wasn't as if either of them planned to settle down for a quiet life in some out-of-the-way province, raising children and chickens. (Her mind veered aside for a moment. Did they raise chickens in Austria? She realized she wasn't sure.)

No, they planned to remain right here in the capital of Austria-Hungary, and continue to be engaged in High Matters of State. The one time she'd used that expression in front of Denise and Minnie—"High Matters of State"—their response had been immediate:

"That translates as 'chopping block' in English." That came from Denise.

Minnie's contribution was: "Yeah, but I think they let your family bury the head with your body afterward. Better than what usually happens to common criminals."

Janos turned to Noelle. "Help me out here. Explain to Ferdinand what the USE is likely to offer—and want in return."

Appalled, apprehensive—and a bit thrilled.

Prague, capital of Bohemia

"Yes, I'm comfortable here, Don Francisco. Quite comfortable—as you'd expect of a suite in Wallenstein's own palace. But it's still a prison and you know it perfectly well."

Duke Albrecht of Bavaria turned away from the window and gave Francisco Nasi a look that was more exasperated than angry. That same exasperation had been subtly indicated by his use of the name "Wallenstein" rather than the new title: "Albrecht II, King of Bohemia."

He transferred the same look to the third man in the room. "I also appreciate the amenities that you and your wife Judith provide me with, Mr. Roth. If you might someday include a key that would let me out of here at will, I'd appreciate it even more."

Morris Roth, seated on a chair not far from Nasi's, smiled but said nothing. Since there was really nothing to say in response to that remark.

Albrecht sighed and turned back to the window. With his hands clasped behind his back, he looked down at the very impressive gardens that formed the centerpiece of the palace Wallenstein had had built in the previous decade. "What am I more concerned about, however, is the fate of my two sons. Who are also being held in captivity—and in their case, Mr. Roth, by your people, not the Bohemians."

Roth cleared his throat. "Ah... Actually, Your Grace, my wife and I are now both citizens of the Kingdom of Bohemia. That's been true for some time, in fact."

"Please. I'm not taken in by that any more than Wallenstein himself is. He knows and I know and you know—Don Francisco certainly knows!—and probably every butcher and brewer in the city knows that you did that as matter of diplomatic courtesy. In the name of all that's holy, Morris"—for a moment, he lapsed into the friendly informality that usually characterized their exchanges when Roth visited—"you were born in the future. In what you yourself believe to have been a different universe altogether. You were, are still, and always will be an American, regardless of what nationality you adopt for official purposes."

Morris said nothing in response to that, either. Instead, he tried to shift the discussion back to the duke's children.

"I assure you, Albrecht, that the commitment of the United States of Europe to religious freedom is unwavering."

"Really?" The younger brother of Bavaria's ruler turned his head and gave Roth a skeptical glance. "Then perhaps you can explain why Michael Stearns—with the agreement of that party he established, the Fourth of July group—has conceded to Gustavus Adolphus' demand that every province of the USE be allowed to create an established church."

It was Morris' turn to look exasperated. "Mike did that for practical reasons—and it's irrelevant to your two boys anyway. They're being held—ah, are guests—in Bamberg. Which, I remind you, is the capital of the State of Thuringia-Franconia, a province which does *not* have an established church."

"Until the next election."

Roth made an impatient gesture. "Your Grace, please stop playing the naïf! You're an astute observer of political affairs and you know perfectly well the Fourth of July Party will be returned to office in the SoTF—probably with an even bigger majority than they enjoy right now. If you want to call your sons prisoners—or hostages, whatever term you prefer—so be it. But they are still in the care of their tutor, Johannes Vervaux—who is a Jesuit, as you well know. No one is or will be interfering in their education. No one is or will be making any attempt to coerce them into abandoning Catholicism. For Pete's sake, Albrecht! The president of the SoTF—and the likely next prime minister of the USE—is Ed Piazza. Who is a Catholic himself."

Without looking away from the window, Albrecht raised his hand in a placating gesture. "Yes, yes, I know. I am not trying to be offensive, Morris. I am simply concerned."

"Sure. They're your kids and you miss them. Frankly, if it was up to me I'd have them sent here, along with their tutor. But..."

There wasn't anything further he could really say, other than: *But Gustav Adolf is calling the shots here and he was born in this century and this universe and he doesn't have any qualms about using two kids as hostages.*

Which...wouldn't help the situation. And which was something the Bavarian nobleman knew perfectly well already.

Nasi now cleared his throat. "Albrecht, we came here today for a reason."

The duke turned away from the window again, hesitated for a moment, and then moved over to take a seat in a chair facing Nasi directly and Roth at something of an angle.

"Let me guess," he said. "You want to begin a discussion—completely tentative, with no formal or official sanction whatsoever from anyone in position of authority—on the question of whether I might be willing to agree to supplant my brother on the throne of Bavaria. Assuming you can remove him from that throne, either by force or by his agreement to abdicate."

The man who'd once been Mike Stearns' spymaster and now ran a private espionage service that was probably the best in Europe shook his head. "That assumption is a given, Albrecht. One way or another, Maximilian is going to go. If it has to be done by force..."

Nasi shrugged. Morris Roth picked up the train of thought. "If your brother's forced off the throne—whether he lives or dies, and under those circumstances I wouldn't place great odds on his survival—then Bavaria will come under the direct administration of either the USE or Sweden. That'll be something of an argument, I think. From Gustav Adolf's point of view, Bavaria is almost as much of a problem as a conquered territory as a still-independent one."

Albrecht smiled, without much humor. "Yes. Even as greedy as he is for absorbing new territory, does he really want to ingest that big a population of Catholics?"

Nasi and Roth both nodded. "Exactly," said Nasi. He nodded toward Morris. "The situation is a bit the same as always exists with us Jews. For an enlightened ruler, having some of us around is an asset. Having too many..."

"Can be a problem," his fellow Jew completed. "I think you're probably right that Gustav Adolf feels the same way about Catholics. He already has a lot of Catholics in the USE, but they're still a distinct minority—even in Thuringia-Franconia. Add in Bavaria..."

He shrugged. "Catholics would still be a minority in the nation as a whole, but they'd now have a province that was almost entirely Catholic. That wouldn't bother me or any up-timer, but the emperor's Lutheran tolerance only stretches so far."

There was silence in the room, for a few seconds. Then Albrecht said, in a voice as cold as the expression on his face: "My brother murdered my wife with his own hand and caused the murder of my oldest son. You can boil him in oil for all I care. Let us begin from there."

Chapter 8

Magdeburg, capital of the United States of Europe

This time, the plane landed with only a couple of slight bumps and came to a halt where and when and in the manner it was supposed to. Gretchen was still relieved when the plane finally came to a stop. Even the short period when it was driving across the tarmac on wheels under its own power made her nervous. For some reason, Eddie called it "taxiing" even though the exercise had no relationship Gretchen could determine with the famous postal service of Thurn and Taxis.

She hadn't liked flying the first time she did it, she hadn't liked it this time, and she didn't imagine she ever would.

That said, they had gotten from Dresden to Magdeburg in about an hour. It would have taken her several days on horseback and longer if she'd walked.

"Thank you," she said politely, after Junker helped her to the ground. "The trip was very... uneventful."

Eddie grinned. "Not pleasant, though, I take it."

She shook her head. "I don't think I will ever..." She broke off, seeing what looked like a small mob headed in their direction.

"What's this?" she wondered.

"Your greeting, I imagine."

Gretchen frowned. "Why are this many people coming to meet me?"

Eddie studied her for a moment, with a quizzical expression on his face. Then he grinned again. "I will say this, Gretchen

65

Richter. It is perhaps the most reassuring thing about you that you really don't know the answer to that question."

Her frown deepened. "That makes no sense at all."

Eddie left off any reply. By then, the lead elements in the procession had come within greeting distance and they'd sorted themselves out as a separate group from the rest. Tentatively, Gretchen classified the four coming forward as the actual delegation, while the others were simply servants or assistants of some sort.

"Frau Richter," said the worthy at the head of the column. "Welcome to Magdeburg. I am General Lars Kagg. The emperor asked me to provide you with an escort to the royal palace."

The general was wearing the sort of apparel you'd expect from a court official, not anything that resembled a military uniform. But that was no cause for surprise. The Swedes—this was true of most German rulers as well—made no sharp distinction between military and civilian posts. Officials of either sort were expected to be at the disposal of the state and prepared to assume whatever responsibilities were given them, in whatever location they were instructed to place themselves.

Kagg had a booming way of speaking, but he seemed courteous enough. Gretchen tentatively ascribed the loudness of his voice to nature rather than to any attempt on the general's part at intimidation.

Kagg turned partway around and gestured to the men just behind him. "If you would allow me to make some introductions..."

The first man he brought forward was, like Kagg himself, somewhere in early middle age.

"This is Colonel Johan Botvidsson. He's serving me at the moment as my aide-de-camp."

The name was familiar. Tata had mentioned the man to Gretchen a few times. He'd been one of the Swedish general Nils Brahe's aides when Brahe had been administering the Province of the Main. As Gretchen recalled, Tata's impression of him had been favorable.

"And this is his aide, Captain Erik Stenbock." As had the colonel before him, Captain Stenbock acknowledged her with a stiff little bow. The stiffness was simply the Swedish court style, not an indication of any particular attitude.

Stenbock was quite a bit younger than either Kagg or Bot-vidsson. He seemed to be in his early twenties.

General Kagg now gestured at the fourth man in the group. "And this is Erik Gabrielsson Emporagrius."

Kagg assigned Emporagrius no specific post, rank, title or position, which Gretchen found interesting in itself. From subtleties in the general's demeanor that she would have found it impossible to specify, she got the sense that—unlike the two military figures he'd introduced, to whom he seemed quite favorably inclined—he had no great liking for this fourth fellow.

At first glance, Gretchen had assumed Emporagrius to be close in age to Kagg and Botvidsson. But looking at him more closely she realized that was due to the severe expression on his face, a sort of facial acidity that made him seem older than he really was. She didn't think he was actually much older than thirty or so.

Emporagrius returned her gaze with an unblinking stare. He made no gesture with his head that bore even the slightest suggestion of a nod.

The introductions completed, Kagg now gestured at the gaggle of servants standing a short distance away.

"And now, Frau Richter, we have carriages ready to transport you to the palace."

There were plenty of towns in Europe where riding in a carriage was likely to result in bruises—sometimes even broken bones. In such places, people would choose to ride in litters suspended between two horses rather than risk direct contact with the ground transmitted by unforgiving wheels. Most of Magdeburg's streets were hard-packed dirt, but the main streets of the capital were superb, compared to those of any town or city in the continent except those of Grantville.

Another surprise awaited Gretchen once they arrived at the palace. The chambers that Kagg ushered her into amounted to a suite. She'd been expecting something more closely akin to a room that a servant might occupy.

Why were they doing this? Gretchen's ingrained hostility toward the aristocracy—and kings and emperors were just top shelf nobility—made her suspicious.

They were trying to soften her up! Fool her into...into...

At that point, her sense of humor came to her rescue. Yes, no doubt all these courtesies were designed for the purpose of softening her up. But she remembered Mike Stearns once making the quip: "If I was scared to death of being softened up, I'd never bathe. Is it really better to stink?"

She turned to Kagg and said: "Thank you. This is very nice. When am I supposed to talk to the emperor? And where?"

"The 'when' depends on you, Frau Richter. The emperor thought you might want to rest for a bit after the—ah—ardors of your travels."

Gretchen made a little snorting sound. "What ardors? I admit that flying makes me very nervous, but it's about as physically strenuous as sitting in a rocking chair. I am ready to meet with the emperor whenever..."

She'd been on the verge of competing the sentence with "whenever it suits His Majesty." But that seemed excessively subservient.

"Now, if he wants," she concluded.

Kagg nodded. "In that case, please follow me."

There were enough servants of various sorts in the palace that at least some of them rushed ahead to warn the emperor that she was coming. So, by the time Kagg ushered her into an even more palatial suite—this one a meeting chamber, though, not a sleeping one—Gustav Adolf was awaiting her in a chair, alertly observant as she came in.

They'd never met before, in the sense of being introduced, although on three previous occasions they'd been in the same room together. On the first of those occasions, Gustav Adolf had been standing over the corpse of the Croat cavalryman whose skull he'd split open with the sword in his hand. And the sword had been dripping blood, unnoticed by the Swedish king, onto the trouser leg of Gretchen's husband, who was lying on his back with a wound in his shoulder.

That memory brought Gretchen up short, for a moment. She'd come into the chamber braced for a fight, but now she found herself disarmed. Whatever else—whatever divided them, whatever disputes they might have—she owed this man her husband's life. And, probably, the lives of hundreds of children who'd also been in the high school that day. It was not likely that, on their own, Gretchen and Dan Frost and a busload of police cadets could have driven off the thousand or so Croats who were assaulting the school. Not without Gustav Adolf and the hundreds of cavalrymen he'd brought in time.

She cleared her throat. "Your Majesty, I do not believe I ever thanked you for saving my husband's life. That day at the school in Grantville."

The emperor's eyes widened. "I wasn't aware that I had, Frau Richter." Then, as the memory came to him, he snapped his fingers. "Yes, now I recall! You were the young lady who was clutching the fellow that Croat was about to cut down. Ha! I never realized until this moment that you and she were the—ah...the same Gretchen Richter."

Gretchen couldn't help but smile. "The notorious Gretchen Richter, you meant to say."

Gustav Adolf made a little dismissive gesture. "Notorious, yes—but notorious to whom, exactly? I am not unaware that you were the central figure in holding together the population of Amsterdam when they successfully resisted the Spanish besieging the city. Today, of course, we are on quite good terms with those same Spaniards—not allied, no, but still on good terms. But would we have had that outcome without you? Probably not, I suspect."

He seemed to sit a bit straighter. "And I am certainly not unaware that you were—no one doubts this at all, certainly not Ernst—" He nodded toward a figure sitting in another chair off to the side. Gretchen was a bit startled to see that it was Ernst Wettin. She'd been so preoccupied with the emperor that she hadn't noticed him at all.

"—the central figure in holding Dresden firm against the threat of Banér." The imperial jaw tightened. "Who followed Axel into treason."

His momentary dark mood vanished almost at once. He gestured toward a third chair, which was positioned approximately equidistant from his own and that occupied by Wettin. "But please, take a seat. We have much to discuss."

As she sat down, Gretchen glanced over her shoulder and saw that Kagg had left the room. Except for two servants standing by a doorway—not the one she'd come in but one that was too distant for the servants to overhear their conversation—the three of them were alone in the room.

So. Apparently this was to be a genuinely private and informal discussion. That had been one of the possibilities, but the one she'd least expected.

As soon as she was seated, the emperor went straight to the point.

"I have a proposal to make," he said. "Not to you alone—not by any means—but I am starting with you because if you are not willing to accept the proposal the rest will be pointless."

She braced herself. The most likely proposal she could imagine would be something on the lines of: *You, Frau Richter, must go into exile, preferably to someplace in the New World. In exchange, I will make this or that concession to your band of radical malcontents.*

"The proposal is this. I will agree to remove imperial administration from Saxony, Mecklenburg, the Oberpfalz and Württemberg. I will also allow Württemberg to form its own province separate from the rest of Swabia. And, finally, I will allow all four provinces to become self-governing with a republican structure of some sort."

For an instant, a look of exasperation came and went on his face. "One of the reasons I'm agreeing to this is to save myself the grief of trying to referee the claims of far too many Hochadel to these areas. But the main reason is to see if you and I can reach . . . what to call it? A *modus vivendi*, let us say."

Gretchen's knowledge of Latin ranged from poor to dismal. Some of her uncertainty must have shown because Ernst Wettin spoke up, for the first time. "His Majesty is using the Latin phrase the way the up-timers do. It refers to an arrangement—something of an informal agreement, if you will, but still binding—that enables parties with conflicting interests or goals to nonetheless coexist peacefully and without resort to violence on either side. This arrangement may be temporary—it usually is—but it can also last indefinitely."

Gretchen looked back at Gustav Adolf. "I see. And what would you want from me in exchange? By 'me,' of course, we're referring to the Committees of Correspondence."

"Actually, no—or at least, not entirely." The emperor leaned forward and fixed her with an intent gaze. "Much of this is specific to you. What I want in exchange—will insist upon, in fact—is that you must agree to run for election as the governor of Saxony."

Of all the things Gretchen had foreseen as possibilities, that one had never occurred to her even once.

"*Me*? *Governor*?" She almost gasped the words. "But—whatever for?"

Gustav Adolf nodded at Ernst Wettin. "I will let him explain. Since it was his proposal to begin with." He grinned and barked out a laugh. "Ha! And be sure I was just as astonished then as you are now. What a mad idea!"

He leaned back in his chair, still chuckling. "But ... one with great merit, once he explained."

Gretchen looked back at Wettin.

"It's quite simple, really. I've spent months with you in Saxony now. Me as the official administrator of the province—and you as the person who really wields the power." Wettin shook his head. "The arrangement is simply untenable, Gretchen. It must be settled—whichever way. The formal power must coincide with the real power, or government itself becomes impossible. Certainly in the long run."

"But ... but ... I have been assuming all along, Ernst, that if Saxony became a republic that you yourself would run for governor."

Ernst nodded. "And so I will. I would say 'with the emperor's permission' but he's already given it to me."

"More precisely, I insisted on it." Gustav Adolf pointed at Wettin with a large forefinger. "Make no mistake about it. Ernst Wettin has my confidence and I will certainly be urging all Saxons to vote for him instead of you."

He grinned again. "Ernst tells me, though—I find this quite shocking!—that the pigheaded and surly Saxons are likely to ignore me and vote for you instead. If you run, that is."

"And if you don't," said Wettin, now leaning forward himself, "here is what will happen. The Fourth of July Party will certainly run a candidate, but they won't garner more votes than I will. They don't have much of an organization in Saxony, as you know. I estimate we would each wind up with about thirty percent of the vote. The rest ..."

He shrugged. "The Vogtlanders will probably pick up fifteen percent or so. The reactionaries—assuming they manage to form a common front—could pick up perhaps ten percent. If they run as squabbling individuals, which is more likely, they'd wind up with less."

Gretchen's Latin might be wretched but her arithmetic was excellent. She'd had no trouble following the calculations. "That leaves fifteen to twenty percent."

"The church, I think. In one form or another."

She followed that logic also. Saxony had a solidly Lutheran population and the clergy commanded a great deal of respect. Everyone who was uncertain would tend to listen to their pastors— would seek them out for advice, in fact.

"A mess, in other words," Wettin concluded. "No one would have a majority. I'd probably have a plurality, so if we adopted an American-style governor structure—what they call the presidential system—I'd become the new executive outright. If we adopted the more common German system wherein a republican province's executive is not separate from the legislature—the parliamentary system, in the up-time lexicon—then I'd have to negotiate with others to form a cabinet."

He threw up his hands. "And wouldn't that be a delight! Assuming the Fourth of July Party is the opposition and the Vogtlanders bloc with them—which they generally would—I'd have to form a coalition with pastors and reactionaries. The first of whom tend to be impractical when it comes to world affairs and the others..."

He smiled now, albeit thinly. "There's an American quip I'm fond of—which they stole from a Frenchman, I think. 'They have learned nothing and forgotten nothing.' That summarizes perfectly, I think, the state of mind of the nation's reactionaries. What would really happen, of course, is that effective power would continue to be in your hands. It's just not workable, Gretchen. Either I rule or you rule—one or the other. Straightforward and visible to all."

Gretchen had already seen the flaw in the logic. "Then why not simply ask—insist, if you will—that I leave Saxony altogether?"

She looked away from Wettin to Gustav Adolf. "There'd be a great deal of unrest if you did, but it wouldn't rise to the level of violence. Not unless I called for it, and I'm not that stupid. That would be—"

She managed to cut herself off before saying: *would be playing into your hands.*

The emperor nodded, as if with satisfaction. "It's nice to be negotiating with someone who's not a fool. You're right, of course. You could rouse the people to rebellion against a brute like Banér, who was threatening a massacre. But against Ernst? Or even worse, against me? When all we asked was for one person to please leave the province?"

But she'd already left all that behind because she'd finally realized the true nature of the proposal.

She was quite startled. She wouldn't have thought that an emperor—first among nobles—would be that shrewd and astute.

He probably wouldn't have come up with the idea on his own, of course. But he'd been shrewd enough and astute enough to be persuaded by Ernst Wettin.

"You don't *want* me to leave Saxony," she said. "You *want* me to stay."

She gave Wettin a look that was almost accusatory. "Because you think I'd win the election."

"In a landslide, if we have a presidential system." Wettin shrugged. "More complicated, with a parliamentary one, since you'd have to run officially as a member of a party rather than as an individual. But that would just add a minor curlicue. The Fourth of July people would be delighted to have you take up their banner. But if you chose to you could simply run as the candidate of the Gretchen Richter Party."

She looked back at the emperor. And, for the first time in her life, had a sense of what a wild lion or tiger felt when they confronted a tamer.

Gustav Adolf apparently sensed her thoughts because his expression became quite sympathetic. "Don't think of it as being housebroken, Frau Richter—or may I call you Gretchen, in private?"

Mutely, she nodded.

"This is something that Michael Stearns has always understood, you know. Eventually, a revolutionary must either"—he looked at Wettin—"what's that crude but charming expression he likes?"

"Shit or get off the pot."

"Yes, that one." He turned back to Gretchen. "Once you become powerful enough—which you are, today, certainly in Saxony—then you must decide. Either try to overthrow the existing power or claim it for your own. But what you cannot do—not for long—is try to straddle those two options."

"You want me to become *respectable*." The word came out like an accusation.

She could see that Gustav Adolf was doing his best to suppress another grin. "Ah...Gretchen. I am told there exists a painting of you done by no less an artist than Rubens that hangs in the royal palace in Brussels. Apparently the king in the Netherlands, as he likes to style himself, thinks it makes a useful cautionary reminder."

She sniffed. "Yes, I've heard about that."

"And in that painting—"

"My tits are bare. Yes, I know. I remember quite well. It was a cold day and I maintained that pose for hours. What is your point?" A bit belatedly, she remembered to add: "Your Majesty."

"My point is that I think no matter how long you live you will never have to fear the horrid fate of slumping into dull and undistinguished respectability."

"I will need to think about this," she said.

The emperor nodded. "Yes, of course."

"And I will need to discuss it with other members of the Committees of Correspondence here in Magdeburg. That will include, you understand, Spartacus and Gunther Achterhof."

"Yes, of course. May I also suggest you discuss it with Rebecca Abrabanel. And Herr Piazza also, if you choose. He's resident here."

"Yes, of course," she said.

The emperor rose. "That's it, then. When may I expect an answer, Gretchen?"

She came to her feet as well. "Soon."

He smiled. "Just as I thought."

Chapter 9

Upper Bavaria, just south of the Danube

The Scots cavalryman came racing toward Jeff Higgins at a speed which he considered utterly reckless given that the horseman was galloping across an open field rather than a well-groomed racetrack. He'd ascribe the man's deranged behavior to his Celtic genes; these were the same people, after all, who saw no problem in walking through wild vegetation in kilts and thought bagpipes were an instrument of musical entertainment. But Jeff had seen plenty of German, Spanish and French cavalrymen do the same thing—and Polish hussars would do it wearing heavy armor, which made them certifiably insane.

The Scotsman arrived at Jeff's side, pulled up his horse, pointed in the direction from which he'd come and said something which Jeff interpreted—more or less—as: "The bastards are over there! Bavarian cavalry! A mile away!" Linguists would probably insist that the man was speaking a dialect of English, whereas Jeff considered it the equivalent of a foreign tongue altogether. By now, though, he'd had enough experience with Mackay's troops to be able to make some sense out of it.

"Which way are they headed?" he asked.

The Highlander understood real English much better than Jeff understood his language—his "dialect," rather. He rattled off something in reply which Jeff interpreted as *the cowardly bastards are running away from us.*

Translating that derisive remark into coherent military tactics meant that the enemy scouts were probably doing what they were supposed to do once they made contact with the enemy, which was to report back to their commanders. Just as this Highlander had done himself, no doubt ordered to do so by Alex Mackay.

Jeff turned toward one of the two men riding just behind him who served as his couriers. The man was close enough to have heard the Scotsman's words himself, but Jeff wasn't sure how well he'd have understood them. "Report to General Stearns that Colonel Mackay has encountered Bavarian cavalry. They're apparently engaged in reconnaissance since they retreated as soon as contact was made."

The man raced off—galloping his horse just about as recklessly as the Scotsman had done. And yet he seemed to all appearances to be a sober and levelheaded Westphalian. Jeff sometimes wondered if there was an unknown characteristic of horses—a parasite, perhaps, or maybe a virus—that infected people who spent too much time in close proximity and caused them to lose their minds. He determined—again—to spend as little time on horseback as he could manage.

In a civilized historical period, he'd have been able to send a report to his commanding general using a radio while seated in a natural form of transport like a Humvee—hell, he'd settle for a World War II era Jeep, for that matter. In this day and age, though, officers were expected to ride horses. And while the army did have radios at its disposal, there still weren't enough yet—or enough qualified radio operators, which was often more of a problem—to make them a widespread form of communication. Jeff's Hangman regiment did have its own radio operators, as did every regiment and artillery battery. Unfortunately, the operator Jeff regularly used, Jimmy Andersen, was somewhere a few hundred yards back—where he'd been ordered to stay so as not to risk the regiment's one and only headquarters radio. Jeff would have had to send a courier to the radio operator in order to relay the message, and if the courier had any trouble finding Jimmy—which he almost certainly would since an army of more than ten thousand men on a march through a seventeenth-century countryside on seventeenth-century so-called "roads" was anything but neat and orderly—it would take the message longer to get to General Stearns than just having the courier do the whole thing himself.

Such were the realities of "combined technology" as the basis for military operations. Sometimes it worked. More often than not, it was a muddle. Sometimes, a sorry joke.

As he did whenever he found himself sliding into what he called *early modern angst,* Jeff pulled himself out with a memory of Gretchen. In this instance—O happy remembrance—with an image of the way she'd looked the morning after they reencountered each other when the Third Division relieved the siege of Dresden. She was smiling up at him while lying in their bed wearing absolutely nothing, which—O happy coincidence—was exactly the costume he'd been wearing himself at the time.

They'd been a little reckless the night before. Gretchen was normally as disciplined as a Prussian martinet when it came to maintaining the rhythm method of so-called birth control. But... It wasn't every day, after all, that husband and wife were reunited right after escaping death and destruction, which they'd both faced the day before.

Another memory came to him now, of the way Gretchen had looked just a few weeks ago on the morning he'd left with the Third Division to march to Regensburg. Looking at him—fully clothed, this time—with a smile on her face that was perhaps a tad rueful but mostly just what Jeff thought of as *Gretchen Richter taking life as it comes.*

"I think I'm pregnant again," she'd said. "Won't be sure for a while, but I think so."

By now, she'd probably know one way or the other. But how she'd get the word to him while he was on campaign was uncertain.

Jeff could remember a time—though it was a bit vaguely, now, because it was back up-time—when the possibility that a wife might have another child would be a source of either great joy and anticipation or anxiety and doubt. Leaving aside the pack of children whom Gretchen had adopted, she and Jeff already had two kids of their own. Jeff wasn't the natural father of the older boy, Wilhelm. But he'd been an infant, less than a year old, when Jeff and Gretchen had gotten married so the issue was irrelevant. Jeff was the only father Willi had ever known.

But in this as in so many ways, the attitude of people born and raised in the seventeenth century was rather different. In an era of haphazard birth control methods and high infant mortality, people had a much more pragmatic attitude toward bearing and raising children. It could sometimes seem downright cold-blooded to up-timers.

Down-timers were less reliant on the nuclear family than up-timers were accustomed to. It was taken for granted that children would spend much of their time growing up with other relatives and even, for well-to-do people, with nursemaids, governesses and tutors. In some of the more extreme cases, parents might see very little of a child of theirs from the time it was weaned until it finished his or her education.

Jeff and Gretchen had done the same thing—which Jeff, at least, often felt guilty about. Gretchen...not so much, possibly because her bona fides as a surrogate mother were so well established.

For the whole year they'd been out of the country before and during the Baltic War, their children had been taken care of by Gretchen's grandmother Veronica. Then, after they got back and Veronica made it crystal clear that she was done with babysitting, they still had plenty of caregivers in the big apartment complex they moved into in Magdeburg.

The children were left entirely in the hands of caregivers after Jeff went off to war and Gretchen moved to Dresden. It hadn't been until the crisis was over—not more than two months ago—that she'd gone back to Magdeburg to fetch their two boys and bring them back to stay with her. The adopted children had remained behind, since they were much older and all of them by now had settled into work or education situations they didn't want to change. The only one of the original group who would have been young enough to come with her, little Johann, had been joyously reclaimed by his natural family a couple of years earlier.

From here on in, hopefully, things would settle down. Jeff and Gretchen had discussed the matter—along with a number of CoC leaders—and everyone had agreed that Gretchen would stay in Dresden rather than moving back to Magdeburg. Willi and Joe would now be raised mostly by their mother, with their father helping out whenever he wasn't on active duty.

And now, it seemed, another child might be added to the mix. Gretchen's reaction to the news hadn't been quite a relaxed shrug, but pretty close. Jeff was doing his best to take his cue from her. And...having only middling success. There was a part of his brain—he thought of it as the part labeled "raised on too many up-time anxieties and touchie-feelie TV talk shows"—that kept shrilling at him: *Bad parent! Bad parent! Your children will grow up to be drug addicts, derelicts, serial murderers and hedge fund managers!*

To Jeff's surprise, the same courier he'd sent out now came racing back. More time must have passed than he'd realized, while he was musing on things gone by and things still to come. Looking around, he saw that the regiment had indeed made a fair amount of forward progress. It was easy to lose track of exactly how far you'd gotten when you were in the middle of an army on the march.

"The general says we will continue toward Ingolstadt," said the courier.

That was the answer Jeff had expected. There'd been a meeting of the Third Division's staff and regimental commanders before the march began, where Stearns had explained that he intended to threaten to close on Ingolstadt from the east along the south bank of the Danube, while General Heinrich Schmidt and the SoTF's National Guard closed in from the north. Hopefully, the maneuver would force the Bavarians to abandon the city rather than run the risk of being encircled and trapped in a siege. Both Stearns and Schmidt thought there was a good chance of success, since Duke Maximilian had to be mostly concerned now with holding Munich.

The courier reached into his coat and pulled out a letter. It was just a small sheet of paper folded twice and sealed with a blob of wax. General Stearns must have received the letter and given to the courier to bring to Jeff.

Even before he opened it, Jeff was sure it had to be from Gretchen. No military communication would be sent in this manner.

Sure enough. The message was short and to the point.

Yes. If it's a girl, we name her Veronica. You pick a boy's name.

Above Ingolstadt

"Head for the nearest hedgehog pit, Stefano," Tom Simpson ordered, pointing down and a bit to the left. The sky was mostly overcast but there was plenty of light. Those didn't look like rain clouds; they certainly didn't indicate a storm front.

Having made two runs over Ingolstadt already, in both of which they'd been fired upon with no serious damage resulting,

Stefano was a lot more relaxed than he had been before. He still wasn't what anyone would call nerveless and steely-eyed, but he managed to keep his twitching to a minimum and he didn't fudge on the steering—he headed straight for the nearest hedgehog pit.

Which...didn't fire on them at all. It wasn't until they passed almost straight overhead that the reason became apparent: the guns were gone. The rails on which the gun carriages would have rested remained in place, and *something*—furniture? logs?—was covered with canvas. But as an active and functioning antiairship emplacement, the hedgehog had been gutted.

"It worked," Tom said, his voice full of satisfaction. "They're pulling out. Stefano, head for the bridge across the Danube."

As the airship veered to the south, Tom examined the city below them through his binoculars. In particular, he was looking to see what had happened to the four ten-inch naval rifles that he, Eddie Cantrell and Heinrich Schmidt had spent a truly miserable three months hauling across Germany a year and a half earlier. The guns had been removed from the wreck of the ironclad *Monitor* with the purpose of using them against Maximilian of Bavaria in case a siege of Munich developed. In the event, the Bavarian issue had taken a back seat to more pressing conflicts and the guns had wound up being left in Ingolstadt for later use. They'd been there when Ingolstadt was retaken by Bavaria thanks to the treachery of the 1st Battalion. Tom had been forced to leave them behind when he led the surviving loyal troops out of the city on their four-day march to Regensburg. They hadn't even had time to salvage the artillery unit's 12-pounders, much less the enormous naval guns.

But now, it seemed, they were going to get them back—or two of them, at any rate. Tom could see the two rifles that had been positioned on the north wall to face Schmidt's SoTF forces. But when he looked for the two rifles that the Bavarians had positioned to cover the Danube...

"Gone," he muttered. "I was afraid of that."

Captain von Eichelberg was standing right next to him, close enough to hear. "They can't possibly get those guns down to Munich," he said, frowning.

Tom lowered the binoculars and shook his head. "No, they wouldn't have even tried. I'm sure they spiked them and then pitched them—well, rolled them, more likely—into the river. We should be able to salvage them, but it'll take some time."

He turned to the radio operator, who was standing a few feet away. "Make contact with General Schmidt. And then I'll want to speak to General Stearns."

Then, to Stefano: "Cut the engines for a bit." The noise made by the four lawnmower engines made talking on the radio impossible, and Tom didn't want to fall back on laborious Morse code communication. One of the nice things about airships was that the wallowing beasts could just float for a while.

Tom's reports were brief and to the point, and would produce very rapid results. Now that he knew the city was undefended and the two naval rifles were no longer a factor, Schmidt would march his National Guard directly into Ingolstadt. They should have the city under control within a day or two.

Meanwhile, since his maneuver had succeeded in its purpose, Mike Stearns would redirect the Third Division to the south. There was no chance he could reach Ingolstadt in time to intercept the retreating Bavarians, so he would move to invest Munich as soon as possible.

As for Tom himself, Stearns ordered him to remain behind in Ingolstadt and get the naval rifles salvaged as soon as possible.

"They'll have spiked all four guns, General," he told Stearns. "And if they did a competent job, we'll need to machine them out."

"*Yes, I know. I'll have some machinists detached to you. There would have been plenty in Ingolstadt, but . . . not any longer.*"

The Bavarians would have either murdered them or—more likely, unless the commander was totally incompetent—taken them in captivity down to Munich. Skilled metal workers were valuable, especially in time of war.

"I should be able to get two of the guns in operational condition fairly soon," Tom said. "But the two in the river will probably take quite a bit of time."

"*I understand. Stearns out.*"

Before they even got to the bridge, Tom could see the Bavarian forces passing across to the south bank of the river. Their formations seemed pretty ragged—so ragged, in some places, that they couldn't really be called "formations" of any kind. This didn't look like an orderly retreat so much as a semi-rout. At a guess, the Bavarian commanders had tried to organize a disciplined withdrawal but had gotten overwhelmed—at least partly—by panicking soldiers.

He was guessing again, but he was fairly sure the mercenaries in the 1st Battalion had been the ones driving that panic.

"Do we bomb the bridge, sir?" asked Captain von Eichelberg.

Tom shook his head. "No, Bruno. It's tempting..."

Which it certainly was. The bridge was packed with enemy soldiers, who were barely moving because the bridge itself formed a bottleneck. As targets went, you couldn't ask for anything better.

"But what if we succeeded too well and brought down the bridge? Or damaged it enough to make it impassable? We want the Bavarians *out* of Ingolstadt, we don't want to pen them into it."

"I understand that, sir. But there's little chance these bombs we're carrying would be powerful enough to do that."

He had a point. They weren't carrying incendiaries because of the risk of starting fires in Ingolstadt. The USE and SoTF forces wanted to capture the city as intact as possible. So they were armed simply with antipersonnel ordnance—what amounted to giant grenades.

"You're probably right, Bruno, but I still don't want to risk it. Besides, the troops strung out on the road are almost as good a target."

He pointed farther to the south, to the narrow road along which most of the Bavarian soldiers were moving. "Head there, Stefano. We'll see if there are any artillery units we can target."

As Stefano complied, Tom turned to von Eichelberg and said: "I suppose we ought to come up with some more military-sounding order than 'head there.' You're the old pro. Do you have a suggestion?"

The captain squared his shoulders and looked very martial. "In the finest old professional soldier tradition, I hereby—what's that American expression—pass the back?"

Tom chuckled. "Pass the buck."

"Yes, that one. This being one of those—what do you call it?—upward technology weapons—"

"High tech."

"Close enough. I feel it is incumbent upon the up-time officer to develop the proper phraseology. Sir. I would just make a hopeless muddle out of the project."

"That's some pretty impressive buck-passing, Captain."

"I do my best, Colonel."

✦   ✦   ✦

Once it became clear that the oncoming airship was targeting his unit, Captain von Haslang ordered his men to abandon the guns and move off the road into the neighboring fields. There was no point losing soldiers as well as equipment. The airship would pass over them too high for musket fire to be effective. His own guns, designed for the purpose of shooting at them—he'd learned that the up-time term was "antiaircraft fire" or "ack-ack"—would have been able to reach them. Quite easily, in fact. But the guns were clumsy to deploy and effectively impossible to aim. There was no chance he could get them ready in time to fire on the airship. It would arrive overhead within a minute or two.

So, none of his men were killed. One was injured, not by enemy fire but by tripping over something and spraining his wrist in the fall.

As for the guns...

Happily, they came through mostly unharmed. The bombs dropped by the airship were rather large but had been designed as antipersonnel munitions. Shrapnel that would kill or mutilate a man did mostly cosmetic damage to cannons. Even a small two-inch gun weighed more than a quarter of a ton.

Several of them were dismounted, of course. Two of the carriages were ruined and would need to be replaced; half a dozen more would need to be repaired. But that was simple carpentry work, and there'd be plenty of carpenters in Munich.

Von Haslang finished his inspection and looked up at the sky. By now, the enemy airship was more than a mile away, headed toward Regensburg.

"Bastards," he heard one of his artillerymen say.

"We'll have our chance at them soon enough," the captain said in response. "They'll come to Munich, don't think they won't."

Chapter 10

Vienna, capital of Austria-Hungary

"So we are in agreement, then?" Janos nodded toward Noelle. "She and I will serve as your envoys to—" He hesitated, but only for a second. However much Ferdinand might detest the necessity, Wallenstein's new status now had to be formally acknowledged.

"To King Albrecht of Bohemia," he continued. "I, as your official envoy to the Bohemian monarch; Noelle, as your unofficial envoy to elements in his court."

That was a roundabout way of saying *to the very rich American Jewish couple Morris and Judith Roth, who have a lot of influence over that bastard Wallenstein and—perhaps more to the point—largely determine the way Americans everywhere look on the bastard at the present time.*

There was a valuable reminder there, if—no, when; the emperor was an intelligent man when he wasn't in a surly mood—Ferdinand had the sense to consider it. Whatever grievances he or Austria had against Wallenstein were miniscule compared to the grudge Americans could hold against him if they chose to do so. The bastard had once tried to slaughter all of their children, after all—yet the Americans had had the wisdom and forbearance to make peace with Wallenstein later, when the circumstances changed.

Ferdinand had been holding his breath long enough that his face was starting to turn red. Now, he exhaled mightily.

"Ah! I almost choke on the thought!"

Janos smiled. "If it eases your soul, Ferdinand, I will be glad to keep calling him Wallenstein when we're speaking privately."

"Please do." The young emperor's hands tightened on the armrest of his chair. "'The bastard' will do nicely, as well. So will—" He gave Noelle a somewhat wary glance.

She grinned at him. "The asshole, perhaps?" They were speaking in German, not Amideutsch, so the term she used was *Das Arschloch*. "Or perhaps I might introduce Your Majesty to one of our American expressions"—here she slipped into Amideutsch—"the dirty rotten motherfucker."

Ferdinand burst into laughter. Like most members of the Habsburg dynasty he had an earthy sense of humor. That was something that often surprised Americans who'd never had personal contact with Habsburgs. They tended to view Europe's premier dynasty as a pack of inbred and sickly hyper-aristocrats—as if such a feeble family could have dominated the continent's politics for so many centuries, since Rudolf of Habsburg became Rudolf I, King of Germany, in 1273.

Janos was very pleased by the emperor's reaction—and learning, yet again, that his American betrothed's somewhat prim physical appearance disguised a spirit that was bold and decisive. This was a woman who had once slain a torturer who was threatening the life of her partner by shoving her pistol barrel under his jaw and blowing his brains out. She'd done that, not because she was bloodthirsty but because she was a terrible shot with any sort of firearm and hadn't wanted to risk missing.

What had struck Janos the most, when she'd told him that story not long after they'd first met, was the incredible presence of mind that had taken—for anyone, much less a woman with little experience with violence. Drugeth knew many veteran soldiers who, placed in that same situation, would have blasted away wildly.

Of course, none of them would have been as terrible a marksman as Noelle. Her inability to hit anything more than two feet away with a pistol was quite remarkable.

After the emperor's laughter died away, Ferdinand gave Noelle a very approving look and said: "I like that. So, yes, in private—just among the three of us—I'd enjoy calling Wallenstein the asshole or the motherfucker. Better still! The motherfucking asshole."

He looked back at Janos. "Are you still sure it's wise to fly to Prague?"

"The danger is minimal, Your Majesty," Noelle said. "I've flown with Eddie a number of times. He's a very good pilot and his plane is well-built and—by now—quite well tested. It even survived a crash in Dresden with no harm done to anyone."

Ferdinand waved his hand dismissively. "I'm not concerned about the physical danger. I'm thinking of the diplomatic risk. Herr Junker is Francisco Nasi's pilot, and while Don Francisco is not formally connected with the asshole's court, he is—second only to Don Morris—the most prominent Jew in Prague. Which is the most prominent Jewish city in Europe. The world, for that matter. And everyone knows that the Jews and Wallenstein are closely allied."

Noelle had a frown on her face. Ferdinand would see in that frown nothing more than thoughtful concern. By now, though, Janos knew her well enough to understand that the expression was disapproving as well. Like most Americans he'd met, she had firm opinions on what they called "anti-Semitism" and she was interpreting the emperor's remarks as an expression of that attitude, at least in part.

And... At least in part, it probably was. Dealing with Noelle had forced Janos to consider his own attitude toward Judaism. Eventually, he'd concluded that some of his views of the religion and its practitioners were no better than unthinking prejudices. Leaving moral issues aside, Drugeth disapproved of prejudice of any kind for practical reasons. A prejudiced man was likely to behave stupidly.

He understood, however, something that Noelle didn't. Her grasp of the complexities of European diplomacy was still largely that of a novice, at least at this royal level. What Ferdinand was really expressing was not a bias against Jews but a distaste for appearing dependent in any way on someone whom most people would perceive as a close ally of Wallenstein.

"I don't think it's really a problem, Ferdinand," he said. "Or, if it is a problem, it's one that speaks to our relationship to the USE. Regardless of who owns the airplane and who flies it, almost anyone in Europe who looks up and sees an airplane passing overhead immediately and automatically thinks: *Americans.* That is just as true of Bohemians as anyone else, and the fact that when the plane lands one of the disembarking passengers"—he nodded toward Noelle—"is an American will reinforce the impression."

Noelle issued a peculiar sound, something of a cross between a choke and a laugh.

In response to the emperor's quizzically cocked eyebrow, she said: "I don't believe you've ever seen the airplane in question, Your Majesty."

He shook his head. "In the sky, once—at least, I believe it was that particular aircraft. But not up close, no."

"Well, you will soon, after Eddie gets done with his current shuttle diplomacy with the—ah—Saxons and Gustav Adolf." Janos was amused to see the deft way she avoided mentioning the specific Saxon being shuttled about. For the emperor of Austria as for most members of the continent's royalty, the name "Gretchen Richter" was what Noelle called *a scandal and a hissing*. Best to leave it unspoken in their presence.

"Anyway, when you do," Noelle went on, "you'll see that another American is very prominently portrayed on the plane itself. It's what we call 'nose art' because the painting is placed somewhere on the nose of the aircraft. There's often—usually, in fact—a title that goes with it."

"Ah." Ferdinand leaned forward in his chair. "There's something here you find amusing. I can tell—I'm learning to interpret your expressions. You'll make quite a good diplomat, by the way. So what is this portrait and this title?"

"The title is *Steady Girl*—that's an expression that refers to a sort of betrothal—and the portrait is of Denise Beasley. She is one of my junior associates and Eddie Junker's betrothed. Well... 'steady girl,' I suppose I should say. They're not betrothed—yet—in the legal German sense of the term."

The emperor's head was slightly cocked, and he had a half-smile on his face. "You're still not telling me everything. Why is this so amusing? Ah, I have it! This portrait is not what you'd call a formal one."

"Uh...no." Noelle fluttered her hands. "Nothing like—like... ah..."

Janos had never seen the aircraft up close himself, but he had enough sense of what Noelle was groping for to provide some assistance.

"Nothing like Titian's 'Venus of Urbino' or Cranach's 'Judgment of Paris,'" he provided.

"Oh, no, nothing like that! Just, ah...well. Denise is very

beautiful and, ah...the American expression is 'leggy.' We'd call the portrait an example of pin-up art. That refers to...ah..."

She was floundering again. Ferdinand smiled and made another dismissive gesture with his hand. "Never mind the details. What you're saying, I take it, is that no Bohemian—or anyone else—who sees that plane landing at Prague's airfield is going to associate the craft with an alliance between cunning Wallenstein and even more cunning Jews."

"Ah...No. They won't. Between me and the picture of Denise—mostly the portrait—they'll be thinking 'Americans.' Well, Ameri-canesses."

Ferdinand leaned back, his expression now thoughtful. "That will be good enough, I think. I simply cannot afford to look as if I am in any way relying on Wallen—the motherfucking asshole—for anything."

Magdeburg, capital of the United States of Europe

"I think you should do it," said Gunther Achterhof. Seeing the look of surprise on Gretchen's face, he smiled. Thinly, but it was a genuine smile.

"Yes, I know," he said. "Shocking, to see Gunther Achterhof agree to something. But I'm just stubborn, I'm not stupid. I have understood for some time now that the situation we have in the nation is unstable and can't last. If I had any doubts on the matter, the business with Schardius and Burckardt settled them."

The names meant nothing to Gretchen, and her expression must have shown that. Galiena Kirsch, one of the other CoC leaders present in the room, leaned over and said: "You'd left for Dresden by then. It was a big murder case that caught the attention of the whole city. We almost got involved directly—and did, at the very end—but we mostly left it to the new police force to handle."

"You can only be the informal power for so long," Gunther went on. "If you push it too far, you wear out the public patience. People like stability and order, especially over an extended period of time."

Most of the other CoC leaders were frowning. One of them—Hubert Amsel—spoke sharply. "What are you suggesting, Gunther? That we disband our organization?"

"No, of course not. What I'm saying is simply that we have to understand the limits within which we must operate. As a political *movement,* we continue to have a great deal of respect among our people and a very large following. But we now run the risk of seeing that erode if we try to extend our moral authority too far, if we try to assume the content of legal authority without accepting the form of it as well."

Gretchen was paying close attention, now. She'd had so many clashes with Gunther over the past year that she'd half-forgotten how shrewd the man could be. There was a reason he was the undisputed leader of the largest CoC in the world, located in the heart of the powerful new nation which the CoCs had played an important role in creating.

"I'm not quite following you, Gunther," said Eduard Gottschalk.

Achterhof frowned. The expression was not one of irritation but simply concentration. The sort of half-scowl a man gets on his face when he is trying to figure out how to explain something for the first time.

"Let me use the Schardius and Burckardt case to make my point," he said. "We almost intervened directly, especially after that terrible killing when the steam crane blew up."

Gretchen had heard about that incident. A horrible accident on a construction site. Dozens of men had been killed. But she hadn't realized it was connected to a murder investigation.

"But we didn't." He looked around the table. They were meeting in the kitchen of one of the apartments in the building that Gretchen and her husband had purchased with the money they'd gained—completely to their surprise—by David Bartley's speculations on their behalf in the stock market. The apartment building doubled as the informal headquarters of the capital's Committee of Correspondence.

"Why?" he continued. "We were certainly tempted. But we had enough sense to realize that if we pushed the police aside to handle it ourselves there'd never be an end to it. And did we really want to be a police force? Spending half our time and energy—not to mention funds—investigating robberies and such that had no political importance whatsoever?"

He leaned back in his chair. "No. We helped the police when they asked for it but we let them handle it. And that's the lesson, comrades. We can either be a political movement or an official government body but if we try to be both at the same time we'll do neither well and we'll lose our effectiveness."

He let that sink in, for a moment. Gretchen, who had been uncertain herself as to the course of action they should pursue in Saxony, found his arguments persuasive.

Galiena spoke up again. "But if we agree to have Gretchen run for office..." Her troubled expression suddenly cleared up. "Ah. I see. She does not run as a representative of the Committee of Correspondence in Saxony. She simply runs as—as..."

Her voice trailed off. "As what, exactly? Just herself?"

"That depends on what sort of republican system we want," said Gottschalk. "Parliamentary or presidential—or perhaps I should say, gubernatorial. If we want Saxony to have a gubernatorial system, Gretchen can run just as herself, as an individual candidate for the office of governor."

Before he'd even finished, every head around the table— including Gretchen's—was being shaken.

"No, no, we don't want that," said Hubert Amsel. "We want a parliamentary system. It's more democratic."

Gretchen had the same reaction, although she knew both her husband and most other Americans would have been puzzled by it. The up-timers, as a rule—Mike Stearns was one of the few exceptions—tended to prefer presidential systems since it was what they had been accustomed to. Because they had so much influence in the region, the State of Thuringia-Franconia had adopted a presidential structure, as had the New United States that preceded it.

But most down-timers, at least those drawn to the CoCs, felt differently about the matter. To them, a "president" and a "governor" were hard to distinguish from a king and a duke. Granted, the posts were elective, not hereditary—but the same was true of any number of institutions which reeked of their medieval origins. The Holy Roman Emperor had been elected, too. That didn't make him any less of a tyrant, did it?

So, everyone at the table shared Amsel's attitude—but Gretchen was by no means the only one who saw the immediate problem.

"If it's a parliamentary system, then Gretchen has to run as part of a party," said Galiena. "Which party? Or are we going to turn ourselves into one?"

"No!" exclaimed Gunther, barely beating out the "nos!" coming from Gretchen herself and Eduard Gottschalk. "Mixing up our movement with a party would be almost as bad a mistake as mixing ourselves up with a government body."

That was Gretchen's assessment also. She glanced around the room and saw that there was clearly general agreement on this point.

That left simply . . .

"There are two choices," she said. "And only two, practically speaking. I either join the Fourth of July Party and run as one of its members, or we create an entirely new party."

Amsel shook his head. "Which would simply be the Committees of Correspondence wearing a disguise everyone would see through immediately. No, I think the only practical choice is for Gretchen to join the FOJs." He pronounced the name as spelled-out letters—*F, O, J*—not as an acronym.

Gretchen almost laughed, seeing the slight moues of distaste on everyone's mouths. She was pretty sure her own lips were pursed in the same manner.

Why? There was really no clear reason. Doctrinally speaking, the FoJ Party and the CoCs were very close on almost all important matters. But that still left a definite if hard-to-specify distinction between the two.

Her husband Jeff Higgins had once expressed it with an Americanism: *Over here, we have the student council advocating all the right things. Over there, we have the roughnecks in their black leather jackets with cigarettes dangling from their lips agreeing with almost everything the student council says but sneering that they're a bunch of wimps and goody two-shoes.*

That was a silly way of putting it, but . . . there was some truth to the witticism.

"I'll join the Fourth of July Party tomorrow," she announced. "I'm meeting with Rebecca Abrabanel before my audience with the emperor so I'll do it then."

She paused, looking around the table to see if anyone had any objection. Seeing none, she moved to the next item on the agenda.

"We can be certain that Gustav Adolf is going to raise the issue of an established church—not just in Saxony but in Württemberg and Mecklenburg also."

"Not in the Oberpfalz?" asked Galiena.

"It's possible, but I doubt it. What should our stance be?"

"No compromise!" said Gunther forcefully. "We insist on freedom of religion in all republican provinces!"

It was oddly relaxing, Gretchen found, to have Achterhof back in his normal role.

"I disagree," she said. "Here are my reasons..."

After the meeting was over, she waited in the courtyard to speak to Spartacus.

"You never said a word in the meeting, Joachim—not one. Why?"

Joachim von Thierbach—who used the public identity of "Spartacus" as his *nom de plume*—shook his head. "I'm considered the intellectual in this bunch. The 'theoretician,' they call me, when they agree with something I say. But they're always a bit suspicious of me, at least here in the capital."

Gretchen chuckled. It was a very dry sound. "Yes, I know. The Magdeburg CoC takes its cue from Gunther and he's...how to put it? If he were a pastor, the Americans would call him a fundamentalist."

Von Thierbach's chuckle had more real humor in it. "Of what they call the 'fire and brimstone' persuasion!" He shrugged. "I thought it was important that they come to the conclusion they did on their own. And then when Gunther agreed with your proposal—right away; I was quite startled!—I saw no purpose in my adding anything."

Gretchen nodded. "So you agree, then? Yes, I know you voted in favor, but I want to be sure the vote wasn't a grudging one."

"It wasn't at all." He paused for a moment and looked aside, at nothing in particular, just as a way of collecting his thoughts.

"Please keep this confidential, but Rebecca Abrabanel has asked me to read her manuscript as she's been preparing it, in order to provide her with my reactions. In effect, she's using me as a sounding board for the CoCs as a whole."

"Yes? And what do you think?"

"Have you read Alessandro Scaglia's *Political Methods and the Laws of Nations*?"

Feeling a bit guilty, Gretchen shook her head. "No, not yet. I own it, but..." She made a vague gesture indicating the many tasks and burdens she had on her shoulders—which, in fact, she did.

"Take the time to read it, Gretchen. In essence, Rebecca's book is a response to Scaglia. Some of her argument is polemical in nature but much of it is agreeable to Scaglia's main premise—which I would summarize as his advocacy of reaching the same end point that existed in the Americans' universe but doing it without the chaos and destruction of a series of violent revolutions."

Gretchen made a face. "A fine sentiment—but try getting Europe's kings and noblemen to agree."

"Exactly Rebecca's point. You might say that where Scaglia argues for a long, slow glide to what he calls 'the soft landing,' Rebecca believes that so-called 'glide' will never land at all without a great deal of what she calls 'encouragement from below.'"

He chuckled again, with unmistakable humor this time. "They're both calling for the same end result—well, more or less—but they differ rather drastically on the proper pace and the mix of political forces required. To get back to the point, though, one of the things Rebecca stresses is the need for the representatives of the lower classes to get their hands directly on the levers of power. Being a 'movement' is fine. It's always where it starts. But in the end, the goal is to *move* society. Not just call for doing so. Not just demand that it be done. *Do it.*"

He made a little bow. When his head came back up he was grinning. "So. Since you don't like 'president' or 'governor,' what title would you prefer? How about 'dominatrix'?"

"Very funny. I was thinking about 'chancellor,' maybe."

"Oh, that's so—so—what the up-timers call 'white bread.'"

"I *like* white bread."

"Sure. Everybody does. How about 'She Who Must Be Obeyed'?"

"*Enough!*"

"See? It's the perfect title."

Chapter 11

Royal Palace
Magdeburg, capital of the United States of Europe

This time, when Gretchen was ushered into the presence of the emperor, two things were different. The chamber was much smaller, almost intimate in its dimensions, albeit as lavishly furnished as you'd expect in a royal palace. And they were quite alone. There were not even any servants in the room; just a small bell resting on a side table next to Gustav Adolf's chair with which he could summon one if desired.

To Gretchen's surprise, the emperor rose to greet her when she came into the chamber. She was no connoisseur of imperial protocol, but she was quite sure that was unusual. Don Fernando—even when he had simply been the cardinal-infante, not the king in the Netherlands—had never risen to greet her when she came into his presence. Neither had his wife Maria Anna, nor the Archduchess Isabella, nor Fredrik Hendrik, the prince of Orange.

Gustav Adolf was smiling a bit ruefully when he resumed his seat. "I am training myself, you see. Well . . . being honest, I am letting my daughter's governess train me. That's the up-timer, Caroline Platzer. Have you met her?"

Gretchen shook her head. "Not so far as I can recall."

"She is what they call a 'social worker.'"

Gretchen tried to make sense of the term. "She works at . . . managing social affairs?"

94

"Not exactly. The way Caroline describes the profession herself—I assure you the crudity is hers, not mine!—is that social workers are the grease that helps a society's axles turn more easily." He shrugged. "I'd think she was at least half-mad except that she can work magic with my daughter where no one else has ever been able to. The princess' ladies-in-waiting are well-nigh hysterical over Caroline's methods, but...they work. And none of their methods ever did anything but make my intelligent and headstrong daughter a veritable terror."

The emperor turned his head a bit to the side, in order to give Gretchen a sideways look. "Are you aware of Kristina's history—her future history, I mean, as recorded in the American books?"

"Yes, in broad outline. She succeeded you, it did not go well, and eventually she abdicated, converted to Catholicism and went to live in Rome." Gretchen tried to keep a smile from showing, but failed. "There was this, too. Apparently her headstrong manner never changed. There's a story in one of those books—so I'm told; I did not read it myself—that when the guests at a celebration she held in her villa in Rome refused to leave when ordered—"

"Ha!" Gustav Adolf clapped his big hands on his knees. "Yes, I read it! She ordered her household guards to fire on the unruly lot. Slew several of them, before the rest obeyed and left."

He chuckled softly, and shook his head. It was an oddly fond gesture, given that it was that of a father reminiscing—using the term very, very crookedly—on his daughter's murderous temper. "Caroline is good for her. And so is her betrothed, Prince Ulrik. I am very much in favor of that."

Again, he gave her that sideways look. "Are you?"

Gretchen hadn't been expecting that question. Her initial reaction was to issue some sort of meaningless inanity—*of course I am in favor of anything that puts the princess at ease*, that sort of twaddle—but she decided that would be a mistake. Instead, she took a few seconds—more like ten—to really think on the matter.

"Yes," she said finally. "When we—by 'we' I mean the Committees of Correspondence—decided to welcome Kristina and Prince Ulrik when they came to Magdeburg during the Dresden Crisis, we understood what it meant. For all intents and purposes, the CoCs were giving their consent to the United States of Europe's remaining a monarchy. I was in Dresden myself and did not participate in the discussion, but I agreed with the decision."

She took a slow, deep breath. "That decision is now essentially irrevocable, given that Your Majesty has lived up to your end of the...what to call it?"

"I rather like Ernst Wettin's term. *Modus vivendi.* And you're quite right. The CoCs, at least tacitly, have agreed that the USE will remain a monarchy. And the monarch in question"—he poked his chest with a thumb—"has agreed that the imperial rule will be bound and circumscribed by constitutional principles."

He now bestowed an outright grin on her—and quite a cheerful one. "Of course, that leaves both of us with plenty of room—everyone else, too! the FOJs, the Crown Loyalists, the reactionaries, oh, everyone—in which to maneuver and bargain and quarrel."

He planted his hands on his knees again. "So. Which will we be doing today, Gretchen? Bargaining or quarreling?"

"Bargaining, I hope."

He extended an open hand, with the palm turned up. The gesture invited her to lay out her proposals.

She took another deep breath, but not a slow one. She was determined to do this straightforwardly and firmly.

"First, I agree to run for the top executive position in Saxony. We will be advocating a parliamentary republican structure for the province, I should add."

The emperor nodded. "In that case, you will need to be representing a specific political party. That would be..."

"I joined the Fourth of July Party this morning. I was—well, there's no actual 'swearing in'—accepted in the presence of Rebecca Abrabanel, Ed Piazza and Matthias Strigel."

"As authoritative a group as anyone could ask for." Gustav Adolf shifted his hands from his knees to the armrests of his chair and looked to the side for a moment. "You are being wise, I think. Please go on."

"Second, on the issue of citizenship. Since the coup attempt by Chancellor Oxenstierna failed and the assembly in Berlin has been declared—by you yourself—as having no legal authority, the provisional citizenship standards established by Prime Minister Stearns remain in place. Those will be the standards that apply in the special elections in Saxony, Mecklenburg, Württemberg and the Oberpfalz."

She paused, cocking an eye at the emperor to see if he wanted to argue the point. But all Gustav Adolf did was nod his head and make another little gesture with his hand. *Not a problem, please go on.*

Now, they came to what she was almost certain was going to be the proverbial bone of contention.

"On the issue of the established church. We propose the following. The Oberpfalz—assuming the populace agrees, of course—will have full freedom of religion. Complete separation of church and state."

Again, she paused, and looked at the emperor.

"Agreed," he said. Then, making a face: "I don't care for it, but the Oberpfalz has been such a mess for so long due to *cuius regio, eius religio*—one ruler after another changing the region's official denomination—that trying to establish a church now is probably hopeless. Please continue."

"Mecklenburg and Württemberg"—she had to keep her lips from tightening here—"will have Lutheranism as the established church."

Gustav Adolf's eyes widened a bit. She didn't think he'd foreseen that concession from the Committees of Correspondence. Then, of course, his eyes narrowed considerably. In negotiations of this sort, what one hand gives the other will promptly try to take back.

"And Saxony?" he asked.

She sat up a bit straighter. "We propose a compromise. What you might call a semi-established church. Lutheranism will be recognized as the province's official church and will therefore be entitled to financial support from the provincial government. But all other religions—that includes Judaism as well as all varieties of Christianity—will not be penalized in any way."

The emperor's eyes were now fairly close to being outright slits. "I fail to see the point. We have already banned all forms of religious persecution anywhere in the United States of Europe."

Gretchen had grown so relaxed in the presence of Gustav Adolf that she had to restrain herself from snapping: *don't play the fool!* As if she were arguing with one of her own comrades.

Which the emperor, as cordial as he might be, was decidedly *not.*

"Your Majesty, I'm not simply speaking of persecution as such. There are other ways in which nonofficial denominations can be penalized. In Hesse-Kassel and Pomerania, for instance, only the established churches can have churches on the street. Other Protestant denominations have to maintain their churches inside courtyards, with no visible sign of their existence. And Catholics and Jews are required to maintain their places of worship on the upper floors, not on the street level. We want none of that in Saxony. The Lutherans can have their tax support. But that is all. That is the only additional benefit they would enjoy."

She stopped and waited for what she expected to be a royal outburst. Gustav Adolf had quite a famous temper, when he unleashed it.

And, indeed, the emperor was glaring at her. His big hands gripped the ends of the armrests, the knuckles standing out prominently.

To her surprise, he took a deep breath and exhaled it slowly. Then, still more to her surprise, he got a peculiar expression. It was almost...

Foxlike? Yes—insofar as the term was not absurd, applied to such a heavy face.

"I will agree on one condition," he said abruptly.

"Yes?"

"If you win the election and become the governor of Saxony—or whatever term you choose for the post—we will face the awkward situation of having the chief of state of a province with an established church who does not belong to that church—in fact, belongs to no church at all."

His expression now became self-righteous; so much so that Gretchen suspected he was putting on an act. "That's quite unacceptable! So my condition is this—you must cease this unseemly quasi-agnosticism and join a church. The Lutheran church would be ideal, of course. But I will settle for any other—"

She interrupted, trying her best not to seem too foxlike herself. "But—Your Majesty!—as you perhaps may not know, I was raised—"

"*Except* the Catholic church!" he boomed. "I've got too many blasted Catholics in the USE as it is!"

He leaned back in his chair. "That is the condition, Gretchen. Pick a Protestant church—and not one that is too disreputable, like the Anabaptists. A Reformed church is acceptable. We have that already in Hesse-Kassel and Brandenburg."

She considered outright rebellion, but...

It was not an outrageous condition, given what the emperor was prepared to allow in exchange. And, besides, did it really matter that much any more?

Well...

Yes. Some stubborn root at the very heart of Gretchen Richter was choking on the idea. Not because she cared about doctrinal issues—which she never had, even when she'd been a young Catholic girl—but simply because she was being *forced.*

She was about to refuse when a very foxlike thought came to her. What if...?

Yes. That would do.

"Very well," she said. "I accept. But I will need a bit of time to make my choice."

Gustav Adolf waved his hand expansively, magnanimously. "By all means! So long as you have made your choice before you take office."

He rose to his feet. "That assumes, of course, that you win the election. Which I most certainly hope you do not, since you are a notorious agitator and the fellow running against you, Ernst Wettin, is a far more sensible sort."

He was smiling when he said it, though.

She spent that evening giving a full report to a large assemblage in Rebecca Abrabanel's town house. Several of Magdeburg's CoC leaders were present along with the people from the Fourth of July Party.

The idea she was considering with respect to the church she'd wind up joining herself, however, she discussed with no one except Rebecca.

Who thought the idea was both charming and shrewd. As she put it: "It's a way to goose the emperor without his being able to take umbrage."

She then had to explain the bizarre way Americans had turned a goose into a verb.

The next morning, Eddie Junker showed up at the townhouse. "Where are we flying to now?" he asked. "Back to Dresden?"

"Later. First we go to Grantville."

Once they were in the air, heading south, Eddie asked Gretchen: "How long will you be in Grantville?"

She didn't answer immediately because they'd encountered some turbulence. Her left hand was clutching the side of her seat. Her right hand had been clutching the door handle but she'd snatched it away when she realized that if she had a sudden spasm caused by—whatever—she might inadvertently fling open the door—never mind that the wind pressure would be working entirely against that possibility—and then fling herself out of the airplane for no good reason known to man, God or beast.

All her knuckles were bone white. Her jaw was clenched. Her eyes were wide but fixed straight ahead as if she were gazing into the maw of hell.

"Oh, relax," said Eddie. "Turbulence in the air is nothing to worry about. Look at it this way. If you were on a ship at sea you'd expect to be riding up and down with the waves, wouldn't you? In fact, if you *weren't* you'd be in trouble."

He waved a hand, indicating the atmosphere through which they were flying. "That's all this is, too. We're just riding waves in the air instead of in water. It only seems dangerous because you can't see these waves."

"It's not the same at all," Gretchen said, through still-clenched teeth. "If a boat comes apart and drops me into the water, I know how to swim. If this airplane falls apart and drops me into the air, I don't know how to fly."

After the turbulence had died down and Gretchen had relaxed a bit, Eddie repeated the question.

"I'm not sure," she said.

"An hour? Two hours? A day? Two days? A week?"

"At least a day. Maybe two. I don't think it should be longer than that."

Eddie nodded. "Fine. I need to fly Noelle and Janos Drugeth from Vienna to Prague as soon as possible. I got the message from the radio operator at the Magdeburg airfield just before we left. So after I drop you off in Grantville, I'll take care of that business before I return. It shouldn't take more than a day."

Gretchen said nothing. They'd run into turbulence again.

Grantville, State of Thuringia-Franconia

The door was opened by a woman whom Gretchen knew to be in her early eighties but who didn't look it to her down-time eyes. Gretchen's grandmother Veronica was only sixty-one, which many Americans still considered to be "middle-aged," but she looked older than the woman standing in the doorway.

They'd encountered each other any number of times when Gretchen was living in Grantville after her marriage to Jeff, but she couldn't recall that they'd ever spoken directly. As always, Gretchen was struck by the old woman's hair. Snow-white but still full, and extremely curly. It was not hard to understand why she'd been the inspiration for Ewegenia, symbol of the Franconian League of Women Voters during the Ram Rebellion.

"Veleda Riddle?" she asked by way of a formal greeting. "I am Gretchen—"

"I know who you are, dear." Veleda smiled. "The whole world probably does—well, Europe, anyway—at least by reputation."

Holding the door open, she moved aside and gestured for Gretchen to enter.

"Come in. Would you care for some coffee? Tea? Broth?"

Gretchen was about to refuse politely when she realized she actually did have a desire—a craving, more like—for a cup of coffee. Her nerves were still a little unsettled from the flight.

And if anyone in Grantville was likely to have good coffee, it would be Veleda Riddle. She was one of the handful of "grand old ladies" among the up-timers. Her son, Chuck Riddle, was the Chief Justice of the Supreme Court of the State of Thuringia-Franconia and while she was now a widow, her husband had been one of Grantville's few practicing lawyers and had made a better living than most residents of the town before the Ring of Fire.

"Yes, please. Some coffee would be nice."

After she'd taken a seat in the living room and Veleda returned from preparing the coffee in the kitchen, Gretchen said: "I was sorry to hear of the recent passing of your husband, Mrs. Riddle."

Veleda handed her a cup of coffee and sat down on the couch positioned at a ninety-degree angle from Gretchen. She had a cup for herself, from which she took a sip before responding.

"I miss him, I surely do. But we all have to pass someday and Tom made it to eighty-four before he died." She smiled, in fond reminiscence. "On his eightieth birthday I remember him telling me, 'Okay, hon, I made it as far as anyone can ask from the Lord. I figure whatever's left is gravy.'"

She took another sip of coffee and set the cup down on the aptly named coffee table.

"And now, what can I do for you, Gretchen Richter?"

Once Gretchen had explained the purpose of her visit, Veleda drained her cup of coffee.

"Oh, my," she said, cradling the cup in her lap.

She stared out the window for a time.

"Oh, my," she said again.

Chapter 12

Mainburg, Bavaria

"We could parachute in," said Captain Wilhelm Finck. He leaned over and pointed to a spot on the big map spread across the table in Mike Stearns' HQ tent. "I think this location would be possible, although we'd have to overfly it first to make sure it isn't too heavily wooded."

Mike thought about it, for a moment. The idea was tempting. The location Captain Finck suggested was close enough to the Amper River for his team to make the reconnaissance before a Bavarian cavalry unit could find them. Unless they had bad luck, at least—but that was always a given in war.

"You need a Jupiter, am I right?"

The Marine captain shook his head. "Not necessarily, sir. A Jupiter is the only airplane big enough for a parachute drop by more than one or two men. But we could do it from the *Pelican* as well."

Mike frowned. "That thing would be visible for miles. There's no way to use it for a mission that needs to be surreptitious."

"It depends on the time of day, sir. If we make the drop very early in the morning, there will be enough light for us to see but the airships won't be very visible from the ground—and we certainly won't be, falling over the side. If any Bavarian soldier does spot the airship they'll simply think it's on a reconnaissance mission."

The captain was right, probably. But it was still one hell of a risk.

Looking at Finck's face, as the captain continued to gaze intently at the map, it was obvious that he wasn't concerned about the danger involved. Although it was part of the USE's marine forces, Finck's unit—officially the 1st Reconnaissance Company, First Marines—was more closely analogous to what the up-time U.S. military would have called special forces. The unit had been formed in response to the disastrous attempt to invade the Danish island of Bornholm two years earlier during the Baltic War.

Like all such special forces—Mike had met a few during his stint in the U.S. Army up-time—the men who joined them were adrenaline junkies. They simply didn't have what Mike considered a normal and sane level of caution and risk assessment—which was something, given that he himself was a former prizefighter and had never lost any sleep over mining coal for a living.

"All right, Captain. We'll make the drop. How soon can you be ready?"

Finck shrugged. "That really depends more on when the *Pelican* can be placed at our disposal than it does on us, sir. Me and my men can be ready by tomorrow morning."

"Tell Franchetti—no, tell Major Simpson to tell Franchetti—to give you top priority."

Mike smiled, a bit crookedly. The up-time military he'd known—for sure and certain some of the tight-ass commanders he'd suffered under—would have had conniptions if they'd been dealing with the Third Division's realities of life. Mike had what amounted to his own tiny little air force consisting of one airship, the *Pelican,* and on occasion—nowhere nearly often enough, as far as he was concerned—he also had one of the USE Air Force's warplanes at his disposal for a few days. Always one of the two Belles, never the newer and more advanced Gustavs. Those were reserved for General Torstensson's use in the Polish theater.

Mostly Mike was dependent on the *Pelican* for what he whimsically thought of as his "air operations"—and never mind the fact that the *Pelican* was a civilian airship being leased by the State of Thuringia-Franconia rather than the USE government. And never mind the fact that it was operationally commanded by Major Tom Simpson, who was an USE artillery officer with no formal ties of any kind to the air force or the SoTF's National Guard.

What the hell, the set-up worked. *If it ain't broke, don't fix it.*

"When we find a good place to cross the river, sir, what do you want us to do?" Finck asked. "Return or stay in place?"

"Stay in place, if you can do so without being spotted. But don't take any unnecessary risks, Captain. There'll only be a handful of you and even allowing for your weaponry"—Finck's unit was armed with lever-action .40-72 carbines—"you'll be overwhelmed by any sizeable enemy force."

"Yes, sir. Shall I be off, then?"

"Yes. Good luck, Captain."

After Captain Finck left the tent, Mike turned toward Lieutenant Colonel Thorsten Engler. "When the time comes for us to cross the river, even if we have the element of surprise—and if we don't we probably won't try it at all—you can be sure and certain the Bavarians will throw every cavalry unit they have available at us. We'll be depending on you to hold them off."

Thorsten nodded. His flying artillery unit could be used against infantry—and had been, on several battlefields—but they were specifically designed to counter cavalry. They were not as mobile as a cavalry unit but had much greater firepower at their disposal.

They were useless against fortifications, however, which was one of their drawbacks. Any infantry unit that had the time to build good fieldworks could drive them off as well.

"How wide is the Amper, General?" asked Leoš Hlavacek, the colonel in command of the Teutoberg Regiment.

Mike turned toward Tom Simpson, who'd come back the day before from a reconnaissance mission over the terrain between Ingolstadt and Freising. He'd taken the risk of having the *Pelican* fly no more than a hundred yards above the ground so he'd gotten a good view of everything. He'd particularly concentrated on the Amper, since that tributary of the Isar was the main geographical obstacle the Third Division was going to face in their march on Munich.

Tom made a waggling motion with his hand. "It varies. In a lot of places it's not even a 'river' so much as it is a braided network of little streams."

"How little?" asked Georg Derfflinger. He commanded the division's 3rd Brigade and, at twenty-nine, was the youngest of the Third Division's brigadiers. "If they're narrow enough and shallow enough, we might be able to cross without having to put up a bridge. Maybe just a corduroy road to keep the men's boots from getting soaked."

Simpson looked skeptical. "It's possible, but I wouldn't count on it. I was up in the air, not down on the ground, so I can't be sure. But from the way it looked, those places where the Amper divides into a network of streams are swamps. We could wind up getting mired down. I think we'd do better to cross someplace where there are solid banks we can anchor a bridge on. Keep in mind that's a pretty small river. I didn't see any place where it was wider than maybe ten yards."

He started to add something and then closed his mouth. Mike suspected that Tom had been about to make a comment that might have struck the down-timers as American chauvinism. By Tom's standards as well as Mike's—any American's—the rivers in Europe seemed pretty dinky. Mike hadn't seen the Rhine yet, so he couldn't judge if it lived up to its world-famous reputation. But neither the Elbe nor the Danube did, for North Americans accustomed to such rivers as the Mississippi, Missouri and Ohio, although Mike had been told that the Danube was a lot more impressive farther east than he'd seen it.

In the United States he'd come from, a body of running water the size of the Amper would probably have been called a creek rather than a river. But Mike had enough military experience by now to understand that it didn't take much of a body of running water—call it a river, a creek or whatever you chose—to pose a serious obstacle to an army more than ten thousand strong that was operating with the sort of equipment available in the early seventeenth century.

The march on Munich from Regensburg posed one major geographical problem for the Third Division. They could easily cross over to the Isar's south bank somewhere between Dingolfing and Landshut, where the Bavarians had no sizeable forces to oppose them, and then follow the river all the way down to Munich.

The problem was that in the year 1636, Bavaria's capital was a far cry from the metropolis it would eventually become. In the time period Mike had come from, Munich straddled the Isar. But today, the city was located entirely north of the river. So arriving at Munich on the south bank would do them no good at all. To be sure, the Isar was narrow enough that they could bombard the city's walls from the south bank. But sooner or later, once a breach was made, they'd have to cross it—right in the face of the enemy, entrenched in the city's fortifications.

No, they had to stay on the Isar's north bank all the way down—but that posed the problem that they'd first have to cross the river's main tributary, the Amper. Hopefully, Captain Finck and his men would find a good spot to do it. They needed some-place the Third Division could reach easily—while the Bavarians could be held at bay long enough—and which had solid enough footing and enough forest in the area—groves, at least—to build the bridges they'd need for the purpose.

He'd have given a lot to have just one or two APCs with him. The vehicles weren't amphibious but they'd do splendidly to drive off enemy cavalry while his engineers threw up the bridges. But in his infinite wisdom—being fair about it, the damn Polish king was being just as pigheaded about keeping the war going—Gustav Adolf insisted that all the functioning APCs had to remain with Torstensson's forces around Poznań.

"Might as well wish for one or two M1 Abrams main battle tanks, while I'm at it," Mike muttered.

"I didn't catch that, sir," said his adjutant, Christopher Long.

"Nothing. Just dreaming the impossible dream."

USE naval base
Luebeck

Admiral John Chandler Simpson believed very firmly—as you'd expect from someone raised in the high church Episcopalian tradition—that a man who used profanity thereby demonstrated his inferior intellect and primitive grasp of the glorious English language. But, as he lowered the message from Veleda Riddle he'd just finished reading—the parsimonious old lady had even paid to have it sent by radio transmission, which indicated how agitated she was—he couldn't help himself.

"Well, fuck me," he said.

Grantville

It was hearing someone else express her own deepest qualms that finally settled Veleda Riddle's mind.

"But she's not one of *us!*" exclaimed Christie Kemp.

The statement stuck in Veleda's craw, as the saying went—all the more so because she completely agreed with it. The woman was not only "not one of us," she was so far removed from "us" that she might as well have been living on Mars.

That was to say, one of the many planets He had created.

"Christie," she said, trying to keep her tone from being too disapproving, "we are a church, not a country club. I think we need to keep that in mind."

"I agree with Veleda," said Marshall Kitt.

"So do I," added his wife Vanessa.

Christie threw up her hands. "Fine! But you need to face some facts, people. We are *not*—not, not, not—prepared to deal with this. We have exactly one priest—well, that we're compatible with—and he's not leaving Grantville. We have no bishop who could ordain more priests, leaving aside that snot Robert Herrick whom Laud saw fit to make the bishop in Magdeburg. Herrick's a goof-off anyway and we all know it. That means we're still completely dependent on Archbishop Laud, who is—pardon my Baptist—an asshole who won't give us the time of day. Even if he weren't, he's in the Netherlands."

She had a point, as crudely expressed as it might be.

"I will write to him again," Veleda said.

Amsterdam, the Netherlands

"That pestiferous woman!" Laud exclaimed. He held the radio missive clutched in his fist and waved it under Thomas Wentworth's nose. "She's at it again!"

"I just came in the door, William," Wentworth said mildly. "On what I intended to be a simple personal visit. What has you so agitated?"

Politely, he didn't add *this time,* as he so easily could have. Exile was a wearing state of affairs for anyone, but his friend the archbishop of Canterbury handled it with particularly poor grace. Perhaps that was due to his age. Laud was now sixty-three and was likely to be feeling his mortality pressing down on him. So much still to do—and now, so little time left in which to do it.

Laud heaved a sigh and sank back into his chair. "It's the American woman, Veleda Riddle. I've told you about her. She keeps pestering me to give the Americans their own bishop. I've already sent them some priests! Well. Two priests—and I made one of them the bishop in Magdeburg. And there are only a very small number of American so-called 'Episcopalians' anyway. What do they need a bishop of their own for?"

Without waiting for Thomas to reply to that—clearly rhetorical—question, Laud raised his message-clutching fist again and waved it about.

"I'll tell you! I'll tell you! They intend to break away from the authority of the true Anglican church, that's what! I'm not a fool, you know. I've read the history books. In their world the archbishop of Canterbury was just a so-called 'first among equals.'"

He broke off for a moment, glaring at the inoffensive wall opposite from him. "They called it the 'Anglican Communion.' Each national church having its own separate identity and authority, with only token acknowledgement given to the English fountainhead of the church."

Wentworth had heard this all before—more than once. "Oh, leave off, William!" he said impatiently. "Why do you even care, other than as a matter of personal pride?"

"You don't understand, Thomas. They're not part of *us*."

Wentworth took a seat on the small divan under the window. "No, they're not. I *have* met some Americans, you might recall. But the way I see it, that's all the more reason to let them go their own way."

He leaned forward, planting elbows on his knees. "William, we have more than enough problems to deal with. One of them—do I need to remind you, of all people?—being to place you back in Canterbury where you belong. Why in the world would you want to pile onto your shoulders this additional distraction?"

Without moving his arms, he spread his hands wide. "So let

them have their bishop, why don't you? Then, hopefully, they'll go on their way and that woman who aggravates you so mightily won't bother you any further."

Laud said nothing for a minute or so; he just continued to glare at the wall. Then he sighed again.

"I suppose you're right." He rose to his feet and moved toward his writing desk. "There's this much of a blessing, at least. The ancient harridan made a specific recommendation once. If I can find it..."

He rummaged among the papers piled around the desk.

"Ah, here it is." He handed the letter over to Wentworth. "This will spare me the nuisance of having to send someone to investigate the possibilities."

Wentworth scanned the letter quickly. When he got to the name of the man whom the Riddle woman had recommended, his eyebrows rose.

"Well, he certainly has the pedigree," he said.

"In that case, I'll send the appointment by radio transmission." The expression on Laud's face was mischievous; indeed, it bordered on being malicious. "They call it a 'collect call,' you know."

He reached for the bell on a side table and rang for his secretary. "I can't actually ordain him over the radio, of course. That requires a laying on of hands. But I can appoint him bishop-elect and make the appointment widely known."

Regensburg

Tom Simpson wouldn't have paid for the radio message, except for the name of the sender. What would the archbishop of Canterbury want with him?

It took no more than a few seconds to read the message. A few more seconds to re-read it. At least a minute, though, for the meaning to finally register.

"Well, fuck me," he said.

As he headed toward the entrance, the radio operator called him back. "There's another message coming in for you, Major Simpson."

Tom turned around. "From who?"

"Your father, it says."

After Tom read that message, the situation became much clearer.

"I swear to God," he muttered, as he emerged back onto the street, "if you planted that woman in the middle of the Gobi desert—oh, hell no, plant her in the middle of Antarctica—she'd find an apple cart to upset. Take her maybe two minutes, tops."

His wife's reaction when she read the message from Laud was a variation on the theme.

"Oh, fuck no! Tom, you can't accept!"

He made a face. "I'll have to check with Veleda or somebody else who'd know the protocol. But I'm not actually sure I *can* refuse. Legally speaking—well, ecclesiastically legally speaking—I think this is more like being conscripted than volunteering. You know how it is in this day and age—half of your top clergymen are political appointees."

"I don't give a damn! I don't want my husband to be a fucking bishop! I'm just a trashy country girl hillbilly! I want to get laid once in a while!"

Tom laughed. "Episcopalian clergy aren't Catholics, honey. They—we—don't take vows of celibacy."

"Doesn't matter! How can I possibly screw a goddam bishop?"

His grin widened. "Come here and I'll show you."

An hour or so later, Rita was much calmer. Not quite mollified, but close.

"Well, I guess there's one upside to the whole thing," she said, her head nestled on his shoulder.

"Hmm?" Tom's eyes were closed. He'd have been purring, if humans were equipped to do so.

"You can get Ursula out of our hair. Send her to Dresden to do her proselytizing. Let her drive Gretchen Richter nuts. It'd serve her right since this is all her fault in the first place."

His eyes opened. "I'm not sure I have the authority to do that. Ursula is just laity, not clergy."

"Says who?" Rita levered herself up on an elbow and looked down on him. "Your church ordains female priests. I know it does."

"Well, yeah—up-time. But here..."

His eyes were wide open, now.

Rita laughed and slapped his chest. Which was like slapping a side of beef. "Oh, Laud will have a shit fit! Welcome to the seventeenth century, way-too-smart-for-his-own-good husband of mine. What should we call it? Hey, I know—the Bishop Wars."

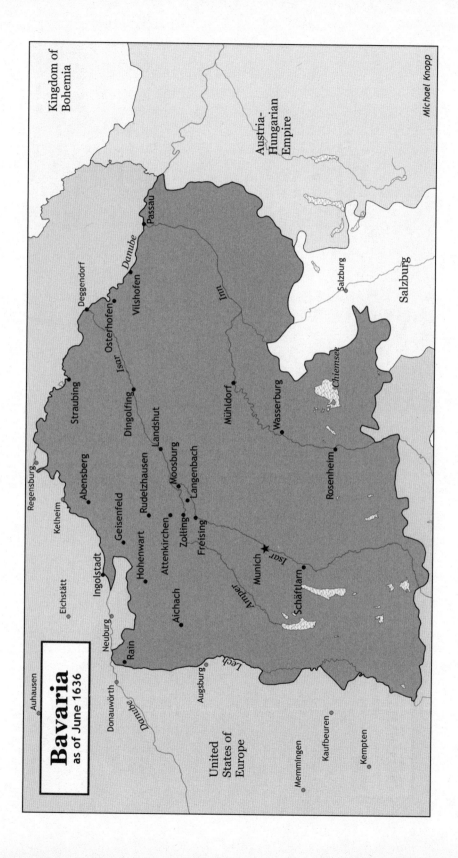

Bavaria
as of June 1636

Kingdom of
Bohemia

Austria-
Hungarian
Empire

Michael Knopp

Salzburg

Salzburg

Chiemsee

Auhausen

Regensburg

Kelheim

Eichstätt

Neuburg

Ingolstadt

Donauwörth

Danube

Rain

Lech

Augsburg

Memmingen

Kaufbeuren

Kempten

United
States of
Europe

Aichach

Hohenwart

Geisenfeld

Abensberg

Straubing

Deggendorf

Danube

Osterhofen

Isar

Vilshofen

Passau

Dingolfing

Landshut

Rudelzhausen

Moosburg

Langenbach

Attenkirchen

Zolting

Freising

Isar

Munich

Ampler

Schäftlarn

Mühldorf

Wasserburg

Inn

Rosenheim

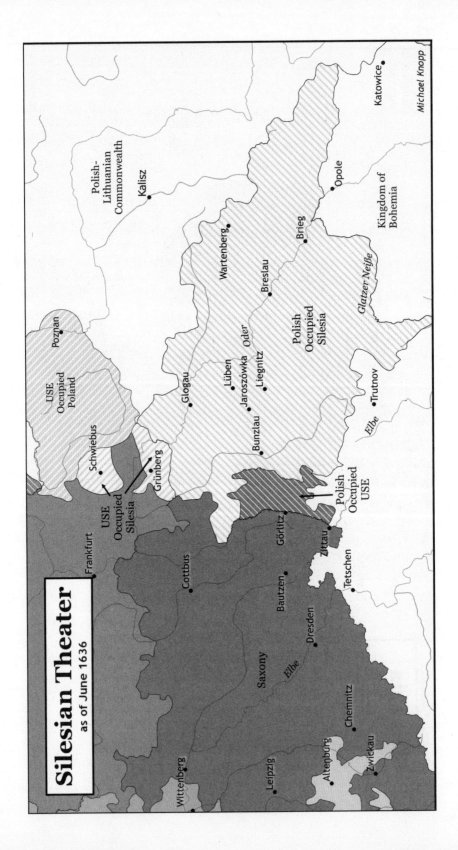

Silesian Theater
as of June 1636

Michael Knopp

Polish-Lithuanian Commonwealth

Kalisz

Katowice

Opole

Brieg

Kingdom of Bohemia

Wartenberg

Breslau

Glatzer Neiße

Poznan

USE Occupied Poland

Polish Occupied Silesia

Glogau

Lüben

Jaroszówka

Liegnitz

Oder

Trutnov

Schwiebus

Bunzlau

Elbe

Grünberg

USE Occupied Silesia

Polish Occupied USE

Frankfurt

Görlitz

Zittau

Cottbus

Tetschen

Bautzen

Dresden

Saxony

Elbe

Chemnitz

Wittenberg

Leipzig

Altenburg

Zwickau

Part Two

May 1636

The sudden blood of these men

Chapter 13

Lower Silesia, near Boleslawiec

By the time he got to the outskirts of Boleslawiec—or Bunzlau, as the town's mostly German inhabitants called it—Jozef Wojtowicz was in a quiet rage. Once he'd gotten beyond Görlitz, which marked the easternmost outpost of Saxony, the area he was passing through had quickly come to resemble a war zone—and a very recent war, at that.

What infuriated him was that the destruction had not been caused by Poland's enemies but by soldiers who were officially employed by King Wladyslaw to protect the area. That would be the army commanded by Heinrich Holk, a man who had one of the worst reputations of any mercenary in Europe—which was saying a lot, given how low that bar had been set by now.

Holk had been employed by the elector of Saxony, John George, right up until the moment that Gustav Adolf invaded Saxony and John George had need of his services. At that point—he might have taken ten minutes to decide, but probably less—Holk immediately fled across the border into Lower Silesia and offered his services to the king of Poland.

Who, for reasons known only to himself and God, had chosen to accept them. Jozef's best guess—which did not mollify his anger in the least—was that Wladyslaw had been preoccupied with the threat that Gustav Adolf posed to Poland and had no troops he was prepared to send into Silesia to deal with Holk. So, he hired him instead. In essence, he bribed Holk to leave him alone.

The up-timers had a term for this sort of arrangement. They called it a "protection racket." Which wouldn't perhaps have been so bad if Holk had been an honest criminal and satisfied himself with the bribe. Instead, he'd made no effort to keep his soldiers under control and they'd set about plundering the countryside.

And that was *another* thing which enraged Jozef. Silesia was a borderland between the Germanies and the Slavic nations, and had been for centuries. At one time or another Silesia or parts of it had been under the control of Poland, Bohemia and Austria. Its inhabitants were a mix of Germans, Czechs and Poles. The rough rule of thumb which held generally through most of the region was that the towns and cities were heavily German, sometimes with a Czech and/or Jewish element, and the countryside was mostly Polish.

The largest city in Silesia was Wroclaw, known to its mostly-German inhabitants as Breslau. By 1518, the city had joined the Protestant Reformation but a few years later, in 1526, it came under the control of the Catholic Austrian Habsburgs. Until the Bohemian revolt of 1618, however, the Habsburgs had allowed a considerable degree of religious freedom. Thereafter, Ferdinand II had imposed his harshly Catholic policies over the area, although the brunt of those policies had initially been borne by Bohemia more than Silesia.

The war itself—what the up-time histories called the Thirty Years War—didn't reach Silesia until 1626, when it was invaded by a Protestant army under the command of the German mercenary Ernst von Mansfeld. In response, the Austrians sent their mercenary commander Albrecht von Wallenstein to drive Mansfeld out, which he did—and followed by imposing his own harsh rule.

And then, just five years later, Wallenstein himself rebelled against the Habsburgs and restored Bohemia's independence with himself as the new king. At the same time, he laid claim to all of Silesia—but that had been mostly a gesture, since the Polish monarchy seized Lower Silesia and Wallenstein was too preoccupied with the Austrian attempts to restore Habsburg rule to pay much attention. All he really cared about was Upper Silesia, anyway, which was still largely under his control.

And there things stood. Most of the peasants were Polish Catholics, who lived in reasonable amity with the inhabitants of the towns and cities, who were mostly German Lutherans. Both

Poland and Bohemia claimed to rule Silesia, but the Bohemians made no attempt to enforce their claim except in some immediate border areas and the Polish claim was enforced by a German mercenary thug whose real allegiance was to lucre and liquor.

As stinky situations went in the already quite smelly continent of Europe, Silesia was a veritable cesspool.

The worst of it was borne by the Polish peasants. The German towns and cities generally governed themselves and had sizeable militias at their disposal. Jozef thought Holk's army was large enough and strong enough that it could have overrun any of the cities of Silesia except possibly Breslau—but only at a significant cost. That was the sort of cost in blood and treasure that even very competent mercenary commanders tried to avoid. Holk and his men satisfied themselves by extorting bribes from the towns to leave them alone and periodically ravaging the villages.

As he passed through one small and deserted village, Jozef's angry musings were interrupted by an odd little sound. Turning quickly in his saddle, he saw a small foot vanish around the corner of a house—not much more than a shed, really—that hadn't been as badly damaged as most of the village's buildings.

That had been a child's foot. He got off his horse, tied it to a nearby post, and went to investigate.

Coming around the corner, he saw the foot again—the foot and most of the leg—sliding under a pile of debris that looked to be the burned remains of another shed.

"Come out, child," he said in Polish. "I won't hurt you."

Moving slowly, making sure to keep his hands outstretched a bit so the child could see that he held no weapons, he advanced on the shattered and burned wreckage.

As he got close, he heard a little whimpering sound. He leaned over and—carefully, he didn't want to dislodge a pile of wooden slats to fall on whoever was hiding there—lifted the largest of the intact boards and peered beneath.

Looking up at him, their faces full of fear, were two small children. A boy and a girl. The boy was perhaps six years old, the girl no more than four. From the mutual resemblance, he was pretty sure they were brother and sister.

"Where is your family?" he asked.

The children stared up at him, mute and silent.

He moved the board entirely aside. "Come out, children. I won't hurt you, and you must be hungry. I have some food."

He glanced around the village square—such as it was, which wasn't much—and saw there was no well. "And water," he added. There was a stream fifty yards away that the village had probably used as its water supply. But the children would have been too frightened to leave their hiding place except at night—and possibly not even then.

The children seemed paralyzed with fear, still. Jozef knelt down and gave the girl's face a gentle caress. "I won't hurt you, I promise. But you can't stay here forever. Come with me and I'll take you someplace safe."

He had no idea where that might be, but he couldn't simply ride off and leave them here. They were too young to survive for very long on their own. The boy might, but the girl would surely die.

"Why does God seem to have such a grudge against poor Poland?" he muttered. Jozef had an insouciant temperament and was generally good-humored. But by now the contrast between Poland's feckless rulers and the people he'd come to know in Dresden was becoming downright grotesque. Were he not a son of Poland and quite attached to his homeland, he'd have instantly traded King Wladyslaw and the whole miserable worthless Sejm for a printer's daughter named Gretchen, a former tavern maid named Tata, and a one-time gunmaker become quite a good officer named Eric Krenz.

The children were still frozen in place, like two little statues. Josef got back on his feet, leaned over, and picked the girl up in his arms. She did not try to resist, nor did she make any sound.

"Don't hurt Tekla!" the boy cried out, reaching out his hand. "Please don't!"

His Polish had a heavy rural accent, but was obviously his native tongue.

Jozef cradled the girl in one arm and reached down with his other hand. "I won't hurt her. Or you. Now come, boy. We have to leave here. What's your name?"

Hesitantly, the boy reached up, took Jozef's proffered hand and levered himself upright.

"I'm Pawel. Pawel Nowak."

"Where is your family, Pawel?"

The boy looked distressed. His eyes moved toward one of the wrecked buildings and then shied away. "Gone. All of them except me and Tekla. They killed my father and uncle. My older brother Fabek also. My mother...I don't know what happened to her. The soldiers took her away. I think she was hurt."

By the end he was starting to weep. So was the girl. Jozef put an arm around Pawel's shoulders and drew him close, while cradling Tekla more tightly.

So he remained for a while, until the children were cried out.

"Come on, now," he said. "We have to get moving."

"Where are we going?"

"We'll spend tonight in Boleslawiec." Since the children were Polish, he used the Polish name for the town. "After that...I have to get to Wroclaw."

Pawel's eyes widened. "But that's so far away!"

The distance from Boleslawiec to Wroclaw wasn't actually that great. Perhaps eighty miles—certainly not more than a hundred. A few days on horseback, no more. But for a Silesian village boy, it would have seemed almost as far away as Russia or France. If he even knew where those countries were located, which he probably didn't.

After some experimentation, Josef found that the best way for the three of them to ride was with Pawel sitting behind him holding on and Tekla perched on his lap. It was awkward and it was going to be uncomfortable for all them, especially the poor horse. But at least today they didn't have very far to go.

Tomorrow and the days thereafter...were tomorrow and the days thereafter. There were advantages to having Jozef's temperament. He wasn't given to worrying overmuch about what the future might hold.

He found a fairly decent tavern in Boleslawiec that had a room to rent. The food was mediocre but edible. The biggest drawback to the situation was that the tavern's barmaids seemed quite friendly but with two children in tow he found himself unable to proceed as he normally would.

So, he retired for the night sooner than usual. When he got back to the room he'd rented, he found that Pawel and Tekla were already sound asleep. They were cuddled together so tightly that he'd have more space on the bed than he'd expected.

First, though...

He'd already placed the batteries in the radio before he'd left Dresden. So all he had to do was place the antenna out of the window. Then, patiently, he began spelling out the Morse code.

Poznań, Poland

"You wanted me, Grand Hetman?" Lukasz Opalinski didn't quite come to attention—Polish military protocol was fairly relaxed about such things—but his tone was respectful and alert. Koniecpolski was not in the habit of summoning one of his junior officers on a passing whim. Something important must be brewing.

The top commander of the army of the Polish-Lithuanian Commonwealth looked up from a piece of paper in his hand. Silently, he extended the hand to give the paper to Lukasz.

In radio contact again. In Bunzlau. Need to meet with someone in Wroclaw. Have two children need care. Nephew.

"*Two* children?" Lukasz couldn't keep from laughing out loud. "I wouldn't have thought even Jozef could have sired two bastards in the time he's been gone."

Koniecpolski smiled. "I don't understand about the children either. But if he says he needs to meet with someone, we must see to it. My nephew is brash but he's no fool."

Lukasz had already thought ahead. "I'm free at the moment—not much for a hussar to do in this sort of siege—and I've been to Wroclaw. I wouldn't say I know the city well, but I do know it."

Koniecpolski nodded. "Off you go, then. It's about a hundred miles or so. If he's in Boleslawiec with two children you'll get to Wroclaw about the same time he does." The grand hetman frowned slightly. "I don't know why he used the German name for it."

Lukasz shrugged. "They're a rude and abrupt folk, so their names are usually shorter. That matters when you're using Morse."

"Ah. I hadn't considered that." Koniecpolski was aware that there was some sort of code usually involved in radio transmission, but he'd probably never actually heard it used. He would have simply been given already-translated messages.

Lukasz was in very good spirits on his way out. Sieges were *boring.*

Lower Silesia, between Legnica and Wroclaw

"There's someone up on the hill," Tekla said. Her tone was anxious. "In the trees. I think they're trying to hide."

"I see them," said Jozef. He'd actually spotted the men before the girl had, half a minute earlier. The "hill" she referred to was more of a slight elevation just a few yards off to the left side of the narrow road they were following. The landscape was mostly flat, as was generally the case in the basin formed by the Oder river. They were quite a ways north of the Sudetes mountains which formed most of the southern border of Silesia.

But there were occasional rises in the terrain, often wooded, and at least three men were on the one just ahead of them. They were indeed trying to hide—none too adroitly—and it was quite obvious the reason they were doing so was because this clumsy effort was their idea of an ambush.

Jozef felt a fierce surge, almost one of exultation. His fury had been building for days and he'd finally have someone to unleash it upon.

But first, he had to take some care of the children.

"Tekla, Pawel, I'm going to stop very soon and you both have to get off the horse." He nodded toward some brush off to the right a short distance away. "Go hide in there. Keep your heads down."

"What are you going to do, Uncle?" Pawel asked nervously. In the three days of their travels, Wojtowicz had undergone a transition from scary stranger to nice man to Uncle Jozef.

"Make these bad men go away. Far away."

Oh, so very very far away.

He brought the horse to a halt. "Now, children. Off you go—and on the right side of the horse, where they can't see you well."

Pawel was on the ground in less than two seconds. He reached up to catch his little sister as Josef lowered her with one hand.

His right hand, unfortunately. But he didn't think it was really going to matter because with his left hand he was already drawing out one of the two pistols he carried at his waist.

He thought the world of those weapons. Even with the money provided him by Grand Hetman Koniecpolski, Josef hadn't been able to afford actual up-time pistols. But these were close to the next best thing: Blumroder .58 caliber over-and-under double-barreled caplock pistols. He'd opted for the longer eight-inch barrels despite the extra weight and somewhat more awkward handling because he wanted to be able to fire from horseback—while moving, at a canter if not a gallop—with a good chance of hitting his target.

He'd been able to practice a fair amount with them, too, before he left Dresden. After his participation in the sortie that marked the height of the battle between the besieged forces and Banér's men trying to get back into the trenches, he no longer bothered hiding the fact that he'd trained as a hussar.

He watched while the children scurried off into the shrubbery, without so much as glancing at the wooded rise where the ambushers were waiting. He didn't need to. Part of the training he'd gotten—which had been reinforced by his later experience as a spy—had been to quickly scan and memorize terrain and whatever forces might be located there.

There were three beech trees crowning the rise, all of them mature with thick trunks and plenty of room for horsemen beneath the lower branches. It was the sort of place careless and lazy soldiers would pick for an ambush. They'd have done better to use one of the groves of fir trees that dotted the terrain.

As soon as the children were out of sight he spurred his horse and charged the rise, angling to the right in order to take as much advantage of the road as he could before the final moments.

Part of his mind registered the squawks of surprise—there was some fear there, too—coming from the men half-hidden among the trees. But he paid little attention to that. His concentration was now visual, keeping everything in sight, in his mind's eye—where everyone was, how they were moving—how many were there?

Three, he thought at first. But then a fourth man came out of hiding and began running away on foot. Clearly, the fellow hadn't been expecting this reaction from a lone traveler with two small children—and wanted no part of it.

He was a dead man, but Josef ignored him for the moment. He'd already shifted the pistol from his left hand to the right and taken the reins in his left. He now guided his horse off the road and straight up the rise into the trees.

The pistol came up—the range was less than ten yards now—and he fired.

His target jerked and yelled something. Now six yards away. He fired again and the target went down.

He shoved the empty pistol into a saddle holster—quickly, the range was down to three yards and one of the men was aiming his own pistol—and drew the one on his right hip.

Then he rolled his upper body down next to his horse's flank. The enemy's shot went somewhere over his head. The fool should have tried to shoot the horse.

He was back up again. Visualizing everything. One enemy was clambering onto a horse—and not doing a good job of it. He must be rattled. A second was fumbling with his pistol—probably the one he'd just fired, proving himself a fool twice over.

Josef drove his horse over him, trampling him under. Distantly he heard the man scream but he was now concentrated on the one getting onto his horse.

He ducked under a branch and came up right next to him. Fired. Fired. The man slid out of the saddle, smearing blood all over. The horse panicked and raced off, dragging him from one stirrup. If he wasn't dead already he would be soon, being dragged like that.

Jozef wheeled his horse around. The man he'd just trampled was moaning and clutching his belly. Something in his body had been ruptured, probably. He'd keep for a while.

The first man he'd shot was lying on his back, staring up at the sky with lifeless eyes. The second shot had passed through his throat.

Josef wheeled his horse back around and set off after the man trying to run away. By now, he was perhaps thirty yards distant.

The fleeing soldier didn't stop and try to stand his ground, the way he should have. He just kept running—as if he could possibly outpace a warhorse. Lukasz had told Josef that routed infantry usually behaved this way but he hadn't quite believed him.

Stupid. Jozef's saber was in his hand. It rose and fell. The fleeing soldier's head stayed on his body but not by much. Blood gushed from his neck like a fountain.

On the way back, Josef stopped at the rise, got off the horse and finished the business with the trampled one. He used the man's uniform—such as it was—to clean the saber blade.

Then he walked his horse back to the bushes where the children were hiding.

The boy stood up before he got there. "Were those the men who killed my father and the others?" he asked.

Jozef shook his head. "Probably not, Pawel. But they belonged to the same army. Holk's men."

"I'm glad you killed them, then."

"So am I." He tried—probably failed, though—to keep the ferocity out of his voice.

Tekla came out of the bushes and rushed up to him. He held her for a while, until she stopped crying.

"Come now, children," he said finally. "We want to reach Wroclaw by nightfall."

Chapter 14

Vienna, capital of Austria-Hungary

"So that's him, huh?" Denise and Minnie studied the Austrian archduke across the room. He was engaged in an animated discussion with another man. "His Royal Highness Damn-My-Balls-Hurt," Denise continued.

Judy Wendell, the young lady who had been responsible for that emphatic rejection of the archduke's advances, shook her head. "He's not that bad a guy, actually. Most of the time, I enjoyed his company well enough. It's just... You know. Monarchy. I mean, *real* monarchy, not that show business stuff we had with Queen Elizabeth and Princess Diana and all them back up-time. These guys get raised really weird and it goes to their heads. The girls too, although they don't seem to get as screwy. Women are more sensible than men under pretty much any circumstances."

Denise and Minnie nodded, indicating their full agreement with that proposition. They then went back to studying the royal person in question. "And he's a *bishop* on top of everything else?"

"I'm not actually sure about that," Judy said. "Everybody refers to him that way, as the prince-bishop of Passau—he's also the prince-bishop of Halberstadt and Strassburg and Bremen, too, they say."

"Hey!" Denise protested. "He's got a lot of nerve. *We* control Bremen and Strassburg."

"That's not how it works," Minnie corrected her. She wasn't

exactly what anyone would call a studious girl, but she did pay
more attention to what their employer Francisco Nasi explained
to them about the political situation in Europe than Denise
usually did. "The pope hands out those bishoprics like candy,
whether he actually controls them or not. They call it *in partibus
infidelium*, which is a fancy Latin way of saying 'in the land of
the unbelievers.'"

She cocked her head toward Judy. "What did you mean when
you said you weren't sure about that?"

"I'm not sure he's actually a bishop—the way the church means
it. Somebody told me that technically he's just the administrator
of the bishoprics. That way he gets to collect the revenues—from
Passau and Halberstadt, at least—but he hasn't taken any holy
vows or anything."

"As he proved when he tried to stick his tongue down your
throat," snorted Denise.

Judy grinned. "Oh, hell, girl, we're in the year 1636. The
freaking *popes* in this day and age will try to stick their tongues
down your throat."

"And stick you elsewhere with other parts," Minnie agreed. She
said that with no outrage or indignation; just the way she might
have said *roses are red, violets are blue.* She had the seventeenth
century's pragmatism in full measure. "He's kind of cute," she
added, still examining the royal fellow across the room.

Denise frowned. "Are you kidding? With that long bony nose
and the Habsburg lip?"

The three girls spent a few more seconds in study.

"I gotta say I'm pretty much with Denise on this one, Minnie," Judy said. "I mean, Leopold's not ugly or anything, but I'd
hardly call him 'cute.'"

Again, they resumed their critical examination. Archduke
Leopold Wilhelm, the brother of the current Austrian emperor,
Ferdinand III, was a young man—he'd turned twenty-two a few
months earlier—and on the tall, slender side. He had dark and
wavy hair parted in the middle of his head, which was long
enough to spill over his shoulders. His narrow face was decorated
with a Van Dyke beard.

In all fairness, Denise's accusations were not wide of the
mark. The prince did have a long and bony nose and his heavy
lower lip could have been put on display in a museum with a

caption saying: *If you ever wondered what the famous Habsburg lip looked like, this is it.*

"Come on," Judy said, starting across the floor. "I'll introduce you."

Even as brash as she was, Denise lagged behind. "You sure? I mean..."

"Relax," Judy said. "The emperor himself laid down the terms of the peace treaty between me and Leopold. Of course, nobody said anything to me directly. But he's been on his best behavior ever since and everybody here at court pretends like nothing ever happened. The French call it *sang-froid.*"

"Cold blood," Minnie translated. Despite—or perhaps because of—the little formal education she'd received in Grantville's school system, Minnie spoke several languages quite well. Her wanderings with Benny Pierce had been linguistically fruitful. Minstrels tended to be a migratory bunch.

The parquet floor they were moving across seemed about the size of a basketball court to Denise. The chamber—it might be better to call it a reception hall or even a ballroom—was almost entirely devoid of furniture. Down-timers, at least those in the upper classes, were more accustomed than Americans were to spending large amounts of time in social occasions on their feet rather than sitting down.

As if to compensate for the absence of chairs or tables, practically every square inch of the walls—and they were tall, too, since the ceiling was a good twenty feet above the floor—were covered with paintings. The great majority of them were portraits, and the great majority of the portraits seemed to consist of representations of various members of the centuries-old and farflung Habsburg family.

As they neared Leopold and his companion, the prince spotted them coming and broke off his conversation. When they drew up next to him, his expression was simply one of calm and relaxed attentiveness.

Despite herself, Denise was impressed. *Sang-froid* indeed!

"Your Serene Highness," the archduke said politely. Whatever he might have personally thought about his older brother's decision to elevate all the Barbies to noble status at the end of the previous year, nothing showed but affable courtesy. Of course, the grandiose titles they now held—Denise had to keep herself from spluttering at the idea of Judy Wendell as a "serene high-ness"—carried a lot less weight than they sounded. It was a court title and didn't mean you ruled anything.

"May I introduce my companions, Your Royal Highness?" Judy said. After she'd done so, the prince gestured at his companion, a good-looking fellow who appeared to be about thirty years old. "This is Adriaen Brouwer, a Flemish artist who arrived here in Vienna recently. He was recommended to me by my sister Maria Anna."

Again—and again, despite herself—Denise was impressed. The sister being referred to was now the queen in the Netherlands, having married her Habsburg cousin Fernando less than two years earlier. Fernando was the younger brother of the king of Spain, who was—to put it mildly—less than pleased at Fernando's presumption in declaring himself "the King in the Netherlands."

It was easy for up-timers to think lightly of the Habsburgs, with their odd-looking lower lip and their inveterate habit of marrying their own cousins. But if Denise had gotten nothing else from the tutelage of Francisco Nasi, it was that only an imbecile underestimated the Habsburgs.

There were now three separate powerful realms in Europe ruled by Habsburgs—Spain, Austria and the Netherlands—and their monarchs were no farther apart from each other than one degree of separation. King Philip IV of Spain was the older brother of King Fernando I in the Netherlands, who had married Maria Anna, the sister of Ferdinand III, the emperor of Austria-Hungary.

Austria and the Netherlands got along quite well, these days. Spain and the other two . . . not so much. Like many big and sprawling families, there was a lot of what you could call dys-functionality involved. Being fair about it, the Habsburgs weren't nearly as screwed up and dysfunctional as Grantville's very own Murphy family—as Noelle would be the first to tell you. There was a reason she'd changed her last name to Stull.

There was this difference, though, Denise had to remind herself. When the Murphys fell out with each other, the worst that happened was that Francis Murphy tried to shoot Noelle's mother Pat at the funeral of Pat's new-except-he-was-really-old-boyfriend Dennis Stull's mother because Pat was his ex-wife and she hadn't paid her respects to Francis' father after he died. In any case, he missed and the bullet hit the body of old Mrs. Stull so he only got charged with mutilating a corpse.

If the Habsburgs fell out with each other, a good part of Europe would go to war with casualties likely to be in the hundreds of thousands.

It would have been hard for Archduke Leopold Wilhelm to have chosen between Judy Wendell and Denise Beasley with regard to which of the two young women was more beautiful. Perhaps for that very reason—reinforced by his still vivid memory of Judy Wendell's knee coming up to his groin—he found his interest drawn more to the third member of the female trio.

She was quite a contrast. To begin with, Minnie Hugelmair was clearly a product of his own seventeenth century. Leaving aside her accent, quite different from the distinctively American accent of the other two girls, Hugelmair had any number of subtle behavior traits which made her origins clear in ways that Leopold could not have specified exactly but which were unmistakable.

Except for one trait, now that he thought about it. The girl's face had been disfigured at some point in her life. Judging from the scar that ran from her hairline down through her left eyebrow, she'd been struck by some sort of object which had destroyed the eye as well. In its place she had a remarkably well-made glass eye which, however, neither moved with her good eye nor had an iris of the same color. Her good eye was hazel; the glass one, blue.

An up-time girl would have been devastated by the loss, not so much due to the practical difficulty of having only one eye but because of the distortion of her appearance. They were odd that way, the Americans. They didn't hesitate to spout the most outlandish opinions and comport themselves in sometimes exotic forms of behavior. But any deviation from what they considered proper bodily standards was viewed with unease, sometimes verging on horror. That seemed to be especially true of the women, from what he'd been told and what he'd seen himself.

They made sure their teeth were perfect, no matter the pain and the cost involved. Their hair had to be just so. They fretted endlessly over their weight. He'd even heard that some of them underwent surgery to have features like noses brought into line with what they considered the proper form.

Hugelmair, clearly, suffered little from that unease. Her left eye might not move properly, but since the rest of her did she wouldn't worry about it. What was, was. What was done, was done.

She was quite a pretty woman, the scar and the glass eye aside, with a sturdier frame than either of the two American girls she was with. He wondered who she was and where she came from.

"Is there any new word about the Turks?" Denise asked.

Leopold nodded. "They're coming. There's no longer any doubt about it. We haven't received specific word yet, but they would have probably started their march within the past week."

"Are you going to try to fight them before they reach Vienna?" The American girl—so typical of them!—didn't seem to find anything odd in her asking such a question of a member of Austria's royal family. For a moment, Leopold was tempted to order her arrested for being a spy.

But it was just a fleeting whimsy, probably brought on by his residue of anger at Judy Wendell. The guards standing by the entrance to the hall would certainly obey him if he gave the order—he was an archduke of Austria, after all, in direct line of succession to the throne should his brother Ferdinand and his children die for some reason. But the order would soon be countermanded by Ferdinand himself and Leopold would be soundly berated, albeit in private.

However annoying the Americans could sometimes be, in the present circumstances the Austrian emperor was determined to stay on good terms with them. An invasion by the Ottoman Empire was nothing to take lightly, and the Austrians were going to need allies. Only the USE and Bohemia were close enough to provide assistance quickly, and relations with Bohemia were very tense. Their best chance at getting an ally was with Gustav Adolf.

Who, for his own reasons, made every effort to stay on good terms with the Americans also.

"Why are you looking at me funny?" Denise asked. Leopold had been told the girl was very brash, which was apparently true.

"He's thinking about having you tossed into the dungeon for spying," said Minnie, "but warning himself not to do it because that'd cause a mess. Me, I think he ought to go ahead and do it anyway. Denise, you're my best friend but sometimes you've got the sense of a chicken."

Denise gaped at her. "What do you mean?"

Minnie mimicked her friend's voice, adding what Leopold presumed was an exaggerated overlay of American dialect. "Are y'allllll gonna go on out and whup on them there Turks right off or are y'alllll gonna wait until they mosey on up a bit before you start walloping on 'em?"

She then slipped back into her normal speech. "That's what they call a 'state secret,' Denise. You can get yourself arrested asking those kinds of questions from a cobbler or a fishwife. Much less asking an archduke."

"Oh." Denise grimaced. "Sorry, Your Highness. I hadn't thought of that."

By now, Leopold was quite amused. "Think nothing of it. The proper appellation is 'Your Grace,' by the way. The only persons in Vienna at the moment whom you'd call 'Your Highness' are my nephew Ferdinand and my niece Mariana."

He nodded toward a corner where Queen Mariana occupied the only chair in the chamber. A three-year-old boy was standing next to her with a scowl on his face, presumably caused by the impertinence of his year-and-a-half-old sister who was occupied in tugging at his sleeve. "You'll find them over there."

"Now that I've put Denise in her place, Your Grace," Minnie said, "I'm actually interested in the answer myself. Are you planning to fight the Turks before they get to Vienna, or do you figure you'd fare better to just wait until they've besieged the city?"

She gave him a gleaming smile. Her teeth were in good condition, he saw. He wondered if that was due to nature alone or if she'd gotten help from one of the American tooth-doctors.

What did they call them? "Dentists," if he remembered right.

"If you want to have me arrested," Minnie continued, "you can probably do it without there being any big trouble. I won't object too much unless you put me in a dungeon that's got rats. I really don't like rats."

He burst into laughter. "I wouldn't think of it!"

Looking around, he saw a number of curious looks being sent his way. For whatever quirky reason, that made up his mind concerning the issue at hand.

"We'll wait until they invest the city," he said quietly. "They outnumber us badly and the terrain to the southeast is often marshy. Our troops would be likely to get bogged down and we'd suffer bad casualties. Here..."

He looked around the chamber, as if he could see the walls of the city beyond. "Vienna withstood Suleiman a century ago and according to the American history books we will—would have—withstood the Ottoman Empire again in 1683. We'll take our chances with a siege now, as well."

He bestowed a big smile of his own on the girl. "You'll pass that information along to Don Francisco, I assume?" It wouldn't do to let her think he was ignorant of her association with the Jewish spymaster in Prague.

"Yes, I will." The gleaming smile didn't fade a bit. "But I'm sure he knows already."

That...was probably true, Leopold had to admit. By now the "secret" plans of Austria's high command had spread through enough of its notoriously sievelike court that he could only hope the Ottomans still didn't know as well.

Partly in order to deflect the discussion onto a safer topic, but mostly because he wanted to continue talking to Minnie, Leopold said: "You should really get out of the habit of calling them 'Turks,' you know."

The gleaming smile was replaced by a slight frown. "Why? They *are* Turks, aren't they?"

"Not exactly—and it also depends on what you mean by a 'Turk.' It's true that the Ottoman Empire had its origins in the Turkish tribes who migrated into Anatolia after the Seljuks defeated the Byzantines at the Battle of Manzikert. But what really holds it together is the Ottoman dynasty—and that dynasty by now is more Balkan than it is Turkish. It you wish to give them any specific tribal identity, you'd do better to call them Albanians."

"Huh?" said Denise. "How does that work?"

"Their royal customs are very different from ours," Leopold explained. "The Ottoman emperors sire their children on the women of the harem—who are often recruited from the Balkans. Succession is usually passed on to the oldest son, but not always. There are powerful factions in the Ottoman government, who often use one or another of the younger sons to give themselves more leverage. The disputes can become so contentious that they threaten the normal rules of succession—as we saw recently in the years leading up to Murad becoming sultan.

"It's not just a question of lineage, either," he added. "For the past century—at least—a good half of the Ottomans' grand viziers have been Albanians and most of the rest have been of *devşirme* origin."

"Devsh—" Denise fumbled with the term. "What's that?"

"It is the custom by which the Ottomans recruit Christian boys, almost always from the Balkans, and then convert them to Islam and indoctrinate them to serve the dynasty. Most of them become janissaries. Others enter the civil service. They provide the Ottomans with a body of capable and loyal servants who have no ties to the Turkish nobility. To be honest, that's one of the big advantages they have over us. Their government is better-organized; more efficient."

Leopold looked around the chamber again. His expression must have become a bit sour, because Minnie laughed and said: "Getting envious, are you?"

When he looked at her, the gleaming smile was back. "I don't blame you," she said. "If I had to deal with noblemen all the time I'd go mad."

"Absolutely bats," her friend Denise agreed.

Leopold wondered what bats had to do with the matter.

They were interrupted shortly thereafter by one of the very noblemen in question, a ponderous and pontificating fellow who buried Leopold under a litany of woes involving the depredations and criminal activities of Wallenstein and his accomplices. Leopold didn't doubt that the woes were woeful and that Wallenstein indeed behaved criminally—he was a traitor under sentence of death, was he not?—but it was never made clear what the nobleman wanted Archduke Leopold to do about it.

Soon after the fellow began his peroration the two American girls and their one-eyed companion politely took their leave and departed for greener or at least less voluble social pastures. Leopold was sorry to see them go—even Judy—but didn't blame them in the least.

Eventually, the nobleman left also. Only the Flemish artist remained behind.

Since Leopold had already agreed to place Adriaen Brouwer on a retainer before the three girls showed up, he felt no hesitation in employing him for a nonartistic purpose. And why should he? The Habsburgs had a long tradition of employing artists in other capacities, as witness the many times Peter Paul Rubens had served as a diplomat for the dynasty.

"I'm curious about that one girl, Adriaen."

"One of the Americans?"

"No. The girl with one eye. Who is she? Where did she come from? How and why is she so closely attached to the Americans?"

The artist's nod was so deep as to almost constitute a bow. He understand how these things worked.

"I shall find out, Your Grace."

Chapter 15

Royal Palace
Magdeburg, capital of the United States of Europe

Gustav II Adolf wasn't quite squinting at Rebecca Abrabanel with suspicion but someone who didn't know him as well as she did might think he was. To some degree, that was because the position of the man added so much weight—what her up-time husband Michael called *gravitas,* stealing from the Latin—to anything he said or did that it was easy to inflate a chuckle into a belly-laugh. Or a slight narrowing of the eyes into a glare of dark suspicion.

King of Sweden, Emperor of the United States of Europe, High King of the Union of Kalmar. It was enough to make even a Habsburg envious.

"Surely you didn't resign your seat in Parliament just in order to be able to visit your husband," he said.

Rebecca fluttered her hands. "Oh, no, of course not. Even though I really haven't seen very much of him since you made him a general."

His narrow-eyed gaze moved down to her belly. "Seen him often enough, I'd say. You're pregnant again."

Rebecca was neither surprised nor taken aback by his bluntness. Her friend Melissa Mailey had told her once of the delicate and discreet customs of up-time monarchs of a later era than this one. Apparently there had been one queen—Victoria, she was called—who became outraged whenever anyone so much as suggested that human beings were not actually ethereal spirits.

137

Kings and queens in the seventeenth century, though—emperors too—lived much closer to the mud and muck of practicality. Thankfully, while Michael and Rebecca were very prominent political figures of the day, the legitimacy or lack thereof of their offspring was of no great concern to anyone. If she'd been royalty in line of succession, not only would she have had to give birth in the presence of onlookers and witnesses, she'd have had to conceive the child under the same scrutiny.

"Well, yes, I am pregnant again." She was tempted to add that was thanks to Gustav Adolf himself. After Michael had brought the semi-conscious emperor to Berlin following his terrible injury at the Battle of Lake Bledno, he'd then spent a few days with her in Magdeburg before resuming command of the Third Division in Bohemia. Very pleasant days, those had been; the nights, even more so.

But that would be impolitic. Gustav Adolf had come to terms, more or less, with the ongoing disability that he was subject to periodic seizures. But he didn't like to be reminded of the episode that had produced that disability. Technically, the Battle of Lake Bledno was one of many victories he could add to his roster of such. But he knew perfectly well—as did his opponent in that battle, Grand Hetman Koniecpolski—that from any strategic point of view the outcome had been entirely to Poland's advantage. Gustav Adolf had been incapacitated for months, the USE had been plunged into a near-civil war, and Poland had been given a precious half-year to strengthen its defenses. There was no longer any realistic prospect for the USE to win a quick and decisive victory over the Polish-Lithuanian Commonwealth.

"But, no, of course I didn't resign my seat just to be able to visit Michael. We want Ed Piazza to be the next prime minister if we win the election, and legally that requires him to be a member of the House of Commons. So I gave up my seat in order to provide him with one."

"I doubt if there is a single burgermeister anywhere in the Germanies who would believe that twaddle, Rebecca. Piazza could have run for special election in any number of districts that are perfectly safe for the FOJs. Dietrich Essert's seat in Mecklenburg, for instance, or Reineke Bäcker's in Thuringia. Either one of them would have been perfectly happy to step down for Piazza."

Rebecca was not surprised by Gustav Adolf's detailed knowledge of her party's inner workings. He'd be even better informed concerning the Crown Loyalists. The moderate Hesse-Kassel/Brunswick/Wettin wing, at least, if not the outright reactionaries.

"I see I can't deceive you," she said, smiling.

"You're trying again—right now," he accused. "You're about to come up with some other illogical explanation."

Well...yes, she had been.

She'd *told* Ed this wouldn't work.

Nothing for it but the truth, then. "The plan is for me to become the new secretary of state. Assuming we win, of course."

"Ha!" His big hand smacked the armrest with a meaty sound. "I knew it! I knew that had to be the reason! Anything else would have been a waste."

With a much more genial expression, he leaned back in his chair in the small reception chamber he liked to use for meetings of an intimate and informal nature. "I approve of the scheme. I'll deny ever saying that—and in a high dudgeon, too!—should it become public. But you'll make an excellent secretary of state for the nation. Better than Hermann has been, for a certainty."

He was referring to the existing secretary of state, Landgrave Hermann of Hesse-Rotenburg, the younger brother of the recently deceased ruler of Hesse-Kassel. Mike Stearns had appointed him secretary of state as a gesture of political goodwill and after he'd been replaced as prime minister by Wilhelm Wettin in the 1635 elections, Wilhelm had kept Hermann in the post. That would probably have been a temporary measure except that the instability which gripped the USE after the emperor's injury at Bledno pushed the issue to the side.

"Being fair to Hermann," Rebecca said, "he never wanted the post to begin with."

"Yes, I know. And I have no great complaint concerning his performance. It's been adequate. But I won't be sorry to see someone with real talent at the work taking over the position."

Rebecca's eyes narrowed a bit. "I have to admit, Your Majesty, I am surprised by your reaction. I would have thought you'd prefer a Crown Loyalist secretary of state."

Gustav Adolf chuckled heavily. "I would prefer an *actual* royal, if I lived in a perfect world. If I could make the decision, I'd appoint Prince Ulrik."

"He'd be very good."

The emperor shrugged. "But we have a constitutional monarchy, and while I am prepared and willing—Ha! Watch me!—to gnaw at the edges of it, I have accepted the basic principle. So, a political party must choose the new secretary of state and at the moment..."

He looked aside, his gaze seeming to lose a bit of its focus. "Again, were this an ideal world—one I'd prefer, at least—I'd be more comfortable with people like Amalie Elisabeth running the government. Not herself, of course. She'd have to abdicate as the landgravine and run as a commoner and I'd expect my pagan ancestors' Fimbulwinter to happen before that does. But people of like mind, I mean."

His eyes came back to her, now in sharp focus. "But that's neither here nor there, as your husband likes to say. We live in tumultuous times and at least for the moment the Crown Loyalists are still in great disarray. You and your Fourth of July Party will win the coming election, I am quite sure of it, and"—his massive shoulders heaved another shrug—"it may be just as well. For a time, at least."

He rose to his feet, signaling an end to the interview. "And now I have other business I must attend to. Please give my best regards to your husband, Rebecca."

She rose and curtsied. "I shall, Your Majesty."

When she brought her gaze back up, she saw that Gustav Adolf's expression seemed a bit surprised.

So did his tone of voice. "I actually mean that, you know."

Wallenstein's Palace
Prague, capital of Bohemia

"You'll have to excuse my longitudinality," said Wallenstein. "Is that even a word, I wonder?"

He was lying on his back in the big bed he'd had placed in one of the audience chambers in his palace. His head and shoulders were propped up by several pillows so that he could look at the people he was talking to, and he had a small short-legged writing table perched across his middle. The former mercenary general and now ruler of Bohemia was a semi-invalid—more like a three-quarter invalid—but he still kept constantly busy.

His American nurse and sometime bodyguard Edith Wild wasn't happy about that. But there were limits to how far even her fearsome self could bully Wallenstein.

He was an odd man in many ways, Noelle had come to realize in the days since she and Janos had arrived in Prague. He could be utterly reptilian in his ruthlessness, as he'd demonstrated just a few years earlier when he launched the Croat raid on Grantville and its high school, yet also quite solicitous of the well-being of those around him. His ambitions were great; going far beyond Bohemia itself. Morris and Judith Roth had already told Noelle and Janos of Wallenstein's long-term plan to ingest as much of Ruthenia as he could manage, after securing his control over Upper Silesia. Janos was also certain that he had ambitions on Austria's Royal Hungary as well, or at least parts of it.

Yet except in formal proclamations it was clear that he preferred the name Wallenstein to that of King Albrecht II. He was invariably courteous to those around him, except on the very rare occasions when his temper rose. And with his closest confidants—Noelle had never witnessed this herself but she had been told about it by Judith—he insisted on being called by his given name Albrecht rather than by any of the many titles he held or appellations he could claim.

There weren't many people who enjoyed that privilege, of course. His wife, Isabella Katharina von Harrach. The commander of his army, General Gottfried Heinrich Graf zu Pappenheim. And a handful of close advisers, which included Morris Roth.

(Not Judith, though. As she'd said to Noelle, smiling wryly: "You can't expect miracles from a man born in the last century—by which I mean the *sixteenth* century. You can't even call Wallenstein a male chauvinist because he'd be mystified by the term. What does a man have to be 'chauvinistic' about? he'd ask. Nature's way is what it is, that's all.")

Without waiting for an answer to his rhetorical question, Wallenstein moved right to the subject on his mind. The man was courteous, yes; but he was not given to casual conversation. His mind was always on his affairs.

"What have we reached agreement on, and what still remains to be settled?" he asked.

The question was posed to Janos. Wallenstein didn't ignore Noelle in these discussions. He listened to what she had to say—even carefully, so far as she could tell. But whenever the discussion became focused, began to come to a conclusion of some sort, Noelle could tell that Wallenstein was excluding her from his thoughts. It was as if she no longer existed in the room. His attention was entirely on Janos.

She found that annoying, to say the least. But... push came to shove, it was just a fact that it was Janos Drugeth and not she who could speak authoritatively for Austria-Hungary. Wallenstein could have been as polite and attentive toward her as possible and it would remain the case that in the end he'd still have to get the answer—or even the question—from Janos.

Before answering, Janos took the time to draw up a chair from the ones against the back wall and sit down close to Wallenstein's side. Noelle drew up one of the other chairs but she didn't bother to move it very far from the wall. Wallenstein wouldn't notice where she sat one way or the other, and this way she could enjoy the breeze coming in through the open window. It was a beautiful spring day.

Edith insisted on keeping that window open all year round except for winter and whenever it rained. That was in direct defiance of the established wisdom of the doctors of the time, of course, but by now Edith had the full and complete confidence of Isabella Katherina. Wallenstein's wife was a rather quiet and retiring sort of person—except where the health and well-being of her husband and children were concerned. At such times she could turn into a fair imitation of a dragon and send the doctors scurrying off lest their learned beards get burned away.

"What we have reached clear agreement on is the following," Janos said. "First, Austria will recognize the independence of Bohemia and yourself as its rightful king. Second, no claims for damages will be made by either party, nor will either party sanction or in any way assist any such claims from third parties. That includes—"

Noelle ignored the next stretch of the discussion and just enjoyed the breeze and the sight of the Hradcany rising above the city. Prague Castle, as it was also known, was a sprawling edifice on top of a hill—collection of edifices enclosed by a more-or-less continuous wall, it might be better to say—that dated back to the founding of the city in the ninth century. It had been built up over time, century after century, as one architectural style succeeded another. Noelle's personal favorite of the many structures in the Hradcany was the Gothic cathedral of St. Vitus, whose spires she could see from where she was now sitting. She'd spent many hours in that cathedral since they arrived; some of them praying; some of them in the confession booth; but, mostly, just enjoying the peace and serenity of the great cathedral's quiet interior.

Her contemplations were broken when a phrase from Janos made clear that they'd finally moved beyond the—necessary, necessary, yes, certainly, but still incredibly boring—establishment of the limits of post-settlement legal proceedings.

"—regard to military affairs, Bohemia agrees to come to the aid of Austria if"—he might as well have said *when,* in light of the news report coming from Vienna but Janos was a diplomat, after all—"it comes under attack from the Ottoman Empire. For its part, Austria-Hungary agrees to come to the aid of Bohemia should Bohemia be attacked by the Polish-Lithuanian Common-wealth. For these purposes, 'attack' shall include any movement of Polish forces into Upper Silesia but not Lower Silesia."

They'd spent a full day arguing over that distinction. Having Morris Roth as a close confidant to both sides brought advantages either way. One of the benefits Janos and Noelle had gotten was that they knew from Morris that while Wallenstein laid claim to all of Silesia it was really only Upper Silesia that he cared about. There was the additional problem for him that depending on how the war between the USE and the PLC unfolded, the USE might very well claim Lower Silesia and he had no desire at all to come into conflict with Gustav Adolf.

No, Wallenstein's ambitions lay to the east, not the north. If he could take Upper Silesia from the Poles—including the city of Katowice—then he could encroach still further on the PLC's south-ern lands. He could take—or try, at least—parts of Lesser Poland and Galicia, and if he could hold those then he could move still further into Ruthenia. Starting from his Bohemian and Moravian base, Wallenstein planned to create a new empire in eastern Europe, most of it in the area her universe had known as Ukraine.

Morris Roth called it "the Anaconda project." He supported it because it was his hope that in the course of that eastward expansion, Wallenstein could undermine the conditions that, in the universe the Americans came from, produced the Cossack rebellion of 1648 led by Bogdan Chmielnicki.

The rebellion had several names in the history books. In those devoted to the history of Judaism it was sometimes called the Chmielnicki Pogroms, and it was probably the worst mass slaughter of Jews between the Roman-Jewish War of the first century and the Nazi Holocaust of the twentieth.

Could Wallenstein do it? Noelle had no idea. But it was not something she or Janos had to deal with right now.

Janos now arrived at today's bone of contention. "That brings us to the issue of Royal Hungary and Bohemia's claims to it."

"To *part* of it," Wallenstein countered. "Only those portions of Royal Hungary which would eventually—"

"In a universe that will now never exist," interrupted Janos.

"—become part of Slovakia, which properly belongs to Bohemia and Moravia, as is implied in the very name 'Czechoslovakia'—"

"Another country that would exist only in that other universe and even in that universe"—Janos' voice had a lilt of triumph in it—"would soon cease to exist anyway."

Wallenstein glared at him. But then, looked away. And then, cleared his throat.

"I would be prepared to pay compensation—some *reasonable* amount—to whatever Austrian or Hungarian notables might lose some estates as a result."

Janos grinned at him. "'Nice try,' as the Americans would say. Yes, my family's lands are mostly in and around the town of Homonna which is indeed inconveniently located in that portion of Royal Hungary that you wish to claim as your own."

His grin went away. "You can't bribe me, Your Majesty. It may be that Austria-Hungary will eventually cede parts of Royal Hungary to Bohemia—in exchange for other considerations, be sure of it. But one of those considerations will not be paying me and my family what would amount to a bribe."

Wallenstein might have looked a bit abashed, for a moment. A very little bit and a moment that lasted less than a second, to be sure.

He cleared his throat again. "I do not propose to dispossess you or your family, Janos. You would always be welcome to remain as landowners within Bohemia."

"Yes, I understand. But that would create the sort of problems for me that Prince Karl Eusebius von Liechtenstein has to dance upon, like hot coals. On Monday he's a taxpayer owing allegiance to you and on Tuesday he owes it to Ferdinand of Austria. Then back to you on Wednesday and Thursday, and back again to Austria for the weekend. Awkward, that is—ten times as much for me, who is one of Ferdinand's closest advisers."

He glanced out the window to gauge the time of day. Noelle had given him a good watch; not an up-time device but still one that could keep the time accurately within ten minutes each day. But Janos still didn't really trust the thing.

"We've accomplished enough for today, I think." He rose and looked down at Wallenstein. Then, in a considerably softer voice, he added: "You look tired. Get some sleep. We will continue this on the morrow."

Wearily, Wallenstein nodded his head—a movement that only covered perhaps an inch or so.

"Tomorrow," he agreed. His eyes were already closed.

Chapter 16

Dresden, capital of Saxony province

"We are all here, I think." Gretchen's eyes scanned the room, looking to see who might be missing from what, borrowing from her husband Jeff's American lexicon, she thought of as a "summit meeting."

She wasn't using the phrase properly, but she liked it anyway. In the universe the up-timers came from, a summit meeting had been an encounter between bitter enemies who were still determined to keep their hostility from erupting into violence. Violence on the scale of direct and outright war between them, at least. From what Jeff had described to her, there had been plenty of wars-by-proxy all over the globe. In some ways, that universe and her own seemed much alike.

This meeting she had called in the Residenzschloss the day after her return to Dresden was something quite different, a meeting between allies rather than a meeting between enemies. Granted, there was some antagonism among the various elements in the alliance, but it was on a fairly mild level. Most of it derived from the prickliness of the Vogtlanders, who had what Jeff would have called a chip on their shoulder. That was especially true of their central leader, Georg Kresse.

Gretchen found their attitude irritating, because it was based entirely on unthinking resentments and suspicions—essentially, the ingrained distrust of country folk for what her husband called "city slickers." Gretchen found the term simultaneously amusing and annoying. Amusing because it was, well, amusing. Annoying because the city slicker upon whose person the Vogtlanders' misgivings were primarily focused was herself. That was to say, a printer's daughter who had been born and raised in the small town of Grafenwoehr in the Oberpfalz.

True, some of her comrades and close advisers could lay claim to urban upbringing. Tata was born and raised in Mainz, and Eric Krenz in Leipzig, both of which were definitely cities and one of which—Leipzig—even had two famous universities. But their personal origins were hardly patrician: Tata's father was a tavern keeper and Eric had been born into a gunmaker's family.

The Vogtlanders had no real grievances of a specific nature, whatever their vague unease about dealing with urbanites might be. Gretchen had made it a point to lean over backward to accommodate them. She'd done so from the very beginning, once Kresse brought his Vogtland irregulars down from the mountains to join the fight against the Swedish general Banér. She'd given the Vogtlanders—all the farmers and village folk living around Dresden—disproportionate representation on the Committee of Public Safety, the emergency council she'd created to organize the city's defense against Banér and his army.

Kresse was one of the people in the room, along with his chief lieutenant Wilhelm Kuefer. Anna Piesel was with them as well. She was Kresse's betrothed but also a leader of the Vogtlanders in her own right.

"So what was the outcome of your audience with the emperor?" asked Kresse. The question was stated abruptly, but that was simply his manner. The tone of his voice had carried no hostility and not more than a faint trace of skepticism.

Gretchen reached down into a small valise she'd brought into the room with her and pulled out a sheaf of papers. The sheaf was divided into four-page reports held together by staples. When she'd visited Veleda Riddle in Grantville she'd mentioned how much she admired the up-time stapling devices and the old lady gave her one along with a box of staples. A welcoming gift, she'd called it, to the world's most recent convert to the Episcopal church.

Gretchen had been amused, because it was apparent from Riddle's demeanor that she thought Gretchen might have wanted a different sort of gift. A machine gun, perhaps—no, better still: a guillotine! At one point, Riddle had made some cautioning noises about the perhaps-inappropriate title Gretchen had chosen for her emergency organization in Dresden. Most Americans, in Gretchen's experience—her own husband being no exception—had an abysmal grasp of history. But that did not seem to be true of Veleda Riddle. She knew French history, certainly.

Gretchen handed the sheaf to Tata, who was sitting next to her. "Start passing these around, please." More loudly, so everyone could hear, she added: "This is a full report on what came out of the meeting."

Kresse could refer to her session with Gustav Adolf as an *audience*, if he chose, but so far as Gretchen was concerned it had been a meeting between equals. Equals in the eyes of God and equals by the rights for all people she intended to spread across the Germanies, and then Europe, and then—although she probably wouldn't live that long—across the entire world.

Not, admittedly, a meeting between equals in terms of immediate power and influence. But that was a matter of fact, not principle—and facts could be changed.

Eric Krenz was staring down at the sheaf in his hand with a look of distaste. The Saxon had an almost comical abhorrence of reading anything beyond technical manuals. "Can't you just summarize what's in it?" he asked.

"Quit whining," said Tata, who was already starting to read the second page of the report. In sharp contrast to the man who shared her bed every night, the tavern keeper's daughter adored reading. She spent any spare money she had in one of the city's two bookstores. Eric never complained about the habit, however. Whatever his own attitude toward reading might be, he was a firm adherent to that ancient piece of male wisdom: *happy wife, happy life.*

True, he and Tata were not married. But Eric would be the first to tell anyone that the principle had wide application. And Gretchen thought it was just a matter of time before he started pestering Tata to bring their relationship into greater alignment with the customs of men and the prescriptions of the Lord. For all their badinage and squabbling, the two of them did seem to get along well.

Tata flipped the page over and started on the next. "So far, it's pretty straightforward and amazingly clear for an imperial decision. *Point one*. Saxony is recognized as a self-governing province of the United States of Europe. Direct imperial administration will remain in the hands of Ernst Wettin but only until the election is held and the results are tallied. *Point Two*. The structure of the province of Saxony shall be that of a parliamentary republic. The executive office of chancellor will be filled by whichever party or coalition of parties wins a majority of the vote. *Point Three*. The province of Saxony shall have a Lutheran established church supported by provincial revenues, with the understanding that all other denominations including Catholics and Jews may practice their faith openly with no penalties or restrictions and—oh, now this is fascinating!—if the chancellor of the province is of a different denomination than Lutheran then for the period the chancellor is in office that denomination will also be considered an established church and may share in the province's revenues in proportion to its share of the population of the province."

She looked at Gretchen. "Where did *that* come from? It's sort of an upside down version of *cuius regio, eius religio*."

Kresse was frowning, as he studied the page. "I don't really see the point to it. We're all Lutherans here."

Anna Piesel gave him an elbow in the ribs. Startled, Kresse looked up.

"Oh," he said. He gave Gretchen a slightly guilty look. "I forgot that..."

The frown returned. "But I thought you'd left the Catholic church. Surely you're not thinking—"

Gretchen's temper was rising a bit. Sometimes Kresse really got on her nerves. "Let me make something absolutely clear to you, Georg"—her eyes swept the room with a hard gaze—"and anyone else who has any doubts about it. If I choose to return to the Catholic church I will do so and if anyone thinks they can infringe upon my rights—" Her voice was starting to rise.

"*Gui-llo-tine, gui-llo-tine,*" Eric said, in a singsong voice, with a grin on his face.

Gretchen glared at him. He shrugged. "Just saying."

Her swelling anger began to subside. She gave it a couple of seconds and then turned back to Kresse.

"No, Georg, I am not planning to return to the Catholic church. I have every *right* to do so, mind you. But..."

She ran fingers through her long, blonde hair. The sensation reminded her again of her vow to get it braided so as to keep it from getting in her way. The vow was only semi-serious, though. Jeff loved her hair the way it was, and while Gretchen wouldn't go so far as to adopt the motto *happy husband, happy life,* she'd allow that there was quite a bit of truth to it.

"I want to belong to a church again," she said quietly. "Some people are content without being part of a denomination, but I am not. The Catholic church..." She shook her head. "Is no longer an option for me. And I don't care for most of the Protestant churches."

She gave the people assembled in the room a look that fell just this side of hard. "That includes the Lutheran church, and if that offends any of you, so be it. I've thought about it a lot over the past year or two, and I decided I want to belong to an American church. So I chose the Episcopalians."

Kresse's frown was back. Could the man manage to let an hour go by without it? "The Episcopalians are an English church."

To her surprise, Eric Krenz responded. "No, they're not, Georg. They originated from the Anglican church but they've been independent for more than two centuries." He waved his hand. "In that other universe, I'm talking about. What you have today in our universe is a complicated situation where over there"—he waved again, more or less in the direction of the British Isles—"you've got a big pack of down-time English clerics and kings and Puritans and whatnot squabbling with each other, and over here"—he now gestured more or less in the direction of Grantville—"you've got a very small pack of up-timers who share a lot of doctrine and most emphatically do not share a lot of attitude with the English."

By now, everyone in the room was frowning—Gretchen too—trying to follow Krenz's summary of religious evolution spanning two universes and twice that many centuries.

Which...

Wasn't bad, actually.

"What he said," stated Gretchen.

As she usually did, Tata remained behind after the meeting adjourned. More unusually, Eric did also.

"How do you come to know so much about the Episcopal church?" Tata asked him.

Eric's expression became shifty-eyed. "Well..."

"Ha!" Tata didn't quite curl her lip. The face she made indicated that she would have except the issue was not worthy of her outright contempt. "Tried to seduce an up-timer once, did you? It went badly, I imagine."

Eric gave her a sulky look. "Anne Penzey. I met her in Magdeburg when Thorsten and I were training in the army. She was, ah, young at the time—"

"*Young*?" said Gretchen. "I know the girl! She couldn't have been more than... That was what, two years ago? She'd have been no older than sixteen!"

"Seventeen," Eric protested. "Almost eighteen, maybe."

"It's not worth getting worked up over, Gretchen," Tata said. "It's true that Eric is a lecher but he's terrible at it so no harm is done." The laugh that followed was more in the way of a giggle. "Look what happened there! Seventeen years old—practically a child, still—and she fended the clumsy lout off with a lecture on ecclesiastical history."

She now moved to the issue actually at hand. "I'm curious myself, though. Why did you pick that American church?"

"It's a little hard to explain. Most of the American churches are... how to say it?"

"Peculiar," Eric provided. "Downright weird, some of them— especially the ones that call themselves pentecostal. There's even one church in Grantville—so I was told, anyway; I didn't investigate myself—where they speak in tongues and play with snakes."

"I'm not sure that rumor is really true," Gretchen said. "Although it might be. Some of the American churches seem a lot like Anabaptists."

She shrugged. "I was raised Catholic. I like the... what to call it? The way Catholics do things. I was told the Episcopalians are much alike, that way. Some of them, at least. The ones they call 'high church.'"

She smiled, then, a bit wickedly. "Especially Admiral Simpson."

"*Simpson*?" Eric and Tata were wide-eyed now. Clearly, both of them were trying to visualize Gretchen Richter and John Chandler Simpson worshipping in the same church and...

Having a hard go of it.

"He *is* on the side of the angels, these days," said Tata. Dubiously.

"I think it's more of a loan," Eric cautioned. "Any day—you never know—Satan might call it in and demand his interest."

Three days later, Tom Simpson came to Dresden. With him, he had in tow a young woman named Ursula Gerisch.

"I'm your bishop," he told Gretchen. "Don't ask me any questions, though, because I'm trying to study up on the job myself. Laud just gave it to me. I think mostly out of pique—probably some spite, too."

Gretchen stared at him. "I thought someone named Robert Herrick was the bishop in the USE."

Tom shook his head. "He's headquartered in Magdeburg. Originally his diocese was named as the whole USE, but now it's being divided. Herrick will wind up with everything that's not part of the so-called 'Grantville Diocese,' as Laud is calling it."

"Which covers what part of the country?" asked Gretchen, frowning.

"I don't know yet. I don't think Laud himself does. But apparently it's going to cover Saxony. I wouldn't worry about it, though. Between you and me, Herrick doesn't really want the job anyway so he won't be underfoot too much. Which is a good thing, from everything I've heard about him."

Gretchen had received an earful herself on the subject of Robert Herrick's shortcomings while she'd been in Grantville.

She moved aside from the doorway to let Tom and Ursula enter her apartment. It was quite a nice apartment, as you'd expect in the Residenzschloss. "I would offer you something to drink but I'm afraid I don't have anything at the moment except some water. Although I could heat up some broth. I've been very busy lately and the boys"—the sounds of two young children playing in another room were quite audible—"don't like coffee and tea. I don't bother keeping it around unless I know Jeff is coming for a visit."

She was babbling a little. A *bishop*? Tom Simpson—huge, affable, cheerful, friendly Tom Simpson, so unlike his father—was now a *bishop*?

Well, why not? They lived in an age of miracles again, as witness the great cliffs created by the Ring of Fire.

"I can't stay long anyway, Gretchen. The only reason I came to Dresden is because we need some special equipment made to get the ten-inch rifles out of the river—never mind the grisly details—and this is the best place to get it done quickly. Grant-ville and Magdeburg have better facilities for the purpose but they're so backlogged with work I decided to come here instead. But I'm leaving first thing tomorrow."

He turned to Gerisch, took her elbow and hauled her forward. "Ursula is the best proselytizer we've got. She's a whiz at it. She agreed to move here and my mother agreed to subsidize her for a while. And if you want to know why a Unitarian is willing to support an Episcopalian missionary, trust me, you really don't want to know. My mother's schemes can confuse the ghost of Machiavelli. Just accept that she is."

He breezed right on, not giving Gretchen a chance to say anything—which didn't really matter since she had no idea what to say anyway.

"We need a proselytizer here in Dresden because until you get enough people to form a congregation there's no point my sending you a priest, which is good because I still have to study up on how I'd go about ordaining one in the first place. Hey, give me a break. I've been a good Episcopalian all my life but it's not as if I paid a lot of attention to how the gears turned. I was a wannabe professional football player and then a soldier after the Ring of Fire."

He finally broke off—for maybe two seconds. "So there we are. Can you put Ursula up for a few days until she finds a place of her own?"

Gretchen nodded.

"Great. I'm leaving, then. I'll see you again . . . whenever. Prob-ably not until we take Munich, though."

And off he went.

Gretchen closed the door and looked at Ursula. The woman had an odd expression on her face. It seemed to consist mostly of unease combined with penance and perhaps a trace of defiance.

"I must warn you, Frau Richter, since you will no doubt hear of it soon anyway. My past is . . . not very reputable."

Finally! A place to rest her anchor.

"Neither is mine," Gretchen said, growling like a mastiff.

Chapter 17

Bavaria, just north of Zolling on the Amper River

General Ottavio Piccolomini lowered his spyglass. "You are certain of this, Captain? If I anchor my plans on your claim and you are mistaken, it could be a disaster. Almost certainly *will* be a disaster because I will have divided my forces."

He spoke in Italian, not German. Most of the officers in the Bavarian army, like Piccolomini himself, were mercenaries and Italian had been something in the way of a *lingua franca* for such soldiers since the late Middle Ages. The transition of military practice from feudal levies to mercenaries employed by a centralized state had begun in Europe with the *condottieri* of the thirteenth- and fourteenth-century Italian city-states like Florence, Genoa and Venice. Many of those Italian traditions were carried on by those who practiced war as a profession, including the language, even after the rise to prominence of Swiss pikemen and German landsknechts in later centuries.

As was true of most mercenary captains, Piccolomini spoke German and Spanish as well as his native Italian—German fluently, albeit with a heavy Florentine accent, and Spanish passably. The reason he was using Italian as the common tongue of the Bavarian forces was not so much due to his own preferences as it was to the heavy Italian element in his army. His immediate staff and most of his commanders were German, but since they all spoke Italian reasonably well he had decided it would be wiser to use that language than run the risk that orders transmitted farther down the line in the course of a battle might be mistranslated.

The officer to whom he'd addressed his question was Johann Heinrich von Haslang, newly promoted from captain to colonel. Shortly after Piccolomini took control of Bavaria's army he had begun a reorganization of the officer corps. Many of General von Lintelo's favorites had been eased out, replaced by officers in whom Piccolomini had more confidence.

His judgment had generally been very good, thought von Haslang—even allowing for the obvious bias he had, being himself one of the beneficiaries of the new regime. Piccolomini was a humorless man, whose thick body and heavy face were a good reflection of his temperament. But he was competent and experienced and didn't seem to suffer from the tendency of all too many mercenary commanders to play favorites with his subordinates.

"I can only give you a conditional assurance, General," said von Haslang. He nodded toward the receding airship in the sky, still quite visible despite now being several miles away. "I have kept extensive and careful records of these vessels. The one we are watching now is the one they call the *Pelican* and it is the one which the USE has maintained in service here in Bavaria since the beginning of the conflict. But they have two others at their disposal should they choose to use them, the *Albatross* and the *Petrel*."

He took off his hat and wiped his forehead with a sleeve. It was an unseasonably hot day this early in May. "Normally, they employ the *Albatross* as something of a general-purpose transport vehicle. It can be almost anywhere in central Europe on any given day. At the moment—but please keep in mind that these reports always lag days behind the reality because—"

He broke off. *Because our pigheaded duke insists on keeping Bavaria's few radios in Munich where they do no one any good at all instead of letting me give at least one of them to our spies...* would be impolitic, even though Piccolomini himself probably would have agreed.

"—because they do," he finished a bit lamely. "But for whatever it's worth, the last reports I received placed the *Albatross* at Luebeck."

Piccolomini grunted. "How fast could they get it back down here?"

Von Haslang shrugged. "That depends on how much urgency they felt, General. These airships operate with hot air and have a very limited range because of the fuel that needs to be expended to keep the air in the envelope heated. Eighty miles or so—a hundred miles, at the most. Luebeck is about four hundred miles to the north."

Piccolomini frowned. "Much farther than that, I would think."

"By road, yes. But I am speaking of the straight line distance which is more or less how these airships travel."

"Ah. Yes." Piccolomini pursed his lips, doing the calculations himself. "So, at least four legs to the trips; probably five or six."

"Six, in this case, General. I know the specific stops they'd make. Each leg would take two to three hours, depending on the winds. If they had fuel ready to go at each stage and made a priority of refueling, they could be back in the air in an hour or so."

"Can they fly at night?"

"Yes, but they try to avoid it whenever possible."

"So, about two days, you're saying."

"Approximately. And unfortunately..."

"That's quite a bit quicker than our spies can alert us"— Piccolomini's heavy lips quirked into what might have been a smile of sorts—"since Duke Maximilian is unwilling to risk the few radios he has out in the field."

He copied von Haslang's hat-removal and use of a sleeve to wipe the sweat off his brow. Added to the heat of the day was the weight of the buff coat the general was wearing—as was von Haslang himself. Most cavalrymen favored buff coats, no matter the temperature. Risking a gaping wound in the torso or even on an arm was not worth the comfort of light clothing.

"And what about the third airship? The *Petrel,* was it?"

"There, we are on firmer footing. They have been using it in their salvage operations in Ingolstadt, trying to raise those two ten-inch guns we tossed into the river before we evacuated."

"It's still very close—closer than the *Albatross,* most likely."

Von Haslang smiled. "Yes, it is—but they've altered it rather drastically in order to lighten it as much possible so they can get the most lift from the envelope. Instead of four engines, it now only has two—and our spies tell me that they keep as little fuel on board as possible for the salvage operation."

He pointed to the still-visible but now very distant airship. "I can't promise you anything, General. But the odds are quite good that the *Pelican* is the only airship we will need to worry about for the next few days."

Piccolomini grunted again. "Better odds, you're suggesting, that what we face against Stearns' forces if we don't take the risk."

"Yes, sir."

After wiping his brow, Piccolomini had kept his hat still in his fist. Now he placed it back on his head. "We'll do it, then." He turned his horse toward von Haslang's immediate superior, General Caspar von Schnetter—who had been a mere colonel a week earlier. He was another of the Bavarian officers who'd enjoyed a promotion.

"You will lead the attack on the enemy's flank, von Schnetter," said Piccolomini. "Remember—speed is critical. We won't launch the attack unless the diversion succeeds in drawing off the enemy's flying artillery—but they don't call them 'flying' for no reason. If you dawdle, Stearns will be able to get them back on his right flank soon enough to face you. And those batteries have a fearsome reputation against cavalry, which is all you'll have at first."

"I understand, sir," said von Schnetter.

"Make sure you do, General." Piccolomini's tone was forceful. "I have heard all too many officers since I arrived in Bavaria spout the opinion that Stearns is simply lucky rather than capable. Maybe so—but only a fool would operate on that assumption. He's won every battle he's fought so far, which in my experience indicates that something more than mere luck is involved."

Piccolomini looked up at the sky, scowling. It was not a clear day; a good third of the sky was covered with clouds. But those clouds foresaged nothing more than an occasional sprinkling.

"I wondered why Koniecpolski chose to attack Gustavus Adolphus in the middle of a storm," he said. "Now I understand the reason. Damn and blast those airships—and the airplanes may be even worse. Your enemy can see everything you're doing."

Thankfully, Gustavus Adolphus seemed to be keeping his few airplanes in the Polish theater. Proving once again—as if the passing millennia had not already given proof enough—that rulers were prone to being pigheaded. If they'd had to face airplanes as well down here in Bavaria...

Rudelzhausen, Bavaria
About ten miles north of Zolling

Ulbrecht Duerr's finger touched a place on the map spread out across the table in the center of the small tavern's main room. "Here, upstream of where the Amper makes that big bend southwest of Moosburg, a bit east of Zolling. That's the place where Captain Finck says a crossing of the Amper would be easiest."

"Anywhere else?" Mike Stearns asked. "And how recent is the information?"

"The information concerning the spot near Zolling is now a day old. There hasn't been any rainfall worth talking about lately and the weather seems to be staying good, so nothing will have changed as far as the condition of the river is concerned." Duerr shrugged. "Of course, there is no way to know if Bavarian forces have moved into the area since Finck was there."

He now tapped a spot on the map that was just north of Moosburg. "This does us little good, of course, but Finck reports there's a place here on the Isar where the river could be easily forded. Cavalry and flying artillery could cross directly, he says, with no preparation at all. For infantry—certainly heavier artillery—you'd want to lay down a corduroy road. But no bridge would have to be thrown up."

"That spot's east of the confluence between the Amper and the Isar. We'd wind up on the wrong bank of the Isar and have to find a place to cross back over again."

Duerr nodded. "True." He glanced up at the ceiling of the room they were in, as if he could see through it to the sky beyond. "The *Pelican* can be back by nightfall and can lay over until tomorrow. We've made a landing place for it. When we move out in the morning we'll have excellent reconnaissance until they have to return."

Mike shook his head. "I don't want to wait, Ulbrecht. I want to keep pushing on, since we still have most of the day left." His own finger tapped a place on the map. "By sundown—well, allowing for enough time to bivouac—I want to be here. This village called Attenkirchen."

Christopher Long tugged at the point of his beard, which was another of the Van Dykes so popular at the time. Mike, who favored a full beard cut short, had never been able to see the logic of the things. Maintaining a proper Van Dyke required almost as much work as being clean-shaven. Why bother?

"I recommend against that, sir. Attenkirchen is a good six—maybe seven—miles south of here. We can certainly make it there by nightfall, in this weather. But we'll be too far away to maintain the security of the *Pelican*'s landing site—and it will be much too late in the day to set up a new one."

Duerr chimed right in. "Which means the *Pelican* will have to continue operating out of Regensburg, and we're getting close to the limit of its operating range unless we provide it with a new secure base."

Mike tried not to let his impatience make him irritable. The more time that passed, the more convinced he became that Bavaria was a distraction, a side show. Yes, Duke Maximilian of Bavaria had a lot to answer for. But the cold, hard fact remained that by now Bavaria had been stripped of most of its former power. That power had always been heavily dependent on Bavaria's alliance with Austria—which Maximilian had shredded with his maniacal response to the flight of the Austrian archduchess who had been supposed to marry him.

And, meanwhile, the Turkish armies were marching through the Balkans toward Vienna. *That,* in Mike's opinion, was where their attention ought to be focused. Instead, practically all of the military power of the nation was tied up fighting either the Poles or the Bavarians, neither of whom posed an existential threat to the United States of Europe. Whereas the Ottomans might, if they could take Vienna.

And the problem there—again! you'd think people would have learned by now—was the damned American history books. Suleiman the Magnificent had failed to take Vienna in 1529, and the up-time history books said the Ottomans would fail again when they tried—would try; might try; could have would have tried; the grammar got insane—again in 1683.

Half a century from now, in another universe—as if that provided any guidance for what should be done *today,* in *this* universe, under *these* conditions.

As bad an influence as the American history books could be, Mike sometimes thought that the influence of American technology was even worse. As witness the reliance his officers were placing more and more on the reconnaissance provided to them by the *Pelican.*

Yes, the airship made a superb observation platform. Much better than airplanes, really. A plane had to spot something while speeding through the air with only one or two pairs of eyes; an airship could effectively hover in place, allowing several observers to take their time examining the landscape below through binoculars and telescopes.

But the damn things had such limits! They burned so much fuel just keeping the envelopes filled with hot air that they could only stay in position for a short time, unless an advance base was created for them. And the problem there was that the craft were so huge and unwieldy that it took time to build a base for them—and then you had to detach a sizeable force to guard the base. Not to mention that they were all but useless in bad weather.

All of Mike's experience as a fighter—first as a prizefighter, and now as a commander of armies—was that if there was any one secret to winning a fight it was to be *relentless.* Hit 'em and hit 'em and hit 'em and hit 'em. Don't stop, don't rest. Push on, push on.

The boxer he'd tried to model himself on when he was in the ring was Rocky Marciano. And while Mike had never thought he had Marciano's talent, he did have the man's temperament as a fighter. Never let up. Once you start, keep on. Hit 'em and hit 'em and hit 'em. If you can't knock them out, wear them down for a while—and then knock them out.

Never let up.

Of course, you had to be strong and in very good shape and be able to take a punch, for that strategy to work. But Mike had all of those qualities and he thought his Third Division did as well. Most of all, he was profoundly distrustful of allowing time to go by in a fight. Yes, yes, it would be nice to have excellent reconnaissance at every waking hour. Why not wish for orbital satellites while you're at it?

"No," he said firmly. "Piccolomini just took over command of the Bavarian army less than a month ago—and he's only had a few days—well, a week or so—to integrate the forces retreating from Ingolstadt. Granted, he's got a lot of experience and a good reputation, but he's not a magician. His C2 is bound to be a little ragged."

"C2"—he'd pronounced it Cee Two—was an Americanism that had by now spread throughout the USE's military. It stood for "command and control."

Duerr and Long were both giving him looks that might fairly be described as fishy.

"So is ours, General Stearns, as many new recruits as we've got," said Long.

He had a point. This campaign against Bavaria was coming on top of the Third Division's campaigns in Saxony and Poland, followed by a march to and back from Bohemia to fight Banér outside Dresden, followed by a march from Saxony to Regensburg. They'd fought their first big battle at Zwenkau in August—less than nine months ago. That had been followed by the savage fighting at Zielona Gora in October and the big battle of Ostra in February. And here they were, just four months later, readying to fight yet another major battle.

They'd lost a lot of men in the process, some of them killed, more of them injured, and a fair number just leaving for quieter pastures. Some of them did so by the rules, but most of them simply deserted. There was no great social opprobrium attached to desertion in this day and age.

Because of its reputation for paying regularly, keeping the soldiers well equipped and well fed, and winning victories, the Third Division had no trouble finding new volunteers to replace the men they lost. In fact, the division was technically over-strength, at almost thirteen thousand men, because of its success at recruitment.

But that came at a cost. To a degree, the Third Division was constantly recreating itself as it went.

"I'm more concerned about our weakness when it comes to cavalry," said Long. "I understand your frustration with the *Pelican*'s limitations, sir. But even reinforced with Mackay's men, our cavalry is terribly understrength. That allows the Bavarians to use their superior numbers in cavalry to overwhelm our own, which—"

"Enables them to move their troops without us being able to spot them," Mike finished for him. "Yes, I know that, Christopher." He ran fingers through his hair, resisting the temptation to tug at it with frustration. "The ideal solution would be to have another airship permanently attached to us that could rotate with the *Pelican*. But we're stretched too much. If only—"

He shook his head, shaking off the pointless wish that Gustav Adolf would come to his senses and end the war with Poland. Being fair to the emperor, even if Gustav Adolf was willing to make peace it was doubtful at this point that King Wladyslaw would be. Part of the reason for the never-ending rancor between the USE and Poland was that the two nations were ruled by two branches of the same Vasa royal family—both branches of which were firmly convinced the other was a pack of scheming bastards who couldn't be trusted. Not for the first time since he'd arrived in the seventeenth century, Mike was reminded of his native state's own reputation for stupid feuding.

Hatfields and McCoys, meet Vasas and Vasas.

"One of these days," he said, "the new hydrogen dirigibles will come into service. That'll help, because they'll be able to stay up a lot longer."

He looked back down at the map and placed his finger on the spot marked *Attenkirchen*. "Here, gentlemen," he said firmly. "By sundown. The *Pelican* will be fueled up and ready to go by sunup, so they'll be here early in the morning."

And then they'll have to leave again in half an hour or so. But he didn't see any point in adding that. Life was what it was. You fought a war with the army you had, not the one you wished for.

Chapter 18

Bavaria, on the Amper River
Two miles east of Zolling

The ducks were what saved Jeff Higgins' life. What bothered him afterward was that he never knew what kind of ducks they were, so he couldn't properly thank the breed with something suitable like erecting a small temple or naming his next child after them.

He and the small scouting party he was leading had just reached the spot on the Amper which Captain Finck had recommended as a good place for a crossing to be made. Jeff had started to come out of the saddle to lower himself to the ground when the flock of ducks—did ducks come in "flocks"? he didn't know—suddenly started squawking—or whatever you called the racket that ducks made when they got agitated—and what seemed like thousands of them lifted themselves out of the river and went flying off.

Startled, his weight resting mostly on one stirrup, he looked to the west and had a glimpse of the oncoming Bavarian cavalry.

He assumed they were Bavarian, anyway—and he wasn't about to stick around to find out. He'd go on that assumption and let the devil worry about the details.

"Out of here!" he shouted, sliding back into the saddle and spurring his horse onto the trail they'd followed down to the river bank. "Get the fuck out of here!"

✧   ✧   ✧

The ducks were mallards and General von Schnetter felt like cursing the things. The waterfowl had alerted the enemy patrol just in time for them to make their escape.

Von Schnetter wasn't concerned about the failure to capture the patrol, in and of itself. What worried him was that the big fellow who'd seemed to be leading them was dressed like an officer—at least, if von Schnetter was interpreting the design and insignia of USE uniforms properly.

The army of the United States of Europe was an outlier in that respect, being the only large military force of the time that insisted on clothing its soldiers in standard uniforms. That actually made it harder to distinguish between officers and enlisted men because the gray uniforms were much the same color and the insignia were hard to differentiate between at a distance. In a properly costumed army, the extra money officers usually spent on their clothing made them stand out more. He himself, for instance, was at that very moment wearing a broad-brimmed hat with a pair of splendid ostrich plumes which nicely set off his bright red shoulder sash.

If that big fellow who'd made his escape was just a scout, it would probably take him and his mates a bit of time to find their commander and pass on the warning, and if the commander was a sluggish sort...

But if he was the commander himself, which he might well have been—von Schnetter was in the habit of leading his own reconnaissance, as he was this very moment—and if he was capable...

"Fucking mallards!" he snarled.

"Form up! Form up!" Jeff shouted, as he reached the sentries he'd posted to guard the flanks of the regiment.

For once, he was thankful for the sword he had to haul around. The damn thing was all but useless for actual fighting but it made for the most dramatic pointer you could ask for. He had the sword in his hand and was waving it in the direction from which he and his three scouts were racing.

He wasn't too happy about that, either, since Jeff disliked being on a horse under any conditions and especially galloping over terrain he wasn't familiar with. Push come to shove, though, he'd prefer falling off a horse even at high speed to getting shot or—worse still—getting stuck like a pig by a damn sword. Unlike himself, there were men in the world who knew how to use the idiotic devices.

"Form up! The Bavarians are here!"

He didn't have time to get the whole regiment into proper formation. Not even close to enough time. But he was able to get three companies in a line with their muskets ready to fire.

No breastworks; no pikemen—against cavalry. This was going to be hairy as all hell. He could only hope that Engler and the flying artillery would come up soon.

Bavaria, near Moosburg
Five miles east of Zolling

At that precise moment, Colonel Thorsten Engler was cursing ducks himself—and wasn't bothering to make fine distinctions between breeds. Being a former farmer, Thorsten knew perfectly well the ducks were mallards. But at the moment, so far as he was concerned, they just belonged to the cursed category of "noisy birds." Between the ones still on the river just a few dozen yards away and the ones who'd taken to the air, they were making such a racket that he couldn't hear anything else.

What he was straining to hear was the sound of horses moving. Or, more likely, the sound of cavalrymen's gear clattering. If there were horses in the area they were moving slowly. Even over the clamor being made by the ducks, Thorsten could have heard the sound of a large group of galloping or cantering horses.

You couldn't see anything, between the heavy growth and the walls of Moosburg. The town wasn't fortified, but like almost all towns and villages in central Europe the buildings were erected right next to each other. Looking at Moosburg from a distance of a hundred and fifty yards or so, he couldn't see anything beyond the walls and roofs of the outlying edifices. For all he knew, there was an entire cavalry regiment gathered in the town square, ready to charge out at any minute.

Or there could be nothing there at all, beyond some frightened civilians trying to hide in root cellars and basements.

The *Pelican* had arrived shortly after dawn, but it had only been able to stay in the area for a short time. The airship was operating at the very edge of its range, this far from its base in Regensburg. By tomorrow or the day after, the SoTF National Guard should have an airship base in operation in Ingolstadt, which would cut perhaps twenty miles from the distance. Better yet, if the Third Division could cross the Amper and secure a beachhead, they could establish an airship base almost right next to their field of operations.

Just before the *Pelican* left—actually, after it was already on its way back to Regensburg and several miles away—it reported what seemed to be significant cavalry movement near Moosburg. General Stearns had immediately ordered the flying artillery squadron to deploy west of the town. He was sending the Dietrich and White Horse regiments from the 3rd Brigade to support them, with Brigadier Derfflinger in command, while keeping the brigade's third regiment in reserve. That was the Yellow Marten regiment, commanded by Colonel Jan Svoboda.

All well and good—once they got here. But Derfflinger's infantry was still a good three-quarters of a mile away, and the artillery units attached to his brigade would be lagging still farther behind. And in the meantime, Thorsten and his flying artillery were on their own.

If they'd been operating in open country, Thorsten would have been less concerned. By now, he had a great deal of confidence in his men, especially the veterans of Ahrensbök. Given enough open space to fire several volleys, he was sure he could drive off any but the largest cavalry force.

Unfortunately, the terrain west of Moosburg was wooded. Not a forest, exactly, but there was enough in the way of scattered groves and treelines to allow an enemy cavalry force to move up unseen until the last few hundred yards—not more than two hundred, in some directions.

If only the *Pelican* were still here...

Bavaria, Third Division field headquarters
Village of Haag an der Amper

The first indication Mike Stearns had that his campaign plans were flying south for the winter was the eruption of gunfire to the west. From the sound of it, a real battle was getting underway.

By the time his units had entered Haag an der Amper early that morning, the little village located a short distance north of the river had already been deserted by its inhabitants. From the looks of things, they'd left several days earlier. Bavaria had been relatively unravaged by the Thirty Years War, especially this close to Munich, but by now people living anywhere in the Germanies—anywhere in central Europe—were hyper-alert to military threats. Every city and town and most villages had their own militias, but except for those of walled cities the volunteer units were only suited for fending off bandits and small groups of plundering soldiers and deserters. As soon as they realized that major armies were coming into the area, the inhabitants would flee elsewhere. To a nearby walled city, if they had privileges there. To anywhere away from the fighting, if they didn't.

In the larger villages, Mike's command unit would seize the best and biggest tavern in which to set up a field headquarters. In smaller villages like Haag an der Amper, there would be no tavern as such. Typically, one of the more prosperous villagers would use one of the rooms on the ground floor of his house as a substitute.

By the time the army was done with such a temporary field headquarters and moved on, the place was fairly well trashed. The structure would usually remain intact, but the interior would be a ruin. Partly that was from carelessness and occasionally it was from deliberate vandalism—although not often if the troops were part of the Third Division. Ever since the atrocities committed by some of his units in the Polish town of Świebodzin, Mike had maintained a harsh discipline when it came to the way civilians were treated.

Mostly, though, the destruction was simply the inevitable side effect of having far too many men wearing boots and carrying weapons tromping in and out of a building that had never been designed for the purpose. Mike had been bothered by the wreckage in his first weeks as a general, but by now he'd gotten accustomed to it. War was what it was.

When the gunfire erupted, Mike's first instinct was to rush to the door in order to look for himself. But he suppressed that almost instantly and turned instead to the radio operator positioned at a small table in a corner.

"Any reports?" he demanded.

The radio operator shook his head. "Not yet, General."

That was a bad sign. Probably a very bad sign. Mike had stationed Jeff Higgins and his Hangman regiment on the division's right flank—and he'd done that partly because that was the flank that was more-or-less hanging out there and blowing in the wind. Jeff was his only up-time regimental commander and he had the only up-time radio operator, his old friend Jimmy Andersen. Mike was confident that, between them, they'd use the radio to warn him of any trouble almost instantly. He *still* had down-time commanders, no matter how many times he snarled at them, whose immediate instinct was to send a courier instead of using their regimental radio.

And now...

"Damnation," Mike muttered. He looked at one of his junior adjutants, who'd also serve him as a courier. "Get over there, Lieutenant Fertig, and see what's happening."

Bavaria, on the Amper River
Two miles east of Zolling

Jeff Higgins wasn't worried about the radio because he assumed Jimmy Andersen would have already sent the warning. His attention was entirely concentrated on trying to keep his formations from disintegrating under the impact of the Bavarian cavalry charge.

They probably would have, despite all his efforts, except that the same partially wooded terrain that was causing Thorsten Engler so much anxiety a few miles to the east was working in favor of the Hangman regiment here. There were just enough small groves, just enough fallen logs, and just enough brush to give his men a bit of cover and impede the Bavarian horsemen.

It was clear very soon, however, that there was no way the Hangman was going to be able to hold this position. Against cavalry...maybe. But Jeff was quite sure this charge wasn't the product of an accidental encounter with a passing cavalry unit. There were too many of them and they'd come on too quickly and in too good a formation. This had been planned.

The Bavarians had outmaneuvered them, it was as simple as that. Jeff was sure of it—and that meant there were infantry units coming up right behind. Probably some light artillery, too. They'd sweep right over them. He needed to fall back, anchor his regiment on the river and just hope that the commander of the 1st Brigade, von Taupadel, was moving his regiments up in support.

Von Taupadel was doing just that, and at that very moment. But moving several thousand men in unfamiliar terrain in response to gunfire coming from a still-unseen enemy is the sort of thing that only happens neatly and instantly in war games.

Unfortunately, von Taupadel did not think of using his brigade radio until several minutes had gone by—perhaps as much as a quarter of an hour. In fairness to him, that was partly because he also knew that both the commander and the radio operator of the Hangman regiment were up-timers, and he assumed they'd already sent a radio message to General Stearns.

Bavaria, near Moosburg
Five miles east of Zolling

Thorsten Engler could hear the gunfire to the west. Each individual gunshot was faint, because of the distance, but that much gunfire can be heard for many miles, especially when it is continuous and never lets up.

Half an hour had gone by since the flying artillery squadron had come into position outside Moosburg—thirty-three minutes, to be exact; Thorsten had a good pocket watch and used it regularly—and there had been no sign of movement in the town. Nothing. Not a dog had stirred.

By now, Engler was almost certain that the cavalry movement the *Pelican* had reported had been a ruse. A feint, to draw the Third Division's attention to its left flank while the real assault came on the right.

He was tempted to send a patrol into the town to find out what was there, but he wasn't quite ready yet. If he was wrong, they'd get slaughtered.

He'd wait five more minutes. In the meantime...

Thorsten turned to his radio operator, who was in place right behind him. Whether because he was betrothed to an up-timer or simply because—this would have been his own explanation, had anyone asked—he wasn't a dumb fuck mired in military traditions and attitudes which he didn't have because he was a sensible farmer—Engler never forgot to use the radio in an appropriate and timely manner.

"Send a message to General Stearns," he commanded. "Tell him I think the report of cavalry movement in Moosburg was a feint."

Bavaria, Third Division field headquarters
Village of Haag an der Amper

Mike read the message through once, quickly. He didn't need to read it again because he'd already come to the same conclusion himself.

He'd have cursed himself for a blithering overconfident reckless fool except he didn't have the time. He still didn't have a report from the Hangman regiment. It was too soon for a report to be brought by a courier and the fact that no radio report had come in meant that Higgins had either been overrun or something had happened to the radio.

Either way, that meant Higgins—at best—had been driven away from the spot on the Amper which Captain Finck had recommended for a river crossing. Which meant...

The Amper could be crossed there from either direction. Which meant...

Piccolomini had feinted on the right—his right; Mike's left—to draw his attention that way. He'd then taken advantage of the *Pelican*'s departure to launch a surprise attack on the Hangman.

Mike tried to visualize the terrain. The area along both sides of the river was wooded. If the Bavarian commander had moved the troops up either the night before or very early that morning—probably the night before, while the Third Division had been setting up camp—then they could have been in position and hidden when the *Pelican* arrived. The airship had only been able to stay in position for half an hour before it had to return to Regensburg.

As soon as it left, Piccolomini had launched the flank attack. But he couldn't have gotten enough men onto the north bank to have any hope of rolling up the whole Third Division. No, he'd use the same ford that Finck had found to move most of his army across, now that his cavalry had driven back the regiment guarding Mike's right flank.

Which meant...

Ulbrecht Duerr summarized the situation. "They'll try to get enough men north of the Amper to roll us up. We need to fall back and anchor ourselves on Moosburg. Which means we need to take Moosburg *now*."

Long shook his head. "That's asking the flying artillery to take a terrible risk. The volley guns are all but useless in close quarter street fighting. All Piccolomini has to have done is left a few companies in the town to bleed them white."

Mike had already reached that conclusion himself. And, for the first time since the gunfire erupted, found his footing again.

"I think we've got a bit of time, gentlemen," he said. "We're going to rope-a-dope. That's *if* the Hangman's still on its feet. Damn it, why haven't they gotten in touch?"

Chapter 19

Bavaria, on the Amper River
Two and a half miles east of Zolling

Lieutenant Colonel Jeff Higgins was staring down at the reason his regiment had not gotten in radio contact with divisional headquarters.

His radio specialist, Jimmy Andersen, still had his hands clutched around his throat. Lying on his back just outside the entrance to the radio tent, in a huge pool of drying blood. His eyes looked like a frog's, they were bulging so badly.

"Jesus wept," Jeff whispered. Some part of his mind knew that—if he survived this day himself—Jeff would be weeping too, come nightfall. Jimmy Andersen had been one of his best friends since...

He tried to remember how far back. First grade. They'd met in first grade. They'd both been six years old.

It was obvious what had happened. Jimmy had heard the gunfire, come out of the tent to investigate—not even a radio nut like Jimmy Andersen would have sent a message before doing that much—and a stray bullet—dear God, it had to have been almost spent, at that distance—had ruptured his throat. The last two or three minutes of his life would have been a horror, as he bled out while choking to death. The only slight mercy was that he'd probably fainted from the blood loss fairly soon. From the looks of it, the bullet had nicked the carotid as well as severing his windpipe.

A freak death. But they were always a feature of battles. It would have probably happened right at the beginning, when the initial Bavarian charge allowed them to come within a hundred yards of the radio tent. Right now, the enemy cavalry had pulled back a ways and the front line—such as the ragged thing was— wasn't close enough any more for a bullet to have carried this far.

What had happened to the assistant radio operator? Jeff looked around but didn't see him. He'd probably just run off, panicked by the surprise attack and the still greater surprise of seeing his immediate superior slain like that.

"Should I contact HQ, Colonel?" asked one of Jeff's adjutants. That was...

Jeff's mind was foggy and this was one of the new recruits to the regiment. It took him two or three seconds to pull up the fellow's name.

Zilberschlag. Lieutenant Jacob Zilberschlag. He'd been commissioned just two months earlier, and was the first Jewish officer in the division. Probably the first Jewish officer in the whole USE army, for that matter. Mike would have made a place for him.

More to the point, Zilberschlag was one of the few officers who knew how to use a radio.

"Yes, please, Lieutenant. Get General Stearns. I need to speak to him—and *quickly.*"

While he waited for Zilberschlag to make contact, Jeff shook his head in order to clear his brain. He had no time right now to let Jimmy's death fog up his thoughts.

The situation was... stable, sort of, but that wouldn't last long. The Hangman regiment had been caught by surprise and battered bloody, but they'd held together long enough to survive the initial clash. Their one bit of good fortune was that they'd only been fighting cavalry and they'd never broken and run. Routed infantry got slaughtered by cavalry, but if they could stand their ground it would be the cavalry that eventually broke off first.

Yes, the fighting had been one-sided but not *that* one-sided, especially after the first five minutes passed and the regiment was still hanging together. The Bavarian cavalry had taken something of a beating too. A bruising, at least.

Jeff could see the river, not more than twenty yards away. The enemy cavalry had pulled back a few minutes ago. That almost certainly meant that they'd been ordered to cover the infantry who'd now be crossing over the from the south bank—right where Captain Finck, bless his miserable special forces black heart—had suggested would make a good place for an army to do that.

Which meant the Hangman regiment had to retreat. *Now.* Fall back a third of a mile or so, however far they had to in order to link up with the 1st Brigade.

He looked back down at his old friend's corpse. He'd have to leave it here. There was no time for a burial party. Hopefully, they'd be able to retrieve Jimmy's body later. Or if the Bavarians wound up in possession of the field, maybe they'd bury him.

But Jeff didn't think they'd be in possession, when everything was said and done. Tonight, maybe. Not tomorrow, though.

The Bavarians had caught them flat-footed, sure enough. The Third Division's commander had screwed up, no doubt about it. But that was all over and done with—and the battle was just getting started.

Jeff's money was on Mike Stearns. Fuck Piccolomini and Duke Maximilian and the horses they rode in on.

"General Stearns wants to talk to you, Colonel." Zilberschlag now had the radio case mounted on his back. He came over, handed Jeff the old-style telephone receiver and turned his back so Jeff wouldn't have to stretch the cord.

"Yes, sir," Jeff said.

"What kind of shape are you in, Colonel?"

"We're pretty beat up. I figure we've lost..." Jeff tried to estimate what the regiment's casualties had been. That was bound to be guesswork at this stage. He also knew from experience that casualties usually seemed worse than they were until all the dust had settled and a hard count could be made of those who were actually dead, those who were wounded—and, of those, how many were mortally injured, how many would recover fully and how many would have to return to civilian life. It always surprised Jeff a little how many people came through what seemed like a holocaust completely uninjured. He'd done it himself in several battles now.

But wild-ass guess or not, the general needed an answer. "I figure we've lost maybe twenty percent of our guys, all told. Most of those are wounded, not killed, but they're out of the fight now."

"Not good, but better than I feared. How's your morale? Your men's, I mean. I know yours is solid. It always is."

Jeff felt a little better, hearing that. He had a tremendous amount of respect for Mike Stearns. It was nice to know that the man had a high regard for him as well.

"We're solid, General. We held 'em off and now the guys are mostly pissed."

"*All right. Here's what I want you to do...*"

After Stearns finished the quick sketch of his plans, he asked: "*Any questions?*"

Jeff's answer came immediately. "No, sir. Our part's about as simple as it gets. Hook up with von Taupadel, hunker down along the river, and hold the bastards in place while you do all the complicated stuff."

"That's pretty much it. Is there anything else?"

Jeff hesitated. This wasn't really part of military protocol since the commanding general of a whole division didn't need to be told every detail of the casualties they'd suffered, but...

"Jimmy Andersen was killed, Mike."

There was silence on the other end of the radio for a moment. Then Stearns said: "*I'm sorry, Jeff. I truly am.*"

"War sucks, what can you say? Hangman regiment out."

Bavaria, Third Division field headquarters
Village of Haag an der Amper

Mike stared down at the radio receiver he still held in his hand.

Jimmy Andersen dead...

The Four Musketeers, the kids had liked to call themselves: Jeff Higgins, Larry Wild, Jimmy Andersen, Eddie Cantrell.

Four teenagers, close friends in the way that geeky boys in a rural area will stick together—the more so because all four of them had lost their entire families in the Ring of Fire. For one reason or another, their folks had all been out of town that day in April 2000 when it happened. There'd been just the four of them, playing Dungeons & Dragons in the Higgins' family mobile home.

Five years later... and now half of them were gone. Larry Wild had been killed in the Battle of Wismar on October 7, 1633. And now Jimmy Andersen was gone, also killed in combat.

He looked up at Christopher Long. "What's the date?" He'd lost track. *Middle of May* was all he could remember.

"May 14, sir."

"1636." For some obscure reason, Mike felt the need to include the year.

Jimmy Andersen would have been . . . what? Twenty-three years old? That was Jeff's age, Mike knew. His birthday had been in March. March 22, if Mike remembered right. Gretchen had sent Jeff a cookie—which hadn't arrived until the next month, naturally.

His thoughts were wandering, and he couldn't afford that. Not now. Not today. But before Mike shoved them aside he allowed a spike of sheer pride to race through his soul.

Everything he'd always believed had been confirmed over the past five years. Every ideal, every tenet of political belief, every guide to personal and social conduct. Mike took no credit for any of them, because like most people born and raised in the United States he'd grown up with those beliefs and ideals. What he *did* take pride in—and take credit for, to the extent he shared in that credit with thousands of other people—was that when a small town in America had been ripped off its foundations by a cosmic catastrophe and tossed into a maelstrom, the people of that town had risen to the challenge. And they'd done so by holding fast to their beliefs and ideals—no, more; championing them for everyone—rather than abandoning them.

Along the way, lots of compromises had been made, sure. Mike himself had been personally responsible for a good number of them. Things sometimes got ragged around the edges. But that was the nature of political affairs—hell, any human affairs. Marriages only survived by the willingness of people to compromise.

Still, all things considered, they'd done well. Damn well. And paid the price for it, too. Somewhere around thirty-five hundred people had come through the Ring of Fire, and by now—just five years later—at least five hundred of them were gone. Mike didn't know the exact figure, and felt a moment's guilt that he didn't.

Most of those people had died because, like most rural towns in economically depressed areas, Grantville had had a disproportionate number of elderly residents, many of them in poor health. Anyone dependent on up-time medicines that couldn't be duplicated down-time—and most of them couldn't—was gone by now.

The others, though, had died in the line of fire, doing their duty. Some of them had died fighting tyranny; others had died fighting one or another of the diseases that ravaged this era.

Larry Wild had died at Wismar and Jimmy Andersen here at Zolling. Derek Utt had died in the Rhineland, fighting the plague. So had Andrea Decker and Jeffie Garand. The list went on and on, and it would keep going on.

Mike tried to remember the famous line from Abraham Lincoln's Gettysburg address. *That cause for which they here gave the last full measure of devotion*, he thought it was.

His people. They'd always been his people. Now more than ever.

"General?" Ulbrecht Duerr's voice broke through his musings.

Mike turned. "Yes, Ulbrecht, I'm here."

He grinned then, and though he didn't know it—then or ever—that savage grin brought instant cheer to every soldier in the tavern who saw. They'd come to know that grin, this past year.

Mike slapped his hands together and advanced on the map spread over the table.

"Gather round, gentlemen. Another stinking duke is going down."

Chapter 20

Moosburg
Six miles east of Zolling

"It's clear, Colonel Engler," said Alex Mackay, getting down from his horse in front of Moosburg's Rathaus. The city hall, as was the case in almost all German towns, was located on a square. Quite a small square, in the case of Moosburg. As if to make up for it, the Rathaus was a rather imposing edifice, three stories tall with a square tower rising up another fifteen feet or so in the middle.

"The whole town is clear." Mackay pointed to the east with a gauntleted hand. "I'm not certain, but I think the Bavarian cavalry the *Pelican* spotted came from across the river and have now returned to the south bank of the Isar. It's wetlands below the confluence with the Amper, but from the looks of it, I think if you went a mile or so above the confluence, maybe even half a mile, you'd find a decent place to ford the Isar."

"You're right," said Thorsten. "We just got word over the radio. That special Marine unit that scouted the area said there's a ford right above the confluence where cavalry and flying artillery can cross without any aid. They think infantry and artillery would be better if we laid down a corduroy road, though."

Alex had removed his hat in order to wipe his brow with a sleeve. Thorsten's last words arrested the motion, however.

"We?" he said, sounding alarmed.

178

Thorsten grinned at him. "I hate to be the one who has to pass this on, Colonel Mackay, but our instructions come directly from General Stearns. *Major* General Stearns, you may recall."

Mackay jammed the hat back on his head without ever wiping his forehead. That minor discomfort had clearly been quite forgotten, in light of this new and profoundly horrid forecast.

"Don't tell me. We have to secure the ford—and then *we* have to build that wretched corduroy road."

Engler's grin felt as if it was locked in place. "And it gets better—for us, not you. General Stearns' orders were for the flying artillery squadron to set up in position to repel any possible cavalry attack while—"

"The puir downtrodden cavalrymen have to get off their horses and engage in manual labor." Mackay's Scot brogue, normally just a trace after so long on the Continent, was easing back into his voice along with his disgruntled mood.

"Indeed so." Thorsten spread his hands, in a placating gesture that would have placated absolutely no one, forget a professional cavalry officer.

"Fuck you *and* the horse you get to keep riding on, Thorsten," said Mackay. "A profound injustice is being committed here."

Bavaria, Third Division field headquarters
Village of Haag an der Amper

The radio operator looked up from his notes. "Colonel Engler reports that the ford has been seized and that his squadron is setting up a defensive perimeter while the cavalry prepares the crossing for infantry and artillery."

"And in such good cheer they'll be doing it, too," said Christopher Long. The smile on his face fell short of outright evil, but by a hair so thin that only a theologian could have split it.

Duerr chuckled. "Cavalry hate being impressed as combat engineers."

"Speaking of which..." He turned toward Mike Stearns, who was pointing out something on the map to Brigadier Ludwig Schuster, who commanded the division's 2nd Brigade.

"General Stearns, pardon me for interrupting, but where do you want our combat engineers to be and doing what?"

Stearns glanced up and then pointed at Schuster. "I want them—all of them; Mackay's cavalry can lay down a simple corduroy road and screw 'em if they can't take a joke—to go with Ludwig. He and his whole brigade should get to the ford above Moosburg and be able to cross it by nightfall."

Duerr hesitated—but challenging his commander was his job, when he thought a mistake was being made. Thankfully, Stearns didn't react as badly as some generals did to being questioned. Not badly at all, being honest about it.

"Is that wise, sir? If von Taupadel and the Hangman—which is already pretty bloodied—can't hold back Piccolomini, you'll have no reserve at all."

He nodded toward the entrance of the tavern. The door had been propped open—more precisely, had been smashed open and was now hanging by one hinge—partly to let in some air and partly so the staff officers inside the headquarters could monitor the fighting that was starting to rage farther up the Amper as more and more of Piccolomini's troops crossed the river.

"I have to say I agree with him, General Stearns," said Schuster. "Let me leave the Lynx regiment behind."

Stearns' brow was creased with thought. Duerr had no difficulty understanding the issues he was weighing in his mind. On the one hand, the Lynx was a solid regiment and its commander, Colonel Erasmo Attendolo, was a very experienced professional soldier. If Derfflinger did wind up needing reinforcement, they'd be good for the purpose.

On the other hand, the Lynx also had something of a reputation for being fast and agile—at least as infantry regiments went. They weren't what anyone would call "foot cavalry," but they could move faster than any other regiment in the division except Carsten Amsel's Dietrich regiment.

Which, by no coincidence, Mike had already ordered to be the first infantry regiment to cross the Isar above Moosburg, as soon as Mackay's cavalry had the corduroy road in place.

Ulbrecht Duerr had now served under General Stearns for almost a year—and it had been a year in which Duerr had seen more combat than in any of the previous years of his long career as a professional soldier. That was partly because his new commanding general was without a doubt the most aggressive commander he'd ever served under.

That aggressiveness could be a problem, sometimes. Stearns would always tend—to use an American idiom—to "push the envelope." He'd take risks that skirted outright recklessness, as he had at the Battle of Ostra, when he ordered the Third Division to attack the army commanded by the much more experienced General Banér in the middle of a snowstorm.

He'd won the Battle of Ostra—and decisively. That same aggressiveness had now got him into trouble, though, when he'd advanced on Piccolomini without having adequate reconnaissance. But he proposed to turn the tables on the Bavarians by continuing to be aggressive, not by pulling back. He'd hold them in place with one of his brigades and the wounded but still fighting Hangman regiment, while he crossed the rest of his army to the south bank of the Isar—and would then march them downstream a few miles and cross back onto the north bank somewhere above Freising.

If it worked, the Bavarians would find themselves in a very difficult place. Stearns would now have most of his army between Piccolomini and Munich. He could go on the defensive and force Piccolomini to take the risks involved with offensive operations. And Piccolomini would have very little time to make his decision because he had more than enough cavalry units to know that Heinrich Schmidt's National Guard of the State of Thuringia-Franconia had crossed the Danube from Ingolstadt and was coming south as well.

Under a different commander, Ulbrecht Duerr would probably have been reduced to a gibbering fit by now. But one thing he'd learned as the months went by was that Stearns' aggressiveness worked in large part because he'd forged his army in that same mold. Simply put, the Third Division of the army of the United States of Europe had the best morale of any army Duerr had ever served in. It was a *fighting* morale, too, not just the good cheer of a unit whose officers did well by them in garrison duty.

What it all came down to were two things:

Could Derfflinger and Schuster, with the flying artillery to shield them against cavalry, make it across the Isar and back across a few miles downstream before the Bavarians clearly understood what was happening?

Duerr thought the answer was . . . *Probably, yes.*

The Third Division was a marching army. They'd been able to

outmarch every enemy force they'd faced. They couldn't outpace
cavalry, of course, but they didn't fear cavalry. Not with the flying artillery to shield them—and, by now, after Ahrensbök and
Ostra, the soldiers of the Third Division considered Colonel Engler
something of a modern day reincarnation of the medieval heroes
in the Dietrich von Bern legends. *Dragon? Coming up, roasted
on a platter. Enemy cavalry? You want that parboiled or fried?*

Second question: Could von Taupadel and the Hangman hold
Piccolomini's army on the north bank of the Amper? For long
enough—which Duerr estimated would take the rest of today, all
of tomorrow and at least part of Friday. Call it two days. That
was a long time for a battle to continue. On the positive side,
they could slowly withdraw to Moosburg—in fact, that was no
doubt what von Taupadel was already doing. It was hard for an
army to break off contact with an enemy that seemed to be in
retreat. Of course, on the negative side, it was also hard for an
army trying to pull back not to disintegrate and begin a full-
scale rout.

Which was no doubt the reason—Duerr was guessing, but he
was sure he was right—that von Taupadel would move his three
regiments forward and let the Hangman fall back into a reserve
position. They needed the rest—and very few soldiers in the
Third Division would be willing to risk annoying the Hangman
by trying to scamper away from the fighting. That was likely to
be lot riskier than dealing with sorry Bavarians.

The answer to that question wasn't even *probably*. Ulbrecht
was quite sure that part of Stearns' plan would work. Especially
with Higgins as the anchor. In a very different sort of way than
Thorsten Engler, the Hangman's commander had developed a
potent reputation as well, among the soldiers of the Third Division.

Thorsten Engler's reputation was flashy and dramatic. The
man himself would have been astonished to learn that he had
that reputation, but indeed he did. And why not? He'd wooed and
won one of the fabled Americanesses, captured not one but two
top enemy commanders at Ahrensbök, been made an imperial
count by the emperor himself—*and* had personally decapitated the
Swedish troll Banér at Ostra. (Using the term "personally" with
some poetic license. The head-removal had actually been done
by some of his volley guns—but he *had* given the order to fire.)

There was nothing flashy and dramatic about Higgins. He was

a big man, true—quite a bit bigger than Thorsten Engler—but he was the sort of large fellow who was always running to fat, especially when he wasn't on campaign. His belly tended to hang over his belt, his heels tended to wear out the cuffs of his trousers, and without his spectacles he was half-blind. He was in fact as well as in his appearance a studious man; more likely when he was relaxing to have his nose in a book than in a stein of beer.

But he had that one critical quality in a commander. The worse the fighting became, the more desperate the battle, the calmer he grew. He was a steady man at all times; steadier, the less steady everything around him became. A rock in rapids; a calm place in a storm.

His men rather adored him, actually. "The DM," they called him behind his back, referring to an obscure Americanism that Duerr had never been able to make any sense of. But it didn't matter, because he understood the humor—and more importantly, the superb morale—when they said that "when the DM smiles, it's already too late." That was always good for a round of chuckles; sometimes, outright laughter.

And there was this, too. Higgins had one other critical quality, for the commander of a regiment that considered itself the elite regiment in the whole of the Third Division—which, by now, considered itself the elite division of the whole USE army.

He was Gretchen Richter's husband. The Hangman had an even higher percentage of CoC recruits than the Third Division as a whole—which had a third again as many CoC recruits than the army's average. Prestige, indeed.

New CoC recruits to the Hangman, after their first encounter with the regiment's commander, were prone to ask: *What does Gretchen see in him, anyway?* To which the response was invariably: *Stick around and you'll find out.*

With Higgins anchoring the Hangman and the Hangman anchoring the 1st Brigade and the 1st Brigade anchoring the entire plan...

Ulbrecht Duerr was in a very good mood, he realized. Amazingly good, given that the morning had begun with a near-disaster brought on by an overly-confident and too-aggressive commander who now proposed to correct his error by being even more confident and aggressive.

Ulbrecht Duerr had been born in Münster, the son of a baker.

As a boy he'd been somewhat awed by the nobility's august status. As an old professional soldier who'd encountered dozens of noblemen professionally, he didn't have much use for dukes, any longer. There were some exceptions—Duerr was quite partial to Duke George of Brunswick—but Maximilian of Bavaria was not one of them.

Bavaria, the Isar River
About two miles northeast of Moosburg

For the last stretch of the work, Thorsten Engler had relented and used some of his own flying artillerymen to finish the corduroy road, allowing Mackay's cavalry to get some rest. He hadn't done that from the goodness of his heart, though. He wanted cavalry—rested, alert cavalry—to be scouting ahead for him when he and his squadron moved toward their next fording place.

The term "flying artillery" that was generally used to refer to his squadron was another piece of poetic license. It was true that because the volley guns were so light, they didn't need many horses to haul them around. Two was enough, four was plenty, and the six that were normally used were simply so that replacements would be available if—no, when; it was inevitable on a campaign—some of the horses were killed or lamed.

All of the soldiers were mounted as well. Some would ride on the carriage horses, others would accompany the wagons carrying the ammunition and equipment, and still others including all the officers would ride their own individual mounts. In short, the squadron was much more mobile than an infantry unit.

But they were still hauling gun carriages and wagons around—and even a light gun carriage drawn by only two horses is an awkward way to conduct forward reconnaissance. Not to mention that if they ran into an enemy cavalry unit without some warning they'd still be trying to set up their guns when the enemy started sabering them down.

So Thorsten wanted cavalrymen—defined as: one man on one horse with at least one weapon he could bring immediately to hand—to be scouting ahead of him. *Well* ahead of him. Half a mile, a mile—better yet, two miles.

                    ✧   ✧   ✧

And then, as it turned out, they could have dispensed with the cavalry screen altogether. By sundown they'd found the second ford they needed right where Captain Finck had said it would be, about seven miles upstream on the Isar. Roughly halfway between Moosburg and Freising.

They hadn't encountered a single Bavarian soldier along the way. Not one. Not a sign of one. It was by then obvious that General Stearns' counter-move was something the Bavarian commander Piccolomini had simply never considered. As so many commanders before him had done in the long history of war, Piccolomini had assumed that his opponent would do the same thing he would do.

Engler hadn't discussed the general's plans with him, but by now he'd come to know Mike Stearns fairly well. One of the things he recalled was Stearns telling him that mercenaries usually had predictable faults.

"They're too conservative by nature," he'd said. "Or let's say they're too conservative because of their economic position. War is a trade for them, not something they do because of ideals—or because of hatreds and bigotries, for that matter. I don't think they're even conscious of it, most of the time, but they're always guided one way or another by a consideration of profit or loss. What do we gain or lose—not for our cause, but for *us*? And if the answer is, not enough for the potential loss we might suffer, they simply won't do it. And what's even more important, I think, is that they'll assume—also without even thinking about it—that their enemy won't do it either."

The ineffable grin had come, then. "Whereas I damn well might."

Thorsten didn't have enough experience yet himself to decide if Stearns was right or wrong in general. But today, at least, he'd been right.

As an added bonus, soon after they began setting up their positions, Captain Finck himself and his Marine unit appeared. Materialized, as it were, out of nowhere.

"We saw you coming," Finck explained to Engler and Mackay. He pointed to a small wood perhaps four hundred yards away. "We weren't sure who you were at first, so we hid out there."

Mackay and Engler looked at the grove, then looked at Finck, then looked at the western horizon where the sun had just disappeared, then at each other.

"We've been here setting up our camp for at least two hours," mused Mackay. "Two hours of hard, unrelenting labor."

"While you, expert scouts—'special forces' they call you, if I am not mistaken," Thorsten pondered, "couldn't manage to determine who we were and cross a few hundred yards—that's what? a quarter of a mile? don't you have to prove you can run to the moon and back in fifteen minutes to qualify for your unit?—until the sun was setting and we have to retire for the night."

Finck smiled at them. "We just got orders on the radio from General Stearns. At the crack of dawn—no, even before then—we have to be heading upriver again. He wants us to scout Freising to see how quickly and easily Piccolomini might be able to fortify it. So we'll have to retire early—now, in fact. Good luck, gentlemen."

He nodded toward the northwest, where the sound of occasional gunfire could still be heard.

"For what it's worth," Finck said, "the fighting mostly died away by mid-afternoon. We couldn't actually see anything, since at this point the Amper's at least two miles north of where we are. But all the indications are that Piccolomini and von Taupadel are squared off against each other, with von Taupadel anchored in Moosburg. This is just a guess, of course, but I'd say that right about now the Bavarian commander is a grumpy man."

Bavaria, village of Haag an der Amper

Captain Finck was wrong. Ottavio Piccolomini wasn't grumpy, he was worried. Everything today had gone the way he'd planned, for the most part. The resistance of the enemy had been more ferocious that he'd hoped for, but he wasn't thrown off his stride by it. He'd already known from the reports he'd read and interviews he'd done of men who'd fought the Third Division that whatever else Michael Stearns might be as a military commander, he was certainly tenacious.

Bavarian casualties had been higher than he'd wanted, but not ruinous. The enemy's had certainly been worse. The ground that Piccolomini and his soldiers had crossed as they drove the invaders back into Moosburg had been littered with corpses, mostly enemy corpses. There'd been so many of them in some places that he'd ordered his soldiers to pile them up in stacks. They'd have to bury them in mass graves once the fighting was over.

Yes, everything had gone well this day. Not as well as he'd hoped, certainly; not even as well as he'd planned. But Piccolomini was too experienced a soldier to be surprised by that. War was what it was: at bottom, chaos and ruin. You could hardly expect it to fall into neat lines and rows.

Seated at the same table in the same tavern that he was all but certain his counterpart had occupied earlier that day, Piccolomini looked around. He finally realized what was worrying him.

The place was too neat. There was almost no litter. The door to the tavern had been smashed aside at one point, probably by an impatient officer who'd gotten jammed in the doorway when the door closed on him unexpectedly. But someone had taken the time to repair it before they evacuated the place.

Not much of a repair; just a piece of leather nailed in place. But why bother at all?

"Do you have any further orders, General?" asked one of his adjutants.

Piccolomini gazed at the repaired door for another second or two. "No," he said. "Just be ready to move out tomorrow morning. Early. I want to launch our first assault on Moosburg as soon as the sun's up."

Chapter 21

Moosburg
Six miles east of Zolling

For Jeff Higgins and his Hangman regiment, the second day of the Battle of Zolling started off well and kept going that way—as of eleven o'clock in the morning, at any rate. The 1st Brigade's commander, von Taupadel, had ordered the Hangman to take positions well inside the town itself and fortify them. If von Taupadel's three regiments found themselves forced to retreat from their positions on the western outskirts of Moosburg, he wanted them to be able to retreat to the east of the town while being covered by the entrenched Hangman.

Moosburg hadn't been badly hit by cannon fire, so the Hangman had to build the fortifications partly by tearing down otherwise-undamaged buildings. Jeff felt a bit of guilt over that, but not much. Bavarian troops—more precisely, troops employed by the duke of Bavaria; most of them weren't Bavarian themselves—had conducted themselves in such a foul manner for years that none of their opponents had any empathy for them or the realm that paid them. Jeff Higgins and most of the soldiers in his regiment understood on some abstract level that the average inhabitant of Bavaria had no control over the actions of Duke Maximilian or the forces he put in the field. That understanding was probably enough to restrain them from committing atrocities against civilians they encountered—of whom there had been a few, including one entire family hiding in a cellar, whom they'd escorted safely out of town. But they would have had to possess a superhuman level of restraint to extend that same mercy to buildings as well. And if that meant that eventually the residents of Moosburg would return and discover that their homes and businesses had been partially or fully wrecked, so be it. Better that, than a righteous and upstanding soldier in the righteous and upstanding army of the righteous and upstanding United States of Europe should have his brains spilled by a musket ball because he hadn't possessed sufficiently adequate cover when the foul minions of the still-fouler duke of Bavaria launched their assault.

Which they did, right at sunup. But—so far, at least; it was still short of noon—the 1st Brigade was standing its ground. So, the worst that the Hangman faced was some hard labor and suffering some minor casualties: one man's helmet dented and his senses sent reeling by a canister ball; one man's cheek sliced open by a piece of splintered stone sent flying by an errant cannon ball; and one man's leg broken by the collapse of part of a wall that the same cannon ball struck and from which the splinter derived—but it was just his fibula, and a clean break at that.

Bavaria, on the Isar River between Moosburg and Freising

Thorsten Engler had found the night that had just passed rather nerve-wracking, and the following morning had been even worse. He'd decided to have his flying artillery squadron use the ford to cross over the river and establish themselves on the north bank. They'd had no time before sundown to erect fieldworks, however, and he hadn't wanted to risk doing so thereafter. The moon was almost full but the visibility still wasn't good enough for soldiers to work.

Besides, Thorsten didn't want a lot of noise, and there was no quiet way to cut down enough trees to build a bridge big enough for thousands of infantrymen and artillery units to cross over. There had been no sign as yet that they'd been spotted by any Bavarian forces and he wanted to keep things that way. So, once the squadron crossed the river and took positions he had sentries posted and ordered the rest of the men to get some sleep.

They started work just before sunrise, as soon as there was

enough daylight to see what they were doing. They would still be making noise, of course, but hopefully the sounds of the battle on the Amper would drown it out. While they worked, Mackay and his cavalrymen maintained patrols that would warn them of any approaching enemies.

There were none, thankfully. Without an infantry shield, Engler and his volley gunners were at a terrible risk. Flying artillery had tremendous offensive power, especially against cavalry. But if they had to go on defense they were more vulnerable than just about any military force. They lacked the ability of infantry to hunker down in defensive positions. A man can fit into a foxhole or a trench or hide behind a tree or even a fencepost; a volley gun and its crew can't. And they didn't have the ability of cavalry to just ride away from danger. Volley gun carriages were too clumsy to make good getaway vehicles, and while the horses could be detached and ridden, they had no saddles. There were precious few gunners who could stay on a galloping horse that he was trying to ride bareback.

So, the volley gunners worked like demons until the fieldworks were finally erected, a little after eight o'clock in the morning. Thereafter, they could relax a bit—physically, at least, if not mentally. With the rate of fire experienced volley gun crews could maintain, and fighting behind shelter, they would be extraordinarily hard to overrun unless they ran out of ammunition—and that wouldn't happen for hours.

By then, of course, the enemy could move up their own light artillery units and once they began firing the squadron would be forced back across the river. Even three-inch guns and six-pounders would quickly reduce the fieldworks they'd been able to erect.

But by then, the bridge would be finished. Unless the 1st Brigade and the Hangman at Moosburg collapsed entirely, forcing Stearns to bring back the other two brigades, the lead infantry regiments from the 2nd and 3rd Brigades would have made it to the ford and begun crossing the Isar as well. Thorsten and his engineers had designed the flying artillery's fieldworks so that some infantry units could take places immediately while other units expanded the fieldworks down either side of the riverbank. By nightfall of that second day of the battle, they'd have a well-nigh impregnable position on the north side of the Isar.

Bavaria, the Isar River
About two miles northeast of Moosburg

Mike Stearns was feeling fairly nerve-wracked himself, a sensation he found particularly aggravating because he was so unaccustomed to it. As a rule, he didn't worry overmuch. He didn't have the fabled temperament of *Mad* magazine's Alfred E. Neuman—*What, me worry?*—but he had been blessed with very steady nerves and a sanguine disposition. Since he'd been a boy, his operating assumption as he went about his life's affairs was that things were generally going to work out well, if for no other reason than that he'd damn well see to it that they did.

Perhaps for that reason, he'd never spent much time gambling. He enjoyed an occasional night of low-stakes poker, but simply because of the social interaction. Before the Ring of Fire, he'd been to Las Vegas twice, on his way to Los Angeles and on his way back. He'd fiddled with the slot machines for a while, on his first trip, more out of mild curiosity than anything else. On his second and final visit, he'd spent about an hour at a blackjack table, despite the fact that he found that particular card game quite boring. He'd done it from a vague sense of obligation that since he'd taken the time to pass through Las Vegas he owed it to someone—maybe himself, maybe the goddess of luck, who could say?—to do some Real Gambling.

So, gamble he had, losing about fifteen dollars in the process. When he walked away from the table he didn't mind having lost the money but he did mildly regret the waste of his time.

The problem with gambling, from Mike's point of view, was that a person was *voluntarily* placing himself at the vagaries of chance. That just seemed monumentally stupid to him. No one except a hermit could get through life without at one point or another—usually more than once—giving up hostages to fortune. But it was one thing to have your destiny kidnapped by forces beyond your control, it was another thing entirely to go looking for the bastards so you could hand yourself over to them.

He felt firmly—*had* felt firmly—that there were only two circumstances when a person should do anything that rash: when you got married, and when you had children. Even then, the degree to which your fortunes were no longer in your own hands was restricted. You *did*, after all, get to pick your spouse, so if the marriage turned out sour it was mostly your own screw-up. And you *did,* after all, occupy the parent half of the parent-child equation, so if your kids wound up being dysfunctional, you were probably the main culprit involved.

And now, on May 15 of the year 1636, Mike Stearns was realizing that he'd just made the biggest gamble of his life. True, he'd thought and still did that the odds were in the Third Division's favor. Pretty heavily in the division's favor, in fact. Nevertheless...

There was a chance that the 1st Brigade might collapse under the pressure of the Bavarian assault that had been going on since the day before. Yes, the brigade was a good one, full of veterans of the Saxon campaign, some of whom had been at Ahrensbök as well. True also, they were fighting on the defensive behind solid fieldworks and could always retreat into Moosburg if necessary. True as well, they had the Hangman regiment—probably the division's best—in reserve.

They were still heavily outnumbered, and facing an army that was also largely made up of veterans and with an experienced and capable commander. So it was a gamble.

If the 1st Brigade collapsed, Mike's whole battle plan went up in smoke. He'd have no choice but to bring the rest of his division back across the Isar in the hope that he could keep von Taupadel and Higgins and their men from being slaughtered. Whether he could do that in time...

...Was another gamble, and one with fairly long odds against success. That was the reason he'd decided to stay at the ford on the Isar just downstream of Moosburg, while he sent the 3rd Brigade and most of the 2nd Brigade up the river to find the ford that Colonel Engler was holding for them. Mike was keeping the Gray Adder regiment with him, to provide cover for the 1st Brigade if they needed to retreat from Moosburg and cross over the Isar.

That would leave the entire Third Division strung out for miles along the banks of the Isar, from the ford below Moosburg to the ford between Moosburg and Freising. Strategically that would leave him with a mess, since he'd be on the wrong side of the river for an assault on Munich. But if the 1st Brigade was broken at Moosburg he'd have a much more pressing tactical mess on his hands, and the fact that most of his forces would now be across the river from Piccolomini's army would put them in a good defensive position. With Heinrich Schmidt coming south with the SoTF National Guard, Mike was sure that Piccolomini wouldn't risk making an assault on the Third Division across the river. He'd just withdraw up the north bank of the Isar and take up defensive positions at Freising or somewhere south of there.

So Mike wasn't likely to face a disaster no matter what happened. But if his plans failed, he'd have led his army into a pointless and brutal killing field due to his own overconfidence. Jimmy Andersen and hundreds of other soldiers would wind up in graves whose headstones might as well read *Here lies a good man, killed because his commanding general was a cocksure jackass.*

Maybe the worst of it was that Mike might kill hundreds more of his men because he was *still* gambling like a cocksure jackass.

He'd know by nightfall, one way or the other.

Bavaria, on the Isar River between Moosburg and Freising

Thorsten Engler didn't think he'd ever in his life felt quite as much relief as he did while watching Colonel Amsel's Dietrich regiment coming across the bridge onto the north bank of the Isar. Within minutes, the infantrymen were taking positions behind the fieldworks that the flying artillery had hurriedly set up.

And, naturally, complaining bitterly that the fieldworks were just the sort of ramshackle crap that you'd expect lazy and pampered artillerymen to set up, while the infantry set about correcting all that was wrong, subtracting all that was useless, and adding almost everything that would actually do any good if it came to a real fight.

Very satisfying for them it was, no doubt—and the flying artillery couldn't have cared less. Insults from infantrymen were of no more moment than mist in the morning or the chattering of tiny rodents. Who cared?

What Thorsten *did* care about was that by the time the Dietrich regiment had taken positions and the Lynx regiment began coming across, there was no longer any realistic prospect that the Bavarians could overwhelm the flying artillery even if they did finally arrive in force. Which—

They still hadn't. In fact, so far as Thorsten could determine, the Bavarians remained completely unaware that the Third

Division had—in almost the literal sense of the term—stolen a march on them.

That blissful ignorance—blissful for the Third Division, at any rate—ended a little after noon. Alex Mackay, accompanied by a small party of his cavalrymen, came cantering across a field toward the new fieldworks. By the time he arrived, both Thorsten and Brigadiers Derfflinger and Schuster had ridden out to meet him.

"They finally spotted us," Mackay reported, twisting in his saddle and gesturing to the rear with his hat. He did so in the effortless manner of someone who'd been riding horses since he was a boy and had been a cavalryman his entire adult life.

"We encountered a Bavarian cavalry patrol about half a mile back. There was no clash, though. Clearly enough they'd already spotted your fieldworks. As soon as they saw us they took off. They'll be giving a report to Piccolomini within the hour."

"All good things come to an end," said Thorsten. His tone was philosophical, however. By then, the Lynx regiment had extended the fieldworks farther down the Isar in both directions, a good half of the Yellow Marten regiment had crossed the bridge and the White Horse regiment had arrived and was waiting its turn.

They'd be waiting for a while, though, because the field artillery units were also arriving and Derfflinger and Schuster were both determined to get them across the Isar as soon as the Yellow Marten finished its crossing.

Derfflinger took off his hat. He did so neither to point with it nor to give his head some respite—the temperature was quite pleasant that day—but to swat away some insects. The advantage to riding a horse was that it rested a man's legs; the disadvantage was that the great beasts invariably attracted pests.

"It looks as if the general's gamble will pay off," he said. "Between you and me and the flies, I had some doubts for a while there."

"Never a dull day in the Third Division," said Schuster agreeably. The statement was patently ridiculous—the Third Division had as many days of tedium and routine as armies always did. But all four men gathered there just north of the Isar understood the sentiment.

Bavaria, on the north bank of the Amper River
Just west of Moosburg

"You're certain, Captain?" Piccolomini demanded. *"Absolutely* certain?"

The cavalry officer nodded firmly. "We got a very good look at them, General. We were there for at least ten minutes before their cavalry patrol spotted us." He nodded toward the slip of paper in Piccolomini's hand. "I made those notes right there on the spot, sir. There's a lot of guesswork, I grant you, but I'm positive about the essence of the report. The enemy has several thousand men on the north bank of the Isar."

He gestured toward the southwest. "About three, maybe four miles that way, sir. Not too far from the village of Langenbach."

Piccolomini squinted in the direction the man was pointing. The narrowed eyes weren't due to sunlight, of which precious little made its way into the interior of the tavern, but to thought.

Not much thought, however. It was now quite obvious what Stearns had done. He'd trusted in the forces he'd left in Moosburg to hold the Bavarian army at bay while he made a forced march, forded two rivers—or rather, forded the Isar in both directions—in order to place most of his troops across Piccolomini's line of retreat.

The maneuver was bold to the point of being foolhardy. Piccolomini would never have even considered it, himself.

But...blind luck or not, the maneuver had succeeded in its purpose. Piccolomini now had no choice but to retreat south of Freising—and he'd have to do so in a forced march himself, in order to skirt the forces Stearns had gotten across the river.

Grimly, he contemplated his options. They were...not good. After fighting hard for two days, his men had suffered a lot of casualties. Not as many as the Third Division—although today's fighting had evened the score quite a bit, since the Bavarians had been the ones fighting on the offensive. But between those losses and the rigors of a forced march which would last at least two days, Piccolomini knew perfectly well that his men wouldn't be able to fight another battle a few days from now at Freising.

They might be "able," but they certainly wouldn't be willing. His men were all mercenaries and they'd be disgruntled. Already *were* disgruntled, he didn't doubt. Piccolomini could and certainly would claim that he'd won a tactical victory here at Zolling. But mercenaries didn't care much about such ways of scoring victories and losses. They'd fought—fought hard—and bled a lot, and a number of them had died. And what did they have to show for it?

Nothing beyond a march back to Munich, the same city they'd marched out of just a few days before. They'd be sullen, and Duke Maximilian—whose temper was always unpredictable these days—might very well discharge Piccolomini before they even reached Bavaria's capital.

So be it. Piccolomini had probably burned his bridges with the Austrians when he'd accepted Maximilian's offer, but there was still Spain. With all the turmoil their cardinal-now-pope Borja had stirred up in Italy, there were bound to be employment opportunities.

Perhaps France, though... With this new King Gaston on the throne and what looked like a possible civil war in the making...

"What are your orders, General?"

Pulling himself out of his ruminations, Piccolomini looked around and saw that most of his adjutants had gathered around by now. He tossed the slip of paper onto the table in the middle of the tavern.

"We have to retreat. Back to Munich. Make sure the ford we've used is well defended. I doubt if the USE forces in Moosburg will make a sally, but it's always possible. Once we're back across the Amper—"

On his way out of the tavern, Piccolomini stopped for a moment to study the leather strip someone had used to repair the door.

Then, shook his head. "He just got lucky, that's all," he muttered to himself, and went to find his horse.

Wondering, all the while, whether he really believed it.

Chapter 22

Bavaria, on the Amper River
Two and a half miles east of Zolling

That evening, after searching for the Hangman regiment's commanding officer for half an hour, Mike found Jeff Higgins digging a grave. Part of him was irritated that a colonel was engaged in simple labor that he could have assigned any soldier to do. For that matter, he could have just let the three soldiers he had helping him dig the grave while he went about doing what he was supposed to be doing, which was commanding more than a thousand men. (One thousand, two hundred and seventy-one, to be exact, as of the start of the battle. All of the Third Division's regiments were over-strength; none more so than the Hangman.)

But Mike said nothing. He didn't have to remove the tarpaulin covering a corpse next to the grave to know whose body it was. Or had been, he supposed, if you believed in an afterlife. Mike didn't and he knew Jeff didn't either, but he wasn't sure about Jimmy Andersen.

He got off his horse and went to stand by the grave. It was already at least four feet deep.

"Do you have a coffin?" he asked.

Jeff stopped digging and straightened up, leaning the shovel against the side of the grave. "No, and I'm not waiting until we can get one. I doubt if there are any civilians within ten miles of here." He looked up at his commanding general and made a face. "I'm being self-indulgent already, so I'm not about to tell my men to start playing carpenter—assuming they could find the tools anyway. Besides..."

He waved his hand in a gesture that encompassed everything around them. "There are hundreds of corpses in the area. Most of them are ours, but the Bavarians left some behind too. We can't make coffins for more than a handful of them, so I don't see any point in trying to pick and choose."

Mike looked around. He'd noticed on his way here from Moosburg that there were fewer corpses strewn about than he'd expected to see. "Where..."

Jeff rubbed his forehead with a forearm. That wiped away some of the sweat, at the expense of smearing a little mud on his face. "The Bavarians stacked them up in piles." He nodded toward the corpse under the tarpaulin. "I found Jimmy in one of them. He was kind of... well..."

He shrugged. "He'd been there almost two days and he was getting a little ripe. But at least his body was still intact. Some of the corpses—a fair number of 'em—were in pieces."

Mike reached down a hand. "Come on out of there. Your men can finish the grave and we need to talk."

Jeff took his hand and Mike helped lift him out of the pit. Then he walked away a few steps so the two of them could talk privately.

"I'm sorry, Jeff," he said. This was not a time for military formalities. "I fucked up pretty bad, and if I hadn't Jimmy would still be alive."

Jeff shook his head. "Don't beat on yourself, Mike. If generalship was easy, everybody and their grandmother would be calling themselves Napoleon and Alexandra the Great. Jimmy's death was a fluke. The bullet that killed him wasn't even aimed at him. It just came in out of nowhere at exactly the wrong time and place. The same thing could happen to you or me or anyone on any given day in a combat zone. War sucks, period. It's just the way it is."

There wasn't anything to say in response. Jeff was right, on all counts. Which still didn't make Mike feel any better.

"Besides," Jeff continued, "the real problem is the same one it's been since the USE put its army together. It's not you, it's that we don't have enough cavalry. Half the time we're stumbling around half-blind, and some of the time we might as well be completely in the dark."

"Yeah, I know. I've put in another request—"

"It ain't gonna happen, Mike," Jeff interjected, "and you know it as well as I do. The Third Division's at the bottom of any stinking nobleman's list, when it comes to 'cavalry jobs wanted.' So I think we need to go outside the box. What we need is our own airplane. Or airship, if we can get our hands on a hydrogen one. These hot air jobs are fine for a lot of things, but they purely suck when it comes to providing us with reliable reconnaissance."

"I've thought about it myself, but I don't know where we'd find one. I had David check with Kelly Aviation, since everything Hal's building is already signed up by the air force. But they don't have anything free, either."

"What about an airship?"

"There's nothing suitable being built in the USE, that I know of. There might be something underway in the Netherlands, but King Fernando will have first dibs on whatever gets built."

Jeff chuckled heavily. The sound had very little humor in it. "So have your wife twist his arm. She *is* figuring on being the next secretary of state, right? Or am I supposed to believe that silly bullshit that she stepped down for Piazza because nobody else was available?"

Mike chuckled as well. "My lips are sealed. But... Next time I see her, I'll see what I can do."

The soldiers digging the grave starting climbing out of the pit. "We're finished, sir," said one of them. "Six feet, like you said."

Mike and Jeff went over and looked down. Then, as if they were of one mind, each of them took one end of the tarpaulin-covered figure lying next to the grave and lifted it up.

In the end, Mike wound up lowering Jimmy into the grave himself. He did so by the simple expedient of climbing in and having Jeff and another soldier hand the body down to him. They didn't have any ropes to lower the corpse and the alternative of just pitching him in wasn't acceptable to either of them.

After he positioned the body as best he could, Mike climbed back out, hoisted by Jeff and the same soldier. The other two soldiers started shoveling dirt over the body.

"Hold on," Jeff ordered them, raising his hand. "I want to say a few words."

"Do you need a Bible?" Mike asked. "That's one thing about a down-time army. Every other soldier will have one."

Jeff shook his head. "Jimmy wasn't religious, Mike. None of us Four Musketeers belonged to a church except Larry Wild. He was raised in the Church of Christ but he didn't really hold to it any more. There's a passage from Ecclesiastes that Jimmy always liked, though, and another one from Romans that Larry Wild recited to us once and all four of us agreed we held to it. I recited it after I heard that Larry had been killed and I still have it memorized."

He moved to the edge of the grave, lowered his head a bit and, with his hands clasped before him, said the following:

"For everything there is a season, and a time for every matter under heaven. There's a time to be born, and there's a time to die. For none of us lives to himself, and none of us dies to himself." He took a breath and added: "Go in peace, my old friend Jimmy Andersen. And if you do find anything over there, try not to screw up, okay?"

He stepped back from the grave and nodded at the two soldiers with shovels. As they went back to filling the grave, Jeff turned to Mike. "What do we do for a headstone? There aren't any masons left in the area either."

Mike had been pondering the same problem and had already come up with a solution. "Just remember where this grave is and hammer a stake with Jimmy's name into it. We'll replace it with a headstone when we get a chance."

"What about the rest of the soldiers? We can't dig individual graves for everybody."

"No, we'll have to bury most of them in mass graves. But..."

He was thinking ahead, still. "After the war's over—this war, anyway—we'll turn this whole area into a military graveyard. There'll be headstones lined up in rows for every soldier who died here, even if they're not right where the man was buried. Like we did at Arlington and Gettysburg and—oh, hell, lots of places—back up-time."

"The Bavarians might not like that idea."

Mike's face had a very hard expression, now. "Ask me if I give a fuck. By the time we finish with them, the Bavarians will damn well do what we tell them to do. We'll build a graveyard here and they will maintain it thereafter. They'll pay for the upkeep too, the bastards."

He went to his horse and got back in the saddle. "Get your men ready, Colonel Higgins. I want to start our march on Munich at first dawn."

"Yes, sir."

After he'd seen to it that his regiment was fed, and had whatever shelter could be scrounged up—luckily, it didn't look like it was going to rain that night—Jeff indulged himself one last time. In clear violation of military rules and regulations, he had the regiment's radio operator send a message to the Residenzschloss in Dresden.

He didn't bother sending it in code. The Bavarians already knew they'd killed USE soldiers that day, so what difference did it make if they knew the name of one of them?

Jimmy Andersen was killed yesterday.

He didn't add anything along the lines of "may God have mercy on his soul." Gretchen was religiously inclined and he wasn't. They'd known that about each other almost since the day they first met.

It had been what movie producers would have called "meet cute," assuming they were producing a horror movie. Jeff had helped Gretchen haul her sister and some other girls out of an outhouse where she'd hidden them from rampaging soldiers.

Wannabe rampaging soldiers, rather. Jeff had held them off long enough for Mike Stearns and the APCs to get there. He hadn't been alone, though. Larry Wild had stood next to him, and so had Jimmy Andersen and Eddie Cantrell.

He and Eddie were the only ones left. He wondered where Eddie was, now. Somewhere in the western hemisphere, the last he'd heard. Eddie had lost a foot in the years since then. On the other hand, like Jeff himself he'd gained a wife so he was still ahead of the game.

"Is there any further message, Colonel?"

Jeff thought about it, for a moment. Then he shook his head. "No, that will be all."

Anything he'd add to that—*I miss you; I love you*—Gretchen already knew. And while Jeff was willing to violate the rules and regulations when one of his oldest and best friends had gotten killed, he didn't see any point in trampling the rules and regs and dancing on their grave.

Besides, Duke Maximilian might not know that the commander of one of the regiments that was about to lay siege to his capital was married to the most feared revolutionary in Europe. Maybe that secret would be his undoing, in some manner as yet unforeseen and unforeseeable.

"They don't call me the DM for nothing," he muttered.

Dresden

Gretchen didn't receive the message until the following morning. When she did, she immediately left the Residenzschloss and went looking for Ursula Gerisch.

It took her a while to find the woman. When she did, Ursula was just coming out of a grocery. The store, like most such in seventeenth-century European cities, was on the ground floor of a narrow building pressed up against buildings on either side. The owner and his family would live upstairs.

Ursula was looking very pleased with herself. That meant she'd made another convert—or made significant progress in that direction, at least. Gerisch had made herself quite unpopular with the city's Lutheran pastors since she arrived. Whether it was in spite of her disreputable past or because of it—Gretchen preferred the latter explanation, herself—Ursula was an extraordinarily good missionary.

Ernst Wettin had privately told Gretchen that several of the pastors had come to him to register their complaints, but he'd shrugged off the matter. First, he'd pointed out to them, the emperor himself had agreed to place unusual restrictions on Lutheran privileges in Saxony. And secondly, the pestiferous Gerisch creature was proselytizing on behalf of a creed which was subscribed to not only by Admiral Simpson—that would be the same admiral whose ironclads had leveled the walls of Hamburg along with a portion of Copenhagen—but by Gretchen Richter as well.

Yes, *that* Gretchen Richter. *You hadn't heard?*

As soon as Ursula came up to her, Gretchen got right to the point. "We need our own church."

"Yes, I know. But I don't know of any vacant ones." Gerisch looked dubious, adding: "I suppose we could take up a collection and see if we could buy one of the existing churches..."

Gretchen shook her head. "None of these Lutheran pastors

would sell to us. The problem's not the money, anyway. I could afford to pay for it myself, if need be."

That was something of an exaggeration. She and Jeff were quite wealthy now, measured in the way David Bartley and others like him gauged such things. But most of their wealth was tied up in the stock market or the apartment building they'd bought in Magdeburg. They didn't have much in the way of liquid assets.

It didn't matter. Gretchen had figured out a solution. All the Lutheran pastors in Dresden would shriek their outrage and Ernst Wettin was bound to wag his finger and express solemn disapproval—for the public record, at least. She didn't think he'd really care that much, personally.

But the reason none of that mattered was because the only person who could have seriously objected was the elector of Saxony, John George, who was no longer of this sinful earth.

"There's a chapel in the Residenzschloss," she explained. "It's ours now."

Gerisch stared at her. "Said who?"

"Says me. Round up as many church members as you can find and let's...well, I suppose we can't say 'consecrate' it because we don't have a priest yet. But we'll do our layman best."

She had no idea if what she was doing was part of accepted custom, tradition or ecclesiastical law according to the Episcopal church. But she didn't care very much because the church she now belonged to was not the Church of England but the Protestant Episcopal Church in the United States of America. And since the United States of America did not exist in this universe, Gretchen figured her church would soon enough transmute into the Protestant Episcopal Church in the United States of Europe—and who could say what customs and traditions and ecclesiastical laws that church would eventually adopt?

Dresden customs and traditions, if Gretchen had anything to say about it.

Which, she probably would. She hadn't leveled any fortified walls or brought down any royal towers, true. But she could lay a reasonable claim to having leveled an entire province. She'd turned a stinking dukedom into a republic, hadn't she?

There was no service, when they all gathered in the chapel that afternoon, because they had no priest. Gretchen just proposed that all of them there—which was herself, Ursula, and eleven other people, all but three being women—say their own quiet prayers.

She did so herself.

Dear Lord, please care for the soul of Jimmy Andersen.

Gretchen hadn't been that close to Jimmy herself. He'd been a quiet man, very introspective. But she knew how much he'd meant to Jeff.

And please care for my beloved husband, who is still in harm's way.

And would be, possibly for a long time to come. But Gretchen felt greatly relieved. She hadn't prayed in ...

How many years had it been? Five years since she'd met and married Jeff. Two years before that, since her father had been murdered in front of her and she herself turned into her rapist's concubine.

Seven years it had taken her, before she was finally able to forgive God. Long years for her; but, of course, not even a moment for Him who moved in such mysterious ways.

Amen.

Eventually, she'd find a priest who could explain it all to her and put everything in proper theological context. She was quite sure that it was inappropriate for a mortal to forgive God. But those were what her husband would call optional technicalities.

They didn't call him the DM for nothing.

Chapter 23

Breslau (Wroclaw), Lower Silesia
Poland

Because the city had been ravaged by plague a few years earlier, Wroclaw's population had declined since Jozef Wojtowicz had last visited it as a boy of twelve. The population had been somewhere around forty thousand people then; today, he doubted if it still had as many as thirty thousand. There were empty buildings everywhere he looked, many of which had badly deteriorated. Still, the city showed plenty of signs of life. He thought it was probably growing again, in prosperity as well as population.

And, again, he was unhappily aware that little if any of the improvement had been due to King Wladyslaw or the Sejm. The emergence of the United States of Europe as a powerful realm in central Europe had brought most of the chaos unleashed in 1618 to a halt. The economy of the area had started rapidly improving as a result, partly driven by the influx of up-time technologies and financial methods.

Wroclaw was a mostly German city, and had been since the Mongol invasion four centuries earlier had destroyed the original Polish settlement. The ties of language as well as kinship made it easier for the city to absorb and reflect the growth taking place to the west. That had been true even when neighboring Saxony had been ruled by the Albertine branch of the Wettin dynasty, whose last elector had been John George. Now that it was for all practical purposes ruled by Gretchen Richter and her CoC comrades, Jozef expected western influence to expand even more rapidly.

Which was something else he had mixed feelings about. On the one hand, he approved of most of that influence. The thing that bothered him was that very little of it was Polish in origin. Still worse was that, so far at least, he'd seen no indication that Poland's rulers were receptive to it, other than in some narrowly military applications.

Jozef didn't consider himself an intellectual—certainly not in the pretentious manner that the hothouse radicals he'd encountered in Mecklenburg used the term. But unlike most members of his szlachta class, he read a great deal. Partly that was due to his own inclination; partly to his responsibilities as the central figure in Koniecpolski's espionage operations in the USE. Among other things Jozef had made a point of reading were the history books regarding Poland which the up-timers had in their possession.

There weren't many of them, unfortunately. Grantville had been a small town. Although its population had a fair number of residents of Polish origin, none of them had been recent immigrants. Such people had an attachment of sorts to their Polish ancestry, but it was sentimental in nature, not analytical, focused heavily on the Pole who had been the then-in-office pope and a trade union leader named Lech Walesa. They knew little of their homeland's history prior to then, and much of what they thought they knew was inaccurate or downright wrong.

Still, there had been a few books in Grantville. The one he'd found especially helpful was Norman Davies' *God's Playground*, a two-volume history of Poland. The second volume was not particularly germane, since it covered the period after 1795—a date in the universe from which the Americans had come, whose ensuing history would now be completely different. But the first volume had been enormously enlightening—so much so that Jozef had paid to have a copy of it made and sent to Stanislaw Koniecpolski.

Had the grand hetman read it? Probably not. Jozef loved and admired his uncle, but he was not blind to the man's limitations. On a battlefield—at any time or place in the course of a military campaign—Koniecpolski's mind was supple and resourceful. But when it came to political affairs, social customs and economic practices, the grand hetman was set in his ways. Nothing Jozef or his friend Lukasz Opalinski said or did seemed to have much effect on the man's attitudes.

Since Jozef hadn't been able to figure out any way to meet surreptitiously in a city to which both he and Lukasz were foreign, he'd seen no reason to even try. Better to have two obvious strangers who apparently knew each other to meet openly and even volubly in the city's central square in the middle of the day. The very public nature of the encounter would do more to allay possible suspicion than anything else.

The fact that Jozef had two small children perched on his horse would help as well. Whatever dark and lurid images Wroclaw's residents might have of what spies and other nefarious persons looked like, a young man accompanied by two children would not be one of them.

Thankfully, when Lukasz appeared in the square he was not wearing anything that indicated he was a hussar. He was armed with both a saber and two wheel-lock pistols in saddle holsters, but that would not arouse any suspicion since he'd obviously been traveling and the countryside could be dangerous. Jozef's friend was an intelligent man, but he'd spent all his life in the insular surroundings of Polish nobility, an environment that scrambled the brains of most of its denizens. In his more sour moments, Jozef thought the flamboyant wings that hussars liked to attach to their saddles when they rode into combat said more about the contents of their skulls than anything else.

They met in the great market square known as Rynek, in front of the Gothic town hall that the city's Polish residents called the Stary Ratusz and its German ones called the Breslauer Rathaus. They were not far from the Oder, but the river couldn't be seen because the square was lined with buildings. The area was busy, as it always was on days with good weather.

Other than some passing glances, however, no one paid them much attention. Just to further allay whatever vague suspicions might arise, Jozef made it a point to dismount not far from the stone pillory positioned southeast of the town hall where miscreants were flogged. Would a criminally inclined person dawdle in such close proximity to the scene of his own possible mortification? Surely not.

Pawel slid off the horse, allowing Jozef to dismount. Once he'd done so, he reached up and lowered Tekla to the ground. By then, Lukasz had dismounted also.

"So these are the children, eh?" The big hussar leaned over, hands planted on his knees, and gave them both a close inspection. Solemnly, they stared back up at him. "They don't *look* much like you, Jozef."

"Very funny, Lukasz. Just the sort of dry wit one expects from a scion of one of Poland's most noble families." He looked down at the children, waved in Lukasz's direction, and said: "This is Lukasz Opalinski. He'll be taking care of you from now on."

"*No, Uncle Jozef!*"cried out Pawel.

"*Noooooooooooo!*"was Tekla's contribution.

"This is not going to go well," Lukasz predicted.

Regensburg

"I don't care," Rita said. "I'm staying here with you." Her voice started rising as she came up on her toes. "I do not want to go to fucking Amsterdam. It's halfway across Europe, for Chrissake!"

Tom Simpson was better versed in geography than his wife, as you'd expect of a field grade army officer. Measuring Europe in its longest dimension, from the Straits of Gibraltar to the Ural Mountains, the distance was a little over three thousand miles—call it an even three grand, for the sake of simplicity. The distance from Regensburg to Amsterdam was...

Somewhere between four hundred and five hundred miles, Tom estimated.

Call it five hundred.

"It's actually not more than one-sixth of the way across Europe, hon," he said mildly.

"That's how the crow fucking flies! I'm not a crow—and you said yourself we don't have a plane available, which means—"

She began counting off on her fingers. *Thumb.* "First, I've got to ride a fucking horse all the way to Bamberg. *Forefinger.* Then—if it's working, which half the time it isn't because it's got to cross the whole fucking Thüringer Wald and something's always breaking down—I've got to take a train to Grantville.

Middle finger. Then, I've got to take another train all the way to Magdeburg."

"Oh, hell, Rita, that's not more than—"

"Shut the fuck up! I'm not finished." *Ring finger.* "Now I'm stuck on a barge wallowing down the Elbe for hundreds of miles—"

"It's maybe two hundred, tops."

"Like I said! Hundreds of miles. Then—" *Little finger, triumphantly raised above her head.* "I've got to get on a fucking boat and sail all the way down from Hamburg to the North Sea and all the way around half of Europe—okay, fine, a third of Europe—to get to Amsterdam."

She lowered her hand. "And all this for *what?* Buying or leasing a fucking blimp about which I know absolutely squat. That's why you're sending Heinz and Bonnie. They know what to look for and what to look out for. About all I know about stupid fucking blimps is that they're big, they're clumsy, and they fly. Sort of."

Not for the first time since they'd gotten married, Tom was grateful that he'd been blessed with a phlegmatic temperament. Rita had not been so blessed. She was extremely affectionate, generally easy-going, and in most respects a delight to be around. But when she got agitated—as her brother Mike had once put it—her hills rose high and her hollers sank low. And she hollered a lot, with a liberal use of the Old Tongue.

It was no use pointing out that by now Rita actually had a lot of experience with dirigibles—more than enough to know perfectly well that they weren't looking for "blimps." It was true that Heinz Böcler and Bonnie Weaver knew more than she did, especially about some of the mechanical issues involved. And while none of the three had any experience with hydrogen-filled balloons, both Heinz and Bonnie had studied up on the subject while Rita had pointedly refused to do so.

All that was beside the point—and Rita knew it perfectly well. She'd spent a whole year locked up in the Tower of London because of what she herself sometimes called the *Early Modern Era Realities of Fucking Life.*

"Nobody is going to sell or lease a brand new hydrogen-lift airship to a pastor's son and an up-timer with uncertain credentials," he said. "Not unless they plunked down enough gold or silver to cover the entire cost, which we don't have. That means we'll have to use credit, which they don't have and you do."

"Are you fucking kidding? I don't have any income worth talking about and you get paid what that cheapskate emperor scrapes up now and then."

Actually, by seventeenth-century standards the army of the USE paid its officers and enlisted men reasonable wages and paid them reasonably on time. Granted, "by seventeenth-century standards" was a bit like saying that by alley-cat standards the garbage can behind June's Diner held gourmet food.

Tom shook his head. "That's got nothing to do with anything and you know it as well as I do. What *matters* here is that"—he started counting off his own fingers, also starting with his thumb—"First, you're Mike Stearns' sister. Second, you're Admiral Simpson's daughter-in-law. Third—"

"Fuck all that! I don't care!"

He left off finger-counting in order to run said fingers through his hair. "Yeah, but King Fernando will care, and Queen Maria Anna will care, and Archduchess Isabella will care, and while whatever Dutch financier you wind up having to deal with might not care he *will* care that the Royal Trio care. Half of being a successful businessman in the here and now is staying on good terms with Their Majesties."

Rita glared at him. But she didn't say anything and she'd stopped cussing, so he figured they were making progress.

"I don't know what to wear," Bonnie Weaver said. Whined, rather. She had her hands planted on her hips and was studying the contents hanging in her closet. Which had seemed adequate enough, the day before, but now seemed like a pauper's hand-me-downs.

A royal audience, for Pete's sake. What do you wear to a royal audience? More to the point, how do you get around the fact that you obviously don't have anything suitable for the purpose?

Johann Böcler looked up from packing his own valise, which he had spread open on the bed. As was often true of the man, he had a frown on his face. If anyone in the world had a temperament that was the exact and diametrical opposite of Alfred E. Neuman's, it was Johann Böcler. The man could and did worry about everything.

That could have driven Bonnie nuts except that Heinz, unlike most worrywarts, never took it out on the people around him.

And he didn't worry about anything that didn't have a clear and practical focus—as the very bed his valise was on demonstrated.

Bonnie and Heinz had started sharing that bed as soon as she accepted his betrothal. From the standpoint of seventeenth-century German custom, the betrothal settled the issues of moral propriety. Whether or not Heinz's Lutheran deity took the same relaxed and practical attitude toward the matter was unknown, and would presumably remain so until Johann Heinrich Böcler became one with eternity. But that problem was neither practical nor focused so he didn't worry about it.

So, very pleasant and often delightful nights she'd been having, lately.

"What are you concerning yourself about?" he asked. "All you need—all we need—for the moment is clothing for travel."

"But . . . When we get to Amsterdam—Brussels is what I'm actually more worried about—it's a *royal court*, Heinz!—then what am I going to wear?"

He squinted at her, as if he were studying a puzzle. "Why are you worrying about that now? When we get to Amsterdam, we'll buy whatever we need for Amsterdam. When we get to Brussels, the same."

She transferred her exasperated hands-planted-on-hips glower onto Heinz. "And with what money, pray tell?"

He shook his head. "What does prayer have to do with it? The Lord does not provide such things. But our employers will."

He dug into the valise and came up with a thick envelope. "In here, I have letters of recommendation from David Bartley, Michael Stearns, Jeffrey Higgins—there's even one from President Piazza, although it's just in the form of a telegram. But that should be good enough."

"Letters of recommendation are one thing. Hard cash is another."

The squint deepened. A puzzle, indeed. "No one at this level pays for anything with cash, Bonnie. If you tried, in fact, you'd be immediately suspect."

She stared at him for a moment, then pursed her lips. "Do you mean to tell me that I've entered a world where if you have to ask what something costs you can't afford it anyway?"

"I have no idea what that means. And it doesn't seem to make sense in the first place. If you have to ask what something costs then you are being careless because you should have found out before you asked." He dug into the valise again and came up with a much, much thicker envelope. "In here I have all the specifications we need to acquire a suitable airship for a suitable price. I don't expect to ask anything except the projected date of delivery."

He could take practicality to extremes, sometimes.

Breslau (Wroclaw), Lower Silesia
Poland

As Jozef rolled up the antenna he'd run out of their window earlier that night, Lukasz read the message.

Again. He wasn't really "reading" it any longer, he was just gloating over it.

"To Dresden! A city I've always wanted to visit!"

Grand Hetman Koniecpolski must have had his radioman right by him, because he'd given them a response within half an hour.

Lukasz to stay with you. Go back to Dresden. Children will be safe there. Report again when possible.

"And sieges are so *boring*. You have no idea, Jozef."

"I've been through a siege, thank you. In Dresden, as it happens. I wasn't bored at all. I was terrified the whole time."

Lukasz looked up from the radio message in his hand. His lip was already curling into a proper szlachta sneer of disdain.

"Of that Swedish oaf Banér?"

Jozef finished rolling up the antenna. He went to hide it away in his saddlebag, being careful not to wake the two children cuddled together on a cot in the corner.

"Oh, I wasn't concerned about *Banér*," he said. "I was worried about Gretchen Richter."

"Pfah!" Lukasz's lip curled still more. "A woman!"

Now finished with the saddlebag, Jozef came back across the room and gazed down upon his friend.

Jozef had spent a lot of time in Grantville, much of it watching the movies the Americans had brought across time and space. He liked most of them and adored some.

"Be afraid, Opalinski," he said darkly. "Be very afraid."

Chapter 24

Freising, Bavaria

When Mike awoke, he saw that Rebecca had risen before him. She'd already brewed some tea and was sitting at the small table in the corner of the bedroom writing something in her notebook. That would be her manuscript she was working on. The deadline she'd set herself for completing it was approaching and she was becoming increasingly twitchy on the subject. Mike thought that was a little silly, since the deadline was entirely a self-proclaimed one, not something her publisher had established.

Even if the publisher had established a deadline, it wouldn't have mattered that much. Book publishing in this day and age was quite unlike what it had been in the world Mike had come from. There, an author signed a contract and got an advance against projected royalties, in return for which she or he promised to deliver a complete manuscript by such-and-such a date.

None of that applied in this case. The publishing house they planned to use was simply the largest publisher in Magdeburg—and the distinction between "publishing house" and "print shop" was essentially nonexistent. The publisher/printer, a man by the name of Martin Gemberling, was an Alsatian from Strassburg who'd gotten his start working with central Europe's first newspaper publisher, Johann Carolus. He'd agreed to print Rebecca's book whenever it got finished, but that was the beginning and end of his commitment. No money had been advanced, no contract had been signed, no publication date or manuscript deadline had been established.

Rebecca had received a lot of money in the form of a loan advanced against her projected royalties from the book. That loan had not come from any publisher, however, it had come from her massive and extended Abrabanel family. Mike wasn't even sure which specific members of the family had come up with the money. The Sephardic Jews who'd been driven out of Spain at the end of the fifteenth century had their own methods and customs when it came to record-keeping, which were obscure to outsiders because they had been designed that way to make it more difficult for gentile rulers to extort money out of them. It was often unclear which members of the family were wealthy and which were not.

Under normal circumstances, Rebecca was a heavier sleeper than Mike was. He was usually the one who woke first and had the tea or sometimes coffee ready for her when she arose. But between his weariness due to the rigors of the campaign and her own edginess regarding the book, she'd gotten up first both mornings since she'd arrived in Freising.

It hadn't taken her quite as long to get here as she'd expected. Once she got to Ingolstadt, she'd found that the *Pelican* was there and was about to relocate to Freising. By then, the Third Division had taken over the town and set up a protected airship base just north of it. The Bavarian resistance that Mike had expected had never materialized. Apparently, General Piccolomini had decided not to contest the territory north of Munich any further and had withdrawn his forces into the Bavarian capital in preparation for a siege.

Mike was delighted that she'd been able to squeeze in an extra day on her visit. He'd be leaving on the morrow, since he wanted to get the siege underway as soon as possible. If she'd arrived on her original projected schedule, they wouldn't have had time to do much except deal with pressing political affairs. As it was...

He stretched languorously and began the lengthy and arduous process of getting out of bed. The night before had been eventful in its own way and he was feeling the aftereffects.

His wife, sadly, was not sympathetic to his plight. "You'd think *you* were the one who was pregnant, the way you're grunting like a sow and moving about like one." To pour salt into the wound, she hadn't even looked up from her notebook. "*I* somehow managed to perform my wifely duties last night—"

"'Duties!'" Mike scoffed. "You sure didn't seem all that—"

Rebecca drove right over him. "Despite being somewhat encumbered from the results of a fairly recent wifely-duty performance—quite an excellent one too, I was told, from someone who ought to know since it was you—and yet I *still* managed to rise with the sun and get to work while you slumbered half the morning away."

Mike looked at the one window in the room. Judging from the angle at which the sunlight was entering, it was still shy of eight o'clock. "You've got a harsh definition of 'half the morning,' my dear."

Rebecca finished whatever she was writing and finally looked up. There was now a gleaming smile on her face. For perhaps the thousandth time since he'd met her, Mike felt a little stunned by how beautiful she was. Granted, some of that was the bias of a besotted husband. But only some of it.

"There is some tea," she said softly. "Not too bad, either."

"What kind is it?"

"Probably best not to ask. Trust me, it is really rather good. Fairly good. Well, not bad. Not actively bad."

"My hopes are falling by the second," Mike muttered. But he got up, got dressed, and made himself a cup. He still much preferred coffee to tea, being in this respect an unreconstructed American. But in the years since the Ring of Fire he'd grown accustomed to the hot beverages that generally served the seventeenth century in its stead.

A thin broth was the most common beverage people drank, in the here and now, when they weren't drinking something alcoholic. Tea was now available, too. Mike was hoping coffee use might keep growing, but he feared the worst. Tea came from the Far East, along routes the Ottoman Empire couldn't easily cut. Coffee, on the other hand, was either grown in areas under Ottoman control or in areas the Turks could interdict. He was fairly sure that the availability of coffee in Europe was about to take a nosedive.

"Stupid war," he muttered, as he took his first sip of tea. Which was...not actively bad.

"Which one?" Rebecca asked. "War, I mean."

Mike used the cup to point to the window, which faced to the east rather than the south but would serve the momentary purpose. "This one. Against Maximilian."

Rebecca closed her notebook and laid down her pen. "He *is*—and has been for years—a malevolent force in Europe's affairs."

"Yeah, he's a complete asshole, duly certified as such by the Pan-Europe Asshole Registrar's Office, which—gee, what a surprise—is headquartered in Munich since that city has the highest concentration of assholes per capita in the entire continent. But he's still a piker, nowadays. Without its traditional alliance with Austria, Bavaria just isn't big enough to threaten anyone. Not seriously."

"The city council of Augsburg—and for certain the commander of the city's militia—would beg to differ with you," she pointed out.

Mike drained his cup and set it down on the narrow ledge that served the room for a kitchen counter. "Yeah, sure, but Augsburgers are always twitchy about Bavaria because they're right on the border. The fact remains that they're one of the USE's officially recognized imperial cities, they're well-fortified and what difference does that make anyway seeing as how the nation they're a part of is about to lay siege to Bavaria's own capital?"

For all the banter in their exchange, Rebecca had been listening closely. "I know you are concerned about the Ottomans, Michael. What I do not quite understand is why you are so concerned. They *did* fail in 1529, after all. And your own history books say they would fail again when they tried to take Vienna a second time—"

He waved his hand as if he were swatting at an insect. "In 1683. If I've heard that once, I've heard it a thousand times. But here's what I also know."

By then, he'd taken a seat on the bed and was leaning forward with his forearms on his knees. "People get so enamored with those damn up-time history books that they forget the other guy knows how to read too. By all accounts I've ever heard, Murad IV is the most capable sultan the Turks have had in a long time. Probably since Suleiman—whom they didn't call 'the Magnificent' for nothing. What are the odds that a man like that won't have been examining the records and drawing his own conclusions from it?"

Rebecca was no stranger to playing the devil's advocate, whenever her husband wanted to seriously discuss something. "By those same accounts, Michael—each and every one of them, so far as I am aware—Murad has decreed that the stories of people from the future are malicious fables, a sign of witchcraft, and cause for summary execution should anyone repeat them. That hardly sounds like a man determined to squeeze every drop of knowledge that he can from your history books."

Mike chuckled heavily. "Yeah, I've heard the same reports. But let me ask you something, sweetheart. If you were Murad and you wanted to launch secret weapons projects based on up-time knowledge *and* you didn't want your enemies to realize you were doing it, what sort of decrees would you make?"

His wife's expression remained exactly the same. Calm, still, attentive—and rather detached. "I would decree that the stories of people from the future are malicious fables, a sign of witchcraft, and cause for summary execution should anyone repeat them."

"Exactly. So would I. Well...if I was a ruthless despot, anyway. Which is exactly what Murad is."

Mike rose to his feet and went to look out the window. He did that from long habit, not because there was anything to see except the wall of an adjacent building. "I don't believe it for a minute," he said softly. "I think the Ottomans have been working around the clock, preparing for this assault on Austria. However authoritarian their government might be, it's also probably the most efficient one in the world. This side of China, anyway. Their empire is huge and they have enormous resources and manpower."

Rebecca went back to playing devil's advocate. "Somewhat cruder technology than Europe's, though, as a rule. At least, cruder than the best Europe can produce."

Mike's shrug was as heavy as his chuckle had been. "I've heard that also, and although I'm a bit skeptical I'm willing to accept the assessment. But I'm not all that impressed by it, either. The Russians who fought the Nazis in World War Two also had a cruder technology than their enemy did. But guess who won? That's because the Russians played to their strengths. Their weapons may have been crude, but they worked and they made a lot of them and they were willing to take the casualties to wear down their enemy."

He turned away from the window to look at her directly. "And that's exactly what I think Murad is planning to do. I think he *does* have airships. Not planes, no. But planes aren't really that useful in fixed, siege warfare. Not the ones we can build today. For that, airships will do just as well and they can be primitive as all hell—as long as the Turks have plenty of them. Understanding that 'plenty' is always a relative term. We've got a handful at our disposal. All they need—"

"Is a few handfuls," she finished for him. "And you think the same will be true with other weapons."

"Yes. We know they have Hale-design rockets. They used them in massed barrages against the Persians. You can expect plenty more where those came from. By now, I'm as sure as I am of anything that Murad will have equipped thousands of his troops with rifled muskets. Once you understand the principle of a Minié ball, designing a gun that can fire one isn't hard. I'm sure they'll be cruder than ours or the French Cardinal, but they'll do. They'll do."

He went back to looking out the window. "I don't know what else the Ottomans will bring to Vienna, but there'll be something, you can bet on it. Maximilian of Bavaria is a vicious son-of-a-bitch but he no longer poses any major threat to anybody except people dumb enough or unlucky enough to work for him. Murad IV, Sultan of the Ottoman Empire...he's something entirely different. He *could* pose an existential threat to us. Or his successor could, if he succeeds in taking Vienna and keeping it."

"You think we should close down the war with Bavaria, if we can get some sort of acceptable political settlement," she said. It was a statement, not a question. "And then move at once to aid Austria."

"Yes. In a nutshell. That's what I think we should do." He shrugged again. "But Gustav Adolf doesn't agree with me and he's calling the shots, at least for now."

Rebecca rose. "Michael, if you are right then you will be proven right within a very short time. Three months, at the latest. We are already near the end of May. By now, the Ottoman march will be well underway. They have to seize Vienna rather quickly or they will be caught by the coming of winter. Which means that if Murad's plans are as you suspect, we will see them unfold at some point over the summer."

He knew his wife very well by now. She was leading him

somewhere. Part of the reason Mike loved Rebecca was that he knew she was smarter than he was. At least in terms of what he thought of as raw brainpower. He suspected he was her equal and probably her superior in some aspects of what people called emotional intelligence.

"What are you getting at?" he asked.

"Go around Gustav Adolf's back. Without directly defying him, lay whatever plans you can that will help you get to Austria as soon as possible, and will keep you from getting any more entangled here in Bavaria than is absolutely necessary. It seems silly to have Major Simpson go to all this trouble to bring four naval rifles to Munich when two would serve the purpose, while the other two remain where they can be brought into Austria quickly. Even ten-inch naval rifles can be floated down the Danube on a barge."

"Already thought of that. What else?"

"You need to get an airstrip built here in Freising as soon as possible."

"I'll see to it. What else?"

"I would devote a lot of thought to the subject of barges. Flat-bottomed boats even more so. Marching an army takes time. Floating them down the Isar and then down the Danube seems much more efficient."

She had a point. But...

"How many flat-bottom boats and barges can there be in Bavaria?" he wondered.

"I have no idea. But I think the better question is: how many boat-builders are there in Bavaria—the southern Oberpfalz too— who might be available to make more?"

The area had been ravaged by war, lately. That always produced a lot of people who were looking for work. Only some of them needed to be experienced boatwrights, just enough to guide the others.

"You're right. I'll get David Bartley working on it right away. I love you."

Rebecca got a long-suffering look on her face. "I foresee more wifely duties in the near future."

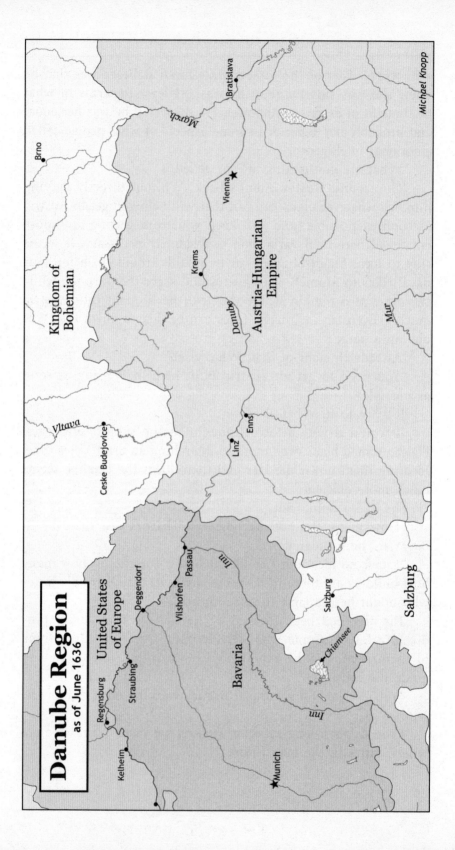

Danube Region
as of June 1636

Brno

Kingdom of
Bohemian

Vltava

Ceske Budejovice

Regensburg

United States
of Europe

Kelheim

Straubing

Deggendorf

Vilshofen

Passau

Inn

Inn

Bavaria

Munich

Chiemsee

Salzburg

Salzburg

Enns

Linz

Danube

Austria-Hungarian
Empire

Krems

Vienna

Bratislava

March

Mur

Michael Knopp

Part Three

June 1636

There burns a truer light

Chapter 25

Prague, capital of Bohemia

On their last night in Prague, Janos Drugeth came to Noelle's suite. When she opened the door and let him in, he had a peculiar expression on his face. If she hadn't known him better, she would have thought him to be undecided about something—no, more than that. He seemed downright indecisive.

An optical illusion of some sort. By now, Noelle had learned that Janos was a complicated man in many respects. But the one thing he wasn't, ever, was indecisive.

Clearly, though, he wanted her advice about something. So, despite the late hour, she ushered him into the small chamber that served her as a salon of sorts, and invited him to sit.

Right after he did so, a servant hurried into the room, looking a bit disheveled. Her name was Ilona and she'd already retired for the night since Noelle had told her she wouldn't be needed again until the next day.

Noelle looked from Ilona to Janos. "Would you like something? A glass of wine?"

"No. Well. I suppose... Yes. I would."

Noelle had never seen him like this. She turned to Ilona and said, "Bring us two glasses of wine, please. I'll have one also."

She didn't understand what was causing Janos to be so unsettled, but she figured if she had a glass of wine with him that might help settle his nerves. She drank little in the way of alcoholic beverages, although she'd found her consumption rising as time passed. In this as in so many ways, the seventeenth century's standards were different from the ones she'd been accustomed to in the world of her birth.

Janos remained silent until Ilona returned with the glasses of wine. "Are you going to want another glass later?" she asked him.

Again, he seemed indecisive. "I don't ... Ah. I am not sure."

Fascinating. But there was no reason to keep Ilona up. The poor girl seemed tired.

"Go back to bed, Ilona," she said. "I know where the wine is, if we need more later."

The servant seemed a bit scandalized by the notion that her mistress could pour herself a glass of wine. But she said nothing; simply curtsied and left.

Noelle turned back to Janos. By then, he'd already drained half the glass—which was also quite unlike him. Drugeth, like almost all noblemen Noelle had encountered since the Ring of Fire, drank a lot of wine in the course of a day. But he stretched it out, so that he never seemed tipsy. She didn't think she'd ever seen him guzzle half a glass like that.

Fascinating. What was on his mind?

She went straight to the point. "Something is bothering you, Janos. What is it?"

"Ah..." He drained the rest of the glass in one swallow.

"Would you care for some more wine?"

He raised the empty glass and stared at it for a moment. He seemed a bit startled that it was already empty.

"Ah, no." He set it down on the side table next to his chair. That motion, at least, was decisive. "The reason I came here tonight is because tomorrow we will fly back to Vienna."

She nodded. Janos had finished his negotiations with Wallenstein that afternoon. Nothing further could be settled until he spoke with Ferdinand to get the emperor's approval to the terms he and the king of Bohemia had finally thrashed out. Eddie had flown the plane into Prague that same afternoon and would be ready to fly back out as soon as Janos and Noelle arrived at the airfield.

"Once we get to Vienna," Janos continued, "we will be staying in the Hofburg and as I'm sure you remember, it is rather crowded."

"To say the least," she said, smiling. The type of buildings that up-time Americans thought of as "palaces," like Versailles, generally dated from a much later period. There was a travel guide to Vienna in Grantville's public library that Noelle had looked at before coming to Austria, and the "Hofburg" it depicted—much less the later and still more elaborate palace called Schönbrunn—was a far cry from what existed in the year 1636. Like most palaces in this time period, the Hofburg was a ramshackle structure, parts of which dated back to the thirteenth century.

As lavish as the furnishings might be, the Austrian royal palace was overflowing with people. Between the royal family and live-in courtiers and a horde of servants, it had a population density that reminded Noelle of some of the poorer trailer parks she'd seen in West Virginia. Kids everywhere; dogs everywhere; people idling on every stair stoop.

It finally dawned on her what Janos was skittering around, like the proverbial cat on a hot tin roof. She felt her own face getting warm.

"Oh," she said. "You're worried we, ah, won't have any privacy."

Janos smiled crookedly. "I can't say I'm 'worried' about it, exactly. It is an absolute given that we will have no privacy."

His expression became solemn. "One of the things I will try to persuade the emperor to do is to remove the royal family to Linz. They should not be there when the Ottoman army arrives. Once the siege begins, it may prove impossible—it will certainly be difficult—to get them to safety. And you should go with them." She started to protest but he held up his hand in a sharp gesture. "Please, Noelle! There is nothing you can do in a siege, and a great deal you can do elsewhere."

"Will you be staying?"

"That will be up to the emperor. I suspect he'll have other assignments for me, though, since he has Baudissin and other officers to lead the garrison. Once the royal family leaves the city, morale is likely to suffer, but the remedy for that is to have one of the younger family members volunteer to stay behind. That would be Leopold. Possibly Cecilia Renata as well."

The logic was cold-blooded, but she understood it. The two oldest of Ferdinand II's four children were the current emperor Ferdinand III and his sister Maria Anna, now married to Fernando, the king in the Netherlands. Ferdinand III had already sired a son and a daughter, and Maria Anna was reported to be pregnant. Even if that pregnancy did not come to term, Maria

Anna was safely ensconced in Brussels, half a continent away from the oncoming Ottoman army.

That left the two youngest siblings, Leopold and Cecilia Renata, as something in the way of supernumeraries so far as preserving the dynasty was concerned. Having one of them stay in the capital during the siege would help the morale of the defending forces.

She brought her mind back to the subject at hand. There was no way that her marriage to Janos could be moved forward. No date had even been set yet, since the looming siege would make the sort of huge semi-official—more like three-quarters-official—ceremony impossible to organize.

Noelle had been taken aback when she realized what Janos and Emperor Ferdinand had in mind for the wedding. She still found it surreal that anyone was deluded enough to think that one Noelle Stull, née Murphy, was a suitable subject for the sort of weddings she'd never seen except on television.

Abstractly, she understood the logic here as well. Janos Drugeth was one of Austria-Hungary's most prominent noblemen and known to be one of the emperor's closest friends and confidants. Any marriage in which he was one of the participants was bound to be a major quasi-state affair, if for no other reason than to satisfy the always-tender sensibilities of the Hungarian aristocracy. The fact that he was marrying an American added a certain frisson to the business. There was still a wide range of opinions on the part of Europe's aristocracy on the subject of exactly where Americans should be placed in the established social hierarchy. A number of Austrians had settled on the formula of referring to all Americans by the appellation "von Up-time"—an expression which Noelle thought was ridiculous and which she knew both Mike Stearns and Ed Piazza actively detested.

But whatever their attitude might be, one thing was clear: Americans were all celebrities. Back in the day, some people had fawned over Zsa Zsa Gabor, some people had found her ridiculous or even contemptible, and most hadn't cared very much one way or the other. But everyone had heard of her.

Of course, there were celebrities, and then there were celebrities. Some were movie stars known the world over; others were minor figures known only in a particular locale. So it was with Americans also, here in the seventeenth century. Nobody thought of the local American souse of a handyman as the prince of anything. But the fact that he was American was still a matter of note.

The changed reality had snuck up on Noelle, but she was now a lot closer to such people as Mike Stearns or Ed Piazza or Melissa Mailey in the pantheon of *American Legendary Figures, Large and Small*, than she'd been a year ago. She wasn't very happy with the change, either. But...

Her thoughts were skittering away again.

When in doubt, Noelle usually found refuge in bluntness.

"I'm a virgin," she said abruptly. She could have added the qualification *technically speaking* but saw no point in detailing the complex behavioral permutations of her relationship with a former boyfriend who'd never come through the Ring of Fire so he couldn't gainsay her anyway. The way she figured it, append-ages other than The One didn't count.

Janos' face was stiff. "I did not ask," he said.

"Yes, I noticed. And I appreciated it. But since it looks as if my, ah, maidenly status is about to change, I figured you ought to know that I'm likely to fumble around the business. Some."

That broke his wooden expression. "I am not concerned about that in the least!"

"Okay, then." She rose to her feet and extended her hand. "Follow me."

He came to his feet and took her hand. Then he hesitated. "I do not—are you concerned about—how to put it?"

"Getting pregnant? It's not likely, tonight. But it doesn't matter because I hold to our church's teachings on the subject of birth control. If I get pregnant, so be it."

He was still hesitant. "I may not—it's possible—that I will not survive this war."

"I understand that. In which case I might wind up with a so-called illegitimate child on my hands, even though I think coupling the words 'illegitimate' and 'child' is grotesque."

She grinned, then. "Quit stalling, buddy. You started this, I didn't—but the girl is willing."

She didn't expand that to *willing as all hell* because that might be blasphemy. In the seventeenth century, you never knew.

Prague's airfield—you call hardly call it an "airport"—was located just beyond the walls of the "New Town," the section of the city known in Czech as Nové Město. To get to it you had to pass through the Horse Gate, so named because the area adjacent to it within the walls was the Horse Market. The Horse Market would eventually be renamed Wenceslas Square, assuming the history of this universe remained faithful to the nomenclature of another.

Which...it might or might not. In the Americans' universe, the name change hadn't taken place until the revolution of 1848. But in this universe, it might never happen at all or it could happen at any moment. The city's Jews were now often referring to the Jewish quarter as the "Josefov," in honor of the emperor Joseph II in another universe who would emancipate Prague's Jews in his Toleration Edict of 1781. Given that in this universe the city's Jews had already been emancipated a quarter of a millennium earlier by King Albrecht II (aka Wallenstein), that renaming seemed impolitic as well as absurd.

But, such was the nature of terminological upheavals produced by cosmic catastrophes. As had been said more than once, the Ring of Fire had a lot to answer for.

Eddie Junker had the *Steady Girl* fueled and ready to go shortly after sunrise, because Noelle had told him the day before that she and Janos wanted to get to Vienna as early in the day as possible. So he was disgruntled—*he'd* risen an hour and a half before dawn—that they didn't show up until late in the morning. By his very excellent watch, 10:06 AM, to be precise.

Seeing the way they held on to each other as they neared, which he coupled with their slow progress, constant nuzzling and generally vacuous expressions, he made certain deductions and came to certain conclusions.

He was still ticked off. Getting up at 3:30 in the morning was a wretched business and those responsible needed a really good excuse to justify their own failure to match the schedule. A major earthquake, an outbreak of plague, the apocalypse, something of that nature. Getting laid just didn't cut the mustard, even if Noelle had waited a preposterous amount of time to take care of the business.

"Are we *finally* ready to go?" he demanded, once they had reached the plane.

There was no answer. They were back to nuzzling again.

"This is getting ridiculous," said Eddie.

Chapter 26

Vienna, capital of Austria-Hungary

The young woman on the stage finished the piece she was playing with a flourish, both vocally and with the fiddle itself. The
audience in the reception chamber burst into applause.

Some of the applause was tentative, tepid, even tremulous.
The audience was mostly made up of Austrian and Hungarian
nobility, who were not accustomed to this sort of music. Some
of them were dubious that it qualified as "music" at all. But
since the performer was closely associated with Americans, even
if she was not American herself, they extended her the benefit
of the doubt.

Others, though, had no doubts at all. No sooner had Minnie
Hugelmair finished her rendition of "The Wabash Cannonball"
than Denise Beasley and Judy Wendell both jumped to their
feet and started whooping and hollering to go along with their
hand-clapping.

The audience stared at them for a second or two, unsure
whether this unseemly display should be the cause of further
applause or disapproving silence. But that issue was settled a
moment later, when Archduke Leopold rose to his feet and joined
the clapping—though not the hollering and whooping—followed
almost immediately by his sister, Archduchess Cecilia Renata. It
took the assembled audience, most of whom were well-trained
courtiers, no time at all to mimic their betters.

Minnie did a bow coupled with a curtsy of sorts—something of a truncated one, since she had both hands engaged with the fiddle and the bow—grinning in a manner that was just as unseemly as the music itself. Those who knew her well, which now included Judy as well as Denise, understood that the grin was largely derisive. Minnie Hugelmair had no illusions at all concerning her position in the eyes of Austria-Hungary's aristocracy—and didn't care in the least.

When her eyes—eye, rather—met those of Leopold, the grin transmuted into something a lot more friendly. She hadn't decided yet what sort of relationship she might wind up having with the youngest of the Austro-Hungarian empire's four royal siblings, but of one thing she was now certain. Unlike most of the people feigning applause in the room, Leopold's applause was genuine. And unlike most of the people in the room, Leopold understood that she was an actual person.

Not very well, to be sure. He had been born and raised in a manner that made such an understanding difficult. But she was willing to give him credit for trying. He was having a definite influence on his sister, too.

All four of the siblings were close to each other, from what Minnie and her friends had been able to ascertain. That was probably due in part to the fact they were close in age. Ferdinand, now the emperor, had been born in July of 1608. The other three had all been born in the month of January—of the year 1610, in the case of Maria Anna; 1611, in the case of Cecilia Renata, and 1614 in the case of Leopold Wilhelm. Less than a six year spread, all told.

The fact that Leopold was favorably inclined toward Minnie had made Cecilia Renata less skeptical of the ragamuffin and her friends than she would have been otherwise. That lowered guard, in turn, had led her to become better acquainted with Judy Wendell. Up until then, Cecilia Renata had very mixed feelings about the beautiful young American. On the one hand, she'd been just as outraged as any other proper aristocrat at Judy's astonishingly rude treatment of her brother Leopold Wilhelm when the archduke had made physical advances on her. On the other hand...

He was also her younger brother and who knew better than his closest sibling—especially a sister!—just how richly deserved that rebuke had been. True, Judy shouldn't have kneed him in the testicles. That was very crude. But she was a commoner, so what could you expect? Cecilia Renata could remember plenty of occasions in her childhood when she'd been sorely tempted to do the same.

Well...perhaps not knee him in the testicles. But hit him on the head? Oh, surely. Punch him in the nose? Yes, that too.

Once Cecilia Renata became better acquainted with Judy Wendell, she found herself becoming friends with the girl. She was a few years older than the American—twenty-four years of age as opposed to Judy Wendell's eighteen years. But Judy had a dry, sardonic wit that Cecilia Renata enjoyed and which resonated with her own detached and acerbic view of most of the people around her. Being a member of the royal family who lacked much in the way of direct power but had a great deal of indirect influence had made Cecilia Renata skeptical of most people's motives. When they fawned on her they usually wanted something.

Judy Wendell never fawned on Cecilia Renata—nor on anyone else, so far as she could determine. The young American knew she was gorgeous and accepted that in the same spirit she accepted the sky being blue and water being wet. It was just a fact—an enjoyable one, in this case—but nothing she took credit for herself, any more than she'd take credit for the color of the sky or the wetness of water.

Cecilia Renata knew that she herself was not beautiful. She didn't think she was ugly, certainly, and everyone agreed that she had very lovely red hair. But she also shared her brother Leopold's long, bony nose, even if she didn't have as pronounced a lower lip as most Habsburgs. And, like Leopold, she was on the tall and gangly side.

When you were royalty, however, appearance didn't matter very much. Someone would marry you even if you looked like a troll. But that too, in its own way, strengthened Cecilia Renata's sometimes mordant outlook. Trust nothing anyone says to you, especially about yourself, unless you know them very well.

She was becoming more and more inclined toward getting to know Judy Wendell very well.

At the reception, following the performance, most of the gathered nobility fell back into comfortable habits and ignored Minnie Hugelmair completely. This suited her just fine because there weren't that many people there whom she had any desire to talk to anyway.

She started with Denise, as she usually did. "You should leave with Eddie," she told her, in a tone that made the statement an outright command.

Which, naturally, made Denise bridle. The girl did not react well to instruction, especially coming from someone who was no farther up Denise's mental pecking order than her best friend. Anybody except a jerk heard what her best friend had to say, but that didn't mean you had to listen to her.

"Why?" she demanded immediately. "Are *you* planning to leave?"

"No. Why should I? Don Francisco doesn't need both of us to report back to him. And while it's true my reports are better than yours—more concise; better organized; way less commentary—yours are still good enough for what he needs to know right now." She slipped into a slightly singsong tone, as if reciting something memorized. "Yes, boss, the Ottomans are coming to Vienna, there is no doubt about it in anyone's mind. The Viennese are worried but they're not as worried as they ought to be. They keep thinking that the up-time history books are some sort of magic talisman. *Didn't happen in 1529; wouldn't have happened in 1683; so how could it happen now?* That kind of silliness."

Denise glared at her. "You just want to stay because you're scheming. About that stupid fucking prince."

"First, he's not a prince. Except in a few places—I'm quoting the immortal words from *The Princess Bride*—that word does not mean what you think it means. Leopold Wilhelm is an archduke."

"Same thing. Close enough."

"Not the same thing. And to quote other immortal words, close only counts in horseshoes and hand grenades."

"You've never played horseshoes in your life."

"Of course not. It's amazing how many stupid games you Americans came up with. Football! Thankfully, most of them didn't make it through the Ring of Fire. Secondly—"

Minnie ignored her friend's splutter of outrage at this grotesque denigration of American games, which was ridiculous anyway because Denise's opinion of football was abysmal and so far as Minnie knew she'd never played horseshoes once in her life.

"—you can't call it 'scheming' because a scheme implies that you're trying to pull a fast one on someone who'd never agree to what you want him to do if you just proposed it straight up and you know as well as I do that Leopold's got the hots for me. The problem, him being an archduke, is that he can't figure out how to approach the subject on account of the last time he put the make on an up-timer he got his balls mashed."

"You're not an up-timer."

"I'm an honorary up-timer. You've said so yourself about a thousand times."

Denise looked sulky. "I don't think I said that more than once or twice. Maybe half a dozen times. Tops."

"Still true—and what's more to the point, Leopold agrees with you. That's why he's scared of me. Which—we're up to point three now—is why I need to stay in Vienna so I have the time to decide if I want to pursue it myself—which I probably do, since I still think he's pretty cute—and, if so, I'll need the time to educate him in the proper ways of a man with a maiden."

"You're not a maiden. Not even close!"

Minnie gave her friend a look of pity. "I'm speaking in poetry, not prose. I can do that because I'm a singer."

Elsewhere in the room, two other people were having another dispute on the subject of leave-taking.

"There is no reason for you to stay, Cecilia Renata. Having one of us remain in Vienna during the siege is quite good enough."

Leopold Wilhelm tilted his head so he could look down his nose at his sister. That did less good than it might have with someone else, because Cecilia Renata was no slouch herself in the down-nose-looking department. True, he had the advantage of four inches in height, but that was easily offset by her advantage of three years of age.

The noses being evenly matched, Leopold tried sentiment. "I won't be able to concentrate on my duties, because I'll be so worried about you."

"I am not planning to stand on the walls with a musket, Brother. If it makes you feel better, I can have the cellars under the outer wing stocked with supplies so I can take shelter there during especially heavy bombardments."

That . . . wasn't a bad idea, actually. The cellars were deep enough to provide protection from any cannon fire, certainly. And in the very unlikely event that the Ottomans managed to breach the walls and make an incursion into the city, they would also provide his sister with an excellent hiding place. The entrance to the cellars had been disguised when it was built for precisely that purpose.

That wing was a portion of the imperial palace that was not directly connected to the rest of the Hofburg. It had been built in the middle of the last century, and its original purpose had been to provide separate housing for crown prince Maximilian. His father, Ferdinand I, suspected his son and heir of Protestant sympathies and wanted him quarantined from the rest of the family.

In the event, Maximilian had remained faithful to the Catholic church, and when he succeeded his father as Holy Roman Emperor in 1564, he transferred his residence to the Hofburg proper. In the years thereafter, the outer wing had been used for a variety of purposes, one of them being a place for Leopold to begin accumulating the collection of art which he intended to become one of the best in Europe. He'd only gotten started on the project, of course.

Thinking of his nascent art collection . . .

Regardless of whether Cecilia Renata stayed in Vienna or left, it would be a good idea to move his art collection down into the cellars. A stray cannonball might do unspeakable damage.

But that was a matter to be dealt with later. For the moment, he still had an obstreperous sister to deal with.

Sentiment having failed, he fell back on logic.

"The whole point of having me remain behind in the capital while our brother and his heir leave for the safe refuge of Linz is because, being male, I can assume command of the city's forces. You, being female, cannot. So what is the purpose of having you stay as well?"

"That's pure twaddle. The command of the city's forces will actually be in the hands of General Baudissin and other experienced commanders. I know it, you know it, every soldier knows it—or they'd be sleeping a lot worse at night, not meaning to disparage my little brother's nonexistent military reputation—and probably every street urchin knows it as well."

A low blow. Accurate and true, but low.

Happily, at that very moment the oldest of the four siblings appeared at their side. Cecilia Renata, despite being a woman, did not actually have to obey Leopold. But she did have to obey Ferdinand III, emperor of Austria-Hungary, king of Croatia (and still formally king of Bohemia as well, at least until Drugeth returned from Prague and a new treaty was signed).

"Brother," Leopold said, lowering his nose just enough to indicate with disapproval their sister, "who is also the emperor of Austria-Hungary and holder of at least two pages worth of additional titles when written in Chancery copperplate, tell Cecilia Renata she has to leave Vienna when you do."

"Brother," said Cecilia Renata, "tell Leopold Wilhelm he's being an officious ass. I'm staying. That's all there is to it."

Ferdinand III, emperor of etc., etc., etc., had simply come over to enquire as to their respective states of health. He looked at Leopold, then at Cecilia Renata, back at Leopold, back at Cecilia Renata, shook his head and walked off.

"You see?" The female nose elevated in triumph.

"He's a fucking prince—fine, archduke. Same difference. He'll take advantage of you."

"How does 'advantage' come into the simple matter of whether I screw him or not?"

"He's up here"—Denise raised her hand high—"and you're way down here." The left hand waved about as low as she could place it.

"Only if that's the position we assume. I could be on top of him, instead. Or he could be—"

"Cut it out!"

Minnie smiled. "I appreciate your concern. But I can't help wonder where that concern was hiding when I was cavorting with the hostler in Dresden who built the airstrip for us."

"That was different. Godeke was a commoner. Like my boyfriend Eddie. Not a damn prince—fine, fucking archduke—taking advantage of you."

Minnie squinted, as if she were trying to decipher very fine print. "You Americans are just plain weird, sometimes. If the hostler had gotten me pregnant, I'd have been in a difficult position since Godeke was a nice guy but I had no desire to marry him. So I would have had to raise the kid with no help beyond what little I could squeeze out of him in a court of law, which was maybe three turnips. Nineteen-year-old hostlers earn what you call squat and I wouldn't even go that high."

She turned her head to contemplate the person across the room who was the nexus of their quarrel. "Whereas if *he* sires a bastard on me I'm sitting what you'd call pretty for the rest of my life."

"He'll abandon you! He'll say the kid isn't his!"

"Why in the world would he do that?" Her squint got even squintier. "Royal scions always have bastards, everybody knows it—including and maybe even especially their wives. If anything, it's an advantage all the way around. From a prospective bride's point of view, it proves he's fertile. From an established wife's point of view, it means maybe he won't be pestering her except when he needs an heir."

Minnie shrugged. "But it's all a moot point, anyway. First, because right now I'm still just thinking about it. Second, because I have the needed supplies to avoid getting pregnant if I decide to go ahead—as you know perfectly well, since I got them from you in the first place. And, thirdly, because I don't give a damn—no, let me expand that into full blasphemic proportions: I don't give a good God-damn—what the theologians say about birth control."

All Christian denominations in the seventeenth century except some of those imported by the Americans disapproved of contraception, and had since the second century of the Christian Era. It wasn't just Catholics, either. Both Martin Luther and John Calvin had weighed in against the practice.

Minnie, however, was a free-thinker on this as on pretty much any and all questions of a cosmological, cosmogenic, spiritual, theological, doctrinal, sacerdotal, ministerial, sacred, sacrosanct and sanctified nature and didn't care what any establishment had to say on the subjects. She figured her glass eye gave her all the authority she needed to make up her own mind.

She brought that glass eye to bear on Denise, to drive home the point. While, with the other—the one that actually worked—she glanced around to see what Archduke Leopold Wilhelm was doing.

At the moment, he was trying to pretend he wasn't looking at her.

Splendid. The likelihood that the answer would wind up being "yes" moved up a notch.

When she brought the real eye back to Denise, she saw that her friend was still being sulky.

"And what about you?" she demanded. "What if *you* get pregnant?"

"Eddie would do the right thing," Denise said stoutly.

"Well, of course he would. But that's the whole problem in a nutshell, isn't it? What's the 'right thing' for a pilot to do when he hasn't got a pot to piss in except that empty bottle Eddie keeps in the cockpit for when he can't hold it in?"

"That's not true!" Denise said hotly. "Eddie's got—got—lots of stuff. Well, his family does, anyway. And besides, I don't care. Neither should you. It's the *principle* of the thing."

Minnie was back to squinting. Very, very fine print.

"How did you Americans get so weird? I've read that famous Constitution of yours. Three times. I don't remember any place where it says that it's forbidden to ever be practical about anything. Is there a secret amendment, maybe? Written in invisible ink or something?"

Chapter 27

On the Isar River in Bavaria
A few miles north of Munich

Tom Simpson surveyed the Isar River, paying particular attention to the two barges moored to the nearby dock, each of which was carrying a ten-inch naval rifle. The barges were more like big rafts than anything else. The Isar was very shallow in a lot of places. That was part of the reason it had taken them so many days to get the rifles down here.

"Let me see if I can translate my commanding general's Newspeak into some resemblance of the King's English," he said, turning to face Mike Stearns. "After I've spent weeks busting my ass—well, okay, I'm an officer; busting my ass busting grunts' asses—in order to get you the naval rifles the Bavarians spiked and in the case of two of them tried to drown, you want me to figure out ways to slow down our progress with the two still-soggy bastards."

Tom jerked a thumb at the two rifles on the barges. "Or do you want me to roll these over and dump them into the Isar? That way, we'll have four soggy bastards."

Mike Stearns pursed his lips thoughtfully. "I'm sure there's something in military regulations that prohibits subordinate officers from being excessively sarcastic."

Tom grunted. "Probably would be, if the USE military had a Uniform Code of Military Justice, which we don't. So that means down-time rules apply and since I'm your brother-in-law I get to be sarcastic. I'm afraid the major general is just going to have to suck it up."

"Since you insist on speaking the King's English, your assessment is pretty much correct." Mike nodded toward the two guns on the barges. "Those will do fine for starting to beat down Munich's walls."

"Go faster with four of 'em."

"I don't *want* it to go faster. We're not going to be launching any assaults so casualties will be light and almost all of them will be Bavarian because those ten-inch rifles have a much longer range than anything the Bavarians can shoot back with. We can take our time reducing the walls. If we speed it up that just means I have to order a ground assault sooner and I'm still hoping to avoid that altogether."

Tom didn't say anything for a few seconds. Then, sighing a little, he took off his hat and ran fingers through his thick hair. "You're playing a risky game, Mike. If Gustav Adolf figures out that you're stalling him, there'll be hell to pay."

"Not... exactly. Or maybe I should say it's not that simple." Mike removed his own hat and copied Tom's fingers-through-the-hair movement. "Gustav Adolf is a very smart man and about as experienced a general as any alive. I'm sure he's *already* figured out that I'm slowing everything down. But what he thinks and what he knows—and can prove—are two different things, and the political risks cut both ways. His authority is solid on the surface but it's still spongy-soft on the inside, because of everything that happened after Lake Bledno. He can't afford an open clash with me—not for a while, at least—over something that's so murky he can't prove that I'm guilty of anything."

He put the hat back on his head, wishing for a moment that military protocol didn't insist on the blasted things. In cold weather, hats were splendid. On a warm day in late May, coupled with a uniform that was too heavy for the season to begin with, they were a damn nuisance.

But, customs were customs—for no institutions were as rigid as armies, except maybe some churches. So, the hat went back on his head. Generals had to sweat just like grunts did.

Not as much, of course. They got to ride horses and were exempt from manual labor. But they had to sweat some.

"Besides, I'm not actually that sure just how bound and determined our emperor is to squash Maximilian like a bug," he added.

Tom's eyes widened a little. "I thought he was hard as nails on that subject."

"Officially, yes." Mike barked a little laugh. "I've seen him do his inimitable roar on the subject in front of a room full of officials and courtiers. When he wants to, that man can bellow like nobody's business."

"I've heard him," said Tom, wincing. "But you're saying you think it's an act?"

Mike shrugged. "With Gustav Adolf, you can't ever be sure. He's got intimidation down to a science and he's usually playing the power game on several levels—simultaneously, mind you, not sequentially."

"I'm not sure what that means."

"There was bound to be at least one Bavarian spy in that room, who heard Gustav Adolf swear that he would see Maximilian's corpse trampled under oxen and the remains scattered to the winds."

"An actual *spy*? Really?"

Mike shrugged again. "Define 'spy.' I doubt if there's anyone at court in Magdeburg who's the Bavarian equivalent of James Bond. But someone who's willing to let his palm get greased for information, from time to time? By persons whose identity and purpose remains carefully unstated? There's probably a dozen of those."

"Point."

"So Maximilian is sure to know that Gustav Adolf has vowed to have him die a horrible death, which means—maybe—you never know with that bastard either—"

"That he'll be more willing to cut a deal. Gotcha." Tom took a deep breath and let it out slowly, then grimaced.

"Okay, boss. One slowdown coming up. You do realize I'm going to have to let some of my men in on it? I can't fake it entirely on my own."

"Yeah, I figured that. But I think we've got at least a month before Gustav Adolf starts making a fuss about it."

"That long?"

"Oh, yeah. Even without screwing off, it took you this long to get just one of the guns out of the river—and it was the easier of the two."

Tom's expression was on the sour side. "Ten-inch guns are

heavier than hell and the Danube's a muddy river. It didn't take long before they were buried in the river bed—if you want to call that muck a 'bed'—and we're working with seventeenth-century technology. What slowed us down the most, though, was that you didn't leave me more than skeleton crew to do the work."

"Oh, come on! You had a bigger crew than that. I figure it was closer to a starving-concentration-camp-inmate-sized crew."

"You did that on purpose," Tom said accusingly. "I can see it all now."

"I *did* have a major campaign on my hands against one of the most redoubtable armies in Europe. I *did* face a very competent and experienced opposing general. I *did* need every good artilleryman I could get my hands on."

"Yeah, yeah, yeah—and I'm sure you pointed all that out to the emperor in your reports. At great length."

"Actually, no. Gustav Adolf knows me too well. If I'd droned on and on about how tough I had it, he would have gotten suspicious right away."

"Well...true. Your style when it comes to stuff like that is more along the lines of 'piece of cake' and 'consider it done.' My wife—that would be your sister, who's known you her whole life—thinks you sometimes suffer from overconfidence."

"So does my wife," agreed Mike, "except Becky usually leaves off the 'sometimes' part."

Freising, Bavaria

After inspecting his wife and daughter's new quarters—which were his too, technically, but he figured he wouldn't be there very often on account of the cavalry patrols he'd be leading—Alex Mackay pronounced them adequate but no better, marched to the open door and stood in the doorway glaring at the inhabitants of the town beyond. Best to dishearten the Bavarian swine right off, lest they begin entertaining notions of rebellion against their new rightful masters.

And mistresses—even if the one whose well-being he was particularly concerned with had a lackadaisical attitude.

"Oh, leave off, Alex!" Julie scoffed. "There's nobody out there for you to scowl at in the first place."

It was true that none of Freising's indigenous residents were visible from the doorway, but that could be due to their cunning. Bands of them might be out there lurking in cellars and whatnot, just waiting for nightfall when they would sortie and commit unspeakable depredations—

"Leave off, I said!" Julie now had her hands planted on her hips and was scowling even more fiercely than her husband. "The town's been swept twice and there aren't more than twenty people still living here—because they're all too old to move around much anymore, or they're immediate family members who had the gumption to stay behind to take care of their old folks and what you *ought* to be doing is figuring out how they might get a little help."

Mackay's shoulders hunched slightly, as if he were bracing himself against a gale. "I'm a cavalry officer," he muttered.

"So what? You can't engage in Christian charity without losing your spurs or something?"

She pushed into the doorway, forcing Alex to the side, then pointed a finger at those portions of Freising that were visible. Which wasn't all that much, since the domicile the USE army had sequestered for Alex and Julie's use wasn't on either of the town's little squares. All that could be seen was a narrow street—not much more than an alley, really—and some nondescript buildings much like the one they were in. Most of those, as was true of buildings everywhere in Freising, had been seized by the Third Division to provide housing for its officers and men. In the distance beyond, perhaps two hundred yards away, they could see a church spire rising above the roofs.

"There's a whole family still there one street over—no, two streets, depending on what you call a 'street.' A husband who's got some sort of disability, I think from an accident, his wife who's holding everything together, her mother, who's so frail I think she'd blow away in a breeze, her mother's second husband—not her dad, her stepdad—who's even more frail than Grandma is, and five kids of whom two are orphans she took in. *That's* what your"—here she did a fair imitation of Alex's brogue—"'desp'rate Bavarian blackguards' actually look like."

She lowered the finger. "The oldest kid's a girl named Mettchen, somewhere around sixteen years old. I already talked to them and Mettchen will be coming over every day to help me out with whatever I need." The finger of accusation became an open hand, palm up. "For which we are going to *pay* them, so cough up, buddy."

"Well..."

"Yes, I insist."

"Well..."

"Do I need to drag out the Wand of Womanly Wrath?"

"Well...."

The town's Rathaus had been one of the very first buildings in Freising seized by the Third Division. Sieges of a major city like Munich were protracted affairs, and the division's command-ing general had seen no reason his troops shouldn't enjoy their stay in Bavaria as much as possible, within the necessary limits dictated by military discipline.

So, the tavern in the Rathaus' basement was operating at full capacity, around the clock. There wasn't much food left, and wouldn't be until the supply barges coming down the Isar arrived. By now, units of the SoTF National Guard had taken control of the Danube all the way down to Passau, well past the confluence of the Danube with the Isar. That provided the Third Division with an excellent water route to bring all its supplies.

But if the food was low, the beer wasn't. Since the Hangman regiment had been established in the first place as the Third Division's disciplinary unit, it had been placed in charge of the Rathaus. From the point of view of the regiment's commander, Lieutenant Colonel Jeff Higgins, that had the up side of provid-ing him with the best quarters in the town. On the down side, it meant he was now in charge of a bunch of drunks.

Would-be drunks, anyway. He'd established a limit of three steins of beer per visit and only two visits a day—with records meticulously kept.

And bribes meticulously taken also, he didn't doubt. But by now Jeff's sergeants knew him quite well. The DM didn't mind soldiers enjoying themselves, but if things got out of hand he'd crack down hard so it was best to make sure everything stayed within reasonable limits.

The sergeants' task was made easier by the fact that almost all of Freising's inhabitants had fled and taken refuge inside Munich's walls. The worst disciplinary problems with soldiers

occupying an enemy town or city usually came about when
liquor was combined with the presence of young women. But Jeff
had had his adjutants check and there was only one family with
a teenage girl still in the city—and that family was under the
protection of Julie Sims. Jeff saw to it that the word was passed
around through the whole division.

Nobody in the USE army was going to annoy Julie Sims,
certainly not a unit as heavily made of CoC recruits as the
Third Division. Partly, because they knew what an asset she'd
been to their cause. Partly also, of course, because they knew
that Julie never went anywhere without her Wand of Womanly
Wrath, which no soldier in his right mind—or dead drunk, for
that matter—wanted to have applied to him.

All in all, as Lieutenant Colonel Jeff Higgins relaxed in his
quarters on the top floor of the Rathaus, with his feet propped
up, a book in one hand and a stein of beer in the other, things
were looking good. War still sucked, but some parts of it were
a lot less sucky than others.

Royal Palace
Magdeburg, capital of the United States of Europe

Gustav II Adolf, Emperor of the United States of Europe, King
of Sweden, High King of the Union of Kalmar, contemplated his
next title. Should he stick to the existing "emperor," with a newly
enlarged empire? Rather greatly enlarged, too, since Bavaria was
one of the bigger realms in the continent.

Or should he add "King of Bavaria" to the list? But he only
spent a short time considering that option before setting it aside.
It simply wouldn't do for a Lutheran king to be ruling a Catholic
kingdom. If he was going to exercise direct power over Bavaria,
it would be better to have that power filtered through the USE's
provincial structure.

Except that... For a moment, he silently cursed the religious
compromise he'd made with Mike Stearns. By the terms of that
agreement, Bavaria would be able to create its own provincial
established church if it chose to do so, and he had no doubt
at all the stubborn papists would insist on hanging on to their
superstitious creed.

Better than being "King of Bavaria," certainly, but still not good.

That left...What was the term the English usurper had used? The Oliver Cromwell fellow?

The emperor rose from his armchair and went over to one of the bookcases in his library. This one was devoted entirely to down-time copies of up-time texts from Grantville.

He found the volume he was seeking—*The Century of Revolution,* by someone named Hill—and quickly found the entry he was looking for. As he had many times before, Gustav Adolf silently blessed the American concept of the "index." Since he still had enormous power as the monarch of his own nation, he'd decreed two years earlier than all books printed in Sweden were required to have indexes. Yes, all of them! There'd be none of this up-time slackness about not requiring indexes in books of fiction.

Lord Protector.

He mused on the matter as he resumed his seat. Yes, he thought, that would do quite nicely. *Lord Protector of Bavaria.* The very uncertainty of the term—what exactly is a "lord protector"?—would allow him to sidestep the awkward issue of religion. Let the Bavarian heretics manage their own internal affairs, so long as he controlled the duchy's foreign relations.

That matter settled in his mind, Gustav Adolf decided to re-read the report he'd received yesterday from General Stearns. He rose and went to look for it. That took a bit more time because he couldn't remember which trash can he'd thrown it into after he balled up the report, cursed it mightily—nothing silent there—and threw it away.

After he found it, he unwadded the report, flattened it out as best as possible, and read through it again.

Which didn't take long. Mike Stearns had faults—a great many of them, in the emperor's current mood—but one thing he was not was pointlessly loquacious.

So.

He read through it again.

"I am not fooled," he growled. But he knew perfectly well that Stearns didn't think he was fooled. The man was a duplicitous maneuvering scoundrel, but he wasn't disrespectful. The purpose of the report was not to fool Gustav Adolf but to fool anyone else to whom the emperor might show the report as a way of demonstrating that his now-public clash with the so-called "Prince of Germany"—ridiculous title, not to mention a presumptuous one—was entirely justified.

But...

"Perhaps it's just as well," he mused. Then, rising again, he went over to the small fireplace that was always active whenever he was in residence and tossed the report into the flames. That wasn't the sort of thing he wanted to leave lying around.

Lord Protector. It *did* have a nice ring to it.

Chapter 28

Dresden, capital of Saxony

Gretchen Richter looked from Jozef Wojtowicz to the two small children at his side—the girl was holding on to his leg with both hands—from there to the large fellow named Lukasz Kijek who had accompanied him back to Dresden, back to Jozef, to the children again and back to Jozef.

"I am provisionally willing to accept the idea that you rescued these children from their destroyed village even though I have never previously gotten any sense that you cared for children at all." She lifted her shoulders in a minimalist sort of shrug. "But I long ago learned that most people have unseen depths so it is possible. I am also willing to accept—very provisionally—that you just happened to run into your old friend Lukasz Kijek wandering around in Breslau even though your explanation as to the reason for his being there is ridiculous."

She now shifted her scrutiny to the Kijek fellow. "If he is a grain merchant then I am the queen of Sheba. Within three seconds of entering this room he had positioned everyone in his mind, especially the three men with weapons. So had you, but you told me you'd been trained as a hussar. He is some sort of soldier, and one with a lot more experience than you'd expect of such a young man."

She now looked back at Jozef. "I don't mind that you're lying to me since it has been clear for some time that there are things

247

you're being secretive about. Up to a point, I don't mind people hiding things from me. Whether or not we have now reached that point is what needs to be determined."

The boy standing next to Jozef, who'd been fidgeting all the while she'd been talking, erupted in protest.

"You shouldn't call Uncle Jozef a liar! It's not right! And it's true what he said! He found us after the soldiers killed everyone in our village! And then when four of them tried to attack us he killed them all!"

Jozef rubbed his hand over his face.

"Killed four of them, did he? All by himself. Why am I not surprised?" She shifted her eyes back to Lukasz. "And you, grain merchant. How many men have you killed in the course of ply-ing your peaceful trade? And please spare me tales of fighting off bandits. Bandits do not rob grain boats."

By now, Eric Krenz and both guards standing at the door were on full alert. Gretchen made a little waving motion, indicating they should stand down. "Everyone relax. I am not making any accusations, I just dislike being taken for a fool. What I really want to discuss with you, Jozef, is the report you brought back. If we subtract all the business involving the tall blond cold-eyed fellow with the big shoulders and the still posture, how much of what you told me is true?"

To her surprise, the big "grain merchant" answered the ques-tion. It was the first time he'd spoken since he'd come into her presence.

"All of it's true," he said. He spoke Low German, not Ami-deutsch, and his accent was something of a cross between Prus-sian and Polish. "Except for the part about me, which you're right about. I'm not a grain merchant and never have been. I'm a hussar."

"Why did you lie, then?"

"I wasn't sure of my reception here if you knew who I really was."

"There is only one way to find out, isn't there?" She now scowled at Krenz and the two guards, who'd started to edge closer again. "I said, *relax*. They're not going to attack me—and even if they did, so what?"

She slapped the table that she'd been sitting behind when the two Poles came into the room. It was big, heavy—and interposed between her and them. "By the time they could get around this or move it aside, I'll have shot them both dead."

The Lukasz fellow gave her an intent, quite interested look. "With what?"

"This." She brushed her vest aside, exposing the 9 mm pistol in its shoulder holster.

"That's a very impressive-looking gun. An up-time model, if I am not mistaken." He actually did sound very impressed. "But your tactics are flawed. I wouldn't try to move around the table or push it aside, I'd just ram it straight into you. Pin you against the wall with it. Crush you, probably. I'm very strong; even stronger than Jozef."

"I don't doubt it, but you underestimate my powers of concentration. I'd still empty this whole clip into you and Jozef even if you broke my ribcage. I wouldn't miss many shots, either. Maybe not any. I've become very good with this pistol."

The evenness of her tone seemed to impress him even more.

"Be afraid," she heard Wojtowicz mutter. "Be very afraid."

His friend Lukasz's lips twitched. "I'm beginning to understand why you said that."

"Enough of this," said Gretchen. "Tell me who you really are and we'll just have to see what happens."

"I'm Lukasz Opalinski—yes, that's *the* Opalinski family—and a hussar in the service of Grand Hetman Stanislaw Koniecpolski."

Wojtowicz rolled his eyes. "We're fucked."

"That makes you the sworn enemy of the emperor of the United States of Europe, Gustav II Adolf," said Gretchen. "I would have you arrested even though I strongly disagree with the emperor's policy toward Poland except that you're also the brother of Krzysztof Opalinski, who is an associate of the highly respected Red Sybolt—"

Eric Krenz spluttered a little laugh. "Highly respected by *whom*?"

Gretchen gave him a cold eye. "By me, for one—and every right-thinking member of the Committees of Correspondence." She brought the same cold eye to bear on Opalinski. "Both of whom are known to be agitating for democracy in Poland, which means they are more likely to be enemies of King Wladyslaw than the USE, which in turn means that your position here is complicated and hasty action would therefore be a mistake. So."

She pointed to some chairs lined up against the wall facing the room's windows. "Pull up some chairs. We need to talk."

As they did so, she looked at the two guards by the door. "I think it would be awkward to have Administrator Wettin present at this discussion. And it would only distress him. So one of you step out in the corridor and let me know if you see Ernst coming this way."

Brussels, capital of the Netherlands

Amsterdam was a bust, for all the reasons they'd made Rita come on this stupid trip which was still stupid even if they'd been proven right.

"It's fucking ridiculous," she grumbled, as they got off the train. "They're building the airship in Holland, right? At Hoorn, north of Amsterdam. All the artisans, all the equipment—the money guys, you name it"—she waved her free hand toward the north while she wrestled her valise off the rail car, stubbornly ignoring Heinz Böcler's offer to help—"they're all up there."

She lowered the valise to the ground. It might be better to say, got it down with a more-or-less controlled drop. The thing was down-time made, which meant it was very sturdy but not what you'd call lightweight.

"So why the fuck are we all the way down here in Brussels?" she demanded.

That being a purely rhetorical question, Rita moved right on to providing the answer without giving either Bonnie or Heinz so much as a second's pause in which to insert a response. "I'll tell you why. Because in the seventeenth fucking century—no offense, Heinz; you're okay but your time period sucks—you can't chew gum without getting His Royal Uppitiness to sign off on it."

She paused for a breath of air, her hands planted on hips, and surveyed the train they'd arrived in. It consisted of a very primitive more-or-less open air steam locomotive hauling five equally primitive if not quite as open air coaches, all of it traveling on a single heavy wooden rail with—in some places; not others—thin iron plates attached to the top of the rail to cut down on wear and tear. The locomotive and all the coaches had outrigger wheels that ran on the side of the road to maintain balance. They reminded Rita of nothing so much as the wheels on Conestoga wagons she'd seen—once in a museum; a jillion times on TV.

Heinz had told them that the design was a variation of the nineteenth-century Ewing system that had been briefly depicted in one of the books in Grantville. It moved very slowly, not more than ten miles an hour and usually less. But even at that speed, if you keep it up around the clock, a train can travel quite a ways. The distance from Amsterdam to Brussels was less than one hundred and fifty miles. Theoretically, they could have made it less than a day.

In the real world, it had taken them a little more than two days. The steam engine had had problems. One of the outrigger wheels had broken, almost derailing that coach—not theirs, thankfully. At several places along the way the track had gone askew. Still, it had been kind of interesting and it beat riding horses or (still worse) being hauled in carriages.

They hadn't intended to make the trip on a train at all. The original plan had been to use one of the hot air dirigibles built by the same consortium that was building the hydrogen one. But there were only two of the airships, one of which was in Copenhagen, and the one that was available had promptly suffered engine failure—and of a fairly catastrophic sort. They'd managed to get the problem under control before the boiler exploded, but two of the crew had been hurt and the engine was pretty much a complete write-off.

They could have waited for the airship in Copenhagen to return, but that would have taken a few days and in any event none of them were too keen on riding through the air in a small basket right after seeing how another basket had just gotten partially parboiled.

There was this to be said for the seventeenth century. It made you reassess the way you calculated risks. Riding halfway across the Netherlands on a dinky one-rail train that was kept from falling over by a wooden wheel sounded just peachy.

"Oh, quit crabbing, Rita," said Bonnie. "You're just cranky because you're nervous."

"Well, yeah. No kidding. The last time I got dragooned into being Ms. Well-Connected Ambassadress, I got pitched into one of the world's most famous prisons. They kept me there for a whole year. I wonder what's waiting for us here in the Netherlands. That stands for 'Low Countries,' you know. They say it's on account of the elevation but you gotta wonder a little. Dungeons have a low elevation too."

"Speaking of ambassadors," said Heinz, "here comes your greeting party."

Rita looked in the direction he was indicating. "Jesus H. Christ," she said. Rita had little truck with down-time sensibilities on the subject of blasphemy. "That mob needs a damn train their own selves."

A mob they may have been, but they were a courteous one—excessively so, in Rita's opinion, although she didn't make any objection. She didn't, for two reasons. First, because despite her frequent complaints and protests, she understood that her job on this mission was to be a *di-plo-mat*, the dictionary definition of which included: "a person who is tactful and skillful in managing delicate situations, handling people, etc." Second, because it is hard to be rude to people who are being nice to you. A few people can manage it—more than a few, if they have the benefit of New York or Paris training—but most can't. Rita was in the latter category. There were some disadvantages to being brought up in a place like West Virginia.

When she—she alone, Bonnie and Böcler having been deftly peeled away by courtiers—was brought into the presence of Archduchess Isabella, Rita found herself being quite disarmed. Most people can manage to be polite, with a little effort. The archduchess, when she was inclined to do so—which was not always, by any means—could turn it into an art form.

She was one of the Grand Old Ladies of the European aristocracy, as grand as it can get short of being an outright queen—and for most of her life, Isabella had actually wielded more real power than all but a handful of queens in the continent's history.

She was known as Isabella Clara Eugenia of Austria, although she'd been born in Segovia and was an *infanta* of Spain. Her father had been King Philip II—yes, *that* Philip II, the one who launched the Armada against England and whose reign was considered the heyday of Spanish power. His empire had included territories on five of the seven continents, lacking only Australia and Antarctica, and the Philippine Islands had been named after him. The reference to an empire upon which the sun never sets, which most Americans attributed to the English empire of a later day, was originally coined to refer to Philip's.

Isabella's mother had been no slouch in the royalty department herself. She was Elizabeth of Valois, the daughter of Henry II of France and Catherine de Medici. Isabella's other two grandparents had been Emperor Charles V and Infanta Isabella of Portugal, on her father's side.

While still in her twenties, Isabella Clara Eugenia had been a contender for the throne of France, being advanced for that position by the Catholic party that controlled the *Parlement de Paris*. In the end a different contender seized the throne, the Protestant Henry III of Navarre, who converted to Catholicism after supposedly making the famous quip "Paris is well worth a mass" and became Henry IV of France, the founder of the Bourbon dynasty.

As if in compensation—it was really just another move in the constant strife of dynasties—Isabella was given in marriage to her cousin, Archduke Albert of Austria. The representatives of the two Habsburg branches were given the Netherlands over which they would rule jointly. She was thirty-three years old at the time.

The marriage was a happy one, except for the fact that all three of their offspring had died in childhood. Their joint rule inaugurated a period of relative peace and prosperity in the southern Netherlands, and it was during that period that the great age of Flemish art began, with their patronage of such figures as Pieter Paul Rubens and Pieter Brueghel the Younger.

Albert died in 1621, ten years before the Ring of Fire. Isabella then joined a religious lay order but continued to rule the Spanish Netherlands—the area that the up-timers would think of as Belgium and Luxembourg—until her nephew Cardinal-Infante Fernando reunified the Netherlands during the Baltic War, whereupon she delegated her power to him.

Her formal power, that is to say. Nobody had any doubt at all that Isabella continued to be a major player in the continent's power struggles.

She was a few months shy of seventy years old when Rita Simpson met her in Brussels. In one of the many, many, many examples of the so-called Butterfly Effect, she had now lived three years longer than she would have in the universe that sent Grantville through the Ring of Fire. And, despite her constant declarations of infirmity and predictions of her imminent demise, she seemed as much a force of nature as ever.

Rita never had a clear memory of what she and Isabella talked about in that first meeting—first audience, rather. The archduchess said nothing at all concerning the matter that had brought Rita and her companions to the Netherlands, or anything else that could be considered business. The occasion was purely personal and informal, insofar as the term "informal" ever applied in the presence of Isabella. Even with members of her immediate family, the archduchess maintained a certain reserve—a guardedness, if you will, which was the product of a lifetime spent both watching and participating in the game of empire.

Rita spoke no blasphemies and used no terms not blessed by Good Society. And for a wonder, enjoyed herself.

Rita's verdict on the encounter, as told to Bonnie and Heinz right afterward, was simple and quite West Virginian.

"I liked her a lot. She's a nice old lady. Not gathering any cobwebs, though, I'll tell you that."

Isabella's verdict on the encounter, as told to King Fernando and Queen Maria Anna right afterward, was simple on the surface but not below, and quite what you'd expect from a Spanish *infanta* whose daddy had ruled in five continents.

"She'll do. She's not her brother, of course. Thank God. But she'll do."

Dresden, capital of Saxony

By the time Gretchen finished probing Jozef and Lukasz to see what they might have left out of their report, inadvertently or otherwise, she and they were sitting at the table rather than standing. Several other people had joined them there as well: Tata, Eric Krenz, the CoC leader Joachim Kappel, and the Vogtlander Wilhelm Kuefer.

She leaned back in her chair, with both hands planted on the edge of the heavy table, and gave the two Poles a long, flat-eyed, considering look.

"All right," she said abruptly. "You need to tell me what

you are willing to do for Saxony"—there was a slight stress on *Saxony*—"and what you are not willing to do. Before you begin, I will make clear that I do not expect you—either of you, not just Lukasz Opalinski—to do anything that could be considered opposed to Grand Hetman Koniecpolski."

"Anything opposed to *Poland*," Jozef immediately countered.

"That's too broad," said Gretchen. "Pissing outdoors could be considered opposed to Poland because the wind might blow foreign piss onto sacred Polish soil."

She leaned forward, still with her hands planted on the table. "What do you really care about King Wladyslaw, Jozef? Or that pack of squabbling szlachta who've made the Sejm a byword for incompetence and selfishness?"

Neither Jozef nor Lukasz said anything, but they both had mulish expressions on their faces.

Gretchen shook her head. "And they say we Germans are pig-headed. Fine. I will narrow this down still further. What I want you to do is go back into Poland and spy for Saxony"—again, she emphasized that name—"with particular regard for seeing if Holk has any plans to extend his depredations into my province."

My province. Gretchen was guessing, but she thought that a proprietary term used in such a vaguely monarchical manner might help reassure the two Poles. The Commonwealth of Poland and Lithuania was what Americans would call "an odd duck." It was partly a monarchy and partly an aristocratic oligarchy, with the royal side providing the form of the realm and the oligarchy its real content. But you could never forget what made Poland so unusual, politically. Its aristocracy was a far larger percentage of the population than in any other European country. One in ten Poles could—and did, most surely—call themselves szlachta. Even if, as was very often true, they were not significantly richer nor in possession of more land than their commoner neighbors.

Coupled to the peculiar privilege of Polish aristocracy called the *liberum veto*, which allowed any member of the Sejm to single-handedly nullify any proposed legislation, the end result was a nation whose real affairs were almost entirely managed by way of informal and unofficial channels. People had fierce loyalties to each other, but that abstract entity known as the Polish-Lithuanian Commonwealth got little of it, for all the sentimentality that was so common in Polish politics.

She was pretty sure that most of Lukasz and Jozef's real attachments were to the person of Grand Hetman Koniecpolski—with whom Gretchen had no quarrel. The war that Gustav Adolf had started against Poland was his war, as far as she was concerned. One Swedish Vasa butting heads with a Polish member of the same family for reasons that meant little or nothing to Germany's common folk.

Let them play their stupid royal games up there by the Baltic. Gretchen's concern was with Saxony.

Lukasz and Jozef looked at each other.

"Okay," said Jozef, after a few seconds. "But only as it concerns Saxony and Holk!"

He raised his forefinger in admonishment. Lukasz's came up to join it. "Only as it concerns Saxony and Holk!" he echoed.

Afterward, when they had left the Residenzschloss and the two Poles were alone, Jozef shook his head. "That was very rash, what you did. Telling her who you really were."

Lukasz shrugged. "She'd already figured out we were lying about something. Aren't you the one, O great spymaster, who keeps telling me that the best way to cover up a big lie is to confess to a small one?"

Jozef frowned. It was true that he had said that—yes, often—but . . .

"What really matters here is not my true identity, Jozef," Lukasz continued. "It's *yours*. It's one thing for Gretchen Richter and her comrades to know that I'm a hussar in service to the grand hetman. It's another thing entirely for them to discover that you're his nephew and his spymaster in the USE."

"Well. True."

"We can't trust them!" Eric protested. "Especially now that we know Jozef was lying to us all along."

Gretchen studied him for a few seconds, her expression impassive. Then she shook her head. "What does trust have to do with this?"

Eric stared at her, then at Tata. Then he shook his own head. "Sometimes, Gretchen, you're a little scary."

"You just noticed?" said Tata.

Chapter 29

Magdeburg, capital of the United States of Europe

When Noelle entered the small audience chamber in the royal palace with Janos Drugeth, she was surprised to see the other people already there: Rebecca Abrabanel, Ed Piazza, Wilhelm Wettin and the landgravine of Hesse-Kassel, Amalie Elisabeth. The four of them were seated in a semi-circle facing Gustav Adolf. The two still-empty chairs in the center of that semi-circle made it clear where she and Janos were supposed to sit.

Glancing around, she saw that there were no servants in the room except the one who had ushered them into it—and he was already leaving, closing the door behind him. Clearly, as had Wallenstein, the emperor of the USE had taken to heart the up-time cautions on the subject of letting servants be within earshot whenever critical matters of state were being discussed. So far, Janos had had only partial success in persuading his own emperor to follow suit. Old habits die hard with anyone; harder still, with aristocracy; hardest of all, with royalty.

Gustav Adolf gestured toward the two empty chairs. "Please, sit down. Wilhelm and Amalie, I do not believe you have met Janos Drugeth before now. He is here as an Austrian Reichsgraf and Ferdinand III's envoy."

Reichsgraf, was it? Janos had enough titles he could attach to his name that you'd need a team of horses to drag them around. "Reichsgraf"—the term could be translated as "imperial count"—was a rank that went back into the Middle Ages, and originally denoted someone who held a county in fief directly from the Holy Roman Emperor himself, rather than from one of the emperor's vassals. As time passed, the real content of the title shifted and became detached from land-holding. Some Reichsgrafen held land as such, others didn't. Janos was one of the ones who didn't, although he retained a great deal of land in Hungary deriving from his other positions and ranks in the empire.

The significance of the title as used in this context by Gustav Adolf was subtle but unmistakable. As Reichsgraf Drugeth, Janos was here as Emperor Ferdinand III's direct emissary and was presumed to be empowered not only to speak on his behalf but to make treaties. That also explained the presence of the four central leaders of the two major parties—at least, those parties which were well-enough organized to seriously contest the current election. There were a lot of reactionaries in the USE, some of them with real power and influence. But they'd been so demoralized by the outcome of the Dresden Crisis that they spent most of their time and energy these days bickering among themselves. For the moment, they were a minor factor in the political equation.

With the emperor of the USE and the four central political leaders present, Janos could not only make proposals but could expect them to be agreed to and signed.

Or not. But at least the possibility existed.

Prague, capital of Bohemia

To Denise's surprise, when Eddie landed the plane at Prague's airstrip, her mother, Christin George, was there to greet her. So far as Denise had been aware, her mother was still living in Grantville.

"Hi, Mom!" she said, rushing up to give her a hug. "When did you get to Prague? And what's the reason for the visit? I hope you didn't come all the way here just to see me. 'Cause once I talk to Don Francisco so he can set Minnie and this doofus straight"—the thumb of accusation pointed over her shoulder at Eddie Junker, who was now getting out of the plane—"I'm heading straight back to Vienna. Where everything's happening."

❖   ❖   ❖

Christin George took her time with returning the hug. Her daughter had reacted to her father's murder during the Dreeson Incident the way Denise usually reacted to things—vigorously. She'd thrown herself into working for Francisco Nasi with the same energy that she'd thrown into becoming Eddie Junker's girlfriend.

Christin approved of the boyfriend. Eddie was a solid guy and she thought he was a good influence on Denise. She wasn't sure about the new boss, which was one of the reasons she'd come to Prague.

The main reason, though, was as simple as it got—she and Denise were the only close family each of them had left and Christin wanted them together again. As much as possible, at least. Having Denise for a daughter was a lot like herding a very big and hyperactive cat.

"I *have* talked to Don Francisco, Denise. That's one of the reasons he told you to come back here. I asked him to."

"Mom!"

By that evening, Denise had settled down a lot. First, because the meeting she'd had with her employer—she'd demanded it, of course, right off, and a bit to her surprise had gotten it—had not gone the way she wanted.

"No. You should spend time with your mother. Minnie is quite capable of taking care of herself—better than you are, being honest about it. I don't need two of you in Vienna and I've got another assignment in mind for you."

"Which is *what*? Uh, boss."

"Spending time with your mother. So off you go. *Now*, Denise."

But there were other reasons, too, for her more settled state of mind. First and foremost, just being back in her mother's company after a separation of several months. Denise's father Buster Beasley had generally encouraged her free spirits. Her mother hadn't dampened them, exactly—women who marry bikers in the face of fierce family disapproval are not given to caution themselves—but she had provided Denise with a certain maternal circumference. Denise had always known that she was free to roam a lot, but there *were* limits, mostly set by her mother.

For a kid, that knowledge could be a comfort as well as, occasionally, a source of frustration. Right now, she was finding that maternal presence a great comfort.

Despite her own disapproval of her mother's wayward recklessness.

"You *sold* the business? Sold it outright? Not leased it to somebody else to run it for you? What were you *thinking*, Mom? Yeah, sure, you can live on that for a while but what are you going to do when it runs out? In—what—maybe three or four months. How much did you get, anyway?"

Christin answered the last question first. Denise reacted pretty much the same way her mother had reacted in times past to Denise's explanations of cause-and-effect issues such as why she hadn't come home until three o'clock in the morning.

"Oh, bullshit! Nobody's going to pay that much—that's a fucking *fortune*—for a weld shop and a storage rental facility."

Eddie came back into the hotel room carrying two glasses of wine just in time to hear Denise's outburst. He handed one of the glasses to Christin and offered the other to Denise.

She shook her head but gave him a smile. There was a fine protocol involved here. If he hadn't offered her the wine she'd have bridled that he was treating her as a child. But, so long as he did, she almost always declined. Denise wasn't a teetotaler, exactly, certainly not as a matter of principle. But the truth was that she didn't much like the taste of alcohol.

She never had. Whatever other concerns her mother and father had had about the possible consequences of Denise's sometimes reckless behavior, they'd never worried she'd do something because she got drunk. Because she got pissed off, yes; rebellious, yes; just to prove to some jerk that he was in fact a jerk, yes. Drunk, no.

Having fulfilled his necessary part in the protocol, Eddie—who *did* like wine; and beer; and most spirits, thank you very much— settled down in another chair in the front room of the hotel suite.

For "suite" it was—and in one of the two finest hostelries in Prague.

"You're shooting from the hip again, Denise," said Eddie. "The weld shop and the rental storage facility? *Pfft*." That last noise exuded insouciance. "Whoever bought the property from your mother probably auctioned off all the welding equipment and supplies and tore down the storage facilities."

"Auctioned them off, actually," corrected Christin. She smiled and shook her head. "Didn't get a lot for them, of course. They were basically just sheds with delusions of grandeur. But Buster's stuff sold well."

"Mom! You *sold* Dad's stuff?"

Christin's expression was exasperated. "For fuck's sake, Denise"—Christin George belonged to the Rita Simpson (née Stearns) school of Proper Appalachian Patois—"what was I supposed to do? Keep your father's arc welders and oxy-acetylene cylinders at my bedside?"

"Well..." Denise couldn't really contest the point, but she had a stubborn expression on her face. "Still. Even his stuff couldn't have brought in *that* much."

"Real estate," said Eddie. "The real value would have been in the storage rental property—because of what it sat on. The buildings may have been sheds with delusions of grandeur but they were still buildings and they spread out over a lot of area." He looked to Christin. "How much land did you own?"

"About half an acre."

He turned back to face Denise. "You have any idea how much half an acre is worth these days inside the Ring of Fire?"

"No." Denise's expression got more stubborn. "Neither do you."

He chuckled. "Not precisely, but it doesn't matter. What I do know is that your mother walked away from the sale with enough to set herself up—in style, mind you—almost anywhere *outside* of the Ring of Fire."

A look of sudden understanding came to his face. "That's the other reason you're here, isn't it? This isn't really a visit."

Christin shook her head. "Don't know for sure yet, but probably not. I do want to be closer to my daughter and"—her face became a little drawn—"Grantville's just got too many memories of Buster. I don't want to forget any of them but I don't need to be reminded of them every day, either."

She shook her head slightly, as if to clear those thoughts away. "I wrote to Judith Roth and she talked to Morris and they told me that if I came out here they'd help me get set up with... something. Don't know what it might be yet. There are several possibilities we're looking at."

Once Denise set her mind to being stubborn, she had a lot of what might be called psychic inertia. "If the Roths are being so friendly to you," she demanded, "why aren't you staying with them instead of"—she looked around, clearly preferring to end the sentence with *this dump* except even when she was in full stubborn mode Denise didn't lose her mind.

"This place," she concluded.

Eddie and Christin exchanged a pitying glance. "She's usually much brighter than this," Eddie insisted.

"Yeah, I know, I raised her," was Christin's response. She placed her half-full glass of wine on a side table and leaned forward, looking at her daughter. "Denise, what happens if word gets out in Prague that I'm on cozy terms with Morris and Judith Roth? That is to say, the richest Jews in the city and probably among the half dozen or so richest people of any creed?"

Denise crossed her arms over her chest.

"Come on, sweetie," Christin crooned, as if she were trying to coax a kitten out of hiding. "I know you can answer the question."

"Everybody you deal with will try to double the price."

"More like triple it," grunted Eddie. His glass now being empty, he used it to wave around as a pointer. "This suite is plush, which signals to anybody that Christin's not a piker. But you don't need to be in Roth financial territory to be able to afford it, even for quite a few weeks."

Denise was silent, for a moment. Then she sighed and uncrossed her arms. "Okay. I really am glad to see you, Mom. And I'd like it if you moved here, I really would."

Her eyes got moist. "I just miss Dad awful, sometimes. Really awful."

Her mother's eyes weren't dry, either. "So do I, sweetheart. But life goes on, whether you want it to or not."

"He used to say that a lot."

"Yeah, he did. He was a wise man, in his own way. I didn't marry him because of the bikes and the tattoos, you know."

She grinned, suddenly, and in that moment the resemblance between her and her daughter was almost startling. "I admit they helped. I was a rambunctious kid just like you were. You should have seen the look on my fucking parents' faces the first time they saw Buster! Straddling his bike in his cut-off leather jacket with me perched right behind him."

Denise grinned also. "Welcome home, Mom."

Magdeburg, capital of the United States of Europe

Gustav Adolf rose abruptly from his chair and began striding about the room in front of his assembled audience. Who numbered only six, but the emperor was clearly in a declamatory mood.

"I will summarize it as follows, then," he said. "Wallenstein— do I need to start calling him King Albrecht?"—ignoring his own question, he went on—"and Ferdinand will make peace. Indeed, they will go further and form an alliance within certain limits."

He stopped and peered down at Janos. "Correct me if I oversimplify, but the gist of it is that Wallenstein will come to Austria's aid against the Turks—within limits, of course, he still has Poland to deal with—in exchange for which Ferdinand will back Bohemia against Poland."

Janos nodded. "In essence, yes. The qualifications—"

Gustav Adolf waved his hand. "Yes, yes, they're clear. Also obvious. Austria's commitment does not extend to any actions on the part of Wallenstein—somehow it seems slightly ridiculous to call him Albrecht II—whose purpose is to increase his territory at the expense of Poland. Likewise, Bohemia is under no obligation to support Austria in the event the Ottoman invasion is driven back and Austria seeks to expand further into the Balkans. What is most important to me in all this, however—"

He stopped and glowered down at the Austrian envoy. "Is that *I* am expected to serve as the guarantor of all these agreements. If I agree to this, then I will be enjoined to come to the aid of whichever party has been wronged by the other's failure to live up to its agreement."

A bit daringly, Noelle interjected: "But only in your person as the emperor of the United States of Europe. No commitment is implied on the part of either Sweden or the Union of Kalmar."

She settled back in her seat, bracing herself for an imperial explosion at her impertinence in saying anything at all. Noelle had no official status at this meeting. But the very fact that she'd been invited suggested that the intricacies of seventeenth-century political affairs were at play. Much of what was done in the here and now was based on personal ties, not formal positions. She was betrothed to Janos Drugeth, one of Austria-Hungary's most powerful noblemen, a close confidant of Ferdinand III, and his personal envoy to the USE. Plus—you could never rule out this factor, although its exact importance was always hard to calculate—she was an American. Plus—this was a bit easier to calculate—someone who had in the past served as one of Ed Piazza's informal agents and Piazza was likely to be the next prime minister and thus someone the emperor was going to be dealing with constantly.

So...

As it turned out, she'd parsed the matter accurately. Gustav Adolf transferred the glower onto her, but only for a moment. Then he chuckled. "Europe will just have to hope that you and the reichsgraf don't produce too many children, lest the rest of us be overwhelmed with little Machiavellis."

He resumed his pacing. "What both Austria and Bohemia want from the United States of Europe in return, *in addition* to our serving as the guarantor of the terms of their own treaties, is for us to support them—with military force, mind you—in their struggles with the Poles and the Ottomans."

Again, he waved his hand. "The Polish issue is moot, since we are already at war with the swine Wladyslaw and his minions. But we are *not*—as of yet—at war with the Ottoman Empire. Agreeing to this treaty—set of treaties, rather—would commit me to undertake a war on two fronts, against what is quite possibly the most powerful realm in the world.

"But what do I get in return?" he demanded. He stopped his pacing and went back to hands-on-hips-stooping-over-and-glowering mode. "Very little, it would seem!"

Before anyone could interject he added: "Yes, yes, trade agreements, that sort of thing. The merchants and moneylenders will be happy. But that seems like precious little, nonetheless."

Noelle was tempted to speak again but refrained. There were limits to how far she could put herself forward.

It proved to be unnecessary anyway, because Rebecca spoke up. "Your Majesty, you are pretending to reduce this to a matter of arithmetic when it is actually an algebraic calculation."

Gustav Adolf puffed out his cheeks indignantly. "Pretending! Pretending!"

But Noelle noticed that his complexion hadn't changed any. The emperor was, in this regard, very much a Swede—his skin was pale, except when he'd been campaigning in the field for days. Even then, she'd been told, he just got sunburned, not tanned.

Noelle had never seen Gustav Adolf in one of his famous

furies, but she'd had them described to her. One of the invariable symptoms was that the emperor's cheeks didn't just swell out, his entire face became as white as a ghost's.

But here, now . . . those puffed-out infuriated heavy jowls had their usual color. Pale, yes, but no more than they always were.

"Outrageous!" he went on.

Rebecca's response was the serene smile for which she was quite well known by now. "Please, Your Majesty. I am simply saying bluntly what everyone here—certainly yourself—understands to be true. Regardless of the details, the essence of this set of agreements—what I would call the algebraic equation—is not this or that specific item but the recognition that the United States of Europe has become the central—I do not say 'dominant,' simply central—power in the continent. Once these agreements are signed, we will have formed what amounts to a Triple Alliance at the very heart of Europe. And if we defeat the Turks, which I have every confidence we will, then our alliance becomes the rightful successor to the Holy Roman Empire."

"She's right, Your Majesty," said Amalie Elisabeth, speaking for the first time since the meeting began. Next to her, Wilhelm Wettin nodded his head. Whatever differences might exist between the Fourth of July Party and what was left of the Crown Loyalists, on this point they were in full agreement—better the United States of Europe should be the pivot of European politics than any other realm. For centuries, the Germanies had been so many toys batted back and forth between Habsburgs—Spanish and Austrian both—and the Valois and Bourbon dynasties of France. That era was now at an end.

A bit worriedly, Noelle glanced at Janos. The Hungarian's jaws were tight—he hadn't enjoyed hearing that, not one bit—but he was obviously not going to argue the point, for the good and simple reason that he couldn't. The price Austria-Hungary was going to have to pay to ensure its survival against the Ottoman onslaught was a tacit recognition that it was no longer the axis of power in central Europe.

Gustav Adolf glanced at Janos also. He understood perfectly well that Drugeth's silence in response to Rebecca's statement was in its own way the most emphatic acquiescence he could make.

The puffed-out cheeks resumed their normal form. He did not smile but he did nod his head.

"If we're going to be a triple alliance of the sort you describe," he said, "we should have a name. Even if it's only an informal one." He smiled slyly. "I would suggest 'the Axis' but the up-timers would probably never stop complaining."

Piazza laughed. "That would...have awkward connotations. In another universe, granted, but our history books are everywhere now."

He looked around. "Well, we could swipe from that other history a different way. Call it the Central European Treaty Organization."

Noelle began rolling the acronym around, and did so out loud. In Amideutsch, since that's what they'd all been speaking.

"*Mitteleuropäischevertragsorganization.* Mepo? No, I guess it would be 'Mevo.'"

Everyone in the room mouthed the acronym.

"I like it!" said Gustav Adolf.

That pretty much settled the question, although Ed Piazza was heard to mutter, "I can hear it already. Beware the Mevonian menace. Beware of Mevonians bearing gifts. Beware..."

Part Four

July 1636

They were born poor, lived poor, and poor they died

Chapter 30

Vienna, capital of Austria-Hungary

Judy Wendell summed up the sentiments of the four young women standing on the wall of the city looking to the east. "Well, that sucks."

"What would you be referring to, exactly?" asked Hayley Fortney. The youngest of the four pointed an accusing finger at the columns of smoke rising from Race Track City, four miles away. "The fact that they're burning down everything we built over there, or the fact that there are about a million of them."

"That's a ridiculous exaggeration," said Cecilia Renata. Her tone seemed a lot less confident than the words themselves, though. "My brother—Ferdinand, not Leopold—he's the emperor—told me just yesterday that our spies mostly agree that Murad didn't bring more than one hundred thousand men.

"Fewer," she added stoutly, "than Suleiman brought the last time the Turkish pigs tried this." Cecilia Renata shared none of her younger brother Leopold's fine sense of the ethnic complexities of the Ottoman Empire. Like most Austrians, she figured Turks were Turks and that was all there was to it.

"It's not the number of soldiers that matters," said Minnie Hugelmair, "it's what they might have with them." Her own finger pointed to something farther away than Race Track City. Farther away—and farther up. "Tell me I'm wrong because I've only got one eye even though that eye works quite well. That looks like a dirigible to me."

"Three of them, actually," said Judy. "My eyesight's twenty-twenty."

Hayley and Cecilia Renata were both squinting at the same objects. "They don't look as big as ours, though," said Hayley. "The *Pelican*, I mean. The Swordfish class. We've got three of them too, you know."

Judy was never one given to false optimism. "Let's be precise, here. Miro Estuban has three of them, only one of which is currently leased to the USE army—and it's stationed in Munich. The *Albatross* and the *Petrel* are ... wherever. Not here. We don't have any airships. No planes, either. Not even a Belle, much less a Gustav or a Dauntless. They're all up in Poland, doing absolutely no good flying around Poznań."

Minnie, from her work for Don Francisco, had a much better grasp of military realities than Judy did. "Doesn't really matter, though. None of the planes are able to shoot down airships, and they're too small to carry much in the way of bombs, either. They're mostly valuable for reconnaissance to find where the enemy is and"—she used her chin to point to the huge army moving up on Vienna—"that's hardly at issue now. They're right over there."

She turned to Hayley. "You really ought to get out of Vienna, like you said you were going to."

Hayley was glaring at the distant Ottoman army. Perhaps more than anyone in the world, she'd been the driving force behind creating Race Track City. Now, from the looks of it, the whole place was being destroyed by the Turks. Even the race track—the stands, anyway—looked to be burning.

"You'd think they want to keep it intact," she growled. "Stupid bastards."

"Why?" said Judy. "You've spent the last two weeks stripping everything out of there and moving it into Vienna."

"Well, yeah, sure. The emperor made it crystal clear a while ago he wasn't going to defend Race Track City and I sure as hell wasn't going to leave anything useful or valuable to the fucking Turks."

"So, they're now burning the scraps you left. What do you care?" Judy could be awfully unsentimental some times. Most times.

A man's voice came from below them. "Hayley, we should go now!"

Turning and looking down from the wide ledge they were standing on, they saw Hayley's betrothed, Amadeus von Eisenberg.

He was standing in the middle of the bastion, next to a pile of cannonballs. The expression on his face combined exasperation with anxiety. "The barge is already loaded! Almost, anyway. Everyone is waiting for you!"

"Off you go, girl," said Judy.

Hayley looked uncertain. "I should maybe stay with you guys, what do you think?"

"That's stupid," said Judy. "Cecilia Renata's staying here out of duty and I'm staying because she asked me to stay with her and I've got nothing else to do. Besides, it's a good idea for one of us Barbies to hold down the fort, so to speak. But one is all we need for that"—here, she grinned—"and I don't have a boyfriend fussing at me."

Hayley still looked dubious. "What about you?" she asked Minnie.

Judy provided the answer for that, too. "She's scheming. And since Cecilia Renata's aiding and abetting her schemes, she figures it'd be stupid to leave. Screw the Turks."

Minnie nodded. "It's not every day a girl like me—especially with just one eye left—gets to hang out with royalty."

Hayley's dubious look got a little cross. "That's pretty gross, if you ask me." She gave the young Austrian archduchess a look from beneath lowered brows. "And why are *you* a party to this? Your own brother!"

Cecilia Renata sniffed. "My *little* brother. A sweet enough boy, but he needs to be seasoned. Far better he should get seasoned by Minnie than by one of the airheads"—the Austrian archduchess was quite taken with American slang—"who loiter about my brother's court. Minnie will be good for him."

Hayley stared at her for a moment, then shook her head. "There are times I don't think I'll ever adjust to the seventeenth century. Especially seventeenth-century royalty."

Cecilia Renata gave her a pitying look in return. "I've known since I was five or six years old that I'd eventually get married to someone purely for reasons of state. The same is true for my brother Leopold, most likely. There is not much room in there for the sort of sappy soap opera mush you Americans love to wallow in."

Hayley's sniff was almost as good as the archduchess's had been. "'Sappy' and 'soap opera' and 'mush,' is it? You've never seen any of the three of them. Well, the first two anyway. There might be some Austrian version of mush, but you wouldn't make it with cornmeal."

"I have great powers of imagination, as befits a many-times-great-granddaughter of the Swiss count Radbot of Klettgau, who imagined his line becoming a great dynasty named Habsburg." She smiled cheerily and spread her arms. "And look, here we are.'

"Besieged by the Turks," said Hayley.

"That was unkind."

"Hayley!" shouted Amadeus. "We have to go! Now!"

"All right, all right!" she shouted down. She gave each of the three other women on the rampart a quick hug and hurried down the stairs—or started to hurry, rather. The staircase was so steep that it was more like descending a ladder. After she'd taken two steps, Hayley stopped, turned around, and went the rest of the way facing backward.

Thirty seconds later, she was out of sight.

"So it's just us now," said Minnie. "What should be call ourselves? We need a name. Neither Cecilia Renata nor I could possibly be a 'Barbie.' The whole idea's ridiculous."

"The Sopranos," Judy immediately proposed.

"What's a soprano?" Cecilia Renata asked.

Hoorn, province of Holland
The Netherlands

"That is just so cool," said Bonnie Weaver admiringly. "It's an ingenious idea, too."

Staring at the huge object moored just offshore—pair of objects, rather—Rita had to agree with her. It *was* both cool and ingenious.

One of the big problems with airships was where to keep the enormous things when they were on the ground. You could tether them with ropes in a large enough open area, but that only worked if there wasn't much wind. What you really needed was a hangar, and the problem that posed was twofold. First, in order for even a small airship to fit inside, the building had to be gigantic—*and* it couldn't have any internal support structure or the whole purpose of the edifice would be negated because the airship wouldn't fit inside.

At a bare minimum, the interior dimensions of the hangar had to be five hundred feet long, sixty feet wide and sixty feet high—and it would be much safer to have the width and height be around eighty feet to a hundred feet instead. That meant, given the resources available in Europe in the 1630s, erecting a seven- or eight-story wooden building with no internal supports and only such bracing as could be kept out of the way of the airship.

Hard, though certainly not impossible. But you still faced the problem that getting the airship in and out of the hangar could only be done if the wind was very weak. Any sort of wind—even a gentle breeze—would make the project difficult and dangerous.

The Dutch consortium that was building the airship they'd come to the Netherlands to buy or lease had found a solution to the problem. Their hangar floated on the water. The base of the hangar rested on what amounted to big barges, with access to the airship when it was inside the hangar being provided by gangplanks.

The hangar was moored by anchors set down by the barges. But whenever it was time to bring an airship in or out of the hangar, the anchors could be lifted and the hangar's orientation changed so that the long axis was directly aligned with the wind.

"Is there any place we could build a floating hangar like that in the USE?" Bonnie wondered.

"Certainly. The Bodensee," said Heinz. "It's formed by the Rhine, in Swabia."

Bonnie frowned. "I never heard of it."

"Yeah, you have," said Rita. "It's usually called Lake Constance in English. It's on the border between Switzerland and the USE." Her voice began to rise a little with excitement. "Heinz is right, too. It'd be perfect! It's not that far from Munich, either. Maybe...I don't know..."

"About one hundred and fifty miles. Not even that."

Bonnie pursed her lips. "That'd be well out of range for a hot air dirigible but not for a hydrogen one. Are there are other lakes, Heinz?"

He nodded. "There are a number of other lakes in the USE that would be big enough for an airship hangar—a number of hangars, in fact. The closest one to Munich in our territory that I can think of is the Hopfensee near Füssen. Not much farther away, there is also a lake near Immenstadt. But those are not big towns, so I don't think they'd have the skills and resources we'd need. There are some other lakes that I think are even closer to Munich but they are in Bavaria and currently under Duke Maximilian's control. Outside of Bavaria, other than the Bodensee..."

Heinz fell silent for a moment while he searched his memory. "There's the Steinhuder Meer in Brunswick. It's very shallow, though—I think it averages no more than three or four feet deep. That might be a problem. And in any case it's farther away from Munich than the Bodensee. The same's true for the Lake District in Mecklenburg and Mummelsee and the Schluchsee in the Black Forest. None of them are closer than the Bodensee and most of them are much farther away."

"The Bodensee it is, then," said Rita. "Are there any big towns right on it, where a hangar could be assembled?"

"I think the best site would probably be Bregenz. It's in our territory, now that Tyrol joined us. It's on the side of the lake closest to Munich and I think it's a big town. But I've never visited the area so I'm not sure."

"Why we've got a radio. If the deal goes through, we'll have our people back home start to work on it." Rita started walking toward the nearby buildings near the shore where the headquarters of the consortium were located. "Speaking of which, it's time to negotiate. Hear me roar. Okay, I'll probably be sweet-talking most of the time. Figure of speech."

Bonnie and Heinz actually did most of the talking, since they knew a lot more about airship construction than Rita did.

"...engine we finally bought is a Chrysler 3.8 which can produce a little over two hundred horsepower." The Dutch engineer rattled off the specs as if he were native born to the late twentieth century. "Of course, we have to use a 2.5 to 1 gear reduction..."

Rita ignored the rest of it. She'd never been much interested in automobile engines even up-time, and most of the discussion between her two companions and the Dutch airship builders might just as well have been in Greek. She was pretty sure the term "3.8" referred to the size of the engine in...liters? Something like that. And she knew that when car engines were used for aeronautical purposes the RPM usually had to be reduced using one or another type of gearing system. Beyond that, she was lost.

But the details weren't her job. Her job was to keep her mouth shut so she didn't goof up anywhere, look solemn and parsimonious, and—most of all; essential!—look like she was the sister of one Michael Stearns, former prime minister of the USE and now one of its leading generals and often known by the informal title of the Prince of Germany.

That was the hardest part, actually. Memories kept coming to her of her brother *As Only A Sister Knew Him*. Mike at . . . what had he been? Fifteen years old, if she remembered right. Coming home from school with a black eye and a split lip and badly skinned knuckles.

Their mother had given Mike a proper chewing out, with their father glowering at him. Then, after she left, Jack Stearns had leaned over and whispered to his son—but she'd heard!— "Next time, Mike, don't swing for the bastard's head with your fist. You'll just cut yourself up. The way to do it—"

He'd spotted six-year-old Rita listening with interest and had shooed her off.

Then there was the time Mike came home—

"Rita?"

Belatedly, she realized Bonnie had now called her name twice. "Ah . . . Yeah. Yes. What . . . Ah, yes?"

"We need a decision here. Do we want a crew of between twelve and fifteen people—that would be optimum—or do we want to cut back on the crew in order to expand the fuel tanks? We could go as low as a crew of six if we really needed to, although they think going below eight starts being problematic."

Rita would have been delighted to fob off on this question too, but it fell within the parameters of "operational issues." Technically, that was her bailiwick.

She spent some time pondering the matter. Partly that was to enhance the image of *Big Shot's Sister, thinking deep thoughts*. Mostly, though, it was because she actually had to think about it.

"What's the range the way it is?" she asked. "Let's assume a full crew of fifteen."

The Dutch engineer who'd been doing most of the talking— Maarten Kortenaer was his name—waggled his hand. "It can vary quite a bit, you understand, depending on the wind and other factors. You would also need to specify the speed and the fuel load. But figure that your range will be somewhere between six hundred and nine hundred miles."

She went back to pondering. She was tempted to go for the full crew option, because a range of six hundred miles between refueling was already far better than the hot air dirigibles could manage. A round trip distance of three hundred miles—no, make it two hundred and fifty to allow sufficient loiter time over the target...

She tried to visualize a map of central Europe. Assuming for the moment that the home base of the dirigible was on the Bodensee, they could possibly even reach Vienna. Come close, for sure—and cover all of Bavaria. Then, once Mike squashed Maximilian, they could shift the base to one of the lakes in Bavaria and they'd easily be in range to cover Vienna itself and its surroundings.

But...

The problem wasn't the fuel itself so much as the hydrogen. By now the USE had a lot of facilities that were able to handle gasoline and kerosene. Producing large quantities of hydrogen, though, was a new challenge.

"How much hydrogen leaks out?" she asked. "Let's say, over a one-week period."

The answer was long-winded and convoluted, with lots of qualifications and variables, but the gist of it seemed to be *we don't really know yet.*

"All right," she said, finally. "Let's split the difference. We'll figure on a crew of ten which can be expanded if need be. I'm assuming most of the weight of the fuel is the actual fuel weight, not the weight of the fuel containers."

"Oh, yes," said Kortenaer. "The weight of the containers is about fifteen percent of the weight of the fuel itself."

Rita nodded. "And they don't take up a lot of space—certainly measured against what's available."

That was one of the big differences between hydrogen and hot air dirigibles. Hydrogen was comparatively stable and you didn't have to keep heating it up. That meant that you could locate the vessel's cargo space, engine compartments, crew quarters, fuel tanks, radio station—almost everything—on the keel, *inside* the envelope, instead of having to place it on an external gondola. You still wanted a control car hanging down from the envelope, but that was just for the sake of greater visibility. All you needed there was room for one or two pilots, a navigator, and some navigation equipment.

Rita had been astonished when she got inside the airship being built in Hoorn and was given a tour of the interior. The area available for people, equipment and cargo was *huge*. It was more like being on a cruise ship than an aircraft.

Of course, space was one thing; lifting capacity, another. Still, the rigid airship being built in Hoorn was far superior to anything the USE military currently had in service.

"How soon will the ship be ready?" she asked.

They'd already negotiated the terms of the lease—and lease it would be, not a sale. The Dutch weren't admitting anything openly, but it was by now obvious to Rita and her two companions that the real power behind the consortium was the king in the Netherlands, Fernando. He wanted the airship to stay in his possession in case he needed it against...

Whichever enemy might show up. The most likely one would be his older brother, King Philip IV of Spain. The airship would make a splendid bombing platform that could throttle the English Channel if another Spanish Armada should happen to show up.

Fernando was willing to lease it to the USE for the time being, though. First, because there really didn't seem to be any immediate threat to the Netherlands coming from any quarter. Both the Spanish and the French had other and more pressing problems on their hands and the USE was on reasonably friendly terms—which stood to get even friendlier because of the airship arrangement.

And, second, because leasing the airship to the USE would give the vessel and its crew what amounted to a baptism by fire. They could learn what the ship could and couldn't do in a real war without the Netherlands having to actually declare war on anybody.

"We could have the ship operational in..." The Dutch engineers spent a couple of minutes in quiet consultation. Then Maarten Kortenaer looked up and said: "Two months. At the beginning of September."

Rita nodded. "That should do."

Amsterdam, the Netherlands

There was a radio message from Mike Stearns waiting for them when they got back to their hotel rooms.

Ottoman army has reached Vienna. They have airships. At least three. We need that Dutch ship ASAP.

"Big brothers are such a pain in the ass," said Rita.

Chapter 31

Outside Munich, capital of Bavaria

"How did Admiral Simpson tear down the walls of Hamburg in a few hours," Mike Stearns wondered, "when the same guns don't seem to be making much of a dent in the walls of Munich?"

The captain in charge of the battery got the long-suffering look common to artillery officers when called upon to explain that cannon are not, in fact, magic wands.

"First of all, sir," he replied, "the walls of Hamburg that Simpson fired upon weren't torn down because he wasn't trying to breach the walls. He was sailing through Hamburg on his way to the North Sea. He just damaged them in the process of doing what he was really after, which was silencing the batteries Hamburg had on the river."

He took a deep breath. "Second, the walls he faced on the river weren't the full-scale star fort walls that he would have been firing on if he'd been investing Hamburg from landside"—here a forefinger waved about—"like we are. Third—"

"Never mind," Mike grumbled. "I'll take your word that there's a logic to it. Even if it does seem weird."

Christopher Long chimed in. "General, there's a reason every big city in Europe spends a fortune—not a small one, either—surrounding themselves with star forts. The fact is that this style of fortification works well against the kind of big guns generally available to us." He nodded toward the nearest of the two ten-inch naval rifles, positioned in a berm about fifty yards away. "These are much better than most and eventually the explosive shells they fire will produce a big enough breach for us to launch an assault. But we only have two of the guns available so far because of the problems Major Simpson has been having salvaging the other two."

Mike had the grace to tighten his lips and keep his mouth shut. He didn't blush, though, which by rights he should have. Tom, following Mike's orders, had managed to get the two remaining naval rifles out of the Danube. His men had drilled out the spikes and cleaned them up, and then shipped the guns down the Danube to the confluence with the Isar.

Where, alas—the details remained unclear, but war is well known to be hell—the barge had capsized and spilled both guns back into the river.

Mike had had the good sense, however, not to cite Clausewitz in the brief message reporting on the mishap to Gustav Adolf. *Everything in war is simple, but the simplest thing is difficult...*

Would not have been well received.

There was no point in Mike grumbling at his artillery officers, anyway. He was just restless. He didn't really want a big breach opened up in the walls of Munich. He just wanted to keep the pressure on Duke Maximilian while he hoped Rebecca—someone, anyone—could finally persuade Gustav Adolf to accept a political settlement with Bavaria.

"Keep up the good work, Captain," he said, and left to make a nuisance of himself somewhere else.

Sieges were frustrating, aggravating, and most of all—*boring*.

Vienna, capital of Austria-Hungary

"Wow," said Judy Wendell, raising the lamp in order to get a better view. "I've heard of safe rooms, but this is..." She smiled wryly. "A royal palace version of it, I guess."

Cecilia Renata rose from the crouch she'd assumed to inspect one of the casks. "That wine is still good, I think. What is a 'safe room'?"

After Judy explained, both Cecilia Renata and Minnie Hugelmair shook their heads.

"No, not really," said the archduchess. "The way you describe a safe room, its purpose is to prevent anyone from breaking into it until help can arrive." She made a little circular motion with her finger, indicating their surroundings. "This is not safe at all, not that way. If an enemy can break into Vienna, they can certainly break into these cellars. This is just a hiding place, that's all. You would only be safe so long as no one knew you were here."

"Speaking of which," said Minnie. "Who *does* know about these cellars? Besides you and us and Leopold."

Cecilia Renata pursed her lips thoughtfully. "Everyone in the royal family, of course. A few officials—but all of them left with the emperor. I don't think there's anyone in Vienna except the three of us and Leopold who knows they exist."

"That can't be true," said Judy, trying to keep the exasperation out of her voice. *Royalty!* It seemed almost impossible for people raised the way they'd been to remember that servants were real live actual all-the-way-around people just like they were. And so were workmen.

"You didn't build these cellars yourselves," she continued. "It must have taken dozens of men to do it. Hundreds, probably. I mean—*look* at it." She raised the lantern again and swung it back and forth, shedding light into various corners.

It wasn't possible to see all of the area, or even most of it. These were cellars—cellars, plural, not one cellar—and there were at least four separate rooms. Quite possibly more, since there were dark areas Judy hadn't explored yet.

"Oh, them." Renata Cecilia shook her head. "They all made solemn oaths to remain silent. But it doesn't matter because none of them could still be alive, Judy. This wing of the palace was originally built in the middle of the last century as a home for Maximilian II before he became the Holy Roman Emperor. These cellars would have been put in at the same time. And he died..."

She frowned. "In the year 1576, I think. That was sixty years ago—and he was fifty years old when he died. Or forty-nine, I don't remember."

"Doesn't matter, either way," said Judy. "Everyone who worked on the cellars has to be long gone by now."

Which didn't mean they hadn't told friends or members of their families about the cellars, solemn oaths or not. But they probably wouldn't have told very many people, and those people would have been sworn to silence also. Those vows no doubt got broken, too. But by the time a century went by, the well-known telephone game effect would have distorted the passed-on memories beyond recognition, and there'd be several different versions of them.

Mentally, she shrugged. The world wasn't a perfectly safe place; never had been, never would be. But as hidey-holes went in a city under siege by a mighty and malevolent enemy, this was pretty damn good.

There were some drawbacks, of course. The lighting sucked. More precisely, there was no lighting at all except that provided by four very narrow slots in the tower near the entrance—and that light didn't penetrate into the cellars because the disguised door that provided the entrance to the cellars two floors below those slots was kept tightly shut. Not only shut but bolted and wedged from the inside. Even if someone suspected there might be an entrance and poked and pried, they wouldn't be able to budge that door. In fact, they wouldn't even be able to determine that it was a door in the first place.

On the positive side, that meant that any light being generated inside the cellars by lamps or candles wouldn't leak out, either. On the negative side, that also meant that the ventilation was wretched. Air passages had been built into the design, but no provision had been made for circulating the air. On the *really* negative side, that meant—

Minnie emerged out of the gloom. "I pried open the lid and looked into it. That oubliette in the corner of the next room hasn't been used in maybe a hundred years. So it's not stinky. On the other hand, if we ever do have to use it..."

She made a face. "This would get really foul down here."

Judy looked around, again holding her lamp up. "Are these barrels all full of wine?"

"Yes," said Cecilia Renata. "They get changed every decade or so."

Judy pounced. "By who? They'll know about the cellars."

"By one of the officials who left with the emperor for Linz."

The archduchess seemed to believe it, too. Amazing. Did anyone really think a court official hauled heavy casks of wine in and out of a hidden cellar all by his lonesome?

Royalty. They'd just have to hope whoever did the actual work would keep their mouths shut—if they ever wound up having to use these cellars at all, which everyone kept assuring Judy they wouldn't.

She found that kind of amazing too. You'd think people who'd been born and raised in a century where all cities had huge fortifications surrounding them wouldn't be so blasted optimistic about everything.

She forced her mind back to the issue at hand. "We couldn't possibly drink all this wine. Not even if we were holding nonstop parties down here. So if the time ever comes, we can just pour one of the casks down into the shit pit. That ought to cut down the smell and help sterilize the crap."

Cecilia Renata shook her head. "I don't think that's a good idea. And we don't need to find out because"—she pointed to a small stack of casks off to one side—"those have lime in them. That's what you use to keep the smell down."

That would probably also reduce the danger of infection, Judy reflected.

"What about water?" she asked. "Wine would be better for drinking but you'd need to wash yourself too."

Cecilia Renata pointed to the entrance to the cellar they were in. "There's a small channel in the far room—opposite the one with the oubliette—that collects rainwater into a cistern. When it fills up, it overflows into another channel that carries it outside. It's not much use in the winter, though."

Judy tried to imagine the condition that water would be in, during a dry spell, after sitting in a cistern for days or even weeks. Thankfully, there'd be plenty of wine. Drinking that water pretty much guaranteed you'd come down with dysentery or something even worse.

"Bah!" she suddenly exclaimed. "We're getting carried away here, ladies! If it ever looks like the Turks are going to break into Vienna, I vote we just evacuate the city like anybody else with half a brain."

Cecilia Renata nodded. "I agree. There is already a provision for that, too. Leopold told me—in fact, he's in charge of it. He and a Captain Adolf Brevermann. If the Turks breach the walls we will evacuate everyone on barges in the Donaukanal."

Judy was skeptical how well that would work. It was true that the Ottomans had so far made no attempt to cross over to the north bank of the Danube or even onto the strip of land between the river and the canal that formed the northern limit of Vienna. That might be on account of the steam barges the Austrians had, which had originally been built to ferry people to and from Race Track City. The Austrians had armed two of them with small cannons. But Judy had her doubts. She was no soldier, but she suspected that if Sultan Murad IV could get one hundred thousand men from Belgrade to Vienna, he could sure as hell get across a river, steam barges or no steam barges.

Most of the city's civilians had already been evacuated, except for eight thousand volunteers—almost all of them men—who had stayed behind to support the garrison, which was now a little over fifteen thousand strong. The defenders were heavily outnumbered, but they had the great advantage of fighting behind some of Europe's strongest fortifications.

What everyone was hoping, of course, was that the USE and perhaps Bohemia would send troops to relieve the siege. But no one yet knew if that might happen, although rumors were flying everywhere.

"Your brother is in charge of that?" asked Minnie. Her expression was a little pinched. "With a captain. Let me guess. The captain will lead the evacuation while Leopold will lead the delaying action."

"That's what he told me," said Cecilia Renata.

"That's stupid!" Minnie protested. "He's playing at being a general! He has no military experience. He's supposed to be a *bishop*, for Christ's sake." Minnie, from her long and close association with Denise, had picked up American habits when it came to blasphemy.

"Which is exactly what *I* told him," agreed the young arch-duchess. "But you know what he's like, Minnie. Well, maybe you don't yet. Whenever he thinks his honor is involved, he becomes as stubborn as a mule and his—what do you call it? That thing that measures how smart you are?"

"IQ," Judy provided. "Stands for 'intelligence quotient.'"

"Yes, that thing. Leopold's IQ drops below that of a mule, at such times. Sometimes, below that of a beetle. He says if it comes to an evacuation under fire that military skill won't be as important as simply keeping morale steady. Which he claims he can do better than anyone—certainly a mere captain—because he's a member of the royal family. All he has to do is not panic, he says."

Minnie's face got really pinched, then. After a short silence, she said: "He's probably right, you know. The fucking idiot."

"He's an idiot for being right?" Judy tried to follow the logic.

"No. He's an idiot for listening to himself being right."

Race Track City
Four miles east of Vienna

The corpses were beginning to smell, which was all to the good so far as Murad was concerned. The Ottoman sultan had ordered the three officers in command of the janissaries who'd seized Race Track City and set fire to it to be hanged for disobeying his direct order that no captured persons or buildings were to be harmed except by his command.

He'd given that order, in part, because he wanted the buildings for his own use. He'd planned to use Race Track City to quarter a large number of his soldiers. Now, they'd all have to make do with tents, since the only edifice which had survived—a factory of some sort, making what looked like buttons—had been turned into his military headquarters.

In part, he'd also ordered strict discipline to be maintained because he had hopes of winning over a portion of the conquered population. There probably wouldn't be many, of course. These Austrians were Catholic Christians, not Orthodox ones like the many subjects of the Ottoman Empire who provided the sultan with most of the troops handling the new weapons. But if Murad could gain the allegiance of even a few, that would be helpful. The chances of doing so would be greatly diminished if they or their families had been abused.

Mostly, though, Murad had ordered the executions because he was determined to use this campaign to break the resistance of the janissaries and bend them to his will. The janissaries were still a formidable military force, but in the long years since they'd been created by Murad I, two and a half centuries earlier, the elite corps had grown increasingly fractious and independent. They and the *sipahis*, the traditional Ottoman cavalry corps, had become too independent of the sultan's control.

But if Murad's plans worked, Vienna was going to fall like no great city had fallen in centuries. Not at the end of a protracted siege, but in a few short days—possibly just one day. Murad was an enormously powerful man, physically, and in battle his favored weapon was a mace so large and heavy that few other men could have wielded it. He would break Vienna's resistance by using his army like that same mace—with one great blow.

The new weapons and the new military units would be the key to that victory. None of them were janissaries, and none were sipahis. Many of them were Christians and Jews, who owed their new status entirely to the sultan.

A slight cough drew Murad's attention. Turning, he saw that Halil Pasha had arrived in response to his summons.

"Begin the sapping operations," he ordered, then watched carefully to see if the former governor of Egypt seemed hesitant to obey. The man was extraordinarily capable but given to pointless tenderness.

That trait had made him very popular in Egypt. Indeed, after Murad summoned Halil Pasha back to Istanbul three years earlier, the shopkeepers in Cairo had been impertinent enough to close their businesses for a week in mourning. Murad had responded by stripping Halil Pasha of his possessions and exiling him on Cyprus.

Only briefly, though, and just to make a point. The man was too capable not to use him.

But there seemed to be no reluctance on Halil Pasha's part to do as Murad bade him. He simply bowed and left to carry out the command. Halil was one of the few men who were privy to Murad's plans in their entirety. He knew, therefore, that sending out sappers was sending men into great danger from which many would not return—and for no purpose other than subterfuge. Murad was going to overwhelm Vienna's resistance by sheer force and violence, not undermine its walls by the slow underground warfare of sappers against counter-sappers.

But the Austrians would be expecting sappers. Indeed, they would already have begun their own counter-sapping operations. If they encountered no Ottoman troops they would become suspicious.

Their suspicions might not lead to anything. Probably wouldn't, in fact. With a few exceptions, Austrian commanders were not imaginative. But there was no reason to take the risk, simply to save the lives of a few dozen sappers.

Kasim Bey was waiting for him also. Murad motioned him to come forward.

"How soon?" he asked.

Kasim Bey shook his head. "It is hard to be sure, My Sultan. The big problem is the armored wagons. If we could dispense with those..."

"No." Murad's answer was quick and firm. "I do not expect them to be very useful if they actually have to fight. No more than you do, Kasim Bey. But they will strike terror in the hearts of the Austrians. For that alone, I want them here."

"That may cost us as much as an extra week, My Sultan."

"I understand. We have to wait another week anyway, for the *katyushas* and the main airship fleet to arrive. An additional week will not matter. We will still only be in August. You are dismissed."

With another hand gesture, Murad summoned the Şeyh-ül-Islâm's acolyte. He'd forgotten the man's name.

"The ruling?"

"My Sultan, my master is even now writing the *fatwa*. Given that the infidels have already been seen to use fire weapons in war, the flamethrowers and incendiary bombs may be used, provided that they are employed in a lawful manner."

Murad was irritated that Zekeriyyâ-zâde Yahyâ Efendi had chosen to remain in his tent and send an assistant rather than present the ruling himself. The Şeyh-ül-Islâm was the empire's greatest scholar and normally remained in Istanbul. But Murad had required him to accompany the expedition to Baghdad as well as this one. Partly that was to improve morale; partly to keep an eye on the man.

But the matter was not important enough to force the scholar to appear before him. Both Murad and the Şeyh-ül-Islâm had known what the ruling would be for the last several months. The purpose of this little exercise was simply to have it stated in public, in front of the officers and officials assembled in Murad's headquarters. For that purpose, the acolyte would do as well as the Şeyh-ül-Islâm himself.

"And how may they be employed lawfully?"

Some of Murad's irritation must have been evident in his tone, for the assistant seemed to twitch for a moment. That was hardly surprising, given that Murad had executed the current Şeyh-ül-Islâm's predecessor. The man had been notoriously conservative and Murad needed a ruling that would allow him to use the new weapons his artisans had developed from their study of the American texts.

"First, the flames may only be used against fortifications," said the acolyte hurriedly, "for Allah alone may use flames against people. But if the flames endanger infidels who fail to flee, then their deaths are on their own heads."

That was the critical part of the ruling. For all practical purposes, it made the use of the new fire weapons legal under any circumstances likely to arise. The incendiary bombs were less useful than explosives on a battlefield and the flamethrowers were too unreliable. Their principal function was against fortifications.

But there was another matter of importance, which Murad wanted to have stated in public also.

"And what else?" he asked.

"The Şeyh-ül-Islâm also recommends that the weapons be wielded by *zimmis* so that Muslims in the heat of battle are not tempted into error by the innovations."

Murad nodded solemnly—as if he had not already put that provision into place. The zimmis—Jewish and Christian citizens of the empire—who manned his armored wagons and airships and provided much of the katyusha force were completely dependent on his goodwill. Unlike the janissaries and the sipahis, they had no other anchor in the empire.

And now he had the imprimatur of Şeyh-ül-Islâm Zekeriyyâ-zâde Yahyâ Efendi on his decision to have the new weapons operated by zimmis. The janissary and sipahi officers in the headquarters had all heard the acolyte say so—and explain that the ruling was to protect the souls of his Muslim soldiers. A good and just sultan could have no higher responsibility.

"You are dismissed," he said to the acolyte.

After he was gone, Murad climbed the stairs to the second floor of the factory. There was a large window that provided a good view of Vienna.

He spent a few minutes looking at the city. Not planning anything, just gazing and pondering a question whose answer had not yet come to him.

What would he rename Vienna, after he'd taken it?

Chapter 32

Jaroszówka, Lower Silesia
Northwest of Legnica (Liegnitz)

"I wish I had my armor and my lance," said Lukasz Opalinski, peering over the hedge.

"Why not wish for your saddle wings while you're at it?" said Jozef. He was crouched beside Lukasz, studying the village of Jaroszówka—what was left of it, which wasn't much. The raiders had set fire to most of the buildings. "It's sad, to see a mighty hussar brought so low."

Lukasz's only response was a dignified sniff. "Just try to keep up with me. Do you see any more?"

Wojtowicz shook his head. "There's just the five of them. Might be one or two more, but they'd be too drunk to stand, much less ride."

"Let's go, then." Still crouched over, Lukasz moved toward the horses, which they'd left behind them in a meadow. The hedge was atop a slight rise which kept the meadow out of sight of the village.

They hadn't bothered to tether their mounts. They were both well-trained warhorses.

They walked the horses out of the meadow toward a small grove of trees. They'd be able to stay out of sight of the small party of soldiers in the village until they launched their attack. The distance from the grove to the village was less than a hundred yards. Their mounts were coursers, who could have covered that distance in seven or eight seconds even if Lukasz and Jozef had both been wearing heavy hussar armor. Wearing only buff coats, they'd probably reach their target in no more than six seconds.

Six seconds is a long time for a trained and alert soldier to react to danger. But the small detachment from Holk's army in Jaroszówka was anything but alert, however well trained they might or might not be. At least one of them was visibly drunk. He was struggling to get onto his horse while his companions made jokes and jeered at him.

After they reached the grove, they saddled up and took a moment to reorient themselves. They could see the village again from here, through the trees. The soldier who'd been trying to get on his horse had apparently fallen in the process and one of his mates was getting off his own horse to help him. The other three were still laughing. One of them had a jug of something— not likely to be water—which he brought to his lips.

"Now," said Lukasz. An instant later he had his courser charging out of the grove.

Jozef followed, making no effort to catch up with his friend. He was content to remain a few yards behind. Wojtowicz had a great deal in the way of martial skills, as he'd demonstrated on several occasions over the past year. But he wasn't in Lukasz's class on a battlefield.

Besides, his friend was new to the fury that Jozef had been experiencing since he first went into Silesia from Dresden. It would do him good to unleash it.

Lukasz hadn't drawn either one of his pistols from their saddle holsters. He was clearly planning to start with his saber—and probably end with it also.

Jozef, being a proper sort of spy and assassin, had no such romantic inclinations. He'd had one of his Blumroder .58 caliber pistols in his hand before they'd left the grove.

It was almost comical, the way Holk's men gaped at them as they approached. The one who'd been dismounting to help his comrade was so startled that he fell off his horse and landed on the man he'd been planning to assist. Both of them went down in a heap, their horses skittering away.

The one with the jug wasted several seconds looking around trying to find a place to set down the jug without breaking it—no easy task when you're perched in a saddle high off the ground. By the time he finally accepted reality, dropped the jug and reached for one of his pistols, Lukasz was twenty yards away and would reach him in less than two seconds.

The mercenary fumbled the pistol trying to pull it out of the saddle holster. The gun slipped out of his hand and fell to the ground. But Opalinski's attention was entirely on the man's two more alert companions. Both of them had pistols in hand by the time he arrived—but they were prevented from using them by the befuddled jug-dropper. What the man should have done was just gotten out of their way. Instead Lukasz drove his courser right toward the man's own warhorse, causing it to rear and impede the line of sight of the others.

Both men fired their pistols anyway. One bullet went flying off somewhere unknown. The other one struck the rearing horse. It was just a graze, nothing serious, but it frightened the already startled horse. It threw its rider right out of the saddle and raced off.

Lukasz reached his first target. The soldier was wearing bits and pieces of cheap-looking plate armor, whose main components were a cuirass and spaulders. Lukasz swung his saber. Up, over, down, like a flash of lightning. The blade passed just below the edge of the right spaulder and cut the man's arm off about three inches above the elbow. The blade still had enough power to pass through the arm completely and hammer the cuirass. It didn't penetrate that armor but the blow drove the man out of the saddle. Between the horrible blood loss and the impact when he struck the ground he was no longer conscious.

Before the first man had even left the saddle, Lukasz had slashed at the other soldier. That man brought up his heavy wheel-lock pistol in an instinctive effort to shield himself, but the hussar was skilled as well as very strong. His blade didn't strike the pistol but the hand holding it, which it cut in half just below the line of knuckles. The pistol was sent flying. The soldier gaped at what was left of his hand, which was the thumb and perhaps two-thirds of the palm.

He didn't gape long. Lukasz brought his horse back around and another swing of the saber slashed through the man's neck, opening the right carotid and almost severing the spine. He fell to the ground, mortally wounded and losing consciousness rapidly.

Two seconds earlier, Jozef had come within five feet of the tangled cluster of two men on the ground. Oddly, the one who was almost back on his feet was the drunken one. Jozef shot him in the top of the head. The heavy bullet drove the man right back down onto the one who'd tried to help him and knocked him flat again.

Since he was momentarily obscured, Jozef shifted his aim and trotted his horse over to the man who'd fumbled with the jug. He was still lying where his mount had pitched him before running off. The wind had apparently been knocked out of him, because all he did as Jozef drew near was stare at him with bulging eyes while his mouth gasped for air.

Jozef leaned down from the saddle to get a better aim and shot the man in the throat. When he straightened and looked over to Lukasz, he saw that his friend had dismounted and was now striding over to the last conscious survivor. That poor soul, whose entire contribution to the melee had been trying to help his drunken companion and getting knocked down by him for his efforts, had just heaved the fellow's corpse off and gotten up on one knee when Lukasz arrived.

Opalinski was extraordinarily strong. That saber strike decapitated the man and sent the head flying at least five yards away.

"That's all of them, I think," said Lukasz. He glanced around quickly, then moved over to check the first man he'd struck down. The fellow was unconscious and it was obvious from the blood pumping out of his severed arm that he'd soon be dead. But Lukasz ended the process by a quick, accurate stab of the saber tip, which opened the soldier's neck as well.

When he straightened up, his face was paler than usual. That was the residue of controlled rage, Jozef knew, not horror at the deaths he'd caused. In the mood Lukasz was in after days traveling through the ravaged countryside of Lower Silesia, he had no more compassion for any of Holk's men than he would have had for wolf spiders.

Less, actually. Opalinski wouldn't have gone out of his way just to destroy some spiders.

They didn't spend much time investigating Jaroszówka, once they'd made sure there weren't any survivors.

As usual, when Holk's soldiers passed through a village, they'd killed everyone who'd been foolish enough to stay—or too infirm, in the case of the old couple whose corpses Jozef found. The only other corpse they discovered, in one of the huts that had only partially burned, was that of an infant who'd been bundled up and stuffed under a cot. From the looks of the gaunt body, the child had died of natural causes not long before the raid. Starvation, most likely. Her kin would have buried her but they'd had to escape the village too soon. So, they'd tucked her out of sight, hoping they might be able to return and bury her properly later.

Jozef and Lukasz spent the rest of the day digging graves for the old couple and the child and burying them. Since they didn't know any of their names, they just erected three crosses and carved "unknown" on them. Then, after staring down at the little girl's cross for a few seconds, Lukasz had added another carving on the vertical piece.

Murdered by Heinrich Holk, was what it read. Her family wouldn't have been starving if his men hadn't plundered the area.

They spent the night just outside the village, preferring their tent to sleeping in the wreckage. After they awoke and had breakfast, Lukasz spoke his first words since carving the girl's cross.

"I'm sick of this. We have to do something, Jozef. Almost all the people those swine are killing, raping and plundering are Poles. They don't go into the big German towns."

Idly, Jozef poked at their little fire with a stick. "There is a solution. But you won't like it."

Opalinski's jaws tightened. He'd obviously figured out already what Jozef was talking about.

"She won't kill anyone who doesn't need killing," the hussar said. "And since Lower Silesia is already being ruled by Germans—Holk's pigs in the countryside and the towns are already mostly German—I'd rather have our Saxons doing it. I can't say I trust them, exactly, but..."

Jozef finished the thought for him. "They can't be any worse than what the king and the Sejm have done."

Lukasz sighed, and ran fingers through his blond hair. "I used to think my older brother Krzysztof was a stupid hothead. I'm not so sure, any longer." He let a few more seconds go by and then added softly: "I've always hoped that the grand hetman would eventually take a stand. But I've given up by now."

Jozef left off poking with the stick and tossed it into the fire. "My uncle is fixed in his ways and his habits, Lukasz. He's great on a battlefield, but for this—" He made a vague gesture with his hand. "He's simply no use. I hate to say it, but it's the truth. We're on our own."

There was silence again, for several minutes. Then Jozef got a quirky little smile on his face.

"We'll have to lie to her. Which is not easy. Are you up for it?"

Lukasz got a fair imitation of the same smile on his face. "What do you mean, 'we'? You're the master spy. I'm just the thick-headed hussar. So you do all the lying and I'll just glare and look furious. Which I know I can manage because I *am* furious."

Magdeburg, capital of the United States of Europe

Rebecca had transformed one of the chambers in her town house into what she called the *war room*. That was the chamber where she and her aides had plotted and schemed and planned and organized the election campaign. With the elections now having started, she intended to continue with the same effort except more tightly focused. All that now needed to be done was captured in a banner hanging high on one of the walls: GET OUT THE VOTE

It was a rather small chamber, given the importance of what happened in it. She'd deliberately chosen it for that reason, after the experience of a few days trying to run the campaign out of the big salon that the Fourth of July Party used for its leadership meetings.

Meetings were fine and splendid things. In their proper place. Rebecca had been sorely tempted to hang a banner in that room, however, this one saying: TOO MANY COOKS SPOIL THE BROTH

But that would be impolitic. So, she'd simply created a war room too small and cramped to satisfy anyone except diehard plotters, schemers, planners and organizers. And let the declaimers and the pontificators enjoy themselves in the big salon.

One of her aides came into the room. More precisely, squeezed her way through the partially open door that was blocked from further inward progress by the back of a chair of another aide squeezed up against a table tabulating the most recent reports from Mecklenburg and Pomerania.

Rebecca glanced up from her own tabulations. As usual, she was perched on a stool in the corner that had the one—very narrow—window in the room. She preferred being by the window because of the light that came through it, not the view. All the window looked out on was an alley.

"Yes, Catharina?"

The young woman—the aides were mostly young women—minced her way over, trying to avoid all the reports piled up in stacks on the floor, then extended her hand to give Rebecca a note. "It's the latest news from Werner."

That would be from Werner von Dalberg, the FoJ Party's candidate for governor of the Upper Palatinate. Unlike some of the MPs, Werner was a skilled organizer in his own right.

Rebecca read it quickly. It was terse, as von Dalberg's prose always was.

Still looking up. Good turnout in Amberg. Excellent in Regensburg. Will be complaints about Ingolstadt.

That last was a given. Most of the inhabitants of Ingolstadt since its liberation were soldiers, and most of them in the SoTF's National Guard. They'd have cast absentee ballots for their home province but a good number of them would also vote in the Oberpfalz. Quite improperly, but their attitude would be *we did the fighting so we ought to be able to vote in the city we liberated too.*

She and Werner had made sure that signs had been posted at all polling stations informing voters that if they were a resident of another province they couldn't vote in the Upper Palatinate as well. But that was just for the public record, since no one was going to waste their time telling armed soldiers that they couldn't vote if they wanted to.

In the end, if the Crown Loyalists filed a formal complaint, Rebecca was sure the courts would rule that all votes in Ingolstadt had to be invalidated and a new vote taken. But they probably wouldn't even bother to file a complaint. From the signs, the FoJP's victory in the Oberpfalz was going to be by such a large margin that the votes in Ingolstadt didn't matter anyway.

Rebecca adored elections. It was too bad they couldn't be held more often. Once a month would be nice. Of course, you'd never get any actual governing done, but this was so much more fun.

Dresden, capital of Saxony

"You're sure?" Gretchen asked. "Absolutely certain?"

"Of course not!" exclaimed Jozef, doing his best to sound aggrieved and much put upon. He almost threw up his hands with exasperation but decided that would be overdoing it. You had to be careful, lying to Richter. It wasn't right that a woman should be that good-looking and that smart at the same time. But ... there it was.

He sighed—again—and tried—again—to convey just the right mixture of confidence in his conclusions and quibbling in his logic. "Everything I've told you comes from conversations I overheard in taverns between some of Holk's soldiers. But some of them were officers and one of them was even a colonel."

"How do you know he was a colonel? Holk's army doesn't use standardized insignia."

She knew too much, too. How did she find out these things?

"Because they called him 'colonel.' Colonel Bentzen or Bensenn, I didn't quite catch the name."

He'd just have to hope the damn woman didn't have a roster of Holk's officers to check that against. She almost certainly didn't, but with Richter ...

"Where was that tavern?" she now asked. "You told me Holk's men generally stayed out of the cities."

"It wasn't a city. Not even a big town. It was in Chojnów, between Boleslawiec and Lignica." He used the Polish names of the towns to reinforce his image as a stubborn but upright native of the Polish-Lithuanian Commonwealth.

Richter glanced at Lovrenc Bravnicar, the Slovene who commanded the small cavalry force that was part of the loosely defined Saxon army-in-creation.

"I've been there once," he said. "I've even been in the tavern he's talking about. At the time—that was ... four years ago, or so, it had about five hundred inhabitants. Since then an epidemic passed through so the population would be smaller. That's probably why Holk stationed some units there. They could find billets in abandoned homes."

Gretchen looked back at Jozef. Then at Lukasz.

"You haven't had much to say," she observed. But she didn't press for an explanation from the hussar. Instead, she went back to studying the map of Lower Silesia that she'd had spread over the table in her headquarters.

"What do you think, Ernst?" she asked.

The small man sitting at one end of the table was frowning. Until perhaps three minutes ago, he'd been intently studying the same map.

"I see no reason they wouldn't be telling us the truth." Ernst Wettin glanced at the two Poles facing Gretchen across the table. "But I don't think that matters anyway. Whether Holk is really planning to attack Saxony or not, just having him there across the border poses a constant threat."

Richter nodded. "What I think, too. Here's the problem, though. If we march into Lower Silesia and take it"—her finger came down on a spot on the map—"we have to go as far as Breslau and take it also. Otherwise our position will be completely unstable. And if we do that, then we've not only seized the biggest city in Lower Silesia. For all practical purposes, we've seized the entire area. From Poland, mind you, which *is* the nation that formally claims it."

Wettin shrugged. "Yes, and so what? We're already at war with Poland. The emperor certainly won't object if we take a chunk out of Poland, especially since the population is so heavily German and Lutheran."

He gave the two Poles a glance that was more dismissive than apologetic. "Meaning no offense to anyone here."

Jozef tried to look suitably annoyed at the obvious slight. A bit hard, that, when he was also trying to suppress a grin. *This was going to work!*

"I'm for it," said Bravnicar. "Fighting Holk in Lower Silesia is the perfect exercise for forging our provincial army."

Jozef could see from her changed expression that that argument was having an impact on Richter as well. Provinces in the USE were allowed to have their own military forces, which were under the authority of the provincial chiefs of state. He suspected that Gustav Adolf wasn't all that pleased with the arrangement, but given the disorganized nature of the Germanies over the past many centuries it would have been impossible to get provincial leaders to agree to form the United States of Europe out of the Confederated Principalities that had preceded it if Gustav Adolf hadn't been willing to accept that provision.

That created a problem for the newly minted province of Saxony, however. The closest remnant to a provincial army that still existed was the rump force that the mercenary general Hans Georg von Arnim had left behind in Leipzig when he marched the rest of his army to Poland to join Torstensson's two divisions besieging Poznań.

Nobody in Dresden—not Richter, not Wettin, and certainly not the Vogtlanders—trusted those mercenary troops. Granted, they'd been well behaved and the city of Leipzig was glad enough to have them. But nobody thought they'd be much use if Saxony ever had to fight a serious enemy.

A new provincial army—that was what was needed. But it would have to be assembled out of disparate bits and pieces. Vogtlander militias, Bravnicar's cavalrymen, the units under Eric Krenz's command that Mike Stearns had left in Dresden.

Jozef hadn't really thought about it, but he now realized that the Slovene cavalry officer was quite right. Fighting an army like Holk's, which was barely distinguishable from a small horde of Tatars or Cossacks—with the vices of both and the virtues of neither—would make an ideal military exercise.

He glanced at Lukasz and saw that his friend was getting excited himself by the idea. He was a hussar, of course. You expected them to salivate at the prospect of fighting, like mastiffs.

"All right," said Richter. "We'll do it. Ernst, you should lead the expedition."

Wettin shook his head. "No, you should."

That was the only time since he'd met the woman that Jozef had ever seen Gretchen Richter taken aback by anything.

"*Me?* But..." She looked quite lost. "I'm a *woman*."

"So was Joan of Arc," replied Wettin. "If you lead the expedition, then what we have is a righteous crusade against wicked invaders of the sacred soil of Saxony. If I lead it"—he shrugged—"we just have a scheme by one branch of the Vasa dynasty to despoil another branch. Which do you think will play better in the nation?"

She stared at him. "That is... very cunning."

The little nobleman smiled, slyly. "Of course, it's also possible I'm scheming to have you eventually burned at the stake. Which is what happened to Joan of Arc in the end, you may recall."

She kept staring at him, for a few more seconds. Then she smiled back, just as slyly.

"I'll take my chances," she said.

Chapter 33

Prague, capital of Bohemia

Eddie Junker had been apprehensive, when he returned to Prague, that he'd find his girlfriend Denise unhappy. Denise had such a sanguine outlook on life that she was normally in a good mood. It was almost as if she dared the universe to try tampering with her disposition so she could smack the big bastard around and set it straight.

But that same disposition meant that she didn't handle tedium well. And, unfortunately, Denise tended to define study as *boriiiiing*. The girl was quite intelligent, but she relied overmuch on that native ability.

Eddie had known, when he brought Denise back to Prague, that her employer Francisco Nasi had come to the conclusion that Denise would be of limited use to him so long as her formal education remained as scanty as it was.

Granted, Nasi defined "scanty" idiosyncratically. Most Europeans of the day—and all Americans—considered a degree (or "diploma," in the up-time lexicon) from the world-famous Grantville high school to be very prestigious. Not, perhaps, equal to a degree from a university in some respects—but in many others, actually superior. Anyone with any sense, for instance, would have far rather gotten medical care and advice from someone who'd graduated from Grantville High and then went on to study medicine in the program jointly run by the SoTF Tech and the University of Jena, than from someone who had an officially more advanced degree in medicine from a down-time university.

True, true, the down-time doctor could explain to his patients in several languages including Greek and Latin exactly what was wrong with them, where the graduate of Grantville High probably spoke only English or German and Amideutsch. So, had you survived, you could have enjoyed reading your death certificate in one of the languages of learning, written in a very fine hand, instead of being still alive but holding in your hand nothing but a scrawled and almost illegible note discharging you from a hospital.

But those issues were of little concern to Francisco Nasi. What he needed were agents who were well-versed in the political complexities of Europe and its immediate neighbors—first and foremost, the Ottoman Empire. That meant learning a number of languages; immersing oneself in the minutia of court intrigue in the many courts of the continent, recognizing and understanding the details of military organization and ordnance, the list was quite long.

It did include training in the use of codes and cyphers as well as all the other little tricks of a spy's work known as tradecraft, which brightened Denise's spirits considerably. The more so when she turned out to have a genuine knack for it.

"I'm not surprised," was her mother's not-altogether-admiring comment when Denise bragged about her proficiency at tradecraft. "You were always good at getting away with stuff. Drove me and your dad crazy, sometimes."

At no point, however, not even when she looked at the list of languages she was going to have to learn, did Denise become melancholy. That was because Nasi had realized long since that having Denise back living with her mother was his recipe for success. His invitation and backing for Christin George's move to Prague had not been disinterested.

So, after Janos Drugeth and Noelle Stull disembarked from the airplane and he'd seen to it that the craft was being properly maintained and refueled in the airstrip's new hangar, Eddie made his way to the address Denise had provided him in a radio dispatch. He found himself before a rather large and attractive house across the river in a very nice section of the Mala Strana. He'd just started up the stairs leading to the entrance when the door opened and Denise emerged. The enthusiasm of her greeting could not have been improved on.

Denise's mother appeared in the doorway, smiling.

"Welcome home, Eddie," she said. He realized then that he had just stepped into a new stage of his life.

Hoorn, province of Holland
The Netherlands

As they followed Maarten Kortenaer while he guided them on a tour of the airship, Rita Simpson had to remind herself periodically not to issue "oohs" and "aahs" as the Dutch engineer pointed out features of the vessel. It was unlikely at this late date that he'd report the appreciative noises back to the heads of the consortium and they'd crank up the price of the lease in response, but... you never knew. No one had ever accused Dutch businessmen of being slow to look for a profit anywhere they could find it.

It was hard, though. The usual problem for an up-timer when a down-timer proudly displayed some product of their craftsmanship was the opposite—making properly flattering remarks in response to something that was a poor cousin to one or another up-time device.

Just recently, for instance, Kortenaer had proudly shown her the new aqualator the consortium had acquired to help the engineers with their calculations. On one level, the water computer was impressive simply because of the intricacy of the design. Or, more precisely, because it was so clumsy compared to what she still thought of (inappropriately, she was told) as a "real computer" that you could actually *see* the complexity of the design. In comparison, an up-time motherboard didn't look like much of anything to a lay person except a jumble of incomprehensible electronic components.

Still, she knew how much more slowly fluidics worked compared to the electronic calculations any up-time computer could handle—or, for that matter, the trusty Texas Instruments pocket calculator she'd brought on this trip to double-check the figures anyone offered her. Nice people, the Dutch; very polite. But when you were dealing with Dutch businessmen you really wanted to double-check everything, just so they knew you were doing it and were therefore not tempted to engage in chicanery. She thought of it as her contribution to keeping people from eternal damnation, even though she was pretty sure the Dutch considered swindling no more than a venal sin. Not really perilous to the soul like blasphemy or working on the Sabbath.

True, there were exceptions to the rule, and some of them could be spectacularly exceptional. She and Bonnie Weaver and Heinz Böcler had been given the chance to visit Rembrandt— yes, that one: *the* Rembrandt who'd had paintings displayed in dozens of major museums in the universe Rita had come from. She'd even seen some of them personally, when she'd gone on a three-day school trip to Washington, D.C. They'd visited the National Gallery, which had several of Rembrandt's paintings. The only one she remembered was "The Apostle Bartholomew." She'd been struck by the way Rembrandt depicted him wearing what she assumed was contemporary clothing instead of whatever people wore in the Near East two thousand years ago.

In the here and now, Rembrandt was still shy of thirty years old. And, like so many artists whose work had survived in the up-time books—Rubens had been effectively paralyzed as an artist for quite some time because of it—he was simultaneously gratified and exasperated. What does an artist who *would* be famous do when he *wouldn't* be famous yet—but was famous, now, simply because he *would* be in another universe?

And, worst of all, could actually see images of paintings he hadn't done yet. In many cases, hadn't even thought of yet. What does he do? Create those same paintings over again?

A few did, in fact. Agnes O'Malley had picked up a book on the Italian artist Guido Reni in a museum she'd visited on the West Coast shortly before the Ring of Fire. Apparently she'd been taken by some of the images, especially the cover image of "Bacchus and Ariadne."

Agnes had died early in 1634, being in her late seventies by then, and her daughter Aggie had donated the book to the Grantville library. By pure happenstance, Reni himself had come to Grantville a short time later while the book was still on display as a newly acquired item. When the library refused to sell it to him, Reni had spent days at one of the tables there copying sketches of his own work he hadn't done yet, which included what was probably his best-known painting—best-known in another universe, not his own—titled "Saint Michael Archangel."

Rita had been told by her husband that Reni had been holed up in his studio in Bologna since he'd left Grantville, doing what amounted to duplicates of his own work. What Tom had found particularly amusing about the man's peculiar obsession was that he'd done "Saint Michael Archangel" originally in order to gain favor with the Barberini family—one of whose members was now Pope Urban VIII—by giving the figure of the devil trampled underfoot by Saint Michael the face of Cardinal Giovanni Battista Pamphili, a prominent member of a family hostile to the Barberinis.

Unfortunately for Reni, Urban VIII was now on the run after Borja's *coup d'etat* in Rome the previous year—and the Pamphili family were long-time partisans of the Spanish faction in the Vatican which now held power.

"He'd better hope Borja never finds out about that painting he's trying to duplicate," Tom had said, chuckling a little. "Or he's toast."

Most artists, however, were of Rubens' mind on the subject. They went out of their way not to duplicate work they'd done— would have done, however you wanted to say it; grammar got pretzelized by the Ring of Fire—but sought out different subjects.

Rembrandt had gotten intrigued by the betrothal of Bonnie and Heinz, especially the juxtaposition between the up-time Baptist—a creed that was just beginning to emerge down-time— and the Lutheran born in this era. Perhaps that was because Rembrandt himself had come from a mixed family, his father being a member of the Dutch Reformed Church and his mother a Roman Catholic.

Whatever his reasons, Rembrandt had insisted that the couple had to pose for him whenever they were in Amsterdam. And then, as he neared completion of the work, he'd come up to Hoorn for the final stages.

"Talk about weird," had been Bonnie's assessment of the situation. "I can absolutely guarantee you, Rita, that if anyone had asked me to predict my future back in April of 2000, just before the Ring of Fire, 'being someday in a portrait by Rembrandt' would not have made the list anywhere. Not even the millionth entry."

The airship they were touring was another exception to the rule. There was simply nothing like this up-time. There hadn't been since the great era of the ocean-crossing zeppelins in the

1930s, which was brought to an end by the *Hindenburg* disaster in 1937. No aircraft except jumbo jets in Rita's time had had the space on board that this Dutch zeppelin did—and it was modestly sized compared to something like the *Hindenburg.* That 1930s era airship had been eight hundred feet long, with a diameter of one hundred and thirty-five feet; the corresponding dimensions of the airship Rita was touring were half that—four hundred and fifty feet long; fifty feet in diameter—and the envelope volume was far smaller.

It was still huge, compared to any up-time airliner Rita had ever flown in. *Forget cramped seats in coach!* The thought was almost gleeful. This airship had an actual *dining room.* A small one, granted. But there were still tables with comfortable chairs around them—and best of all, what would be a spectacular view once the zeppelin was in the air, since there was an entire bank of windows along one side of the chamber.

True, the windows themselves were a bit weird. Making large flat panes of glass was difficult for seventeenth-century technology, so the window panes of the airship were of the type common in the era: a crosshatch of small diamond-shaped panes, each of which was only a few inches across.

Who cared? When the time came—very soon, now—for them to take command of the airship, they'd be just about the only people in Europe traveling to a war zone in *style.*

When the tour was over, Kortenaer asked the question whose answer Rita and Bonnie and Heinz had been wrestling with for days.

"Have you decided what to call her?" he asked. "We still have time to paint the name on the envelope."

The obvious solution would have been to title her the *Gustav II Adolf.* You could never go wrong in this day and age flattering monarchy. But Rita and Bonnie had bridled at the idea, and while Heinz favored it—ever the practical junior official whose father was a Lutheran pastor—he wasn't prepared to fight over the issue.

They'd then spent a day plowing through Greek and Latin mythology, adopting and discarding one name after another: *Mercury, Daedalus*—*Icarus* was a nonstarter, of course—*Pegasus* and *Phoenix.* For a while, Rita had championed *Dragon,* for no particularly good reason except she was getting cranky. Probably for the same reason, Bonnie had spent an hour or two plumping for *Thunderbird.*

Finally, Heinz had saved the day by applying the tried and tested principles of the junior bureaucrat: *find the established rule; failing that, invent one.*

"I think all airships in the service of the USE military should be named after cities. So we should name this one the *Magdeburg.*"

"The *Dresden,*" Rita and Bonnie countered simultaneously.

"Are you actively *trying* to pick a fight with the emperor?" Heinz complained.

He...had a point.

"Okay, fine," said Bonnie. "The *Magdeburg* it is."

"The *Magdeburg,*" Rita announced.

The Dutch engineer nodded. "And would you like that spelled out in Fraktur?"

"Yes," said Heinz.

"No way," said Rita and Bonnie.

Wallenstein's Palace
Prague, capital of Bohemia

"That leaves simply the matter of Royal Hungary," Janos concluded, setting down the papers he'd been occasionally consulting as he summarized the provisions of the treaty.

"I repeat my offer, Janos," said Wallenstein. The three-way negotiations between Austria-Hungary, the USE and Bohemia had gone on long enough that they'd gotten to be on first-name terms by now. At least, Drugeth and Wallenstein had. Janos still wouldn't have dreamed of calling Gustav II Adolf anything but "Your Majesty."

Drugeth nodded. "And I appreciate it, Albrecht. But I still feel it would produce a very difficult situation for me to be simultaneously owing allegiance to you as well as the emperor of Austria-Hungary. And there's no other way I could retain my lands in Royal Hungary after the transfer to Bohemia. So I must decline."

Lying propped up on his bed, Wallenstein studied him for a moment longer. Then he gave his head a wry little shake. "That sort of loyalty is rare. I hope your monarch appreciates it."

Janos shrugged. "I believe he does. But it doesn't really matter whether he does or not. A man with principles does not choose his course of action based on the likely reward or punishment."

"You will lose most of your property—your income with it—as soon as the treaty is finalized." Wallenstein glanced at Noelle for a moment. "And you are soon to be married again, with a family to care for."

Noelle usually spoke little at these sessions with Wallenstein. Today, she hadn't spoken at all. But now, she did.

"Janos' income will be quite sufficient," she said firmly. "You perhaps forget, Your Majesty"—she wasn't about to refer to Wallenstein any other way—"that I was born and raised a commoner in a small town. I am accustomed to getting by—getting by quite well, in fact—on fairly limited means."

Wallenstein now subjected Noelle to the same intent study. She reminded herself that it never paid to underestimate this man. Yes, he had most of the unthinking prejudices and biases of his time and place. But he was also extraordinarily intelligent and able to set aside those attitudes when he made the effort.

"You are looking at the matter too narrowly," he said. "Yours will probably not be a morganatic marriage, you know. Ferdinand hasn't ruled on the question yet, but my guess is that he will rule the way Janos has asked him to. If he does, that means you will have responsibilities you would not have if you were simply Janos Drugeth's spouse."

Noelle was uncomfortably aware of that already. She'd urged Janos not to make an issue of it, but he'd gotten stubborn and pressed his case upon the emperor. That put Ferdinand in something of an awkward position, because Austria-Hungary had still not clarified the legal position of up-timers in terms of the empire's class structure. The device of referring to them as *von Up-time* had become a fairly widespread custom, but was still not a matter of settled law.

"There is a simple solution to all of this," Wallenstein said abruptly. "Your wedding will happen after the treaty is signed and the Slovakian portion of Royal Hungary is transferred from Austria-Hungary to Bohemia. During that period, I will ennoble Noelle as the countess of Homonna." He waved his hand. "For services rendered to the crown of Bohemia, which is true enough. I can do that because I'm the king of Bohemia and if anyone objects they will regret it."

For just that moment—cold, cold moment—Noelle got a glimpse of the man who had ordered the Croat raid on Grantville and its high school.

"There, Janos," Wallenstein went on. "All problems are solved. Ferdinand is spared the need of making a final ruling on the class status of up-timers—not for long, I suspect, but that's his headache—and you get your family's lands back but with the sufficient—what's that handy American expression?"

"Cover," Noelle supplied. "Or fig leaf."

"Yes, that. With the cover that the lands are really your bride's, not yours, so you can evade the necessity of swearing allegiance to me."

He gave Noelle a smile that had a sly edge to it. "Of course, she will have to do so."

If he'd thought to catch her off guard, the attempt failed. Noelle had figured that part out already.

She'd have to hold her nose, figuratively speaking. But the Roths had already sworn allegiance to Wallenstein, and so far as she could tell neither one of them had started growing horns or hooves so she could probably get away with doing it, too.

"Of course, Your Majesty," she said. Her own smile was very sweet. Dripping with honey. Well, saccharine.

Chapter 34

Deggendorf, Bavaria
At the confluence of the Danube and Isar Rivers

When Major Tom Simpson returned to the headquarters he'd set up in one of the smaller taverns of Deggendorf, he was surprised to see Ursula Gerisch waiting for him. Surprised—and not pleased. At the moment, his attitude toward religion in general was not as genial and relaxed as it usually was. Having to keep the peace between the more ardent CoC members in his unit and the SoTF National Guard company which Heinrich Schmidt had detached to aid him in the salvage work and Deggendorf's Catholic population was trying his patience.

The problem was the so-called "Deggendorfer Gnad." It was one of the more popular pilgrimages in the Catholic areas of Central Europe, and drew somewhere around forty thousand people to the town every year.

So far, so good. Unfortunately, the event that had initiated *this* pilgrimage had not been the sort of thing—apparitions of the Virgin Mary, usually—that had begun the pilgrimages at Santiago de Compostela, Altötting, Medugorje and Czestochowa, and would do the same at Fatimah and Lourdes in later centuries.

No, the Deggendorfer Gnad had begun as a result of a pogrom against the city's Jews two hundred years earlier. The real cause of the massacre had almost certainly been the high debts the town's residents owed some Jewish moneylenders. But it didn't take long before the bloody deed was disguised by a very different legend that turned the slaughter into an act of piety.

Tom had seen the inscription in Deggendorf's basilica himself, after some irate soldiers had brought the matter to his attention:

> *In the year of the Lord 1337, on the day after Mich-*
> *aelmas, the Jews were slain. They had set fire to the*
> *town. Then the body of God was found. This was seen*
> *by women and men and the building of the house of*
> *God was begun.*

The bit about "finding the body of God" was obviously a reference to the charge of host desecration, which was almost as popular as blood libel as a way to whip up Christian fanatics and bigots. Too many years had gone by to determine exactly what had happened, but it didn't really matter.

On the one hand, the Bavarian establishment—secular and religious alike—had come down squarely in support of the pilgrimage. That had been true going back to Heinrich XIV, the duke of Bavaria at the time, who had promptly forgiven the citizens and allowed them to keep the loot they'd plundered from the city's Jews. And it was still true: one of the strongest current supporters of the Deggendorfer Gnad was none other than Duke Maximilian's younger brother Albrecht, whom Tom knew Mike Stearns wanted to make the new duke of Bavaria if Maximilian could be forced to abdicate.

On the other hand, the army of the USE—the National Guard of the State of Thuringia-Franconia wasn't much different, in this respect—was heavily CoC in its composition and attitudes. Those were the soldiers who were now ruling the roost in Deggendorf—everywhere in northern Bavaria—and a fair number of them had joined the army right after participating in the so-called Kristall-nacht slaughter of anti-Semites all over the Germanies after the Dreeson Incident.

And they were perfectly willing to visit the same treatment upon the be-damned foul medieval bootlicking lackeys who infested Deggendorf.

Just what Tom needed. Holding back a pogrom of pogrom-celebrants with one hand while he tried to raise two great heavy monster naval rifles from a river bed where (cough cough) an unfortunate accident had sent them plunging.

For that reason, the sight of Ursula Gerisch sitting quietly at a table in the corner of the tavern did not lift his spirits. What did *this* religious fanatic want?

Fine, he was overstating the matter. Excessively enthusiastic convert to his own church, how's that? There was probably something in Episcopal canon law that forbade outright fanaticism.

There was no point in stalling, though. Ursula Gerisch was nothing if not persistent. So he marched over, looked down at her—loomed over her forbiddingly, being honest about it—and said sternly: "What do you need, Ursula?"

The look the young woman gave him was odd. It seemed to be part-reproachful and part-beseechful. But mostly, it seemed hopeful.

"Is it true, what I read?" she asked. "In one of the pamphlets that Frau Riddle sent me."

Veleda Riddle was sending her *pamphlets,* too? Just what the world needed. A well-informed fanatic. *Excuse me, excessively enthusiastic convert to my own church.*

Ursula hurried on. "The church—your church—now my church, too—will ordain women as priests. Is this true? In one of the pamphlets, there are pictures of women priests. I saw them with my own eyes."

For a brief moment, Tom had an image of himself—his huge hands, rather—throttling the life out of a white-haired old woman.

The image was fleeting; gone before even one second had elapsed. He felt a moment's guilt, even—although that didn't last much longer.

There was no evading those upward-looking, imploring eyes.

He sighed, pulled out a chair, and sat down at the table across from her. Then, slowly and carefully, he removed his hat and set it gently on the table.

"Yes, Ursula, it's true. The Protestant Episcopal Church in the United States of America, of which"—*God help me*, but he didn't say it out loud—"I am a bishop, started ordaining women as priests back in..."

He couldn't remember the exact date. '76? '77? Somewhere in the mid-70s.

That would be the mid-*nineteen hundred* seventies. Most assuredly not the mid-*sixteen hundred* seventies—which were still forty years off in the here and now.

Which meant a quarter of a millennium off, in whatever you called "real cultural time."

"About thirty years ago," he said. "That was up-time, you understand."

Ursula nodded. "Yes. I do not envy you, Bishop Simpson. Having to make a ruling as to how up-time canon law applies to us." She gave him a gleaming smile. "But I am sure you will come to the correct decision."

She rose and curtsied. "I must be off. I have to get back as soon as possible."

"Get back..."

"To Dresden. I told Gretchen I would bring her the news as soon as I spoke to you." And off she went.

The tavern keeper came up. "Would you like a stein of beer, Major?"

Tom didn't normally drink while he was on duty; which, technically, he still was until... He pulled out his pocket watch. Two more hours.

Screw it. "Yes, please."

The tavern keeper went to fetch it.

Tom weighed the likely results if he did...

Archbishop Laud would probably have a stroke.

The Anglican Communion would be stillborn in this universe.

Then he weighed the likely results if he didn't...

Would Gretchen Richter lead a schism and separate the Protestant Episcopal Church of the Province of Saxony from the Protestant Episcopal Church of the United States of Europe?

Does a she-bear shit in the woods?

"Well, fuck me," he said.

Dresden, capital of Saxony

"This is utterly ridiculous! Do you hear me, Krenz? *Ridiculous!*"

But Eric stood his ground. Didn't even flinch. "It is *not* ridiculous, Gretchen. I've been in a battle. More than once! You haven't. On a battlefield, you need to wear armor. It's not enough to just have a helmet."

Gretchen glared at him. "Stop making things up. I've seen the uniforms you wear. The most you ever have is a buff coat."

"Well, of course. *We* were just volley gunners. Or later, when I got promoted, I was an *infantry* officer." He made a motion with his upper body as if he were about to dive. "You need to be able to get down on the ground quickly. But you—*you* are the commander in chief. *You* will need to be up on a horse. Way up where the enemy can see you—and they'll be shooting at you, don't think they won't."

He turned to the two Poles standing near, both of whom were grinning.

"You tell her."

Jozef Wojtowicz managed to get the grin off his face before Gretchen could transfer the glare onto him.

"He's basically right, Gretchen," said Jozef. "Unless you plan to command from all the way in the rear."

"Which is not wrong, you know," added Lukasz. "Grand Hetman Koniecpolski doesn't lead charges himself. He hasn't for many years."

"I'm not planning to lead any cavalry charges either," said Gretchen, almost hissing the words. She jerked a thumb in the direction of Lovrenc Bravnicar. "He'll be the one doing that."

Jozef glanced at Eric Krenz. Seeing the look of appeal in the young officer's face, he sighed and ran fingers through his hair. "Gretchen, you're talking as if you were going to be commanding a real army. But you aren't. You're going to be trying to herd—well, not cats, no. But you're going to be trying to get groups of men who have very different experiences and customs, and have never fought together, to act as if they were an army. Which they are not. Not yet, anyway."

"That means you have to be seen," said Lukasz. "*Really* seen. Not just glimpsed now and then but seen by everybody and seen all the time. And there's no way to do that on a battlefield without the enemy being able to see you as well. They *will* try to kill you."

"And that's where the armor comes in," said Krenz hurriedly. "You won't be *close* to them, Gretchen. They'll be shooting at you from far away. Far enough that good armor will stop even a bullet. Or shrapnel from an artillery shell that lands nearby."

Gretchen gave Krenz a hard look for a few seconds, then transferred the look to the two Poles. And then, softening a bit—just a bit—her eyes went to Tata.

"What do you think?"

"I think you should wear the armor," came the immediate response.

Gretchen shifted her gaze to look at the assembled pieces that, properly fitted and shaped, would eventually form a suit of armor that would fit her.

"I will feel ridiculous," she predicted. "*Ridiculous*."

"That's all right," said Tata. "Only still alive people feel ridiculous."

The proverbial gleam came to Gretchen's eyes. She gave the two Poles a sudden grin.

"You're making me nervous, Gretchen," said Jozef.

"Me too," agreed Lukasz.

"If I'm to be a commander who has to appear in front of all on the field of battle, then surely I need bodyguards. Gustav Adolf has bodyguards, doesn't he? So! Who better to serve as my bodyguards than two hussars? In *full* armor."

She turned the gleaming gaze onto the armorer in whose shop this was all taking place. "Can you make hussar armor?"

He frowned. "Yes, I suppose. But it's very expensive. Is Saxony going to pay for that along with your own armor?"

"No, I'll pay for it myself. I'll sell some stock. I have lots of stock." She actually had no idea how to turn stock into liquid cash, but she'd send a telegram to David Bartley. He'd do it for her.

"Gretchen!" protested Lukasz. "We can't!"

"Why not?"

"Because—because—" He looked to Wojtowicz for help.

"It will look bad, Gretchen." Jozef indicated himself and Lukasz with a quick flick of his thumb and forefinger. "We're Poles. We can't be seen fighting on your side against... Well, technically, Holk's army is in the service of Poland."

"That's a lie and you know it. And the solution to the problem is obvious. Fly a Polish battle flag from your lances." She looked back at the armorer. "You *do* have lances, don't you?"

"I can make some," the armorer replied. He gave the two Poles a dubious look. "But they won't be those peculiar lightweight Polish things. They'll be real lances. German-style lances."

"Lances are lances," Gretchen proclaimed, never having held one in her life. "Big long spears. That'll do well enough to hold a banner. And these two probably won't have to do any fighting anyway because"—her eyes truly were gleaming—"my armored awesomeness will surely cause the enemy to flee as soon as they lay eyes on me. And my two Polish hussars."

Lukasz and Jozef looked at each other. Then Jozef shrugged. "I suppose if we ever get put on trial before the Sejm we could claim we were just passing by and saw what we mistook as an allied army fighting a horde of what looked like unregistered Cossacks..."

Lukasz wiped his face with a large hand. "Stop, Jozef. Just stop."

Grantville, State of Thuringia-Franconia

"Telegram for you, Mrs. Riddle." The teenager standing on her porch handed Veleda a piece of paper that had been folded over twice and sealed with a blob of wax. The blob had then been stamped with the design of the telegraph company, a particularly ornate symbol because the lettering was in Fraktur.

"Thank you." Frowning—who would be sending her a telegram from—she checked the return address—someplace called Deggendorf? She had no idea where that was.

She opened the telegram and read it. By the time she finished, which was only a few seconds because it was not a long message, the frown had vanished. Replaced by very wide eyes and a startled look.

"Oh, my," she said, then hurried inside to the telephone.

"Vanessa? Veleda here. We need to have a church meeting. Yes, the whole church. Except for Father Barneby. I'll explain why at the meeting."

"This is insane!" said Christie Kemp. "Utterly insane—and now I understand why you didn't want the Reverend to be here, Veleda. He'd have had a fit."

"Why is it insane?" countered Marshall Kitt. "We had female priests up-time. St. Thomas á Becket Church in Morgantown had one. She'd been there for—" He looked at his wife Vanessa. "How long was—"

"That was up-time!" Christie half-shouted. She threw up her hands for emphasis. "Up-time! In case you hadn't noticed, we're down-time now. *Nobody* has female clergy here and now. You hear me? Nobody! Not even the Unitarians in Transylvania."

Veleda eyed her skeptically. "How do you know anything at all about a church in Transylvania?"

Christie waved the objection aside. "I don't need to know the specifics. It's obvious. If we Episcopalians try to ordain a woman priest we'll be the laughingstock of the continent—if we're lucky!"

Marshall Kitt leaned back in his armchair and gave Kemp a hard look. "Let me see if I've got this straight, Christie. If any woman is going to get ordained in the Episcopal church it'll be this Ursula Gerisch woman. And she'll get ordained in Dresden because she'll presumably have the support of Gretchen Richter. That would be the same Gretchen Richter who held off the Spanish army at Amsterdam and Banér's army at Dresden, and is now likely to get elected as the chancellor of Saxony. So I really don't think it's too likely that anything worse than being laughed at will happen to us—and ask me if I give a good God-damn what some benighted backward jackass thinks of me and my faith."

"She a dangerous radical!"

"Well, yeah. I thought that was the point I just made."

USE naval base
Luebeck

Admiral John Chandler Simpson's wife Mary happened to be visiting him when the telegram arrived from Veleda Riddle. After reading it, the admiral handed it to her.

"You'll love this," he said.

Mary Simpson read through it twice. "I don't see what all the fuss is about." She gave her husband a rather arch look. "I'm sorry if it took you Episcopalians until the 1970s to finally get around to it, but we Unitarians ordained our first female minister all the way back in 1871. That would be *eighteen* seventy-one. Celia Burleigh, her name was."

"Yes, dear, I know. You've told me before." His patient tone was replaced by a more mischievous one. "But I will point out that 1871—that would be *eighteen* seventy-one—is exactly two hundred and thirty-five years from *now*. That would be the year *sixteen* thirty-six. Not even your precious Socinians have female clergy, so far as I know."

Mary pursed her lips and tapped them with the rolled-up telegram. "I'm pretty sure you're right. I think the very first female clergy—well, since the very first centuries when there's some evidence of women serving as priests—came out of the Society of Friends. The Quakers, as they're usually called. But I don't think they even exist yet, and if they do it'd only be in England. Hmm..."

"You're making me nervous, Mary."

"I think I may visit Dresden soon. Our son probably needs some encouragement"—she gave her husband a very mischievous smile—"seeing as how he's now a bishop. First one ever in the family, I believe."

Chapter 35

Magdeburg, capital of the United States of Europe

"We have certainly won a majority in the House of Commons, that much is clear already." For a moment, Rebecca continued to study the big map of the USE hanging on the wall of the meeting room, and then stepped over to the blackboard next to it.

"As far as the provinces are concerned, here is what we know so far."

She began writing in big, clear Roman letters. No Fraktur here.

> *PROVINCES SURE TO ELECT*
> *FOURTH OF JULY MAJORITIES*
> > *Mecklenburg*
> > *Magdeburg*
> > *Saxony*
> > *Thuringia-Franconia*
> > *Württemberg*
> > *Oberpfalz*

"So, six out of sixteen," said Constantin Ableidinger. "What we expected—but it does mean we'll be in a definite minority in the House of Lords."

Rebecca shook her head. "You're jumping to conclusions. Wait until I finish." She went back to writing.

PROVINCES SURE TO ELECT
CROWN LOYALIST MAJORITIES
   Westphalia
   Brunswick
   Hesse-Kassel
   Tyrol

PROVINCES SURE TO ELECT
REACTIONARY MAJORITIES
   Pomerania

"Huh!" exclaimed Ableidinger. "That can't be right, Rebecca."

"What? That Pomerania would be run by a pack of medieval hooligans?" demanded Charlotte Kienitz. "What rock have you been hiding under, Constantin? We all knew Pomerania would—"

He waved a big hand irritably. "No, no! I'm not talking about Pomerania. Back up. I was referring to the list of provinces who'll be electing Crown Loyalist majorities. There can't just be those four. What about Jülich-Berg, the Upper Rhine and the Province of the Main—and Swabia, for that matter?"

Rebecca's face might have held just a trace of annoyance. Just a trace, though. The young Sephardic woman was a natural diplomat.

"Please, Constantin. Patience. I'll get to them."

He settled back in his chair and she added one more province to the list of those which would be electing reactionary leaderships:

Brandenburg

"Now we get to the provinces you were wondering about," said Rebecca. She went back to writing on the blackboard.

PROVINCES WHERE THE
ELECTION IS STILL UNDECIDED
   Jülich-Berg
   Upper Rhine
   Main
   Swabia

Finished, she set the chalk down. "Based on the returns so far, our best guess is that the Crown Loyalists will wind up with majorities—rather slim, but still clear majorities—in the provinces of the Main and the Upper Rhine."

"And Swabia? Jülich-Berg?" asked Ableidinger. Charlotte Kienitz scowled at him. So did just about everyone else packed into the room.

"Let's start up a chant," proposed Albert Bugenhagen, the mayor of Hamburg. "Constantin, be quiet! Constantin, be quiet! Let Rebecca finish!"

The chant was immediately taken up by most of the people there.

"CONSTANTIN, BE QUIET! CONSTANTIN, BE QUIET! LET REBECCA FINISH!"

The one-time leader of the Ram movement, currently a Member of Parliament from a district in Franconia, grinned. "I make no promises," he said. "Silence does not come naturally to me."

"Understatement of the century," muttered Charlotte. "Please go on, Rebecca."

"Swabia is turning out to be a surprise," Rebecca said. "We thought the Crown Loyalists would probably win the same sort of majority they look likely to win in Main and the Upper Rhine. Instead, it looks as if *we* might win the province—and by a surprising margin."

"How sure are you?" asked Matthias Strigel, the governor of Magdeburg province.

Rebecca looked to the side and gestured at a young woman standing against the wall. "I will let Gisela explain. She's the one on our staff who's been following Swabia the closest."

She gestured again. "Come, Gisela. Don't be shy."

A little uncertainly, the young woman stepped forward and came to stand beside Rebecca in front of the big blackboard. Then, realizing where she was, she moved over a bit to stand in front of the map. "Is there..."

Rebecca pointed to a wand hanging by a nail. "Use that as a pointer."

Gisela took the wand in hand. "Swabia is a hard province to follow because it's so spread out. When Württemberg became its own province"—she placed the pointer on it—"what seems to have happened politically is that different regions in Swabia next to it became heavily influenced by the three big imperial cities in the area, Strassburg, Ulm and Augsburg."

Quickly, Gisela tapped the spots indicating the imperial cities in question. Strassburg and its large hinterland were on the western border of Swabia, nestled between Burgundy and Lorraine. Augsburg, whose hinterland was much smaller, was on the opposite side of the province, right on the Bavarian border. Ulm, also with a large hinterland, was more-or-less in the middle of Swabia, abutting Württemberg.

"Ulm is solidly Crown Loyalist in its sympathies," Gisela continued, "and their attitudes affect this whole area of Swabia"—the wand swept up and down along the edge of the imperial city—"especially to the south, near Tyrol. But Strassburg and Augsburg have become more and more favorable to our party over the past period."

"Strassburg, too?" asked Kienitz. "I knew that was true of Augsburg."

"Oh, yes." Gisela smiled. "There seems to be a rough rule of thumb that applies most everywhere in the United States of Europe—well, except for in Brandenburg and Pomerania. The closer an area is to a war zone or a possible war zone, the more likely they are to be favorable to the Fourth of July Party."

"But—" That came from Strigel, who was frowning in puzzlement. "I realize that nobody has much trust in Bernhard of Saxe-Weimar—well, I suppose I should call him Grand Duke Bernhard, since we've officially recognized his County of Burgundy—and there's been some chaos in Lorraine lately. But that was caused by the French who look to be starting their own civil war, since Louis was murdered and Gaston made himself the new king. It doesn't seem to have much to do with us."

Rebecca issued a soft laugh. "You underestimate the power of romance, Matthias."

"What does that mean?"

"It is widely known in Strassburg—all of western Swabia, I imagine—that we recently sent Captain Harry Lefferts into Lorraine to help Duchess Nicole restore peace to her principality." She spread her hands, as if offering something up for inspection. "You see? Wherever there is trouble with foreigners, you are always better served to send someone like Captain Lefferts. What good are Crown Loyalists for that?"

"It's the same thing that's affecting the election in Jülich-Berg," said Gisela. "People haven't forgotten the destruction caused by Hessian troops when Wilhelm V tried to seize Bonn and Cologne.

There's a lot of hard feelings still—but it also reinforces the attitude that the Fourth of July Party is a lot more interested in fighting enemies than it is in grabbing stuff for itself."

"Do you really think we might *win* in Jülich-Berg?" asked Ableidinger.

"No way to know yet," said Rebecca. "Jülich-Berg is a new province so it still does not have much experience with organizing elections and tabulating the results. Swabia is not much better. So it will be a while before the final results are in. My guess is that the Crown Loyalists will wind up winning the election in Jülich-Berg, but by a slim margin."

"But you're sure about the general outcome?" asked Strigel.

"Oh, yes," said Rebecca. "Here, I'll show you." She picked up a rag and wiped off the chalk marks she'd made earlier, then started writing afresh.

PERCENTAGE OF VOTE PER
PROVINCE FOR FOJP
  Magdeburg (80%)
  Mecklenburg (70%)
  Saxony (70%)
  Thuringia-Franconia (65%)
  Württemberg (60%)
  Oberpfalz (60%)

"These are rough estimates, of course. But we don't expect them to vary by more than five percent either way." She went back to writing.

Westphalia (45%)
Brunswick (40%)
Hesse-Kassel (40%)

"Huh! We got that much in Hesse-Kassel too?" said Ableidinger in his booming voice. "I would have thought—"

"CONSTANTIN, BE QUIET! CONSTANTIN, BE QUIET! LET REBECCA FINISH!"

Ableidinger laughed—boomingly. But he did shut up.

Rebecca wrote the name of the last definitely Crown Loyalist province.

Tyrol (20%)

"As you can see," she said, "the only province where the Crown Loyalists have run up the kind of super-majorities that we have in most of our provinces is Tyrol." She shrugged. "Which became part of the USE very recently, and has never—so far—had much in the way of a CoC or FOJ presence."

She set down the chalk again. "So, yes, there is no doubt that we will have an absolute majority in Parliament." She bestowed a smile on Ed Piazza, who was sitting in his usual seat at the middle of the big table in the center. "All hail our new prime minister!"

"ALL HAIL! ALL HAIL!"

The room burst into laughter. Ed made a face.

When things had settled down, Rebecca resumed speaking. "The results from the imperial cities favor us as well," she said.

Once again, she used the cloth to erase the blackboard. "Here are the results from there. These are quite accurate, by the way. By now, all of the imperial cities can produce quick and accurate election tallies. I will rank them in order."

Magdeburg (88%)

That produced a big cheer. Rebecca ignored it and kept writing.

Luebeck (72%)
Hamburg (64%)
Augsburg (57%)
Strassburg (52%)
Ulm (45%)
Cologne (43%)
Frankfurt am Main (38%)

"Again, we see the same pattern. Our majorities are simply greater than theirs, almost everywhere. The only real exception is Tyrol."

"What about Pomerania and Brandenburg?" asked Charlotte.

Rebecca softly slapped her hands together to brush off the chalk. "I won't bother writing it down. For one thing, because those two provinces are very slow about tallying the election results. Our best guess at the moment is that the Crown Loyalists will get somewhere around one-third of the vote, we will get one-tenth—if we're lucky—and a not-so-small pack of reactionaries will wind up with a clear majority. Whether or not they'll be able to form actual functioning government majorities is anybody's guess. Probably, in Brandenburg; probably not, in Pomerania."

"Who would run the province, then?" asked Bugenhagen.

"For all practical purposes, Pomerania has been directly administered by the Swedes for years. I expect that to continue, with one or another reactionary as the official governor of the province." She smiled, rather sardonically. "Knowing Gustav Adolf, he will make sure it is some docile eighty-year-old dimwit."

That got another laugh from the whole room. As did Ableidinger's follow-on quip: "A deaf, dumb and blind octogenarian! Our emperor is no slouch!"

Ed Piazza had not been participating in the jests. Instead, he'd been scribbling in a notebook. He now looked up, his lips pursed, and issued a whistle of surprise.

"I think we may even wind up dominating the House of Lords. Assuming we get the imperial cities added to it—which we ought to, if we wind up with the kind of majority in the House of Commons that Rebecca thinks we're going to get."

"How is that possible?" asked Strigel, frowning. "Most of the provinces have hereditary or appointed heads of state."

"It's more complicated than that," said Piazza. "Rebecca, can you put what I read up on the blackboard? Thank you."

As Ed began reading from his notes, Rebecca transferred the information so everyone in the room could read it.

> *PROVINCES WITH ELECTED*
> *HEADS OF STATE*
> > *Magdeburg*
> > *Mecklenburg*
> > *Saxony*
> > *Thuringia-Franconia*
> > *Württemberg*
> > *Oberpfalz*

PROVINCES WITH HEREDITARY
HEADS OF STATE
   Westphalia
   Brunswick
   Hesse-Kassel
   Tyrol
   Jülich-Berg

"So far, as you can see, the split falls exactly along party lines. The six provinces with elected heads of state are all Fourth of July, the five with hereditary provinces, all Crown Loyalist except for possibly Jülich-Berg." He grinned, very cheerily. "One of the side effects of Gustav Adolf settling accounts with John George of Saxony and his brother-in-law the former elector of Brandenburg is that those two provinces no longer have hereditary rulers. Saxony is now a republic and Brandenburg—at least for the moment—is under direct imperial administration.

"Now, moving right along... Rebecca, would you please list the provinces under direct imperial administration?"

She put them up on the blackboard:

   Pomerania
   Brandenburg
   Upper Rhine
   Main
   Swabia

After she finished, everyone contemplated the list for a while.

"Huh," said Ableidinger. "We have six, the Crown Loyalists have five—and our sneaky way-too-smart emperor has the remaining five by proxy. Did I say 'proxy'? No, no—a hundred times, no! The cunning of the man knows no bounds. He *is* the head of all five of those states, as—what are the titles? I forget. 'Duke of Pomerania' is one of them."

"It doesn't matter," said Piazza. "Constantin's quite right. Essentially, the House of Lords is divided almost equally into thirds: one-third us, one third the Crown Loyalists, one-third Gustav Adolf."

He leaned forward in his chair. "But now look what happens

if we add the eight imperial cities to the House of Lords. Rebecca, if you'd do the honors..."

Again, she had to erase everything on the blackboard to make room for the new material.

IMPERIAL CITIES, PARTY
AFFILIATION FoJP
   Magdeburg
   Luebeck
   Hamburg
   Augsburg
   Strassburg

IMPERIAL CITIES, PARTY
AFFILIATION CROWN LOYALIST
   Ulm
   Frankfurt am Main
   Cologne?

"We are actually not sure how Cologne will line up politically," Rebecca said. "The same issue is involved with Jülich-Berg. One the one hand, Duchess Katharina Charlotte is the hereditary ruler of the province and as such someone we would expect to be inclined toward the Crown Loyalists. On the other hand, she has had a very recent unpleasant experience with Hesse-Kassel, whose current ruler Amalie Elisabeth is one of the recognized central leaders of the Crown Loyalists. In addition, she is Catholic and the city of Cologne is very staunchly Catholic.

"It makes for a complicated situation. The area is politically rather conservative but is also Catholic and has just recently fought what amounted to a war against Protestant Hesse-Kassel—and all of the Crown Loyalist leaders and provinces are Protestant. So Katharina Charlotte and Cologne might very well look toward us for protection of their religious freedoms. We will just have to see what happens."

"But for the moment," said Piazza, "let's assume that Jülich-Berg lines up with the Crown Loyalists. What does that leave us, in terms of seats in the House of Lords?"

Strigel had been doing the arithmetic and provided the answer. "We still don't have a majority but we certainly have a clear plurality: Out of a total of twenty-four seats, we have eleven—and if either Jülich-Berg or Cologne sides with us on any question, we will have half the votes. This is *much* better than I expected."

"Yes, it is," said Piazza. "Especially because on a number of issues—not all, of course—we can expect Gustav Adolf will be more inclined to side with us than with the Crown Loyalists. Let's start with this. He is sure to be favorably inclined to our position that Harlingen and Bremen should be added as imperial cities, because that would strengthen the USE's naval position. And, for somewhat different reasons, both of those would be strongly FOJ in their political sympathies. Probably at least as much as Hamburg."

"Which would give us a clear majority in the House of Lords," said Strigel.

"Yes," said Piazza. "Although—a cautioning note, here—in the House of Lords the emperor is always going to have a lot of influence. If he were strongly opposed to us on some issue, I don't have much doubt he'd be able to sway enough of the imperial cities to outvote us."

"What's the situation with Oldenburg?" asked Charlotte Kienitz. "If it gets added as a province, it'll vote against us in the House of Lords. Maybe not in the Commons, though."

Piazza looked at Rebecca to provide the answer.

"The negotiations continue," she said. "Count Anthony Günther is of two minds, it seems. On the one hand, he dislikes the Danes and he's certainly not inclined toward becoming part of the Netherlands. That makes him lean toward joining the USE as a province with himself as the hereditary head of state. The problem—as so often—is the history books. The up-time ones, I mean. The details are unknown, but it seems that he had no offspring because after his death Oldenburg was absorbed by Denmark. If true—remember that the American records contained no specific details—then the rulership of Oldenburg if it becomes a province of the USE would pass into the hands of the Vasa dynasty. Which, to put it mildly, does not please the count of Oldenburg."

She shrugged. "Ideally, from his point of view, Anthony Günther would keep Oldenburg an independent principality, as he has done quite successfully since he became the count more than thirty years ago. But that was only possible because of the chaos of the time and the fact that he was able to play one power off against another. With the consolidation of the USE and the reunification of the Netherlands, doing so is no longer realistic and he knows it. But he keeps stalling and I imagine he will do so until the war with Poland ends. At that point, Gustav Adolf will have his army free again and by then he will have lost all his patience with Anthony Günther."

She smiled. "In short, expect a hurried settlement at that point. But not before—"

Hearing the door to the room open, Rebecca broke off and turned to see who was coming in. It was Wilda Scherer, one of her assistants.

"Yes, Wilda?" said Rebecca. "What is it?"

The young women hurried toward her, a telegram in her hand.

"More election results?"

"No, it's from Vienna." Scherer glanced down at the paper. "Well, from Linz." She thrust the telegram into Rebecca's hand, as if she desperately wanted to get rid of it.

Rebecca read the message.

"Oh, dear God," she said.

Part Five

August 1636

Their works drop downward

Chapter 36

Vienna, capital of Austria-Hungary

There were five of the Ottoman airships, it turned out, not three. They came toward Vienna slowly; to all appearances, simply drifting with the wind.

Archduke Leopold Wilhelm peered intently through his spyglass. Each of the airships had something suspended below its gondola. The things looked like big baskets, hanging from ropes. What were they?

Perhaps more to the point, what were they *for*?

"What's the matter, Your Grace?" asked Minnie Hugelmair. She was standing next to him on the bastion, looking over the wall at the slowly approaching Ottoman forces. Their front ranks were still more than a mile away—too far for cannon fire to be effective.

He lowered the spyglass and frowned. "They've got something..." On an impulse, he handed Minnie the spyglass. "See what you can make of it."

As Minnie brought the telescope to her one good eye, Cecilia Renata pushed forward. She and Judy Wendell had been standing a little behind Leopold—where he'd asked her to stay. The archduke wasn't happy that she was here at all. He'd only let the three women join him on the bastion after getting his sister's promise that they'd leave as soon as any firing started.

"What's the matter?" Cecilia Renata repeated.

Before he could answer, Minnie spoke. "They've got what look like great big baskets hanging maybe twenty yards below the gondolas. I'm guessing, but I think—yes, there goes the first one."

She handed the spyglass back to Leopold. "They're producing smoke. I read about the tactic in one of the books in Grantville. It's usually used by naval vessels. Up-time, I mean."

By then, Leopold could see it for himself. Four of the baskets—no, all five now—were producing great billows of white smoke.

He assumed it was smoke, anyway. It looked a lot like fog.

"Is it poisonous?" he asked.

Minnie shrugged. "We'll find out soon enough." Not for the first time, he was struck by the girl's attitude. Hugelmair had probably never read Seneca or Epictetus or Marcus Aurelius—although you could never be sure, with her—but they would have envied her calmly stoic view of things.

"But I don't think so," she added. "The up-timers did use poison gas in at least one of their wars, but they fired them from cannons." She pointed her finger at the slowly nearing airships. "They didn't want to be too close to the stuff. If that's poison gas and the wind shifts, everyone in those gondolas would be dead."

She lowered the finger and shook her head. "I think this is just smoke. But what that means is that they're trying to hide something from us, and whatever that 'something' is can't be anything we're going to be happy about."

Leopold was already unhappy—acutely unhappy. Nothing about this Ottoman assault had made any sense to him, since an orderly had awakened him before dawn.

To begin with, it was coming too soon. The Ottoman trenches were still much too far from Vienna's walls. Any assaulting troops would have to cross hundred of yards of open ground, right in the face of massed cannon fire. They'd only begun their sapping operations, less than three weeks ago—and then, didn't seem to be pushing them energetically.

It was possible that Murad was being reckless—that had been the opinion of most of Leopold's military commanders, at any rate—but Leopold thought it was unwise to assume that your enemy was making a mistake. Maybe he was, maybe he wasn't. Better to assume that he wasn't, however, and try to figure out what he might be undertaking that you hadn't foreseen.

By now, the five smoke clouds had drifted forward and a

little downward. They'd also spread out and were beginning to merge. Within a short time, that would be a solid wall of smoke, obscuring everything from about three hundred yards high right down to the ground.

He didn't bother shouting any orders, though. He could hear officers already doing so, all along the walls. The gist of their orders was simple: *Be alert! For... whatever!*

Following the armored wagon, Uzun Hussein felt like snarling—not at the still-distant Christian enemies on the walls of Vienna but at the Christian bastards manning the wagon right in front of him.

His anger derived partly from simple rivalry. Like all janissaries—he was sure the sipahis felt likewise—Hussein resented the new military units the sultan had created. Most of those soldiers were unbelievers. Christians from the Balkans, as a rule, but there were some Jews from Istanbul as well.

Whichever they were, none of them had any business preceding janissaries into battle.

Yes, yes, he and his fellow janissaries had been assured that the new units, the "special forces" as they were called, would not be supplanting the janissaries when it came time for the climax of the battle, the cut and thrust of sword and spear. But all that meant was that the janissaries would do most of the bleeding and dying, while the stinking infidels shrank away to the sides after doing their "special work."

Mostly, though, Hussein's resentment of the soldiers manning the war wagons had a crude and simple source. The wagons broke down constantly—and when they did, who got to do the mule-work of pulling and pushing and digging them out?

The janissaries, that was who. While the "special forces" did their "special work" that didn't require any sweating.

The wagon just ahead of him slewed sideways. The left front wheel—this was the third time since the assault began!—had gotten jammed into something again. Rabbit holes, badger burrows, almost anything could cause trouble for the wheels despite their width.

The problem was that the wheels were relatively small in diameter and the weight of the wagons they bore was immense. They did not handle rough surfaces well.

One of the Christian swine stuck his head out of the hatch

just to the side and in front of the cannon. "We need a push!" he shouted.

"I'll give you a push," Hussein muttered. He hefted his musket slightly. "Push this right up your ass."

But he didn't, of course. He would have been executed if he had—and, almost as bad, would have soiled his precious new musket. Like all janissaries who'd been supplied with the weapons, Hussein adored his new musket. It was a muzzle-loading flintlock, not one of the breech-loading caplocks that some of the troops had been issued. But it was easy to load, because of the special new Murad ball—so-named because it was said the sultan had invented it himself. Which he might have, for it was a truly ingenious design. The ball was slightly smaller than the bore of the musket and had a flange that expanded when the gun was fired. That made it practical to rifle the bore, greatly improving the weapon's accuracy, without having to force the ball down the barrel. Hussein could fire three rounds a minute with it. Three rounds a minute! And still be able to hit a target twice as far away as he could have with the muskets he'd been accustomed to using.

So, he just set the weapon down and went to lend a shoulder to the effort.

Abraham Zarfati began to relax. Despite what the chymists had told the airship crews, he'd been worried that the smoke they were producing would be noxious—possibly even deadly.

It wasn't pleasant, certainly. While most of the smoke was borne ahead of them by the wind, some of it eddied upward and back. They were running the engine as slowly as possible and in reverse, producing just enough thrust to retard the ship so it stayed behind the smoke instead of running with it. But the process was difficult to control and sometimes they overtook the billowing clouds.

The smoke stank, no question about it. But it didn't interfere with breathing and didn't do more than cause some tearing of the eyes on occasion.

The effect would be worse on the soldiers on the ground, if they had to charge through the smoke. Still, especially with the help of the damp facecloths they'd been provided with, they should be able to get through with no great difficulty.

And there was this added benefit to being one of the crews assigned to create the smoke clouds: once they were done and had dropped the smoke baskets, they'd be out of the fight for some time. They'd have to return to their base, flying into the wind with not-very-powerful steam engines, in order to land, refuel, and load either regular or fire bombs, depending on what their commanders ordered. By the time they got back to the walls of Vienna, the assault would have either succeeded or been driven off. Either way, it was not likely the airships would be in any real danger.

That suited Abraham just fine. He was a sensible Jew. Let the idiot janissaries beat their chests and extol the glories of martial exploits. He'd volunteered for the sultan's new aerial force in order to learn skills that he expected to be quite valuable for him and his family once the war was over.

Of course, there'd be another war afterward. There always were, with sultans—and with this one more than most.

But the thought wasn't hostile; not even grudging. No man in his right mind wanted to anger Murad, for to do so was almost certain to lead to his death. But in most ways the new sultan was capable, and even fair-minded. He was certainly a great improvement over his predecessors.

"I can see the walls now!" shouted Isaac Capsali. He was leaning over the side of the gondola and pointing ahead.

Abraham joined him. And . . . saw nothing.

"Where?" he demanded.

"I *saw* them," insisted Isaac. "But then the smoke swirled back around."

He might be right. Most likely, he'd caught a glimpse of one of the outlying bastions.

Either way, it didn't matter. They'd be out of this battle before much longer.

The Christian katyusha gunner Stefan Branković was a lot more unhappy with the smoke obscuring everything on the ground than was the Jew above him who was creating that smoke. His unhappiness didn't derive from the stink, which he barely noticed, nor did it stem from the irritation of his eyes. The problem was as simple as problems ever got—he couldn't see what he was doing.

More precisely, he couldn't see *where* he was doing it.

"Are we in range?" asked his assistant, Vuk Milutin. He waved at the smoke swirling around them, as if that paltry gesture could make anything clear.

"How should I know?" snapped Stefan.

The *mülazım* in command of their katyusha *bölük* emerged out of the smoke, looking rather infuriated. "Idiot generals and their idiot—" The mülazım broke off the angry sentence when he saw Stefan and Vuk. He'd been talking to himself, not intending to be overheard by any of his soldiers. Unlike many of the Muslim officers appointed over the Christians, he tried to lead, rather than just command. His insistence on using the new titles was an example—most of the commanders of the other bölüks still wanted to be called *bölük başı*, at least when the sultan was not around.

"Have you seen any of the range markers?" he demanded.

An object about the size of a watermelon—but much heavier—came falling through the smoke and struck the mülazım on the top of his helmet, driving him straight to the ground. The sound of his neck breaking was quite audible.

Stefan and Vuk stared down at the officer's corpse. The thick linen sack full of gravel had gotten impaled on the spiked helmet which the katyusha units used and now covered his whole head. Sticking up from it was a slender pole atop which was a small banner. The insignia on the banner read: *200*.

That stood for two hundred kulaçs—a *kulaç* being roughly equivalent to the height of a tall man, about six feet.

"We're in range," said Vuk, quite unnecessarily.

"Shut up and give me some help." Stefan was already unhitching the katyusha cart from the two horses who'd been drawing it. "No—better yet, find the hostler."

Vuk looked around, with a helpless expression on his face. You couldn't see more than a few yards in any direction.

"How am I supposed to..."

"Never mind. Just hold the horses yourself. I can get the katyusha ready."

The rockets were already in their racks, so all Stefan had to do was attach the fuses. The problem would come later, after the first volley was fired. Reloading a katyusha rack was a job for two men. If the hostler hadn't appeared by then, they'd have no choice but to leave the horses to their own devices and hope the silly beasts didn't run off.

Which they wouldn't, if all they heard was the sound of the rockets being fired. They were accustomed to that by now. But if Austrian shells started landing nearby, there was no telling how the horses would react.

But that was a problem for later. At the moment, Stefan's main concern was to have their katyusha ready to fire when the signal came. The *binbashi* who commanded the katyusha force was a harsh man, quick to inflict corporal punishment on anyone he deemed a slacker. It was unlikely that he would know exactly which katyusha units had failed in their duty, given the smoke that obscured the entire battlefield. But... you never knew.

Soon, Stefan had everything ready, the smoldering slowmatch in hand. There was nothing to do now but—

The sound of clashing cymbals penetrated the smoke quite clearly. At least *something* had gone according to plan.

He touched the slowmatch to the fuse. Within two seconds, all eight rockets were headed toward the walls of Vienna.

"Hurry!" shouted the Christian whose head stuck out of the hatch. "They'll be starting the assault soon!"

"Fuck you, you stinking—" One of the janissaries next to Uzun Hussein raised up, looking as if he were ready to attack the bastard. Hussein was sympathetic, but this was no time for a brawl.

"Shut up!" he bellowed. "Everyone—*push.*"

Whether because this last effort was fueled by anger or simply because they'd managed to get the wheel partway out of the hole, the armored wagon suddenly surged forward. Now back on more-or-less level ground, the machine rumbled toward Vienna.

"Maybe we'll get lucky and the Austrians will hit it," said the same man whom Hussein had had to silence. "A good solid ball from a big cannon ought to do the job."

"Shut up," Hussein repeated. His tone wasn't sympathetic at all, this time. It was just as likely that a cannonball striking the heavily armored wagon would glance off and strike down some janissaries instead. Leaving that risk aside, he wanted the wagon functioning once it got to the enemy's bastions. The war machine's cannon was something of a joke, so far as Hussein was concerned—more for show than anything else. It wasn't a big cannon, firing a ball no heavier than four pounds. What good was that against a well-built star fort?

But the flamethrower... That was a different matter. It was a fiendish weapon, more properly wielded by djinni than men. Even if the empire's legal scholars had ruled its use legitimate, Hussein was glad that he wasn't the one using it. Let a Christian or a Jew lose his soul instead.

To Leopold, the rocket barrage came out of the smoke wall as a complete surprise.

It shouldn't have. The top Austrian commanders had all been briefed by Janos Drugeth's spies. They'd been told to expect rockets—lots of them—along with a few airships and at least a thousand rifled muskets.

But Leopold had been more concerned about the rifles than anything else. The Austrian infantry still wasn't equipped with any, except for a few in the hands of snipers. He was skeptical that they had the accuracy claimed: good up to five hundred yards, one of the spies claimed. He thought that was doubtful for anything other than an American rifle—and only an up-time made one, at that.

Rockets were notoriously temperamental weapons, and very hard to aim. So if the Ottomans did use them, Leopold had expected plenty of advance warning.

But he hadn't foreseen the smoke. And if he'd been told that the Ottomans had the so-called "Hale" design for their rockets, he'd forgotten.

So he wasn't expecting a big barrage of rockets fired from no more than four or five hundred yards away, which came out of the smoke with almost no warning—and many of which actually hit their target.

It was a big target, of course. Hundreds of yards of bastions and curtain walls, all of them protected by a glacis. But there were a lot of rockets, too.

Still, it was just pure blind bad luck—ridiculously bad luck— that one of the rockets sailed right over the bastion wall and exploded no more than ten yards from Leopold and his three female companions.

The only thing that kept any of them alive was that the

timed fuse didn't go off until the rocket was already past them, so most of the shrapnel kept flying forward and peppered the ground below the bastion—where, happily, no one was standing.

One piece of shrapnel removed Leopold's hat and sent it sailing toward the moat. Two more pieces—very small ones, luckily—struck Judy Wendell. But, luckily again, they struck her on the hem of the riding jacket she favored when venturing outdoors. No damage was done except to the jacket itself, and even that wasn't much.

The piece of shrapnel that struck Cecilia Renata, on the other hand, was quite sizeable and it struck her directly on the side of her head. The only thing that kept her alive was that she wore her thick red hair curled up in two big buns covering her ears, and today she was also wearing a broad-brimmed hat to protect her fair complexion from the sun.

She went down like a stunned steer, blood oozing into the hair on the right side of her head.

Minnie got to her within three seconds, with a kerchief in hand that she began wrapping around the archduchess' head to stem the blood loss. No arteries had been severed, but head wounds always bleed badly. She probably had a concussion as well.

A moment later, Judy was kneeling next to her, helping to hold the dressing while Minnie finished tightening it down.

Leopold's contribution was to stare at them. Being fair to the young man, there was nothing he could do that Minnie and Judy weren't already doing—and he was, technically, in command of the whole garrison.

Even if that was mostly a formality, he still couldn't abandon everything else in order to attend to his sister. For a quarter of a minute or so, his thoughts skittered around like a drop of water on a hot skillet.

Minnie got to her feet. "Nothing more we can do, right now— but we have to get her out of here. Judy, you take her left side."

Between them, the two young women got the unconscious archduchess' arms slung over their shoulders and started down the ramp leading up to the bastion wall.

"Be careful!" said Leopold.

Without looking around, Minnie waved her hand. The gesture could have meant anything between *will do, master!* and *you worry about yourself, fellow.* But Leopold knew Minnie well enough by now to know which end of that range was most likely.

He turned back to face the still-invisible enemy, somewhere out there in the smoke. What would they do now?

Another hissing barrage of rockets arrived. None of them landed near Leopold, and a quick glance backward assured him that none of the rockets posed any danger to his sister and her companions. By now, the three women were off the bastion and hurrying toward the city itself—insofar as the term "hurrying" could be applied to two women carrying a third like a limp sack of grain.

A new sound came to his ears. Something... odd, but also oddly familiar.

After a few seconds, he realized what it reminded him of. That was the same sound that the "Sonny Steamer" had made, racing around the track at Race Track City.

Something was coming, driven by a steam engine. He was quite sure a day which had started badly was about to get worse.

Chapter 37

Vienna, capital of Austria-Hungary

Judy Wendell came to a stop. "This isn't going to work," she said, breathing heavily.

Minnie Hugelmair, who had Cecilia Renata's other arm over her shoulder and was also supporting the archduchess with an arm around her waist, took a few deep breaths herself. She was a bit shorter than the American girl but she outweighed Judy by at least twenty pounds and was stronger. Still, she too was half-exhausted by now. Carrying a limp human body is hard work, even shared between two people.

Minnie glanced around. They were within the city itself now, no longer in sight of the fortifications, and had a large two-story building shielding them from rockets.

"Let's set her down," she said. A few seconds later, they had the Austrian archduchess sitting on the ground, propped up against the wall of the building.

She didn't look good. Not only was she still unconscious, but her face was very pale and her breathing was rapid and shallow.

"I think she's in shock," Minnie said.

Judy was already taking her pulse and had her other hand on Cecilia Renata's forehead. "I'm almost sure you're right," she said. "Without a sfigmawhoozit—I can never remember how to pronounce the word for a blood pressure gadget—there's no way to be positive. But her pulse is weak and rapid and so is her breathing. She's cold and clammy, too."

She removed her hands from the archduchess' forehead and wrist. "Good enough for government work, as they say."

Minnie snorted softly. "As *Americans* say. In this day and age, you're better off doing shoddy work for a private party than trying to swindle the government." She made a chopping motion with the edge of her hand against the side of her neck. "You up-timers just had slack and soft-hearted governments."

Judy made a face. "You've got a point. I can remember a carefree and happy time before the Ring of Fire when I barely knew what 'shock' was, much less how to diagnose and treat it."

She sat down and propped herself against the wall next to Cecilia Renata. "What should we do, Minnie? We've got to find someplace we can give her emergency care. She needs to be lying down with her feet up, and kept warm."

Minnie was rested enough to stand up and walk to the corner. Peering around it, she first looked toward the fortified walls. But there was nothing to see in that direction because the smoke now completely obscured the view. Looking the other way, she could see the spire and the roof of the imperial palace.

She came back to where Judy and Cecilia Renata were sitting. The archduchess had slumped a bit sideways, with her head resting on Judy's shoulder. But her eyes were now open and she seemed at least half-conscious.

Minnie knelt down next to her, on the opposite side from Judy. "Your Grace?" she asked.

Cecilia Renata's eyes turned toward her. The movement seemed to be coordinated and both pupils were the same size. Minnie had also been trained in first aid and she knew that was a good sign.

"Where are we?" the archduchess asked. Her voice was weak, but clear. "What happened?"

Then, before Minnie could answer, Cecilia Renata's eyes bulged a little and her cheeks started to swell. Recognizing the signs, Minnie managed to scramble out of the way before the archduchess vomited.

"Well, that's one royal outfit which is going to need a good cleaning," said Judy. She'd sidled away herself. "And I'd say that makes it definite—she's got a concussion, all right. We have *got* to get her somewhere safe."

Minnie pointed to the north. "We can make it to the Hofburg. That's the best place I can think of."

Since the archduchess seemed to be done with vomiting,

Minnie wiped off her face with a clean part of the hem of the same royal skirt. "Up you go, Your Grace. We need to get moving."

Once again, she and Judy got under Cecilia Renata's shoulders and got her onto her feet. This time, thankfully, the young archduchess was able to bear much of her own weight. They started moving toward the Hofburg.

The rocket barrage had finally ended. By the time it did, Archduke Leopold had made his way to the headquarters set up by his military commanders in a chamber beneath the southernmost bastion of the walls. They'd positioned it there because they'd thought that was the most likely place the Ottomans would attack.

They'd been wrong, but not by much. Murad had actually aligned his forces a bit farther to the west. Presumably he'd done so in order to give himself a wider front across which to send his troops in an assault.

"The rockets didn't do much damage," said General Wolf Heinrich von Baudissin, the top commander of the garrison defending Vienna. His tone was dismissive. "A few men killed here and there, some buildings—civilian buildings—destroyed. Our fortifications were not damaged at all."

"Then why did the Turks use the rockets in the first place?" asked Colonel Raimondo Montecuccoli. "I think we'd be foolish to underestimate them."

Leopold was inclined to agree with him. He'd become quite impressed with Montecuccoli over the past few weeks. The Italian cavalryman was young for his rank, only twenty-seven. But Leopold would have been a lot happier if he'd been in charge of the garrison instead of Baudissin.

Baudissin was a Lusatian, now in his late fifties, the quintessential "grizzled and experienced commander"—as he never tired of depicting himself. Although a Protestant and someone whose military experience had mostly been in service to Protestant realms—with Denmark, Sweden and then Saxony—he was, like most professional officers of the time, quite willing to serve a Catholic monarch.

He had the advantage and disadvantage of not being mentioned in any of the up-time history texts. Advantage, because there was nothing bad to report about him; disadvantage, because nothing good was said, either.

It was difficult if not impossible to draw any conclusions

about his absence from the historical record. He might simply have died before he became sufficiently prominent. In any event, the American texts were notoriously sketchy about the history of central Europe in this era. In the end, Emperor Ferdinand III's decision to hire him had been driven mostly by necessity. There was something of an acute shortage of experienced generals available for service to Austria. Wallenstein had rebelled and the two generals who'd led the conspiracy against him—Piccolomini and Gallas—were no longer available either. Piccolomini had chosen to work for Bavaria and Gallas had gotten his brains shot out by the American sharpshooter Julie Sims at the Battle of the Alte Veste.

In retrospect, Leopold thought that hiring Baudissin had been an unwise decision on his brother's part. But no one had foreseen how quickly the Ottomans under their new sultan would launch an invasion. Wallenstein's successful rebellion had placed a premium on loyalty, when it came to the Austrian emperor's attitude toward his generals. And, whether competent or not, no one thought that Baudissin posed the same sort of threat to the Austrian crown that Wallenstein had.

If for no other reason, because he wasn't bright enough. Leopold's brother had even said that to him, once.

Leopold cleared his throat. He was normally hesitant to speak up at these command meetings. Regardless of his position as an archduke in line of succession and his formal status as the overall commander of Vienna's defense, Leopold was very well aware of his age—*twenty-two*—as well as his vocation—*bishop*—and his military experience—*none*.

"The rockets have still had an effect on our troops," he said. "That was quite obvious to me on my way over here. Between the smoke and the rockets—that bizarre noise coming from the Turkish ranks isn't helping either—they're pretty badly shaken. I think we need to shore up morale."

Baudissin didn't curl his lip, or make any other visibly derisive sign. But it was quite clear that he was paying no attention to the archduke's cautions.

Leopold caught the eye of Montecuccoli. The Italian officer made a slight face, accompanied by a little shrug, as if to say: *I agree with you, but I'm not in charge.*

Technically, Leopold *was* in charge and—technically—he could relieve Baudissin of his command right here and now.

But... He shrank from that course of action. If for no other reason, the impact on a garrison that was already wobbly of having its commander summarily relieved in the middle of a battle—and replaced by who? Leopold? A not-that-well-known and very young officer like Montecuccoli?—was likely to make things still worse.

"Murad just did it to bolster the morale of his own troops," Baudissin went on, his tone firm and confident. "The Turks will now go back to proper siege techniques."

His finger came down on a portion of the map spread out across the table in the center of the room. "They'll start extending their trenches here, while"—his finger moved over a bit—"their sappers concentrate here, closer to the canal."

He certainly sounded as if he knew what he was talking about.

On the way back to their base, Abraham Zarfati made sure that his airship was at least three hundred kulaçs above the ground. If they followed the plan, the oncoming airships that would be dropping bombs on the fortifications would be flying very low—not more than one hundred kulaçs.

Supposedly. But Abraham was an airship commander himself and he knew that the natural inclination of an airship pilot was to avoid flying too low. That was true even without the added incentives of smoke that obscured visibility and the possibility of enemy gun fire.

The smoke would be worrying the bomb ship pilots. Supposedly— that treacherous word, again—the smoke should have cleared away by the time the bombing airships arrived over the fortifications. But that depended largely on the wind, and Abraham was pretty sure the wind had died down quite a bit. There could still be a lot of smoke in the area when the new wave of airships arrived.

That would not be his problem. But he didn't want to run any risk of colliding with an incoming airship whose pilot was hedging his bets.

No one had any idea what would happen if two airships collided—which was exactly where Zarfati wanted to leave that particular bit of knowledge: "Result unknown." Eventually someone would probably find out. Let it not be him.

Hearing his engineer muttering something, Abraham turned to see what the problem was.

"Trouble?"

"Not as such," replied Joseph Culi. He was scowling at the steam engine in the center of the gondola. "I just wish the sultan would let us adapt one of the American designs."

Out of reflex habit, Abraham glanced around quickly. That was silly, of course. Some of the airships had Muslim commanders, but everyone on board this one was a Jew. Still, you needed to be careful on the subject of the Americans. Or "up-timers," as they were also called. Sultan Murad IV was willing—no, eager—to modernize his army, and to do so he had no choice but to look to the American texts for ideas and inspiration. Nonetheless, he had still not rescinded the official proscription against any reference to Americans.

"This stupid thing is *slow*," Joseph growled.

"Reliable, though," countered Abraham.

"So is a mule. And I bet I could hang a mule over the side and let its farts drive us along—probably as fast as this thing does."

Abraham chuckled. The steam engines the sultan had ordered put in use for his fleet of airships were based on a design that was almost a century old and of entirely Muslim origin. The great astronomer Taqi ad-Din Muhammad ibn Ma'ruf ash-Shami al-Asadi had devised the plans for such an engine, although he'd never actually tried to build one, so far as anyone was aware. But the design had still existed in his book, *The Sublime Methods of Spiritual Machines*, and Murad had seized on it as the basis for his engineers to develop a suitable airship engine. Abraham suspected the sultan had chafed at the necessity to rely on machines developed by infidels and saw this as a way to at least partially counter that taint.

Taqi ad-Din's machine had been a steam turbine designed to rotate a spit for cooking meat. He'd also designed a steam-operated six-cylinder water pump. To serve the purpose for which Murad had commanded them, the Ottoman engineers had combined and transformed those designs into an engine that could turn the propellers that drove the airships.

The Ottoman-designed engine did have some good points. It was reliable, it didn't break down often, and the thrust could be easily reversed with a simple gear shift. The boiler was run at lower pressures than on American designs of the same size and wall thickness and thus operated with a greater safety margin.

But it was also quite a weak engine. So weak, in fact, that the airships couldn't operate in any sort of strong wind. As far as Abraham was concerned, though, that was a disguised advantage. Fine for the sultan—down there on the ground—to order his airships to fly in the face of strong winds. Better for Zarfati and his crew to be able to refuse such an order on the simple grounds that it couldn't be carried out due to mechanical realities.

"I can see one of them now," said Isaac Capsali. Abraham joined him near the prow of the gondola and looked over the side to where the pilot was pointing.

Sure enough, the huge bloated shape of another airship was passing below them—and quite safely below them, he was pleased to see.

The smoke was much thinner, too.

"I think the sultan's plan might work," said Isaac, sounding surprised.

It *was* surprising. Zarfati had never heard of "Murphy's Law" but he was a Jew and thus automatically attuned to its wisdom. The whole history of his people could be described as the unfolding of Murphy's Law across millennia.

The rabbis wouldn't approve of that thesis. But Abraham Zarfati was a skeptic by nature. Which also, of course, made him doubtful that Sultan Murad's plots and schemes wouldn't go awry themselves, sooner or later.

Not his problem, though. Not today, at least.

"Where do we go now?" wondered Judy. She looked around the oddly deserted courtyard outside the palace. Normally, there would be a number of guards standing around. They must have all been pressed into manning the walls once the Ottoman attack began. The only person she could see was an elderly servant, who was now starting to come toward them.

"My rooms," said Cecilia Renata, speaking barely above a whisper. The words weren't slurred, which was a good sign, but the archduchess was looking pretty haggard. She'd vomited again on the way; the sort of dry heaves that were worse than what Judy thought of as a run-of-the-mill upchuck.

Judy and Minnie looked at each other over the archduchess' bowed head. For the last stretch, they'd once again had to support Cecilia Renata on their shoulders.

"Do you know where they are?" Minnie asked.

"Yes, if I remember the way," Judy replied, sounding none too confident. "Cecilia Renata was with me both times I went there, though. I just followed her."

Thankfully, by then the servant had arrived. Some quick questioning ascertained that the old fellow did know the way there. He headed into the palace, leading the way.

Hobbling the way, to be precise. He wasn't moving very fast. But that didn't matter because Judy and Minnie couldn't move any faster than he was, not with the archduchess' arms draped over their necks.

Getting up the stairs to the upper floor was a royal pain in the ass, but at least Judy had the satisfaction of knowing that this pain in the ass really did qualify as "royal." And from there it wasn't far to the archduchess' chambers.

They lowered her onto her bed. Judy got her under the covers while Minnie gave the servant instructions to make some sort of broth for Cecilia Renata. She needed to get something back in her stomach, even if she did heave it up again.

After the servant left, Minnie and Judy looked down on their charge. The archduchess' eyes were closed, now.

"I think we're not supposed to let her fall asleep," said Minnie. "Not with a concussion. She might not ever wake up."

Judy shook her head firmly. That part of her first aid training she did remember clearly, in the way someone will remember it when a false notion is dispelled.

"Nah, that's a myth. Pure bullshit. As my instructor said, if falling asleep with a concussion caused someone to fall into a coma then we'd always be in the middle of a coma epidemic." She shook her head again. "As long as there aren't any internal injuries to worry about—and she just got whacked in the head, it's not like she was in a big car accident—then she can sleep as much as she needs. Fatigue and drowsiness are symptoms of a concussion, so it's not surprising."

Minnie looked relieved. "Good, because I wasn't looking forward to having to stay awake all the time to make sure she did."

She moved toward a partially open window. "It sounds a lot quieter out there. Maybe the attack's over."

When she reached the window, she swung it fully open. She

was facing southwest, right toward the enemy—although Minnie couldn't see them from here.

Judy came and joined her. "I hope you're right. But I wouldn't count on it."

Minnie pointed toward the distant sky. "See that line of clouds? Looks like there might be a storm coming. Maybe that's why they called it off."

Judy followed her friend's pointing finger. She had two eyes, where Minnie had only one—and her eyesight was better, to begin with.

"Those aren't clouds, Minnie."

"Huh?" Minnie squinted, which Judy found a bit amusing because she only squinted her good eye. All she needed was a monocle.

"Then what—? Oh, fuck."

Judy nodded. "'Oh, fuck' is right. As in, I think we're about to be."

Chapter 38

Vienna, capital of Austria-Hungary

They were close enough for the final assault to begin. But the officers ordered the janissaries to wait until the airships arrived and finished their bombardment of Vienna's walls. Uzun Hussein was normally impatient at such moments and just wanted the fighting to start. But right now he was weary from the last struggle to get the miserable armored wagon moving again after it got stuck in another hole, so he was grateful for the rest.

If it had been up to him, the war wagon would have been left to rot in that hole. They'd begun the attack with eight of the things, and by now only three of them were still functioning. Two had gotten hopelessly stuck. Two more had suffered mechanical failures. And a fifth had destroyed itself when the steam engine that drove it exploded.

That wagon had been close enough for Hussein to see what happened. The zimmi commanding the war wagon had been perched in the cupola's hatch when he started screaming and tried to climb out of the wagon. He hadn't gotten far before a blast of steam hurled him completely out and down onto the ground. His pants had been blown off and the bottom half of his body was a parboiled ruin.

It took him a while to die, shrieking with agony. He'd have been better off if he'd been trapped inside the wagon with the rest of the crew. They would have all died immediately when the engine blew up. Hussein didn't know exactly how the steam engines worked—and didn't want to know, either—but he'd been told they needed a tank full of boiling water that had to be kept at just the right temperature. Not hot enough, the machine wouldn't work; too hot, the tank—the "boiler," they called it—would erupt.

Hussein didn't care much what happened to the war wagons, especially since the crews were all Christians. Not even the commanders were Muslim. The sultan was said to adore the stupid things, but they were so ungainly and temperamental that Hussein couldn't see that they had much use in a real battle.

Perhaps he was wrong. They'd find out soon enough, when the assault started. Those who were more familiar with the war wagons than Hussein claimed the engines were so powerful that the wagons could climb up the glacis protecting the walls. He was skeptical of the claim, after seeing how much trouble the machines had just crossing flat ground. On the other hand, the glacis probably wouldn't have the same sort of holes and obstructions that had been causing the problems on the open terrain.

They'd find out soon enough.

Leopold stared up at the line of approaching airships. His stomach felt hollow. The Austrians had been completely fooled. They'd thought the Ottomans had only three airships—then, five, when the smoke screen was laid down. Instead, they had...

"How many are there?" he asked Montecuccoli.

The Italian officer standing next to him lowered his spyglass. "There are ten in the first line, with another five coming behind them. Add the five which laid down the smoke, and there are a total of twenty—assuming that's actually all of them." He shook his head. "How did they do it? There can't possibly be enough goldbeater skins—not even in the entire Ottoman empire—to make that many huge balloons. Envelopes, whatever they call them."

Leopold tried to remember the briefing he'd gotten from Drugeth's spies. "I don't think they need to use goldbeater skins, although those are best for the purpose. Cotton covered with varnish will work, I believe. Silk would be better, if they can get it."

Montecuccoli sighed. "It doesn't matter. However they did it, they did it. The evidence is right in front of our eyes. The question now is: what are they planning to do, and what do we do in response?"

Leopold had been going over the same briefings in his mind, with that very goal in mind.

"They're going to drop bombs," he said. "They can stay right above us and we won't be able to do much about it if they stay too high for us to shoot at them with muskets. Maybe cannon, but..."

"We don't have enough time to figure out how to use cannons for the purpose," said Montecuccoli. "I suspect that would require specially designed weapons to be effective. All we have is what we have now."

Leopold was still thinking ahead. "They'll be able to clear the troops off the walls. They can't keep bombing for very long, but they'll be able to keep it up long enough to hammer our men into paste."

"What I think also," said Montecuccoli, nodding. "We have to get the men off the walls and into shelter. When the bombing is over, they can rush back out to fight off the ground assault—which you know will be coming right on the heels of the airship attack."

"You're right. Give the order, Colonel."

Montecuccoli began to move toward the cluster of couriers who had been trailing after them as he and Leopold did their inspection tour of the fortifications. He'd give them the orders and they'd begin to pass them down the line. But before he could get there, another courier came racing up the stairs leading to the bastion.

"*Stand your ground! Stand your ground! General Baudissin has given the order!*" the courier started shouting. He pointed toward the oncoming fleet of Ottoman airships. "Use volley fire from muskets! Don't try to use the cannons!"

Looking a bit helpless, Montecuccoli turned back to face Leopold.

Who, for his part, spread his hands in a gesture of similar helplessness.

Montecuccoli hurried over to him. "You can relieve him of command and take it yourself, Your Grace," he said.

Leopold had already considered that possibility, but...

He shook his head. "It's not realistic, Colonel." He pointed at the airships. "Even if Baudissin did not resist the command, the Ottomans will be here before the transition of leadership could be completed—before it could really even have begun. All that would result is chaos."

Montecuccoli studied the nearing enemy vessels, stroking his beard as he did so. After perhaps three seconds, he made a face. "You're right, I'm afraid. But this order is madness. The men will be completely unprotected from any bombs dropped upon them. And at the height those ships are sailing—flying, whatever you call it—they can hardly miss."

"By the same token, Colonel, they'll be low enough that we should be able to hit some of them with musket fire. That part of Baudissin's order is sensible enough, at least."

"Yes...although it will depend on how those hulls—whatever they're called—are armored. Or should we fire on the big balloons that hold them up?"

Leopold tried to remember the briefing the spies had given them. The Ottoman airships were now close enough that it was clear they were using hydrogen, not hot air. The gondolas had no burners that he could see. Hydrogen was supposed to be a very flammable gas, but if Leopold remembered correctly, it was not actually that easy to set on fire with musket balls alone. And because of the curvature of the balloons, balls which stuck them might simply be deflected.

"Aim for the baskets hanging underneath," he ordered. "As low as they're flying, I think we can penetrate their floors and kill at least some of the crews."

By now, the knot of couriers had spread out and passed the order along to all the soldiers in the bastion. They were beginning to assemble on the top floor of the fortification, with muskets in hand. Some of them were holding their guns in such a gingerly manner that Leopold almost laughed. Those would be artillery-men. Many of them hadn't fired a musket in years; a few of them, perhaps never at all.

He looked back up at the sky. The Ottoman airships were only a few hundred yards away now. They looked enormous. Even though Leopold knew that most of their volume was simply empty space filled with gas, their sheer size still produced an instinctive terror. It wouldn't take much, he knew, for the Austrian soldiers to begin panicking.

"*Now! Now! Now!*" shouted the *çorbacı* in command of Hussein's *orta*. Hundreds of janissaries in the regiment-sized unit began their charge on the Austrian bastion nearest to them. All across the line on the southern side of Vienna's walls, other ortas came forward to join them.

"Charge" was something in the way of poetic license. The janissaries had five hundred yards to cross before they reached the base of the glacis and they were carrying rifled muskets as well as kilij or yataghans, the Ottoman saber and sword. They were not wearing armor as such, but their uniforms were heavy and it was a fairly hot summer day. If they tried to run before getting much nearer, they'd just be exhausted by the time the fighting started.

In any event, the janissaries in Hussein's orta were still under orders to accompany the war wagon. The miserable machine was slow under the best of circumstances, even when it wasn't breaking down or getting stuck. Any man in good condition could walk faster than it could move, although he'd have to push himself a little.

The cannons on the enemy fortifications began firing almost immediately, as Hussein had expected. They were well within range. But he was struck by how light the fire was. And, for the first time, began to wonder if the sultan's plans might actually work.

As an experienced veteran, he'd been skeptical, despite his general admiration for Murad. By rights, they should have spent at least another month extending the trenches closer to Vienna's walls. And like all the janissaries, since they had had to protect the men doing the digging, Hussein knew that the efforts of the sappers had been desultory. The sappers he'd talked to himself even suspected that their work was mostly just for show.

But now...

The key, he understood instantly, was the fleet of airships passing overhead at that very moment. The huge war devices were bound to unsettle the enemy—Hussein found them unsettling himself. If the officers were right in their estimates, what was now happening on the walls of Vienna was that most of the enemy troops were being assembled to fire musket volleys on the approaching airships.

That might be tough on the airship crews, of course. Hussein didn't have the experience to know, one way or the other. But he didn't care because every Austrian soldier firing a musket at an airship was an Austrian soldier who was not firing a cannon at him. And besides, except for some of the commanding officers, the airship crews were made up of zimmis, not good Muslims. Mostly Jews, from what he'd been told.

Hussein preferred Jews to Christians, but he did so in the way a hungry man will "prefer" a food he doesn't much care for to one he actively dislikes. Every Jew in those airships passing overhead could get killed in this battle and Hussein would not be at all disturbed—not so long as there were more Jews to man the devilish things. He had no desire to do it himself.

But they were past them now, he saw. The airships would arrive over the walls of Vienna several minutes before the janissaries reached the base of the glacis and began the assault itself.

By then, who knew what might happen? Maybe the sultan was right.

Minnie and Judy could hear the sound of the musket fire, as the airships neared the walls of Vienna. From their vantage point in the Hofburg, they couldn't see the fortifications themselves, but the airships were clearly visible. They could even see, on some of them, that they had banners either painted or attached to the huge envelopes. The banners were green with the traditional Ottoman triple crescent design. Underneath the crescents, they could see that something was written.

"What does that mean, do you know?" asked Judy. "That inscription, there." She pointed.

It was now close enough for Minnie to make out the lettering, even with just one eye. But while her knowledge of spoken Turkish was becoming passable, she could barely understand the script at all.

She shook her head. "I have no idea. Nothing good for us, though." She hesitated, looking back at the figure of Cecilia Renata on the bed. Minnie had thought she was asleep, but the young royal's eyes opened and she whispered, "What's happening?"

For whatever reason, that shaky whisper made up Minnie's mind.

She turned back to face Judy. "We need to get out of here. Now."

Her companion frowned, still not taking her eyes from the airships. "And go where? In the shape she's in, we can't possibly make it out of the city. The last group of evacuees left yesterday."

"No, but we can get someplace a lot safer for her in the

palace itself." She stuck her head out of the window and craned it around. But she couldn't see what she was looking for because it was hidden behind a corner of the palace.

"Those cellars we visited." She reached her arm out of the window and pointed toward the corner. "You know, the ones beneath that other part of the palace."

Judy grimaced. "It's dark and musty down there. I bet it's damp, too. Why should we—"

She still hadn't taken her eyes off the airships, so she saw the sudden flurry of objects that began falling from them onto the fortifications below.

She took a deep, sudden breath. A moment later, the rolling thunder of explosions began. And a moment after that, the first great tongues of flame reached up high enough that she could see them. It was almost instantly joined by others—all along the fortifications obscured by the intervening buildings, except for two places where it looked as if there were gaps.

Gaps. Judy was no soldier, but you didn't need to be Napoleon to figure out why the Ottomans had left a couple of places unburned. That was where they'd do their charge on the walls.

Until this very moment, Judy hadn't really been that concerned about the outcome of the siege. Like almost everyone else, she knew the past history and the future history and the repeated failure of the Ottoman sultans to take Vienna. And had let that knowledge—no, not "knowledge," merely supposition—determine her thinking.

"We need to get out of here," she said. "Right now."

She turned from the window and saw that Minnie was already hoisting the archduchess out of the bed.

"What's happening?" Cecilia Renata said again.

"Bad stuff," was Minnie's reply. "Come on, Your Grace. We've got to get you someplace safe. Well, saf-er."

With a little grunt and a heave, she had Cecilia Renata cradled in her arms. Fiddler and singer she might be, but Hugelmair was a strong girl. "Lead the way," she said to Judy. "I'll carry her."

Chapter 39

Vienna, capital of Austria-Hungary

The soldiers on the other bastions began firing as soon as the Ottoman airships were within range—in other words, much too early. At two hundred yards, they could reach the airships with their musket balls, but even firing in volleys most of the balls would miss at that range. Even if they hit, the likelihood that they'd have enough force to punch through the tough wicker was low. All the more so because now that the enemy vessels were closer, Leopold could see that the Ottomans had attached shields to the sides of the gondolas. These were the type of shields the Turks called "kalkans," made of rattan wound around a central metal boss and further strengthened with silk cords. They were quite light but effective. As a second layer of shielding, they added further protection from musket balls fired at the sides of the gondolas.

The floors, on the other hand...

Using his spyglass, Leopold studied the bottom of the gondolas. They were flat, not sloped or rounded, and they weren't shielded.

He lowered the spyglass and turned to Montecuccoli. "I think—"

But the Italian's attention was riveted on the soldiers in the adjoining bastion, who'd just fired their first volley. "*No! You fucking idiots!*" he shouted, cupping his hands around his mouth. "*Wait till they get closer!*"

The officer who seemed to be in command over there obviously heard him, because he made a rude gesture in their direction—and, just as obviously, had no intention of following the advice.

Leopold placed a hand on Montecuccoli's shoulder and gave it a little shake. "Ignore them, Raimondo. We have our own airship to deal with. Wait until it's no more than a hundred yards away—and then have the men aim for the floor of the gondola."

Montecuccoli broke off scowling at the adjoining bastion and squinted at the nearing Ottoman vessel. "Aim for..." He made a face. "These are just muskets, Your Grace. Not very accurate."

"Yes, I know. But we have a hundred of them." He gave a quick glance at the mob of soldiers who'd piled onto the bastion's fighting surface. "More than that, I think. But you need to take command. Their own officers are...well, confused."

Montecuccoli immediately began shouting at the soldiers on their own bastion, and gathering their officers around him. They were relieved to see that someone was in charge and seemed to know what he was doing, even if technically he had no direct authority over them.

Leopold went back to studying the Ottoman fleet of airships. The nearest of them had now started to pass over the glacis and was within a few dozen yards of the fortifications themselves.

The archduke had a gnawing feeling that the same confusion existed everywhere on Vienna's fortifications. Most of the Austrian troops in the garrison were veterans, but in this situation that might be as much of a handicap as a help. They were accustomed to a certain type of fighting, but today the Ottoman sultan was breaking all the familiar rules. It was now clear to Leopold that Murad had never intended to take Vienna by the normal methods of siegecraft. That was the reason he was launching the assault before the trenches had come near, and the reason the Turkish sapping efforts had been so lackadaisical. They had in fact just been for show.

Less than half a minute later, the first Ottoman airship began dropping its bombs, and the Austrian defenders were caught by surprise again. Or, at least, Leopold was—but he was quite sure General Baudissin was also.

The Ottomans weren't dropping normal explosives, they were dropping fire bombs. Big jars full of some sort of liquid that not only erupted into flames as soon as the jars burst on impact, but seemed to cling to everything as well. Leopold wasn't certain, but he thought this was the material that the Americans called "napalm." They also called it "jellied gasoline," if he remembered right. In essence, an up-time and more fiendish version of Greek fire.

It was a terror weapon, which killed as effectively as normal bombs but also spread panic among the defenders. Already Leopold could see streams of soldiers pouring off the bastions, almost as if they were a liquid themselves. He could hear officers shouting commands, ordering the men to stay at their posts. But it was increasingly clear to him that they would fail in that effort. The men were simply too frightened, too uncertain, too confused. As Leopold had feared, Baudissin's insistence that the soldiers remain on the bastions and walls during the airship bombardment was proving disastrous.

A shadow came over him. Startled, he look up and saw that the enemy airship which had been heading toward this bastion was almost overhead. And it was very low, certainly not more than one hundred yards above them. Belatedly, it occurred to Leopold that he was on the verge of being roasted alive, if—

"Fire!" Montecuccoli roared. The sound of the volley came instantly, as if it were an explosion itself.

Looking back up, Leopold thought that the gondola seemed to buck a little. As if struck from below by an ox. Or a donkey, at least.

He brought the spyglass back up and peered through it.

Yes! He could see two—three—four—five—was that a sixth?—hole in the floor of the gondola.

Or thought he could, at least. He really wasn't sure. It was quite dark under there. Maybe he was imagining things.

But then he realized the airship had already passed over them—without dropping any bombs.

Yes!

Moshe Mizrahi stared down at the corpse of the airship's commander, Mustafa Sa'id. He had been . . . butchered was the only term Moshe could think of. One of the balls that came through the floor of their gondola had struck Mustafa right under the chin, taking off most of his jaw and his nose. A second bullet had passed through his groin and ended somewhere in his abdomen.

Moshe forced himself to look away. With Mustafa dead, as the airship's pilot he was now in command of the vessel.

Elijah Frizis was also dead, he saw. He felt a moment's guilt that he was more upset over the death of Mustafa than he was over that of his fellow Jew, Elijah. But Sa'id had been a good fellow, for a Muslim, and a very capable airship commander. Whereas Elijah's best quality had been that his surliness also made him taciturn, so at least you didn't have to try to talk to him. And the reason they'd made Frizis their bombardier was because that job took practically no skill at all. Just a strong back, to pick up the heavy bomb jars. The man had been dull-witted as well as unpleasant.

"What do we do now?"

Moshe turned his head and was relieved to see that Mordechai Pesach was still alive. Leaving aside the fact that Mordechai was a friend, he was also the airship's engineer. As chance would have it—good luck, in this instance—the two men whose skills were most important to running an airship had both survived.

"You're bleeding." said Pesach. He pointed to Moshe's left side. "There. Just below your elbow."

Moshe brought up his arm and was surprised to see that he'd apparently been wounded. He couldn't feel a thing, though, so it must not be serious even if there seemed to be a good bit of blood soaking his sleeve.

"No time for that now," he said. He took a quick look over the side of the gondola. They'd passed completely over the bastion and the fortifications and were now above the city itself.

"We need to climb higher," he said. "Drop some ballast."

Mordechai pointed to the jars lined up on a ledge against the side of the gondola. There was another line of them on the side where Moshe was standing. "Why not just drop the bombs?"

Moshe shook his head. "Not over the city."

"Why not?" demanded Mordechai. "We're not carrying fire bombs. Not even superstitious Muslims have a problem with dropping regular bombs anywhere. And even if they did, it wouldn't apply to us. We're zimmis, remember?"

"That's not the point. These bombs are supposed to be used on the troops guarding the city walls. If we drop them anywhere else, the sultan will be angry." He shook his head again. "Just drop some ballast, that's all. Enough to lift us another fifty kulaçs—no, better make it another seventy-five."

Mordechai grimaced. "And return to base with all the bombs

still on board? The sultan is sure to order us executed if we do *that*."

"We'll drop them when we pass back over the city walls."

"On top of *janissaries*? Why don't we just cut our throat and be done with it?"

"We'll make sure we pass over a part of the wall that's burning. The janissaries will only be storming two of the bastions, remember?"

"How could I forget?" said Mordechai. "Since one of them was the one *we* were supposed to bomb."

Moshe had already thought of that—in fact, he was tempted to turn right around and make another bombing attempt on the same bastion. The problem was that the airship was slow and cumbersome, and by the time they came back over that bastion the janissaries would have started their assault.

He looked back at the bastion in question. From their height, he could see the Ottoman army in the distance beyond.

Then he saw the great cloud of smoke and realized it was all a moot point. Clearly enough, Sultan Murad had spotted the problem and come to his own solution.

"We'll just have to hope for the best," he said, pondering the odds.

On the one hand, Murad was said to be a fair-minded sultan. On the other hand, if he did decide against you he usually had only one punishment. Moshe fingered his neck, wondering what being hung felt like.

Not good, he was quite sure of that. But at least you'd die fairly quickly. And maybe he'd get lucky and Murad would have him decapitated instead.

Stefan Branković hadn't been expecting the order. But he and his men had been ready for it, nonetheless. When you were operating directly under the eye of Sultan Murad, it was not wise to be sluggish. It was *really* not wise.

So when the signal rang out, he and Vuk Milutin had their katyusha cart in motion before the cymbals stopped clanging. Vuk rode the guide horse while Stefan, as the cart commander, rode the back of the cart itself.

The position was more prestigious, but as he had every time before, Stefan envied his partner. Even the skimpy saddles provided for katyusha crews were more comfortable than being jostled and jarred on the back of a cart being pulled by horses.

They were trotting, of course, not galloping. Still, it was all he could do to keep from being thrown off.

Fortunately, they didn't have to go very far. Just four hundred or so kulaçs, enough to get in front of the janissaries and within close striking range of the bastion ahead of them.

Glancing quickly to each side, Stefan saw that the entire bölük was keeping pace with them. By the time they reached the janissaries, the infantrymen had reformed their ranks into lines that the katyushas could pass through. They were arrogant bastards—Stefan didn't know anyone who liked janissaries, even their fellow Muslims—but you couldn't deny they were good at what they did.

They were good at dying, too, Stefan thought cheerfully. Better them than him—although, being a conscientious man, he'd do his best to make sure as few of them died today as possible.

At the mülazım's command, they halted the cart and readied the katyushas. That took very little time. At the next command, Stefan put the slowmatch to the fuse, as did all those to either side. The entire line of katyushas was swallowed up in billowing rocket smoke.

Because of the smoke, Stefan didn't see the effect of their barrage on the bastion. But he didn't really care, anyway. Whatever Austrian soldiers might still be alive up there—they were the janissaries' problem now, not his.

When Leopold saw the hail of rockets headed toward them, he realized in that instant that Vienna was lost.

Or accepted the loss in that instant, it might be better to say. The more rational part of his brain had already realized the Ottomans were going to take the city that day.

"Take cover!" he shouted. But Montecuccoli had already given that order. The men were crowding against the walls on the bastion, sheltering as best they could from the oncoming missiles.

Belatedly, it occurred to Leopold that perhaps he should follow his own advice. He barely made it to the wall before the rockets began striking—and then, had no choice but to huddle against the backs of the men already there. Fortunately for him, the rockets proved to be rather ineffective against fortifications like these. For one thing, they were inaccurate. Many of them plunged harmlessly into the glacis, others struck the walls but the warheads were not powerful enough to break those heavy fortifications. Others sailed overhead and landed somewhere behind, while still others veered completely aside.

Out of that entire barrage, only three rockets struck onto the bastion fighting surface itself—and one of them at the very far edge. The warheads were using timed fuses, and those were always a bit haphazard. This missile didn't explode soon enough, so almost all of the shrapnel sailed off harmlessly.

The same problem afflicted the other two missiles, since they were coming in at such a shallow angle. The one that exploded while it was still passing above did wound several men and kill one outright. But the fuse on the third missile must have been cut much too long, because that missile actually bounced off the bastion surface and was at least thirty yards beyond the edge when it finally exploded. Its warhead did no damage at all, beyond peppering the walls of nearby buildings.

Leopold came to his feet and tried to peer over the walls to see what was happening now. He had to half-climb onto the men in front of him to do so.

What he saw was frightening. A mass of Turkish soldiers—janissaries, from the uniforms—was charging toward the bastion. And in their midst was some sort of bizarre machine. Leopold recognized the noise it was making as the one he'd heard before. He was pretty sure that was a steam engine driving the thing forward.

The machine was what the up-timers called a "tank," he thought. An armored vehicle of war driven by its own engine and armed with a cannon. In fact, he could see the cannon itself—although, oddly, it seemed to be aiming at the glacis in front of it.

He slid off the pile of men he'd used as an impromptu ramp of sorts and looked toward the other bastions on the walls. Most were now enveloped in flames—all of the bastions he could seem except his own and the one on the far west which was almost out of his sight. That one also had a mass of janissaries charging toward it, although he didn't see another tank.

The correct defensive tactic in this situation was obvious. The same flames that had driven Austrian soldiers off the walls and bastions would also act as a barrier against the Ottomans. They needed to rally the soldiers and concentrate them on the two bastions where the Ottoman assault would be taking place.

He saw that Montecuccoli was coming toward him and started to give those very orders. But then, as he looked around, saw that it was already too late. The Austrian troops—everywhere except right here, from what he could see—were already routed. In a panic, they were fleeing away from the walls. By the time they could be rallied, it would be too late.

"The day is lost, Your Grace," said Montecuccoli. "I recommend that you do what you can to lead an evacuation of the city. If we move quickly, I think we can still save many of our soldiers, though not the city itself." He paused, seeming to brace his shoulders a bit. "I will take charge of the defense of the bastion and buy you what time I can."

Leopold shook his head. "Your plan is good but the arrangement is wrong. You organize the retreat, Colonel—get Captain Adolf Brevermann to help you. He's already got boats ready for the purpose. If you encounter Baudissin, assuming the stupid bastard is still alive, tell him I gave the order to do it. I will stay here and organize the bastion's defense."

"Your Grace—"

"That's an *order*, Colonel. I would have no idea how to rally and reorganize men who are already demoralized. I think it is within my capability to do something as simple as tell men already in position to hold steady and open fire." He shrugged. "Raimondo, they are more likely to stay and fight if I stay with them. You know that as well as I do. So now, go and do as I command."

Montecuccoli opened his mouth, closed it. Opened it again. Closed it. Then he gave Leopold a quick, deep bow.

"Your Grace," he said. He turned and hurried off the bastion.

But Leopold didn't watch him once he was sure Montecuccoli was leaving. He had his own soldiers to rally.

"To the guns, men!" He remembered he was bearing a sword and drew it out of the scabbard. "To the guns!" he repeated, waving it around and feeling a bit silly. He was supposed to be a *bishop*, not—not—

What had been that Roman's name? Horatius, if he remembered the legend right. Horatius at the bridge.

Whether it was the sword-waving, or perhaps because his voice had not wavered, or perhaps because he was an archduke of Austria—perhaps because he was a bishop, who could say?—the men held firm. They were loading the cannons and making ready to fire.

He wondered if he'd be remembered as long as Horatius.

Leopold at the bastion.

Probably not. Horatius had survived and his Rome had gone on to dominate the world for centuries thereafter. Leopold was pretty sure he was going to die today and would enjoy the same posterity as the Greek noblemen who led the defense of Constantinople when the Ottomans seized that city.

What were their names?

Who knew?

Who cared, for that matter?

Chapter 40

Vienna, capital of Austria-Hungary

As his airship drew nearer to the fortifications after having made a long slow turn over Vienna, Moshe Mizrahi could see what was happening again. The assault against the westernmost of the two bastions that had not been struck by fire bombs had stalled. From what he could tell, he thought the airship assigned to bomb that bastion had either failed entirely in its mission or had only dropped some of its bombs on the soldiers guarding it.

If those soldiers had fired as effective a volley as the one that had struck his own airship, Moshe was not surprised. It was now clear that the officers commanding the airship force had seriously underestimated the risk posed by musket volleys if the vessels flew too low. In the future, they would either need to fly at a greater altitude or attach some sort of armor to the gondola floors—preferably both, as far as Moshe was concerned.

Mordechai Pesach came up next to him. "How's your arm?"

Moshe glanced down at the bandaged limb. They'd had enough time while the airship was coming around to attend to that problem, and the bleeding seemed to have stopped entirely.

"Hurts," he said, "but not too bad."

Mordechai pointed to something in the distance. "Look! Their armored wagon is way back there. Not even close to the bastion."

Moshe saw that he was right—and, again, was not surprised. He'd been doubtful the war machines would work that well. Being driven by a steam engine while floating through the air was one thing. Driving such a great heavy brute of a wagon across land, something else entirely.

Mordechai now pointed to a different bastion, farther to the east. That was the second of the two bastions that had been left unharmed by fire bombs, so that the janissaries could storm them. It was the bastion they were supposed to have bombed. "Look at that war wagon, though!"

Peering in that direction, Moshe could see that a war wagon had managed to reach the glacis without breaking down and was now starting to climb it. He couldn't help but wince with sympathy for the crew. The steam engine driving the wagon was based on an American design, which was quite different from the one driving his airship. The secret to the greater power generated by those engines was mostly crude and simple—they ran the boiler under much greater pressure. If it exploded, in the close confines inside that wagon...

At least they'd die quickly. In horrible agony, but it wouldn't last long.

He shook his head, shaking off the thought at the same time. It looked as if the assault on that bastion was going well. He and Mordechai needed to concentrate on the bastion just ahead of them. The janissaries were still far enough away from the glacis that if they dropped their bombs accurately, they wouldn't hit any of the Ottoman soldiers—and might even clear the way for the assault to succeed. That would go a long way toward improving their status in the eyes of the sultan, if Murad was angry over the failure of their first bombing run.

"How high do you think we are now?" he asked Mordechai. "Over the bastion, I mean, once we come over it."

Pesach pursed his lips, gauging the matter. "About seventy-five kulaçs, I'd say. Certainly not more than a hundred."

"That's what I figure also—and it's too low. The only way we can be sure of hitting the target is to stay right above it without moving, and I'm not taking any chances of getting hit by another volley. So let's drop some more ballast. I want to be at least one hundred and fifty kulaçs above the bastion. At that height, even if they hit us, I don't think the balls will penetrate the gondola."

"Let's hope you're right," said Mordechai.

✧   ✧   ✧

For a while, Leopold thought they might be able to drive back the Turks. The Austrian cannons were slaughtering the bastards, the way they were coming such a great distance across open ground with nothing to shelter behind.

It was the tank that turned the tide. Once the armored wagon started up the glacis, the Austrian soldiers got very anxious. There was something unnerving about the way the machine slowly and stolidly kept coming. Bullets bounced off it—even being hit a glancing blow by a cannon ball didn't seem to faze the thing.

Thing? It seemed more like a living creature, full of malevolence.

Still, Leopold kept the men steady enough—until the tank was no more than twenty yards from the walls and a Turkish soldier emerged from the central hatch holding some sort of peculiar-looking tubular device. A torch of some kind?

The tube spouted a long tongue of flame that reached all the way over the walls and fell on some of the men sheltered there. They began screaming hideously, running toward the stairs leading off the bastion. Still alight, like moving torches.

Leopold realized instantly that the Ottoman weapon was using some variety of Greek fire—napalm, whatever. And he realized at the same time that it couldn't possibly be that effective a weapon. Not just one of them, at least. All they had to do was shoot the soldier wielding it.

"Stand your ground!" he shouted, charging up to the wall and waving his sword. "Fire a volley at the wagon! Kill the bastard!"

But it was hopeless. The men had already been badly hammered by enemy fire. Among the many unpleasant surprises of that day, the janissaries were now armed with muskets that were far superior to what had been expected. Now the morale of the Austrian troops shattered and they started racing off the bastion.

Leopold himself was knocked down by several of the routed soldiers. He might have been trampled except one of them—a very big fellow—took a moment to grab him by the collar and haul him back onto his feet.

"It's no use, Your Grace," the man said. "Just try to save yourself, all you can do now."

And he was gone. After a brief hesitation, Leopold realized he was right and followed the soldiers off the bastion.

What should he do now? Where should he go?

Cecilia Renata. He had to find out what had happened to his sister and the other two women. Do what he could to get them safely out of the city. There might still be time. The Ottomans hadn't surrounded the city, they'd concentrated all their forces against the southern walls. If he could...

If—if—if—

Once he was off the bastion, he started running toward the Hofburg.

To Hussein's astonishment, the final charge up the glacis was unopposed. Until that moment, the Austrian resistance here had been ferocious. He wasn't certain, but he thought it was the armored wagon that had made the difference. If so, the stupid thing turned out to have some use after all.

But he'd figure out later if he owed the zimmi crew an apology. Right now he just wanted to kill some Austrians. The swine had been butchering them and he looked forward to returning the favor.

As soon as he came over the bastion wall he spotted a wounded Austrian soldier trying to lever himself upright with a musket. Hussein rushed at him with his yataghan. Finally, he'd be doing the butchering.

But the man collapsed back onto the stone floor and Hussein's swing went wild. He tripped over the Austrian and almost fell himself. Now furious, he spun around to deliver the death stroke.

The muzzle of the musket was pointing right at him, held by the enemy soldier as he lay on his back. The Austrian's finger pulled the trigger and Hussein saw nothing more.

"Let's do it," said Moshe. He and Mordechai started dropping the bomb jars over the side. The wind was slight enough that they could both work at it for perhaps a minute before having to make adjustments in the thrust to keep them over the target.

The bombs were heavy, each one weighing about half a kantar—a kantar being roughly the weight of a woman or a small man—and they had to be lifted off the ledges they were resting on and over the side. But for two men working together, the work could be done quickly.

As they did so, Moshe saw that one of the ledges had been struck by a musket ball. He hadn't noticed earlier. Those ledges had been added despite the additional weight in order to keep the bomb jars from rolling about. But he now saw that the ledges also served as additional shields. If the jars had simply been resting on the floor of the gondola when the musket balls punched through, it was very likely at least one of them would have been shattered.

Would that have been enough to explode it? Probably not. But Moshe tried to imagine what would happen on an airship carrying fire bombs, if one of those jars was burst by enemy fire. Even if the impact didn't set the liquid afire, you'd still have the gondola floor awash in the hideous stuff, with an open flame no farther away than the steam engine.

Which, yes, you could shut off. And then what? Be adrift and completely helpless before the wind.

"We need to armor these things better," he grunted, as they heaved another jar over the side.

"We're starting to drift," was Mordechai's only response.

They didn't drift much, though—not at all, so far as the Austrian soldiers two hundred and fifty yards below them could tell. They'd fired two volleys at the airship, but at that height only half a dozen balls had struck anything—all but one, the envelope—and none of them had done any damage.

The height from which they were being dropped meant that the bombs weren't hitting all that accurately, either. At least a third of them missed the bastion entirely. But enough of them fell to complete the demoralization of the troops manning that part of Vienna's fortifications, and they began to run also. Within less than a minute, all of them were routed off the bastion.

Murad's telescope was so large that it needed a tripod to hold it steady. But the sultan didn't mind the cumbersome arrangement. Even at that distance, a bit more than a mile away, he had an excellent view of what was happening on the walls of Vienna.

Both of the targeted bastions were now clear, and one of them was already being seized by his janissaries. The other, the one which had just been bombed by the returning airship, would be very soon.

He stooped a bit, in order to raise the angle of the telescope. It took him a few seconds to bring the airship into view. When he did, the inscription on the side of the envelope was quite visible, because he was looking at it from an angle.

He'd ordered the airships to be named after Ottoman victories. This one was the *Chaldiran,* in honor of the great triumph more than a century earlier over the Safavid heretics of Persia.

He stood up straight. "Have the crew of the *Chaldiran* brought before me after they land. Along with the crew of the *Esztergom.*" That had been the airship which had failed in its mission to bomb the bastion that the *Chaldiran* had just struck.

"Bring them here, My Sultan?" With a little nod of his head, the officer indicated the sultan's headquarters tent.

Murad smiled, very broadly. "Certainly not!" He pointed to the city in the distance. "Have them brought to me in my new palace. What the Austrians used to call the Hofburg."

When Leopold reached the Hofburg, all he found were some looters—three civilians who'd stayed behind to help in the defense of Vienna and who had apparently now decided to reward themselves with some of the palace's valuables before escaping the city. All the other civilians Leopold had seen on his way here had been racing to get out of Vienna before the Turks got their hands on them.

As soon as the looters spotted Leopold, when he entered the palace, they fled. They looked almost comical doing so, the way they were weighted down with ungainly treasure. One of them was even carrying a table piled high with his gleanings. He wasn't moving any faster than a man could walk.

"Idiots," Leopold muttered. As slowly as they were moving, they probably wouldn't make it out of the city before the Turks caught them. At which point they'd lose everything they'd stolen and probably their lives in the bargain.

But he had much more important concerns than a trio of looters. He raced up the stairs, heading for his sister's chambers.

She wasn't there—but from the look of her bed, she had been. And not so long ago, he thought.

He was sure Minnie and Judy were still with Cecilia Renata. They were not women who would abandon her in these circumstances.

So where had they gone? Were they trying to flee the city?

Possibly—but not probably, he thought. Not given his sister's injury. Instead, he suspected they'd made for the safety of the cellars in the detached wing of the palace. He'd go search for them there.

If he did, though . . .

He hurried to the window and looked out. He couldn't see

the fortifications, but even at this distance he could hear the sounds of the Ottoman victory. The enemy would be pouring over the walls, except in those places where the flames from the fire bombs still hadn't died down.

The worst of the sounds were the screams of wounded Austrian soldiers who hadn't been able to escape and were now being butchered by the janissaries. But there weren't very many of those. Mostly what he heard were the triumphant shouts of enemy soldiers.

They'd be at the Hofburg very soon. If he took the time to search the cellars looking for Cecilia Renata, he'd have to stay there even if he didn't find her. There wouldn't be time to escape from Vienna.

So be it. The cellars would make an excellent hiding place. And if he could...

He just had time, he thought. He ran out of the room and raced up the stairs to the next floor. Then down a long hallway and around a corner and he found himself in the radio room.

The radio was still there, he was relieved to see. He gathered it up in his arms, after detaching wires which did...whatever they did. Leopold knew very little about how radios actually worked. But he'd have plenty of time to learn, he figured, since he'd be trapped in those cellars for weeks.

At least. Maybe months.

Some small treacherous part of his brain added in a whisper: *maybe forever.* But he paid it no attention.

He hurried back down the stairs and out into the courtyard. There, he paused for a few seconds, listening intently.

The Turks were getting close, he thought. But he still had time to make it into the cellars. Burdened by the radio—which was bulky and clumsy more than heavy—he wasn't able to move faster than a sort of brisk half-shuffling trot. But he didn't have all that far to go.

Still, he was relieved once he reached the detached wing. Again, he paused for a moment, this time not listening but looking around carefully, to make sure no one was watching him. He couldn't afford to be seen entering—not even by other Austrians, who could be questioned if captured by the Turks. If the Ottomans ever suspected that there were hidden cellars here, they'd surely find them no matter how well disguised the entrance was.

But he saw no one. He turned and entered; then hurried toward the stairs leading to the upper floors of the tower. The hidden entrance to the cellars was located one floor above, and two floors below the small chamber at the top of the tower with its four narrow windows.

He had to be careful, here. He couldn't afford to leave any trace of his passage, and if he dropped anything he'd have to make sure—

"Leopold!"

Startled, he looked up and saw Judy Wendell at the next landing, peering down at him around a corner in the stairwell. She had a strained look on her face—and, he was a bit startled to see, a pistol in her hand.

Which was pointed at him. But she lowered it right away.

"Hurry!" she said. "Do you need help?"

He shook his head. "No, just make sure the door is open. It's ... cumbersome."

The door was designed to be cumbersome, of course. It was very heavy, with stone facings that matched the stone work of the stairwell. The door opened outward, so that once it was closed there would be no way to smash it in—or even to realize a door was there—without smashing in a good portion of the stone wall. It was then held shut not only by several latches but by an ingenious arrangement of bolts and chains that allowed someone inside to tighten down the door to the point where it would be quite impossible to pry it open, or even to see that a door existed.

When he reached the door, Judy was holding it open. After he passed through, she came behind him and started to pull it shut.

"Not yet," he said, starting down the staircase beyond. He was moving slowly and carefully, because he couldn't see very well. "That's the only light we have until we get some candles or lamps. There are a lot of them down here, you know. Is my sister with you?"

"Yes. Minnie's taking care of her at the moment."

"How is she?"

"She's been better. But she'll be all right, I think." Judy was now following him down the staircase. Once they reached the floor of the cellar she pointed to the left. "They're in that chamber. I'll go back up and keep watch."

As he neared the chamber, moving very slowly and feeling his way in the darkness, he could see a bit of light ahead. Minnie must have at least one candle burning.

She had two, as it turned out. And, like Judy, was waiting for him with a pistol in her hand—but not pointed at him, thankfully.

"I just wanted to be sure it was you," she said, rising from her chair and returning the pistol to some hidden recess in her garments. He hadn't realized she had one in her possession.

Cecilia Renata was lying on a narrow bed next to Minnie. She was asleep, he saw.

He looked around and spotted a sort of narrow table—more like a tall bench, perhaps—against one of the walls. He went there and, with a small sigh of relief, set the radio down.

Minnie had come over with him, a candle in hand. She held the light over the equipment he'd brought, inspecting it. Judging from the knowing expression on her face, she understood a lot more about radios than he did—which wasn't saying much, of course.

"Very nice," she said. "But you forgot to bring an antenna. And there's no battery."

Leopold had heard of "antenna" and "battery." But he couldn't remember what they did or even what they looked like.

Minnie must have seen the helpless look on his face, because she smiled and patted him on the cheek.

"Never mind, you did good," she said. "We'll figure something out."

The pat on the cheek was quite outrageous, for someone in her position to administer to an archduke of Austria. The hand placed firmly on the back of his neck and the long kiss that followed were even more outrageous.

But Leopold didn't mind, under the circumstances. At all.

Eventually, to his regret, the kiss ended. Minnie patted him on the cheek again and began walking toward the entrance to the cellars. "Come on," she said. "We've got to get that door sealed so no one knows we're down here."

He followed after her. "I still can't believe it," he said. "We withstood Suleiman for weeks—and would have done the same—did do the same—whatever—when the Turks came again fifty years from now. Then. Whenever."

They reached the stairs and started up, moving slowly with just the one candle to light the way.

"And now," he continued, trying not to wail, "we've lost the city after such a short siege!"

Minnie stopped abruptly and turned to look back down at him.

"What are you talking about?" she said. "The siege of Vienna has just begun."

Chapter 41

Magdeburg, capital of the United States of Europe

When Rebecca entered the small audience chamber in the palace, she found Gustav Adolf half-slumped in a chair. The expression on the emperor's face was complex: chagrin mixed with belligerence, overlaid by a sort of stolid resignation.

"Your husband was right and I was wrong. You may gloat for half a minute," he said. "No more than that, however, or I will become—what's that up-time expression? 'Testy,' I think. Which doesn't make any sense, when you think about it. How is aggravation a test? But I often find American expressions to be absurd."

"As do I, Your Majesty," said Rebecca, keeping her expression bland. "For instance, what could possibly be the meaning of 'cut the mustard'?"

"I forgot," he said. "You never gloat, do you?" He indicated a nearby chair with a meaty hand. "Please, have a seat. Piazza is right. You will make a superb secretary of state. Which is good, because your first assignment begins immediately."

As she lowered herself into the chair, Rebecca allowed a little frown of concern to crease her face. "The results of the election are not actually final, Your Majesty. Until then—"

"Be damned to all that!" It was a testimony to the emperor's short temper that he skirted blasphemy. "No one doubts that the Fourth of July Party won a clear majority—and I haven't time for petty republican foolishness. If Wettin objects, I'll toss him into the palace prison."

He pointed a thick finger at the floor. "It's down there, don't think it isn't! I made sure of that when I approved the architect's plans for the palace. It's even got a toilet. That's for the guards, of course. The prisoners can make do with chamber pots!"

Rebecca had to fight down the urge to smile. She knew about the small dungeon that Gustav Adolf had incorporated into the palace when it was constructed. She also knew that the only use the emperor had ever made of it was to lock up one of his mastiffs when the beast got unruly. But he'd let the dog out after only two hours.

No one in the world took Gustav II Adolf lightly. The man could be ferocious, at times. But he really didn't have the makings of a true autocrat—certainly not one along the lines of Ivan the Terrible or Caligula.

"You do not actually have the authority to do that, Your Majesty," Rebecca said mildly.

His savage frown was replaced by an equally savage grin. "Says who? I remind you, Frau Abrabanel, that although that we have a constitution the specific powers and limits upon them of the monarch are stated only vaguely and subject to wide interpretation." He slapped his hand on the armrest of his chair. "I make sure of that, hah! Which means that any major dispute will need to be settled in the courts."

The frown reappeared. "Courts which your scheming husband did his best to pack with republican malcontents and quibblers when he was prime minister, I grant you that. But all judges have one characteristic in common, revolutionary rascals or not."

The grin reappeared. "They deliberate very, very slowly. So by the time the courts finally rule that I exceeded my authority as emperor when I tossed Wilhelm Wettin into my dungeon and I have to let the wretch out, you will already—no, long since—have made a settlement of the Bavarian issue."

He fluttered his hands in a shooing motion. "So be off and about it, Rebecca. I will settle for that bastard Maximilian going into exile—anywhere he wants as long as it's outside the USE and not on its borders—and replaced as duke by his brother Albrecht. But make sure Albrecht understands that Bavaria will henceforth be a protectorate of the United States of Europe. That includes stationing a small USE garrison—fine, fine, it can be an expanded ambassadorial guard—in Munich."

Rebecca opened her mouth. Closed it. Then, after a brief hesitation, nodded her head.

Put that way...

"What about Regensburg?" she asked.

Gustav Adolf glowered fiercely at... nothing in particular. "It remains—now and forevermore—within the jurisdiction of the Oberpfalz. If the Bavarians object, tell them that's the price of starting and losing a war. No, no! Add that they can be thankful I don't seize all of northern Bavaria down to the line of the Amper River—which—"

He wagged a thick admonishing finger. "You can tell the Bavarian swine I'm sorely tempted to do anyway."

Again, he made the shooing motion with his hands. "And now, again—be off!"

As soon as Rebecca left the emperor's presence, she went straight to the palace's radio room. She made no attempt to disguise her movements nor did she use any code in her transmissions other than the approved imperial code. Neither subterfuge would have had any point. Gustav Adolf would certainly find out where she'd gone—he'd expect it, actually—and while she could use a code he couldn't decipher, that would cause more trouble than it would be worth. Not to mention the nuisance of having to transmit a coded message via a radio operator who had no understanding of what he was saying and was almost sure to garble the message.

The first message was to Michael:

Gustav Adolf agrees to Bavarian settlement. Maximilian to go into exile outside the USE and not on its borders. Albrecht to replace him. Bavaria to become USE protectorate.

She saw no point in further elaboration. Her husband was quite capable of reading between the lines and taking the needed military measures.

She sent the exact same message to Noelle in Prague. Noelle would relay it to Janos Drugeth, Duke Albrecht and Wallenstein.

The message she sent to Vienna was more diplomatic:

Emperor Gustav II Adolf has decided to reach a settlement with Maximilian, if possible. The duke to go into exile and be replaced by his brother Albrecht.

She saw no need to rub the Austrian emperor's face in the fact that Bavaria would henceforth be a satellite of the USE. Ferdinand was smart enough to figure that out for himself—and quite smart enough to understand that protesting the fact would be pointless.

That immediate task done, she contemplated her next course of action. And, almost immediately, realized that there was a problem she had completely overlooked in the just-passed discussion with the emperor. So, she had the radio operator send yet another message to her husband:

Will need airfield ready for operation ASAP in Freising.

Then, back she went to the audience chamber. Fortunately, while Gustav Adolf had already left he had only done so to attend to what were euphemistically referred to as "personal toiletries." No matter how august the imperial personage might be, some tasks simply couldn't be relegated to a servant.

He returned a short time after she was ushered into the chamber.

"Did you forget something?" he asked, lowering himself into his seat. Rebecca, for her part, had decided to remain standing. She told herself, firmly, that was not for the sake of being able to flee the imperial presence in great haste—even though she was sure Gustav Adolf was not going to react well to her next . . .

What to call it? *Proposal* was not strong enough, certainly, but *command* was preposterous. One did not "command" Gustav II Adolf, Lion of the North, King of Sweden, Emperor of the United States of Europe, High King of the Union of Kalmar—you could now toss Lord Protector of Bavaria into the title salad—to do anything.

She settled for *elucidation of stern necessity to the royal understanding.* In her own mind only, of course.

Sure enough, after she explained her reason for returning, the emperor glared up at her fiercely.

"Your husband put you up to this!" he accused.

"No, he did not, Your Majesty. I simply—"

It was time for a change in their relationship, she realized. As the secretary of state of what was, after all, Gustav Adolf's government, she could neither afford nor tolerate maintaining the same formalities she had always adhered to prior to this moment.

So, she threw up her hands with exasperation, plopped herself into a chair facing the emperor, and exclaimed: "Gustav, it is long past time you gave up this pointless stubbornness on the subject! Those warplanes serve no purpose buzzing around in northwestern

Poland. Fine—keep one of them—no, two, in case one requires maintenance—to alert Lennart in the unlikely event that Grand Hetman Stanislaw Koniecpolski goes mad and attempts a sortie from Poznań. But that's all Torstensson needs up there!"

The glare on Gustav Adolf's was replaced by look of concentration. "No, Lennart needs at least three. One—as you say—as a reserve in case maintenance is needed. *When* maintenance is needed, rather, since it always is with those complex machines. One to maintain a patrol around Poznań—that's as much to fray the Poles' nerves as anything else. Another to patrol farther afield, in case that bastard Wladyslaw tears himself away from his whores in Warsaw long enough to organize an army to march to the relief of Poznań."

He grunted softly, a sound that suggested mollification. "I admit I could probably now spare the rest of the planes. Both Belles, certainly, and at least one of the two Dauntlesses."

"*One* of the Belles," Rebecca countered. "They're not much use for anything except reconnaissance. Michael will need real warplanes to fight those Ottoman airships."

"Nonsense!" bellowed Gustav Adolf. "The truth is that none of our so-called warplanes will be of any use against airships—or other warplanes, if the Turks ever manage to build any—and you know it as well as I do!"

He was . . . right about that. Nonetheless, Rebecca wanted the best planes she could get for her husband and the forces he'd soon be leading against the Ottomans.

"Still, the Gustavs and Dauntlesses might be of use against the armored wagons the Turks are reported to have. The Belles . . ." She shrugged. "They are simply too small, too light."

"Nonsense!" he bellowed again. "Must I remind you that it was a Belle that destroyed a Danish warship at Wismar?"

She shook her head. "Only because Hans Richter rammed the plane into the ship after he was wounded. If he had simply used the Belle's missiles instead of turning the plane itself into a missile, he would have done no more than superficial damage."

The emperor really did have a magnificent glare. His heavy brow loomed over his icy blue eyes like a cliff; the eyes themselves peered down that big heavy nose like the eyes of a raptor—and somehow he even managed to impart a sense of fury into those glacier-colored irises. Rebecca was quite impressed.

She was also certain that it was mostly for show. Always

hard to tell with Gustav II Adolf, of course. But she was willing to take the risk.

"Let Michael have one of the Gustavs and both Dauntlesses," she proposed, "along with one Belle. That will leave Lennart with the other Belle and two Gustavs—enough for his purposes."

The glare lasted for perhaps another three seconds. Then it was replaced by a look of calculation. A look of cunning, you might also say.

"I will agree—on one condition. Go talk to those two pestiferous airplane designers in Grantville. They will listen to you. Tell them they must—*must*, you hear?—stop their petty squabbling and combine their resources. We need warplanes that *can* attack airships—and other planes, soon enough. Someone will build them; the French, if not the Turks."

She stared at him, dumbfounded. "But...why me? I know nothing about airplanes."

"You know how to get people to do things." He grinned, suddenly. "As you have just demonstrated once again."

He made that same two-handed shooing gesture. "Now, go. Go. I will tell Lennart to send a Belle and the two Dauntlesses to the Third Division as soon as an airfield is ready to receive them in Freising. You *did* tell your husband to build one immediately, I assume?"

"Ah...Yes, I did."

"Such an efficient woman. Now, off you go."

Once in the corridor outside the audience chamber, Rebecca started muttering to herself. "So which one of us, exactly, just got done maneuvering the other?"

With Gustav II Adolf, that was always hard to tell.

Freising, Bavaria

Mike Stearns handed the deciphered radio message to Christopher Long. "See to it, Christopher. And do it quickly."

His adjutant stared down at the message. "Ah..."

Mike chuckled. "Get Jeff Higgins to advise you."

"He knows how to build an airfield?"

"Probably not. But he's a geek so he'll figure it out."

✧   ✧   ✧

Jeff shook his head. "Geek, is it? Figure it out. That's an insult to geekdom."

Long's frown seemed to be permanently affixed to his face by now. "What *is* a 'geek,' anyway?"

"You wouldn't understand if I explained. It's a geek thing." Jeff pursed his lips. "The reason it's an insult to geekdom is because geeks like stuff that's complicated and building an airfield is about as simple as it gets. There are only..."

He paused for a moment, adding them up.

"Three things involved. First, find a flat piece of land that's at least four hundred yards long—five hundred would be better—and between twenty and thirty yards wide. Second, it needs to be manicured. That means carefully swept for any sort of obstructions and those need to be removed. Any rock bigger than a piece of gravel; any and all tree stumps; any logs or even big sticks—anything that a plane's landing gear could stumble over. Third and last, do whatever you can to make the surface as hard as possible."

Long's frown hadn't budged. "And that is done...how?"

"In a perfect world, we'd macadamize the surface. That means covering it with crushed stones. Well, basically. Some kind of binder helps, too. But we haven't got time for that. I'd recommend you start by finding some heavy wagons and driving them back and forth across the surface until you've compacted it. Then..."

He got an evil-looking smile on his face. "It won't kill the guys to get in some marching practice. We can start with my regiment. After you're done with the wagons, we'll march the regiment up and down the field for a while. Then, while they rest, have another regiment take the Hangman's place. Keep doing that until the surface looks as compacted as it's going to get. Then give the airstrip another manicure and finish by raking everything as flat as you can get it."

Long nodded slowly. "All right. I think I grasp the basic principle. You're right—it isn't really all that complicated."

Jeff's heavy upper lip curled into a sneer. "Damn insult to geekdom, what it is."

Prague, capital of Bohemia

Janos Drugeth's expression was almost haunted. "I can't believe..." He shook his head. "Never mind that. The immediate problem is that we don't have enough planes for our purposes. We only have Nasi's. We need another."

"We'll just have to make do with what we have, until another plane becomes available," said Noelle. "The most pressing thing is to get you down to Linz. That airfield will be ready soon, yes?"

"Ferdinand says so." Janos managed a smile of sorts. "Of course, whether or not an emperor of Austria is an expert on airfields is a proposition that could easily be debated. But I'm sure he has experts advising him."

Noelle refrained from pointing out that the courtiers of a seventeenth-century monarch probably had as little expertise on the subject of *airfields, construction and proper maintenance thereof,* as the monarch himself. They'd just have to make do what with they had.

"Eddie can fly you down when the airfield's ready. In the meantime, he can get me..."

She began faltering at that point. Janos chuckled, humorlessly.

"Get you and Albrecht and his two children—he'll want that Jesuit tutor of theirs, too—into a plane that can't hold that many people," he concluded.

She ran fingers through her hair. "We'll just have to do it in stages. I'll fly to Amberg and pick up the kids. The tutor will have to wait—or he can get his own butt down to Freising from Amberg on horseback. It's not *that* far. Once I drop the kids off—"

"Into whose care?"

She waved her hand. "Details, details. I'll figure that out later. Then I can have Eddie fly me back to Prague to pick up Albrecht."

"Who has not yet agreed to any of this—and you won't be here to negotiate with him."

Noelle snorted. "We'll see about that. Follow me, O great count of Hungary, and do your best to look like a vampire."

She headed for the door.

"What is a 'vampire'?" he asked.

The Bavarian nobleman didn't need much in the way of persuasion, as it turned out. Perhaps that was due to Noelle's way of approaching the subject.

"Here's how it is, Albrecht," she began. "You can either finally agree to this deal and come with me—not now; maybe a couple of days—to Bavaria, where you'll be reunited with your sons and become the new duke—understanding that Gustav Adolf is in no mood to dicker about the 'protectorate' part of the deal and if you're wondering what 'in no mood' means think of a very big bear with a very sore tooth—or you can stay here in Prague and rot the rest of your life away while Gustav Adolf gobbles Bavaria up whole. You've got five minutes to decide."

She made a display of looking at her up-time wristwatch. It was simply a piece of jewelry, these days, since the battery had died more than two years earlier. Albrecht probably even knew that himself. But it was still an impressive gesture.

"I need more time to consider the matter," Albrecht protested.

"Sorry, but you haven't got it. Four minutes, fifty seconds left."

Albrecht turned toward Janos. "This is most precipitous!"

Drugeth shrugged. "It's out of my hands, I'm afraid." He nodded toward Noelle, who was peering intently at the watch as if the device were still functional. "The USE is in charge of it now, and she's their emperor's envoy."

"Four minutes, thirty seconds. Time's running out, Albrecht."

"See?" she said, after they left. "That wasn't so hard. I knew he'd be reasonable about it."

"In much the same way a man facing the headsman's ax will come to his senses," mused Janos.

"Oh, that seems like a melodramatic way of putting it." She displayed her wrist triumphantly. "All I had was a watch that doesn't work."

Chapter 42

Lower Silesia, near Legnica (Liegnitz)

By the third day of the expedition, Gretchen had come to detest
her armor with a bone-deep passion.

She had been prepared for the weight of the miserable stuff.
In fact, she'd curled her lip at the prospect of hauling around
forty to fifty pounds of steel. Leave it to men—the boastful, whining, bombastic, histrionic gender—to pontificate on the crushing
weight of armor.

Forty pounds—fifty pounds, even—pfah! It was well distributed
across the entire body. Nothing at all like the burden of carrying
a child on one hip and a basket of laundry on the other, which
any stalwart girl could manage by the time she was twelve.

No, it wasn't the weight. It was the *heat*.

They were in the middle of August, and while Lower Silesia
did not have a particularly hot climate, August was still August—
the peak of summer. The sun beat down on her steel armor from
dawn to dusk. She might as well have been wearing an oven.

Worse than the armor itself was the padding underneath
it. The gambeson she wore beneath the steel was essentially a
quilted jacket, which was the last thing any sane person would
wear in mid-summer.

But wear it she must. She'd initially rebelled and tried to wear
the armor without it, but she'd given that up after a few minutes.
To begin with, the armor had been designed to fit over a gambeson,

382

so it was too loose without it. Just walking around—clumping around, rather—was enough to risk bruises. If she ever actually had to use the armor to fend off a weapon, the impact would simply be transmitted by the armor itself, without the padding.

She started sweating by sunup and sweat all day.

She itched.

She stank.

In the evening, when she removed the armor and gambeson, she expected to see chunks of soggy flesh being peeled off as well. To her surprise, that had never happened.

Yet. She was sure it was only a matter of time.

It was no wonder Poland's warrior class, the szlachta, behaved like so many idiots. What could you expect of people who voluntarily roasted themselves every day? It was a wonder they had any brains left at all.

That was especially true because the most horrid part of wearing armor was the stupid helmet. Bad enough for her body to be half-melting; even worse was that her brains were being parboiled.

And she couldn't *see*. All she had was a narrow slit to look through. Never mind that her eyes were half-blinded anyway by the sweat pouring off her brow. Even if her forehead had been as dry as a bone it was like trying to move around while looking through a keyhole.

A wide keyhole, fine. It was still a keyhole.

She swiveled her head around—that was the only way to see anything that wasn't directly in front of you—and looked for Opalinski and Wojtowicz. Her two so-called bodyguards had ridden ahead a few minutes earlier to scout the terrain.

"So-called bodyguards" because if they'd really cared about guarding her body they never would have forced her into this idiotic armor to begin with. Gretchen thought she was far more likely to kill herself by falling off her horse because she couldn't see where the dumb beast was putting its hooves than she was to get killed by an enemy soldier.

She'd been glad to see the two Poles ride off. Stupid cheery bastards. Despite the fact that he was wearing armor himself, Opalinski had even been singing for a while. Some Polish drinking song—she knew enough of the language to figure out that much—which was undoubtedly as crude and silly as any German drinking song.

(American drinking songs were even worse. Her husband had once forced her to listen to a song called "Ninety-Nine Bottles of Beer on the Wall." Thankfully—he'd probably saved himself from getting divorced—Jeff couldn't remember any of the lines after disposing of the ninety-seventh bottle.)

It took Gretchen a while to spot Jozef and Lukasz, since she could only inspect a narrow slice of the surrounding terrain through the eye slit in her helmet. But eventually she did.

Good. They were at least two hundred yards off. Even if they raced back immediately and started nattering at her she could get a few minutes' worth of relief.

She undid the latches and took the helmet off her head, then shook her head vigorously so that her long hair, which had been pressed into a sodden mass, could blow free in the breeze.

What a relief!

A flash of yellow in the corner of his eye drew Jozef's attention. He looked in that direction—like Gretchen, he had to swivel his head to do so—and then hissed his displeasure. If he hadn't been wearing a helmet, he would have shaken his head with disapproval as well.

"The damn woman's taken off her helmet, Lukasz," he said, loudly, so that his companion could hear him. Opalinski was riding ahead, perhaps five yards distant.

Lukasz reined in his horse and turned to look. He, too, had to swivel his head to do so. Fortunately, the armor that all three of them were wearing was quite well made. Poorly crafted armor could result in helmets that could barely be swiveled at all. A man had to turn his whole body around—or that of his horse—in other to look in a new direction.

When he saw the far-off little splash of yellow, he grunted. "I can't say I really blame her. Try to imagine what your head would feel like in a helmet if you had hair like that."

If he hadn't been wearing plate armor, he would have shrugged. But, like head nodding and head shaking, that gesture was futile at best when you were cocooned in steel.

"Let's leave her be for a few minutes before we insist that she put it back on," he said. "I want to get to the crest of this rise ahead of us and see what's beyond."

He set his horse into motion. Jozef made ready to do the

same, but paused to give the distant blonde figure a last glare of censure.

The glare was replaced almost instantly by widened eyes.

"*Lukasz!*" he shouted.

Captain Philipp Asch lowered his spyglass. "It's her," he said. "It's *got* to be her."

Standing next to him in the ramshackle barn, Lieutenant Otto Bierman was squinting through a crack between two boards in the wall. He had no spyglass and was near-sighted to boot, so all he could really see was a vague splotch of yellow a few dozen yards away.

"Are you sure you recognize her?" he asked, frowning.

Asch issued a little snort of exasperation. "How could I recognize her when I've never met her? But what other blonde-haired woman would be riding a horse out here, wearing fancy armor like that? She's good-looking, too, just like people say."

Unlike his subordinate, the captain had quite good eyesight and the woman wasn't all that far away. In the spyglass, he'd gotten a very good look at her.

"Let's go," he said. "Her ransom's got to be good—and Holk will give us a bonus himself if we bring her in."

"What about those two Polish hussars that were with her?"

Asch shook his head. "Who knows? They've ridden off anyway. She was probably negotiating something with them. I said, let's go."

He jammed his own helmet onto his head. It was nowhere close to being as fancy a helmet as the one the woman had removed, just the common sort of lobster-tailed pot helmet known as a *zischagge*. Like many low-grade mercenary officers, Asch was a commoner who couldn't afford a better helmet. He'd been born in a small town in Swabia, the son of a cooper. If they could capture the notorious Richter and collect a ransom, he'd be richer than he'd ever been in his life—or even dreamed of being.

"Now, Bierman," he half-snarled. His lieutenant was prone to being slow-witted.

None of the other men in their unit had gotten off their horses when they entered the barn, which they'd done as soon as they spotted the trio of oncoming riders. So at least Asch didn't have to chivvy them into the saddle as well. It would be stretching a point to say his men were "ready." They were no worse than the average cavalryman in Holk's army, but that wasn't saying much.

Still, they'd do. The woman was alone now. Even if the pair of hussars decided to come to her help, which Asch thought was not likely, he wasn't too concerned about it. Hussars could be ferocious in battle, true enough. But there were still only two of them—and he had eleven men with him. Two against twelve. Those were hopeless odds, even for hussars.

A few seconds later, he led the charge out of the barn. Within three seconds of emerging, he spotted Richter.

She hadn't moved very far. She couldn't be more than seventy yards off.

Splendid. This would all be over within a minute or two.

Gretchen's eyes were drawn immediately to the group of horsemen piling out of the barn she'd noticed earlier. She hadn't paid much attention to it, since it was half-ruined and obviously abandoned. Neither had Lukasz nor Jozef.

Stupid—all three of them. An abandoned barn made as good a hiding place for enemies as a functioning one. Better, actually, since there'd be no nervous livestock to make warning noises.

But what was done was done. She had no more than a few seconds to decide what to do.

Trying to escape from them was not an option. Not for her, at any rate. Gretchen wasn't inept in a saddle, but she was no horsewoman, either. If she tried to gallop away from cavalrymen, she'd most likely just spill herself on the ground.

Within two seconds, in fact, she'd decided the horse was a liability altogether. With an agility that would have astonished her if she'd been thinking about it, given the armor she was wearing, she was out of the saddle and back down on the ground almost instantly.

Then, she slapped the horse on its rump to get it out of the way. She didn't much like horses but she had no great animus against the beasts, either. No point in getting it killed, even leaving aside the fact that she didn't want a panicky horse in her vicinity. She had enough trouble as it was.

All that had taken perhaps five seconds since she'd spotted the cavalrymen. They had covered half the distance between them, by now. She had only a few more seconds before they'd be upon her.

Happily, she had three factors working in her favor.

First, the stupid helmet had gone flying off somewhere so she could see what she was doing.

Second, she'd drawn the line at wearing armored gauntlets, so her hands were unencumbered and her fingers were nimble.

And, third, she'd bullied the armorer into making an addition to her cuirass that he'd considered an affront to both dignity and martial style. You couldn't exactly call it a "shoulder holster"—it was more in the way of a pouched breast plate—but it served the same purpose, and did so quite well. She'd made sure of that.

Her nine millimeter pistol was now in hand—and she had two spare magazines if she needed them in the not-exactly-a-breast-plate's match on the right side of her cuirass.

It was a Glock 17, the same one her husband had given her shortly after their marriage five years earlier. It had belonged to Jeff's father. Gretchen had been trained in its use by Grantville's police chief, Dan Frost, and had become a very good shot.

Gretchen *adored* her nine millimeter pistol—never more than this very moment.

She saw no point in trying to find shelter. There wasn't any worth talking about on this stretch of what had once been farmland, and a suit of plate armor is hardly suited to agile leaping about. Best to just stand there, take a solid two-handed firing position—thankfully, the armor had been well enough made to allow for that also—and wait for the enemy to arrive.

Which she figured they would in about...

Three seconds.

Lukasz and Jozef were driving their horses toward her with all the recklessness and superb horsemanship that Polish hussars possessed. But it was already obvious they wouldn't reach her in time. The first of the small mob of enemy cavalrymen were almost upon her.

Asch had been in the lead for most of the charge, but toward the end two of his cavalrymen surged ahead of him. They were both very good horsemen—better than he was, though he certainly wouldn't have admitted that publicly.

All the greater his shock, then, when both men suddenly came out of their saddles. He had a glimpse of one of them as he fell. Blood was gushing out of his throat.

What happened? He had a memory of some sort of very loud ripping sound.

His mount shied away from the falling corpse and carried him right past the woman in armor. As he wheeled the horse around, he heard that same peculiar ripping sound.

Another one of his men was falling out of his saddle. His cheap cuirass was soaked in blood.

Again, the ripping sound—and, again, one of his cavalrymen slumped in his saddle. But now Asch was able to see the odd gun in Richter's hand as it jittered about, and he suddenly understood that what he was hearing was the sound of multiple shots being fired one right after another. Asch realized that he was looking at one of the famed up-time pistols. "Semi-automatics," they were called, if he remembered right.

He'd never encountered one before. He'd heard tales of their astonishing rates of fire, but he'd dismissed them as myths; or gross exaggerations, at least.

He shouldn't have, perhaps. Asch had been one of the soldiers on the Stone Bridge at Prague who'd tried to cross in the face of Jews and students organized by a few Americans. But he'd been far in the rear and hadn't personally witnessed the rockets that had broken the charge. None of the firearms had had a particularly unusual rate of fire, so far as he could remember.

Another cavalryman came charging at her but this time Richter killed the horse. He wasn't sure how many shots she fired to do it. Three, four—perhaps even five?

The horse's knees buckled and the rider was spilled right onto Richter. She managed to lunge aside far enough that only her midriff was struck by the falling cavalryman. Still, even wearing that splendid plate armor, she was knocked down and had to be shaken by the impact.

Not *that* shaken, though. Even lying on her back, she managed to bring her pistol to bear and shoot the man who'd knocked her down. Right in the face. The bullet passed through his upper teeth and out the back of his head.

Asch saw his chance and drove his horse toward her supine body. He would trample her and worry about making the capture later. The ransom would be the same regardless of her condition, so long as she was alive, and it wasn't likely that being trampled would kill her outright—not wearing that armor, at least.

She looked up at him as he came and that frightening pistol came up also. He ducked his head.

This time he heard the shots quite distinctly. *One. Two.*

His horse buckled and down he went. All thoughts of Richter vanished. Asch was far too experienced a cavalryman not to know how dangerous falling off a moving horse could be. All his attention was now concentrated on landing on the ground without breaking his neck.

The first thing he did, of course, was throw away his own pistol. Landing on top of a cocked wheel-lock was a good way to get killed.

The horse trampled Gretchen before it fell—which was probably just as well, since otherwise the whole weight of the great brute might have landed on her. Still, even wearing a steel cuirass, having a horse's hoof slam into your ribs was no fun at all.

Fortunately, the breath wasn't knocked out of her. Everything was sheer chaos by now. For her, at least, and she could only hope the same was true for her enemies. All her attention was concentrated on getting a new magazine into her pistol. She'd used up the seventeen rounds she'd started with.

Jozef could no longer tell what was happening. He and Lukasz had crossed more than half the distance already, but the fracas was obscured by the fact that Lukasz was a better horseman than he was and had gotten ahead of him. It didn't help that he was so blasted big, either, especially wearing armor. It was like trying to peer around an elephant—while galloping at full tilt yourself.

Jozef was a very good equestrian, if not in his friend's league. Still, most of his attention had to be devoted to the simple task of staying in the saddle. Falling off a horse that was moving close to thirty miles an hour was a sure way to break some bones, one of which might well be part of your spine.

Lukasz had a better view of what was happening and was such a superb horseman that he didn't need to concentrate entirely on staying in the saddle. So he'd seen Gretchen get knocked down.

But what he could also see was that the men attacking her were confused themselves as to what was happening. Several of them had been killed, in a manner that many of them probably didn't even understand. Two horses were now also down, along with the corpses of the men.

Horses are big animals and big animals are leery of stepping on treacherous terrain. In their none-too-capacious brains, corpses and carcasses qualified as *treacherous terrain,* so all the surviving horses were jittery.

Jittery horses make for jittery riders, and jittery riders tend not to pay close attention to what's happening around them because they're preoccupied with staying in the saddle. Besides, "what was happening around them" by now consisted mostly of horses jittering around.

In short, it was almost comical to see the way Gretchen was left alone for a few seconds. Deadly seconds in which she rearmed her very deadly pistol.

She came back up—not to her feet, just to her knees—assumed that peculiar two-handed firing stance, and started killing again.

Lukasz was almost there. He lifted the lance out of its holster and set his own killing stance.

Gretchen shot one of the bastards—twice, maybe three times—before another one of them took aim at her. His pistol fired and she was sent sprawling again, spinning half around from the impact of the bullet on her cuirass.

It was a hammering blow. The wind still wasn't knocked out of her, but she was half-stunned.

So, she was in perfect position to see the final moments of Lukasz Opalinski's charge.

Jeff had told her once of his own experience being charged by a mounted Polish hussar. He'd escaped being killed—barely—but his friend Eric Krenz had gotten wounded in the process.

"What's it like?" he'd said to her. "It's fucking terrifying, that's what it's like. Being lanced by a Polish hussar is right up there with—with—hell, I don't know. Being charged by a really pissed-off elephant with really big tusks, maybe."

Indeed, so. In that last split second before the lancehead speared its target, Lukasz looked enormous. She could only imagine how he looked to the man he was about to kill—who, for his part, was just staring at him with his mouth wide open and his face as pale as a sheet.

The lance took the cavalryman in the chest and drove through the buff coat as if it was a child's jacket. Three feet of the spear came through the other side—including, incongruously, the red-and-white Polish banner he'd attached to it. Both the lancehead and the banner were coated in blood and gore.

Lukasz made no effort to hold onto the lance. To the contrary, he pitched it aside as soon as the spearhead passed through his target, which had the effect of hurling the dying man onto the ground and out of Lukasz's way. By the time the man came out of the saddle, Lukasz had already drawn his saber.

Which also looked huge. That was hardly surprising, since by the standards of one-handed swords it *was* huge. You could make fun of a lot of things about Polish hussars, but their fighting skill was not one of them.

That skill didn't run toward subtlety, though. The saber struck another cavalryman on his right thigh and cut through to the bone. The pain and shock paralyzed the man. His guard lowered, Lukasz's next strike cut through the flange of the man's lobster-tailed pot helmet, severed his spine and sent him flying out of the saddle.

Lukasz—she had no idea how—managed to duck a pistol shot and then came back up with the saber rising high above him.

Down it came, like an ax. That man's helmet was split in half, the pieces falling aside, while the blade went several inches into his skull. From the sound of it, though, Gretchen thought the man was actually killed by having his neck broken from the force of the blow.

Lukasz was immensely strong. One quick twist of his wrist freed the saber from the skull it had imbedded itself in, and another quick twist tossed the man's corpse aside.

Then Jozef arrived. Gretchen was obscurely pleased to see that he was a man with her own inclinations when it came to weaponry. *To hell with that medieval crap.* He had his own pistol in hand and started shooting.

Within a few seconds, it was all over.

After dismounting, Lukasz moved through the bodies littering the ground to see if there were any survivors. The horses had all run off by now except the two Gretchen had killed.

One of the men who'd been shot was still alive. But he wouldn't be for much longer so Lukasz severed his carotid artery with a thrust of the saber. Under the circumstances, it was a mercy killing.

Another cavalryman was almost entirely unhurt, except for having the wind knocked out of him. His left forearm might be broken too, from the way he was cradling it. Lukasz checked to make sure the man was unarmed, and then told him: "If you move more than three inches in any direction, I'll cut your head off."

That would hold the fellow, he judged. He checked the rest of the corpses while Jozef tended to Gretchen. The woman had obviously been battered about, but none of her injuries were life-threatening.

Served her right, anyway, being as reckless as she had taking off her helmet.

But...

Lukasz Opalinski was a very experienced soldier, given his still-young age. Gretchen Richter had been attacked by a dozen men, only one of whom had survived.

He'd killed three of them and he thought Jozef had killed two more. The rest—six, all told—had been killed by Richter herself.

He knew very few hussars who would have survived, in her position, even with the help of that fearsome up-time pistol. That had taken the sort of cool nerve and concentration in battle that not many men could manage.

He wasn't sure he could have done it himself.

Gretchen waited, more or less patiently, until Wojtowicz and Opalinski finished berating her. She figured she owed them that much.

Eventually, they finished. By then she was back on her feet, aching all over but apparently with no permanent injuries.

She would admit that the armor had kept her from having ribs broken by a horse trampling on her, and had kept a bullet from passing through her torso. But if she'd been wearing the stupid helmet she'd have been unable to shoot accurately.

More to the point, she'd been going about this whole business wrong from the very beginning. That was what came of listening to men whose shaky grasp on practical reality had been shaken still further by their faith in military superstitions.

"Fine, I shouldn't have taken off the helmet. But I never should have been wearing it in the first place. We're doing this all wrong. Chasing all over trying to find Holk and fight him. It's stupid."

The two Poles frowned at her.

"How else can we find the bastard?" asked Lukasz.

"Make him come to us. I will show you."

She pointed at the one surviving mercenary. By now, he was sitting upright. Still cradling his forearm, which was almost certainly broken, not that Gretchen or her two companions had any sympathy for the swine.

"Bring him. He might know something."

Neither she nor Lukas nor Jozef bothered to speculate on whether or not the man would talk. First, because he was a mercenary. Of course he'd talk.

Secondly...

Opalinski went over to their captive.

"Be afraid," he told the fellow cheerfully. "Be very afraid."

Chapter 43

Freising, Bavaria

"You're sure?" Mike Stearns asked, his tone of voice insistent.

His brother-in-law got an exasperated expression on his face and lapsed out of military protocol. "For Christ's sake, Mike, will you please stop fretting about it? We'll be fine. The last thing Piccolomini's going to do is order a sortie. Right now—bet you dollars for donuts—the only thing he's pondering is where to find his next job. Seeing as how this one is clearly coming to an end."

Mike looked away from Tom and spent a few seconds studying the distant walls of Munich. They were starting to look pretty ragged. The relentless pounding of the two ten-inch naval rifles, for weeks on end, had turned large stretches of the Bavarian capital's fortifications into not much more than rubble. They were at the point where launching a mass frontal assault would be on the agenda very soon—except that Mike was on the verge pulling the Third Division out of the siege and beginning the march into Austria.

Beginning the ride into Austria, it would be better to say. By now, he had close to a hundred barges assembled in Freising. The vessels were anything but uniform, either in size or carrying capacity. But he figured he had enough to carry the whole 1st Brigade as well as the Hangman regiment down the Isar to the confluence with the Danube near Deggendorf. From there, the troops would transship onto larger craft which would take them down the Danube to their final destination at Linz, which had become the new capital of Austria.

They needed to get there quickly. No one doubted that as soon as he felt he had Vienna under control, Sultan Murad would leave a garrison to hold the city while he marched most of his huge army up the Danube to crush the final pocket of Austrian resistance. If he could manage that, he would win the war, not simply Vienna.

Murad had to be stopped at Linz. That was the best that could be done for the moment, but Mike thought it would prove to be good enough in the end. So long as the Austrians held Linz and Emperor Ferdinand was kept from being killed or captured, the fight could continue without the morale of the allies being too badly hammered. But if they lost Linz—and with it all of Austria—Mike wasn't so sure of that. Everyone was astonished at the speed and ferocity of the Ottoman onslaught. Even Mike himself, being honest about it, for all that he'd warned people of the danger of underestimating the Turks.

He looked back at Tom Simpson. "All right. You'll still have the 2nd and 3rd Brigades for a few more days. By then General Schmidt should have arrived with the SoTF National Guard. Between them and the two regiments I'll leave behind—"

"—we'll be fine. Like I said, quit worrying." He made the same sort of two-handed shooing motion that Gustav Adolf had used with Rebecca. "Go, will you? *Sir.*"

The last word came with a smile as well as an emphasis. Mike couldn't help but smile back.

"Fine. I'm off."

On their way down to the docks, his adjutant Christopher Long asked him a question.

"Dollars I understand, as part of a wager. But what is a donut?"

Mike explained, then added: "My wife claims we stole the idea from Jewish bagels and just made it unhealthy. She might be right."

As he had many times in the past, Long got a long-suffering look on his face. "What is a bagel?"

Munich, capital of Bavaria

Ottavio Piccolomini had been worried himself that Duke Maximilian might order a sortie, once he realized that Stearns was starting to withdraw some of his forces from the siege. There would be no useful purpose to such a sortie, though. Even if the Bavarians managed to dislodge the remaining USE forces, they couldn't possibly destroy that army. The approaching forces of the State of Thuringia-Franconia would intervene before they could do more than inflict some casualties—and they'd suffer plenty themselves while they were about it.

No, by this point, Piccolomini's main concern was to keep his army as intact as possible. The war was lost, no matter what he did. From his point of view, the best outcome would be a negotiated settlement where Maximilian went into exile and was replaced by his brother Albrecht. There was really no longer any reason for the duke to reject that outcome, since his only heirs were Albrecht's two sons unless he remarried and sired more offspring.

But, first, Maximilian didn't have enough time left for that alternative. And, second, he lacked the desire anyway. The ruling duke of Bavaria was now sixty-three years old, heartsick at the loss of his wife Elisabeth of Lorraine, and still further disheartened by the treachery of his betrothed, Maria Anna of Austria. He spent most of his time in prayer, these days, paying little attention to the affairs of his duchy.

Piccolomini was fairly sure—he certainly hoped—that Maximilian would accept a political settlement if one was offered to him. The fact that Stearns was now withdrawing some of his forces would seem to indicate that Gustav Adolf was finally opting for that solution also, probably because of the unexpected Ottoman victory at Vienna.

Assuming that to be the case...

Piccolomini needed to plan for his own future. Any political settlement the USE would accept with Bavaria would certainly result in a sharply reduced independence of the duchy, even if it wasn't simply absorbed entirely. That meant a much-reduced Bavarian army as well, and the likelihood that the USE would allow Piccolomini to remain as its commander was essentially nil.

The best outcome for him would be to negotiate his withdrawal, along with that of most of his men, as part of the settlement. He could extract as many as ten thousand soldiers, possibly, which he could take with him wherever he went. A mercenary general with an army at his disposal could always get a much better deal with a new employer than a general on his own.

So. Where to go?

Italy, he thought. The Spanish recklessness in overthrowing Pope Urban VIII was producing tremendous unrest in the peninsula. Cardinal Borja, the new self-proclaimed pope, could use Piccolomini's services. And since the Spanish crown had thrown its support to Borja, they'd presumably be willing to foot the bill. Whatever weaknesses and failings the Spanish kings might have, they always had the silver fleets from the New World to rely on.

All things considered, his situation was actually quite good. True, he'd lost the war. But he could claim a tactical victory at Zolling, which would make him the only general in Europe who'd ever defeated Stearns on a battlefield. Given how much of Europe's royalty and aristocracy detested the American upstart, Piccolomini thought he was eminently employable.

Grantville, State of Thuringia-Franconia

Rebecca gave the two aircraft designers an exasperated look of her own. "Can the two of you stop squabbling for a moment? I cannot spend much more time on this. I need to get down to Freising so I can begin negotiations with Duke Maximilian."

Hal Smith and Bob Kelly both had the grace to look embarrassed. After a moment, Hal cleared his throat and said: "Rebecca, trying to keep Bob and me from disagreeing is just hopeless. Maybe if he weren't such a stub—"

"Hal!" exclaimed Rebecca, almost barking the name. "I said: stop squabbling."

"He's right, though," said Bob Kelly. He placed his hands on his thighs and pushed himself back in his chair. Then he smiled a bit. "We can't even agree on which of us is the stubborn one. I admit, that's probably like trying to pick which mule is the most ornery."

He shrugged, without moving his hands from his legs. "Look, let's do it this way. Hal goes ahead with his pusher design and I'll concentrate on building the two-engine Mosquito-style plane I think would be best for our purpose. The government can buy either one it wants, once the prototype is ready."

Hal grunted. "Or both, like you guys wound up doing with the Dauntless." There was a note of grievance in his voice. Rebecca knew that Hal was still annoyed that the USE government had decided to expand its little air force by buying two of Kelly Aviation's new Dauntless planes instead of putting in another order for his tried-and-tested Gustavs.

But there was no point in stirring up that issue. She had enough to deal with, as it was.

She looked from one of them to the other. "Just to be sure, in case the emperor asks me to explain. You are both convinced that it would be a mistake to try to develop a single-engine tractor plane whose gun would either fire through the propeller by using a—I forgot what you called it—?"

"Synchronization gear," Hal and Bob said, simultaneously.

"Yes, that. Or to mount guns on the wings, where there would not be any risk that the bullets would strike the propeller."

Again, simultaneously, both men shook their heads.

"Synchronization gears are tricky to get right," Bob said, "and if you mess it up you've got a real problem on your hands. In the universe we came from, they didn't get them working smoothly until the Second World War. But we don't have anything like the kind of industrial base they had."

"The problem isn't just the synchronization," added Hal. "Putting guns on the wings won't work either. The machine guns we can build right now are pretty damn crude and they malfunction a lot. The truth is, we need a two-man crew to operate a real fighter. One to fly the plane and one to fire the gun—and get it working again when it messes up. Trying to pile a synchronization gear on top of that is like putting lipstick on a pig."

Rebecca chuckled. She'd heard that American expression before but still found the image amusing.

"I see," she said. Again, she looked back and forth between them. "So the way you will each handle it is that Hal Smith's aircraft will have the gunner positioned forward of the pilot—"

"Forward and below," qualified Bob. "That way the pilot's forward line of sight isn't obstructed."

"Christ, that thing's going to be a tub," muttered Kelley. "Slower'n molasses."

"It won't be slower than an airship!" snapped Smith in reply. "Which, you might recall, is the specific mission involved. And at least I'll get it built in time to do some good—which is more than you'll be able to say after your fancy damn sorta-Mosquito runs into the design problems it's bound to have because you're too ambitious like you always are. I'm telling you, Bob—"

"Enough!" said Rebecca. "Each of you will approach the problem in the manner you prefer. As we are all agreed."

She rose from her chair. "And now I must be off to deal with a much easier task than this one. That would be negotiating a peace settlement with the most vicious duke in the continent. Goodbye, gentlemen. I wish you both great success."

At least the two men had the grace to look a bit guilty as she made for the door. But before she'd finished closing it behind her, they were back to squabbling again.

Eddie was waiting for her at the airfield. Before Rebecca climbed into the cockpit, she took a moment to admire the nose art. Most people who saw the *Steady Girl* illustration—men, especially—were struck by the pulchritude of the model. But Rebecca was more impressed with the skill of the painting itself.

That skill was not surprising, of course. The illustration had been painted on the plane by Artemisia Gentileschi, one of the few artists of the time who had still been remembered in the world Rebecca's husband had come from.

"Munich, right?" said Eddie, after Rebecca was in her seat and he had her properly buckled down.

"Well, Freising, actually."

Eddie waved his hand casually as he settled into his own seat. "What I meant. Same direction."

Rebecca mused on his words for a while, as he got the plane into the air. Eventually, she decided not to worry about it. Surely, the man wouldn't fly the aircraft as casually as he depicted its destination.

Prague, capital of Bohemia

"I wish you were coming with me," said Noelle, trying not to sound too whiny as she said it. She brought down the lid of her small trunk and closed the latch, then looked around the bedroom to see if she had overlooked anything.

Janos smiled and put his arms around her. "I would not fit, anyway. The *Dauntless* only seats three people."

That was true enough. The third seat in the rear of the fuse-lage was narrow even for one person, if they were heftily built.

"And I have to get down to Linz as soon as possible," Dru-geth continued.

Noelle nuzzled his shoulder. "We need more aircraft," she complained. "It's ridiculous, the way everyone has to rely on Nasi's private plane. Why didn't anyone else have the brains to buy a plane? It's not as if Francisco's the only rich man in Europe. He's not even close to being the richest, either."

Janos didn't bother with a reply, since Noelle knew the answer as well as he did. Airplanes in the here and now were still being built on a one-off artisan basis. Even craft that were supposedly all of the same type—a Gustav, or a Dauntless, or a Belle—were actually quite individual in their construction. Each engine was different, salvaged and adapted from one or another up-time automobile.

He'd once seen a photograph of an up-time aircraft assembly line, taken during what the Americans called their second world war. Quite marvelous, it was—but there was nothing like that in the year 1636, and wouldn't be for quite some time.

Francisco Nasi had gotten his airplane at just the right time, right after Bob Kelly had finished a Dauntless but before he'd begun fiddling with it as he invariably did. The man was an incorrigible perfectionist. A short time after Nasi bought the plane, the USE air force finally agreed to buy the other two that Kelly was working on. That had exhausted the man's inventory.

Noelle wasn't quite done with grousing. "It's all Gustav Adolf's fault," she continued. "It's absolutely idiotic the way he insists on keeping all the Air Force's planes up in northern Poland, where they serve no purpose at all."

There was no point saying anything in response to that, so Janos didn't. Noelle was right, of course. But as the Americans said in one of their quips: *that and fifty cents will get you a cup of coffee.*

He'd inquired, once, as to the precise value of "fifty cents." After being told, he'd been almost as astonished as he'd been at the sight of a World War II aircraft assembly line. There had really been a time—would be a time—when a luxury item like coffee could be purchased for so little? The sheer scale of the universe from which the up-timers had come was an endless source of bemusement. It wasn't simply that their edifices and their machines had been huge; so had been the world-wide trade network that enabled them to create those structures—and ship coffee in such bulk that even the poorest man could afford to buy a cup almost on a whim.

Noelle drew back and pushed him away gently. "Okay, enough pissing and moaning. Seeing as how you're the bold and daring cavalry commander, *you* get to haul the trunk down the stairs."

"I'll stumble and break my neck," he whined.

"Suck it up, buddy."

Eddie arrived in Prague the next day, after having delivered Rebecca to Freising.

"I'm starting to feel like a damn bus driver," he complained to Noelle, as he helped her into the cockpit. He'd been the one who had to muscle her valise into the cargo compartment at the rear of the fuselage, of course. Noelle had insisted she was much too weak for such an enterprise and Janos Drugeth—no fool, he— had decamped as soon as the plane landed on Prague's airstrip.

Her betrothed had urgent business, Noelle had said—a claim that Eddie didn't believe for a minute, since he'd be back to fly Drugeth down to Linz as soon as the Austrians there got the new airstrip finished. That shouldn't take more than a few days, which would give him the time he needed to shuttle Albrecht, his two sons and their tutor down to Freising and then bring Noelle back to Prague where Nasi would give her whatever new assignment he had in mind.

Which would almost certainly be going to Linz to rejoin Drugeth so Nasi could keep his finger in that pie as well as all the others he was meddling with.

Some people got all the luck. Eddie was just the damn bus driver. At least he got into Prague fairly often so he could spend time with Denise.

Chapter 44

Magdeburg, capital of the United States of Europe

Ed Piazza gazed at his image in the full-length mirror positioned in the hallway entrance to his apartment. He and his wife Annabelle lived on the second floor of a three-story residential building located in the southwest area of Magdeburg's Neustadt. (The "New City," in English parlance). Their apartment building had been recommended to them by Mary Simpson, who lived just three doors away on the same street. For Ed and Annabelle, both avid opera fans, the clincher had been that the apartment was within easy walking distance of the city's Opera House.

The image in the mirror gazed back at him—at least, insofar as he could see anything of the face beneath the broad-brimmed hat sporting an ostrich plume.

"Christ, I feel stupid," he said. "I sure don't envy Morris Roth, having to wear a ridiculous get-up like this every day."

"Better get used to it," said Annabelle, standing just behind him and a bit to his left. Her tone of voice was noticeably lacking in sympathy. "For what it's worth, I agree with Judith Roth. Middle-aged men with expanding bellies and thinning hair look a hell of a lot better in fancy seventeenth-century outfits than they ever did in up-time suits."

"Hey!" Ed protested. "My hair's as thick as ever even if it's mostly gray now."

Annabelle plucked the hat off his head, exposing the skull beneath. "That forehead's at least an inch higher than it was when we met."

402

"Well, almost as thick," Ed qualified. His eyes moved down to the image's midriff. "I won't argue about the belly. Which is not my fault, anyway! Back in the day, when I was an honest high school principal, I was on my feet a lot. Now that I'm a no-good rotten politician, I spend most of my day sitting on my butt."

"You should start loitering in back alleys with your hand outstretched for bribes. That'd give you a little exercise, at least."

Ed sniffed. "Not how it's done in the here and now. Corruption's an entirely sedentary affair. No exercise required at all, except throttling your conscience—and even that's just pro forma."

He tugged at the bright blue sash that crossed his chest from his left shoulder. "I admit I don't miss having to wear a damn tie."

"Enough preening," said Annabelle. She seized her husband by the shoulders and began steering him toward the door. "The emperor awaits, and you don't want to be late."

"And that's another thing," Ed complained. "Why do we have to have the only monarch in Europe—hell, probably the whole world—who thinks punctuality is a virtue?"

Once down in the street, they found a carriage waiting for them. The vehicle belonged to the Marine Corps, and had a Navy captain standing by the open door waiting to help them in.

Ed frowned at him. "Is this part of the protocol, now? And when did you get here from Luebeck?"

Captain Franz-Leo Chomse smiled. "The admiral's wife suggested to the admiral that I might be helpful. There being no pressing need for my services at the moment in Luebeck, Admiral Simpson sent me down here. As for the issue of protocol, so far as I know there isn't anything established yet."

After they climbed into the carriage, Chomse came in and closed the door behind him. "If I might make a suggestion, though," he said, "now that the awkwardness of having a Crown Loyalist prime minister is behind us, I would recommend that you establish the Marine Corps as the official guards of the prime minister's person and residence."

He nodded politely at Annabelle. "And family as well, of course."

Ed sighed. "Let me guess. Simpson put you up to this. Or Mary did."

"The admiral himself, with regard to the position of the Marines. Mrs. Simpson did suggest, however, that it was perhaps time to establish an official residence for the prime minister. The down-time equivalent of Number 10 Downing Street, was the way she put it. She said she saw no need for the more flamboyant alternative of erecting a White House."

"Oh, wonderful," said Ed. "An official residence which will no doubt be within walking distance of Government House and the Royal Palace instead of the Opera House."

"I would imagine so," said Chomse blandly.

There was a serious issue beneath the badinage, though. A whole set of issues, in fact. Ed Piazza was about to become the third prime minister of the USE, but in a number of ways he would be the first one who was fully legitimate. Mike Stearns had simply been appointed to the post by Gustav Adolf when the USE was formed in late 1633. And while the second prime minister, Wilhelm Wettin, had been elected to the position, his administration had very quickly become embroiled in the plot hatched by the Swedish chancellor Oxenstierna to overthrow the USE's regime after the emperor sustained his incapacitating head injury at the battle at Lake Bledno.

The administrations of both Stearns and Wettin would always have an asterisk attached to them—in the minds of the populace, at least, if not the official histories. Piazza would be the first prime minister of the USE chosen in a fair and reasonably untainted election whom no one suspected of having any schemes in mind beyond governing the nation—or having any attachments to anyone else who might have such schemes.

True, he was known to be close to Mike Stearns, the man now often called "the Prince of Germany." But if Stearns had wanted to seize power, he would have done it at the height of the Dresden Crisis, after his defeat of Banér at Ostra. The fact that he had voluntarily resumed his position as the commander of the Third Division once the emperor had regained his senses amounted to his assurance to the nation that he had no such designs.

In the universe the Americans had come from, it was said by historians that perhaps the greatest boon George Washington had given the nation he'd helped create was the way he left office. In a different way, Mike Stearns had done much the same thing after the Dresden Crisis.

But legitimacy is always aided by props and buttresses. One of those, however small it might seem, was to have the chief executives of a nation reside in an official dwelling, instead of anywhere they might choose to waft about.

"Cheer up, dear," said Annabelle. "Look at it this way. Princess Kristina adores musical performances so it's just a matter of time before she insists on having operas—musicals, oratorios, you name it—performed regularly at the Royal Palace. Which we can walk to."

"With a pack of Marines surrounding us any time we go outside," muttered Ed. "Great."

"As opposed to the pack of CoC toughs that Gunther Achterhof makes sure we have surrounding us any time we go outside where we live now. What's the difference?"

Ed couldn't help but smile. The solicitude of the city's Committee of Correspondence for his and Annabelle's health and well-being had a slightly comical edge to it. Since Piazza hadn't had any official status in Magdeburg—technically, he was still the President of the State of Thuringia-Franconia and technically he still lived in Bamberg, the SoTF's capital—he'd felt it would be inappropriate to ask the national government to provide him with any official assistance.

So, Gunther Achterhof had made good the lack. And if having a bunch of CoC activists as bodyguards and assistants was a bit like having a pack of bikers doing the job...

Well, what the hell. He'd certainly never worried about being assaulted by irate reactionaries, had he?

The carriage drew up before the Royal Palace.

"And here we go," he said. "O brave new world, that hath such rituals and protocols in it."

"Stop grousing," said Annabelle. "And make sure you don't knock off your ostrich plume getting out of the carriage."

The ceremony itself went flawlessly. Gustav II Adolf, Emperor of the United States of Europe, King of Sweden, etc., etc., etc., appeared in the audience chamber moments after Ed arrived. He was dressed in a costume that was an order of magnitude fancier than Piazza's—and wore it with an ease that was at least two orders of magnitude greater.

Long and ornate sentences issued from the monarch's mouth, the gist of which was:

I need a new government. Are you willing to organize it?

Not quite as long or quite as ornate sentences issued from Ed's mouth, the gist of which was: *Yup.*

To which Gustav II Adolf replied, stripping away the dense verbiage:

Have at it, then. You can leave now.

"See?" said Annabelle, after they emerged from the audience chamber. "That wasn't so bad."

"Where would you like to go now, Prime Minister?" asked Chomse.

Ed didn't have to think about it. "To the Government House. The radio room. I need to send Rebecca a message."

That was just a short walk across Hans Richter Square, followed by climbing four flights of stairs once they were in Government House. For obvious reasons, the radio room had been placed on the top floor.

Ed paused to take a brief rest on the third floor. At the age of fifty-five, climbing a bunch of stairs wasn't as easy as it used to be. His wife, who was eleven years younger than he was, waited patiently. Unlike her husband, she wasn't breathing any more heavily than usual.

"How long are you going to be my factotum?" he asked Chomse.

The navy officer shrugged. "As long as you need me. I assume you'll have your own staff put together shortly."

"Take me about a week, I figure. Okay, then. Make a note. See about getting an elevator installed."

"Sissy," said Annabelle.

"I'm just thinking about the convenience of elderly guests we might have."

"Liar," said Annabelle. "I can remember when you were an honest straight-talking school principal instead of a sleazeball politician. It's kind of sad, really, the way some people lose their moral rectitude along with their hair."

Ed gave Captain Chomse an appealing look. "Isn't there some sort of protocol governing how sarcastic wives are allowed to be once their husbands reach a certain social elevation?"

"Judging from the way Mrs. Simpson speaks to the admiral, no. I believe what she'd say in this situation is: 'suck it up.'"

Annabelle burst out laughing.

The message Piazza sent to the Third Division's radio station in Freising was short and sweet:

*You're it, Becky. It's official. Secty of State. Get that
bum out of there ASAP.*

Munich, capital of Bavaria

"I'm afraid the duke is indisposed," said Ottavio Piccolomini. "He
asked me to begin the negotiations with you on his behalf." He
motioned toward a nearby chair. "Please, won't you sit down?"

As Rebecca took her seat, she considered the implications of
the general's short statements.

The duke is indisposed. Translation: *He doesn't want to deal
with it himself, which means he's not going to resist whatever
settlement is reached. Not very hard, at any rate.*

He asked me . . .

Why would he ask a military figure to negotiate a political
question?

Translation: *All of Bavaria's top officials are either fleeing
Munich*—which would be quite easy, since Michael had made no
effort to surround the city—*or they've gone into hiding and are
trying to stay out of sight in case the settlement winds up being
a savage and punitive one.*

Which meant that, for all practical purposes, Bavaria's government had disintegrated under the combined pressure of the siege
and the expectation that Maximilian's resistance was at an end.

To begin the negotiations . . .

The key word was "negotiations." The use of it meant that
Piccolomini—as well as Maximilian himself, presumably—was not
going to quibble over what was transpiring. If they wanted to stall,
Piccolomini would have used a term like "discussion" instead.

So.

Since Piccolomini was the key figure in all this, on the other
side, Rebecca decided that a diplomatic opening statement was
called for. Michael would have put it more crudely: *Start by but-
tering up the son of a bitch.*

"My husband asked me to extend his respects. Your command
of Bavaria's forces was superbly adroit in the recent battle. He
also asked me to extend his appreciation for your consideration
in handling the USE's dead and wounded soldiers."

Neither of those statements was a lie, after all, leaving aside the slight fib involved in saying Michael has asked her to make them. He'd done no such thing. On the other hand, if she'd asked him, he would have, so as fibs went it was a pretty minor one.

Piccolomini nodded his head, a bit ponderously. "Please thank him for the kind sentiments, and return my own respects."

There was a slight pursing of the Italian general's lips when he said that. Rebecca suspected that Piccolomini was fibbing a lot more than she had. If he'd been able to express himself with complete honesty, he'd probably have said something like: *Tell your husband he's one lucky bastard and next time he pulls a reckless stunt like that he'll surely get a thrashing at the hands of a real professional general like me.*

But Piccolomini's record in the history books as an accomplished diplomat in his own right—not to mention Machiavellian schemer—clearly had some substance to it. So, he said none of that.

Rebecca was guessing, but she was fairly certain that Piccolomini had his own interests in this parley. If so, it would be best to entwine those into the talks right from the start.

"I must begin by making clear that Emperor Gustav Adolf believes firmly that any settlement with Bavaria must include a settlement of your own status and situation as well as that of your troops."

Piccolomini nodded his head again—a quick, short nod, this time, not a slow and ponderous one.

"Yes, I agree. What does he have in mind?"

So, she'd been right. A good place to start. A superb one, in fact, given what she could offer.

"You and all your men will be guaranteed safe passage out of the city. You may keep your personal property, including horses and weapons. Field artillery, also, if they belong to you or your officers rather than Bavaria."

Piccolomini made a face. The expression was a complex one, though. There was clearly satisfaction—even pleasure—at the generous terms. But also, apparently, he felt some trepidations. Or reservations, at least.

"Not all of my soldiers will want to leave, Frau Abrabanel. Most of them are foreign mercenaries—Italians, mainly—but a fair number are resident in Bavaria. Some were born here, others have settled and made attachments. Wives, children, that sort of thing."

Rebecca considered the matter, for a moment. She had been given no precise guidelines on how to handle the issue.

"How many of your men do you think would want to stay?"

"At least three thousand. More likely to be close to four thousand."

"But no more than that?"

"I shouldn't think so." He got a thin, cold smile on his face. "There's been a fair amount of desertion since the siege began, especially of soldiers who've been in Bavarian service for five years or more."

Translation: *Any Bavarian soldier whose service went back to the slaughter at Magdeburg is scared of what will happen to him if he falls into the hands of the USE army. As well he should be.*

That seemed to make for a good point of departure.

"Let me propose the following, then. Any soldier in your army who wishes to remain behind in Bavaria may do so—provided he can provide documentation that his service in the duke's army goes back only three years or less."

"That will exclude most of the officers," said Piccolomini. But he was simply making a statement of fact, not registering a protest.

Rebecca shrugged. "Those are the terms. It will take a week or so to organize the transition of authority, so those officers who are forced to leave will have a bit of time to resolve their affairs."

"Not enough time to resolve them very satisfactorily," said Piccolomini. "Most of them have families and some of them have businesses they will need to sell."

But, again, it was an observation, not a protest.

"The massacre at Magdeburg casts a long shadow, General." Rebecca's tone of voice was even colder than Piccolomini's smile had been. "I have very little sympathy for them—and I can assure you that the soldiers of the USE army and the National Guard of the State of Thuringia-Franconia will have none at all. You know as well as I do that regardless of what orders may be given them by their commanders, at least some of the soldiers will take personal vengeance on anyone they suspect was a participant in the sack of Magdeburg."

Piccolomini just nodded in response. Clearly, he had no intention of resisting the provision, which was hardly surprising. The larger the army that Piccolomini could march out of Munich, the better would be his prospects for future employment.

He'd go to Italy, almost surely. Most of his men came from Italy, and the job situation for a mercenary commander was better there at the moment that anywhere else in the continent.

Well...Anywhere else that would be safe for Piccolomini. If he fell into the hands of Wallenstein, he was a dead man.

"Let us now discuss the disposition of Duke Maximilian," said Rebecca. "Our terms are as follows..."

Freising, Bavaria

"Encode and send the following to Prime Minister Piazza, please." Rebecca laid down a note in front of the radio operator.

> SETTLEMENT MADE STOP MAX TO GO INTO
> EXILE IN ITALY STOP WILL LEAVE MUNICH IN
> SEVEN DAYS STOP PICCOLOMINI AND MOST OF
> HIS SOLDIERS TO ESCORT HIM STOP ALBRECHT
> TO ENTER THE CITY THE NEXT DAY STOP
> WHAT YOU WANT ME TO DO STOP

She settled down with a book. Piazza would be responding soon. His response came almost immediately:

> GO TO DRESDEN STOP
> WHAT IS GRETCHEN DOING STOP

Rebecca stared at the decrypted note.

What is Gretchen doing?

Rebecca had no idea what he was talking about. The last news she'd gotten was that Saxony's Fourth of July Party—with Gretchen Richter now as its recognized leader—had won at least sixty percent of the vote and was now in control of the province.

Ah, well. Rebecca had a superb governess and staff looking after her children and she'd never visited Dresden. It would be almost like a vacation.

With Gretchen Richter. Doing something.

Not exactly a relaxing one, of course. More like a danger sport sort of vacation.

Chapter 45

Hoorn, province of Holland
The Netherlands

Maarten Kortenaer stared at Rita Simpson. The Dutch engineer's eyes weren't actually bugging out, but they were certainly doing a good imitation of it.

"But . . . That's not possible!" he protested. "All the histories—those are *yours*, you know"—his tone became accusatory—"say that the Ottomans failed to seize Vienna—*again*—when they tried in . . ."

His eyes became slightly unfocused, as a person's will when they are scouring their memory.

"1684, I believe."

"1683, actually," Rita responded. "In a *different* universe." She had to struggle a little not to snarl the words.

Kortenaer looked back down at the radio message she'd handed him. "You are sure about this?"

"Of course I'm sure about it!" Again, she had to fight down an outright snarl. *D'you think I'd fake something like this as a joke, you fucking—?*

She took a deep breath. "I assure you the radio message we received"—she pointed at the note in Kortenaer's hand—"is quite legitimate. And, as you can see, was sent by Emperor Gustav Adolf himself."

She was pretty sure that was pushing it. Unless she missed her guess, the message had actually been sent by her sister-in-law,

411

Rebecca Abrabanel. The radio operator had told her the message came from Munich, not Magdeburg. But Becky would have cleared it with Gustav Adolf, so it wasn't more than a technical fib.

Before Kortenaer could say anything further, the door to his office opened and one of the officers of the consortium came into the room. Rita had met the man a couple of times but she wasn't quite sure what his name was. His given name was something like "Hubert"—maybe Hubrecht—and his last name started with an "O" but that was all she could remember.

He, too, was holding a radio message in his hand. He placed it in front of Kortenaer. "This one is from King Fernando himself," he said, "so there's no doubt about it."

He spoke in German rather than Dutch, perhaps as a matter of courtesy to Rita. Her Dutch was lousy but her German was quite good by now—allowing for the fact that "German" was an umbrella term for a jillion dialects, some of which were not mutually comprehensible except in writing. That was a good part of the reason Amideutsch had spread so rapidly. It tended to serve as a lingua franca.

Kortenaer read the message, puffed out his cheeks, and raised his hands in a gesture that suggested helplessness.

"Very well," he said. "We'll have to make do as best we can." He gave Rita a stern look. "You understand that we will have to leave behind all of the armaments we discussed."

Rita nodded. She wasn't perturbed by his statement because she'd always been skeptical that the rockets the Dutch planned to fire from racks slung beneath the gondola would work anyway. They were so preoccupied with making sure the rockets couldn't ignite the airship itself when they were launched and would fly reasonably straight that they completely ignored the itty-bitty problem that they had no guidance mechanism whatsoever. Rita thought the chances of the rockets hitting another airship ranged from dismal to nonexistent.

Besides, if she was correctly interpreting a separate message that her brother had sent to her—she hadn't shown this one to the Dutch—then Mike had a different weapon system in mind entirely: Why else would he have instructed her to stop in Freising and pick up one Julie Mackay, née Sims?

Kortenaer was still looking stern and gloomy. "No rockets, not even any bombs."

Rita wasn't concerned about the lack of bombs, either. By now, the methods and materials needed to make bombs designed to be dropped from airships were readily available in the USE. But one thought did occur to her.

"What about the armor we talked about?" she asked.

She almost laughed, seeing the war of expressions on the Dutch engineer's face. Clearly, his aggrieved perfectionist's soul wanted to tell her—sternly and gloomily—that the armor as well would have to be left behind given the unseemly haste with which his customer wanted his product delivered. But whatever his personal inclinations might be, Kortenaer was an honest man. So, after a momentary hesitation, he nodded his head.

"Yes, we can bring it with us. We will have to install it on the flight itself, but we should have enough time for that. The armor is not, after all, particularly complicated."

That was putting it mildly. The "armor" was simply sheets of thin steel—more precisely, a few sheets made by welding together a number of smaller pieces. The manufacture of sheet steel in large dimensions was still in its infancy in the Netherlands. The stuff wouldn't keep a bullet fired by a large-caliber up-time rifle from penetrating, but it should be pretty effective against ground fire from down-time muskets, even rifled muskets.

"We're set, then," she said. "How soon can we lift off?"

She wasn't sure if *lift off* was the right way to put it. Aeronautics was also in its infancy in this brave new world of hers, but already the people involved in the new industry were becoming just as fussy and anal-retentive as sailors were when it came to proper terminology.

No, no, no! That's not a "floor!" It's called a "deck!" And never mind that both things served exactly the same purpose. You stood on them. Thazzit.

From the slight wince on Kortenaer's face, she suspected that she had in fact used the wrong words. But all he said was: "Tomorrow morning."

A field outside Vienna

Moshe Mizrahi wanted to look away, but didn't dare. From the standpoint of Jews and Christians, Murad IV was a great improvement over previous sultans, but he was still a sultan. Despite his reputation, from what Moshe had seen Murad was not cruel for the sake of cruelty, nor did he seem to take any personal pleasure in the punishments he meted out. But the sultan was still utterly ruthless and never hesitated to make an example of someone if he thought that would stimulate others to greater effort and tenacity.

On the positive side, Murad also never hesitated to hand out rewards and promotions, either, if the sultan felt that someone had conducted himself well. Moshe's presence here at the execution field was a testament to that.

Yesterday, Murad had promoted him to the rank of *kolağası* in what the sultan called the *Gureba-i hava*. The name of his air force was supposed to be an honor, with its similarity to the *Gureba-i yemin* and *Gureba-i yesar*—two of the *altı bölük* cavalry units—but Moshe wondered if the sultan was not also making a joke about the preponderance of Jews in its ranks. After all, the root of Gureba was *garib*, and certainly the Muslims considered him and his fellows to be garibs—strangers. Nevertheless, his promotion made Moshe one of the three immediate subordinates of the Gureba-i hava's commander, a Muslim Albanian *binbaşı* named Şemsi Ahmed, and the only Jew of that rank.

A high honor, indeed, but it came with a price. Moshe's airship, the *Chaldiran*, was the vessel Murad had designated as the execution platform for the surviving members of the crew of the *Esztergom*. The logic was simple, brutal—and very like Murad. The crew of the *Chaldiran*, with Moshe Mizrahi in charge after the death in battle of the airship's Muslim commander, had recovered from their casualties and gone on to fulfill their mission. The crew of the *Esztergom*, on the other hand, despite suffering lighter casualties—only the commander had been killed—had fled the field of battle without inflicting any harm at all on the enemy.

So, the crew of the *Esztergom* would be thrown out of the *Chaldiran*, in full view of the entire complement of the new air force. Over a field close enough to the walls of Vienna that plenty of other Ottoman soldiers would be witnesses as well.

At least Murad had not insisted that Moshe and his engineer, Mordechai Pesach, had to carry out the execution themselves. Three burly janissaries would be the ones who muscled the surviving members of the *Esztergom*'s crew over the side of the gondola. Those condemned men were all fellow Jews, so Moshe was profoundly thankful for that small mercy.

If mercy it was, at all. Sultan Murad had probably made that decision at least in part to avert the possible risk that a pair of Jews might be tempted to save three other Jews by simply flying away and deserting to the Austrians. The risk was admittedly slight, since all of them had family in the homes that the sultan had provided for the Jews of the air force—homes that were guarded by janissaries within the confines of the walled compound established for the air force. The *Esztergom*'s crew had returned, after all, despite the near-certainty of punishment. But the sultan took no chances.

Moshe did his best to ignore the pleas and screams of the first member of the *Esztergom*'s doomed crew, as he was lifted and forced over the side. The man struggled fiercely after his hands and feet were unbound. Sultan Murad had ordered the restraints removed before the men were jettisoned, probably because he thought the sight of a man plummeting to his death while thrashing and flailing would be more effective than the sight of one falling like a sack of meal. But against three janissaries each of whom was larger and stronger, the man's efforts were futile. In less than ten seconds, he was plunging to the ground one hundred kulaçs below.

The second crew member was untied and hauled to the side of the gondola. He made no effort to fight back, nor did the one who followed. Neither would Moshe himself, if he'd been in their position. All they had left now was the dignity of their final moments, before their bodies were turned into broken, mangled bloody paste.

Throughout, Moshe watched what happened. He wanted to look away, but there was a fourth janissary on board. The *bostanji başi*—the commander of the sultan's gardeners, who harvested heads as well as flowers for the sultan—was in charge of the execution, but he'd spent most of his time watching Moshe. The sultan would want to know if his newly promoted Jewish kolağası was tough enough to carry out his duty.

Would Murad order Moshe similarly executed, if he looked away? Probably...not. But with this young and energetic sultan, it never paid to take such risks.

Finally, it was over.

The bostanji başi stepped over to Moshe and slapped his shoulder lightly. "Back to base." He smiled. Thinly, but it was a definite smile. "The sultan will be pleased by my report."

After returning to their base and seeing to it that his airship was properly moored to its mast—the huge hangars the sultan had ordered erected would not be finished for some time yet— Moshe turned to his commander. Şemsi Ahmed had been there to oversee the process.

"What was done to the families of the *Esztergom*'s crew?" Moshe asked. It was a dangerous question to ask, but he felt compelled to do so.

After giving him a hard look, Şemsi Ahmed replied. "The Sultan did not order the men cast out of the air force when he ordered them cast out of your balloon. Their deaths were during the campaign, so the orders I sent were that the families were to be treated as if their men had died on campaign. They had to leave the houses they had been given, of course, but they received the death benefit."

Moshe was startled. What Ahmed had done could conceivably mean his own execution if the sultan found out and took it poorly. If so, the argument that he was simply following procedures would give Ahmed the same protection against the executioner's sword as holding up the paper on which the rules had been written would when the blow descended.

Yet, looked at from a different angle, Ahmed's action had been very shrewd. He had just cemented the personal loyalty of his airship crews, the great majority of whom were Jews.

"Everything according to the regulations, then," Moshe said. "Nothing worth mentioning."

"Exactly so."

In point of fact, Şemsi Ahmed had taken no risk at all. His action in sheltering the families of the *Esztergom*'s crew had been quietly ordered by the sultan himself. Murad IV had many qualities. Ruthlessness was one, certainly. But so was shrewdness.

Freising, Bavaria

"Does Suhl have a radio station yet?" Julie Mackay asked the young soldier who was currently staffing the Third Division's radio center in Freising.

"I'm pretty sure... Hold on, let me double-check." He flipped through the pages of a notebook on his table. That didn't take more than a few seconds, since it was a slim volume.

"Yeah, there's one. I've never sent a message to them, so I don't know if someone will be there right now. It's the middle of the day, you know."

Julie tried not to glare at him. "It's only—what?—two hundred miles? Not even that!"

The operator shrugged. "That's still not line of sight. We're in the Little Ice Age, you know. The Maunder Minimum's just getting started. That means—"

Julie bit off her immediate response, which would have been *screw the damn Maunder Minimum.* "Yeah, yeah, I know," she said abruptly. "Radio doesn't work that good in daytime. Fine. You got a pad I can use?"

He pulled out a standard radio message pad and handed it to her, along with a pencil. She wrote her message in block letters.

> FROM: JULIE MACKAY
> TO: DELL BECKWORTH
> HAVE YOU GOT A LIGHT 50 FOR SALE? I NEED
> ONE ASAP.

She placed the message in front of the operator. "Can you send that message in the evening window?"

He looked down at it and nodded. "Yes. I don't know how soon you'll get an answer, though. That'll depend on who's running things up there. We man this radio round the clock, twenty-four seven, but... Civilians, you know."

Under other circumstances, Julie would have found that statement both amusing and, in some respects, significant. In the seventeenth century, soldiers were generally the people considered to have slack and lackadaisical habits. This soldier's attitude—he was a down-timer, too; a Westphalian, judging from his accent—was a reflection of the Third Division's morale.

That took some of the edge off her anxiety, but only some. She was pretty sure her Wand of Womanly Wrath wasn't going to cut it, if the Ottomans had armored their airships.

Dammit, she needed an elephant gun!

Vienna, capital of Austria-Hungary

At the crack of dawn—what she judged to be the crack of dawn, more precisely; she couldn't see anything beyond what the light of the candle in Leopold's hand provided—Minnie began the elaborate process of opening the door leading to the secret cellars in the palace.

She moved slowly, so as not to make any noise. It took a while, but eventually she had the chain that held the door tight loosened and removed, and undid all the latches. Then, holding her breath, she pushed the door out.

Not far, though—no more than half an inch. Then she waited, listening. After a minute or so, hearing nothing, she pushed the door out another half inch. Then she waited again.

On the third push, she moved the door out a full inch. A very faint trace of light began to show.

She waited, listening. She could now hear some sounds, but they seemed distant; their origin undiscernible.

"Go ahead," Leopold hissed. "I think it's safe."

He was probably right, but Minnie wasn't willing to risk opening the door all the way yet. She did move it a couple of inches, though. For the first time, a crack appeared that allowed her to peer through into the staircase beyond. She could hear much better, too.

Again, she waited, ignoring the slight sounds coming from behind her that indicated the archduke's growing impatience. But, after another minute had gone by and nothing was heard that suggested the nearby presence of anyone, she finally opened the door all the way.

She had gauged the dawn correctly, as it turned out. The light was pale, but provided more than enough illumination for her and Leopold to climb the two flights that led to the small room in the tower that had windows. As they did so, Judy moved down to the floor below and kept watch. So far as they could determine, this outlying annex of the palace was unoccupied by anyone except themselves. That wasn't really surprising, since this detached wing was no longer used for anything except storage.

Once Minnie and Leopold got to the top of the tower, each of them—carefully, very carefully—brought an eye to one of the narrow window slits and looked out onto the city beyond.

What struck Leopold was the devastation which the cursed Turks had visited on his beloved city.

What struck Minnie, on the other hand, was how comparatively little devastation there was.

Leopold had led a sheltered life, most of it in Vienna—a city which had, up until now, suffered no damage from the long years of war since the Bohemian crisis almost two decades earlier. Minnie had led a life which had not been sheltered at all, and had done so in areas of the Germanies which had been badly ravaged.

"Horrible," he whispered.

"Not too bad," was her contribution. "But we'll have to wait a while. It still won't be safe to venture out there."

Leopold looked away from his window to stare at her. "Why would we venture out at all?"

"The radio. We need to get back in touch with our people. Denise will be worried sick about me and I couldn't even begin to count the number of people who'll be fretting over you."

Uncertainly, Leopold looked back out of the window. "Are you sure we need that antenna and the battery?"

"Oh, yes. We might—not likely, but it's possible—get by without the antenna. But without the battery, the radio is just so much junk."

He winced. Minnie smiled and moved away from her window slit. "Not your fault, Leopold. These things happen. Now, come. We've seen what we needed to see. Let's get back into hiding."

Ten minutes later, the door was shut and tightly sealed again.

"How long do we need to wait?" she wondered.

"At least a month," said Judy.

"Perhaps two weeks," said the prince. "Murad will be leading most of his army out before long, I'm sure of it. He'll want to take Linz and the rest of Austria. Once he's gone, there'll only be a garrison left. By then, people will have started moving around and one of us can blend in."

Minnie was inclined to agree with Leopold. Either way, though, they'd be spending a lot of time down in these cellars.

With little in the way of lighting and still less in the way of anything to do. She'd already made up her mind, though, so she wasn't too concerned about it.

Fifteen hours later, when everyone agreed it was time to go to bed, Minnie followed Leopold into his corner of the cellar and slid under his bedding.

"What if you get pregnant?" he asked, very softly.

That was certainly a possibility, if they stayed down here long enough. She'd brought some birth control supplies into the cellars that she'd hurriedly snatched from her room in the palace, but they wouldn't last very long.

Minnie was not given to pointless worrying, however. If it turned out they would be trapped here for the better part of a year, she figured they'd have a lot worse things to deal with than a squalling baby.

"Hush," she whispered, and began the proceedings.

Chapter 46

Breslau (Wroclaw), Lower Silesia
Poland

"Why does she want to come here?" Tata asked, looking over Gretchen's shoulder to read the newly arrived radio message.

Gretchen shrugged. "She's the new secretary of state. I assume she wants to advise us or scold us or both."

She gestured toward Eric Krenz, calling him over. "We need an airfield built," she said, handing him the message.

"Why me?" he whined.

"Just do it and don't argue," said Tata. "It'll keep your men out of trouble, which they're bound to get into otherwise, the way they're getting soused at the Rathaus every night."

That was quite unfair, actually. Eric had been maintaining good discipline over his soldiers. There'd been more trouble from the Vogtland irregulars, who weren't as accustomed to obeying orders as the army regulars that Krenz commanded.

But not all that much trouble—certainly not by the standards of armies occupying cities in what the Americans called the Thirty Years War. The Vogtland commander, Georg Kresse, could impose his will on his men whenever he wanted to, and he had started to do so after a couple of incidents of looting shortly after the Saxon army seized Breslau.

Or marched into Breslau, it might be better to say. The city council and inhabitants hadn't tried to put up a fight, despite

Breslau's significant fortifications. Whatever misgivings they might have about letting the Saxon army come into the city, they were a lot more worried about Holk and his mercenaries.

The worst incident had involved three of Lovrenc Bravnicar's cavalrymen, who'd gotten drunk on the second day of the occupation and tried to rape the daughter of a tavern keeper. The girl's father had intervened and gotten a bad beating for his effort, but the effort had been enough to provide the time it took for Lukasz Opalinski—who'd been quietly drinking in an adjoining room in the same tavern—to get involved in the affair.

A tavern keeper was one thing; the big hussar, something else entirely. Lukasz broke the neck of one of the cavalrymen and beat the other two senseless. The next day, Gretchen ordered the two still-unbroken necks to join their departed fellow at the end of a rope.

And, the same day, she'd ordered all of the Slovene officer's cavalry to leave the city and start patroling the countryside. Bravnicar hadn't objected because, first, it was a good idea anyway; and, second, Gretchen was Gretchen. *She Who Must Be Obeyed.*

Thereafter, there'd been very little trouble. That was probably assisted by Jozef Wojtowicz's clever idea of displaying Gretchen's armor in the main room of the Rathaus. The two quite noticeable dents in the armor served to remind the soldiers enjoying their beer that the woman who now ruled the city had recently killed half a dozen of Holk's mercenaries herself, despite being shot and trampled in the process.

She Who Must Be Obeyed. The joke was heard often, now. Gretchen still found the witticism irritating but she no longer tried to stifle it. There was no doubt it served a useful purpose.

"She might cause trouble for us," Tata said, after Eric left.

"Rebecca?" Gretchen shook her head. "She's more likely to be of help, I think. That is one very smart woman. And we've got a tangled mess on our hands."

Tata smiled. "Speaking of which, you'd better get ready for the big—what should I call it? meeting? brawl?—in the Rathaus two days from now."

Gretchen made a face. "I'm sure it won't be so bad," she said, not sounding confident at all.

"Maybe you should put your armor on for it," Tata suggested.

"That's not funny."

"I wasn't joking."

Freising, Bavaria

The Belle taxied to a stop and the pilot shut off the engine. Before the propeller had stopped turning, the airfield's ground workers had already set the wheel chocks. The pilot climbed out of the cockpit, unhooked his leather aviator helmet, and stripped it off his head. Long brown hair spilled out across...

Her shoulders.

Rebecca was startled. She knew the USE Air Force had female pilots—several of them, in fact—but she hadn't expected one of them to be assigned to be *her* pilot.

She wasn't sure what her feelings should be on the subject. Was the assignment of a female piloting a Belle something she should take as a subtle slight? Should she be angry about it? Nervous about it?

Angry at herself for feeling any of these things? Not for the first time since the Ring of Fire, Rebecca felt simultaneously exhilarated and annoyed by the up-timers' attitudes on the subject of what they called "women's lib."

Exhilarated because of the many openings provided for women like herself. Annoyed because those openings were so often... Well, annoying. Life in the days before the Americans arrived had in so many ways been much simpler.

As the pilot came over to her, Rebecca saw that she was a young woman. Somewhere in her mid-twenties, at a guess, even allowing for the excellent teeth possessed by so many middle-aged Americans.

"Hi," the woman said, extending her hand. "I'm First Lieutenant Laura Goss. Colonel Wood assigned me to be your pilot for what he calls 'the duration.' Near as I can tell, that means I'm at your disposal for as long as you need me."

Goss was short, by American standards—not more than five feet tall, Rebecca estimated—and on the stocky side. Her eyes were brown, very close to her hair in color. Her face was roundish, and while not ugly was not what anyone would call especially pretty, either.

But then she grinned, which livened her appearance quite strikingly. Tentatively, Rebecca thought she'd like the woman.

"Don't take either me or the old Belle here"—she pointed over her shoulder with a thumb—"the wrong way. Colonel Wood's not snubbing you. The Belle's like me. Neither of us are glamorous but we're both reliable and steady. In particular, since we're likely to be going every whichaway, the Belle handles rough airfields better than either a Gustav or a Dauntless. And I've got what you might call a soft touch."

Her hand made a swooping motion, as if it were a porpoise bounding through the water. "Easy up, easy down. That's me. Some of your hot-shot pilots—all men, natch—will rattle your teeth every time they land."

Rebecca smiled back. "I am certain you will be superb at the job. Are you familiar with the airstrip at Dresden?"

Goss shook her head. "No. But I'm told it's in good shape so I don't foresee any problems. That's where you want to go, I take it. How soon?"

Rebecca turned her head and pointed to a valise next to the wall of the control tower. "Right now, if possible."

"Let me gas up first," said Goss. "I'm not sure what the fuel supply situation is in Dresden these days."

Less than an hour later, they were in the air and flying northeast.

The takeoff had been very smooth, just as Goss had promised, not that Rebecca had all that much experience with airplanes. She knew her husband disliked flying, but she herself found it quite delightful. The turbulence they occasionally encountered was simply stimulating.

"How soon will be there?" she asked after a short while.

"Two hours or so, depending on the winds. It's a little over two hundred miles. Of course, that's assuming we don't run into any bad weather or Turkish interceptors."

Rebecca glanced at her.

"Just kidding," said Goss, again with that splendid grin. "The weather's not likely to change in the next couple of hours, and if the Turks have any fighter planes they're keeping them well under wraps."

That last quip was not as amusing as Goss thought it to be, Rebecca reflected. The Ottomans had already shown themselves to be quite proficient at keeping new weapon systems a tightly-held secret.

Still, she thought the likelihood they'd leapt so far ahead of the USE when it came to aircraft design was almost nil. The great strength of the Ottoman Empire when it came to such matters was its huge resources and well-organized government. Just as her husband had predicted, the Turks had produced weapons and weapon platforms that were less sophisticated than the best Europeans could produce—but they'd work, and there would be a lot of them.

The rest of the voyage passed smoothly. They encountered neither bad weather nor enemy interceptors.

The airfield at Dresden was rather crude, compared to the ones Rebecca had experienced at Magdeburg and Grantville. But, again just as she had predicted, Goss landed the plane deftly and with no mishaps at all.

There was a delegation to greet Rebecca, led by a startlingly ugly man by the name of Joachim Kappel. Rebecca knew who he was, although they'd never met. One of Gretchen Richter's top lieutenants—but ranked no higher than fourth or possibly even fifth, as these things could be calculated.

Which meant that Richter had taken both Agathe Donner—"Tata," as she was called—and Eric Krenz into Silesia with her.

"Lovely," she said.

Kappel looked startled for a moment, and then grinned. "Been a long time since anyone called me that," he said. "Not since I was maybe two months old. Usually they call me 'the troll.'"

Rebecca was simultaneously embarrassed and amused. She hadn't intended to say that loud enough for anyone to hear.

While she'd been talking with the delegation led by Kappel, Laura Goss had been having her own quiet talk with someone whom Rebecca took to be in charge of the airfield. The lieutenant finished with the conversation and came over to her.

"We can refuel here but it'll take a day or so. I don't recommend flying on to Breslau until we do. They might have their airfield ready by now—not likely, but they might—but I'd be astonished if they have any refueling capability as yet. I don't want to leave here without being topped up."

Rebecca decided that was just as well. Taking two or three days to assess the situation in Dresden while Richter was absent was probably a good idea anyway.

As it turned out, however, assessing the situation in the city and the whole province took much less time than that. That was because when she arrived at the Residenzschloss she discovered that the acting chancellor of Saxony whom Gretchen had put in charge of the province while she was gone was none other than ...

The man she'd just decisively trounced in the recent election, Ernst Wettin, duke of Saxe-Weimar.

"Yes, it's a bit odd," he said, smiling. "Gretchen trusts me, you see—within limits, of course, but I'm hardly likely to exceed those limits under these circumstances. My apologies, by the way, for not meeting you at the airfield. I had some matters I had to finish dealing with. Would you care for some refreshments?"

Two hours later, Rebecca felt she had a good sense for the state of the province. In a word, solid. In a few words, steady and not unsettled.

"It helps a great deal that the emperor sent General von Arnim and most of his army to Poland," said Ernst. "That removed any large military force in Saxony that the CoC people and the Vogtlanders might have felt posed a threat. The soldiers remaining in Leipzig are enough to maintain order in the city but no more than that."

He shrugged. "In truth, the biggest problem I face is that Dresden's Lutheran pastors continue to be agitated."

"Agitated? By what?"

She had the definite sense that Wettin was suppressing a grin. "By the competition posed by Richter's new Episcopal church," he said. "They're quite aggressive in their proselytizing, just as the Mormons are in Franconia. Saxony's been Lutheran for a long time. The pastors have gotten stodgy, I fear."

On the evening of the second day after their arrival in Dresden, Lieutenant Goss got word over the radio that the airfield outside Breslau was in good enough condition for them to make the flight. By then, she'd gotten the Belle refueled as well.

They took off the next morning, shortly after dawn. The flight would be another short one—by direct flight, Breslau was less than two hundred miles away—and Rebecca wanted to have a full day available to her after she arrived. Knowing Gretchen Richter as well as she did by now, five years after the Ring of Fire and having gone through the Spanish siege of Amsterdam with her, Rebecca was sure she'd need it.

Wherever Gretchen Richter went, excitement was sure to follow. The woman was like a force of nature. Sometimes benign; more often...

Not so much.

Always exciting, though. The truth was, although she'd never have admitted it to anyone, Rebecca had enjoyed the siege of Amsterdam.

Well, not "enjoyed," perhaps. But it had certainly been interesting. She was sure the situation she was about to enter would be, as well.

Breslau (Wroclaw), Lower Silesia
Poland

"Do not aggravate me any further on this issue," Gretchen said warningly. "It is settled. You understand? *Settled*. Any farmers in Lower Silesia who choose to take advantage of our offer will be given shelter behind the walls of Breslau—*and* Liegnitz, *and* Glogau, *and* Lüben *and* Bunzlau—whether you like it or not."

The town notables who were crowded in the Rathaus' main room began muttering to each other. The sound reminded Rebecca of the buzz of bees in a hive.

Gretchen pointed at the figure of Lukasz Opalinski, who was standing not far away. The hussar was wearing his full suit of armor, with his helmet nestled in the crook of his arm and a truly brutal-looking saber in a baldric slung over his shoulder.

Rebecca was quite sure Gretchen had instructed him to wear that armor. He looked enormous, like something out of medieval legend.

"If you don't like the fact that those farmers are almost all Poles, not Germans," Gretchen continued, "take your complaints to him. He's Polish, too. He can negotiate with the incoming hordes and settle whatever squabbles might arise."

Opalinski now smiled at the crowd. In formal terms, you could call that smile "benign." If you were a village idiot.

Rebecca had been at the meeting since it began, in mid-afternoon. So far, though, she'd simply played the role of an observer. But by now she thought she had a good enough sense of the situation to intervene.

Gretchen's strategy was clear, simple—and in its own way, as brutal as a hussar's saber. By throwing open the gates of Lower Silesia's fortified towns to the province's peasantry, she would entice the Polish population to flee the countryside and take shelter within their walls. That would strip Lower Silesia of any sustenance for Holk and his mercenary army, unless they began farming themselves—which they were about as likely to do as turn into swans.

The truly fiendish part of Richter's scheme, however, was her disposition of the livestock. The cattle and swine would not be taken into the towns, but would be rounded up and kept in pens just beyond the fortified walls. If Holk and his men wanted to become rustlers, they would have to come near the urban areas they had so far generally avoided.

That would create the conditions for a pitched battle between Richter's motley forces and those of Heinrich Holk. A battle which Richter herself clearly thought—no, seemed utterly certain—she would win and Holk would lose.

Was she right?

Rebecca did not have the experience to gauge the military probabilities. But she'd been at Amsterdam and she knew what Gretchen had done at Dresden in the face of Banér's army, which had been far more fearsome than Holk's.

So, it was time to intervene. The main thing needed here was to infuse the new allies—which they were, whether they liked it or not—with confidence.

She rose to her feet and raised a hand. "If I might say a few words, Gretchen."

Richter immediately stepped back a pace or two and gestured for Rebecca to come forward.

Once Rebecca was facing the crowd, she waited until they fell silent, which took very little time. By now, they would have been informed who she was and what she represented.

In case there was still any uncertainty, though...

"I am Rebecca Abrabanel, the Secretary of State of the United States of Europe. I am also the wife of Michael Stearns, the commanding general of the Third Division of the USE's army."

She waited a few seconds, for that to sink in. Her status as the wife of the Prince of Germany was likely to carry more weight in this crowd than her official position. The political revolution that had swept across most of the Germanies over the past few years would have bypassed the German towns of Lower Silesia, for the most part. Their populations were certainly not medieval, any longer, but neither were they what anyone in their right mind would call progressive.

Raw power, though—that they understood.

"My husband is now marching his forces to come to the aid of the Austrians. Meanwhile, most of the USE's army continues to wage war against King Wladyslaw of Poland."

Translation: *You won't get any help against Holk from the armies of the USE, but you don't have to worry about any Polish retaliation for whatever you choose to do, either. Which leaves...*

Gretchen Richter, Chancellor of Saxony. And now...

This was going to be *such* a nice touch. Rebecca was really quite pleased with herself. As soon as she'd gotten the idea, the night before, she'd had a quick exchange of radio messages with the emperor. Gustav Adolf had been pleased with the idea himself, as you might expect.

"I recommend, therefore, that you accept the authority of"— she motioned to Gretchen—"Chancellor Richter of Saxony. Whom Emperor Gustav II Adolf has also just appointed as the Lady Protector of Lower Silesia."

Gretchen stared at her. Which was not surprising, since she was hearing about this new development at the same time as the crowd of town notables in the Rathaus.

"And do exactly as Chancellor Richter tells you to do," Rebecca concluded.

"This is absurd!" Gretchen exclaimed, as soon as the door to the room was closed and they had some privacy. "What in the name of creation is a 'lady protector'?"

"You are," said Rebecca.

Lukasz Opalinski and the other Pole in Gretchen's retinue, a man named Jozef Wojtowicz, had followed them into the side room, along with Tata and Eric Krenz. As soon as he entered the room, Wojtowicz had started grinning.

"It's brilliant, Gretchen," he said. He flipped a thumb and forefinger back and forth between himself and Opalinski. "And it makes things a lot easier for me and Lukasz."

She frowned at him. "How does it do that?"

Opalinski had eased himself into a chair, which was a somewhat elaborate process when wearing a full set of hussar armor. "It does that precisely because no one has any clear idea what the title means. 'Lady Protector of Lower Silesia' is a much—ah, less problematic, let's say—personage for we Poles to follow than the leader of a USE province." He cleared his throat. "The USE being a nation with which, technically speaking, Jozef and I are at war."

"Awkward, that is," agreed Wojtowicz. "But who could object if we took up arms in the service of the Lady Protector of Lower Silesia to put a stop to the depredations of mercenary outlaws?"

Richter was now glaring at the two Poles. "That's ridiculous, too! The silly title was given to me by the emperor of the USE, remember?"

Lukasz waved his hand airily. "Yes, yes—but so what? Who's to say that given a peace settlement between the USE and the Commonwealth of Poland and Lithuania—which is bound to happen, sooner or later—King Wladyslaw won't agree to anoint you with the same title himself? At which point we'd have what amounted to a joint protectorate between Poland and the USE over the much-abused and downtrodden region of Lower Silesia."

He sat up straight in the chair, his expression becoming more serious. "The point is, Gretchen, the title doesn't make Lower Silesia a province of the USE. That means its status can be negotiated when the time comes—but in the meantime, you now have the authority to get that wretched pack of so-called patricians"—he waved toward the main hall of the Rathaus—"to do what you want them to do."

He now looked over at Rebecca. "Brilliant idea. Was it yours, or Gustav Adolf's?"

"It was hers," Gretchen said, sounding a bit sour. "Had to be. The woman is much too smart to let run loose like this."

Rebecca just looked serene.

Part Six

September 1636

What does the mountain care?

Chapter 47

There was a large crowd waiting for Mike Stearns—or, rather, waiting for the motor boat which brought him. As they neared the docks, it became obvious to Mike that most of the onlookers were far more interested in ooh-ing and aah-ing over the Bass Cat Sabre than they were in him.

As he deftly brought the boat up to the pier, Sergeant Melchior Dietrich of the 1st Reconnaissance company gave Mike a sly grin. "Don't take it personally, General," he said. "You have to remember this is the second time I've made the trip to Linz."

Mike smiled. "And you couldn't resist showing off, the first time."

Now the Marine sergeant's expression became solemn, to the point of lugubriosity. "Oh, no, sir. I wouldn't do something like that. No, I put on a display of the boat's speed—top speed's almost sixty miles per hour, you know—because the boat's pilot insisted that he had to experience the maximum speed so he could properly gauge the time we'd need to avoid obstacles."

"I thought *you* were the pilot."

Dietrich got that unmistakable look of the connoisseur overhearing someone using improper terminology concerning his obsession. "Oh, no, sir. I'm not the pilot, I'm the *helmsman*. The pilot's an Austrian fellow who knows the Danube from here—actually, all the way from Passau—down to Vienna."

Mike knew the Marines had hired a local to guide them as they sped up and down the Danube. The Sabre was a two-seater with not much in the way of carrying capacity. He'd ordered it brought down by airship from Grantville to provide the Third Division with a riverine reconnaissance capability. Of course, it had doubled nicely as a way to bring the Third Division's commander down to Linz in style.

"And naturally you had to do the demonstration right here in front of Linz's population and the royal court because your Austrian pilot knew this stretch of the river by heart."

The sly smile came back to the sergeant's face. "Exactly so, sir."

As he always did when dealing with Marines, Mike felt simultaneously admiring and irritated. There was no question the Marine Corps had panache. That helped cover the fact that it was ultimately a military unit with more in the way of political clout than any clear function.

In truth, the main reason the Marine Corps had been established not long after the Ring of Fire was because Americans—and the inhabitants of Grantville were no exception—had an emotional attachment to them that stemmed from their own history.

Given the realities of war in the 1630s, however, the sort of full-capacity army that the Marine Corps had been up-time—they'd even had what amounted to their own air force—had little purpose. What marines were *really* needed for was the task that had been their original one, centuries earlier: to provide naval vessels with a complement of marksmen used in battle against other black-powder vessels in close quarter combat, and a landing force for small scale shore operations.

That was certainly how Admiral Simpson had envisioned them, initially. But in one way or another, that simple function had gotten frayed over time. Rebecca had used Marines to provide Princess Kristina and Prince Ulrik with a bodyguard when they came to Magdeburg during the Dresden Crisis, partly because they were what was available and partly because they had fancy and glamorous uniforms.

Naturally, in the time-honored manner of military units going back to the charioteers of the pharaohs, the Marines had kept pushing for more roles, especially ones that had some glamor attached to them. Hence the origin of the very unit to which Sergeant Dietrich was attached as a "transport auxiliary," the 1st

Reconnaissance company—which was still the *only* reconnaissance company the Marines had, and Mike was sure that Admiral Simpson was doing his level best to keep it that way. When the fiasco at Bornholm had shown the need for such an outfit, the Marines had muscled their way into the position, shoving aside the claims of the Army.

Simpson had backed them, initially. Lately, though, the admiral was starting to make noises about organizing an entirely separate unit of what he defined as "maritime marines like they're supposed to be" which would be called the Naval Marines and would be under the direct and no-damn-fooling thumb of naval commanders.

He'd probably get it, too. Inter-service rivalry was alive and well in 1636, and Mike thought only a fool would underestimate John Chandler Simpson's skill at bureaucratic knife-fighting.

Not his problem, though. As men held the boat against the dock by lines, Mike was helped out by an Austrian officer. "Welcome to Linz, General Stearns," the man said.

"Glad to be here." Once he'd gotten solid footing on the pier, he turned to look down at Dietrich. "Where did you leave your pilot, Sergeant?"

"Here, sir. I know the stretch of river between here and Passau well enough by now." He nodded toward someone in the crowd. "He's right over there, in fact."

"Off you go, then. I want regular radio reports from as far down the Danube as you can get without taking any real chances."

"Yes, sir."

Mike turned back to the officer who'd helped him out of the bass boat. "Where to, now?"

"The emperor awaits you, General. General Pappenheim is here also."

"Already? How did he—oh, right. It must be nice for Wallenstein, having what amounts to his own private plane."

"I believe it's Don Nasi's plane, actually."

As if a man as shrewd as Francisco Nasi would risk annoying the new king of Bohemia, who'd just recently emancipated the city's Jews—and Prague probably had the largest population of Jews anywhere in the world.

But Mike didn't say that aloud, of course. "Lead on, then."

Chiemsee (Bavarian Sea)
Bavaria

"And there it is," said Tom Simpson, after he and his small unit reached a crest in the landscape. From that vantage point, they could see all of the Chiemsee, with the majestic line of Alps rising in the distance to the south.

"How big is the lake, Major?" asked Captain Sebastian Bleier. "I'm from Nordhausen, near the Harz mountains. This is the first time I've ever been to Bavaria."

"According to the information sent me from the Grantville library, the Chiemsee's got a surface area of about thirty square miles. The greatest depth is a little over two hundred feet. It's the biggest lake in Bavaria."

"More than big enough for our purposes," said the combat engineer officer, nodding. "A bit far away from the theater of operations, though."

Tom shrugged. "It's about one hundred miles from here to Linz; two hundred, to Vienna. That's well within the *Magdeburg*'s range. The only alternative would have been to build the hangar on the Traunsee, on the border between Salzburg and Austria. But that had two big drawbacks. First, it would have taken us much longer to get there, even if the archbishop of Salzburg was cooperative—which he probably wouldn't be. Paris Reichsgraf von Lodron's made almost as much of a religion of his neutrality as he has of his Catholicism."

He paused to admire the scenery for a moment.

"The second reason?" Bleier prompted.

"The Traunsee's located on the Traun river, which is a tributary of the Danube."

"Good water transport, then. That would be an advantage for us."

Tom shook his head. "Sadly, the Traun joins the Danube a few miles *downstream* of Linz."

"Ah."

"Yeah. Ah. Depending on how the fighting goes, that could be under Ottoman control, if they can push right up to the walls of the city. So it'd be easy for them to send an expedition up the river to destroy our airship base. No, we're better off playing it safe by building the hangar here."

With his hands planted on his hips, he scanned the shoreline. "The biggest problem we've got is that, according to the Grantville library, there aren't any sizeable towns on the lake. We'll have to make do with whatever village carpenters and artisans we can round up."

Captain Bleier's eyes widened. "Village carpenters—to build a structure five hundred feet long and seventy feet tall?"

"Yeah. Ain't life a bitch? I'm sure we'll wind up having to import almost all of our labor force. But they have to have loggers around here, and"—he waved his hand, indicating their heavily forested surroundings—"we've obviously got no shortage of wood."

Tom's expression became somber. "The really big problem lies elsewhere."

"Which is?"

"How did an innocent and upstanding artillery officer get dragooned into being a miserable combat engineer?"

Bleier grinned. "The same way you got dragooned into being an air force officer. The commanding general is your brother-in-law and he trusts you." The captain shook his head, in an exaggerated gesture of disbelief at the folly of others. "The problem with you Americans is that you think nepotism just brings advantages. Which is nonsense. Just ask any innocent and upstanding Reichritter's son"—here he slapped his chest—"who got dragooned into upholding the family's honor by enlisting in the USE army. And *then* got assigned to the engineers because he'd made the mistake of being proficient at mathematics."

He, too, paused for a moment to admire the distant Alps. "Just as you say: Ain't life a bitch?"

Freising, Bavaria

When she saw the man climbing out of the gondola of the *Albatross,* Julie Mackay was surprised. She hadn't expected Dell Beckworth to bring the rifle *himself.* The guy had to be . . . what? Sixty, maybe? Like most people in their early twenties, Julie considered that age to be more-or-less synonymous with *teetering-at-the-edge-of-the-grave.*

As she went over to greet him, she saw one of the *Albatross'* crew hand a long and obviously heavy package down to Beckworth. She hurried her steps in order to lend him a hand.

But before she could get there, Beckworth had the package resting on the ground next to him and had turned to greet her.

"Hi, Julie." He patted the side of the package. "Here it is. But like I warned you over the radio, the only one I had left was this prototype. It's a heavy bastard—just about fifty pounds. I cut twenty pounds off that for the later models."

"The heavier, the better, Dell, from my point of view. It'll cut down on the recoil. I only weigh about one hundred and thirty-five pounds."

Beckworth grimaced. "You sure you don't want me to shoot it? I'll be going with you, y'know."

Julie stared at him. "Since when?"

"Since my boss said it was okay—he's a good patriot; anything for the war effort—and since your boss said it was okay."

She frowned. "I don't have a boss." Her voice started to rise a little. "And if you talked to Alex and either you or he thinks he's my 'boss' just 'cause he's my husband, well, let me tell you—"

Beckworth raised a placating hand. "Not him. I got Mike Stearns' okay to come along."

That brought Julie up short. Of course, Stearns wasn't her boss, either.

Or was he? Technically, Julie was now a mercenary soldier, having been contracted by the Third Division—fine; what they called a handshake contract and so what? both she and Mike were West Virginians; good enough—to do some fancy shooting for them. If Julie understood the legal technicalities, that still didn't make Stearns her "boss" but it did obviously give him some say-so in the matter.

She squinted at Beckworth. "Don't you think you're a little old to be involved in combat?"

"Too old! Young lady, I'm only fifty-five and I'm in good health. Besides, it's not like I'm going to be coming out of the trenches and charging across hundreds of yards of open ground. This is what they call 'aerial combat,' which is a fancy way of saying you're fighting while sitting on your butt."

She glanced over at the gondola. "I think we'll be standing, actually, but...Okay, I take your point."

He gave her a friendly smile. "Julie, this here piece is what you call custom-made. It's a one-off, not a mass produced rifle like the ones you're used to. Even if you do all the shooting, I think you'll still find me handy to have around. And you'll need a spotter anyway."

He nodded toward the *Albatross.* "I got a suitcase in there with some clothes and a good pair of binoculars—and my eyesight's still about twenty-twenty."

"Well..."

"*And* my toolbox."

That clinched it. Dell Beckworth was a top-flight gunsmith, and he was right about the quirkiness you were likely to run into with handmade guns, especially ones that were on the outer edge of performance. The Beckworth Light 50 was the closest thing Julie could find in her new universe to the .50 caliber BMG that had been the gun of choice for long-range snipers going back to the Vietnam War.

Back up-time, they'd wanted the gun for its incredible range. She wanted it for its striking power. If the Ottomans had armored their airship gondolas, she was pretty sure her usual rifles weren't going to be enough for the job.

"Okay, then," she said. "Want help carrying that?"

"'Help,' my ass. I've got my own luggage to deal with. You're the shooter, you can damn well carry it yourself." With an evil grin, he released his hold on the upright package and gently gave it a push. The package began toppling toward her.

"*Timmmmmmmmber!*" he called out.

Linz, capital-in-exile of Austria-Hungary

As the awkward silence continued, Mike Stearns got a wry smile on his face. *Leave it to the coal miner to have to do the dirty work.*

He rose to his feet. That wasn't necessary from an acoustic standpoint, since there were only half a dozen men in the room, and they were all sitting fairly close together. But he'd learned long ago that standing gave someone a certain edge in a situation like this.

"Meaning no disrespect to His Majesty, but I do not believe the example of the first battle of Nördlingen—we're speaking here of a battle fought in an entirely different universe under very different conditions than the ones we face—can provide us with much in the way of guidance."

That was the politest way Mike could figure out to say that the proposal just advanced to place Emperor Ferdinand III in direct overall command of the allied forces bordered on idiocy.

And went well over the line when it came to toadying. The proposal had been advanced by Rudolf von Colloredo—Rudolf Hieronymus Eusebius von Colloredo-Waldsee, if you wanted to go all tails and black tie about it—who was not-so-subtly maneuvering to get himself promoted to the rank of field marshal.

Von Colloredo was the highest-ranking officer in the Austrian army, of those who had survived the Ottoman seizure of Vienna. No one knew exactly what had happened to the previous Austrian commander, General Wolf Heinrich von Baudissin, when the Turks overran the garrison. He had presumably died in the fighting, although he might have been captured. Either way, he was no longer in position to exercise any sort of command.

Which was probably just as well, in Mike's opinion. Another of the men in the room was a young Italian officer by the name of Raimondo Montecuccoli, whom the emperor had just promoted from colonel to general. Montecuccoli had led the evacuation that had saved about half of the men in the Vienna garrison and an even larger percentage of the civilian population of the city.

For which, upon his arrival at Linz, he had been rewarded by being arrested on the orders of General von Colloredo and charged with either treason or mutiny—von Colloredo didn't seem to know which applied better to the circumstances. Fortunately for Montecuccoli, Emperor Ferdinand had placed his friend and adviser Janos Drugeth in charge of the investigation. Drugeth had interviewed a number of the surviving soldiers, three of whom had been present on the bastion and heard Archduke Leopold order Montecuccoli to organize the evacuation while the archduke remained to command the defenders.

Mike had spoken privately to Janos on the matter and knew that the Hungarian nobleman's opinion was that von Baudissin's leadership at the critical moment in the assault had been disastrous, just as Montecuccoli had depicted. Still, no one could deny the man's personal courage. By several accounts of survivors, von Baudissin had joined the soldiers whom he'd ordered to stay on the walls and bastions when the Ottoman airships started bombing, and had most likely died with them.

None of the men present in the room, in Mike's opinion,

were good candidates for being in overall command of the military forces. It was true that Ferdinand and his Habsburg cousin Cardinal-Infante Don Fernando had led the imperial forces which decisively defeated the Protestant allies at the battle of Nördlingen in 1634. Leaving aside the fact that had happened in a different universe, the situations weren't at all analogous. Most of the imperial forces had been Spanish infantry, who could—in both universes—lay claim to being still the best in Europe. They'd mostly been led by the experienced commander Count Leganés. Furthermore, they'd outnumbered their opponent—which was certainly not going to be the case in the coming battle against the Ottoman army.

Of the other Austrian officers present, none of them fit the bill. Von Colloredo was not only a sycophant, but Mike gauged him to be a plodder at his actual trade—at best. Montecuccoli seemed to have talent, but he was too junior an officer. Janos Drugeth was the best prospect, being a veteran soldier and obviously very capable. But he didn't have any experience commanding really large bodies of men.

The same was true of Mike himself. By now, he was quite confident of his ability to command a division-sized force. But that same experience had made clear to him that commanding an entire army, especially one made up disparate units from allied forces, was another kettle of fish entirely.

That left Pappenheim, the commander of the Bohemian forces present. He'd brought about ten thousand men with him into Austria, the core of which force was his own famous cavalry unit, the Black Cuirassiers.

Pappenheim had as much combat experience as probably any soldier in Europe, much of it in command of sizeable forces. But he'd never been in overall command of those armies and he didn't really have the temperament for it. He was impetuous in battle, a trait which made him undoubtedly fearsome but was not really the most important characteristic for a top commander. For that you wanted judgment, which Mike didn't think was Pappenheim's strong suit.

And, besides, why fiddle around when there was a man available who was the one most obviously suited to the job in the whole continent?

"I propose instead," Mike continued, "that we ask Gustavus

Adolphus to take command of our allied army. We can have him flown down here within a day or two."

He sat down. A small hubbub erupted which be let run its course before saying anything further.

Bluntly, Drugeth posed the critical question. "He is said to be incapacitated by seizures, General Stearns. Is this true?"

"Yes and no. He does have seizures, yes. But they don't come that often—perhaps once every month or two—and they don't usually last very long."

"'Very long' being...?"

"Half an hour. Sometimes shorter, sometimes longer." On one occasion, Gustav Adolf had been incapacitated for a day and half, but Mike didn't see any reason to bring that up.

The men present looked at each other, uncertainly.

Ferdinand spoke up. "Could he bring his doctor with him? The famous Dr. Nichols, I mean?"

"I don't see any reason why not," Mike replied. Seeing the lessening of doubtfulness in the faces around him, he pressed the matter. "There is no reason we can't have someone with him who could assume command for the duration should Gustav Adolf suffer a seizure. Personally, I would recommend"—he nodded toward the Hungarian nobleman—"Janos here. True, he's never commanded an army of this size. But by all accounts he's very steady and he's an experienced soldier. Surely he could maintain the situation until Gustav Adolf recovered."

Everyone—except Janos himself—now looked quite relaxed.

"A splendid proposal," said Emperor Ferdinand.

Freising, Bavaria

"This is the dining room," Bonnie Weaver explained. She gestured toward the windows to the side, which slanted in toward the bottom, since they were flush with the underside of the huge dirigible. "You get a hell of a view once we're in the air."

Julie Mackay looked around the big room in the hull of the *Magdeburg*. "Wow," she said. "And I get my own private cabin, too?"

"Yup."

"Double wow."

Chapter 48

Munich, capital of Bavaria

"It's not fair!" Rita proclaimed, for the third time, as she re-read the radio message—also for the third time.

Noelle was reading the same message over Rita's shoulder. "Sure isn't. I'm not *ready* for this."

Rita gave her a glance that was not in the least sympathetic. "A little late in the game for getting cold feet, isn't it? You've been making cow eyes at that damn Hungarian for—what is it?—two years now?"

"Year and a half." Noelle shook her head. "I don't have cold feet about marrying Janos. I'm just . . . Goddamit, Rita, you had a reasonable wedding in a local church in Grantville followed by a reasonable reception in the high school cafeteria. *That,* I could handle fine."

She jabbed an accusing forefinger at the slip of paper in Rita's hand. "But you know good and well that's not what this wedding's going to be like." Her tone of voice became more high-pitched. "I thought we wouldn't be getting married until . . . I don't know . . ."

"The war was over?" Rita barked a laugh that had very little in the way of humor in it. "The way things are going, by then you'd be in your forties."

She sighed, laid the radio message on a side table and slumped into a chair in the small salon. Then she gave the room a sour examination that lasted for perhaps five seconds.

443

"Typical seventeenth-century so-called 'palace,'" she grumbled. "Is there any decent plumbing? Be serious. Will it be well heated in the winter? Be serious."

Noelle sat down in a chair not far from her. "At least you won't be too crowded here. If it makes you feel any better, I'll be stuck in a palace—using the term very loosely—that's packed to the rafters with people. And probably has even worse plumbing than the Munich Residenz."

Both of them understood the logic behind the message they'd just received.

Rita had been appointed the new USE ambassador to Bavaria. Her qualifications? She was the sister of the guy who'd just been pounding down Munich's walls with the most powerful cannons in the world and could always come back and finish the job if the new duke of Bavaria got out of line.

Noelle had been told to go to Linz where it seemed everyone and their grandmother was planning to hold the biggest wedding of the season—in between making a desperate last stand against the Ottoman onslaught. The reasoning? If Linz could be held, then marrying a prominent up-timer whom Wallenstein planned to ennoble to an even more prominent Austro-Hungarian aristocrat would be a splendid way to help solidify the new Triple Alliance. (They were even starting to call it that.)

"The seventeenth century sucks," pronounced Rita.

"Big time," agreed Noelle.

Chiemsee (Bavarian Sea)
Bavaria

"That thing is...big," said Captain Bleier.

As understatements went, thought Tom Simpson, that one was a dandy. He'd known the dimensions of the *Magdeburg*, of course, since he had to in order to design and build a hangar for it. But abstract knowledge was one thing; seeing the enormous airship up close was something else altogether.

"At least we got the mast finished in time," said Bleier.

That had been their first priority, once they were able to start construction. Building a hangar for the *Magdeburg* was going to take at least six months—if everything went as planned. Tom wouldn't be a bit surprised if it took twice as long, though. The six month estimate was based on the experience of the Dutch, but they'd had a much better infrastructure in place at Hoorn than he had on the shores of the Chiemsee.

Obviously, they had to have something ready long before then that could serve as a base for the *Magdeburg*. A hangar was really only necessary for major maintenance of the airship. They could moor the vessel to a mast in the meantime, although doing so would inevitably result in a faster deterioration of the envelope since it would be exposed to the elements.

So, they'd thrown up a mast just tall enough to moor the *Magdeburg* while personnel and supplies were loaded directly from the ground. They'd work their way backward, so to speak: first, a mast, while they assembled the wherewithal to build the hangar; then, finally, the hangar itself. By the time they were done, the airship base at the lakeside village of Chieming would have become a respectably-sized town.

"Lucky you," said Bleier. "Getting to return to civilization while I remain here in the Bavarian wilderness."

Tom didn't say anything. Truth be told, he had mixed feelings about his reassignment to Linz. On the one hand, he certainly wouldn't miss the primitive facilities here on the Chiemsee. The area wasn't quite a "wilderness" but it came awfully close. He also wouldn't mind at all getting back to his more familiar duties as an artillery officer.

On the other hand, he'd just found out that his wife had been appointed the ambassador to Bavaria. He'd been hoping to see her, but the *Magdeburg* had dropped her off in Freising at the same time it had picked up Julie Mackay. Which meant that Rita would be stuck in Munich while he went still farther to the east.

Once the *Magdeburg* was moored and held steady with lines, Tom climbed aboard the gondola using a rope ladder. Noelle Stull was there to greet him, along with Julie and Dell Beckworth.

"What are you doing here?" he asked Beckworth. Then he waved a big hand in dismissal of his own query. "Never mind. Stupid question. I don't suppose you brought anything more useful than an oversized gun? You know—things like a portable sawmill, maybe a couple of dozen master carpenters. Better yet, somebody who knows what he's doing when it comes to managing construction."

"Not with us, no," replied Beckworth. "But they told us to tell you that the *Petrel* will be coming down soon with some of that stuff. They'll be bringing Walter Goodluck to take over from you, too."

"Good deal," said Tom. "Walter's got experience with this sort of thing, which I sure as hell don't." He turned to Noelle. "Are you in overall charge of this clusterfuck? Pardon my Anglo-Saxon."

She smiled. "If it makes you feel any better, Rita's language was even worse than yours when she got the news."

"My wife's language is *always* worse than mine, when she gets pissed. Difference between being raised High Church Episcopalian and really low church hillbilly. And you didn't answer my question."

"It's not actually clear to me exactly who's in charge of the *Magdeburg*." Noelle nodded toward the three Dutch officers clustered around the controls in the forward end of the gondola. "If you ask them, they'll insist they're just the guys running the airship, not the ones giving the orders as to what it's supposed to do."

Now she pointed above her head, indicating the envelope of the airship. "Bonnie Weaver and Heinz Böcler are up there inside the hull, and they're even more adamant that they're not in charge either."

Tom scratched at his beard. "What about you?"

"Be serious. I'm just the bride getting a lift."

"I'm getting a bad feeling about this," Tom muttered.

Noelle's smile took on a distinctly evil tinge. "At a guess—yup. I'd say Mike's calling you into Linz in order to put *you* in command of the *Magdeburg*."

"Dammit, I'm an artillery officer."

"You need to qualify that statement, Major Simpson," she said. "You're an artillery officer whose commanding general is your brother-in-law *and* you're stranded in the year 1636. In case no one told you, right smack in the middle of the Little Ice Age *and* the Era of Absolute Nepotism."

"The seventeenth century sucks."

"Exactly what your wife and I were just saying."

Linz, capital-in-exile of Austria-Hungary

The Gustav taxied to a stop just a few yards short of the not-so-small crowd waiting to greet its passengers. Either the pilot had a lot of confidence in his skill or he had a blithe attitude on the subject of *Austrian aristocracy, pureed*. Knowing air force pilots fairly well by now, Mike figured the answer was both of the above.

The crowd itself was more cautious. Even after the propeller stopped spinning, no one moved toward the aircraft.

Mike chuckled. *Leave it to the lowly coal miner to be the one to observe proper etiquette*. Then—moving quite boldly, he thought—he strode toward the aircraft.

The passenger door was already opening and Gustav Adolf was emerging. Mike wasn't surprised that the emperor hadn't waited for someone to open the door for him and place the suitable disembarking gear in place—which, in this case, was no more elaborate than a sturdy four-legged stool. Gustavs might be able to lay claim to being the premier warplanes of the era, but the things were no larger than a Cessna 172 Skyhawk or a Beechcraft Bonanza.

The empty weight of the plane was less than a ton. A Gustav carried a pilot and three passengers with a small cargo space in the rear of the fuselage. Or, alternatively, the craft would carry a small payload of bombs or rockets instead of the passengers.

Like a Beechcraft Bonanza and unlike a Cessna Skyhawk, the Gustav was a low-wing aircraft. So, once he got the door open, Gustav Adolf had to clamber over the wing in order to get onto the ground. It was a bit of a drop, though, which was the reason for the courtier who was now hurrying forward with the disembarkation stool in his hands.

The emperor didn't wait for him, though—which, again, didn't surprise Mike. Gustav Adolf was a big man, who tended to gain a lot of extra weight when he wasn't on campaign. That said, he was also quite muscular and athletic and was only forty-one years old. So, allowing for the heft involved—no one would ever mistake him for a gymnast—he got down onto the ground in a fairly nimble manner.

He'd already spotted Mike and now strode forward to greet him, ignoring the courtier who had to move rather nimbly himself to keep from being trampled under by the imperial progress.

448 *Eric Flint*

"This was your idea, wasn't it, Michael," he stated when he came near.

Mike nodded. "I proposed it, yes. No one objected, though."

Gustav Adolf smiled. "Such a diplomat. As good as your wife, sometimes. What you mean is that no one objected once you explained—I imagine you shaded the truth a bit, in the process—that my seizures are not too frequent and don't usually last very long. Provided I had the world's best doctor around, I could manage. Speaking of which..."

He turned back toward the airplane, from which another passenger was emerging. It wasn't Dr. Nichols, though, but his companion Melissa Mailey. "Companion" was the word they'd settled on for public consumption, although Melissa was still prone to referring to herself as "James' squeeze," on those not-infrequent occasions when she felt like goosing proper society. James had proposed marriage to her on at least three occasions that Mike knew of, but Melissa had always declined. The issue, she'd explain, had nothing to do with her sentiments toward James himself. It was simply that she already felt like enough of a sell-out being regarded by most people as in some way analogous to a duchess or some such grotesque personage. The least she could do, she figured, was uphold some small smidgeon of scandal.

By the time she emerged onto the wing and had herself turned around, tentatively waving one foot in the direction of the ground, the courtier had placed the stool in position to receive that foot. But Melissa, despite being slender and in reasonably good condition for a woman in her early sixties, was no athlete at all. Sure of herself in the face of any social or intellectual challenge, she was always a bit tentative when dealing with a physical one.

Gustav Adolf stepped back to the plane and extended his hand. After giving him a quick smile of thanks, Melissa took the hand and got herself down on the ground with that royal assistance.

Mike almost laughed, hearing the little hiss of disapproval coming from the mob behind him. Well, not exactly "disapproval," since one couldn't very well disapprove of a voluntary action on the part of an emperor. The sound managed to mix scandal with astonishment, overlain by a soupçon of censure.

Melissa herself was oblivious to it all. Even five years after the Ring of Fire, the woman's soul was still saturated with the egalitarianism of her upbringing and personal inclination. She'd seen nothing more remarkable in Gustav Adolf's offer of a helping hand than the natural action of a polite younger man toward a woman two decades older than him. The fact that the man himself was (a deep breath needed to be taken here) the Emperor of the United States of Europe, King of Sweden, High King of the Union of Kalmar, Lord Protector of Bavaria—he'd probably be adding something like Overseer of Lower Silesia before the year was out—was irrelevant to her.

The look on the face of the courtier who'd put down the stool and extended his own hand was priceless. Mike really had a hard time holding down the laugh that almost produced in him.

No sooner was Melissa sure of her footing than she looked up and glared at Mike.

"I suppose this was your idea?" she demanded.

He frowned, wondering what...

"Don't play the innocent with me, Michael Stearns! I remember your jackanapes from high school, don't think I don't. My skeleton may be starting to creak but my brain isn't." She jerked a thumb in the direction of Gustav Adolf. "He wouldn't have come up with the notion that I had to come along. Not on his own, anyway, even if he was the one who had me frog-marched onto the plane. Fine, figuratively speaking. Meaning no offense, Your Majesty."

The last sentence had about as much sincerity in it as there was moisture in the Sahara Desert.

Mike glanced at the emperor and spotted the look of amusement in his blue eyes.

"Michael is actually quite innocent in the matter," said Gustav Adolf. "It was his wife who gave me the idea, at the same time as she recommended Gretchen Richter's new title of 'Lady Protector of Lower Silesia.' She was quite right, though. Having you join us in the defense of Linz will impart an additional legitimacy to the enterprise, at least in the minds of that portion of our population whom tact prevents me from labeling the surly and disputatious rabble."

The last phrase came with a wide grin; wide enough to remove any sting from it.

Melissa was now glaring at him. Then back at Mike.

"Your wife!" she said accusingly. "Rebecca! That woman schemes more than—than—" She groped for a suitable historical analog.

Gustav Adolf, with the benefit of a classical education sadly absent in Mike's native West Virginian schools, provided it:

"Queen Olympias of Macedon, perhaps, or Empress Theodora of Rome—no, I have it! Lucrezia Borgia."

"Yes, her! Them."

James Nichols had come alongside and gave her arm an affectionate squeeze. "For whatever it's worth, hon, I'm glad to have you here."

She gave him a look that somehow combined affection with displeasure. "Yeah, sure. In bed, it's great. But sooner or later other aspects of nature will call."

She went back to glaring at Mike. "Go ahead. Tell me the plumbing in Austrian palaces—even in Vienna, much less here—is up to snuff. Go ahead, I dare you!"

"Well..."

"What I thought. Dammit, I'm too old for this."

Chapter 49

Prague, capital of Bohemia

Francisco Nasi contemplated the expression on the face of his youngest employee, Denise Beasley. He was of two minds on the matter she had raised. On the one hand, there could be several advantages to following the course of action she proposed.

On the other hand...

He now looked over to the third person in the room, Denise's mother Christin George, and spent a few seconds contemplating the expression on her face.

Which was, in a nutshell, worried—a sentiment that matched his own. Denise Beasley was a young woman of much intelligence, great energy, and even greater boldness. Over time, she could become a real asset to his work. In the short run, however, her weaknesses tended to cancel her strengths. She relied too much— much too much—on her native wit, and was erratic when it came to intellectual pursuits and her own education. Still worse, her energy and boldness all too readily spilled over into recklessness.

In truth, her best friend Minnie Hugelmair was—had been, perhaps; her fate was still unknown—a much more useful employee than Denise herself.

Still...

He considered, for a moment, the possible advantages to sending Denise to Linz, as she was requesting.

Only for a moment, though. The deciding factor was the face of

451

her mother. Not the worry in the face, but the face itself. Christin George was one of those women whose physical beauty did not disguise the intelligence beneath. In some ways, she reminded him of his distant cousin Rebecca Abrabanel—and, as had been true when he first met Rebecca—Francisco found her immensely attractive.

Unfortunately, he couldn't afford to succumb to that attraction, which was all the more difficult to resist because he was fairly sure the attraction was mutual. By this time, more than four years after he'd left Istanbul to cast his fate with those of the time-displaced Americans, Francisco had shed most of the unthinking attitudes of his youth and upbringing. The idea of marrying a gentile was no longer unimaginable to him—in fact, it wasn't even especially outlandish.

But he couldn't do that while pursuing the goal that he had set himself when he moved to Prague. He'd told everyone at the time—everyone except Morris and Judith Roth—that his motives in doing so had been purely personal. Make a lot of money doing what he knew best, which was intelligence-gathering and influence-peddling. (Call it espionage, if you insisted, but the work was much broader than that.) Find himself a Jewish wife in the largest, probably the wealthiest and certainly the most cosmopolitan and sophisticated Jewish community in the world.

In reality, he'd come to share the Roths' purpose—find a way to avert the horrendous Chmielnicki Pogrom, the coming slaughter of Jews in Poland and Ruthenia that had been the worst episode in Jewish history between the destruction of the Second Temple and the Nazi Holocaust of the twentieth century.

In the world the Americans had come from, the pogrom had begun in 1648, as an offshoot of the Cossack rebellion against the Polish-Lithuanian commonwealth. And while it was a mistake to assume that something would automatically happen in this universe because it had happened in that of the up-timers, the social, economic and political factors that had led to the Chmielnicki Pogrom were just as prevalent in this one and just as difficult to change.

He had discussed the project with the Roths for hours on end. And while much was still obscure and uncertain, some things seemed clear enough.

First, the key was Bohemia, with its large Jewish population and its close relationship with the new Bohemian regime.

Second, whatever Francisco or the up-time couple might think in the abstract of Wallenstein's overweening imperial ambitions, they could be harnessed to their purpose.

Third, Bohemia was not strong enough on its own for what Morris Roth called "the Anaconda project," but it was now allied not only with Austria—that mostly removed a possible barrier—but also with the United States of Europe. The USE was probably already the most powerful nation in Europe, and if it could defeat the Ottoman Empire, or even just hold it at bay, it could prove an enormous asset to their purpose.

Marrying an American like Christin George would probably aid in that regard, but not very much. There was already the great marriage tie between the Americans and Europe's Jews, in the persons of Michael Stearns and Rebecca Abrabanel.

No, much more important was the task of solidifying his prestige and informal authority with Prague's Jewish community. The Roths had already accomplished a great deal in that regard, but they were handicapped by being viewed as outsiders. Jews, yes—certainly; no one in Prague doubted that—but such an odd pair of Jews! They adhered to something they called "Reform Judaism," whatever that was.

It would be up to Francisco, that part of the project. Which meant that, more than anything else, he needed to find a proper and suitable Jewish wife. He'd begun the needed measures some time ago and he thought at least one of the possibilities might soon come to fruition.

So.

"No, Denise. There is no point in your going to Linz." He held up a hand to forestall her gathering protest. "There is nothing you can do to help Minnie—assuming she's even still alive, which she may well not be—and if you're willing to use your head, you know it as well as I do."

"But—"

"*No*," he said forcefully. "Denise, I shall be blunt. I don't trust you—not on this subject. You're likely to do something rash, which will achieve nothing except put yourself at risk."

"Honey, listen to him," Christin said softly. "He's right."

Denise slumped down in her chair, arms crossed over her chest. "What am I supposed to do, then? Just sit here, twiddling my thumbs?"

"By no means," said Francisco. "I do have a job for you—but it's in Lower Silesia, not Upper Austria. I need you"—he now looked at her mother—"and you, Christin, if you're willing, to set yourself up in Breslau. There's nothing you can do in Linz, but the situation in Lower Silesia... Oh, now, that's becoming very interesting indeed."

Christin George was a woman in her mid-thirties; which was to say, far more attuned to matters of a practical nature than her teenage daughter. "Who's footing the bill? And who takes care of our house while we're gone?"

"As to the first, I will cover all expenses involved. As to the second, Eddie will be traveling a great deal—he'll be flying you to Breslau as soon as they've established an airstrip—but he'll be resident in Prague. He can maintain your house for you. I will provide some additional funds for the purpose."

Christin nodded, then cocked her head slightly and regarded Francisco with a look that seemed both amused and...regretful, perhaps?

"It's a deal," she said, rising from her chair. "Let's go, Denise. You've got your marching orders and—what am I, by the way, Francisco? A sub-contractor or your direct employee?"

"Sub-contractor, I think."

"Chiseler. That way you don't have to pay for a pension or medical benefits."

Nasi smiled. "I don't pay my *employees* a pension or medical benefits—no one does—although I will cover all costs if they're injured on assignment. The same will go for you, of course."

"That's right, I keep forgetting what year we're in. 1636 AD—or, what year is it to you Jewish folks?"

"5396," he replied.

"Either way, the side benefits are lousy."

By then, still looking sullen but obedient, Denise had risen and was opening the door. A second later, she'd passed through. Her mother made to follow but, at the door itself, she turned around.

She had that same odd expression on her face. "Just so I know, since I've begun to wonder lately—am I correct in assuming this means we won't be starting to date? Ah, that means..."

"I understand the colloquialism." He nodded. "Yes, that's what it means. If it matters, I'm not too happy about that myself. But..."

She raised a hand, forestalling the need for any explanation.

"I get it, Francisco. The needs of the cause, and all that. If it matters, I can't say I'm happy about it, either. But I understand the situation. Good luck—and I really mean that, by the way."

A moment later she was gone, closing the door behind her. Francisco went back to his desk and sat down. He spent perhaps a minute contemplating the closed door, then sighed, and ran fingers through his hair—which was still black, and still full. He was still in his late twenties, after all.

Less than ten years younger than Christin George. Practically the same age. An ideal match, in terms of levels of experience and maturity. Assuming, that is, that you were not concerned with producing a large number of progeny—which, however, he had to plan for, if he wanted to advance his goal. Of the three Jewish girls his intermediaries were investigating, the oldest was twenty-five and the youngest was fifteen. The most promising prospect, in most respects, had just turned nineteen. He could only hope they'd have something to talk about, and had very little hope their senses of humor would coincide.

If the girl had any sense of humor at all. Christin George's was excellent.

"Damnation," he said. Jews had their own proscriptions concerning blasphemy, but they were less wide-ranging than those of Christians, in some respects.

"The needs of the cause," he reminded himself. Then he went back to work.

Linz, capital-in-exile of Austria-Hungary

Gustav Adolf looked around the table, taking his time to examine each face as he came to it and summarizing his impressions.

Pappenheim. A given. Ferocious in battle, very capable, but also limited in his perspective and given to rashness. He'd make a splendid hammer, though, if the right situation arose.

Von Colloredo. A nonentity, most likely. Certainly not someone to be relied upon. The Americans had a quip that applied here: "Keep your friends close and your enemies closer."

Montecuccoli. A promising officer. Now was the time to test him, but the test couldn't be too exacting. If he failed—if any of them failed—it could prove disastrous.

Drugeth. In essence, the Hungarian would be the emperor's chief adjutant. An assignment he would probably carry out splendidly, if Gustav Adolf was any judge of military character. Which, he was.

That left...

The man they called the Prince of Germany. Perhaps the most unsettling aspect of that informal title was that Gustav Adolf was coming to accept it himself. Not even grudgingly, any longer.

He would be the rock. Everything else would pivot around that surety.

"Here is my plan," said Gustav Adolf.

Less than an hour after the meeting had ended, a courier came to fetch Mike Stearns in his private chambers. Cham-*ber*, single, rather. The population density of Linz was by now akin to Mike's conception of what Calcutta looked like, and that of the so-called "royal palaces" not much better.

There were two royal edifices in the city, actually. One was the "palace" proper, a castle built by Rudolf II. As was usually true in the era, the castle had been an expansion of older buildings, parts of which dated back to medieval times. The other edifice was the town hall, built in the previous century. Emperor Ferdinand had sequestered it for royal use after moving his capital to Linz.

Mike's small chamber was situated in the town hall, for which he was thankful. The plumbing was every bit as primitive as that in the castle, but by now Mike was used to that. He'd been on almost continuous campaign since he joined the army more than a year ago. Still, the town hall had more of a Renaissance flavor to it and less of the medieval gloom of the castle. His chamber had a window in it that actually let in quite a bit of light.

"Yes, what is it?" he asked, after opening the door in response to a polite knock.

"The emperor—ah, Gustavus Adolphus, I mean, not Ferdinand— would like to see you in his quarters," said the courier.

Those were also in the town hall, despite the castle being technically the more prestigious of the two royal buildings. The Vasa dynasty was relatively new, as royalty measured such things, and its members still tended for the most part to retain plenty of Swedish practicality.

"Lead on," said Mike.

When he reached the emperor's quarters—which were quite a bit larger than his, naturally, although the plumbing would be no better—he found that Pappenheim was there as well. Mike didn't know the cavalry commander very well. He'd met him before, on a few occasions, but had never spent much time in conversation with the man. He did know that, much to his surprise, Morris Roth had come to like Pappenheim—*albeit with some reservations*, as he put it.

Gottfried Heinrich Graf zu Pappenheim, to give the man his complete moniker, was of Bavarian birth. In the manner that was so common in this era, both the king and the top general of Bohemia were not Czechs themselves but Germans—and nobody thought much of it. He was a very experienced military commander, and looked the part.

"You sent for me, Your Majesty."

"Yes, Michael, I did. There is something I wish to discuss more privately than I could in the general staff meeting." Gustav Adolf, like Pappenheim, was already seated. He gestured towards a third chair positioned close to them. "Please, have a seat."

After Mike did so, the emperor leaned forward. "Have you ever watched a bullfight? The way the Spanish do it, I mean."

The question caught Mike off guard, and for a moment he groped for an answer. The problem was the historical dimension. He'd once been asked, not long after the Ring of Fire, if he'd like to taste some chocolate. Surprised that chocolate had already found its way to Europe, he'd agreed—only to discover that the frothy drink he was handed didn't taste at all like the chocolate he'd been accustomed to.

"Ah...Only on television, Your Majesty. Not in person. But that was a bullfight in my own time, not—"

"Yes, yes, I understand," Gustav Adolf interrupted, waving a hand. "It is practiced quite differently by the Spaniards of our day. The killing is done by an hidalgo on horseback, using a lance, not—not—what is the name of that preposterous fellow? The one with the silly hat waving a silly cape about?"

"The matador."

"Yes, him. I will say the fellows are brave enough." He turned toward Pappenheim. "Imagine, Gottfried! Killing a bull on foot—with just a sword."

Pappenheim curled his lip. "Stupid."

Gustav Adolf shook his head and looked back at Mike. "Not so stupid as all that. Whether fighting now on horseback or"—he waved his hand again, this time indicating that mysterious other universe from which the Americans had emerged—"in their time on foot, bullfighting has always had one steady feature. No one—no man, be he never so bold—tries to kill a fresh bull. The monster is always bled first, by others."

Mike had no particular interest in bullfighting and had only watched the spectacle on television a few times. But, driven by whatever peculiar mechanisms governed human memory, the name of the men involved came to him.

"They called them banderilleros and picadores, where I came from," he said. "If I remember right, the banderilleros fought on foot and the picador rode a horse. They all did the same thing, though—stick the bull with short spears and lances until it became fatigued from pain and blood loss. Its head would then come down, allowing the matador to run his sword through its spine."

"Exactly so!" said Gustav Adolf. "And so must we do as well, when we face the monster."

He shook his head again. "I am not concerned about the Turkish janissaries. I have every confidence you will hold them at bay, Michael. But the Ottoman cavalry—the sipahis—" Here, he grimaced. "One man measured against another, I am certain Gottfried's cuirassiers are their equal—no, their better. But there will be far more of them."

"How many more?" Mike asked.

"The survivors of the siege claim there were at least thirty thousand sipahis. Many claim there were fifty or sixty thousand—some, even a hundred thousand. Montecuccoli seems the steadiest of the lot, and he estimates the sipahi numbers to be somewhere around thirty thousand."

Mike looked at Pappenheim. "And you have...?"

"Eight thousand."

Mike nodded. He understood the military calculations involved. In the seventeenth century, cavalry was the offensive arm, not infantry. That was beginning to change, under the impact of the Ring of Fire, but for the most part it still held true.

That meant that as long as Murad had a decisively more powerful cavalry—which he certainly did, at the moment—he would always have the advantage in any battle fought on the open field. Of course, no commanding general in his right mind in Gustav Adolf's position would be thinking in terms of offensive operations at the moment, given the huge disparity in numbers between his forces and those of Sultan Murad.

Not at *this* moment, no. But the war was not going to end quickly and there would be many moments to come. If the Swedish king could use the coming battle, where he would be holding a defensive position, to bloody the Turkish cavalry as badly as possible...

"You see the logic?" asked Gustav Adolf.

"Oh, yes, Your Majesty. I will need some time to talk to my men, you understand."

"Certainly."

"You sent for me, sir?" asked Lieutenant Colonel Engler.

"Yes, Thorsten, I did. There is something I wish to discuss more privately than I could in tomorrow's staff meeting." Mike was already seated. He gestured towards a nearby chair. "Please, have a seat."

After Engler did so, the Third Division's commander leaned forward. "Have you ever watched a bullfight? The way the Spanish do it, I mean."

Chapter 50

Gretchen studied the map spread out on the table with a scrutiny that was both intent and annoyed.

"Cowardly bastards," she growled. "And what are they eating, anyway? Grass?"

Eric Krenz shrugged his shoulders. "Holk's army is about as wretched a pack of soldiers as you can find anywhere in Europe, Gretchen. Probably anywhere in the world. I didn't really think they'd be launching assaults on us any time soon."

"I am afraid he's right," said Lukasz Opalinski. He and Jozef Wojtowicz were scrutinizing the map also.

Lukasz was, at any rate. His fellow Pole was pretending to, but it was obvious to Opalinski—probably to everyone else in the room, too; certainly the women—that Jozef was finding it hard not to ogle the two newly arrived females who were sitting on chairs against a nearby wall in Gretchen's headquarters chamber.

Mother and daughter, they were, which was quite evident by their resemblance. Both of them were beautiful, the daughter in the way of girls in their late teenage years, the mother in the way of women now closer to forty than thirty.

Oddly enough, Jozef seemed to be more drawn to the older of the two women. That was not his normal inclination, in Opalinski's experience. Wojtowicz was still shy of thirty himself, having recently celebrated his twenty-eighth birthday. He was usually attracted to women at least five years younger than he and with considerably less in the way of intelligence—something which, in Lukasz's estimate, was not at all true of the older Beasley female, judging from the keen and interested way she was following the discussion.

"We need to draw them out," said Lovrenc Bravnicar, the Slovene cavalryman.

"A standard way of doing that is with cavalry raids," said Opalinski. "But I can't say I recommend that in this situation."

Bravnicar made a face. "No, we're too heavily outnumbered. From what I can tell, at least half of Holk's forces are mounted."

Lukasz smiled. The Slovene couldn't bring himself to call them *cavalrymen*. Which, in truth, many of Holk's men really weren't, despite riding on horses. Their mounts were farm animals, often enough, stolen in the course of plundering raids by infantrymen too lazy to want to march.

In truth, Holk's army was a wretched one. But he had at least two thousand men under his command—probably closer to three—and while Lukasz didn't doubt the superior morale of the forces Gretchen commanded, they were even less of an army than Holk's.

The core of the infantry were the Third Division regulars commanded by Eric Krenz. But there were no more than three hundred of them. Add to that Bravnicar's cavalry—fewer than two hundred—and you had exhausted the total of Gretchen's troops who had experience as part of a real army.

The single biggest component of the forces Gretchen had brought from Saxony were Kresse's Vogtland irregulars. Those numbered somewhere between six and seven hundred men— understanding that included in the term "men" were at least one hundred and fifty women, who might or might not fight depending on the circumstances.

Since they'd assumed control over Lower Silesia's big towns, they'd been able to add a number of volunteers from one or another of the German militias. More had come forward than Lukasz had expected, actually—close to five hundred.

Finally, there were perhaps one hundred Polish farmers who'd volunteered as well. Over time, Lukasz was fairly confident that he and Jozef could expand that number three or fourfold, but it wouldn't happen quickly. Relations between Lower Silesia's German townsfolk and Polish farmers weren't hostile, but they weren't especially close and cordial, either. Each tended to be suspicious of the other, in the way of urban and rural folk from time immemorial.

All told, Lukasz and Jozef had reported to Gretchen just that morning that her army consisted of no more than one thousand, seven hundred soldiers, ninety percent of whom were infantry.

Foot soldiers, rather. Except for Krenz's regulars, you couldn't really call them "infantry."

"Bomb 'em," piped up a female voice from the side. "Bomb the bastards. That'll rile 'em up, you watch."

Everyone turned to look at the one who had spoken, the younger of the mother-daughter pair. Denise, her name was, if Lukasz remembered correctly.

Denise now pointed to a solid-looking fellow standing toward the back of the chamber. That was Eddie Junker, the pilot who'd flown Denise and her mother into Breslau just a short time ago.

"Ask him. That's how we met. I dropped a bomb on him. Well, technically, Keenan dropped it. But I gave the order."

She now grinned. "And, boy, was Eddie pissed about the whole thing. I bet if you started dropping bombs on Holk's shitheads they'd get really pissed too."

Gretchen was now peering quizzically at Junker. "I was not aware that your aircraft was a warplane. I thought it was a civilian one."

The stocky pilot shrugged. "Define the terms. None of the aircraft being made now—not the Gustavs, not the Dauntlesses, and certainly not the Belles—are what Americans would have called 'warplanes' in the world they came from. They're very crude and primitive aircraft modeled on up-time civilian designs which can be adapted to use as weapons platforms—very crude and primitive weapons platforms."

He gave the younger Beasley a look that seemed composed of equal parts affection and annoyance. "Technically, Denise is right. The Dauntless is equipped with mounts—hard points, they're called—to which bombs or rockets could be attached. If we had any, which we don't."

"We can make some," Denise immediately stated. "Don't anybody claim we can't because *I* know how to do it. Well . . .

bombs, anyway. Without venturi any rockets we made would be almost useless—might even be dangerous to us—and so far as I know Breslau doesn't have anything you could really call a machine shop so we can't make them. Bombs, though—those are pretty simple."

Everyone stared at her, including Opalinski himself. It was always a bit tricky gauging the age of up-timers, but most of the uncertainty came from their resistance to normal aging. Except for the generally superior teeth and the absence of such things as smallpox scars, young Americans looked pretty much the same as down-timers of the same age.

The Denise girl couldn't be more than … eighteen? Nineteen, perhaps—certainly not more than twenty. Yet she discussed the manufacture of explosive weapons as casually as she might discuss baking bread.

"She works for Nasi," Jozef whispered in his ear. "Don't forget that. Don't *ever* forget that."

Lukasz wondered if the same was true of the girl's mother. If so, Jozef would be well-advised to stay as far away from the woman as possible.

Gretchen, though, didn't seem in the least bit disconcerted by Denise Beasley's knowledge of the means of mayhem, just interested. "I need a clear answer, girl. Can you make such bombs? Here—in Breslau. With what we have available. I need a precise and realistic answer."

Such was Richter's force of personality that even the brash young Beasley girl seemed taken aback for a moment.

"Well…" She made a face and shook her head. "I can't give you that answer sitting here. I need to get out in the town and see what's available."

"I can tell you what is available," said Gretchen. "We have plenty of gunpowder—black powder, that is. We do not have the makings for iron bombs—not quickly enough—but I'm sure a cooper could make metal straps for a pot bomb that could be attached to the airplane's—'hard points,' they're called?"

"That's right," said Eddie. "And, yes, that ought to work. He'd also have to design a latch that would work on the hard points, so we could drop the bombs, but that shouldn't be too hard. It's not really that complicated."

Gretchen nodded and looked back at Denise. "Given that the

bombs will be dropped from a fast-moving airplane, am I correct in assuming that timed fuses would not be a good idea?"

Denise's eyes widened. "God, no!" she exclaimed. Kresse frowned at that blasphemy, but had the good sense not to protest openly.

"You need contact fuses for these kinds of bombs," Denise continued. "I know how to make those. As long as we've got percussion caps, it's pretty easy."

She glanced around the room. "And if nobody here has any percussion caps, you really have no business being out here at the ass end of the Thirty Years War in the first place."

"We have percussion caps," said Jozef. "I do, at any rate, and I could certainly spare a dozen or two."

"Ought to be enough," agreed Denise. She looked back at Gretchen. "What about gasoline or kerosene? If we've got ten or twenty gallons of that to spare, and some soap—soap's got to exist in a town this size—then I can make some pretty decent incendiary bombs. That'll *really* piss off the shitheads."

Gretchen nodded. "We've got some gasoline stockpiled, yes. Not much, but we can probably provide you with what you require."

"Okay, then." Denise clapped her hands, rubbed them together, and looked around the room again. "Who's good with making stuff, here? So I can show them how to do it?"

"I thought *you* were going to make the bombs," said Gretchen, frowning.

"Oh, no. You need me to be Eddie's bombardier. Target spotter, rather." In a very animated way, the girl started gesturing with her hands, as if making a three-dimensional model of the airplane.

"The way it works with a Dauntless is this," she said. "Up front, you've got Eddie on the left in the pilot seat, flying the plane. He can't do that while concentrating on the target at the same time. Back home—up-time, I mean—our guys could do that because they had these super-fancy Star Wars type helmets that let 'em see everything and coordinate firing at the same time—I saw a documentary on it once—but there's no way Eddie can do that with what he's got.

"So"—her hands now shifted to the right—"there I am, sitting in the shotgun seat. I'm the spotter and the one who decides when to drop the bomb, on account of the guy who *actually* yanks the release trigger is stuffed into that narrow back seat where he can't see much of anything."

Now, she frowned. "Piss-poor design for a bomber, if you ask me. What Bob Kelly *should* have done is design a real bombardier's sight for the girl up front, so she could do the release at just the right moment like they did back up-time during World War II."

Lukasz didn't know anything at all about aircraft design, but he was quite sure that if the Bob Kelly fellow were present he could explain in precise and elaborate detail why the girl's criticism overlooked practical realities. Denise seemed rather charming but he suspected her know-it-all attitude could get tiresome. For his sake, he hoped her pilot paramour had a disposition that was as solid and steady as his body appeared to be.

Denise shrugged. "You work with what you got. But that's why we need a three-person crew. The bombardier proper—that's what I call the guy in the back, on account of he's the one who actually drops the bomb—can be pretty much anybody who can follow orders and has good reflexes."

For the first time since she and her daughter had been ushered into the room, the mother spoke. Her name was Christin George, if Lukasz remembered correctly. As a rule, married American women took their husband's surnames, a peculiar English custom which was not observed on the Continent. She had kept her own, though, it seemed—or perhaps she'd changed it back after she'd been widowed. Lukasz didn't know any of the details, but he knew her husband had been killed during the Dreeson Incident.

"You've got one thing criss-crossed, honey," she said, looking at her daughter.

"What's that?"

"No way am I letting you fly into what amounts to a combat zone. Bad enough you're making bombs, but that horse left the barn a long time ago. I remember the hissy-fit I threw the first time Buster taught you to weld."

"Hey! I'm a good welder!"

"You are *now*, yeah. Your father had you starting at the age of six. You may have forgotten the way you yowled when you screwed up, but I haven't."

"Mom!"

"No. N. O. *No.* You stay right here in Breslau, on the ground. Somebody else can spot targets for Eddie. All that takes is good eyesight, a good sense of relative motions and directions, and the ability to holler '*Now!*' in a clear and piercing tone of voice."

"Mom!" Denise's gaze swept around the room. "Everybody here is a down-timer. None of them have any experience with what flying's like except Eddie and he's got to fly the plane. It'll take any of 'em days—weeks—before they'd be any good at it."

"Bullshit. I've flown in planes way more often that you have, young lady. My eyesight's still twenty-twenty and after spending years riding on the back of a Harley driven by your father I've probably got a better feel for relative motion than anybody this side of the Ring of Fire. And with you for a daughter who mastered foot-dragging at the age of two, I've got '*Now!*' down pat."

And, indeed, Christin George's *Now!* had been clear and piercing.

"Mom!"

"It's settled." Christin looked at Gretchen. "So all you need now is to appoint the guy who yanks the lever in the back seat."

"I volunteer!" said Jozef, smiling widely and as innocently as he could manage.

Like a lamb being led to slaughter, thought Lukasz. The woman was almost a decade older than Jozef and she probably worked for the spymaster Francisco Nasi. Judging by the amused glint that had just come to her eye, she also had no doubt at all of the outcome of any flirtation between herself and the most reckless Pole alive.

Whatever *she* wanted it to be.

"You are an idiot," he whispered to Jozef. But Wojtowicz kept that smile plastered on his face. Much like a death mask.

Vienna, former capital of Austria-Hungary, now occupied by the Ottoman Empire

Minnie finished her examination of the area of the city she could see through the narrow slit in the tower and stepped back a couple of paces. The sun still hadn't come up, this early in the morning, so there wasn't much chance anyone might spot her face in that opening. But there was no point in taking chances, however remote they might be.

"I think Murad's gotten most of his army out of the city by now," she said softly. The Ottomans had begun their march out of Vienna two mornings earlier, but getting that huge an army out of a conquered city and onto the road to Linz would have posed a challenge to the sultan and his officers. For one thing, plenty of his soldiers would have been drunk or recovering from drunkenness. Despite their religion's prohibition against the use of alcohol, Muslim soldiers were no strangers to drink—and the prohibition didn't apply at all to the many Jews and Christians in the Ottoman army.

"Are you sure?" asked Judy, in a whisper. The likelihood that anyone was close enough to hear a voice high in the tower was also remote; but, again, why take chances?

Minnie shrugged. "No, I'm not. But it's very quiet out there, much more than it has been since the Turks took the city. We'll know in a few days. If all that's left is a garrison, then the Austrian civilians still in the city will start moving around and getting back to their businesses. We'll be able to spot them from here."

Judy grimaced. "If there are any civilians left alive," she said, still whispering.

"Most of them will be," said Leopold. Like Minnie, he was speaking very softly but not in the outright whisper being used by Judy. "Murad didn't order a massacre when they took the city. If he had, we would have heard the screaming. In fact, he probably kept a tight rein on his troops because he'd want the city as intact and functional as possible. And he'd be able to do so because the fighting was fierce while it lasted but it was all over quickly. What usually makes soldiers run amok with fury when they sack a city is that they've suffered weeks of bloodshed."

Cecilia Renata came up the stairs from the ground floor, where she'd been moving around carefully, seeing what was available by the carefully shielded light of a small lamp.

"There's a cart down there that ought to suit your purpose, Minnie," she said. "It's a small one made to be hauled by a person, not a horse."

Leopold looked from his sister to his lover. "What purpose?" he asked. "What is she talking about?"

Minnie hadn't raised the subject with Leopold yet, because she knew he'd object to her proposal. "Let's get back into the cellars," she said. Leopold was likely to start raising his voice once she explained.

✧   ✧   ✧

"That's insane!" the archduke said—and, indeed, with a voice that was raised, although you couldn't call it a shout.

"Be quiet!" hissed his sister.

Leopold waved his hand irritably. "Nobody can hear us down here, not with these walls around us."

Cecilia Renata curled her lip. "Then why aren't we asking Minnie to sing for us to help pass the time?"

Her brother ignored that and went back to glaring at Minnie. "It's insane," he repeated, speaking more softly but still insistently.

"You're just acting angry at me because you're mad at yourself for not bringing the battery and the antenna," said Minnie, "which I've already explained is silly because you had no way of knowing we needed them."

That wasn't entirely true. An alert royal scion would have made it a point to learn how the peculiar up-time signaling device worked. But in the nature of things, princes tended to be incurious because they already thought they knew everything. About the only exception to that rule Minnie could think of was Prince Ulrik of Denmark, judging from the tales about him.

Still, there was no point having Leopold any more upset than he already was.

"We have to get the radio working," Minnie went on. "It's the only way we can get back in touch with our people. We've already agreed on that, Leopold—including you."

"Yes, yes, I know I agreed—but I didn't expect you to come up with this mad plan."

"How else can we do it?" she demanded. "Face facts. Neither you nor Cecilia Renata has any idea how to mimic Austrian commoners going about their business. And while Judy might be able to manage—maybe—she's much too good-looking to be moving around a city occupied by foreign troops."

"You're good-looking too!" Leopold said stoutly.

Minnie smiled and patted his cheek. "That's sweet. The difference is that I can disguise my appearance much better than Judy can. Just for starters, I can—I will, too, be sure of it—take out my glass eye. There are other things I can do, the most important of which involves that cart Cecilia Renata found."

The young archduke frowned. "How is that important?"

Minnie explained.

"That's disgusting!" said Leopold.

"Really gross," agreed Judy.

"So *that's* why you were so pleased when I found the bucket," said Cecilia Renata.

Breslau (Wroclaw), Lower Silesia
Poland

"Ready for the trial run?" Christin George asked, after Jozef Wojtowicz opened the door to the apartment he shared with Lukasz Opalinski.

He smiled at her, very toothily. "Yes, indeed. I am looking forward to it. A pity your daughter doesn't have any bombs ready yet."

Christin shrugged. "Trust me, she will soon enough. But today we're just doing a reconnaissance flight to see what's out there and where there might be any suitable targets."

To her surprise, the faces of two young children materialized, shyly looking at her from around Jozef's hips. A boy and a girl.

The girl said something in Polish. Christin could recognize the sound of the language by now but didn't know what any of the words meant.

Jozef said something in reply, caressing the girl's head with his hand.

He looked back at Christin. "She's worried that you're coming to take them away."

"Why would she think that?"

Still gently stroking the girl's hair, Jozef made a face. "She worries a lot. Her few years on Earth have been hard ones, so far. Her name's Tekla, by the way." His other hand fell on the boy's shoulder. "Her brother's name is Pawel. I found them in a destroyed village and ... well ..."

"You took them in. Good for you." She leaned over and gave the two children a toothy smile of her own. "Hello, Tekla and Pawel."

They hid their faces.

So. Jozef Wojtowicz had more parts to him than she'd supposed. That was interesting.

Chapter 51

The confluence of the Danube and the Traun
A few miles southeast of Linz

"Here," Gustav Adolf stated. "We will anchor our position here."

They were standing on the promontory formed by the confluence of the Danube and the Traun. The spit of land was narrow, forming an acute angle projecting out into the flowing water of the two rivers.

"Position the two ten-inch naval rifles here, Major Simpson," the emperor commanded. "They will make it impossible for the Turk to move any troops by boat near the confluence."

He glanced at the big artillery officer and smiled. "The two guns you already have here in the city, by such good fortune."

Neither Tom nor Mike Stearns, who was standing next to him, said anything. Both men tried their best to look as innocent as cherubs.

"When the other two arrive," Gustav Adolf continued, pointing to the north, "we will position them by the bridge. Whatever else, we must hold that bridge. If worse comes to worst, we can burn it, since it's a wooden bridge. But I would much rather keep it intact so we can sortie across the river—and, even more importantly, bring the Third Division and the Black Cuirassiers back across it if necessary."

Mike frowned. "You don't want to position them on the Pöstlinberg?" That was a hill more than fifteen hundred feet high that rose above the city of Linz on the left bank of the Danube.

Gustav Adolf shook his head. "It is tempting, I admit. But I am not at all sure that we will be able to hold Steyregg"—that was the small town just across the river from Linz where Mike's Third Division was taking up positions—"and if we lose Steyregg then we are bound to lose the hills behind it. We will certainly position some of our guns atop the Pöstlinberg—some twelve-pounders, certainly; some twenty-four pounders also, if we can get them up there in time—but I don't want to risk the ten-inch naval rifles. They are irreplaceable and so long as we have them we can interdict the rivers."

Tom was doing his best not to look pleased. The emperor had just said it himself—Tom was going back to being an artillery officer. That wasn't exactly his "first love"—football was—but it beat being a figure-it-out-as-we-go airship commander.

His pleasure lasted for all of five seconds.

"Major Simpson can set up the naval rifles, certainly," said Mike, "but he needs to get back to commanding the *Magdeburg* as soon as possible. His aide, Captain von Eichelberg, is quite capable of handling the guns thereafter."

Stabbed in the back by his own brother-in-law! Where was Early Modern Era nepotism when he needed it?

Gustav Adolf nodded. "Certainly. Speaking of the *Magdeburg*, how soon will she be ready for battle, Major Simpson?"

Tom was tempted to answer *how the hell should I know—I'm a damn artillery officer,* but...he didn't. First, because it would be impolitic, to put it mildly. Secondly, because it would be dishonest. Despite his best efforts to fend them off, the Dutch engineers and Julie kept him informed of every step in their progress or lack thereof.

"We need another four days to get everything ready, Your Majesty. Three days would be manageable. We'd simply have the armor partially established, but with enough coverage to protect the shooters."

"What if the pilots get killed?"

"It's not likely all three members of the flight crew would be killed. If they do come under fire, they can crouch below the windows of the gondola. Unless the Ottomans have better rifles than we're expecting them to have, they won't penetrate the walls. Those had shielding built into them while the airship was still under construction at Hoorn."

The emperor frowned. "I should think armoring the entire gondola would add too much weight." Gustav Adolf enjoyed flying, although not to the extent his daughter Kristina did. But he enjoyed it enough that he'd made it a point to become fairly knowledgeable about the new flying machines.

Tom shook his head. "You're thinking of steel armor, Your Majesty. They're only using that to shield the shooters. The way the gondola proper is shielded is with what amounts to a gambeson covering the entire hull."

"And that is enough to stop a *bullet*?"

"To be honest, no one really knows yet. Obviously, a lot will depend on the muzzle energy of the gun and the range at which it is fired. The hope is that any bullet fired by a normal musket or even rifle won't penetrate or, if it does, will have had most of its energy dissipated."

The emperor looked skeptical—truth be told, Tom was a little skeptical himself—but he simply nodded. "And what if the Ottoman airships arrive sooner than that?" Gustav Adolf asked. "Granted, that is not likely. Between the aircraft we now have flying reconnaissance and that very speedy river boat, we have excellent knowledge of the disposition of Murad's forces. He *could* order an airship assault two days from now—he could order it today, for that matter—but there would be no point since his ground forces couldn't get in position to take advantage of any openings the bombing might create."

That was the great imponderable. No one had much experience with the effect of airships used in a close air support role—and no experience at all with their effectiveness in a field battle. The few times they'd been used so far had been against fixed targets, either fortifications or the one time the airships supporting Tom's retreat from Ingolstadt had carried out a night-time bombing raid against Bavarian cavalrymen bivouacked in a small town.

There were no lessons to be drawn from up-time experience, either. In that universe, airships had not been used in combat roles in a significant way until World War I, and then they'd only been used in two capacities: for reconnaissance and for strategic bombing. No one had used zeppelins on battlefields and so far as Tom had ever been able to ascertain there had never been a single instance of airship-to-airship aerial combat. At some point in the course of World War I, it was possible that men aboard one craft might have fired pistols or rifles at enemy airships. But, if so, Tom had not found any references to such actions.

As had so often been the case in this universe shaped by the Ring of Fire, the combination of up-time knowledge with down-time technological capability produced an uneven and mixed result. On the one hand, airships were much more advanced in their military potential—at the moment; this would change, and might change quite soon—than either airplanes or antiaircraft gunnery were. No airplane yet built was capable of shooting down an airship, and unless the dirigibles flew extremely low they were almost impervious to ground fire as well.

Even in World War I, with a much broader and more advanced industrial base than anything that existed in Tom's new world, it hadn't been until the fall of 1916 that British airplanes were finally equipped with machine guns and incendiary rounds capable of shooting down zeppelins. During the first two years of the war, a number of German airships were destroyed by ground fire, but there did not exist any guns in the year 1636 in this universe that had anything comparable to the antiaircraft capability of their World War I counterparts. And wouldn't be for some time.

Tom knew that was Gustav Adolf's big worry. The emperor was one of the most experienced captain generals of the era—perhaps only Grand Hetman Koniecpolski was his equal, now that Tilly had been killed. He could gauge the capabilities of his infantry, artillery and cavalry, even adding in all the factors produced by the new weaponry.

He could even calculate the use of airplanes, since, for the time being, they were mostly useful simply for reconnaissance.

But airships? Those, Gustav Adolf did not have a good sense for. The giant dirigibles had played the key role in enabling the Ottomans to seize Vienna so quickly. Could they play a similar role here at Linz?

Tom didn't know the answer to that question himself. But he was betting on Julie Mackay and he thought it was a bet he'd be winning soon. He'd know sooner than just about anybody whether he had or not, since he'd have the ringside seat.

Steyregg, on the north bank of the Danube across from Linz

Jeff Higgins and Thorsten Engler were standing on the roof of a house at the eastern edge of the town of Steyregg. Perched on the roof, rather; it was too steep to actually stand erect. The position still gave them an excellent view of the terrain stretching to the east.

The terrain was fairly flat, and had been completely stripped of trees. The absence of trees was common near towns of the period, as it had been in most periods of history when wood was still the principal fuel for fires and cooking. Jeff had once seen a photograph of some part of New England in the nineteenth century and it had looked much the same way.

The hills rising to the north were still fairly heavily wooded, though. That wouldn't have been true this close to a big city like Munich, but Linz had a considerably smaller population.

"Are we going to try to hold the hills?" Thorsten asked.

Jeff shook his head. "Mike says no. We don't have the men."

"That's probably true, but if we don't..." Thorsten pursed his lips. "There'll be no way to hold Steyregg and the north bank if the Turks move into the hills."

"True. But what Mike's figuring—which means Gustav Adolf is figuring, I figure—is that Murad is going to continue with the same tactic that got him Vienna. He'll start with one big hammering blow, right off. Which he'll send across the flats because if he sends that many men into those hills they'll slow down to a crawl."

"And we do the butchering then."

"That's the plan." Jeff shrugged. "Afterward—assuming we beat back the Turks—Murad will probably settle in for a siege. That's when he'll send troops into the hills. At which point we'll have to give up the north bank and retreat across the bridge into Linz."

They fell silent for a while, as they continued their study of the terrain. Eventually, Thorsten pointed to a stretch of land that was flatter than any other. "That's where any cavalry charge will come. It's a narrow front; ideal for the volley guns. The trick will be getting back in time."

He gave his companion a calculating look. "I don't suppose there's much chance I could count on an infantry change by the stalwart Hangman regiment to provide us with protection."

"Sorry, but that'd just expose us to rocket fire even if we could drive off the sipahis. No, I'm afraid you'll have to depend on your own nimbleness. 'Flying artillery,' remember? That, and Pappenheim's men."

Engler grimaced.

"The Black Cuirassiers *do* have a reputation, you know."

"Yes, I recall. Aren't they the ones who started the butchering at Magdeburg?"

Now it was Jeff's turn to make a face. "Well, besides that."

Thorsten looked to his left, where the Steyregg Schloss was quite visible on a nearby hill. "Are we setting up our headquarters in the castle?"

"Where else? It's got the rooms, it's got the elevation, and the plumbing's no worse than the latrines we're digging in the field."

Thorsten's gaze went back to the flattish terrain to the east. The men of the Third Division were busy down there, digging trenches and putting up bunkers. Give them another two days, and they'd be in good condition to face the oncoming Turks. There was no intention to fight a battle here on open ground, not for the infantry and the field artillery. They'd stay in their fieldworks and fight from behind shelter.

It would be nice if Thorsten and his men could do the same. But... "Flying artillery," they were called. Very soon, they'd find out if they could live up to the reputation.

Vienna, former capital of Austria-Hungary, now occupied by the Ottoman Empire

"This has got to be the most disgusting thing I've ever done," complained Judy Wendell. She hoisted another bucketload out of the oubliette in the corner of the far cellar, taking care to move slowly and not spill any of the contents on herself.

Or on her clothing, which would be even worse. They had enough of a water supply in the cellars to manage a spare regimen of bathing. Not every day, of course. But they didn't have enough to do any sort of regular laundry. The only reason their garments weren't getting too foul yet was because they weren't doing anything except sitting around, chatting, and playing endless rounds of word games.

Hadn't been doing anything physical, rather. Until Minnie set them all to work making the necessary—gross; nauseating; loathsome—preparations for her expedition.

"Why couldn't we do this at the last minute?" she said, trying not to whine.

"Stuff has to dry out for a while," Minnie explained, "or it'll be too hard for me to use. I've got to hide stuff in it, remember?"

"Thank you for sharing that. The most disgusting thing I've ever done just got disgustinger."

"I don't think that's a word in English."

"No, it's not. I just added it to Amideutsch, where anything can be a word."

"Please stop talking," said Cecilia Renata, as she finished emptying the contents of the bucket into the cart. Her voice was tight and thin. "I'm almost throwing up as it is."

Leopold appeared out of the gloom. They never had more than one or two lamps and candles burning at a time. For weeks, they'd lived in a sort of perpetual twilight except on the rare occasions when they ventured into the tower.

"How much longer will this take?" he asked. "It's stinking up the whole place."

All three women glared at him. "It occurs to me," said Cecilia Renata, "that this would go faster if we pitched my useless brother into the well."

"True enough," said Minnie. "That'd raise the shit level at least two feet."

Leopold retreated back into the gloom.

Brzeg, thirty miles southeast of Breslau

"I think we may have found the bastard, Eddie," said Christin George. She was looked through a pair of binoculars at the town they were flying past. Or she had been—right now she was studying the small castle perched on a low cliff on the west side of the Oder river.

Jozef Wojtowicz peered through the small window he had available to him in the rear seat of the Dauntless. It was cramped and the visibility was poor. If he'd been as big as Lukasz he'd have been utterly miserable. As it was, he found the experience of flying to be exhilarating enough and nerve-wracking enough that he wasn't bothered too much by his physical discomfort.

"That's one of the Piast castles," he said.

"Who or what are the Piasts?" asked Christin.

"They were Poland's first dynasty. They ruled for more than four hundred years until the last of their kings died. That was Casimir III, the one they called 'the Great.' The Piasts built several of these castles in the area. There's one in Lignica and another one in Gliwice—what the Germans call Gleiwitz."

He struggled to get his head a bit higher. "I think Christin may be right, Eddie. This is exactly the sort of place Holk would set up his headquarters. Can you fly back around? And get us closer?"

"Let's take it in stages," Eddie said, as he brought the plane back around. "I'll start with a fast and not too low approach right over the castle. Tell me what you spot, if anything."

As the plane neared the castle again, Christin could see soldiers coming out of the structure. Stumbling out of it, some of them—one fellow did a silent-era movie pratfall as soon as he came into the courtyard that would have turned Buster Keaton green with envy.

"Yeah, that's got to be them," she said. "Of course, I can't tell if Holk himself is here."

The plane passed right by the square tower that adjoined the castle. More soldiers were coming out of that structure.

Jozef got a good look at it. "I think that's what they call the Tower of Lions. If Holk's in there, that's most likely where he'd be."

"One more time, Eddie," said Christin. "How low can you go?"

"Safely? That depends on several things, but..." He'd been studying the surrounding terrain and nodded toward something below. "I can follow the Oder behind that line of trees until we get close. They won't have enough time after they spot us to get a proper volley ready."

"Assuming those fucks can do a volley in the first place," jeered Christin. "I think half of 'em are drunk."

Drunk or sober, Eddie's assessment proved to be correct. When he brought the plane up over the tree line and swept around the tower, not more than two hundred feet off the ground, they were met by nothing more than sporadic gunfire. Jozef was fairly sure that all of the shots had simply been fired out of pique.

"That's it, then," he said, as they flew back toward Breslau. "One bombing raid coming up."

Chapter 52

Rebecca always found the way Gretchen studied a map to be quite striking, because of the sheer intensity of the blonde woman's scrutiny. It had been more than two years since Rebecca had spent a lot of time in Gretchen's company, during the Spanish siege of Amsterdam. She'd forgotten, a little, the nature of the woman's character when she was facing a major challenge. Someone had once described Gretchen as a force of nature, and there were times Rebecca thought the depiction was quite apt.

This being one of them. Ever since she'd brought her motley army into Lower Silesia and taken control of the big towns, Gretchen had been squeezing the province as if it were a lemon in her hand—bound and determined to force Holk and his thugs out of hiding. By now, at least a third of the province's Polish rural folk had either come into the towns or taken shelter beneath their walls, with more still coming every day. And if Lower Silesia's agriculture and commerce was suffering as a result, so be it. The inhabitants—the Poles even more than the Germans—had grown sick and tired of the mercenary army that was theoretically there to protect them but, in reality, behaved like a pack of thieves and extortionists.

On their own, they would not have put up any resistance. For that, leadership was necessary. And, with the exception of her husband, Rebecca had never met anyone who could project raw leadership the way Gretchen Richter did. It was as if the woman had a fierce halo surrounding her that called out: *Follow me.*

Holk and his men were still refusing to come out to face her challenge. But now, it seemed they might have discovered the beast's lair.

"You're sure?" Gretchen asked, then, immediately, waved her hand as if brushing away smoke. "Never mind, stupid question. But you think there's a good chance of it?"

Jozef Wojtowicz nodded. "It makes sense that Holk would have set himself up in Brzeg, Gretchen. He's just the sort of greedy bastard who'd be taken by the idea of setting himself up in one of the Piast castles, and the one at Brzeg is really the only one that's available. We hold the castle at Lignica, of course."

"There's the one you told me about in Gleiwitz, too," she pointed out.

Lukasz Opalinski now spoke up, shaking his head. "Gliwice's too close to Katowice. There's still a Polish garrison in that town, and even if there weren't Holk has to be worried about getting too close to Bohemia. Wallenstein claims all of Upper Silesia and he might still be angry enough at Holk because of the raid on Prague to launch an expedition against him, if he knew Holk was close by."

Rebecca found the subtle tug-of-war between Gretchen and her two Polish advisers a little amusing. Gretchen invariably used the German name for the big towns with mostly German populations, although she was quite willing to use the Polish names for the Polish-inhabited villages. A fundamental issue of democracy was apparently at stake.

The two Poles, on the other hand, insisted on using the place-names of their own native tongue. A fundamental issue of national pride was apparently at stake.

Rebecca was pretty sure Gretchen was going to win the contest, eventually—certainly if she kept control over Lower Silesia. The policies she was instituting were designed, among other things, to restrain the German townfolk from taking advantage of the current vulnerability of the rural Poles clustering around the towns. For instance, she'd established rigorous price controls and while a black market had inevitably emerged she was keeping it fairly well suppressed.

It helped a great deal, in that respect, that she had the core of Third Division troops under Eric Krenz's command. Those soldiers were German themselves and so could move easily among the town folk—but they were also either CoC in their political disposition or at least CoC-influenced. They might not have much in the way of personal empathy for the Polish refugees, but if Gretchen Richter told her regulars that they should squelch any and all attempts to exploit the refugees, squelch them they would.

It would be interesting to see how it would all turn out, in the end. From veiled comments in the radio messages she was getting from Ed Piazza, Rebecca was now certain that the USE government's policy toward Lower Silesia would be to keep it—perhaps as an outright new province, perhaps as an expansion of the existing province of Saxony, or, assuming a peace treaty was eventually made with Poland, perhaps as a protectorate of some kind.

That would certainly be Gustav Adolf's predilection. And while the initial attitude of the Americans and the Fourth of July Party toward the war with Poland had been skeptical—sometimes even hostile—that attitude was shifting as time went on. Partly that was due to the inherent dynamic of military conflict. Sympathy for an opponent was bound to decline as casualties mounted.

But there was more involved. As the war continued, the attitude toward the Polish regime on the part of the USE's population, including—in some ways, even especially—those under CoC influence, was starting to harden. Whatever its faults and however stunted its democratic and egalitarian principles might be in many respects, the government of the USE was far more responsive to the needs of its population than were the Polish-Lithuanian Commonwealth's king and Sejm.

For all the liberties granted to the Polish nobility and the much-vaunted religious toleration of the PLC, the lot of the commoners was generally wretched and getting steadily worse as the so-called "second serfdom" continued to be forced down the throats of the rural folk. Poland, which had once been among Europe's most advanced and enlightened nations, was increasingly becoming a realm where a relative handful of immensely wealthy and powerful landowners—"magnates," in the Polish parlance—lorded it over a peasantry being reduced to outright serfdom. In Poland now, King Wheat ruled in much the same way that King Cotton had ruled the American South in a different universe.

More and more, therefore, the population of the USE—and even more so its soldiers—were becoming partisans of Gustav Adolf's war against his Vasa cousin. Not because they cared about the dynastic issues involved but simply because they were coming to see the Polish-Lithuanian Commonwealth as yet another bastion of tyranny and reaction, like Spain or the Ottoman Empire.

So, whatever settlement might eventually come out of the war with Poland and Lithuania, Rebecca was now certain that the USE would keep its control over Lower Silesia, in one way or another.

Which meant—whether Gretchen liked it or not—that the Lady Protector of Lower Silesia was going to keep her title for quite some time. Rebecca thought it was illustrative of the irony of human history, that a woman who despised grandiose personal titles was so well suited to them.

As she demonstrated yet again.

"Well do it, then. Eric—Lovrenc—Georg—start assembling the army. We'll start the march on Brzeg the day after tomorrow."

"How much of a garrison do you want to leave in the towns?" asked Georg Kresse.

"None in the smaller ones. Two hundred here in Breslau." Gretchen gnawed on her lower lip for a moment. "One hundred—no, seventy-five should be enough—in Liegnitz. That's it, I think."

The Vogtlander frowned. "No more than that?"

Gretchen shook her head. "We don't need any more than that. It's now clear that Holk has concentrated his forces to the southeast. All of the towns we control—Glogau, Lüben, Bunzlau, all of them—are northwest of Breslau. Holk can't raid them without getting through our people."

Kresse was always stubborn. "He's got a lot of cavalry. He might raid around us."

Gretchen nodded toward Eddie and Christin, who were seated against one of the far walls. "We've got airplane reconnaissance, remember? Unless..." She looked at Eddie. "Is your employer making noises that you have to return to Prague?"

Eddie shook his head. "No. In fact, I just got a message from him this morning ordering me to stay here. 'For the duration,' as he put it. Of course, 'duration' is a pretty vague term and ultimately Don Francisco is the one who'll define it. But I don't see much chance he'll call me back until you've dealt with Holk."

"Good." She now looked at Christin. "And you are supplied with bombs, yes?"

"Oh, yeah. My little girl's been busy. She's having fun, actually. Which probably makes me the world's most disreputable mother, but so it goes."

Gretchen went back to studying the map. "The day after tomorrow, then. At the crack of dawn—no, before then. As soon as there's enough light to see." She did a quick measurement, using her thumb. "In a straight line, Brzeg's about thirty miles from here. If we make twenty miles the first day—I hope for better, but we'll see—then we will be in position to attack the bastards when there's still plenty of light on the second day."

So might a glacier predict its forward progress—except Gretchen would move much faster than a glacier. Rebecca had once heard Ernst Wettin call Gretchen *as ruthless as an avalanche.* It was a grotesque simile, in some ways. In others...

Quite accurate.

Vienna, former capital of Austria-Hungary, now occupied by the Ottoman Empire

"Yeah, I've got some eyeliner," Judy said. She nodded toward the chamber that she and Cecilia Renata slept in. "I've got it in my purse. But why in the world do you want it?"

She gave Minnie an evil sort of smile. "Is the archduke fussing about your appearance? You look fine to me, allowing for too many weeks spent living in a cellar when one week is seven days too many."

Minnie shook her head. "I'm not worried about keeping Leopold interested." A bit smugly: "I'm managing that just fine. But I need to make sure that when I go out into the city I don't get any other man interested. As in, bored Turkish garrison soldier with too much time on his hands and a very low threshold of interest. Taking out my eye won't be enough by itself."

She reached up and ran fingers through her hair. "I'll muck this up good, of course. And I'll stink of shit. But I want to have black teeth, too. The best thing I can think of that I could maybe use for that is your eyeliner. Cecilia Renata has some henna, but that won't blacken my teeth."

"Eyeliner'll work," said Judy. "I used my mom's once on Halloween, trick or treating. She had conniptions when she found out, but it was just because of the principle of the thing. The stuff's not dangerous." She made a little moue of distaste. "And given everything else you'll be doing to yourself, I guess blackening your teeth is small potatoes. Speaking of which, I'm starting to dream about French fries."

"Wouldn't that be a treat?" Minnie was quite fond of the American way of frying potatoes—which were called "American fries" by everyone in the USE except the up-timers themselves.

"How soon are you going?" Judy asked.

"Day after tomorrow."

"I thought you'd want to get it over with as soon as possible."

"I would," said Minnie. "But the shit hasn't dried enough yet."

Judy stared at her. "I can remember a time when I'd get upset if my shoes had gotten scuffed. God, the Ring of Fire's got a lot to answer for."

Steyregg, on the north bank of the Danube across from Linz

Mike Stearns looked around the bunker where Jeff Higgins had established the headquarters for his Hangman regiment. "Looks pretty sturdy," he said.

"I think so," Jeff agreed. "It helps a lot that we could bring the logs down the hill—from not too far away, either—instead of having to drag them across a mile of farmland." He reached up and rapped one of the logs that formed the roof of the bunker with his knuckles. It was a good six inches in diameter.

"I'm pretty sure it'll stand up to rocket fire. Cannonballs too, at least up to twelve pounds." His lips twisted into a grimace of sorts; part hope, part skepticism. "What I don't know is how well these bunkers will do if the Turks start dropping incendiaries on us."

Mike nodded. "For whatever it's worth, none of the reports we got from the assault on Vienna had the incendiaries being delivered by anything except airships. We can't be sure, of course, but I don't think the Ottomans have equipped their rockets with incendiary warheads."

Jeff looked back up at the log-and-mud wattle that formed the roof of the bunker, as if he could see the sky beyond. "Think Julie can do it?"

"We'll find out. The only other way to take out an airship that anyone's figured out, unless they fly low enough for ground fire to hit them, is to try dropping bombs on their envelopes."

"Huh?"

Mike smiled. "Yeah. Jesse Wood had a couple of his pilots look into it. They found a reference in one of the computers—why it was ever on the hard drive is anybody's guess—that the first English pilot who took out a German zeppelin during World War I did it by flying over the airship and bombing it."

Jeff's eyes narrowed, as he tried to visualize how that might work. Then he shook his head.

"With our fuses? Good luck with that."

Mike shrugged. "Yeah, nobody's too optimistic it'll work. But we've equipped all our warplanes with bombs and we'll give it a try. We've got three of them now, since Becky sent her Gustav down here to join the two Dauntlesses."

Jeff was familiar enough with the design of the planes to immediately spot a problem. "The Gustav, maybe, since the pilot can release the bomb himself."

"Herself, in this case. The pilot's Laura Goss."

"Herself," Jeff corrected. "But there's no way it'll work with a Dauntless, with that clunky design Bob Kelly came up with. The guy who actually drops the bomb can't see squat. What was he thinking, anyway?"

Mike shrugged. "I imagine he was thinking of the Dauntless as a civilian plane. I can remember a time, you know, when *I* didn't automatically put everything in a military framework."

Jeff chuckled. "So could I, if I tried real hard. I'd cuss the Ring of Fire again, but..."

"You got Gretchen and I got Becky. All things considered, I figure it was one hell of a deal."

"Yeah, me too."

They were silent for a moment, each man lost in thoughts of his wife. Then Jeff gave his head a little shake to clear it, and said: "Day after tomorrow, you figure? That's when they'll come at us?"

"That's what all the reconnaissance reports are telling us. Day after tomorrow."

Chapter 53

Vienna, former capital of Austria-Hungary, now occupied by the Ottoman Empire

Minnie set out a couple of hours before dawn. She figured she'd get at least halfway to her goal before the sun came up, and was less likely to be spotted than at any other time. Even if she was spotted, the explanation for her presence on the streets was simple and obvious—so obvious, not to mention repellent, that she'd probably never get questioned at all.

In Vienna, as was true throughout central Europe, night soil was collected by a disreputable group of workers. They were a European analog to one of the untouchable castes of Hindu India, although their position in society was not formalized by religion. In most of the Germanies, there were harsh laws governing their work and status. No such laws were in place in Austria-Hungary, but their social position was pretty much the same.

As a rule, the work was done by the men of the caste's families, but that was not a legal requirement, since night soil collection and disposal was not a guild matter. The rule was broken fairly often even under normal circumstances, and was even more likely to be broken after a recent foreign occupation. So having a woman pulling a night soil cart through the streets was not likely to seem suspicious to anyone.

Minnie could disguise her appearance, but the one feature she could not disguise beyond a certain point was her age. She

did her best to behave as a middle-aged woman might, but there
were limits to that ability. For one thing, the cart was heavy,
even only half-full as it was with the substance she and Judy and
Cecilia Renata had loaded into it a few days earlier. Her vehicle
was a hand cart, similar in design to the handcarts pulled across
North America by the Mormon pioneers of the mid-nineteenth
century. She simply couldn't behave in too decrepit a manner, or
she'd never be able to accomplish her purpose.

Oddly enough, though, her greatest worry had nothing to do
with the perils of the journey itself.

"Make sure—*make sure!*—that Leopold doesn't see me when I
get back," she'd whispered to Judy and Cecilia Renata, after she
and they had muscled the cart down to the ground floor and
she was preparing to leave the tower. "I don't ever want him to
know what I looked like."

That was part of the reason she'd decided to leave so early;
earlier, even, than night soil workers usually started their chore.
The young Austrian archduke was a heavy sleeper, and she'd been
able to ease her way out of their bedding without waking him.

Looking at her in the lamplight, Judy had to struggle mightily
not to wince—or gag. Minnie looked . . .

Horrible. Her eyesocket gaped open and she'd done something
to it—Judy didn't know what and didn't want to know—that suggested there was some sort of infection there. Her mouth hung
slack and loose-lipped, exposing just enough of the blackened
teeth to make it seem that she was mostly toothless. Minnie
even managed to shape her lips in such a way as to reinforce
that impression.

Worst of all, in some ways, was her hair. Minnie's hair was
normally quite full, colored somewhere between chestnut and
auburn. It was perhaps her best single feature, from the standpoint of beauty—and the one Judy had wondered how Minnie
could possibly disguise. Everything about her normally cried out:
look! healthy young woman!

She'd managed it, though. She'd used a combination of dust
and ashes to turn the color into a dull gray-brown. Somehow—Judy
really didn't want to know how she'd managed this feat—she'd
turned the fullness of her hair into tangled braids and matting.
The hair just looked plain mangy, now.

And, finally, there was the stench. She smelled—literally, not figuratively—like shit. The odor was detectable within ten feet; up close, it was quite nauseating.

"Remember," Minnie had repeated—three times—"keep Leopold away from me until I've been able to clean up."

Which was going to be a project in itself. Judy had already discussed it with Cecilia Renata and the two of them would spend the time after Minnie left getting her bath ready. They'd use one of the wine casks that was close to being drained, upend it and remove the lid, and fill it with water. There'd be enough wine still left to serve as a disinfectant, and wine was actually quite a good cleaning agent, especially for hair.

So Cecilia Renata had assured her, at any rate. The thought of using wine to shampoo her hair had never once occurred to Judy—and never would have, if she lived to be ninety-five years old, if it hadn't been for the be-damned Ring of Fire.

Of course, if it hadn't been for the Ring of Fire a lot of other things would never have happened to her either, she reminded herself. Good things! Like...like...

Associating with genuine royalty in a cellar while hiding out from slavering foreign conquerors.

"Talk about turning a silk purse into a sow's ear," she muttered.

They dowsed the lamp before opening the exterior door to the tower. Except for a few brief explorations by curious soldiers, the Ottomans had for the most part ignored the detached wing of the royal palace. There was nothing worth stealing beyond some saddles, since the building had been used for the storage of spare lumber, old furniture, tackle and the like. There were valuable items in the wing—extraordinarily valuable, given the passage of time, since they consisted of Leopold's art collection—but they were in the hidden cellars.

There were Turkish officers now residing in the main palace, however. It was unlikely that any of them would be awake yet; and, fortunately, the tower door was not visible from the main palace entrance where janissaries stood guard at all times of the day and night. But a gleam of light could be spotted in darkness where the shape of someone easing a handcart into the courtyard would not be.

It was done within a minute. Without saying a word or

glancing back, Minnie set out, pulling the cart behind her. Carefully, quietly, Judy and Cecilia Renata closed the door and retreated back up the tower to the hidden entrance to the cellars. Not long thereafter, they were back in hiding.

Minnie didn't so much as glance at the main building of the Hofburg, as she passed it by. It was tempting to try to retrieve the battery and antenna that Leopold had overlooked in the palace's radio room, since they were so close, but that would be a mistake. By now, there was a good chance all the remaining radio equipment in that room had been removed and brought to Murad to be turned over to his artisans. But even if the battery and antenna were still there, Minnie thought there was no chance she could make her way through the palace up to the top floor and back without being spotted. And while Ottoman soldiers would probably ignore her if they encountered her on the street or in poor areas of the capital, they certainly wouldn't if they found her in the Hofburg. Night soil generated in royal palaces was removed by servants, not by outcastes.

Her goal lay elsewhere. Following basic principles of their tradecraft, she and Denise had rented a small space—they'd had Eddie rent it for them, rather—in a warehouse halfway across Vienna, not long after they arrived in the city. That was where they had cached their own radio equipment, in case they had need for it later, and that was where she was headed now.

Breslau (Wroclaw), Lower Silesia
Poland

"Remember," Denise said to Jozef Wojtowicz, both her tone of voice and her gaze very intent. "This one"—she pointed to the bomb that two Air Force members were attaching to the hard points on the left side of the plane's fuselage—"is the regular bomb. Just high explosives—well, stretching a point—that'll send out shrapnel."

She shook her head, the gesture expressing quite a bit of pride. "I got some nasty stuff in there. Rusty nails, pieces of broken horseshoes, you name it. Okay, it's probably not as good as real shrapnel, but *still*."

She now stooped over and pointed to the bomb already

attached to the set of hard points on the right side of the fuselage. "That one, though, that's napalm. Well, close enough. It's an incendiary, you know."

Now, she straightened back up and looked at her mother, who had also been following the little lecture. "You got that, Mom?"

"Yeah, it's simple enough. Left side, fireworks; right side, fire."

Christin frowned and looked up at the plane's fuselage. "I never asked, though. Do the release levers match the position of the bombs? What I mean is—"

"Yeah, they do," said Denise. "I checked just to make sure this one worked the same way as the one I was in when me and Keenan Murphy and Lannie Yost...well..."

Her mother chuckled. "When you bombed your boyfriend and Noelle."

"Hey! That's not fair. Eddie wasn't my boyfriend yet."

Jozef reflected that Eddie Junker had to be a brave man, picking Denise Beasley to be his paramour. He wondered what that might imply about himself, given his intense attraction to Denise's mother. Was he also a brave man? Or just, as Lukasz said, an idiot?

But that was a matter for later. For the moment...

He gave Christin the big smile that seemed to come to him automatically whenever he dealt with the American woman. He thought of it as a "beaming" one. Lukasz was just being churlish when he labeled it *a village idiot's sort of smile.*

"So let us be agreed," he said. "Tell me which lever you want me to pull before you give me the signal."

Christin nodded. "Got it. 'Left bomb.' Then—whenever the time's right—I'll holler '*Now!*'"

Eddie stuck his head out of the pilot's side of the cockpit. "Any time you're ready, folks."

Christin and her daughter exchanged mutually admiring looks. "Have at 'em, Mom!" said Denise.

Steyregg, on the north bank of the Danube across from Linz

Mike Stearns lowered his binoculars. "And here they come, just like they did at Vienna. Five airships leading fifteen more—except here they're coming in four lines of five airships each."

"It's a narrower front here, sir," said Raimondo Montecuccoli. He was standing next to Mike and still had his spyglass in place. "I thought they might try to bomb Linz itself, but apparently they plan to focus entirely on our positions here, north of the river."

Mike had speculated on that possibility himself. Linz wasn't a major city even by the standards of the time, but it still sprawled out much farther than Steyregg and the fortified positions the Third Division had built in front of the town. That made it a softer target because whatever antiairship ground fire the defenders of Linz might be able to manage, it would be more spread out than whatever they might have in Steyregg.

Which was not much anyway, being honest about it. They'd briefly considered trying to mount one of the ten-inch naval rifles as an antiairship gun—"briefly," because Major Simpson's reaction to the proposal had been blunt, forceful and profane. He'd pointed out that he had enough trouble mounting the guns in such a way as to enable them to cover both the Danube and the Traun. Trying to add an elevation capacity to the mounts that would be sufficient to shoot at airships was simply impossible.

"If you gave us weeks to do it, maybe," he'd said. "*Maybe*— and I'd make no guarantees even then. There's no way we can do it in a couple of days. As it is, if the Ottomans manage to get a flotilla very far up the Traun we won't be able to bring the guns to bear on them."

"I concur with Major Simpson," his subordinate Captain von Eichelberg said stoutly.

The truth was, for the moment *any* position was a "soft target" for airships, at least as far as ground fire was concerned. True, Mike had assigned the entire Dietrich regiment to serve as his "ack-ack," if and when he gave the order. At that point, a little more than a thousand men would fire a coordinated volley at whatever airship their commander, Colonel Carsten Amsel, chose for their target.

They'd be firing with SRG rifled muskets, too, which had a greater range than most muskets of the era. Still, as long as the airship kept more than three hundred yards above the ground—above four hundred, almost certainly—even a volley of one thousand Minié balls wasn't likely to do much damage except by blind luck.

"They seem to have added some armor, sir," said Montecuccoli.

"The bottom of the gondolas—is 'bottom' the correct term for that?—are now V-shaped. That wasn't true at Vienna."

Mike brought his binoculars back up and studied the feature Montecuccoli was indicating. Sure enough, now that the airships were closer and he was looking more carefully, he could see that the hulls of the gondolas were distinctively V-shaped—more so than any boat he'd ever seen, in fact. The angle the sides of the gondola now formed was roughly ninety degrees.

"That's got to be in order to deflect bullets from ground fire," he said.

Montecuccoli lowered his own spyglass. "It's odd, though. Unless I misunderstood something Major Simpson told us in his briefing yesterday, for all their immense size these airships really don't have that much in the way of lifting capacity. With regard to their—what did he call it? cargo capacity?—even the *Magdeburg* can't carry more than a few tons above the weight of the ship itself along with its crew, fuel, ballast and equipment. And these Ottoman airships are quite a bit smaller than the *Magdeburg*."

Mike understood the point he was raising. An Ottoman airship probably didn't have a net cargo capacity greater than a ton. Any armor they added would have to be subtracted from the weight of their payload. What was the point of flying a well-armored airship over a target when all it could drop once it got there were a few grenades?

"I think that new outer armor is very light, Raimondo," he said. "That's just a guess, but now that I think about it, that's how I'd do it. In fact, whenever we get around to using the *Magdeburg* as a bombing platform—which we won't be doing today, of course—we ought to consider doing it ourselves."

"I'm not sure I'm following you, sir."

Mike lowered his binoculars. "All you need to do is deflect some bullets—basically, if you fly high enough, you just need to be able to handle stray and lucky shots. So you place thin boards at an acute angle, maybe—no, probably—backed with some kind of light padding. Fabric; silk would be even better. Sure, if enough bullets hit the outer armor they'd wind up shredding it, but so what? By then the battle would be over and I'm willing to bet the Ottomans designed the new armor so they can easily jettison it when necessary."

The Italian officer grunted. "I think you're probably right. Clever bastards."

"Never forget the greatest of all military principles, Raimondo."

"Which is...?"

"The other guy's got a brain, too."

Lower Silesia
About ten miles southeast of Breslau

"I *hate* this armor," Gretchen hissed. If her glare had actually been as hot as she imagined it to be, the whole countryside would be starting to smolder.

Which would serve that countryside right, as far as she was concerned! Stupid farmland owned by stupid Poles who managed their affairs so poorly she was forced to set everything straight while wearing this—this—this—

"Argh!" she snarled, then slapped her midriff.

"And I'm five months pregnant, too! You watch—I'll miscarry because of the way this idiotic armor presses on me."

Lukasz Opalinski, riding next to her in full hussar armor— he'd even managed to get an artisan to build him some saddle wings—was not sympathetic. "You would have surely miscarried in that attack if you *hadn't* been wearing your armor. If you'd survived at all, which you probably wouldn't have. Stop whining. Your pregnancy is barely showing even in your normal clothing. And *you* aren't wearing a helmet."

He reached up and slapped his own helmet with a steel-gauntleted glove. "As I am forced to."

"Forced to! Ha! Stupid hussar. I'll bet you bathe wearing that helmet."

Opalinski made no reply. By now, he'd come to know Gretchen Richter well enough to know that she'd get over her foul mood fairly soon—instantly, if any sort of problem needed to be dealt with.

And the fact was, whether the woman liked it or not, that having her wear that bright and distinctive armor—especially without a helmet—was a stroke of political genius.

Not hers, of course. It had been Tata and Eric Krenz who made the proposal—with Lukasz and Jozef immediately supporting them.

❖   ❖   ❖

"They're right, Gretchen," Jozef said. "I can't think of anything that would boost the morale of our forces more than having you lead the army out of Breslau wearing that armor. Without the helmet, so everyone can see your face and that famous hair of yours."

"My hair is *not* famous," she hissed. "That's ridiculous!"

"Yes it is," Tata immediately countered, "after that one surviving Holk asshole told everybody the story of what happened in the fight. Here in Lower Silesia, your blonde hair's as famous as your tits were in Amsterdam. Well, maybe not that much."

Gretchen glared at her.

Tata stood her ground. "They *were* famous. I heard about your tits all the way down in Mainz."

Lukasz had heard that story too, by now. But he judged it would be most impolitic for him to say anything about it. Instead, he tried to get back to the real subject at hand.

"The country folk will be impressed too, Gretchen," he said. "Especially with me riding next to you in my armor—and holding up a Polish battle flag."

They'd been right, however much Gretchen detested her armor. Along every mile of the march since the army left Breslau, villagers had come to gawk at the spectacle. Hundreds of them—each of whom would be spreading the story across the whole countryside.

Gretchen was not exactly a beautiful woman, although she came close. She fell shy of standard notions of female beauty because her features were just that little bit too pronounced. Her nose was a bit too large and beaky, her jaw a bit too strong, her brow a bit too heavy—although it certainly matched the eagle's gaze she so often exhibited.

But she wasn't participating in one of those peculiar American beauty contests Lukasz had heard about. The ones up-time—they didn't hold them here—where they apparently paraded young women around in order to bestow a prize on one of them, in a typically absurd American manner. One moment, the girls were displayed practically nude; the next, they had to display some sort of skill, usually a silly one.

No, Gretchen was leading an army to rid the country of trolls and ogres. For that, the fierce face above gleaming armor and below that long yellow hair served perfectly.

They'd still have to fight a battle, of course. That would be when Lukasz would come into his own. Protecting Gretchen Richter in a fight would be a real challenge.

Perhaps the woman would be sensible this time and stay safely in the rear. Judging from the eagle look on her face, though...

Probably not.

"I *hate* wearing this armor," she hissed again.

Lukasz, however, was delighted she was wearing it, given the situation. He didn't say so, of course. He was a bold and daring Polish hussar, not an imbecile.

Chapter 54

Vienna, former capital of Austria-Hungary, now occupied by the Ottoman Empire

To her relief, when Minnie got to the warehouse where she and Denise had rented a storage bin, the facility was deserted. Her biggest worry had been that she'd find the warehouse owner still present, which would have been awkward. Eddie had been the one who'd actually negotiated with the warehouse owner and paid him the rent; not she and Denise. It would have been seemed peculiar for two women as young as they were to have done so. But even if she had been the one to rent the bin, the owner wouldn't have recognized her anyway, given her appearance of the moment.

If need be, Minnie had been prepared to kill the owner. She would have been very reluctant to do so, because she had no animus against the man. Not to mention that she'd never killed anyone in her life. To her knowledge, at least. It was conceivable—though certainly not likely—that one of the barrel staves she'd thrown at the rioting students in Jena when they started stoning her had struck and killed one of them. (If so, good riddance—those students had cost Minnie her eye and they were training to be theologians; which was to say, more useless than any creatures on earth.)

But, happily, the warehouse was completely deserted. So, she left the dagger in its sheath, hidden on her right thigh, and went to work. They'd never intended for anyone but Eddie to retrieve

495

anything from the storage bin, since neither she nor Denise had foreseen the Turks seizing Vienna so rapidly. But they'd kept a copy of the key in their own belongings.

The lock on the bin appeared to be a simple Slavic-style screw key padlock, only marginally superior to the English-designed "smokehouse" lock. Up-time inspired padlocks were beginning to appear in Europe, but the use of one would have drawn automatic attention in a place like Vienna. This lock had been provided to them by their employer, however, and was quite a bit better than it looked. Nasi had had it made by a Jewish metalworker in Prague, based on a design provided by Morris Roth.

Within a minute, Minnie had the lock open and the chain removed. It took only a bit longer to retrieve the items they'd stored there, one of which was a small two-barreled caplock pistol modeled on an up-time .41-caliber Derringer pistol.

The first thing Minnie did was load the pistol from the contents of a pouch holding powder, bullets, and a short ramrod, and tuck it away in her left sleeve. That done, she felt only marginally safer than she had before, but a lot more sanguine as to her prospects. Minnie did not lack self-confidence. If it came to it, she was fairly confident she could down a single opponent with the pistol and make her escape. If there were two opponents...

Not so much.

Then, making sure the radio equipment was still well-covered with the oilcloth they'd wrapped it in, she began the nasty work. Using a small trowel they'd found among the stored supplies in the cellars, she cleared out enough of the night soil from the cart to make room for the radio equipment and other things she'd retrieved from the bin.

That done, she scooped the night soil back into the cart, covering everything in such a way that it was very unlikely anyone would ever want to poke around in there to see if there were anything hidden.

The trowel, she discarded in a corner of the warehouse. It stank, but the whole warehouse stank a bit. There were plenty of small animals using it for a combined residence and toilet. She didn't think the smell would draw any attention.

And then, off she went, hauling the cart back toward the distant Hofburg. Things were going quite well, she thought. It was still rather early in the morning. The sun hadn't been up for more than two hours. If her luck held out, she'd be back in the cellars before noon.

The confluence of the Danube and the Traun
A few miles southeast of Linz

"I thought they'd begin with this." Gustav Adolf lowered the up-time binoculars he'd been using to observe the Ottoman flotilla advancing up the Danube toward the confluence with the Traun.

"Risky on their part," said General von Colloredo. "I wouldn't have done it, myself."

I am sure you wouldn't, thought Gustav Adolf. *But then, you're not the most capable sultan the world has seen in a century, are you?*

But he left all that unsaid. Von Colloredo wasn't of much use for anything except routine military matters, but there was no point in offending the man.

"If there's one thing Murad has plenty of," Gustav Adolf pointed out, "it's soldiers. And he's already shown that he's willing to take bold risks if there's a chance of winning a quick victory."

With the binoculars now hanging from their straps, he pointed his finger at the end of the tributary and then swept his hand to the right, indicating the whole reach of the Traun as it neared the Danube. "If Murad can get past the confluence and seize the left bank of the Traun, he'll be in far better position to launch direct assaults on Linz. If he can't, then even if—even after, I should say, since there's no way I can stop him for very long—he seizes the north bank of the Danube, we'll wind up with a long siege. And not one that favors him, since he won't be able to interdict all of the waterways down which we can bring supplies."

"I can see the logic, Your Majesty, but the casualties..."

"Will be high, even if he succeeds. Yes, I know—and you can be sure Sultan Murad knows as well."

For a moment, Gustav Adolf's thoughts veered aside. He wondered if Janos Drugeth was correct in his speculation that Murad was deliberately bleeding his janissaries in order to reduce their power in Turkish affairs.

He might be. That was not something Gustav Adolf would ever consider doing himself, but there was really no analog in Europe to the role played by the janissaries in the Ottoman Empire. It was not hard to believe that a sultan, if he was ruthless enough, might follow that course of action.

But there was no point in pursuing that speculation here and now. The battle was about to begin.

He turned his head and called out to the commander of the battery, Captain von Eichelberg. "Are they in range?"

"For the two naval rifles, Your Majesty. Not the rest of the battery."

"Fire on them, then."

Von Eichelberg passed along the order. The artillerymen manning the ten-inch guns had been tracking the Ottoman flotilla since it first came into sight around a bend in the Danube four miles downstream. So it was not more than a few seconds before the first of the guns fired. Followed, three seconds later, by the other.

Gustav Adolf wasn't using his binoculars now, just the sports glasses the Americans had provided him with years earlier. He wanted to see how far off these first shots would be.

Both shots struck their targets. Or at least, one of them did. That shell passed right through the bow of the barge and exploded a split-second later, producing a horrible slaughter among the janissaries packed into the vessel. The other shell had much the same result, even though Gustav Adolf thought it might have struck the bow of its target just below the waterline. The immediate butchery was much less than the first shell produced, but the final death toll might be as bad or worse. The bow of that barge was blown wide open and the waters of the Danube surged in. Within seconds, the barge was sinking.

Some of the janissaries aboard would escape, but most wouldn't. The barge had been traveling down the middle of the river, and in this stretch the Danube was easily a thousand feet wide. Swimming four or five hundred feet was within the capability of a good swimmer, but not encumbered the way these were. Janissaries didn't usually wear armor, but their heavy woolen underclothes and pants were covered by a thick, full-sleeved and knee-length overcoat. Within seconds of being immersed in the river, that clothing would be soaked with water. Short of wearing mail or plate armor, it was hard to imagine something as difficult to stay afloat in. The quick-thinking and more agile janissaries would save themselves—assuming they could swim at all, which many couldn't. The others would surely drown.

The naval rifles were muzzle-loaders and they didn't have the advantage of the hydraulic recoil systems they would have been provided with aboard the ironclads they were originally designed for. So it took a while to reload them—considerably longer than Gustav Adolf was happy with. General von Colloredo was practically dancing with anxiety by the time they were reloaded and back in position.

Fortunately, river barges packed with heavy infantry and moving upstream didn't move quickly either. They'd only gotten a hundred yards closer when the rifles fired again.

This time, one shot missed completely, sending up a spectacular plume of water which did nothing more than drench part of the complement of soldiers in the barge it had been fired at. But the other one made up for it by striking a blow on the adjacent barge that was every bit as deadly as the first shell fired. By now, wide stretches of the Danube were becoming blood-colored.

"Reload!" shouted von Eichelberg.

North bank of the Danube
About a mile west of the village of Langenstein

Atop the wooden tower he'd had erected as an observation platform in his headquarters camp, Sultan Murad stepped back from the telescope on its tripod and straightened up. "Call them back," he said. "I can't afford to lose this many men, even if we could reach the confluence at all, which we might not."

He turned to his aides. "Begin the assault against Steyregg."

Steyregg, on the north bank of the Danube across from Linz

"Get your men ready," said Jeff, to the officers clustered in the Hangman regiment's command bunker. "I just got word over the radio. The river assault's been driven off. That means the bastards will be coming at us next."

He stepped up to the observation slit and studied the enemy in the distance. Not the ones on the ground—he wasn't worried about them; at least, not yet—but the ones he could see floating in the sky.

"Do your thing, Julie," he said, almost whispering.

Aboard the airship Magdeburg
Two thousand feet above Linz

"Okay, they're coming forward," said Tom Simpson. "If they follow the Vienna pattern, that first line will be laying down smoke."

"So we ignore them?" asked Julie.

"I figure. The smoke'll cover the advance of the ground troops, but that's not our problem. We need to take out the airships which will be doing the bombing."

He turned to Gerrit Janssen, who insisted he was only the pilot of the *Magdeburg* even though for all practical purposes, outside of combat, he was the captain. If this were a seagoing naval vessel, he'd have been called the ship master.

"Can we avoid that first line?" Tom asked. "Keep in mind that if we fly over them we'll have to drop down quickly to meet the next line. Firing on those airships from above will be useless, since we'd only be poking holes in the envelope and we don't have any incendiary rounds."

Tom was skeptical that even incendiary rounds would do much good, fired one at a time from Dell Beckworth's elephant gun. In theory, setting fire to an airship using hydrogen for lift should be easy, but he was sure that in the real world it would be a lot less straightforward. The ball not only had to penetrate the envelope— easier said than done, even with a .50 caliber round—it also had to let in enough oxygen to create the right mixture to ignite the hydrogen. Yes, during World War I the British had shot down a number of German zeppelins firing incendiary rounds from airplanes—but they'd been firing machine guns, not single shot rifles.

Janssen considered the problem for a few seconds, then shook his head. "Flying over the first line's not a good idea, *Captain* Simpson." He placed enough stress on the term *captain* to make it clear that they would be following proper naval protocol on board *this* ship, thank you very much. Janssen was just running the craft, he was not commanding it. Tom was—which made him the captain, all other rank considerations be damned.

"We're faster than any of their airships," Janssen continued. "I'm sure of that. I don't know what sort of heathen Moham- medan steam engines they're using over there"—here, his lip curled, bringing his florid mustachio to full attention—"but from what we've seen so far they're pathetically weak. So—"

He pointed through the window to the enemy airships in the distance. All three of them were standing in the bow of the gondola, which gave them an excellent view forward. "We're positioned three miles south of Linz, and about a mile southwest of the river, the way the Danube courses here."

Now he started gesturing with both hands, using them to simulate relative movement and positions. "In order to spread smoke over Steyregg and the positions taken by the Third Divi- sion, the Ottoman tubs will have to fly past our position. As they near the confluence, we will fly across the Traun—coming down to their altitude as we do so—and then cross over behind them. If I'm gauging this correctly, we will pass behind that first line of airships and in front of the second line."

Tom visualized the maneuver. "Crossing the T on them, in other words."

Janssen frowned. The expression was one of puzzlement, not disapproval. It occurred to Tom that the expression he'd just used probably wasn't in tactical usage yet. The guns on warships in this era were so inaccurate that the standard naval tactic, which the Dutch used to great effect, was simply to swarm the enemy and engage in what amounted to a seagoing melee.

He started gesturing with his own hands. "What I mean is that the *Magdeburg* will be passing in front of the second line of Ottoman airships. Shooting from within the hull, where we've set up the tripods, Julie will have a good angle at each of their ships as we near them."

He turned to Julie. "Am I right?"

Her brow was creased with a frown also, but hers was just one of concentration. "Yeaaaahhh..." she said slowly. "I think you're right. We'll find out when we try it."

Then she shrugged. "I'm not too worried about shooting with my regular rifle—which is what I'll start with. Almost any sort of angle will work for me, as long as the enemy's in sight and in range. The problem's going to be with the Beckworth .50." Her own lip curled. "Dell can call that thing a 'Light 50' till the cows come home; it's still bullshit. That thing's a monster. It weighs a ton and it's clumsy to handle. Can't possibly shoot it without a tripod—and the tripod's got to be fixed in the right place."

She glanced at the Dutch pilot. "Meaning no offense, Mr. Janssen, but the next time you design an airship to shoot an elephant gun from, you need to set a continuous rail all along the windows so the tripod can be slid into position after the windows are taken out."

"I'm just the pilot, Madame Mackay. I am not the engineer."

"Whatever." She turned away and headed for the broad-stepped ladder that led into the hull. "You get the ship into position, Mister I'm-Just-the-Pilot. I'll take it from there."

Linz, capital-in-exile of Austria-Hungary

Melissa Mailey planted her hands on her hips and all-but-glared at the Austrian emperor and empress. "You're the ones who insisted I come down here. Your Majesties," she added, remembering the protocol.

"Actually, that was General Stearns' proposal." Emperor Ferdinand smiled widely. "Not that Mariana and I weren't entirely in favor of the notion. We were sure you'd be an asset."

As bald-faced diplomatic lies went, that one was pretty impressive. Melissa was quite sure that the royals who ruled Austria had looked on the idea of having one of Europe's most notorious revolutionaries as one of their guests with something not far from horror.

Nonetheless, they'd gone along with Mike Stearns' idiotic suggestion—and so, here she was.

"All right, fine. But you agreed to bring me in. I gather the theory is that I'll help bolster the morale of the lowlifes."

"The . . . which?" asked Empress Mariana, frowning slightly. They'd been speaking German—the dialect prevalent in Austria, that is—but Melissa had a tendency to blur the lines between all dialects of German and the German daughter language she was most comfortable with, which was Amideutsch. So, without thinking, she'd tossed *lowlifes* into the last sentence. Apparently the term was unfamiliar to Austrian royal family.

Too lowlife, as it were.

She waved her hand. "Never mind. What I mean is that since I'm here, let's make the most of it. The best propaganda pitch I can think of, Your Majesties"—here she focused her attention on Mariana—"is for me and the empress to work in the hospital you've set up to handle the wounded when they start coming in."

She squinted at Emperor Ferdinand. "You did set up a hospital, I trust?"

He was now frowning too, and a lot more deeply than his wife had. "Yes, certainly—there's a big battle coming. But—but—"

He and Mariana stared at each other.

"I've never heard of such a thing!" he protested. "An *empress*? For that matter, even a queen or a provincial princess. Attending wounded soldiers in a hospital?"

He resembled a fish out of water, gasping for breath. Ferdinand III was still a young man—two years shy of thirty—but in that moment he looked like every set-in-his-ways octogenarian in history, hearing a preposterous new idea advanced.

"I know no one expects it, Your Majesty," said Melissa. "That's the whole point. We'll have Mariana and me"—here she pointed to herself with a thumb—"that is to say, the empress of Austria-Hungary and Famous Wild-Eyed Radical Number Five—hell, I might even be ranked number four, these days—working together to tend to our valiant soldiers fighting off the Wicked Ottoman Sultan, and we'll leave for some other time my opinion that the distinction between Wicked Sultans and Virtuous Emperors usually depends on who's beholding whom and from what angle."

"But—but—it could be dangerous," protested the emperor. "Hospitals . . . they have *diseases.*"

"Well, yes. If there weren't any danger the flamboyant propaganda coup wouldn't be a coup at all, would it?" She wasn't sure if the French term *coup* had entered the general European royal lexicon, but if it hadn't it was about time it did, so to hell with it. "But I don't think it'd really be all that dangerous. For one thing, my squeeze—ah, companion—is going to be running the medical show and he'll insist that proper sanitation and antiseptic measures be taken at all times. And for another—"

She shrugged. "Gustav Adolf probably won't be having seizures all that often, so even if one of us does get sick, Mariana and I will still have the world's best doctor tending to us. And we'd be Patient One and Two, since you're the empress of Austria-Hungary and I'm his—ah—companion."

She saw no reason to parse which one of them would wind up being Patient One and which would be Patient Two, should the occasion arise. Let royalty have their delusions.

"So," she said brightly. "What do you say?"

Chapter 55

Piast castle
Brzeg, thirty miles southeast of Breslau

"You both understand what I'm about to do?" Eddie said. He was almost shouting, since he wanted to make sure Jozef could hear him in the back seat over the noise of the airplane's engine.

"Got it," said Christin, speaking in a normal tone of voice because she was seated next to him. From the back, Jozef called out: "Yes, I understand!"

But Eddie wasn't satisfied with a mere acknowledgement. The critical person involved in the maneuver was Christin, since Jozef could presumably be counted on to yank the release levers when she gave the order.

"Repeat it back to me, Christin," he ordered.

Christin George had a personality that was similar to that of her daughter, and if Denise had been sitting there her most likely response to that command would have been something along the lines of: "What, you think I'm too dumb to get it the first time?" But Christin had the advantage of an additional nineteen or twenty years of age, and the maturity that went with it.

The uncertainty of that spread—nineteen or twenty—depended on whose reckoning you used. The Ring of Fire had happened in the month of April in the year 2000, and the town of Grantville had arrived in its new universe in May of the year 1631. So, when they wanted to calculate their age, most up-timers simply transferred the same months into their new calendar. Simplifying, every May—usually May 1—they added however many years had gone by since the Ring of Fire to the age they'd been when it happened.

Christin George had been born in 1968, up-time reckoning, and it was now September of 1636, by the down-time calendar. So, she considered herself thirty-seven years old.

Not every up-timer used this simple and sturdy method, however. In particular, American teenagers approaching what they still considered the magic number eighteen (even though that age had little importance to down-timers) had a tendency to fiddle with the math involved.

As did Denise. She'd been born on December 11, 1987. So, by the standard method of calculating age, she wouldn't be eighteen until December 11, 1636.

Screw that! The way she looked at it, years were years—no matter what month it happened to be. She'd been born in the year 1987, which meant she'd been thirteen when the Ring of Fire happened—*not* twelve and a half, like her mother claimed. So, since yet another May had passed in their new world, *voila!* She was eighteen years old. Nineteen, come December 11.

"We're only going to do one pass at the castle," Christin said amiably, "because you don't want to give Holk and his men time to assemble so they can fire a volley at us. That could get hairy since you're planning to fly very low all the way until we drop the bombs, so we have the best chance of hitting the bastards."

"You got it," said Eddie, nodding. "And I'm starting the descent."

The Piast castle was located on the edge of a low cliff—more like a bluff, really—overlooking the Oder on the west bank of the river. Because of the positioning of the Tower of Lions with respect to the castle proper and the courtyard that adjoined them, they'd agreed that the best approach to drop the bombs to good effect would be to come up the river from the southeast. So, Eddie had circled far around the town of Brzeg and was now flying above the river.

Just above it—there probably wasn't more than twenty feet between the plane's fuselage and the water. From Christin's vantage point in the cockpit, it looked as if they were flying even lower than that. It was both scary and exhilarating.

Luckily or unluckily for him, depending on your disposition,

Jozef couldn't really see the river. The single-person back seat of a Dauntless wasn't simply cramped and narrow, it didn't provide a good view of the countryside below because the windows on either side were small and placed rather high.

Now that he'd become a little accustomed to flying, Jozef envied Christin her much better vantage point in the front seat. He thought he would have enjoyed the sight she was able to look at.

But this was, after all, a combat mission, not a sightseeing tour. So, Jozef put all envy aside and concentrated on the task at hand. Which, in his case, was about as simple as it got: yank up on two levers, in whatever order and at whatever instant Christin gave the command.

"I'm ready!" he called out.

The top speed of a Dauntless wasn't much more than one hundred miles an hour, and they were flying slower than that. That was partly because of the weight of the bomb load. If you assigned Denise Beasley to make bombs for you, it was pretty much a given that the girl would build them right to the upper limit of size and weight. No wallflower, she, when it came to making things go *boom*!

Leaving that aside, Eddie was flying as slowly as he could anyway, without risking a stall. They weren't facing soldiers accustomed to the speed of airplanes, they were coming against men whose traditional gauge of speed had been riding a horse. Whether they flew at eighty miles per hour, or seventy or even sixty—the plane's stall speed was just below that—they'd be moving faster than the trained reflexes of seventeenth-century shooters.

Eddie figured he was doing about seventy miles per hour, in the last mile of his approach. The speed gauge he had was a bit crude, so he didn't want to drop below that lest he risk stalling.

To Christin, as low as they were, it seemed as if they were flying at least twice that fast. She had to force herself to stop looking down at the river racing past them and look up toward the castle they were approaching.

She could see the tower now. It rose perhaps forty feet above the courtyard and was one story taller than the main building of the castle.

"Get ready, Jozef!" she called out. "It won't be long now. It'll be the left lever first, like we planned—and I'll give you a one-two-three countdown."

As best I can, but she left that unspoken. She didn't want to shake Jozef's confidence in her—or her own, for that matter. Christin had very steady nerves, as you'd expect from a woman who'd spent many hours riding motorcycles since she was a teenager. But this was new to her.

"Get ready," Eddie said, almost muttering. "I'm about to— okay, *now*."

He brought the plane up out of the river bed and over the cliff, flying just above the trees lining the Oder. The castle was right ahead of them. They'd reach it in seconds.

Christin could see men milling around in the courtyard—a dozen of them maybe—with more coming out of the castle. Some of them had guns in their hands, some didn't—and from what she could see, the guns themselves were a mismatch. At least half of them looked like big pistols. Those would be wheel-locks, favored by cavalrymen.

Two of the men in the courtyard fired at them with pistols. Given the distance, the speed of their approach and the inherent inaccuracy of smoothbore pistols, they might as well have been throwing stones.

"Almost..." Eddie said.

Christin started the countdown. "Three! Two!"

Eddie veered the plane just a bit, now aiming it toward the Tower of Lions rather than the main castle.

"One! Left—*now!*"

The plane lurched up as the bomb was released. Christin hadn't foreseen that and it threw off her timing just a bit. But she recovered quickly.

"Right—*now!*"

The plane lurched again, and then they were passing right over the tower. Christin was afraid they might even scrape against it, but they actually had fifteen feet to spare. Eddie had a lot of confidence by now in his ability to handle a plane. From his point of view, this had been nowhere nearly as scary as the experience of flying the Dauntless out of Dresden during the siege.

They happened in every war. One term for them was *golden BB*, which first came into common use by American combat pilots during the Vietnam War. But the concept and the haphazard reality behind it went back as far as warfare itself.

The fluke shot, the unpredictable twist, the weird killing.

The two most famous such incidents in American history dated back a century before the Vietnam conflict, both of them taking place during the civil war.

The more ironic of the two happened on May 9, 1864, at the Battle of Spotsylvania Court House. The Union general John Sedgwick was killed by a Confederate sharpshooter right after saying: "They couldn't hit an elephant at this distance."

But the more important incident had happened a year earlier. On the evening of May 2, 1863, returning from a scouting expedition of the Union lines after the first day of the Battle of Chancellorsville, General Stonewall Jackson was mistaken for the enemy by Confederate pickets and shot three times in the confusion that followed. He died of his wounds eight days later. After being told of Jackson's death, General Robert E. Lee commented, "I have lost my right arm."

A golden BB had been responsible for the death of Larry Wild during the Battle of Wismar, when he was struck by a cannonball. Given the speed at which his Outlaw motorboat had been racing and the impromptu haste with which the Danes had fired the cannon, it was just blind bad luck that the ball even came near him.

Not long afterward, in the same battle, Captain Hans Richter died in what became the single most famous incident in the entire war against the League of Ostend. Enraged by the destruction of the Outlaw—he assumed, wrongly, that both his friends aboard the craft had been killed—Richter flew his plane directly at another Danish warship in order to be sure of hitting it with his rockets.

It was a foolish maneuver, however heroic, which resulted in his own death. But you couldn't really call that death a "fluke." His plane was struck by a volley of shots fired at it as he drew near.

And it had happened in this war also, just four months earlier, when Jimmy Andersen had been killed by a stray bullet fired by someone who wasn't even aiming at him.

Now, it happened again.

Heinrich Holk had been relaxing in his chamber on the top floor of the Tower of Lions when the bizarre buzzing sound alerted him that the enemy airplane had returned. Immediately, without taking the time to put on his boots, he leapt up and began racing down the stairs to the courtyard below.

He knew that airplanes could be brought down by ground fire, as rare an event as that might be. He'd been born and raised in Denmark, his father being the commander of the fortress at Kronborg, and spent the first years of his military career fighting against the Austrian imperialists, first under General von Mansfeld and then under General Wolf Heinrich von Baudissin—the same Baudissin who'd just been killed when the Turks overran Vienna. And while Holk had switched sides after the Peace of Luebeck in 1629 and entered Wallenstein's service, he had kept ties with a number of his former countrymen. So, two years earlier, he'd received by mail a detailed account of Hans Richter's death in battle from one of his confidants.

If it could be done by a wretched naval commander, it could certainly be done by him!

"Form up! Form up!" he was shouting, as he reached the ground level and rushed toward the door of the tower leading outside. Seeing him coming, the guard at the door hastily opened it for him.

Holk had just reached the open doorway when the first of the two bombs struck the ground of the courtyard.

Christin George and Jozef Wojtowicz both had excellent reflexes. Still, both of them had been slightly behind the pace at which the action had unfolded. In Christin's case, she misjudged the right time to release the bombs; in Jozef's—who had his eyes closed by them and was just listening for the signal—because even the quickest human takes a split second to translate a shout into jerking a lever.

So, the first bomb missed its intended target. Instead of landing squarely in the middle of the small mob of soldiers clustered in the courtyard, it overshot the mark. The bomb did kill one of them, crushing his skull as it passed by, but it didn't explode until it struck the ground right in front of the now-open door of the tower. Because of the low angle at which the bomb came in, most of the shrapnel was blown straight forward.

It was as if Heinrich Holk was hit by a gigantic shotgun blast. One piece of shrapnel—part of a horseshoe—struck him under the nose and removed the top half of his head. One of his arms and both legs were blown off. Another big piece of shrapnel came into his torso, ricocheted around his rib cage and more-or-less eviscerated him on the way out.

The guard at the door would have been horrified except he didn't have time. The second bomb, the incendiary, passed right through the doorway and exploded inside the vestibule of the tower. In an instant, both the guard and the dismembered corpse of Heinrich Holk were obliterated. For all practical purposes, the bottom floor of the Tower of Lions had been turned into a crematorium.

If Eddie Junker and Christin George and Jozef Wojtowicz had deliberately *planned* the perfect assassination of Heinrich Holk, they couldn't have done a better job. In fact, they had no idea they had killed him—or even hurt him. They didn't really know how much damage the bombs had done, and when Christin suggested they fly back to see, Eddie vetoed the idea.

"We're getting low on fuel," he said. "I don't want to risk it."

In the courtyard outside the Tower of Lions, the little mob of soldiers stared open-mouthed at the raging pyre the structure had become. Some of Denise's homemade napalm had splattered into the stairwell before it ignited, so the flames were already spreading to the second floor. It wouldn't be long—so much was obvious to everyone looking on—before the entire tower was in flames.

"General Holk's up there!" shouted one of the officers, pointing at the top floor.

Another officer cupped his hands around his mouth and shouted: "Get out, General! Get out! Jump onto the roof of the castle! Don't try to come down the stairs!"

As a theoretical proposition, what the officer suggested was feasible. Holk was still a fairly young man, in his late thirties. But years of war—years of carousal and dissipation, even more—made it unlikely that he'd be able to escape safely by that route. Getting out of a window on the top floor would be easy enough, and from there he could reach the roof of the main castle. But that roof was quite steep, there were no handholds except the chimney on the opposite side, and the tiles were not in good repair. One slip and he'd be plunging to his death onto the ground thirty feet below.

But Holk never emerged from the tower.

"Are you sure he's up there?" asked a third officer of the first one.

The man shrugged. "I think so. That's where he usually is in the morning."

Pieces of the tower, some of them still burning, were starting to fall into the courtyard. The men there retreated. By now, everyone in the main castle had emerged and the crowd numbered around sixty.

"Maybe he spent the night with his whore," suggested one of the sergeants. He pointed toward Brzeg. "The one at the tavern."

"Let's go find out." Within a few seconds, most of the soldiers present were heading for the village. Only a handful stayed behind to watch the conflagration.

Which, soon enough, spread to the main building of the castle. Before the day was over, the entire edifice would be a gutted ruin.

Once they reached the village, the soldiers found the tavern's barmaid who doubled as a prostitute for Holk when he was in the mood, and questioned her.

Frightened—she was sure she'd be the one blamed if anything bad had happened to Holk—the woman fudged the truth. The general had indeed spent the night with her, but he'd left early in the morning.

"Where did he go?" demanded an officer. He pointed a finger at the Tower of Lions, now a roaring pyre visible to anyone in Brzeg. "Did he go to the tower?"

To her, that finger was one of incipient accusation. Any moment, those men would charge her with setting the fire.

Granted, that made no sense. But none of those soldiers was especially sensible and the barmaid was not very bright to begin with. Floundering, she came up with an alternate tale.

"He said he was going to Grodków," she blurted. It was the only place she could think of. Holk had mentioned to her once that he kept a small garrison in that town.

Grodków was only twelve miles away. An hour's ride for a man on horseback.

The stables hadn't been attached to the castle, so the horses were safe. The mob charged back and within a short time most of them were mounted up and heading for Grodków. Not more than two dozen stayed behind.

Who went, who stayed, and by what command? In essence, everyone did whatever they chose to do. Holk had never established a clear chain of command in his army. That had been deliberate on his part, as a way of making it difficult for anyone to oust him from his position—which was not unheard of among mercenary companies in the Thirty Years War.

Had he dropped dead right in front of them, whether from a wound or a heart attack, the top officers in Holk's army might have been able to work out an arrangement suitable to all of them over his cooling corpse. But in this atmosphere of uncertainty and chaos, none of them was even thinking in those terms.

A day passed. Many of the soldiers who'd ridden off to Grodków came back to Brzeg, but the uncertainty was not cleared up. No, Holk was not at Grodków—but he *might* have been there. The villagers and the men in the garrison had produced several stories, ranging from *we never saw him* to *yes, he was here but I don't know where he went* to *he went to*—any of three other locations named. Soldiers went riding off to all three.

By now the fire had burned itself out and it had rained for several hours. Soldiers began picking their way through the embers.

They found one skeleton—more precisely, they found parts of one skeleton. Between the heat of the flames and the eventual collapse of the entire edifice, the bones—those which survived at all—had been badly scattered.

Still, it was clear that most of the skeleton was positioned near the doorway. So, that had to be the remains of the guard. There was always a guard stationed at that doorway and the one holding the duty on that day was also missing.

Clearly, therefore, that was him. What was left of him. The rest of the bones they found—pieces of bone; none of them had been intact and many had simply been burned away—were obviously his remains also.

Holk had not been there. He was still alive. But where had he gone?

Word came that an army was nearing Brzeg. A huge army, led by an angel in armor accompanied by hussars flying Polish battle flags.

Clearly, it was time to seek greener pastures. No one even suggested that they engage in a battle. Obviously, King Wladyslaw had tired of their depredations and had sent an expedition to chastise them.

Probably severely. Gibbets and stakes were likely to be popping up everywhere. And if it struck anyone as unlikely that an angel—and where would Wladyslaw find an angel anyway? in *Poland*?—would stoop to hanging and impaling people, they kept their own counsel.

Wars were being fought all over Europe, so it wasn't as if there weren't plenty of employment opportunities. Most of them opted for Russia. There was a civil war brewing there, it was said.

The mystery would never be cleared up. As time passed, Heinrich Holk became one of the legends of Silesia. The troll—the ogre, the bloodthirsty fiend—who came to eat children who didn't obey their parents. A horrible man had become a horrible monster.

Breslau (Wroclaw), Lower Silesia
Poland

"So how'd it go?" Denise asked eagerly, after they disembarked from the plane. "Did my bombs work right?"

"They worked swell, honey," replied her mother. In truth, Christin didn't know one way or another whether the first bomb had exploded. By the time she was able to look back and see the castle they were much too far away to tell. But it was obvious that the incendiary had gone off splendidly. So, in good conscience, she was able to add:

"By now, that castle's just so much charcoal."

"What about Holk?"

Christin shrugged. "Who knows? He might very well not even have been there."

Denise wasn't pleased by that ambiguity. But she wasn't given to moping over contingencies and she was delighted that Eddie and her mother were back and in good health. She'd been a little worried. That was a combat mission they'd been on, after all.

She spent most of the day and the entire evening with Eddie, celebrating. It wasn't until the next morning that she saw her mother again, after she came down to the kitchen in response to the odors of breakfast being cooked.

"Mom!" she cried out, staring at the breakfast-maker.

Christin was sitting on a stool at the table, with a cup of

coffee in her hands—well, coffee wannabe—and wearing a robe. And from the looks of things, nothing else. Except a very satisfied smile on her face.

Denise recognized the robe, since her mother had owned it forever. More to the point, she recognized the *other* robe in the kitchen, since her mother had owned that one forever too and it really didn't fit the person who had it on, which made it blindingly obvious that he wasn't wearing anything at all under it.

"What's *he* doing here?" Denise demanded. She recognized the smile on her mother's face, too, although she hadn't seen it in...

In...

Had it really been that long since her father died? A year?

Closer to a year and half, actually.

"What do you *think* he's doing here?" Christin said acerbically. "I'm not *that* old, young lady. We didn't see any reason we shouldn't celebrate either."

Jozef Wojtowicz turned away from the skillet he was working at, with a smile on his face.

A really wide, self-satisfied sort of smile.

"In Poland, we call breakfast *śniadanie*," he said. "Usually I prefer cold cuts on bread but supplies are tight in Wroclaw so we're making do with sausage. German-style sausage, I'm afraid. But we do have some eggs, too."

"I know we do," she said, almost snarling. "I bought them yesterday while you were gone."

God, that smile was disgusting. He looked like a village idiot who'd hit the jackpot.

Chapter 56

Steyregg, on the north bank of the Danube across from Linz

Since the assault began, Abraham Zarfati had never let his gaze move away from the huge enemy airship for more than a minute. At first, the airship had remained hovering in the same position over Linz, about a mile from the river, and not facing him directly. The vessel had been turned almost broadside to the Ottoman flotilla. He'd hoped that they might simply be assigned to protect the city that was now the new Austrian capital.

But now he could see that the airship was coming around and heading toward them. And he was not a bit surprised to see that the enemy vessel was faster than their own as well as much bigger.

"That thing is *enormous*," hissed Isaac Capsali, who'd come to stand alongside him. "Do you think it's going to ram us?"

"I have no idea what they plan to do," replied Abraham. That was nothing more than the simple, if very uncomfortable, truth. None of the officers and soldiers in the sultan's Gureba-i hava had yet been in an aerial battle between airships. There had been a great deal of speculation and theorizing on the subject, some of it quite wild. But in war, more than in any other human pursuit, practical experience was essential.

And of that, there was none. None at all. Abraham had been told privately by the Muslim commander of the airship fleet that even the American texts—which were officially still labeled "manuals of witchcraft" but were being assiduously studied by scholars assigned to do so by the sultan—carried no record of such an encounter.

Abraham's own supposition was that rockets would probably be the devices used, eventually. He knew that engineers of the Gureba-i hava had already designed and tested several ways of attaching and firing rockets from the airships' gondolas. The key problem to be overcome was the risk of having the initial rocket exhaust set fire to the airship that deployed the weapon. The solution the engineers seemed to be leaning toward was to drop the rocket seven or eight kulaçs before igniting the propellant with a timed fuse. Guidelines would be used to keep the missile level as it fell—basically, four strings feeding through small holes drilled in flanges welded to the fuselages.

Abraham didn't think the rockets would work very well, even if the design proved to be functional. There was no way to guide the missiles once they were fired, beyond the crude mechanism of spinning them. In practice, that meant that rockets were only effective as area saturation weapons—which was exactly the way the katyusha forces used them. But to do that effectively required firing barrages of rockets. Not even the most enthusiastic proponent of using rockets as airship weapons thought the missiles could be fired in volleys.

"It's not coming at us," Isaac said, pointing with his finger.

Abraham saw that he was right. As it drew nearer, the enemy airship was also angling its course to take it between the first and second line of the Ottoman airships—and closer, he thought, to the second line than to his own.

He looked toward the Ottoman airship flying just to his left, to see if there were any messages. But there were none. Not yet—he was sure there would soon be a flurry of them.

The Gureba-i hava had gotten the first radios produced by the sultan's artisans, but they were big and heavy things. Only the commander of the flotilla, Şemsi Ahmed, had been provided with one to take aloft on his airship—and he'd had to leave some of his bombs behind in order to retain the vessel's lifting ability.

Şemsi Ahmed would maintain contact with the sultan with that radio. Whatever orders he or the sultan wished to send to the other vessels in the flotilla had to be transmitted using a semaphore system. The decision had been made to position the commanding airship of each line on the far left of that line, beginning with Şemsi Ahmed's own vessel, the *Pelekanon,* in the fourth and last line. Moving forward, the commander of the third line was Mevlana Kadri, aboard the *Savra.* Moving forward again, the airship on the far left of the second line was the *Chaldiran,* commanded by the only Jew of that rank, Moshe Mizrahi. Moshe would be the commander of the first ships which did actual damage to the enemy by dropping incendiary bombs. All five ships in the first line were only going to be laying down smoke, at least in the initial stage of the assault.

It was a high honor for Mizrahi and Abraham was pleased by it. Truth be told, Abraham didn't much care for Moshe Mizrahi personally, but any honor received by a Jew in the sultan's service was of benefit to all other Jews.

The commander of the front line was Mustafa bin Ramazan, aboard the *Turnadağ.* Abraham's own vessel, the *Preveza,* was the next one over in the line.

Within a short time, the monstrous enemy ship was passing directly behind the *Turnadağ* and the *Preveza,* not more than a quarter of a mile away. Abraham could now see that crew facilities had been built right into the hull of the vessel, not simply placed in the gondola the way the Ottoman ships were designed.

But he didn't spend much time examining the enemy, because the *Turnadağ* was beginning to send semaphore signals. It was time to start deploying the smoke.

Two minutes after the smoke began to billow out from the baskets hanging below the airships in the first line, Abraham heard a sharp cracking sound coming from behind. Followed closely by another, and another, and yet another. He moved to the rear of the gondola to see what was happening. And, soon, came to realize what the enemy's tactics were going to be, in an aerial battle between airships.

Julie had decided to start shooting from the vantage point of the gondola. She wouldn't be able to do that with the Beckworth .50, which Dell had placed in a compartment of the main deck above. The rifle was simply too big, too heavy and too clumsy to deploy effectively in the confines of the gondola.

But as long as she was using her regular rifle, which was a Remington Model 700, the gondola had advantages. The main advantage was that it had a much wider field of fire than she could get shooting from the main deck—360 degrees, in fact, although the slope of the envelope right behind the gondola gave only a very narrow band through which she could fire.

In practice, however, her restrictions would be greater than that. Leaving aside the fairly crowded conditions of the gondola, which she'd have to share with the three members of the flight crew, Tom Simpson, and Dell Beckworth, there was a structural problem. Unfortunately, when they'd designed the *Magdeburg*, Maarten Kortenaer and his fellow Dutch engineers hadn't foreseen the tactic of firing rifles from the gondola or the main deck compartments. So, while they'd made provision to allow some of the windows to be partially opened to let in fresh air, they had not designed the windows to be removed altogether.

That modification had to be hurriedly done while the *Magdeburg* had been en route from Hoorn to pick up Julie at Freising. And they'd only had time to allow for removing about a third of the windows. Still, she'd be able to cover most of her potential targets so long as the *Magdeburg* was within range and at roughly the right altitude.

Once they reached Freising, there was another impromptu change of plans. After they showed Julie the steel sheets they'd brought with them to build what amounted to a well-protected "shooter's house," she vetoed the idea.

"Do we have any reason to think the Ottomans will have sharpshooters of their own?" she asked. To hell with false modesty: "In my league, I'm talking about?"

Well . . . no.

"Then screw it. Trying to shoot from inside a cramped box will be a royal pain in the butt. If it turns out we need it, we can install it later. Eventually, we'll probably have to. But not in this first engagement."

Within range, for Julie using her regular rifle, could mean anything up to one thousand yards. If she were firing from a position on solid ground, at least. She didn't know yet how much the movement of the airship would affect her aim. Less than if she'd been on a boat at sea, certainly; but there was bound to be some unpredictable movement due to turbulence.

In the end, she decided that her outer range with the Winchester would be seven hundred yards; with the Beckworth .50, five hundred yards—although she wouldn't be surprised at all if that wound up being much closer to three hundred yards. Beckworth insisted that he had the huge gun sighted in, but since Julie hadn't been able to do that herself, she was a tad skeptical of the claim. For that matter, she'd only been able to fire a few test rounds from the monster—and she'd done that after they were in the air, firing at passing geese. (Which she hadn't really been trying to hit, anyway. Julie didn't much like geese—who did?—but she had no particular animus against the birds.)

"You're in range, Julie," Beckworth announced.

They'd already settled on taking out the pilots first. Presumably, the Ottomans would have backup pilots on every airship, but those were not likely to be equivalent to the copilot of a commercial aircraft, back up-time. Such copilots were pilots in every respect, who normally spent as much time guiding the aircraft as the pilot did.

There was really no purpose to that on an airship designed for military operations, though. Such vessels were not flying constantly, almost round the clock except for occasional maintenance, with interchangeable crews. Typically, they'd only be flying for a few hours on a specific mission, and their crews would be fixed and invariable, other than to replace members who'd gotten sick or been injured. So why not use the same man all the time to be the established pilot? All you needed was for one, or perhaps two, other members of the crew to get enough training to be able to get the airship safely back if the pilot suffered a mishap.

An overly optimistic attitude, perhaps. But it was an inevitable byproduct of the fact that no one in the world except Mike Stearns and Tom Simpson had seriously contemplated how one airship might be able to take out another in aerial combat—and they'd only thought of it because they knew Julie's capabilities with a rifle.

Three seconds later, Julie fired at the nearest Ottoman airship. That was the one on the far left of the second line of enemy vessels. They'd decided to start by targeting that line of ships because, assuming the Turks were following the same tactics they'd used at Vienna, the first line would only be laying down smoke—as, indeed, they had just begun doing.

"Got 'im," grunted Dell.

Julie had time for one more shot before she'd have to start aiming at the second vessel in the line. But, before she could bring anyone into her scope, all the other members of that crew had ducked out of sight below the gunwale of the gondola.

"What the hell," said Dell. "Try a shot through the hull. You might hit one of them—or something worth hitting, anyway."

Julie thought that made sense. Aiming at a spot where one of the Ottomans had ducked out of sight, she fired a shot about a foot below the gunwale.

By then, the *Magdeburg* was nearing the next airship in the second line of vessels. Julie brought the pilot of that craft into her sights and fired.

"He's down," announced Dell. "Go for the guy with the fancy uniform."

He was presumably an officer—and not as quick-thinking as the crew of the first ship. He was just standing there, his mouth open, staring at the oncoming *Magdeburg*.

She fired again.

"He's down, too," said Dell. He shifted the spotting scope to bring the next airship into view. As they "crossed the T," each ship was getting closer and closer. The third vessel they were nearing was no more than five hundred yards away. And, fortunately, the *Magdeburg* was still riding smoothly. The air was very calm today. Of course, that was part of the reason Sultan Murad had chosen to launch his attack.

Moshe Mizrahi realized instantly what had happened to his pilot, and called out: "Everybody get down! Take cover! They have a marksman on that ship!"

He did so himself, even while still shouting. So, he was in position to see the next bullet pass right through the wall of the gondola—so much for thinking kalkan shields would provide adequate protection—and, as neatly as a tailor cutting off an extra bit of cloth, snipping off the very top of one of the incendiary bombs.

There was a little jiggle—just his airship responding to slight turbulence. But it was enough to send a few drops of the infernal substance inside that bomb flying out of the now-open top and splashing on the deck of the gondola.

He stared up at the bomb, momentarily paralyzed. If it shattered and spilled all of its contents...

The incendiary bombs were essentially just ceramic amphora with a simple fuse inserted into the top spout. The enemy bullet had cut off that top and sent it flying somewhere. Completely out of the gondola, Moshe thought. Glancing around, he couldn't see it or the fuse anywhere.

There was no time to waste. He came to his feet, seized the bomb by its handles, and hurled it over the side. With no fuse, it wouldn't ignite when it hit the ground unless there was a fire nearby. But at least it was no longer a threat to his own vessel.

He heard that distinct *crack* again. Then, a few seconds later, still another.

The airship's engineer, Mordechai Pesach, was at his side by then. Like Moshe himself, staring at the closest Ottoman airship. That was the *Ihtiman*. None of its crew were in sight and the vessel was clearly drifting out of line.

One—probably two—of that crew had been shot. The rest were apparently hiding somewhere in the gondola.

Moshe was in command of this line of five vessels. But how was he to transmit his commands to men who weren't even looking at his semaphore?

"What do we do?" asked Mordechai.

He heard the *cracking* sound again. More distantly. By now, he realized that was the sound of the enemy marksman's rifle and he was beginning to suspect they'd just encountered the legendary American female. The half-mythical monster they called the *Jooli*.

The huge enemy ship was now passing in front of the third vessel in his line, the *Mostaganem*.

Again, the crack. The *Mostaganem*'s gondola erupted in a ball of fire. A moment later, another and much greater ball of fire exploded. Within seconds, the envelope itself was starting to burn.

The lines holding the gondola to the envelope were severed by the intense heat and the gondola—what was left of it—plummeted to the ground many kulaçs below. The fiery envelope drifted away, now completely unguided, and began following the gondola downward, although much more slowly.

"Holy shit," hissed Dell.

Julie stared at the furnace the third Ottoman airship had become, just a few hundred yards away.

"What happened?" she asked.

Dell shook his head. "I'm guessing, but I think that second shot you fired into the gondola after they all ducked down must have hit one of their incendiaries—and then it set off a bunch of others. And if I'm right..."

"To hell with shooting at crew members," Julie concluded. She got a very grim expression on her face. "Okay, change of tactics. Let's see what happens."

The *Magdeburg* continued onward. In less than a minute, they'd be crossing the T on the fourth vessel—and now the range would be down to three hundred yards. If the Turks had any sharpshooters of their own on their airships—she hadn't seen any yet, but who knew?—things were going to get a lot hairier.

"What do we do?" repeated Mordechai.

Moshe glanced at the *Ihtiman*. By now, it had drifted still farther out of line and would have been at risk of running into the *Mostaganem* except what was left of that ship was no longer there. The burning gondola had already struck the ground and the envelope was nothing more than a fireball that would impact the ground itself within a minute.

Thankfully, one of the surviving members of the *Ihtiman*'s crew had gotten back up and was looking at him.

Moshe glanced to the rear of his gondola. The last member of his crew was on his feet also. That was the new bombardier who'd replaced the one killed at Vienna. He'd been cross-trained as a semaphore operator.

"Tell the *Ihtiman* to follow us!" he said, then moved quickly to the controls in the bow of the gondola. He'd also been cross-trained, and would now have to serve as the ship's pilot.

Moshe didn't think there was much hope that any of the other ships in his line would survive the Jooli. But at least his ship and the *Ihtiman* could complete their mission.

Yes, he'd have to answer to the sultan when this was all over. But Murad would forgive a commander whose force had suffered terrible casualties because of enemy action, so long as he kept to his duty. He might even reward him, in fact. He'd have no mercy for a commander who flinched.

Once he was sure he had the *Chaldiran* back under control, Moshe looked to his right and to his rear, to see what was happening to the last two ships in his line.

He did so just in time to see the gondola of the fourth ship, the *Cerbe,* turned into another fireball.

North bank of the Danube
About a mile west of the village of Langenstein

Sultan Murad straightened up and walked away from the telescope. Once he reached the railing of the platform atop his observation tower, he leaned over and shouted down to the three radio operators in the shed they'd erected to shelter their equipment. One of them, as always, was standing in the open in case the sultan had orders for them.

"Send a message to the *Pelekanon,*" he commanded. "Şemsi Ahmed is to cancel the airship assault and bring back his vessels."

The operator hurried into the shed. Not long afterward, he reemerged.

"The binbaşı asks if that is to include the smoke ships," he said.

Murad had been pondering that very issue.

"Yes," he replied. With no possibility of softening the enemy's lines with the airship firebombs, he could see no point in ordering the janissaries forward. They would just get butchered.

What might still be possible would be a charge of his sipahis, following a katyusha barrage. The casualties would be heavy, but the cavalry might be able to cross the open ground fast enough to get in among the defenders.

But limiting visibility would just be a hindrance for that. Horses were skittish beasts. It would be almost impossible to drive them into smoke clouds at any pace faster than a walk. And for such a charge to succeed, they'd need to close at a gallop.

Steyregg, on the north bank of the Danube across from Linz

"They're going back, Tom," announced Dell. "Should we pursue them?"

Tom Simpson looked at Julie. "It's your call, I figure."

She thought about it, but not for long. The fifth and final ship in that second line had veered aside as soon as she'd blown up the fourth ship's gondola. She'd taken a couple of shots at it, but didn't know if she'd hit anything important or any member of the crew. She obviously hadn't gotten any of the incendiaries on board.

By then, her angle of fire had been awkward, because—whether from shrewd calculation or just happenstance—the enemy vessel had climbed as well as veered. After her second shot, which she'd hurried, it had risen out of sight above the *Magdeburg's* envelope.

She was getting a better sense for the tactics involved in these airship-to-airship fights. They'd caught the Ottomans by surprise today, but it wouldn't last. The next time they met, the Turks would be doing their own maneuvering—and they'd have their own sharpshooters aboard.

Of course, they wouldn't be in *her* league. Still, it would be a real fight, next time.

"No, I don't think so. But what's happening to that first line of their airships? The ones laying down the smoke?"

Tom hadn't been paying much attention to them, since they hadn't been the targets. He moved to the bow of the gondola and peered out. "Where are...?"

The Dutch pilot understood the question. He pointed toward the Pöstlinberg. "All five of the smoke ships broke off. They're flying back now, over the hills to the north."

Looking that way, Tom spotted them. "Can we intercept?"

"Maybe the closest one," said the pilot.

"It's worth a try. Let's go for it."

"They probably won't have any incendiaries aboard," Julie mused. "And the crews are bound to have figured out by now that they need to stay out of my sight below the gunwales."

"Time to use the .50, then!" Dell exclaimed, enthusiastically. "They can't drag those big boilers out of sight. I'm telling you, Julie—dollars for donuts—the .50 will punch right through that steel."

"Oh, joy," said Julie, rubbing her shoulder in anticipation.

Dell proved to be right. The first two shots Julie fired just ricocheted off the boiler of the ship they targeted. Through his spotting scope, Dell could see that the bullets had put big dents in it, though. So his enthusiasm didn't flag.

And, sure enough, the third shot struck the curved surface of the steel at just the right angle and penetrated.

There wasn't the spectacular explosion Tom had foreseen. Judging by the feebleness of the Ottoman propellers, he'd already figured out that their steam engines didn't operate at the same pressure and temperature as those designed by the USE or the Dutch.

Still, there was an impressive cloud of steam produced, and they could hear at least one man screaming even at that distance. So they'd done some immediate damage, and regardless of anything else that airship was probably doomed. With no engines, they'd just drift. They'd have to exhaust hydrogen from the envelope and try for as soft a landing as they could manage, without being able to steer the ship.

Good luck with that, in these hills.

"Okay," said Tom. "Let's head back. A good day's work, folks."

North bank of the Danube
About a mile west of the village of Langenstein

Murad had summoned his best combat engineers and weapons designers to join him atop the observation platform.

"We need our own Joolis," he pronounced. "Make them."

Chapter 57

Vienna, former capital of Austria-Hungary, now occupied by the Ottoman Empire

Uzun Hussein was in a good mood, which was quite unexpected. When he'd awakened in the hospital weeks earlier, and recovered enough from his wounds to think about anything beyond the pain, he'd been plunged into anger and resentment. He couldn't remember what had happened to him in the final assault on the bastion, but whatever ball had removed his right eye and cut a deep gouge into his skull—it had been pure luck that he hadn't had his brains spilled out altogether—had left him unconscious for days.

Which meant he'd missed out on all the loot his comrades would have plundered. In Vienna! Capturing this city had been a dream for Ottoman soldiers for more than a century—and now that they'd finally done it, he'd gotten nothing beyond his janissary's pay.

So he'd remained for the rest of his stay in the hospital. Sullen and unwilling to talk to anyone.

Finally, the day before, an officer had come to give him his new orders—and he'd been plunged into still deeper anger and resentment.

His days as a combat soldier, it seemed, were over. He'd be allowed to remain in the janissary corps, but henceforth he would be assigned to police duties. Which paid less than he'd been getting, and had almost no chance for loot at all.

Hussein had had no choice in the matter, so he'd kept silent. If he'd given vent to his fury he'd simply have been punished—and there was no life for him outside the janissaries; certainly not now, when he was one-eyed.

He'd been ordered to begin his new duty the following day.

Still more humiliations had followed this morning. After he put on his janissary uniform—a new one had been provided for him, since the one he'd been wearing during the assault on Vienna had been ruined—he presented himself to his new commanding officer. This was a young *mülâzım* named Hasan bin Evhad, who had no doubt been placed in the military police because he was not capable of any greater assignment.

To his surprise—not to mention outrage—Hussein had been provided with neither a musket nor a yataghan, which were the proper weapons for a janissary. Instead, the mülâzım had handed him nothing but a dagger and a club.

Seeing the expression on Hussein's face, the mülâzım shook his head. "Don't snarl at me. The sultan ordered that no soldier maintaining order in Beç"—that was the usual Turkish name for Vienna—"is to carry any other weapons."

"What if there's trouble?" Hussein demanded.

Hasan bin Evhad sneered. "Trouble with who? The only Austrian soldiers left are in shackles. There aren't more than a few thousand civilians still in the city and they certainly won't be a problem."

"You can't say that. Our own men will be fighting over the women, if nothing else."

The mülâzım's lip curled still further. "What women? There were only a few dozen when we took the city. All of them were whores for the Austrian soldiers and now they're whores for us. If you want a woman, go to the brothels and pay one. Nobody fights over them. Why bother? The price is cheap—even cheap enough for men with no loot."

"No loot?"

Seeing the confusion in Hussein's face, the mülâzım's look of derision was replaced by a friendly grin.

"You didn't know? The sultan forbade all looting when we took the city. He had the order enforced, too—men were impaled, not just hung, if they were caught breaking the order."

Hussein stared at him. That was a gross violation of Ottoman custom. The sultan's soldiers—certainly the janissaries!—were traditionally given three days after taking a city in which they could plunder whatever they could get their hands on, as long as it was movable. That included the city's women. The officers would usually even overlook violations of the Muslim prohibition against alcoholic drink.

But... Murad IV could have managed it, Hussein realized. Already he'd heard other wounded soldiers calling him "Murad the Magnificent." And why not? Their young sultan had succeeded where even Suleiman had failed.

"Why?" he asked.

Hasan bin Evhad shrugged. "Our sultan thinks in big terms. He said he wanted the Austrians as willing subjects, because there was no other way to build the empire he plans to build."

Hussein understood the reasoning, well enough. It was not even especially exotic. Ottoman tradition toward most of their subjects, in the Balkans as much as in Anatolia and Mesopotamia, was to rule with a light hand so long as the conquered peoples refrained from rebellion.

But that came after the conquest, not right in the middle of it!

Hasan bin Evhad shook his head again. "Best you get used to it, Hussein. Now take your club and dagger and go out there and maintain order."

It took Hussein perhaps an hour to get over his surprise and subdued indignation. But once he did...

Ha! He hadn't missed out on the loot, after all!

Served all those other bastards right. The ones who hadn't been badly wounded in the sultan's service.

He adjusted his eyepatch to a jaunty angle and strode down the thoroughfares like a conqueror.

Steyregg, on the north bank of the Danube across from Linz

At that same moment, the katyusha gunner Stefan Branković was experiencing ambivalence of his own. That was produced by the unexpected destruction of several airships and the withdrawal from the field of the vessels laying down smoke. On the one hand, he was pleased that they wouldn't have to fumble their way forward half-blinded by smoke. On the other, the enemy forces who'd be shooting at them as they advanced wouldn't be blinded either.

He tried to resolve his uncertainty by reminding himself that it really didn't matter what he thought. What mattered was what Murad thought because, whether Stefan or anyone liked it or not, they would be obeying him. The sultan was a fair ruler, but "fairness" simply spoke to the man's even-handedness, not to how heavily the hand came down.

The clash of cymbals announced the advance. "May God watch over me..." he murmured, setting his team of horses into a trot. He would have preferred to canter or even gallop, but they still had far to go.

For the purposes of this battle today, the Third Division's artillery batteries had been reorganized under a single command instead of being left to the various regiments they were attached to. Jeff Higgins had some doubts about the wisdom of that decision, but it did have one definite advantage—*he* wouldn't have to be the guy trying to figure out how soon to order the big guns to fire. All he had to think about was how soon to tell his infantrymen to start firing their rifles.

Not any time soon, he figured. Unless the Turks coming forward with their rocket wagons were deaf, dumb and blind or really stupid—or had a commander who was—they'd stop their advance while they were still well out of range of the SRGs. It'd be rockets against twelve-pounders, for a while, with the infantry just there as observers.

Hopefully, observers. Some of them would probably get turned into corpses, though.

In his own command bunker, positioned a hundred yards behind Jeff's and closer to the river, Mike Stearns was studying the same oncoming rocket wagons. He was using binoculars, though, because of the greater distance.

So far, the battle was going well, he thought. The critical thing was that the *Magdeburg* had succeeded in breaking the assault of the Ottoman airships. Only two of the airships had broken through and dropped their bombs, and neither had been able to do a lot of damage.

The bombs dropped by one of the airships had missed the

trenches and bunkers completely, because they'd been dropped too soon. The leading airship had done better, with most of its incendiaries either hitting the Third Division's fieldworks or at least coming close. The fieldworks had been thrown up hastily in the short time the Third Division had had at its disposal after it arrived in Linz. They been primarily designed to handle fire-bombs, at least up to a point. The dirt-covered log roofs over the bunkers hadn't been penetrated by the incendiaries, and while a really large number of bombs being dropped would undoubtedly spill flames into the works, the few bombs that one airship was able to drop just weren't enough.

One bunker had been seriously threatened, but the men in it had been able to escape using the trenches that connected all the bunkers. They'd only lost two men killed and four injured.

It remained to be seen, of course, how well those same bunker roofs would stand up to rocket fire.

Vienna, former capital of Austria-Hungary, now occupied by the Ottoman Empire

Hussein heard the altercation before he turned the corner—long before he turned it. He first heard the woman's screeching while he was still a block away.

He didn't hurry his steps, though. First, because the only women who'd be in Beç these days would be Christians, and he didn't care very much what happened to infidels. Secondly, because the screeching had a tone of fury rather than fear. Whatever was happening around the corner didn't sound like it was an immediate crisis.

When he did round the corner, he came to an abrupt halt. That was not due to the sight in front of him so much as it was the stench. Unfortunately, the wind was blowing toward him and that hideous crone *stank*.

Stank of shit, to be precise, which wasn't surprising given the cart she'd been hauling behind her. A night soil worker, who'd been going about her filthy trade when the two Ottoman soldiers accosted her.

But why had they accosted her in the first place? She'd have nothing to steal so their only interest in her would be carnal.

But who in their right mind would want to have anything to do with this creature?

Neither the woman nor the two soldiers had noticed him yet. So Hussein had a bit of time to study the scene more closely.

Several things became apparent. First, both soldiers were drunk and at least one of them was a Christian—he had a crucifix hanging from his neck. They were probably both Christians, then. Add inebriation to their inherent dull-wittedness and you had at least part of the explanation for their interest in the woman. Zimmis—Christians, especially—would fuck sheep, goats, dogs, almost anything.

The rest of the explanation came from the woman. When Hussein had first seen her, he'd taken her to be a crone because of the missing eye and teeth, and the straggly hair. But now he could see that she was not very old. It was hard to tell, because of the shapeless and filthy garments she was wearing, but he thought she might even have a full figure.

Not that he'd be interested in her, even if she did. She was still a disgusting wretch.

The woman screeched again; something in German, he thought. He wasn't sure, because he didn't speak the language at all. One of the Christian soldiers made a jibe in response, and that was in Serbian which he did understand somewhat.

That same soldier made a lunging gesture toward the woman, as if to grab her. It was half in jest—but only half.

For her part, the woman leaned away, but she didn't run. From the way she had her right hand tucked into her garments, Hussein suspected she had a weapon in there. Some sort of cheap dagger, undoubtedly.

It was illegal for civilians in Beç to own or carry weapons, of course. That had been the very first ruling made by the sultan. But Hussein hadn't actually seen anything and he was not inclined to search her to find out.

Nor was there any need to. This was a minor incident, more of a nuisance than anything else.

He strode forward, immediately drawing the attention of the trio. "Go," he commanded the two soldiers.

They stared at him. One, with a slack jaw; the other—the one who'd tried to grab the woman—with what seemed to be a smirk.

He said something, which he clearly found very amusing.

Hussein didn't understand several of the words, but he thought what the Christian bastard had said was: *look, another one-eye; maybe they're mates.*

He wasn't in *that* good a mood. His club swept up, around and across and the would-be wit found himself on the ground with a bloody nose. It might be broken.

Not that Hussein cared. "Go!" he repeated. The still-standing soldier helped his mate to his feet and the two of them stumbled off.

He turned to the woman. Since he didn't know what the German terms for "go" or "leave" might be, he just waved his hand peremptorily. The meaning of the silent gesture would be clear enough.

Quickly—yes, she was young; no crone would move like that—the woman picked up the handles of the night soil cart and moved away. He made sure to stay well clear of her and was relieved when she was no longer upwind.

He watched her for a block until she rounded a corner. She was headed in the general direction of the palace, which he thought a bit odd.

But a bit odd wasn't odd enough for him to want to get near her again. Perhaps her circuit including buildings in that direction.

No concern of his, any longer. He resumed his patrol.

Steyregg, on the north bank of the Danube across from Linz

The cymbals clashed again. Stefan made to touch the slowmatch to the fuse.

But the commanders had waited too long after the katyushas had gotten into position. The line of enemy berms in the distance suddenly erupted in noise, flame and smoke.

Stefan did fire his eight rockets, though, before the twelve-pound ball cut him in half.

For the most part, the bunkers held up well. The katyusha rockets were much better suited for antipersonnel use than against fortifications, even fieldworks. Only one roof collapsed under the barrage. But it took long enough to come down that, again, most of the men were able to escape through the trenches.

The Third Division's guns did a great deal more harm to the enemy's wagons. Gustav Adolf's armies had always been good with artillery, and the Third Division was no exception.

Had he seen, the USE's emperor would have been pleased. But Gustav Adolf had suffered a seizure just before the gunnery duel began—his first since arriving in Vienna.

He wouldn't have been able to see much, though, even with his binoculars. Since no one had wanted him to take the risk of being north of the Danube when the battle started, he'd remained in position in his own bunker close to the naval rifles on the spit of land formed by the river confluence.

Janos Drugeth was with him when the emperor suffered the seizure. It would have been quite unnerving except for the presence of the American Moorish doctor. Nichols went about the business of tending to the emperor calmly, efficiently—almost matter-of-factly.

Reassured by the doctor's obvious confidence in the outcome, Janos left the bunker and took a position close to the naval rifles' berm—almost atop it, actually—which gave him the best view of the battlefield across the Danube.

The allies had gotten the best of the first two encounters, but Janos didn't think the battle was over. Murad was nothing if not aggressive. Janos was sure that he'd try a mass cavalry charge next. The sipahis would suffer heavy casualties, yes—but there were so *many* of them.

In the distance, he heard the booms of kettledrums—called *kös* by the Ottomans, followed by the clarion call of a *boru*. The sound produced by the Turkish version of a trumpet carried clearly across the river.

Within seconds, all other sounds were drowned beneath the thunder of hooves. Thousands of horses—no, tens of thousands of horses—were coming onto the battlefield. The greatest cavalry charge in living memory was about to begin.

In living memory? Possibly in the memory of any man since Emperor Darius sent his Immortals and Scythians against Alexander the Great at Gaugamela.

Chapter 58

Steyregg, on the north bank of the Danube across from Linz

As the equivalent of a regimental commander, Lieutenant Colonel Thorsten Engler had attended all of General Stearns' staff briefings, including the one where the Hungarian Janos Drugeth had presented the top officers of the Third Division with his best estimates concerning the forces they'd face when Sultan Murad's army reached Linz.

Janissaries: These were the Ottoman Empire's elite infantry, and they would number between twenty and twenty-five thousand strong. Interestingly, Drugeth had learned that Murad hadn't brought all the janissary units that usually went on campaign, bringing some of the *sekban bölüks* that usually stayed in Constantinople as a sort of home guard instead. Murad seemed to have been selective of the units; some had been heavily involved in the disturbances of 1632 and, before that, in the death of Sultan Osman. Those left behind had, for the most part, been less involved.

Sipahis: The traditional Turkish cavalry. At least thirty thousand, possibly forty thousand. About two-thirds of them were the provincial sipahis, essentially feudal levies, whose quality would range from excellent to abysmal. But he had also brought the bulk of the *alti bölük*, the six standing cavalry units. Their quality was uniformly excellent. And again, interestingly, the sipahis of the alti bölük had been involved in the disturbances of 1632, if anything to a greater extent than the janissaries.

Topçu Ocağı. The artillery corps, in which was included the new katyusha rocket wagon units. They would number perhaps ten thousand, which was a huge increase from the days of traditional artillery. Many of the new units were manned by zimmis—non-Muslims—mostly Orthodox Christians from the Balkans. Drugeth had expressed the hope that there would be some friction between the traditional artillery and the new units that would hurt their efficiency.

Akıncı. "In times past," Drugeth had told them, "the units that were called akinci were irregular units, mostly light cavalry. They were raised from the border areas of the empire, where they usually had experience as raiders. They were not given regular pay and they served entirely for plunder.

"What's interesting is that the akinci were disbanded by Grand Vezir Koca Sinan Paşa and absorbed into the *timariot* cavalry over forty years ago. Murad revived the name, which means 'raiders' and which has a sort of romance associated with it, just two years ago for a new corps in the regular army. They're made up entirely of Muslims and are now mostly infantry."

He'd gone on to explain that Murad had been careful to give the impression that they were intended as nothing more than temporary units, even following the tradition of assigning selected janissaries to command some of the bölüks—call them companies—that made up the new force. After all, one of the reasons that Osman was dethroned and executed was that the janissaries feared he was going to supplant them. But many of the companies were commanded by officers not taken from the janissaries but from groups like the bostanjis who were loyal in 1632. And they had been expanded quietly until they numbered perhaps twenty thousand, almost as many as the janissaries.

"The janissaries are jealous of them and insist that they retain their status as the empire's elite infantry—a proposition that Murad seems to accept, judging by his readiness to allow them the honor of serving as his shock troops. Which means, of course, that they're suffering heavy casualties. I think he may be planning to wear them down and eventually supplant them, at least to an extent, with the new akinci."

Cebeci. "This is also very interesting," Drugeth had said. "Traditionally, the cebeci were what you might call technicians more than combat soldiers, being responsible for maintaining and keeping the empire's weapons and transporting them to wherever they were needed. Murad has expanded them drastically and placed them in charge of developing new weapons as well as maintaining the existing ones."

He'd chuckled then, quite humorlessly. "The way Murad seems to view the matter, 'developing' new weapons means training with them—and fighting with them as well. By now, according to my correspondents, the cebeci are eight or nine thousand strong and growing every day. The armored flame-throwing wagons which appeared before Vienna, for instance, were manned by cebeci. They include many zimmis in their ranks although the top officers are all Muslims."

He'd finished with a summary, and a supposition. "All told, Sultan Murad brought somewhere between ninety and one hundred and ten thousand men on this campaign. I am not including in that number any of his naval units or the new air force the Turks have. He will leave no more than ten thousand of those men as a garrison in Vienna, mostly cebeci and akinci with perhaps a thousand janissaries to keep order over them. So, here at Linz, we will be facing approximately eighty thousand men—perhaps as many as ninety-thousand—at least a third of which will be sipahi cavalry."

Then, rather grimly: "I think we can expect Murad to bleed his sipahis badly. If I'm right, he's using this war to rebuild his army; from the inside out, you might say. He'll break the janissaries and sipahis—not destroy them, certainly, but bend them to his will and eliminate their fractiousness—while he raises up new corps and units who have no traditional privileges or ties to the Turkish aristocracy and answer to him alone."

Drugeth had then looked at Thorsten, and Pappenheim. "It will get brutal, I'm thinking. For you volley gunners and the Black Cuirassiers, especially."

By now, with the battle experience he had, Thorsten Engler thought he could gauge the right time to sally his volley guns just by the sound of the oncoming cavalry.

On most fields. Not on this one. Thorsten had faced thousands of cavalry before, but not *tens* of thousands. The sound made by that many big animals running at once seemed more like a vibration than a sound. He found it quite confusing—not to mention disturbing, because the most critical task he had right now as the commander of the volley gun squadron was to gauge the right time to order a sally.

Frustrated, he ran out of the bunker and hurried onto the roof, in order to get a better look at the oncoming enemy.

What he saw startled him. The sound had seemed not loud enough to him, from his position in the bunker, since he'd been extrapolating from his experience at Ahrensbök and other battle-fields. What he realized now was that the Ottoman sultan—or whoever had given the command for this mass charge of sipahis— had made a mistake. Possibly a very bad one.

There simply wasn't enough *room* for thirty to forty thousand cavalrymen on this field. The space available for the Turkish horses wasn't more than half a mile—if that—measuring from the line of trees covering the first hills on the north to the marshy terrain that extended out from the left bank of the Danube. Murad had set up his command center with its observation post too far to the rear. At that distance, even with a telescope, he hadn't gauged the terrain properly. He was probably assuming his sipahis could advance across a front that was at least a mile and a half wide, when what they really had was less than a third of that room.

To make things worse for the sipahis, the terrain was only flat in places. It wasn't hilly, no—from Murad's distance, it had probably seemed quite level—but it was cut here and there by rises, dips and streams. From his position atop the bunker, Thor-sten could see a dirt road whose embankment would provide his volley guns with superb cover—and his squadron could reach it before the enemy could.

"Forward!" he shouted. "All batteries forward!" Most of his men wouldn't have heard him, or not clearly if they did, but Thorsten could rely on his officers to pass the command along.

He rushed back into the bunker, which he'd shared with Jeff Higgins. The commander of the Hangman regiment was waiting for him.

"What's up?" Jeff asked.

By now, accustomed to up-timers and their sometimes peculiar idioms, Thorsten knew better than to glance at the roof to see what Higgins might be referring to. "Murad—whoever—screwed up, Jeff. They're already getting bottlenecked. If your regiment backs us up, we don't have to do a mere sortie. We can position the volley guns in a good defensive position and cut them up. If we have infantry defending us, we can stay there for a *lot* of volleys."

He headed for the rear exit. His horse was being held for him just beyond. "I haven't got time to talk! Check with Stearns if you need to!"

He was gone.

Jeff looked at his radio operator, a young fellow from Hesse-Kassel who had eventually replaced Jimmy Andersen. "You heard, Reitz?" he asked.

The radio operator nodded.

"Call General Stearns. Tell him Colonel Engler thinks he can hold a position forward of the line of bunkers if he has infantry support—and I'm taking the Hangman out there to give it to him. Got that?"

He didn't wait for an answer before charging out of the bunker himself and looking for his own horse.

When Mike got the message, he cursed for maybe three or four seconds before he ran out of his own bunker to climb on top of it.

Unfortunately, his bunker was farther to the rear than the one where Engler and Higgins had been stationed—and its roof was several feet lower. He couldn't see anything; not enough, at least, to gauge whether the assessment of his subordinates was accurate or not.

There was no time to dilly-dally. Whatever he was going to do, had to be done *now*.

"Stick with those who got you here, Mike," he muttered to himself. Then he raced back into the bunker.

He had three radio operators but he ignored them in order to address his two aides, Christopher Long and Ulbrecht Duerr.

"Order all regiments forward. Out of the bunkers and trenches."

Long stared at him. Duerr reacted more quickly. "To where, sir?"

"I don't think they'll have any trouble figuring it out—but they can look for the division's flags."

He had two flag-bearers in the bunkers as well. The mounts for both of them were tethered outside next to his own.

"Follow me, lads." And out he went.

The confluence of the Danube and the Traun
A few miles southeast of Linz

"What are they doing?" demanded General von Colloredo. The words were almost shrieked. He lowered the spyglass and turned to the emperor. "Have they gone mad?"

Gustav Adolf kept his binoculars to his eyes. Partly to see what was unfolding; mostly, because he had no good answer to the question.

Steyregg, on the north bank of the Danube across from Linz

"What are they doing?"

Pappenheim ignored the question asked by one of his officers, for a moment, while he studied the development through his own spyglass. He had a good view of the field east of the town, because his vantage point was in the belfry of the town's church. He had one boot planted on the bell, which he'd cut down to give himself a better view.

It didn't take him more than a few seconds to figure out the answer.

He handed the spyglass to one of his aides. "What are they doing?" he said. His face was creased with a savage grin and his famous crossed-swords birthmark stood out more prominently than usual.

"What are they doing?" he repeated. "They're fighting, that's what they're doing. Order the Black Cuirassiers to mount up."

Vienna, former capital of Austria-Hungary, now occupied
by the Ottoman Empire

When she was within a quarter mile—just a quarter of a mile!—of the detached wing of the Hofburg which held the hidden cellars, Minnie finally had to accept the fact that she'd have to wait until nightfall before she could approach any closer. There were simply too many sentries stationed in the vicinity of the palace. Already, she'd been accosted twice by Ottoman patrols, demanding to know what she was about. Her pretense of not speaking any of their languages—which was mostly true, after all—combined with her appearance and smell, had been enough to avoid any repercussions. But if she tried to get any nearer, that would stop being true.

Fortunately, there were plenty of abandoned buildings nearby. Most of the Austrian population had fled before the Ottomans took Vienna, and the garrison Murad had left behind when he marched on Linz was not big enough to fill the city. Not too far away, she found a deserted bakery that would serve to hide her until the sun went down.

There wasn't any danger that Turkish soldiers might loot the place, either, because it was obvious that they had already done so. After moving her cart out of sight of anyone who might casually look in from the street, Minnie went upstairs to see if there was a bed she could use.

Her good fortune held. There was one. Not in very good shape, and after she'd spent a few hours on it the bed would stink as well as be disheveled. But at the moment all she wanted was some rest.

Hauling the cart halfway across the city and back had been arduous, and there was also the accumulated effect of the tension she'd been under. Despite her anxiety, she was asleep in minutes.

Steyregg, on the north bank of the Danube across from Linz

The first three volleys fired by the squadron were devastating. The oncoming sipahis, already tangled up by their own numbers and the terrain, were being mowed down. What was perhaps even worse was that their horses were being mowed down as well—and in even greater numbers, because they were a much bigger target.

So, the corpses of big animals added still further to the jumble. What was to have been, in theory, a charge of tens of thousands of cavalrymen, was, willy-nilly, degenerating into an infantry battle—and one where all the advantages were on the side of the Third Division.

By the time contact was made between the first ranks of the sipahis and the volley gun squadron, Thorsten had most of his units in good position. They were partially shielded across most of the line by the embankment formed where the road had been dug into the terrain.

The height of the embankment varied from a few inches to almost three feet. What was perhaps more important was that the volley guns were positioned on the road rather than on a field, as was normally the case. A dirt road in the Upper Austrian countryside wasn't much, but it made a more stable foundation for light artillery and one that was much easier to maneuver the guns upon.

After four volleys, a number of sipahis abandoned their horses and charged forward on foot. They were encumbered by heavier armor than janissaries wore and were mostly armed with lances and sabers rather than guns. But there were enough of them to overrun the volley gunners, and their ferocity had been aroused by the casualties their front ranks had suffered.

The volley guns were deadly, but they had one great vulnerability. Once an enemy got close enough, they stopped being useful, and the soldiers who manned them were reduced to being light infantry— emphasis on "light"—and poorly trained in that function to boot.

But by then the Hangman regiment had arrived and taken up positions to guard the volley guns. Against them, armed with their SRGs and grenades, the sipahis had no real chance.

Still, for a while they put up a fierce fight, and groups of them broke through in several places.

Thorsten Engler was close to one of those breaches and rode his horse forward to rally the men.

Which he did quite well, everyone present agreed afterward. But a man on horseback waving a sword around and not paying much attention to what was happening right next to him is at a severe disadvantage when he's attacked by a sipahi wielding a lance whose sole interest and concentration is on killing him.

Thorsten saw the sipahi at the last moment. Frantically, he swung his sword down just in time to deflect the lance thrust away from his ribs—

—and into the flank of his horse. The spear-tip penetrated at least six inches, maybe more. Squealing with fear and pain, the horse rose up and threw Thorsten out of the saddle.

He landed on top of an overturned volley gun. There was a spike of agony running up his spine and he heard, more than he felt, his leg break. Then his head struck something hard and his vision got blurry.

The last thing he saw, vaguely, was the huge shape of his horse as it lost its footing and came down upon him.

The confluence of the Danube and the Traun
A few miles southeast of Linz

"What are they doing?" demanded General von Colloredo. "*What are they doing?*"

Gustav Adolf kept his binoculars to his eyes. Partly to keep from striking the hysterical wretch with them; mostly, because he was fascinated by what he was seeing.

Steyregg, on the north bank of the Danube across from Linz

By the time Mike Stearns and most of the regiments started arriving at the dirt road that had become the front line of the battle, the volley gunners were falling back in disarray—some of them retrieving their guns, many leaving them behind—and the steadiness of the Hangman regiment was getting frayed. Say what you might about the semi-feudal pigheadedness of the Ottoman Empire's sipahis, they were brave men and not ones to flinch from savage fighting.

But they'd suffered terrible casualties by now, and once the rest of the Third Division started pouring fire into them, they began to fall back.

At which point—he'd timed it perfectly—Pappenheim's Black Cuirassiers struck them like a sledgehammer. The cuirassiers began by firing their heavy wheel-lock pistols; then, as the sipahi retreat turned into a rout, went after them with their sabers. At least another thousand sipahis fell, dead or wounded, before Pappenheim pulled them back.

As stubborn as he was himself, Pappenheim had learned some lessons over the years. The imperialist defeat at Breitenfeld had been partly due to the recklessness with which he'd pushed his cavalry charges. Here, facing a much larger enemy army than the Swedes had brought to Breitenfeld, Pappenheim did not make the mistake of over-extending himself.

The Turks had been bloodied today; bloodied badly. But the main body of Murad's army was still in position—and the fearsome janissaries hadn't even fought at all.

The confluence of the Danube and the Traun
A few miles southeast of Linz

Gustav Adolf tucked away his binoculars and turned to Colloredo. "The Third Division is my rock, General. Do not forget it."

He almost smiled when he said it, for all that he found Colloredo annoying. There was an irony here. Gustav Adolf didn't doubt for a moment that the historians would credit him with today's victory, even though he'd had very little to do with it beyond standing on this spit of land and looking properly august.

Well, no, he'd done a bit more than that. Gustav Adolf had been the one who'd made the judgment that Michael Stearns would make a decent general, hadn't he? And the heart of that judgment was that Stearns would be able to make the same judgments himself—which he so clearly had, as today proved once again.

Vienna, former capital of Austria-Hungary, now occupied
by the Ottoman Empire

When she finally reached the entrance to the detached wing of the palace, moving carefully in the darkness so as not to make any noise, the door swung open. Leopold emerged and took the handles of the cart from her; then, gently, nudged her inside. He followed with the cart.

Judy was inside, as was Cecilia Renata.

"What's he doing here?" Minnie hissed. "I told you to keep him away from me until I was clean."

"He insisted," said Cecilia Renata. "You know how stubborn my little brother can be."

By then, Leopold had the cart inside and closed the outer door. He took Minnie by the arm. "Come," he said. "There's a bath ready for you in the cellars."

"The radio—"

"We'll take care of it," said Judy. "You just take care of yourself."

Once they were in the cellars, Leopold helped Minnie get out of her clothes and into the bath. The water was tepid and the wine mixed into it was a little dizzying—or maybe that was just her own light-headedness. Now that it was over, she was starting to shake.

Leopold took her filthy garments into the back chamber and disposed of them in the oubliette. When he returned, he brought some clean cloths with which he began cleaning her.

"You don't have to do this," she said.

"Be quiet."

"I don't want you to see me like this. Or smell me."

"It doesn't matter. Be still."

It took a while. Twice, she had to get out of the tub while Leopold and Judy poured the vile contexts into the oubliette and refilled it with fresh water and wine. But eventually, she was clean again—or at least, as clean as anyone could hope to be when they had to hide out for weeks in hidden cellars.

After drying off, she and Leopold huddled together under their bedding in the chamber they now shared. Minnie began crying. She didn't even know why.

"I've been thinking about it," he said, "for all the time you were gone. I'll just remain a bishop. That way I can't get married to anyone and you and I can stay together."

She stopped snuffling, sat up, and looked down at him. "That's ridiculous. They'll never let you."

"Why not? My brother has heirs, and they're in good health. My oldest sister is carrying on the family tradition in the Netherlands. If need be, Cecilia Renata's still available for a diplomatic marriage, too. I'm the youngest. There's no reason I can't stay a bishop."

"That's ridiculous," she repeated.

He smiled. "Let's not worry about it right now. We're still hiding out from the Turks, remember?"

"You said they weren't really Turks. Make up your mind. And it's still a ridiculous idea."

"You don't like the idea?"

"I didn't say that. I just said it was ridiculous."

"So is going out alone into an occupied city and bringing back a radio in a cart full of shit. But you did it, didn't you?"

She didn't have a ready answer for that.

Chapter 59

Linz, capital-in-exile of Austria-Hungary

The first thing Thorsten Engler saw—quite fuzzily, for a few seconds—was the heavy-nosed face of Emperor Gustav II Adolf beaming down upon him.

His teeth sparkled; his eyes sparkled. Thorsten thought that might be an illusion produced by his lack of visual acuity, but even after he was able to focus clearly, it was apparent that he resided in the emperor's good favor, at least for the moment.

"Well done, Colonel, well done!" Gustav Adolf leaned over and gave Thorsten a hearty clap of congratulation on his shoulder.

Which immediately sent a spike of agony racing down Thorsten's spine.

"*Ahhhhhhhh...*" The emperor stepped back a pace, grimacing with sympathy and apology.

Dr. James Nichols came forward, raising a cautioning hand. "We need to be careful, Your Majesty. I still don't know the extent of the injuries to Colonel Engler's back. He may have muscular-skeletal damage, possibly a slipped disk"—Nichols spread his hands in a gesture halfway between a shrug and a demonstration of life's inherent uncertainty—"any number of things, which we have no way to determine quickly without an X-ray machine. That's on top of his broken ribs, broken leg, and what I'm pretty sure is a ruptured spleen."

He gave Thorsten a quick look of reassurance. "That last issue's probably not too severe, Colonel. The bleeding appears manageable, so I shouldn't have to cut you open. Some rest—that'll take time, of course—will probably allow the spleen to heal on its own."

Gustav Adolf leaned over again; this time, Thorsten was glad to see, while keeping his hands clasped behind his back. He seemed to be studying something on the right side of Thorsten's face with keen interest.

"The wound should do quite nicely," he said. He glanced up at Nichols. "Will the scar be visible enough? Perhaps we should..." He made a gesture suggesting someone sprinkling salt.

Nichols lips tightened. "I don't believe anything but nature's course is either necessary or proper, Your Majesty. Even with the sutures, the colonel's injury will...ah..."

He was obviously struggling to remain polite. More curious than alarmed, Thorsten reached up with his right hand and dis-covered that side of his head was covered with bandages.

"Did I lose the ear?" he asked.

"No," said Nichols, shaking his head. "Although it was a close thing. As it is, you'll have a fairly dramatic scar stretching from just under your ear down along your jaw line."

"A true warrior's mark!" boomed Gustav Adolf. "Perfect for our purpose. And now"—he turned away for a moment, gestur-ing at someone behind him and out of Thorsten's line of sight. "I'd wait to do this in a proper public ceremony, but I'm afraid I can't take the time. That bastard Murad is no slouch. Already he's got infantrymen working their way up the hills toward the Pöstlinberg and I'm sure it won't be long before he's probing down the south bank of the Traun. We're in for a proper siege now, make no mistake about it."

A Swedish officer stepped forward and handed a pair of small boxes to the emperor. The officer still had several other objects in his possession, Thorsten saw, including what looked like a large sash of some kind, colored a bright scarlet.

"Let's begin with these two," said Gustav Adolf, "since they're the simplest. Leave it to Americans! They even have a name for it, you know? 'Minimalist,' they call it."

He set one of the boxes on the hospital bed and flipped open the lid of the other. Then he drew out what seemed to be a silver-colored emblem—a star, perhaps?—hanging from an elaborately decorated wide ribbon.

"This one is the Silver Star, presented by the USE Army for valor in combat." He plopped it down on Thorsten's chest; then opened the other box. "They call this one the Purple Heart, which they give out to wounded soldiers. A clever idea, that. I should have thought of it myself."

The object—a stylized heart-shaped emblem, colored purple— was also plopped on his chest. The emperor turned back to the officer, then brought forward the scarlet sash along with another emblem of some sort. This one was mostly gold-colored and consisted of a squarish variation on a Maltese cross suspended from a large octagonal emblem.

"Clearly, you're not fit yet to wear this the way you're supposed to, so..." Gustav Adolf glanced around, pulled a chair forward, draped the sash over it and placed the emblem-and-cross on the seat.

"They would have given you the Order of the Golden Fleece— the Austrians, I mean—except that's only for Catholics and I was assured that you are"—here the emperor gave Thorsten a beady eye...

"Not Catholic," Thorsten filled in for him. He saw no point in complicating the issue with an explanation of the intricacies of the religious negotiations between himself and his betrothed, Caroline Platzer, who belonged to one of those peculiar denominations the Americans seemed to breed like rabbits. A "Quaker," in her case.

"So Ferdinand came up with this one just yesterday. He couldn't give it to you himself because he's preoccupied at the moment, as you can imagine. But it's a brand new imperial distinction—you're the first to hold it! Congratulations, Colonel Engler. You are now a member of the Imperial Austrian Order of Ferdinand. Eventually he thinks there will be four ranks, he told me, but this will remain the highest: Knight of the Grand Cross. And now..."

He turned back and received yet another item from his subordinate.

"Something from me," he said. A short but heavy chain was laid on Thorsten's chest, to which was attached a medallion, which was also gold but appeared to be blank.

"The Royal Order of Kalmar," Gustav Adolf announced. "You'll have to forgive me for the absence of an insignia. I'm still arguing with the king of Denmark over what it should be. Naturally, that drunken schemer wants the three lions of Denmark, which is preposterous, since it should be the three crowns of Sweden."

The emperor grinned. "My daughter, of course, is advocating for three unicorns. She'd rather have horses but only barbarians use horses for an emblem. Eventually, we'll settle it, at which time you can bring this insignia back and we'll place a proper medallion on it."

From the weight of the thing, the chain had to be made of actual gold. Thorsten tried to imagine what it must have cost.

"And now I must be off!" boomed the emperor. "Again, congratulations, Colonel! I am sure you will acquit yourself as splendidly in your new assignment as you have in this one."

Again he leaned over, this time to shake a large forefinger in front of Thorsten's nose. "And remember! Three, do you hear? Three! I'll settle for nothing less."

And off he went, followed by a small pack of officers. When the room cleared, Thorsten saw that Jeff Higgins had been waiting in the back of the room. He now stepped forward, smiling.

"I'll add my own congratulations," he said.

"Three? Three *what*?" asked Thorsten, feeling altogether bewildered. "What is he talking about?"

"They didn't tell you?" Jeff shook his head. "It's the old saying: there are three ways to do things. The right way, the wrong way—"

"And the Army way," James Nichols concluded, chuckling.

"You're being relieved of your command of the volley gun squadron," Jeff said.

"On account of your injuries," Nichols added. "You're going to need months to recover, Thorsten."

"So they're sending you back to Magdeburg, and putting you in charge of recruitment." Jeff nodded his head in the direction of the door through which the emperor had left. "That's what the 'three' refers to. Three divisions. They want you to raise three new divisions."

Thorsten stared at him. "Three... divisions. *Divisions*?" He started to throw up his hands but another spike of pain stopped him. "We've only got three divisions right now—total. You're talking about doubling the size of the army!"

Jeff nodded sympathetically. "Pretty much. That why they're piling medals and decorations on top of you—not that I don't think you deserve 'em—and why our not-exactly-sentimental emperor is tickled pink over your developing scar. He thinks it'll add a nice dramatic touch."

He leaned over and examined the bandage. "Can't really see much, but... What d'you think, Doc? If we sprinkled some salt in it..."

"Over my dead Oath of Hippocrates," growled Nichols.

Thorsten was feeling a little light-headed. That could be the effect of his injuries, of course.

"Look at it this way," said Jeff. "You'll be able to spend months snuggled up with Caroline."

"Well... eventually," said Nichols. "He *does* have a broken leg, at least four broken ribs, mostly likely a ruptured spleen and God only knows—we won't, for months—what kind of shape his back's in." He gave Thorsten a sympathetic shake of the head. "I'm afraid you and Caroline won't be doing anything more energetic than holding hands for a while."

But he'd be with her again. Thorsten hadn't seen her in months. He felt a lot cheerier.

Naturally, Jeff had to add: "Three divisions. That's only thirty thousand men, you know. Figure at the rate of recruiting fifty men a day—that's only five an hour, figuring a ten-hour day—you'll have it done in... what is that? Two years? A little less?"

"Your bedside manner really sucks," observed Nichols.

Breslau (Wroclaw), Lower Silesia
Poland

After he had the antenna positioned properly, Jozef moved back to the small door leading into the attic—tip-toeing all the way—and listened for any sound coming from below.

Nothing. No sound at all. That was what he expected, since Christin, Denise and Eddie had left less than two hours earlier and shouldn't be back until well after nightfall. Still, it was nerve-wracking.

Just extending the antenna had taken a quarter of an hour. There was still plenty of twilight to make any quick movement noticeable, and the antenna wouldn't work properly unless it extended beyond the open window.

This was the first opportunity he'd had to send a message in more than two weeks. He couldn't afford to waste the opportunity.

Once he had everything ready, he sat and stared at the wall for several minutes. There was nothing to see, not least of all because he'd blown out his candle and the attic was dimly lit.

What was he going to tell his uncle? How could he explain to the grand hetman of the Commonwealth of Poland and Lithuania...

Eventually, he sighed and lit the candle again. As far below the window as it was, no one outside should see anything.

In any event, the message took little time to transmit.

NOTHING TO REPORT STOP

Linz, capital-in-exile of Austria-Hungary

"The way I see it, we'll have one huge advantage," said Tom Simpson.

Mike Stearns cocked his head. "And that is..."

"Our Dutch-built airship is powered by an internal combustion engine. That means no boiler to be blown up."

"They can still shoot it," pointed out Julie.

Dell Beckworth shook his head. "Yeah, but they're more likely to kill us than they are to wreck the engine. We can only put so much armor on the *Magdeburg* before it won't be able to get off the ground at all."

By now, Mike had gotten enough sense for how dirigibles worked as combat vehicles to feel more confident expressing an opinion. "Correct me if I'm wrong, but since we're planning to use the *Magdeburg* in a defensive capacity—at least for now—that means we don't have to carry a big fuel supply. Just enough to get up in the air and fight off enemy airships, right? We're not planning to travel anywhere. And how long can such a battle last? Not more than two hours, I wouldn't think."

He paused to look at everyone sitting at the table in the new building that was being erected to serve as "airship central." Somewhat to Mike's amusement, a turf war had emerged over which service controlled the *Magdeburg*—the air force or the army? Jesse Wood, the commander of the USE's air force, was naturally arguing that his service should be in charge of it. But the army—more specifically, Gustav II Adolf in his capacity as the army's top commander—was pushing back.

Possession, as always, was nine-tenths of the law, and right now the army had the *Magdeburg*. Building a new "operations center" for it was one of the emperor's ways of staking down his claim further. He was no slouch at inter-service rivalry himself.

Mostly, Mike wanted the opinion of the two Dutch engineers at the table. They'd have a better sense than anybody of what the effective parameters were, with regard to the issue he'd raised.

Maarten Kortenaer finished the calculations he'd been doing with a pen and paper and looked up.

"It's a good point, General. If we presume that we only keep enough fuel on board for three hours' flight, then we can add a fairly significant amount of armor to the ship. Enough to protect three members of the flight crew on the gondola, certainly, which is all we need to run the ship for short operations."

"And the gun crew?"

Kortenaer made a face. "That's more difficult to calculate, because it would depend on the size of the weapon, where and how it could be positioned—I'm assuming it will be something too big and awkward for the gondola—and how many armored shooting positions we'd want."

"Four positions," said Dell. "Two aft, two forward, one either side of the keel."

He nodded toward Julie. "And just big enough to protect her. Once we get Julie and the gun in position and loaded, me and the other gun crew guy can retreat back into the interior of the hull. We ought to be safe enough. Our main protection's always going to be that we can outmaneuver them and outrange them. If they get close enough that they can start hitting us with any kind of accuracy, we're probably screwed anyway."

Julie frowned. "What other gun crew member? I thought it was just going to be you and me? The .50's not *that* heavy."

"To hell with that popgun," said Beckworth, grinning. "I'm going to be making a new gun. Ollie Reardon up in Grantville is already machining the barrel for me."

"What new gun?"

He pulled out a sketch and spread it open on the table. "Meet the Lahti L-39, year 1636 version," he said. "I'm modeling it after a Finnish design for a twenty-millimeter antitank rifle they built during World War II. It didn't work against the later and heavier Soviet tanks like the T-34, but it'd take out anything with lighter armor and it made a dandy sniper's weapon. I don't figure the Turks will be lifting T-34s into the air any time soon, so it ought to do the trick."

Mike thought Beckworth's face might actually break in half, as widely as he was now grinning. Gun nuts were just plain weird, sometimes.

Vienna, former capital of Austria-Hungary, now occupied by the Ottoman Empire

Minnie had taken even more time than Jozef had to extend her antenna out of the narrow window in the tower. Below, Judy and Leopold kept watch for anyone approaching the detached wing of the palace where the cellars were located.

When she was finally ready, she nodded at Cecilia Renata and the archduchess lit the small candle she had, carefully cupping it to shield the light.

Once Minnie had tuned to the right frequency, she began the transmission.

RATS EAT CATS

If he was listening and got the message—or, more likely, his operator got it and relayed it to him at once—her employer would be responding within half an hour. If they hadn't heard anything by then, they'd have to retreat into the cellars and try again early in the morning.

"You can put it out," she whispered. Cecilia Renata extinguished the candle.

It was perhaps twenty minutes later that a message was returned. Hurriedly, Cecilia Renata relit the candle while Minnie recorded the message.

CATS EAT RATS STOP CEDAR

"Cedar" gave her the code they'd be using. Minnie had it memorized, as she had all three of them. But it would be a slow and laborious process to answer. Eventually, though, she'd sent the message. Once translated, it would read:

Hidden in secret cellars in palace. Stop. Me, prince, princess— that was technically incorrect, but shorter than "archduke" and "archduchess"—*Judy. Stop. Supplied for months. Stop. Undetected. Stop. No immediate peril. Stop.*

"You can blow it out again," she said to Cecilia Renata, then in a louder whisper sent down the stairs: "Leopold, Judy—come up. We're done."

Once they were safely back in the cellars, Leopold started fretting again. "We should have sent it to our brother, instead. All right, *too,* not instead. It's not right that he doesn't know."

They'd already had this discussion—twice—but Minnie didn't bridle. She understood, and even sympathized, with Leopold's feelings.

"I *can't* send it to Emperor Ferdinand," she said patiently. "All I could do is listen for a frequency on which there was a transmission that I *thought* might be from Linz. And then who would I be sending a message to? Which I'd have to send in the clear because we don't have a code we share. Who knows who'd wind up getting the message?"

"Leave off, Brother," said Cecilia Renata. "Minnie's right."

"Don Francisco will know what to do," said Minnie.

She was pretty sure she was right about that, too.

Ottoman encampment
A few miles southeast of Linz, at the confluence of the Danube and the Enns

In his command pavilion, Sultan Murad IV closed the book he'd been reading, which was a compilation of all the articles and pieces of text his agents had found in the Grantville libraries in which he was discussed or mentioned. By now, he knew the material extremely well and had parts of the text memorized.

...*dead at age 29...*
...*cirrhosis of the liver...*
...*untimely death...*
...*addiction to alcohol...*

He had meant to rewrite the book. Beç had been the beginning. Now, after the setback at Steyregg, he wondered if all he was doing was scribbling over some of the pages.

He set the book on the table in his chamber, right next to

the bottle he'd brought from the palace in Beç—a thing of beauty to hold the German king's wine.

He reached for the bottle and took a swallow of its contents.

Murad's birthday had passed just a few weeks earlier. He was now twenty-four years old.

...dead at age 29...

He stared at the bottle for a time. Then he took another swallow.

Five years.

Chapter 60

Brzeg, thirty miles southeast of Breslau

The Lady Protector of Lower Silesia—a title Gretchen Richter still found ridiculous—was seated at the table in Brzeg's largest tavern where she'd been holding court. That was an expression no one would dare use to her face, knowing how much she'd detest it—but which, of course, also proved the point. Whether she liked it or not, approved of it or not, Gretchen Richter was now the ruler of Lower Silesia.

No one doubted that, certainly not the thousands of mercenaries who'd formerly been in the employ of Heinrich Holk and were now fleeing the province. Lovrenc Bravnicar's cavalry had been pursuing them to the border—bits of them; pieces of them; they were no longer an organized army—but there'd been very little actual fighting.

Gretchen stared up at Rebecca Abrabanel, who'd just entered the tavern and placed a message on the table in front of her.

"I didn't realize you had a radio," she said. Gretchen's tone was at least half-accusatory.

"I am the Secretary of State of the United States of Europe on official business. Of course I have a radio with me. I have had it all along. The Belle is a small plane but it's not *that* small."

Gretchen now looked at the woman standing a few feet behind Rebecca, in the uniform of the USE Air Force. That look was also rather accusatory.

Lieutenant Laura Goss shrugged, without unclasping her hands behind her. "It fits easily in the back. It's one of the came-through-the-Ring up-time models, you know. Nothing clunky about it. And there's no point glaring at me like that. I'm just the chauffeur."

Gretchen looked back down at the message, then back up at the Air Force officer. Her gaze was still on the accusatory side.

"And how did you land here anyway?" she demanded. "We haven't built an airstrip."

Goss issued a derisive little snort. "Airstrip! Do you think the very first Belle took off and landed from an airstrip? Jesse Wood made that first flight and dozens after it from a flat meadow. This part of Poland's got plenty of flat meadows, including one right out of town. I practically taxied down the main street, such as it is. Would have, maybe, if it weren't for that half-baked wall they've got in the way."

Technically, Brzeg was a walled town. Those walls didn't pro-vide much protection against anyone except a band of outlaws, but there was a gate barring the road into the town.

Gretchen now transferred the still-half-accusatory look to Eric Krenz. Who, for his part, shrugged in a manner that was every bit as insouciant as the Air Force lieutenant's had been.

"Don't glare at me either, Gretchen," he said. "I'm still a captain in the USE army. You think I'm going to tell my own secretary of state I'm not opening a gate for her?"

"You are *not* a captain in the USE army," Gretchen said. She rapped a knuckle on the radio message. "Not any longer. You've been promoted to major."

Krenz did not look pleased by the news. "It's just as they say! No good deed goes unpunished."

To most people, a promotion meant additional recognition and prestige. To Krenz, it meant additional work and responsibility.

"She's right, though," said Tata, who'd been standing next to Gretchen at the table. She straightened up from reading the mes-sage. "It also says you're still in command of the troops detached from the Third Division and it says a company from von Arnim's army—excuse me, von Arnim's *former* army—is being sent here from Leipzig and will be under your command as well."

Eric looked gloomier still. "Marvelous."

Tata went back to reading through the message, which, for a

radio message, was unusually long. "The really big news, though…" She shook her head. "I hadn't expected that."

"Me either," said Gretchen, almost hissing the words.

Lukasz Opalinski had been standing against a far wall, doing his best to seem invisible, which was not easy for a man as big as he was. He'd never seen *Star Wars*—never even heard of it, in fact—but his posture and countenance exuded one of the famous lines of dialogue from the movie.

This isn't the Polish hussar you're looking for.

Lukasz hadn't spoken to Jozef in several days. What radio message had he sent to Stanislaw Koniecpolski? What in the name of Jesus—Poles, with their tradition of religious freedom, took blasphemy a lot less seriously than most Christians did— were they *doing* here?

Now, he cleared his throat. "If I might ask, what does the message say?"

Tata glanced at him. "The gist of it—"

Gretchen interrupted her, taking over the summary. "It says I'm confirmed as the so-called 'Lady Protector of Lower Silesia'— which is still an absurd title!—and that the United States of Europe is declaring Lower Silesia a protectorate under its jurisdiction."

Lukasz had feared as much. He and Jozef had just helped the Polish-Lithuanian Commonwealth's sworn enemy to conquer one of the PLC's own provinces.

This is what the Americans would call friendly fire. To which they would no doubt add, *on steroids.* Lukasz still didn't know exactly what steroids were, but he grasped the essence of the expression.

He found himself whistling soundlessly. Would he still whistle so, before they kicked the stool out from under him and the rope seized his neck?

"Now that I have seen to the proper establishment of authority in our nation's new province," said Rebecca, "I must leave. Prime Minister Piazza has instructed me to go to Linz."

Gretchen's gaze now became fully accusatory. "Where your husband—*and mine*, whom I have not seen since he presented me with this"—here she gave her expanding belly a little slap— "are now stationed."

"Indeed." Rebecca smiled. "I shall give Colonel Higgins your regards."

"I want to *see* him."

"I will tell him that."

"There is no justice."

"Of course there is." Rebecca leaned over and tapped the radio message with her forefinger. "Are you not yourself the one dispensing justice, here in Lower Silesia?"

And with that, she departed the tavern.

Shortly afterward, the situation deteriorated. Gretchen Richter was never one to let fury/indignation/resentment/despondency get in the way of her duty.

The town authorities of Brzeg had remained silent throughout Rebecca's visit, but now they came forward and began flooding Gretchen with pleas, protests and demands. Their own German dialect was not so different from the Amideutsch that Rebecca and Gretchen had been speaking that they hadn't been able to understand the exchange.

The heart of it, certainly—which was that Gretchen was their new mistress. And they wanted assurances from her concerning...

Practically everything, it seemed.

Guild practices and customs must be maintained.

Only Lutheran churches could be allowed on the streets.

Jews must be expelled, if any of the Christ-killing dogs had the nerve to show up in Brzeg.

No peasants had any citizenship rights in the town.

They got no farther before the explosion.

Lady Protector of Lower Silesia, indeed. It was understandable if the assembled notables of Brzeg—or Brieg, as they insisted on calling it—soon found that title indistinguishable from *She-Devil From Below.*

Within a quarter of an hour, Gretchen had issued her decrees and sent Tata with a squad of soldiers to the town's printer to have them produced and plastered all over town.

She did spare the guild masters. For the moment. All others fell to the ax.

Complete separation of church and state now exists in Lower Silesia. No churches have any special authority or privileges.

Jews are welcome to enter Brzeg either on business or personal affairs. Hostility toward such persons exhibited in any public manner will be punished.

At that point, two more squads of soldiers were sent forth. One to erect a pillory in the town square. The other to purchase—for a reasonable price; gouging would be dealt with severely—a sturdy horsewhip.

The gate to the town is to be kept open at all times. Day or night, seven days a week. Free entry and exit is granted to all citizens of Lower Silesia—and every inhabitant of the province is now a citizen.

In the event of a military emergency, all citizens of Lower Silesia have the right to seek shelter in the nearest walled city. Authorities attempting to exclude such persons will be harshly punished.

At this point, yet another squad of soldiers was sent forth to find and purchase—for a reasonable price; gouging would be dealt with severely—some rope of suitable length and diameter.

Gretchen refrained from ordering the erection of an actual gallows. But she did assure the assembled notables—all of whom were now clustered as far away from her as they could get—that an experienced carpenter would be assigned to design one. And there were plenty of experienced carpenters in the ranks of the USE army, so she didn't care in the least if the town's carpenters were inclined to cooperate or not.

Until that point, Lukasz was rather enjoying the situation. No Pole objects to seeing haughty German patricians put firmly in their place.

Alas, Gretchen went further. She now turned toward him and issued a new set of commands:

"I'm sick of this. These are the worst ones I've encountered yet, but all of these Silesian town councils disgust me. I want you and Jozef to put a priority on organizing a farmers' militia—a *big* militia; well-armed and well-trained. At least two thousand men. Three or four would be better."

Lukasz tried to think of a way out.

"Most of them won't know any German," he protested. "We'll wind up with a military force that can't speak the national language."

"I'm glad you brought that up. I see we need a new decree."

Henceforth, the official languages of Lower Silesia are German and Polish. All official proclamations and instructions will be issued in both languages or, in areas where only German or Polish is widely spoken, in whichever language predominates.

Military units are not exempt from this decree.

"That should do it," she said.

Breslau (Wroclaw), Lower Silesia
Formerly Poland, now claimed by the USE

When Jozef Wojtowicz got the radio message from Brzeg—Gretchen had a radio also, of course—he threw up his hands.

"The woman is insane! Now she wants me and Lukasz to organize a Polish farmers' militia. A big one—she's talking about thousands of men!"

Christin George cocked her head. "I was under the impression she'd already told you to do that."

Jozef shrugged irritably. "Yes, yes—but I didn't take it all that seriously. Now Lukasz tells me she really wants it done. Read it yourself!"

He handed her the radio message, which Christin read quickly. She didn't have her daughter's aptitude with languages, but by now she was quite familiar with written Amideutsch—although the spelling could sometimes throw her off. No language or dialect of the time was consistently spelled; certainly not one as new as Amideutsch.

Finished, she tossed it back on the table. "You'd better hop to it, then." Adding, with a grin: "But I think we've got time for a quickie."

Linz, capital-in-exile of Austria-Hungary

When he saw the man waiting for him at the entrance to his rooms in the palace, Mike Stearns came to an abrupt halt.

"Francisco. When do you arrive? I didn't even know you were coming."

"Early this morning. Just an hour ago," said Nasi. "I didn't tell anyone I was coming—and it's my hope the news still hasn't spread. Not a great hope, though, since Eddie flew me down.

Airplanes are still rare enough in Linz that the arrival of one always draws some attention."

He nodded at the door. "Please, Michael, may we enter? I'd like to keep my visit as little-known as possible, until we've decided on a course of action."

"Course of—?" Mike shook his head. "Sure, come on in." He stepped forward, opened the door and passed through.

"Foolish of me," said Nasi, chuckling softly, as he followed Mike into the room. "I didn't think to see if it was already unlocked."

Mike pulled up a chair for him and sat on the edge of his bed. The room was small, containing nothing more than a single bed, a small writing table and chair, a clothes trunk and an armoire that was well-made and ornately carved but not spacious. It was just big enough to hold his spare uniforms.

"I saw no point in locking it," Mike explained. "I've got nothing in here worth stealing—not, at least, for anyone who could get through the guards out front—and the locks in this day and age are crappy anyway."

"You didn't bring one of your up-time padlocks?"

Mike shook his head again. "You wouldn't have come here if it wasn't something really important, Francisco. So what is it?"

Nasi set his valise on the floor and sat down. "I have news, Michael. Good news—very good, in fact—but there are major security problems posed."

He went on to explain.

After he was done, Mike pursed his lips. "'Major security problems' is putting it mildly. I presume you didn't tell Denise or Eddie."

"No, of course not."

"Anyone?"

"Just you."

"Nor even the radio operator?"

"He doesn't know the code Minnie and I used."

Mike ran fingers through his hair. "All right, so we can still keep it to the bare minimum. That would be Ferdinand and Gustav Adolf, the way I see it. Well, Rebecca too. We can't cut the USE's government completely out of the loop and she'd kill me when she found out."

Nasi smiled. "I trust Rebecca. Anyone else?"

Bells began ringing outside. Mike's head came up.

"Okay, the wedding's about to start and I'm supposed to be there." He rose to his feet. "You want to wait here or come with me?"

"I'll wait here. If I appear at the wedding, there will be questions."

Mike pointed to the desk, which was designed with a lift top. "I've got a few books in there, if you need something to read."

"Sadly, I already have reading material." Nasi reached into his valise and pulled out a rather thick folder.

"What's that? And why 'sadly'?"

"In here are the relevant documents concerning my three prospective brides. I had a thorough investigation done, so it's fairly voluminous. And 'sadly,' because I've spent too much time with you Americans. I'm afraid I've been infected with your sentimentality when it comes to marriage."

Mike grinned. "True love and all that."

"Exactly so."

Mike turned and placed his hand on the doorknob. Then he paused, as he listened to the church bells.

"And two more," he said.

Chapter 61

Linz, capital-in-exile of Austria-Hungary

Noelle never remembered much about the wedding, except for the huge crowds that seemed to surround them wherever she and Janos went. They *were* huge, too; it wasn't just her imagination. Later, after she had time to process everything, she understood the reason that was so. It would be nice to think she and her new husband were wildly popular, but the actual explanation was both more prosaic and a lot more cold-blooded.

Austria-Hungary had had its back to the wall, until the USE showed up and played the critical role in beating back the Turks in what was being called the Battle of Steyregg. And while Gustav Adolf had been in overall command of rhe allied forces, every one of the most visible features of that victory—the ten-inch naval rifles on the spit, the Third Division; most of all, the huge airship that had driven off the Ottoman fleet of airships—all of them were associated with Americans.

And, now, one of Austria-Hungary's most prominent noblemen and a close friend and advisor of Emperor Ferdinand III was marrying an American. One who, it was said, was close to the USE's new prime minister, Ed Piazza—and just to put the icing on the cake, both the prime minister and the bride were themselves Catholics.

The simmering dispute over the nature of the marriage had vanished. Noelle knew from Janos that Ferdinand had been prepared to rule that their marriage would not be morganatic, and he'd stare down the nobility who objected. But in the event, that proved unnecessary. Just as he had said he would, the moment the treaty was signed between the Empire of Austria-Hungary and the Kingdom of Bohemia, Wallenstein had ennobled Noelle as the new countess of Homonna—with all of the lands down to the smallest pond and patch that her new husband's family had once owned.

Whatever anyone thought of that arrangement—which, to uncharitable souls, could seem as if an upstart king had given a made-up title to an upstart commoner—they were keeping their mouths shut. The debate over the class status of Americans would continue, with the existing set-up pleasing no one but still being something they could all tolerate for the moment.

The Austrian nobility wouldn't have to lock horns with the emperor. That could be a dicey proposition, especially given that the attitude of their Hungarian counterparts was uncertain. On the one hand, Hungarian aristocrats could be just as haughty as Austrian ones; on the other hand, it was one of their own whose marriage was being fiddled with.

For their part, the Americans could let the issue slide for a while longer—"kick the can down the road," in their own idiom. Almost of them disliked aristocratic pretensions and a lot of them purely detested them. Among that number, ironically, was the very man so many people called "the Prince of Germany." But, if pressed, Mike Stearns would insist that the title was merely a whim—a jest, almost. Did any American think that Elvis Presley had really been "the King," after all?

Sooner or later, Noelle supposed, the issue would come to a head. But she was just as glad that she could sidestep it personally. True, if she ever decided she wanted to run for a seat in the USE's House of Commons, her title as the countess of Homonna would be an obstacle. (Presumably—but, here too, the situation was murky. Did a noble title *in another country* disqualify someone from running for a seat in the Commons? The laws were murky.)

The chance that Noelle would ever want to do such a thing, however, ranged from *cold day in hell* to *hell freezes over*. She was, by training as well as temperament, someone who naturally gravitated toward the executive side of government, not the legislative one. And within those executive functions, her liking and strengths ran toward accepting and carrying out assignments. Not—very much *not*—toward running for office so she could decide on someone else's duties.

All things considered, despite the nervousness she'd felt at the start of the day, her wedding went extremely well. It was a long and fatiguing event, of course, as big official weddings always were, especially when they were taking place within the imprimatur of the Roman Catholic church in all its full and formal glory.

But, now, it was over. There was still a bit of an ordeal left, which was the post-wedding reception. This would not be the party-in-all-but-name that American wedding receptions typically were, but a genuine reception—which was to say, the long and tedious process of meeting and greeting all of the many dignitaries who'd come to pay their respects.

Noelle wasn't looking forward to it. But she didn't imagine it would be all that bad, either.

Two hours after it began, she was having some doubts. She wasn't sure she'd ever been so bored in her life. Thankfully, the actual meet-and-greet part was done, but it seemed she and Janos were expected to stand around just in case someone else felt like coming up to them and saying something completely inconsequential.

So, she was relieved when Emperor Ferdinand came up, took both Janos and her by the elbow, and led them away.

"That's enough, I think," he said. "And there's a matter I need you to assist me with."

The three of them did a stately procession out of the public portions of the palace, nodding graciously to one and all as they passed through. The advantage to having the emperor himself as their escort was that very few people—only two, both of whom were inebriated and quickly brushed aside—were bold enough to stop them for a chat.

Less than three minutes later, Ferdinand ushered Noelle and Janos into a small audience chamber.

The first thing she noticed was the other occupants in the room, all of whom were already seated: Gustav II Adolf, Mike Stearns, Rebecca Abrabanel and Francisco Nasi.

The second thing she noticed was that all the seats, including three vacant ones clearly intended for the emperor, herself and Janos, were arranged in a circle.

The third thing she noticed was that there were no servants in the room. No guards, either.

Not one.

Oh, hell's bells, she thought. *This is not good.*

As soon as Ferdinand took his seat, he gave everyone a quick, hard look. "What you are about to hear may not be discussed with anyone—no one—who is not already present in this room. Is that understood?"

Mutely, Noelle and Janos nodded. None of the others did, which Noelle took to mean they already knew what the emperor was about to disclose.

Oh, hell's bells. This is really *not good.*

She wondered if she could make it to the door before someone tackled her. Probably . . . not.

Ferdinand nodded toward Francisco Nasi. "He received a radio message yesterday from Vienna. They are still alive. Unhurt. My brother and sister, and their two companions. The American Judy Wendell and a woman named Minnie Hugelmair. She works for Don Francisco, it seems, and was the one who sent the message."

Janos grunted softly. "They made it to the secret cellars, then?"

"Exactly so," said Ferdinand.

"What supplies do they have?" Janos asked.

Ferdinand looked at Nasi. The Jewish spymaster made a small shrugging gesture. "I don't know, exactly. All the message said in that regard was: 'supplied for months.' Understand that this message was sent in code, using Morse, and they must have been at some risk while sending it so they would have kept it as brief as possible. But I know Minnie. She's as steady as a rock and not given to hyperbole. If she says they're supplied for months, that can be taken at face value."

In for a penny, in for a pound. "I know Minnie too, Your Majesty," said Noelle. "Leopold and Cecilia Renata are fortunate to have her for a companion in this situation."

She glanced at Janos. "If someone could explain . . . what are these secret cellars?"

The explanation took a few minutes. From the attentive way they listened, Noelle thought that these details were also new to Mike, Rebecca and Gustav Adolf. Ferdinand had probably just filled them in on the gist of the situation before Noelle and Janos arrived.

Once the explanation was over, Ferdinand looked to Mike Stearns. "I must ask—is it possible your Captain Lefferts might be able to rescue them?"

Noelle couldn't stop herself from blurting: "Oh, no!"

Everyone looked at her. "Why not?" asked Gustav Adolf. "The captain is the world's—well, Europe's—most accomplished gaol-breaker, is he not?"

Noelle groped for a way to explain, all the while silently cursing herself for not keeping her blasted mouth shut.

"Yes, that's true, but..." She began with a quibble: "Your brother and sister—all of them—are not *in* a gaol, Your Majesty. No one is holding them captive, after all. What they are is in *hiding*. And—and—" She didn't know where to go from there.

Thankfully, Mike took up the slack. "I have to say I'm with Noelle on this one, Your Majesty. Harry Lefferts... How to say it? You want courage, boldness, tenacity—Harry's your man. Cleverness, too. But we're not talking about breaking someone out of prison here. I can't see any way that Harry's skill set is going to be all that useful to us."

"In any event," Rebecca chimed in, "Captain Lefferts is far away from here, on another assignment."

Gustav Adolf cleared his throat. "Indeed, he is. He may not even be on the continent, at the moment." He raised his hand. "But I should say no more about that."

Ferdinand looked back at Mike. "Indirection, you're saying?"

"Yes—and strategic indirection, not simply tactical. Harry Lefferts can head-fake in a fight with the best of them, but we're not *in* a fight. Not yet."

"It is more like a game of go than chess," added Rebecca. Seeing the incomprehension on most faces, she fluttered her fingers. "Go is a Chinese game. A few of the Americans play it and I have watched them. It is more of a game of position than maneuver. Hard to explain—but what I am trying to express is this: What we need to do first of all is determine a way we can insert a rescue team into Vienna. That will almost certainly have to be done through diplomatic subterfuge, however. This is really a task for a very capable agent, not a commando leader."

Again, she fluttered her fingers. "At some point, it may be necessary to bring in what my husband would call 'the muscle.' If so, and if he's back from—wherever he is—Captain Lefferts may be called upon. But we need to begin by choosing the agent."

Everyone now looked at Nasi.

"I agree. And I know just the right person for the job."

He now looked at Noelle.

"I just got *married*," she said. Well, squeaked.

Vienna, former capital of Austria-Hungary, now occupied by the Ottoman Empire

"The name of the person I am thinking of starts with an M," said Minnie.

"Is the person female?" asked Judy.

"Yes."

"Of *course* she's female," said Leopold. "Minnie always picks women when she's defending."

"Just as you always pick men," said his sister, unsympathetically. "Is the person you are thinking of a resident of Europe? Defining Europe as always—west of the Urals, north of the Caucasus."

"Yes," said Minnie.

"Is she active in politics?" asked Judy.

Minnie shook her head. "That question's posed too broadly."

"I'll restate it. Is she a head of state?"

"No."

"Is she married to a head of state?"

"No."

"Does she hold any official title?"

"Yes."

Cecilia Renata pounced. "Does she hold any official *post*?"

"No."

"Ha!" Judy clapped her hands. "Title but no post. That narrows it down to..."

"Thousands of women in Europe," said Leopold. "Assuming that she isn't dead—which we still don't know—in which case the number climbs to tens of thousands of women in Europe."

"You're right, I forgot," said Judy. "Is the woman you are thinking of still alive?"

"Yes."

Leopold shook his head. "That still doesn't—"

"Is she a *real* woman?" asked Cecilia Renata. "Not mythical or legendary."

"Yes."

"I am sick of Botticelli," groused Leopold.

"Would you rather play Ghost?"

"God, no." As an archduke of Austria-Hungary, Leopold considered himself exempt from the third commandment, so long as the blasphemy wasn't heartfelt. "That's the most boring word game there is. Why didn't any of us think to bring a deck of cards?"

"Do you want me to haul out the shit wagon?" asked Minnie. "I'm sure I could find a deck of cards somewhere in Vienna."

Without waiting for an answer to that—oh, so very rhetorical— question, Cecilia Renata pressed on. "Is the person you are thinking of active in the arts?"

"Yes."

"Ha!" Judy clapped her hands again. Vigorously enough, this time, to cause the candle to flicker. In that dim, unstable light, she looked like a predator. "We're hot on the trail! Is this fun, or what?"

Cast of Characters

Ableidinger, Constantin Member of USE Parliament; leader of the Ram movement.

Abrabanel, Rebecca Leader of the Fourth of July Party; wife of Mike Stearns.

Achterhof, Gunther Leader of the Committees of Correspondence.

Albrecht II (Wallenstein) King of Bohemia.

Andersen, Jimmy Radio operator for the Hangman regiment; close friend of Jeff Higgins.

Austria, Cecilia Renata, Archduchess of Sister of Austria-Hungarian Emperor Ferdinand III and Archduke Leopold Wilhelm.

Austria, Leopold Wilhelm, Archduke of Younger brother of Austria-Hungarian Emperor Ferdinand III and Archduchess Cecilia Renata.

Austria, Ferdinand III of Emperor of Austria-Hungary; older brother of Archduke Leopold Wilhelm and Archduchess Cecilia Renata; married to Mariana, infanta of Spain.

Bavaria, Albrecht, duke of	Younger brother and heir presumptive of Duke Maximilian.
Bavaria, Maximilian I, duke of	Ruler of Bavaria; member of the Wittelsbach family; older brother of Albrecht.
Beasley, Denise	Agent for Francisco Nasi; informally betrothed to Eddie Junker.
Bleier, Sebastian	Captain in the USE army; combat engineer.
Böcler, Johann Heinrich, "Heinz"	Formerly private secretary of Duke Ernst of Saxe-Weimar; now employed by David Bartley.
Chomse, Franz Leo	Captain, USE Navy, aide to Admiral Simpson.
Dalberg, Werner von	Leader of the Fourth of July Party in the Oberpfalz.
Donner, Agathe, "Tata"	CoC organizer in Dresden; close associate of Gretchen Richter.
Drugeth, Janos	Hungarian nobleman; friend and adviser of Austrian Emperor Ferdinand III.
Duerr, Ulbrecht	Officer, USE Army; aide to Mike Stearns.
Engler, Thorsten	Lieutenant Colonel in USE Army; commander of the Third Division's flying artillery.
Franchetti, Stefano	Airship pilot.

Gerisch, Ursula	Convert and missionary for the Episcopal Church.
Gundelfinger, Helene	Vice-President of the State of Thuringia-Franconia; leader in the Fourth of July Party.
Gustavus Adolphus	*See "Vasa, Gustav II Adolf"*
Higgins, Jeffrey, "Jeff"	Lieutenant Colonel, USE Army; husband of Gretchen Richter.
Hugelmair, Minnie	Agent for Francisco Nasi; friend of Denise Beasley.
Junker, Egidius, "Eddie"	Employed as an agent and pilot by Francisco Nasi; informally betrothed to Denise Beasley.
Kienitz, Charlotte	Leader of the Fourth of July Party in Mecklenburg.
Koniecpolski, Stanislaw	Grand Hetman of the Polish-Lithuanian Commonwealth.
Kortenaer, Maarten	Dutch aeronautical engineer; one of the designers of the *Magdeburg*.
Krenz, Eric	Captain, USE Army.
Kresse, Georg	Leader of guerrilla movement in the Vogtland.
Kuefer, Wilhelm	Guerrilla fighter in the Vogtland; Kresse's assistant.
Long, Christopher	Officer, USE Army; aide to Mike Stearns.
Mackay, Julie	Sharpshooter; wife of Alex Mackay; neé Julie Sims.

Mackay, Alexander, "Alex"	Cavalry officer in the army of Gustavus Adolphus; husband of Julie Sims.
Mailey, Melissa	Leader of the Fourth of July Party.
Nasi, Francisco	Former head of intelligence for Mike Stearns; now operates a private intelligence agency.
Opalinski, Lukasz	Polish hussar.
Pappenheim, Gottfried, Heinrich, Graf zu	Top general of the Bohemian army.
Piazza, Edward, "Ed"	President of the State of Thuringia-Franconia; leader of the Fourth of July Party.
Richter, Maria Margaretha, "Gretchen"	Leader of the Committees of Correspondence; wife of Jeff Higgins.
Riddle, Veleda	Prominent figure in Grantville and the Episcopal Church.
Saxe-Weimar, Ernst, duke of	Brother of Wilhelm Wettin; administrator for Emperor Gustav Adolf.
Saxe-Weimar, Wilhelm IV, duke of	_See "Wettin, Wilhelm"_
Simpson, John Chandler	USE Navy admiral; father of Tom Simpson.
Simpson, Rita	Wife of Tom Simpson; sister of Mike Stearns.
Simpson, Thomas III, "Tom"	USE Army artillery officer; husband of Rita Stearns; son of John and Mary Simpson.

Stearns, Michael, "Mike"	Former Prime Minister of the Unites States of Europe; now a major general in command of the Third Division, USE Army; husband of Rebecca Abrabanel.
Strigel, Matthias	Governor of Magdeburg province; leader of the Fourth of July Party.
Stull, Noelle	Former agent for the SoTF government, now employed by Francisco Nasi; betrothed to Janos Drugeth.
Vasa, Gustav II Adolf	King of Sweden; Emperor of the United States of Europe; also known as Gustavus Adolphus.
Vasa, Wladyslaw IV	King of the Polish-Lithuanian Commonwealth.
Von Eichelberg, Bruno	USE artillery captain; aide to Major Tom Simpson.
Von Haslang, Johann Heinrich	Bavarian captain, assigned to anti-airship artillery.
Von Lintelo, Timon	Bavarian general.
Wallenstein	*See "Albrecht II"*
Weaver, Bonnie	Formerly a geologist for the SoTF State Technical College; now working as a contractor for Estuban Miro's airship company.
Wendell, Judith Elaine, "Judy the Younger"	Barbie Consortium member; friend and companion of Archduchess Cecilia Renata.

Wettin, Wilhelm,   Prime Minister of the USE;
(formerly Saxe-Weimar,   leader of the Crown Loyalist Party.
Wilhelm IV, Duke of)

Wojtowicz, Jozef   Nephew of Grand Hetman
Koniecpolski; head of Polish
intelligence in the USE; friend
of Lukasz Opalinski.

Acknowledgments

As always, I got a lot of help from many people in writing this novel. I can't possibly thank all of them without turning this into a longwinded essay, but I would like to single out a few people who were of particular assistance:

Stanley Roberts was extraordinarily helpful to me in dealing with all of the Ottoman material. The history of that great and long-lasting empire is both complex and difficult to grasp for anyone who, like me, has never devoted specialized study to it. Stanley, as he has in previous novels, was invaluable in steering me away from errors and toward the things I needed.

Iver Cooper and Kerryn Offord were of great help when it came to the material dealing with airships.

Finally, I want to thank Judith Lyons for her assistance with regard to the Episcopal Church. Institutions—certainly religious ones—always look simpler from the outside than they really are. Judith was very supportive in guiding me through those intricacies and subtleties.

Errors that may remain, with respect to the matters touched upon above or any others, are entirely mine.

Note on the transliteration of Ottoman Turkish Words

Ottoman Turkish was written using a modified Arabic script. As most of my readers will not be familiar with this script, I have elected to transliterate the Ottoman words using the more familiar Roman characters of English, with the addition of some special characters which I define below.

In those cases where an Ottoman word has entered English (e.g., janissary, vizier), I have used the standard English spelling. For less common words, there are several different transliteration schemes that are used by scholars. While for those familiar with them they present a clear guide to pronunciation, for the general reader each has its advantages and disadvantages. Because this book is aimed at the general public, rather than use a single scheme, I have elected to use the transliteration which, in my opinion, will give the reader the best chance of pronouncing the word correctly.

Character	Pronounced like
Â, â	a, but with palatalization of any preceding consonant (this is often described as being pronounced as though there is a y between the consonant and the â)
Ç, ç	ch, as in chocolate
ğ	unvoiced, causes the preceding vowel to be drawn out by a small amount, like gh in light or fought
İ, i	ee, as in see
I, ı	uh, like the u in fuss
Ö, ö	ir, as in bird, like German ö
Ş, ş	sh, as in show
Ü, ü	ew, as in flew